CALLING OF THE DRAGON'S BLOOD

ADAM ORION NORTH

Should A Dragon Fall

Calling Of The Dragon's Blood
Under The Dragon's Shadow
Chasing The Dragon's Tale

Calling Of The Dragon's Blood

EPUB ISBN 978-1-957324-15-9

Paperback ISBN 978-1-957324-17-3

Hardback ISBN 978-1-957324-16-6

Author's Note

It has been brought to my attention that not everyone knows the tale of the cobbler and the elves. Though not pivotal to this book nor any of the ones that follow, that bygone story is referenced early. While the telling of the folklore is widely available, I think it might be best if I provide a brief synopsis for those who are unfamiliar with it.

The tale follows a cobbler (that is a person who makes shoes) who is struggling financially despite being honest and hard working. One day he awakes to find that someone has assembled his shoes while he was sleeping. He sells the shoes, buys more materials, and then leaves the materials out overnight. More shoes are assembled, and more materials bought.

Eventually, the cobbler and his wife decide to hide and spy on whoever is making the shoes. When they discover that the work is being done by two naked elves, the cobbler and his wife make clothes for the elves. The elves take the clothes, dance around, leave, and are never seen again. The cobbler and his wife lived happily ever after.

Personally, I think that the story could have been better crafted. However, I was not consulted.

PART ONE

Prologue

Wind howled through mountains capped in pure cold. High above the world below, a secluded stronghold had been shaped directly into the cliffs. In this place beyond civilization, only a single man drew breath. However, Azamond was never alone in his sanctum. Intricately carved crystal statues attended him silently, each a unique interpretation of human form. Even in their stillness, the life inside them could not be denied. Endowed with animus by the will of the wizard, light pulsed faintly within each of their prismatic chests.

Elevated above his ever vigilant servants, Azamond stood on a scaffolding that he himself had raised from the floor of his resplendent studio. Hand outstretched, the wizard caressed the cheek of his greatest work. Granite yielded under his touch as he shaped the face. He poured more than life into the stone; he gave it love. The effort exhausted him quickly, leaving him unable to finish more than half the face. Despite the cost, he was committed to his work. It was a tremendous undertaking of untold ambition. When completed, his work would be an eternal monument to the power of life itself.

Azamond stepped away from the massive sculpture, moving to lean on the rail of the scaffolding. The wizard appraised his work, pleased at how he had captured the idea of feminine grace.

What he had wrought was only a promise of what would come to be. He sent his will into the scaffolding, causing it to bend and twist upon itself as it lowered him to the chamber below.

The wizard took pleasure at the feel of the stone beneath his feet as he reestablished his connection to the stronghold. Azamond could feel the energies in the air as he worked, but it could never compare to the intimacy of stone. Each of the stones that tiled the floor of the stronghold had been collected from diverse lands. They provided the stronghold with connections to places of power, both known and forgotten. However, to the wizard, they were more than merely a means to power. He regarded every one of them as a separate work of art he must preserve and cherish.

A lithe, crystal form offered its master a rich russet colored robe that had been embossed with golden, geometric designs. Azamond covered his own nude body and then allowed himself a moment to appreciate the beauty of his servant.

An explosion rocked the stronghold, the echoes rumbling through the stone halls. Azamond panicked. He could only think of one thing that might have the raw power to force its way into his home. A being of unstoppable will and dark purpose. A thing that was itself more impossible than the breaching of his domain.

The wizard felt his connections to the world beyond broken as the dark thing approached. He could feel the stones crushed with malicious contempt. Azamond's panic turned to terror. The stronghold began to tremble. He could feel his servants die in violent surges.

He stared into the open entry to the halls beyond. There was nothing he could do. Shattered crystal flew across the entryway in a spray. There was nowhere he could flee. The thing that he feared most entered the chamber. In desperation, Azamond drew on what power was still available to him. He focused on the essence of stone, preparing his defenses.

The crystal servant beside him rushed forward, only to be swept aside in a shower of crystal shards that scattered across the floor. Distant rooms collapsed under the weight of the mountain. Fire struck the wizard, instantly stripping away his defenses. Azamond fell to his knees in torment as the flames took him. He screamed in agony, reaching out in beseech of mercy.

There was no mercy in what had come for him.

One

Belac struggled to remain conscious. Awareness had proven itself elusive, slipping from the grip of his mind like fog straining through his fingers. A bustling tavern in Aldenon was the last of his clear memories, leaving him with the mystery of whether he was the victim of poison, or of violence. He vaguely remembered being on a boat of some kind, but it was exceptionally difficult for him to think at the moment. Regardless of how he may have come to be in his current circumstance, he had no idea where he was. A deep need for self-preservation clawed its way to the forefront of his addled mind and urged him to discover more.

Belac's head rolled to the side and then up. He was being dragged between two appallingly ugly men. Most men were ugly to him, so the information did little to help him determine where he was or what had happened. *It must have been one of the men from the tavern,* he thought to himself. He tried to remember its name and failed. Belac decided that wherever he had been, he must have smiled at the wrong woman.

"Yeah, the elf here I get," one of the men said with the thick accent of sailors. "But why go back for a chest, and a heavy chest at that, filled with stuff he ain't got no use for anymore, and we ain't allowed to so much as open? I ask you that! Way I see it, a box can just as easily sit in a room elsewhere, without us having to drag it."

"True point, and right said," the other man replied as they dropped the elf face down on a cold, stone floor.

Belac attempted to rise, but he was only able to get one elbow under himself before a metal gate slammed shut behind him. *I think I might be in prison,* he speculated grimly. The sound of a bolt locking into place confirmed the elf's suspicion.

"But I ask you this," the second man continued. "You see all the empty we passed getting here? Seems to me, they got cells that want filling. Seems to me, it would be better for us both if they was full up with chest, boxes, and crates before them that hired us get to thinking real clever like on how we should be paid."

"Fine thinking that. But consider this. What..." The first man said as he moved beyond the elf's hearing.

Belac shook his head and a lock of long, black hair fell forward in front of his face. Rolling onto his side and then his back, he tucked the stray lock behind one of his pointed ears. *I liked it better when I didn't know where I was.* His azure eyes gazed up into the shadows that clung to the ceiling of his cell. As his vision adjusted to the dim lighting, pain seemed to seep in through his eyes. *Maybe I should just go back to sleep and hope that I wake up somewhere else.* He closed his eyes and fell into a darkness far greater than the shadows above him.

The scraping of stone on stone brought Belac awake. He sat up and surveyed his cell once more. It looked like what he would have expected an evil dungeon to look like. He was not sure how dungeons in the holy bastions of good differed, but he was convinced that there would be something to tell them apart. *Maybe music or something.*

Walls, floor and ceiling; all were constructed of a dull gray stone that had been poorly shaped into irregular blocks. There was nothing else in the room, no bed, no blanket, no chair, not even a bucket for necessity. *I don't think that I am going to like it here.* The elf put his right hand on the floor and swung his right leg under himself. Then his bare feet pressed down on the cool stones as he rose to a standing position. *Obviously, whoever built this place doesn't have any pride in their work.*

Through the bars that held him prisoner, Belac saw a dim passageway that separated him from a wall of shadowed cells. In the cell across from his own, a crouched shape moved at the edge of the light. A dwarf, unkempt and raggedly clothed, had dug his thick fingers into the loose mortar between the floor stones and pried up the largest of the oblong slabs. *Is he trying to dig his way out? I know that dwarves like tunnels, but that is going to take a really long time.* The dwarf wedged one end of the slab between the bars of his cell door and the stone wall in which it was set. *Oh. Yeah, that's a better idea.* Metal screeched as the dwarf heaved against his stone lever, the lower hinge of the door pulling free from the wall. *It's working!* Hastily, the dwarf moved the slab away from the bars of his cell and then placed it beside the doorway, just out of sight. *Wait. What's he doing now?* Belac watched in confusion as the dwarf inexplicably proceeded to lie down on the recess that had been left by the removal of the floor stone. *Is he going to sleep?!*

"What are you up to, Elf?" asked an angry man in a grimy, blue tunic. "Well?! Don't just look at me like you're stupid, Elf!" The guard kicked the elf's cell door hard enough to make it rattle in its frame. "What are you doing in there?"

Belac had neither seen nor heard the guard's approach, and was at a total loss as to what he should say. "Nothing," the elf ventured.

The guard was unconvinced. "Nothing don't make that kind of noise, Elf. If I have to..." He turned around at the clangoring sound of metal.

With the force of his whole body, the dwarf whipped the floor stone up and across the guard's face. The man fell onto his back in front of Belac's cell. What was left of the guard's face could hardly be described as one. As Belac looked down on the man's ruined face with pity, the dwarf brought the slab down on the guard's head. There was a sick crushing sound, and then there was a floor stone where a man's head had once been. *That is less blood than I would have expected.* Belac was brought to attention by the snapping fingers of the mad little dwarf.

"Hey." The dwarf snaped his fingers again. "Hey, are you with me in there?" the dwarf asked as if he had not just murdered a prison guard in the middle of what the elf felt certain was a very large prison.

Belac turned his head to look down at the dwarf and into his pale gray eyes. *I can never tell how old dwarves are.* Dwarves lived every bit as long as elves, but to Belac, they all looked the way humans did in their middle age. The dwarf was the strangest one that Belac had ever seen. He had the hard face of a dwarf, but in place of a beard there was only stubble. The dark hair that covered his hair was so jagged that it looked as if the dwarf may have cut it himself without the use of a mirror. *Maybe he had to break the mirror and use a shard to get the job done.* Despite being dressed in the same ill-fitting canvas as Belac, the cloth did little to mask the dwarf's stout build.

Upon noticing the dwarf's bare feet, Belac muttered, "We should get shoes." *Making us go barefoot is just mean.*

The dwarf barked a short laugh before bending to collect the jailer's keys. "Right. About that," he said, sorting through the keys. "That's where you come in." After selecting a key, he began unlocking the elf's cell.

Wisely, Belac waited for the cell door to be opened before asking, "Me? What do you want me to do about it?" Then he added, "Hey, wait! Is that some kind of elf, cobbler joke?"

The dwarf laughed softly. "It is now." His laughing sounded almost painful. "No, that's not what I meant. When they dragged you in here, those two fools were complaining about a chest. I'm hoping that you might know where they stored that chest."

Belac slowly shook his head, unsure how the dwarf would react. "I don't even know how I got here. Or where here is for that matter," he admitted as he stepped out of his cell.

Surprisingly enough, the dwarf only nodded his head as if to say that he had expected as much. "Do you think you can lead us back the way you came in? As much as you do remember, that is?"

"Sure." Belac was in fact not sure of that at all. The only thing he was sure of was that he was not going to just stand there next to an open cell and a dead guard while the dwarf ran off, presumably to murder a few more people in protest of such obviously false imprisonment.

The dwarf bent down and shoved the floor stone away from the guard's corpse. He then unbuckled the dead man's belt before standing to secure the belt around his own waist. He pointed down with his jaw. "I don't think it will do much good, but put that tunic on." He reached down and picked up the guard's truncheon. "And try not to get too much blood on it if you can." He slid the truncheon through a leather loop on the belt. "And go ahead and grab his shoes too if you think they will fit."

"Too small," Belac said as he removed the guard's tunic.

"You, or the boots?" the dwarf asked.

"Does it matter?" Belac asked in turn.

The dwarf gave a soft rasp of amusement. "Probably not, but it's hard to know what might matter until it does," the dwarf replied enigmatically. He looked down and made the approximation for himself. Then he grabbed the man's ankle and dragged the body into the elf's empty cell.

Belac grimaced at the bloody tunic, but then put it on over his canvas shift. *This thing smells like old cheese.*

Looking at the elf in his newly donned blue tunic, the dwarf said, "Yeah, that's not going to help even a little bit." He started walking to a nearby corridor. "Let's go."

Belac wondered how he was expected to lead them back the way he had been brought, without actually being able to lead. He decided to not say anything since he did not know where he was going anyway. It quickly vexed Belac that the arrangement worked out so much better than he thought it should have. Whenever they came to a turn or branching, the dwarf would hold up a fist and first cautiously check the corridors for roaming guards before looking to Belac for direction. The dwarf knew what he was doing.

Before long, the elf had no idea which way to go, and he was fairly certain that he could not have found his way back to their cells had he wanted to. Not that he wanted to. He resolved to confess at the next juncture, but when the dwarf held up his fist and stopped their progress, Belac faltered. It was suddenly a vicious looking fist.

"Two guards." The dwarf's voice was low. "Stay quiet."

Stay quiet?! Belac was an elf. Elves were quiet by nature. *Dwarves! Dwarves are the loud ones!* He narrowed his icy azure eyes at the dwarf. He was just about to say something when his demented little companion stepped out into the corridor. Quietly.

The dwarf slid the truncheon from his belt as he casually walked up behind the guard on the left. He jumped up and brought the butt of the weapon down on the back of the man's neck. The guard fell limply, drawing the attention of the other guard. The dwarf swung the end of the truncheon to the right in an upward arc that slammed into the other guard's throat. The guard clutched at his damaged trachea and tried to back away. With his left hand, the dwarf gripped the man's trousers at the knee and then hammered the fisted truncheon into the man's hip. The man was wrenched backward violently, and his head whipped onto the stone floor. Belac cringed at the sight.

The only noises made had come from the blows themselves and the collapse of the guards. Then the dwarf passed through a cased doorway and out of sight. *This is insane! That crazy dwarf is going to run around, murdering everyone! He is going to get me killed!* Belac debated whether he should break away on his own or go help the dwarf. It occurred to him that he had not heard any sounds of struggle from the room ahead. He wondered if something was wrong with his fabled elven hearing.

The dwarf's head popped out of the room and saved Belac the decision. With an impatient gesture, the dwarf waved the elf over. Then he bent down, grabbed each of the dead men by an ankle, and pulled them into the room. Hesitantly, Belac followed.

Two

Belac stepped into a small room, finding a table and chairs on the right, two dead guards in the center, and a dwarf standing next to a pair of storage trunks on the left. *I should have stayed in my cell. I should have waited for the dwarf to go away. And then I should have snuck off in the opposite direction.* Belac closed his eyes. *Now, I'm going to die in this stupid prison.*

"Guard the door," the dwarf said as the elf entered

Belac opened his eyes and looked at the cased opening. "Uhm, there is no door…"

"Fine," the dwarf said, waving his hand dismissively. "Then stand in the door shaped hole in the wall and keep a lookout." He then began dragging one of two large trunks away from the wall.

As Belac moved to comply, he asked, "Why am I on lookout?" Looting sounded much more appealing to him.

Without pausing from his task, the dwarf said, "You have the pretty blue shirt."

"It's covered in blood!" Belac complained. "Anyway, you said that it wouldn't be any help."

The dwarf bent to take hold of the second trunk. "Well, it can't hurt much either."

Belac looked back to find that the dwarf had placed one corner of the second trunk on the lock of the first. "Then, you wear it," he told the dwarf.

"What? That thing would be a dress on me." The dwarf climbed up onto the trunk. "We are trying to avoid detection," he said before jumping up and stomping down on the edge of the trunk.

"Stop that!" Belac hissed at him. "You're going to get us caught!".

Grinning, the dwarf jumped again. This time the hinge holding the lock ripped free from the trunk. He hopped down and shoved the top trunk off the lower one, the clamor loud in the small room.

"We need to be quiet!" Belac complained in a hushed but angry voice.

The dwarf lifted the lid of the unlocked trunk enough to look inside, then he quickly closed it and began to rearrange the trunks. "You are a terrible lookout." He straitened and made a turning motion with one finger. "Look. Out."

"Oh, excuse me all to death!" Belac replied. "I didn't know that you were going to call out to every guard in the prison! What am I supposed to do now? Count how many men come running to kill us?!"

"That would be handy to know," the dwarf answered before stomping down on the rearranged trunks. It only took a single attempt to remove the second lock.

Belac's fingers clawed at the air between him and the dwarf.

The dwarf hopped down, shoved the top trunk off the lower one, and then flipped open the lid of the second trunk. "Right on," he said happily to himself. Raising his voice, he ordered, "Hey, get in here."

Belac glanced out into the corridor. "What about keeping a lookout?"

"We made too much noise. Speed might be more important now." The dwarf began rummaging through the open chest.

"We?! 'We' made too much noise?" Belac was indignant. "Did you even think to try one of the keys?" He bent down, grabbed a set of keys off one of the dead guards, and shook it at the dwarf.

The dwarf frowned. "Do you really think that any of those finger sized keys are going to fit in one of these tiny locks?" He kicked one of the locks.

Belac simply stood there. Something was wrong with the world. Crazy, psychotic little dwarves were not supposed to notice things that an elf could miss.

Irritated, the dwarf huffed. "Are you going to argue about everything?" He pointed at the other trunk with his whole hand. "Put that gear on."

Brightening, Belac asked, "Is that my stuff?"

"Does it matter?" the dwarf asked, still irritated. "It looks like it's better than an old cloth sack and a bloody rag."

Belac narrowed his eyes at the dwarf's back, but then went to the trunk in hope. When he opened the lid, he was amazed to find that his belongings were inside. He briefly wondered who had undressed him. The first image that came to mind was that of a portly fellow with a bald spot. He instead decided to picture three giggling barmaids, and questioned if sometimes the truth was better avoided.

Belac turned his back to the dwarf, disrobed, and dressed quickly in his tailored black trousers and boots. Then he crawled into his puffy white shirt before donning his black leather fencing vest. He was smiling by the time he picked up his sword belt with four blades sheathed in silver accented black leather. On each side was a matching set of rapiers with silvery guards, complemented by slim poniards. Even his coin purse was there. *I might think I was lucky. That is, if I had not woken up in a labyrinth with an insane dwarf bent on mass homicide.*

His mood heightened, Belac strapped on his sword belt. Then he drew on of his rapiers as he spun to face the dwarf and let out a playful, "Ha!"

The dwarf slapped the blade aside and punched Belac square in the gut.

"Stop that," the dwarf admonished.

Bent over, Belac looked up and slightly sideways at the dwarf. He was outfitted in a loose-fitting suit of dull, splotchy gray material that to Belac, did not look soft enough to be called clothing. The loose cloth was held in place by belts of faded leather that secured pouches and an array of sheathed knives. Next to the dwarf's similarly faded leather boots was the strangest backpack that Belac had ever seen. Fashioned from the same materials that the dwarf now wore, the pack was fixed to an odd metal frame next to a wide, leather scabbard.

The dwarf reached into his trunk and took out a long, darkly stained wooden device with a short handle that protruded from one end at an angle. He slid the device into the scabbard on his rucksack and then swung the pack onto his back. After tightening the pack's straps with practiced hands, he walked past Belac and stuck his head out into the corridor. After a moment, he leaned back inside and looked at the elf.

The dwarf seemed to be considering something. Finally, he said, "We need to move."

Belac straightened as best he could and nodded. As he followed the dwarf out into the corridor, the dwarf quickly turned, grabbed Belac's sword belt, and then swung him back into guard room. Belac opened his mouth to ask the dwarf what he thought he was doing, but it was promptly covered by a calloused hand.

A man's voice came from the corridor outside. "How was I to know them other cells would be the wrong ones. They are the same ones we used last time. Seems to me, they should tell a man where he needs to go, before he drags someone off. It's not right I tell you."

Belac could hear them now. For the first time, he was glad that the dwarf was sharp. Initially, Belac thought that the men outside were the same two that had carried him to his cell. However, their conversation soon made it clear that was not the case. He nodded and the dwarf removed his hand.

"Right or not, we got to do it. You think listening to you bellyaching makes it better?"

"Bellyaching you say! You're the one always going on about the place being too big for nothing."

"What do I know about dungeons? Other than: they pay, we work."

Hiding behind the dwarf, Belac waited for the men to pass by the guard room before he dared to peek out into the corridor.

One of the men nodded his head toward a half-conscious man that they were dragging along between them. "I hope you at least know where we have to take this one."

"It's just up round that way. But we can ask the next guard we find and be sure like."

"If we can even find one. They need signs in this place."

"Yeah, with big arrows on them telling the way."

Belac looked down, wanting to judge the dwarf's response. The dwarf, however, was not there. Belac looked back up to see that a dwarf, who looked very much like the little madman he had been following, was walking up behind the three men. The dwarf had a knife in each hand. *He is going to get us killed! I am going to die.*

"Arrows ain't going to help. What, you think there is only one place to go? There would be arrows everywhere, pointing every which way."

"That's why you make them different colors, you stupe."

"Ain't enough colors in the..."

The dwarf drove a blade into the side of the man on the left, causing him to drop the prisoner that he helped carry. When the other man looked over in surprise, the dwarf swiped his other blade across the man's throat. Finally, the dwarf darted back to the first man on the left and stabbed him in the neck. The dwarf pulled his knives free as the man collapsed to the floor, then he looked down at the prisoner. Dressed in the same canvas that had been supplied to Belac and the dwarf, the prisoner was a frail looking man. Dirty and bald, the man appeared to have lived a rough life.

"Grab an ankle," the dwarf told him.

Awake with fear, the old man shifted as if he meant to run. The dwarf's only warning was a slight cant of his head. It was enough. The man did as he was bid, climbing to his feet and then dragging one of the corpses after the dwarf and into the guardroom. Behind them, they left a trail of blood smeared against the stone floor.

Looking at the growing pile of bodies in the guard room, Belac decided that his only hope seemed to be that just the right number of guards ran into them. Enough to give the dwarf someone to murder other than an elf named Belac, but not so many guards that they got past the dwarf and killed that same elf.

Belac motioned with his hands. "Why didn't you just let them pass by? They obviously didn't hear us."

The old man scowled at the elf.

The dwarf mumbled something under his breath that the elf could not quite make out. *It sounded an awful lot like 'stupid elf' was in there somewhere.*

"What was that?" Belac asked. When the dwarf faced him, Belac thought that maybe he should ask fewer questions.

"Where do you think they were going?" the dwarf asked him.

Immediately, Belac understood. *To our cell block.* He narrowed his eyes at the dwarf. *This is his fault. Somehow.* Instead of answering, Belac asked, "Well, do you have to kill everyone? We could have made one of them tell us how to get out of here."

"Not worth the risk," the dwarf explained. "They might sound off an alarm before we convinced them to cooperate. Even then, we would have to trust them to show us or tell us the right way. I'm not all that trusting." He paused for a moment to let that sink in. "Then, after all that, I would still have to kill them anyway."

Belac looked at the old man. "Do you know the way out?"

"I, I believe that I may." The old man was not very convincing.

Still, that was not the answer Belac had been expecting. Movement from the corner of the room made the elf jump back. The pile of bodies was moving. He exhaled deeply at seeing the dwarf tugging on one of the legs.

"What are you doing? We can't take that with us." Belac paused. "We are not taking it with us, are we?"

The dwarf gave another of his painful sounding barks that passed for a laugh. "Some of it, yeah."

Belac stared at the dwarf. He could not fathom what use the corpse could be, but he was certain that he did not want to try running through the halls of the prison, dragging a dead guard like some kind of holiday sled.

"Get his boots off," the dwarf told the elf. Then he pointed at the old man, again using his entire hand. "You. Lose the beggar suit."

Belac looked down at the body. It was one of the two men that the dwarf had clubbed to death. The dead guard let out a moan. *Maybe not so dead.* The dwarf stomped down on the man's head. There was a sickening sound that Belac would never forget. Both he and the old man stared at the dwarf.

"What?" the dwarf asked, his hands held apart in an impatient gesture.

"I thought he was already dead," Belac replied weakly.

"Yeah, I kind of thought he was too," the dwarf admitted. "Must have just knocked him out. Well, he's dead now." He nodded to the body. "Get his pants off too."

"The man does indeed look dead to me," the old man offered a little belatedly.

"Well, then he must be," the dwarf said while removing the guard's tunic. "All must bow before the will of a tribunal." There was something particularly bitter in the dwarf's phrasing.

The dwarf tossed the old man a wad of blue tunic. The old man had the presence of mind to not need to be told what to do with it. Once the old man had changed into the guard's tunic, Belac handed him the trousers and boots.

The old man put the trousers on quickly and then stomped his feet into the boots. To finish the disguise, the dwarf buckled a guard's belt around the man's waist.

Belac smiled. "Now we have a guard that knows the way out."

"Great, let's go," the dwarf grumbled with less enthusiasm than the elf suddenly had.

Before leaving, the old man bent down and grabbed an additional truncheon and a set of keys. He smiled feebly as he tucked them into his belt.

"Good thinking," Belac said to the old man as they followed the dwarf out into the corridor.

Three

Belac thought that the dwarf should have been more inspired, now that they had a guide. "He says that he knows the way out. That's a good thing, right?"

The dwarf glanced at the elf irritably. "If he does. To tell you the truth, I was starting to think that you didn't know which way to go back there." The dwarf gave a small smile and shook his head. "But, that worked out well enough. Maybe this will too."

The old man's back straightened. "What? You think me false?" He looked at the dwarf, trying to gauge his disposition. "Then, why would you follow me thus far?"

In fact, they were not actually following the old man so much as he was following them. They were progressing through the complex much the same as the elf and dwarf had before. The only change was that the dwarf now looked to the old man for direction.

"Be quiet," the dwarf hushed. "I didn't say that I don't believe you. But right now, it doesn't really matter if I believe you or not."

They had come to an intersection of corridors. The dwarf checked left from the right side of the corridor, then right from the left side. Every time the dwarf did this, Belac wondered why he did not just peek around the corners.

The dwarf seemed satisfied, but instead of continuing on, he took a few steps back away from the intersection and faced the old man. "I don't know where I am." The dwarf pointed his hand at the elf. "He doesn't know where we are." His hand moved to the old man. "You say, you know which way to go. Maybe you do, maybe you don't. Without you, we would just have to guess. I haven't taken the time to figure the odds, but I am pretty sure that me guessing would not be much better than taking direction from you. So, that is what we are going to do. Now, be quiet, and pay attention."

Now that Belac had his blades back, he almost wished he could fight openly instead of having to sneak around waiting for someone to catch them. He kept his voice low but asked, "Why are you suddenly so worried? Just a moment ago, you were smashing open boxes, and no one heard anything. This place is huge, and we have seen like what, five guards? Even those sailors mentioned how few guards this place has. It's not like any of the other ones we ran into gave us much trouble." *Whoever had been responsible for the recruiting had some obviously low standards.*

The dwarf was growing more impatient. "Well, 'few guards' still means guards. As in, more than one. It only takes one to sound an alarm. Do you have any idea how many a 'few guards' might be for a place this size? If we want out of here, we need to do it quiet."

The old man, handling the stress poorly, asked, "And where exactly is here!" He waved his arms around dramatically. "It is just a bunch of empty rooms!" He tried to open a nearby door. The rough wood barely moved in its frame. "Locked, empty rooms!"

Belac could not help but grin. "You know, that is kind of what a prison is before they fill it."

The old man gave the elf another scowl, then opened his mouth to speak.

The dwarf spoke first. "Enough." His voice was calm but his tone hard. "Get a hold of yourself, or I will leave you gaged, tied, and unconscious on the floor."

Belac did not doubt the dwarf in the slightest. He had not known him long, but he could still tell that the dwarf was serious. *He might even just kill the old sod.* The elf looked on, wondering if the old man could reign in his growing panic. Belac decided that he liked having the old man with them. He would serve as a type of buffer; someone that the dwarf was more likely to kill before moving on to his elven companion.

The old man nodded.

The dwarf walked back to the intersection and checked it again. He looked back to the old man. "Just point," he instructed.

The old man indicated they should go left. With a short nod, the dwarf set off in that direction. As they followed, Belac inspected the old man. By all appearances, he seemed sufficiently cowed. However, the elf thought that he could sense some hidden reserve in the old man, something held back in waiting. *I guess no one likes being threatened.*

They moved quickly through the prison. The dwarf made no complaints. Therefore, Belac suspected they moved quietly as well. At every crossing and every corner, the elf expected them to run into a group of guards or a patrol of some sort or another. And every time, the anticipation grew stronger. He almost began to dread the empty corridors as much as the thought of discovery. When they finally came to a guard, Belac felt a little let down by the event.

The guard was asleep. Sitting on a stool, leaning back against the wall, the guard was snoring softly. Belac found himself wanting to strangle the man. After having spent so much time and effort trying to stealth their way through the prison, the sleeping guard seemed to mock them. In one simple act of incompetence, the man had somehow invalidated any sense of accomplishment the elf may have had. Never mind the fact that their small group of three were lucky to still be alive.

Belac took a step forward, his eyes intent on the guard. He was held back by the dwarf's grip on the back of his belt.

"Easy there, Buddy." The dwarf was grinning. "Let me check something before you go running off like a crazy person."

Belac turned and narrowed his eyes at the dwarf. *Crazy person? Me?!*

The dwarf must have misunderstood the look. He chuckled and said, "Don't worry. If this doesn't work, I'll let you kill him."

Misunderstanding or not, the sentiment made Belac feel better. *What is wrong with me?* Prison was no place for an elf. That was all there was to it.

The dwarf reached over his shoulder and grabbed the handle of the box-like device that Belac had watched him holster earlier. He pulled the device free from its scabbard and pumped a sliding lever on the underside. With a practiced motion, he unsnapped one of the leather pouches on his belt, revealing two rows of miniature, metal arrows. *Dwarves. Can't even make arrows right.* Without pausing to look, he drew one of the arrows from the pouch. *Can't even call them arrows if you think about it.* He slapped the arrow into a slot on the top of his device and raised it to stare across the top. There was a soft thrak and the arrow shot away too fast for Belac to follow. The arrow took the sleeping guard in the head, throwing him from his seat as the projectile passed through and clanged against the wall farther down the corridor.

The dwarf chuckled as he lowered his strange weapon. "I almost feel sorry for the guy."

It was the old man who responded. "Do not bother feeling any pity for men such as these."

The dwarf gave the old man an odd look. "You know something I don't?"

The old man stared back, obviously confused.

The dwarf tried to clarify. "Something about the guards in particular, that is. Do you know who they are? We didn't think to ask you earlier."

"No. No, I do not know who they are." The old man was still a little perplexed. "Why? Do you know who they are?"

"No," the dwarf said. "Far as I can tell, they are just your average everyday guards. If kind of bad at their job. Most of them are probably decent enough people."

"Wait a moment. You do not think that these guards are bad men? I do not understand. If you know that they are merely doing their job, and you do not believe them to be villains, then how can you be so untroubled in killing them?" His confusion was only growing, and it was making his odd way of speaking more pronounced.

"One has nothing to do with the other. I don't need to hate someone to kill them." The dwarf thought about it for a moment. "Yeah, I have even killed people that I liked before."

The old man stammered, "But, I mean, why would you want to kill them. If they are just doing their job..."

"These guys are between me, and the way out. Between me and my freedom." The answer was simple for the dwarf. "Being the nicest guy in the world won't save you from that."

Somewhat more familiar with the diminutive psychopath, Belac was quite comfortable with changing the topic. "How can you have a crossbow without, you know, a bow on it?"

"It has a lasserite spring," the dwarf told him.

"A Lassa-whats-it?" Belac thought the dwarf might be making words up.

"Lasserite." The dwarf explained, "It gives off more force than you put on it."

"Ah," Belac said holding up a finger. "Magic spring"

"No, it's not..." The dwarf was growing impatient. "Yeah. Sure. Magic."

Belac did not notice the condescension. "That makes it a what? Magic-bow? Spring-bow?"

The old man was more comfortable with the new line of discussion. "No, that cannot be it. It does not have a bow. It would not make any sense for it to have 'bow' in the name."

"What then?" Belac asked. "Magic-spring-arrow-throwing-box-of-death?"

"It's called a springer." The dwarf was exasperated. "Can we move on now?" He motioned around them, reminding the other two where they were.

Returned to purpose, the three continued down the corridor toward the dead guard and the cell block that he had been guarding.

After a couple of paces, the dwarf said, "And they are not arrows. They are called darts."

"Does it matter?" Belac did not think so.

"It does if you want someone to hand you a dart when you ask for one," the dwarf told him. "That is kind of why we give things different names in the first place."

"Fine," the elf conceded. "Just as well, I guess. They don't look much like proper arrows anyway."

"That's because they are not arrows," the dwarf insisted stubbornly.

Four

From directly past the dead man came faint voices and the sound of muffled movement. The old man stepped closer to the dwarf, only to be casually shoved away. He stumbled and almost fell, but the dwarf spared him no attention.

With the same quick movements as before, the dwarf had another bolt loaded into his springer. Belac stopped next to the old man, and watched as the dwarf skulked forward and disappeared around the corner of the next corridor. All Belac could hear was the sound of his own breath. He found himself expecting it to turn to mist. He envisioned the temperature dropping as a hoard of ghost came charging out to avenge their recent murder and to continue guarding the prison even after death. He was more than a little relieved when instead of undead guards, or live ones for that matter, the dwarf reappeared from the corridor.

"Bring the keys," the dwarf told the old man while unloading his springer.

Trying to be helpful, Belac asked, "Do you want me to go get the little metal arrow thing for you?"

"The dart?" the dwarf corrected. "Sure."

As he hurried to retrieve the dart, Belac wondered if being helpful would be enough to keep the dwarf from killing him.

Along the way he picked up a small piece of stone that had broken from the wall when struck by the bolt. The stone seemed more brittle than he would have expected. *Maybe ask the dwarf?* Dwarves were supposed to know about rocks. When Belac picked up the dart, he stared down at the thin blood smeared along its silvery surface. It was a violent reminder that he knew nothing about the dwarf. There was no way to tell if the strange little creature would know anything about rock, or stone, or anything else for that matter. *He is about as much like a dwarf as this thing is an arrow.*

Rock in one hand, dart in the other, Belac turned down the corridor after the other two escapees. The old man was attempting to open one of the cells while the dwarf kept watch. Belac walked up to the dwarf and offered him both the rock and the dart.

"What's that?" the dwarf asked.

"It's a dart. Okay," Belac said, "I get it. It's called a dart."

"I know it's a dart," the dwarf affirmed, taking it away from him. "What's," he nodded to the rock, "that?"

Belac looked at his other hand. "Oh. It's a rock"

The dwarf shook his head. "You are killing me, Elf."

"With a rock?" Belac asked, confused.

"No, not with a..." The dwarf took a moment to compose himself. "Why are you trying to hand me a rock?"

"You broke it off the wall with your dart." Before the dwarf could respond, Belac continued, "Look how brittle it is. Who makes a prison out of something like this?"

The old man clapped a hand to his thigh. "Got it!"

A cell door opened and a slim man with long, dirty blond hair walked into the corridor. His hair fell in front of his face as he looked down and made a show of dusting himself off. Though the attempt had little effect, he seemed satisfied enough when he looked up. He ran a hand through his hair, brushing it back. His face was delicate while still being handsome. He looked very pleased with himself, though it could have simply been that he was just happy to be out of his cell.

Belac had what he felt was a completely reasonable dislike of attractive human males. Humans were meant to be average in every way. *That is what 'average' means.* For as long as humans had been humans, they had possessed a tendency to club to death any other human that was different in any significant way. That the attractive ones might escape this fate seemed unfair.

"Did they at least throw things at you?" Belac asked without thinking.

"What?" The young human was understandably confused.

"Never mind," Belac replied and then turned to inspect the cells on the other side of the corridor.

The elf stepped over to the closest cell to better see into the unlit space. Chained to the wall in the back of the cell, hung a man of imposing proportions. The man was bare chested, displaying the bulging muscles of his upper body and a gaping wound in his mid-section. Blood and organs had spilled down the front of the man and onto the corpse of a dead wolf. The smell of death was still faint. Whatever had happened in that cell, had happened recently.

Belac backed away, not wanting to even consider what might have transpired in that cell. He looked to the other cells, worried what else he might find. Behind him, another cell door opened. The elf dreaded what he might see, but he turned all the same. When he saw the woman that walked out of the cell, Belac thought that he might be imagining things. She was beautiful, with wicked blue eyes that gleamed from behind long bangs of wild, jet hair.

"It was the same key," the old man said, misunderstanding the elf's countenance.

The woman stopped and looked to the other escapees. "Does someone want to tell me what is going on here?" The woman's tone made her question sound more like a demand.

"We would if we but could, my dear," the old man supplied.

"We are in prison," the dwarf corrected.

The woman shifted her weight to her hip. "That's all?"

"I hope not," the dwarf told her.

"You hope not?" the woman persisted.

The dwarf crossed his arms. "Do all of your conversations go like this? Because that sounds exhausting."

The woman glowered at the dwarf.

The old man stepped away and moved to another cell. "Last one," he said as he began unlocking the door.

The cell door swung open. In the back of the cell, a shadowed form rose from a crouch. It was the most frighting thing Belac had witnessed since waking in that strange place. It was not until the creature stepped into the light, that he realized it was a person. *If an orc can be called a person.* Dark eyes were set in a gray face that was masculinity indulged to perversion. His black hair was pulled back into a braid that draped over his left shoulder.

"Why would you open the door?" Belac hissed at the old man angrily.

The dwarf's gruff laugh kept things calm. "Don't worry, Elf. He is not going to eat you."

"Right…" Belac replied unsurely.

"You are not going to eat him, are you?" the dwarf asked the orc. He sounded genuinely curious.

When the orc replied, his voice was surprisingly refined. "Not right this moment." He smiled. It did not help.

That thing belongs in a cage.

Without warning, the orc rushed at Belac, knocking him into the wall. The elf bounced off the wall and then fell onto his backside. *The crazy orc is going to kill us!* The orc ran past Belac, leaving him to watch transfixed as the gray monster charged down the corridor and then slammed through the stone wall at the end. Dust and sound punctuated the orc's exit. There was nothing but darkness in the hole left behind.

"What the..." Belac muttered as he climbed to his feet.

As the escapees walked down the corridor after the orc, the woman had the presence of mind to slide the truncheon from the dead guard's belt. *Beautiful and smart.* While Belac did appreciate how slyly she had taken the weapon, he found it a bit concerning that she did not seem to care that the man she was stealing from was dead. *Or that he has a hole in his head.* The woman would require further consideration.

As the dust began to settle, it became clear that the orc had breached the prison's intended confines. There was a small drop, but a darkened cave waited on the other side. *A way out!* The young man and woman crawled down through the hole in the wall. Without hesitating, Belac followed them down into the dim.

The orc stood tall in the shadows, looking down at a dead guard lying at his feet. The guard must have happened by and seen them escaping. The orc had then stopped him from getting away and raising an alarm. Though, with all the noise that the orc made crashing through the prison wall, it would probably have been better if anyone else had noticed the guard instead.

Belac shook his head. "There is no way that someone did not hear that."

"You think?" the woman asked rhetorically.

Belac narrowed his eyes at her.

From above, still within the prison, the dwarf called down to them. "Hey people, we have to move."

"Sure." Belac gestured around the cave. "But look what we found. A way out."

"No. No, it's not." The dwarf hopped down to join them. "This is a cave. It could go anywhere. Or it could go nowhere. You go wandering off into the dark, you are more likely to die of thirst, starvation, or a broken neck than you are to actually find a way out."

The woman turned toward the dwarf. "But can't you…" she began.

"No," the dwarf interrupted her. "And there is no time for this. We need to…"

The sound of rock shifting above turned into a thundering roar of falling stone. Moved by deep instinct, everyone scrambled away from the collapse. Then the light from the prison was cut off. Not a single ray of hope shone through the cracks.

When Belac had awoke, he had done so in pain, in prison, and with no idea as to why he was there. He could not have imagined a worse situation to be in. That was before the dark.

Five

Never before had Belac known a darkness so complete. His world had become so absent of light that his mind began to fabricate shapes, guessing at what might be there. His head darted left and right in rising panic, vainly hoping that with enough searching he might find some vestige of the light.

There was a ringing in Belac's ears accompanied by a strange howling rush that quickly faded. He started to cough, the sound joined by the coughing of the others.

"I hate you people so much," a dwarf muttered in the distance.

There was the sound of shifting debris as others began to stir. Belac sneezed.

The dwarf raised his voice and said, "Stop. Moving."

There were a few more shifts as the escapees each settled into a more stable position. Belac knew nothing but rock, dust, and the faint ringing in his ears. This was interrupted by the rustling and muttering of an angry dwarf. As the ringing in Belac's ears began to abate, sounds of life became easier for him to make out. They were not particularly happy sounds.

Over the soft sounds of misery, the woman asked, "What happened?"

There was a sharp ping that did not quite harmonize with the fading ringing in Belac's ears. He instinctually turned to the noise, finding the dwarf lit by a pale golden glow. The dwarf stood, kicked a rock to the side, and then held the light above his head. In that moment, the villainous dwarf looked more a messiah bearing an icon of salvation.

"What happened," intoned that new bringer of light. "Is that I made the mistake of letting any of you people out of your cages." With that, the moment was shattered.

The dwarf shouldered his pack and moved over to the elf's position. As the dwarf approached, Belac could see that the light was emanating from some sort of small rod. The dwarf held out a second rod that matched the first but without the glowing light. He tapped the end of the rod on a nearby rock. It produced a ping and began to glow. Though the sound died, the glow remained.

"Here, take this," the dwarf instructed, handing over the rod. "And don't lose it. Those things are expensive."

Right then, light was life. Belac had no intention of losing his. While the rod's composition was a mystery to him, the leather thong attached to the bottom was easy enough to understand. He slipped his hand through the loop and then stood up.

The dwarf began to slowly run the light of his own rod over the elf. "If it starts to go dim, just tap it on something again," the dwarf explained louder than seemed necessary. "If you need to make it stop, you have to hold the bottom end against something solid." He held the rod against a rock in demonstration. "Like this." Then he tapped it once more, and its light returned. "Understand?" he asked, looking to the others.

Oh, right. Not talking to just me. Belac, lost in the dark, captured by the successive light and the hope it represented, had forgotten about the others. *I bet that as long as I don't tell them, I will not have to pretend to be sorry about it.* He held up his rod and let the light play along the walls of the cave. While its shape was much to be expected, small and pitted with darkened alcoves, the color was wrong. The walls were a dark brown resembling the color of saturated rust.

The prison, massive as it was, had been gray. It seemed an extraordinary amount of gray stone when the surrounding rock was brown. *Whatever. I'm not a dwarf. I don't know anything about rocks. Also, I am not running around murdering everything. Proof I'm not a dwarf.*

Two more quick pings, and the young man and woman had light. It was now bright enough for the orc to confidently join them. Another ping, and he too had his own light. Though everyone was covered in dust, they all appeared to have survived the collapse uninjured. That is, until Belac saw the lower half of the old man. The upper half of the man was buried under rubble, while the lower was as still as the stones that had crushed him.

"I am going to want all those back," the dwarf told the others. "Assuming we ever get out of here." He then began running the light over each of them in much the same perfunctory way he had Belac.

Belac suddenly understood. *He is checking for injuries.*

"Have faith." The reassurance came from the young man. "We will all survive this yet."

"No one can have faith in everything," was the dwarf's sour retort. "I think I will save mine for things that are probably true."

Moving her light to search the shadows, the woman asked, "The elder?"

The dwarf pointed behind himself with his thumb. "Dead."

"How can you be so certain?" the woman accused more than asked.

The dwarf gave her an annoyed look. "I am familiar with the condition."

The silence she returned was no less annoyed.

Clearly attempting to change the topic, the man asked, "So…What was with the dramatic halt back there?"

The dwarf was obviously still annoyed. "The one before or after you people got us trapped in a cave?"

The man sighed. "After."

"You mean the one where everyone was blind, disoriented, and intent on stumbling around in the dark until they broke something or caused a larger collapse?" The dwarf was still annoyed. "That 'dramatic' halt?"

It was the woman who spoke in defense. "Hey! This is not our fault."

The dwarf closed his eyes and took a moment to collect himself before speaking. "We need to get moving. Air, water, food. We only have so much time before one of these becomes a serious problem."

"Air?" the man asked.

"We can breathe now, but after that cave in, there is no telling how long until we run out of air or it turns foul." The dwarf was already making his way over to the collapsed prison wall. "It looks like there was an access tunnel that ran along the side of the prison."

The woman was intrigued. "Used to access what?"

Belac guessed, "Maybe to build the prison?"

The dwarf shrugged dismissively. "No way to know. But it has to be the reason the wall fell out the way it did. See here?" He pointed his hand at the obstructing stones.

Everyone watched as the dwarf moved stones away from the corner where the prison rubble met the cave wall. Some, he picked up and tossed aside casually, while others he touched, only to take his hands away without moving the stone at all. Finally, he stepped back and sighed. With his whole hand, he pointed at one of the more sizable stones, one almost as large as the dwarf himself. "We have to move that one." He turned to the others. "I am going to need some help."

Instead of preparing to help, the woman asked, "Why that one?"

"Because it is in the way," the dwarf answered dryly. "And because it is the least likely to cause another collapse and kill us all."

The young man voiced his concern. "Least likely?"

The dwarf shook his head. "What part of, 'Caves are dangerous, and we could all die,' do you not understand?"

Despite the dwarf's words, Belac thought that he could almost detect a trace of humor.

The dwarf motioned to the orc and then the stone. "Come on, help me move this," he said in a tone that dismissed the others.

The orc immediately joined the dwarf in the endeavor. Belac realized that none of them had even thought to help the dwarf when he had been clearing the way. They had all just stood and watched, helpless observers. He could not have expressed why, but he felt this did not bode well for their chances of survival.

In the confines of the cave, the sound of stone grating against rock was loud enough to be worrisome. As the larger stone was tipped out of the way, smaller rocks and debris came loose and fell precariously. The escapees all held their breath in fearful anticipation. Nothing happened.

Then, Belac sneezed. While it did not cause them to all be crushed by a mountain of rock, the elf did find himself having to bear the stares of his companions. Belac held out his hands out in submission and smiled weakly.

"All right," the dwarf said, breaking the stares. "I am going to climb in there first and take a look around. If I can find a way through, the rest of you can follow after me."

The man did not try to hide his suspicion. "Why are you going first?"

The dwarf looked at the man and asked, "Do you want to go first?"

The man looked from side to side, searching the others for support.

"Right," the dwarf continued. "Then, I am going in. You all stay here and try not to do anything."

The dwarf took off his pack and placed it next to the opening. Then he crawled through with more agility than Belac would have expected from a dwarf. For the first time, Belac noticed that the dwarf's legs were longer and more proportionate than was typical for a dwarf. An arm reached out of the opening, grabbed the dwarf's pack, and pulled it back through.

The sudden movement and rustling sound startled the young man. He stepped backward into the orc and bounced off. The man turned and gazed up at the orc, but said nothing. The orc simply returned the silence. Prudently, the man returned his attention back to the opening.

Time became difficult to register as those left behind watched the opening together, left in waiting, uncertain if they would ever breathe free. The dwarf's face popped out of the hole. He appeared far more relaxed than any of the others.

"All right, people," the dwarf said. "There is definitely a way forward on the other side. It is entirely possible that we don't all die horribly."

Dark as his words sounded, they had an immediately positive impact on the others.

The woman, her voice elevated with hope, asked, "You found a way out?"

"Nope." The dwarf sounded undeterred. "I found a way past this cave-in and the certain death of staying here." He paused for effect. "But you can stay here if you want."

The young man stepped forward. "No, thank you," he said as he walked over to the opening and the escape it now represented.

The dwarf shifted his weight and held up a hand in a halting gesture. It was clear that he was not going to allow anyone through until they listened to what he had to say. "You can come through in any order you want," he informed them. "As long as the orc comes last."

"Is that so?" asked the reserved orc in a dangerous tone.

"Yes." The dwarf ignored the tone. "You are too big. You should be able to make it through, but it is going to be a squeeze. I think we might have to pull you the last bit. There's a chance that something is going to get dislodged when we try. If that happens, and this collapses, I need everyone else on the other side of it."

The orc stayed silent, calculating.

The young man gestured to the rough opening. "Can't we just, you know, make the hole bigger?"

Belac was a little surprised by the proposition. Nothing about the man had suggested that he was the type of person to volunteer for anything, much less work. As for Belac, he personally would be quite happy to leave that gray monster of an orc on the bad side of the cave. He glanced over at the orc and wisely said nothing.

"I don't think we can open it up any further." The dwarf explained, "At least, not without making things worse. None of this stone is stable. We keep digging, and there is a real chance that we all die before we ever find another way through this."

Belac believed him. There was a ruthless honesty to the dwarf. Also, his position gave the others little room to argue. The orc believed him too. Belac could see it in the nod that the orc gave and the softening of his features.

"Don't worry," the dwarf added before sliding back into the opening. "I won't kill you on purpose,"

Not helping, Belac thought. The silent laughter of the orc proved him wrong.

Six

Belac admired the orc's composure. While the opening did prove large enough for the orc to pass through, he was completely dependent on the others to pull him. With his arms stretched out and his body elongated, the orc could not have wriggled his way back out, struggle though he might. Had he chosen to struggle, the result may very well have been an avalanche of crushing stone. The others could have left him there, trapped and abandoned, and he would not have had the breath necessary to scream as they walked away.

Belac thought of the old man, buried but not forgotten. The orc too could still share that grim fate. They all could.

When the orc was finally free of the stone crawlway, Belac found himself unexpectedly relieved. His mind, frantically searching for hope and reassurance, let him believe that if the orc had not been crushed beneath rocks and stone, then none of them would be. When the orc stood, Belac even went so far as to clap him on the shoulder in a show of comradery.

The orc regarded him silently.

"Glad you're not dead." Belac meant it.

The orc nodded and stepped past him.

The dwarf had already begun to continue onward. Belac felt that the dwarf should have said something first, given some explanation or instruction. Instead, he had simply walked off, leaving the others to follow or stay there and die. It felt a little inconsiderate. *How hard would it be to say something? Something like, "Let's get moving." "This Way." or "Follow me."*

"Or at least a grunt," Belac said aloud. "It's not hard to grunt. Watch. Gerrrr." *Okay, that was a bad grunt.*

"What is wrong with you?" the man asked him. "Did you hit your head or something?"

"Did I hit my head?" Belac's eyes opened wide. "Yes, I hit my head! I hit my everything! A building fell on me!"

"Now, now, now," the woman said, putting her hand on the elf's back in a calming manner. "It's not as bad as all that. It was only part of the building."

Belac spun around to face the woman. Her blue eyes twinkled. Belac narrowed his own.

Smiling, the woman took hold of the elf's shoulders and gently turned him around before urging him onward. She was clearly enjoying his distress.

Belac resumed following the dwarf. *Crazy woman. How can she be having fun while we are all trapped in a cave with a psychotic dwarf and a bunch of glowing sticks?! All of these people are crazy! The smug human thinks he's smart. The woman thinks she's funny. The orc… is an orc. And the dwarf! The dwarf is the craziest one of all! Sure, he seems all reasonable most of the time. But what he really wants to do is kill everyone!* He was staring at the back of the dwarf's head with so much intensity that Belac suddenly worried that the dwarf, through some kind of mad dwarven sorcery, would notice the attention and turn around in a murderous rage. The elf decided to avert his eyes and began studying the tunnel instead. *I think it would be best to keep that dwarf pointed at anything not elf.*

The tunnel was wide enough that Belac could have walked down the center with both of his arms held outstretched and still not have touched the sides. He was beginning to loathe the ugly, dark brown that held him captive. Not that he cared much for the dull gray blocks of the prison wall to his right. It was easy to see why the dwarf had not bothered to offer the others any directions before he had set off. There was only one way to go. The elf tried to take comfort in the realization that at least he could not get lost. He tried not to focus on the almost complete lack of options.

"Do you think this leads out?" Belac asked the dwarf. However, reassurance from anyone would have been welcome.

"The tunnel?" asked the man in a reply that Belac found supremely unhelpful.

"Yes, the tunnel," the woman supplied. "What else could he possibly have meant?" She waved her hands around. "That is all there is." She pointed with both hands, back toward the rubble. "It is just tunnel," she swung forward, pointing, "and more tunnel."

"Thanks," Belac told her.

She looked at the elf as if he were trying to escape. "And of course, he thinks that there is a way out. Or we hope there is one anyway. How could any of us know? I have never been here before. Have you ever been here before? How about any of you? Anyone?"

No one wanted to answer her, but it was the dwarf who spoke up. "I am not looking for a way out."

That changed things.

The woman tried to change them back. "Yes, you are."

"No. I'm not," the dwarf corrected her with an obstinance found only in dwarves. "What I am looking for is a way back in."

The man asked, "Back into the prison?" He sounded hopeful.

Belac held up a finger. "I would really rather just get out."

"I'm sure you would," the dwarf allowed before explaining. "But as I keep trying to tell you people, caves and tunnels do not go where you want them to, just because you want them to. They had to bring us into the prison somehow. We know there is a way in, so we know there is a way out. I want fresh air every bit as much as the rest of you, and the best way to get it runs back through that maze of prison cells."

Compelling as the dwarf's words may have been, they could not contend with the recessed metal gate that came into view ahead on the left. The dwarf grunted.

"See!" Belac shouted. "I knew he could do it!" *I knew he could grunt!*

"Wrong way." There was resignation in the dwarf's voice.

The woman could not hide her excitement. "We have to check it."

"It's the wrong way," the dwarf said again.

"We don't know that," the woman said, undeterred.

The man rushed ahead to the gate, blowing past the others. "It's locked," he called back. Then he rattled the gate in its frame to demonstrate.

The woman joined the young man and heaved against the gate. It gave a small squeal.

"Wrong. Way," the dwarf repeated.

That was when Belac saw them. He did not know what preternatural sense alerted him, but he would have been dead without it. The first thing he noticed was the golden light reflecting from a set of shadowed eyes in the tunnel farther ahead. They alone would have been enough to give him nightmares. The fangs were worse.

"Beast!" Belac exclaimed with more confidence than he felt. He drew a rapier and pointed.

The others followed the movement, looking away from the gate and to the darkened tunnel. Muscles rippled under the thick, glossy black fur of the hunched beast. However, all Belac could focus on were the fangs; fangs too large in a snarling mouth.

The dwarf turned to the orc and ordered, "Get that open," pointing to the gate with his hand.

Belac continued to stare at the fangs as they split open and the beast let out the sound of tortured souls. The woman stepped forward fearlessly and spun her truncheon in a complicated pattern. Dirty, disheveled, and clad in nothing but bruises and tattered rags, her bravery was something to shame the heroes of history. She was the most beautiful thing the elf had ever seen. Her raven hair streaked out behind her like a war banner as she rushed forward to meet the beast.

As the woman closed on the beast, she leapt into the air, spinning around to bring the truncheon down on the beast's snout. A clawed hand swung out and tore through flesh and bone. The woman crumpled, the damage to her chest too severe for her to even scream. The beast grabbed her head and lifted her limp form up. Then it buried its maw into her chest.

It had all happed so fast, that flash of beauty to blind legend, and then death. Belac found his courage. He found it in rage. The elf charged the beast without thinking. As he did, another beast flew over the first, fangs and tortured roar. Belac stepped to the side and slashed with his rapier. The narrow blade cut through fur and flesh but only scored the bone, the damage superficial.

There was a screech of metal from the gate, answered by more of the bestial roars. The elf was forced to dodge back as the beast took a heavy backhanded swing at him. The attack left the beast's chest open. Belac lunged, his slim blade plunging in up to the hilt. The beast fell on him. Belac had missed the heart. Claws scraped against stone as the beast lifted itself up. Once more, all Belac could see were fangs. *I am going to die.* Laid out on his back under the beast, he stared up at the fangs as they split wide.

A heavy bladed knife thrust upward into the beast's neck. Using the hilt, the dwarf wrenched the mass of fur and fangs away from Belac. Blood gushed on the elf as he scooted out from under the thrashing beast. Terrified, Belac felt a resistance stopping his hand. He looked down and found his hand still in a death grip on his rapier.

His fear had taken him so completely that Belac could not remember how to let go. Determined beyond all reason, he yanked the weapon free. He staggered to his feet and looked from the bent shape of his bloody sword to a violence that matched the beast's.

Standing over the beast, the dwarf viciously stabbed his heavy bladed knife into its chest repeatedly. The visage of the dwarf's face was not one of contorted rage or bloodlust. It was hard and focused and filled with a terrible hate. A hate so strong, only something as stubborn as a dwarf could hold it back. The dwarf did not miss the heart.

"I would rather face fangs," Belac muttered.

The dwarf snaped his attention directly at the elf. The action was so intense it felt like an assault. Belac took a frightened step back, his rapier once more forgotten. The dwarf had dark blood covering his arms, chest, and face.

Belac held his arms out to his sides and said, "I'm not a monster!" fear evident in his voice.

The wail of distant roars pulled both of their attentions down the tunnel and to the dark. When Belac heard that sound of torment and rage, in his mind, he once again saw fangs. Trying to pull himself back from the dark, he looked away. It was then that he noticed three more broken mounds of fur, black and wet. He tried not to look at all the blood.

The man called urgently, "Come on!"

The wails were getting louder, the fangs closer.

"Get behind the gate," the orc said as he himself stepped out into the tunnel.

The dwarf pushed the elf toward the open gate. "Move, Elf!" he commanded impatiently.

Belac ran for the safety of the gate, the dwarf on his heels. The orc followed them both in, dragging one of the dead beasts behind him. Before Belac could form a question, tortured roars pulled his attention away. They were close now. He could hear the claws on stone and almost feel the fangs.

The dwarf slammed the gate shut, the metal clamoring in its frame. "The bolt is broken," he barked.

The orc was forced to raise his voice above the roars. "I had to get it open."

Now, Belac truly could see the fangs. The beasts were piling down the tunnel. The roars tore at the elf's mind. There were too many of them. He could not have begun to count them, but there were far too many of the beasts for the escapees to fight and survive. *Too many…*

Belac's ruined rapier was ripped from his hand. The dwarf took it and lodged it into the gates locking mechanism. It was immediately tested by a beast slamming into the gate. The dwarf pulled the elf back as a clawed hand reached through the bars. Claws raked the air, bodies rattled the gate, and tortured roars promised no escape.

Seven

They fled, pursued by roars and driven by fear. The tunnel they traveled was less than half as wide as the one now filled with claws, fangs, fur, and death. It curved gradually to the right, breaking the beasts' line of sight. At the loss of their prey, the beasts gave one final roar of frustration and rage.

Belac could hear claws on stone accentuating the sound of the pack moving away. "That is a good thing, right?" he asked in desperate optimism.

The dwarf kept his stony eyes on the path ahead. "You are going to need to be more specific."

"The beasts," Belac said in an attempt to clarify. "They are leaving. That's a good thing, right?"

"Sure," the dwarf answered. "As long as they don't know another way around. This tunnel bends back in the direction that those things came from."

Belac said nothing more. He was exhausted and his hands were shaking. He would need rest soon, but he had no way of knowing if the others would wait for him. He hated the idea of having to choose between dying on his feet from exhaustion or being left alone to be eaten by the beasts. Fangs flashed in his mind, and he resolved to shamble on.

The orc came to a halt. "A moment," he requested with polite urgency.

Belac's attention was brought back to the present. He turned around and saw that the orc had continued to drag the beast's bloody carcass along behind him. There was a trail following them as gruesome as the orc's trophy. Belac looked away. The others had stopped as well. They too seemed concerned with the orc's burden. Ahead, the tunnel began to straighten out and there appeared to be a large, jagged opening to the left.

The dwarf looked down at the dead thing that the orc had brought with them. "You can't keep it," he said humorously.

The orc shook his head. "I only need a moment."

The human sputtered, "Why would you bring that?" His hand trembled as he pointed at the body.

The orc reached over and drew one of Belac's poniards from its sheath as if it were a knife in a kitchen block. The action was so casual that it implied the blade actually belonged to the orc, and it was simply the elf's job to carry it around for him.

"Hey!" Belac cried, putting his hand over the empty sheath. He tried to think of something slightly more articulate to say, but the dwarf took him by the arm and pointed him down the tunnel in the direction from which they had fled.

"Try to catch your breath," the dwarf instructed. "But keep a look out. Mostly, listen. I am going to scout ahead a little. I will not be far. Stay sharp."

The word 'sharp' made Belac think of fangs. Fangs and dwarven knives.

The dwarf walked away without waiting for a response. It irked Belac that the dwarf would give orders and then simply expect everyone to follow them. *He's not the boss of me! I don't have to do what he tells me!* Belac wondered why he did it, why he listened to anything that the dwarf had to say. He realized that it was because the dwarf was right. Belac really did not like that.

Belac looked down at the orc busy at work. Dark hands moved with expertise as the orc cut into the beast's flesh. With a swift, practiced ease, the orc was skinning the thing. Belac looked away. He could see the dwarf standing next to the large opening ahead.

Behind the dwarf, in an almost comical attempt at stealth, the young man crept up and began handling the dwarf's pack. Belac was unsure what the man was doing, but it felt wrong. The elf knew that he had to do something about it. So, he began marching toward the strange scene. Before Belac was halfway there, the dwarf pivoted, grabbed the man's wrist, and snapped the man's arm with an upward thrust to the elbow.

The man cried out, backing away from the dwarf. "You broke my arrrr…" He continued to scream as he fell into a vast cavern.

Belac slowed to a dumbfounded stop.

The dwarf leaned out over the edge of the cavern. "Well, that's another light rod I am never going to get back."

In a daze, Belac joined the dwarf. The elf leaned over the edge and looked down where the man had fallen. There was a small, dim light, but the distance was too far to make out the man's body.

"He… He's dead," Belac stammered. *He has to be.*

"Yeah, probably." The dwarf sounded disappointed. "I didn't plan on killing him yet."

Belac moved away from the ledge and faced the dwarf. "Plan on killing him?" He was incredulous. "Yet?" Panic was seeping into his voice.

The dwarf met Belac's stare unthreateningly. "I was hoping we might be able to get some information out of him before we had to kill him," he explained. "The guy was wrong."

Joining them, the orc agreed with the dwarf, "It was his scent."

They wanted to kill the man because he smelled funny?!

The dwarf focused on the orc. "I noticed the eyes."

The orc tilted his head to the side in calculation. It was an oddly reptilian gesture. Satisfied, he nodded. Something passed between the orc and the dwarf. They shared some new unspoken understanding. *Well, I don't understand!* Belac did not like it. It was not just that the two agreed it was completely acceptable to murder people because they smelled funny or looked at one of them strange. It was that they agreed about something else, something to which the elf was not privy.

The dwarf looked at the elf. Then he leaned to the side and looked toward the way that they had come. Then he looked back at the elf. "You have got to be the worst lookout ever," the dwarf said judgmentally.

Belac could not think of anything to say in defense. He glanced out over the ledge into the cavern and tried to think of some way to blame the human. *There would be no harm in it. He's already dead. They didn't like him anyway. They planned on killing him. They did kill him!* "He did it," Belac said quickly, pointing out into the dark cavern.

"He did it?" the dwarf replied dryly.

"It was his fault," Belac corrected himself.

"Right," the dwarf said in dismissal. He turned to the orc. "Are you good?"

"Indeed," the orc affirmed, holding up a bulk of sable fur.

The two walked onward, leaving Belac to follow. The elf found it odd how alluring the glossy black fur was once it had been removed from the beast. He looked back at what was left of the skinned carcass. It was a powerful reminder to stay with the other two. *Unless they plan on killing me too.*

"Do you plan on killing me too?" Belac called after them.

"I don't plan on it." The dwarf did not stop walking.

Belac ran to catch up with the other two. *Do I smell funny?* The tunnel wound left, wrapping around the edge of the cavern below. The path had been carved into the side of the cavern's walls, giving them a view of darkness and demise as they continued on. Having to walk next to what could suddenly be a fall to his death was unpleasant, but at least they were now moving away from the beasts.

The golden glow of the lights they carried played against massive stalactites. The wet glistening rock reminded the elf once again of fangs; fangs that were still hunting them somewhere in the dark. "What are those things?" Belac asked.

The dwarf replied, "You are going to need to be more specific."

"You know exactly what I am talking about!" Belac accused the infuriating dwarf. "I'm talking about those gorilla-wolf-monsters that almost Ate! My! Face!"

The dwarf laughed at him. "Gorilla-wolf-monsters?"

"Yes! Gorilla-wolf-monsters!" Belac would not back down. "Giant animals covered in black fur with claws and fangs." With his hands above his head, he clawed at the air.

The dwarf was not looking at him.

"I know you saw them!" Belac continued. "The orc is still playing with one of the dead ones!" He pointed at the orc violently.

"One of the gorilla-wolf-monsters?" The dwarf did a poor job of holding back his amusement.

"I hope we find one," Belac fumed. "I hope we find one and it Eats! Your! Feet!" He began hopping up and down. "And I am going to dance around. And I am going to point at it. And I am going to say, 'Look! You see it? Do you see that? That's a gorilla-wolf-monster!"

Both the dwarf and the orc were laughing at him now. The orc at least had the decency to do it silently.

The dwarf composed himself and said, "Well, I guess you know what they are called then."

The orc suggested, "You can now tell the story of how you bravely fled the gorilla-wolf-monsters." His face twisted in some orcish approximation of a smile.

Belac said stubbornly, "That is not what they are called."

"It is now," was the dwarf's reply.

"No," Belac tried to redirect. "What are they called?"

"Gorilla-wolf -monsters," the dwarf said seriously before chuckling to himself.

Belac wanted to throw something at him.

"All right. All right." The dwarf made an effort to push his amusement aside. "I don't know what those things are." His tone grew more serious. "But they are dangerous. No question about that."

"Of course, they are dangerous." Belac wanted a better explanation.

"Right," the dwarf continued. "But they do die if you put enough holes in them. Also, they did not seem to coordinate all that well. I know that a tunnel does not always allow for many tactics, but all I saw back there was blind aggression. If they had more intelligence, we would probably be dead."

Mollified, Belac said, "Well, that's something."

"Maybe," the dwarf corrected. "Maybe not. Stupid can be dangerous all by itself."

"We have to call them something," Belac insisted. "Gorilla-wolf-monster' takes too long to say."

"If time is an issue, just yell 'beast' again," the dwarf conceded.

When the pathway reached the end of the cavern, it continued straight, tunneling farther into the rock. It was not until they were once more surrounded by stone, that Belac realized how oppressive the gaping dark had been. It was not only the looming fall, but the dreadful volume of emptiness. It was that the darkness had been so vast, even the magical light that they carried could not hold it back.

The tunnel soon angled down deeper into the rock. While the decline made it physically easier to continue, so too did it press on the elf that they were getting further and further from freedom. Every step down was another into the dark, and one more away from a sun that he may never feel again.

Eight

It takes precious little time before a tunnel gets boring. This is especially true for an elf. Even more so for an elf named 'Belac.' He was bloodied, bruised, exhausted, and in all fairness, lucky to still be alive. Despite it all, he had difficulty thinking about anything other than how ugly the roughly cut tunnel walls were. He looked to the dwarf and found the view no better. The orc, however, was interesting. Disgusting, but interesting none the less. He had half of his sable pelt draped over one shoulder, hanging limply behind him. The other half he worked on. He had been spitting on the underside, then folding the pelt over and rubbing it against itself.

As the orc repeated the process, Belac asked, "What are you doing?"

The dwarf answered for the orc. "He is cleaning the pelt." The dwarf seemed distracted.

"With his spit?" Belac thought that a bit doubtful. "Don't you need chemicals for that? Or is it just salt? Whatever. I'm pretty sure that tanners don't just spit on stuff." He thought that the dwarf might simply not be paying attention. *He might be lost in thought about how ugly this tunnel is. Or maybe he likes it. He is a dwarf. Maybe he likes rock the color of dirt.*

"Orcs can do that," the dwarf said offhandedly. "There is something in their saliva. It works, and it works fast."

The orc grunted in what Belac assumed was agreement.

"That's it?" Belac was unconvinced. "That is all he has to do? Just spit on it?"

"He still needs to scrape it," the dwarf explained. "It's probably best if we stop for that. That should make it a lot easier on him, and we need to stop anyway."

"We need to stop?" Belac asked.

The dwarf looked to the orc. "We will need to stop, right?"

The orc grunted, once more presumably in agreement.

"Yeah, okay," Belac allowed. "But why do we need to stop? I really kind of want to get out of here."

"My guess is that he wants shoes." The dwarf paused and thought. "Or boots maybe."

The orc grunted.

Belac's brow furrowed. "How did you guess shoes?"

"I began with the assumption that the orc is not stupid," the dwarf replied dryly.

The orc gave more of his silent laughter.

Belac did not care for the implication. "And what is that supposed to mean?"

"Calm down." The dwarf chuckled. "What was the first thing you wanted when we met?"

"We should get shoes." Belac had not been thinking intelligently at the time. Still, he decided to leave well enough alone. He could figure out how he was being insulted later.

The orc halted. "This is good."

Belac and the dwarf made room for the orc to lay out the fresh pelt. The orc then used his borrowed poniard to scrape away a nasty pink sludge. He absently flicked the poniard, slinging some of the sickening mess to the side. The elf stepped farther away. Once the orc had finished scraping the pelt clean, Belac was amazed at how quickly the orc fashioned it into boots. Without stitching, they were mostly strips of black fur wrapped around loose cuttings of the pelt.

After finishing the boots, the orc appraised what was left of the pelt and then wrapped up his forearms as well. The orc straightened from his crouch, rising to stand above his companions. Bending backward, he stretched out his spine before straightening once again. Then he twisted and flexed, testing his work.

"All right," the dwarf interrupted. "Enough preening. Let's get out of here."

As they resumed their decent, Belac smiled and asked the dwarf teasingly, "Hey. Do you stiiiiill think this is the wrong way?"

The dwarf turned and gave the elf an irritated look. "The right way is guarded by a pack of gorilla-wolf-monsters."

Belac could not help himself. "Then, are you surrrrre it's the right way?"

"But you never know," the dwarf continued as if the elf had not spoken. "It is entirely possible that we are going to have to deal with another one of those things before too much longer."

The orc asked, "Is that so?"

"What?" was all Belac could manage.

"Oh, yeah," the dwarf answered the orc. "Think about it."

Belac did think about it. He thought about tormented roars and the gleaming of fangs.

The dwarf continued, "Back there, when that gorilla-wolf-monster had the elf down, it slobbered and bled all over him."

Belac looked down at his once white shirt, now stained with dark blood.

The dwarf did not stop. "What if those things were not gorilla-wolf-monsters at all? What if they were something worse?"

Belac knew that they could not really be gorilla-wolf-monsters. He had made the name up. *What could be worse?* "No..." the elf gasped.

"Yeah." The dwarf's tone was friendly. "Have you ever met a werewolf before?"

"No..." Belac's mind raced. *They could have been...*

"Maybe you have," the dwarf suggested. "Fangs, claws, too much hair, and a bad mood. What do you think a werewolf looks like?"

"They are not real." The elf was desperate.

The orc argued, "They looked real to me."

Please...No...

"You know," the dwarf said thoughtfully. "Maybe that was not even a real prison back there. Maybe, just maybe, it was really a werewolf factory."

That would explain it. That would have explained everything. Belac stopped walking. He did not want this. He did not want to turn into one of those things. "But I don't want to be a gorilla-wolf-monster," he said miserably.

The other two stopped and turned to face him. The elf's eyes were wide and watery.

"Go like this." The dwarf opened his mouth and showed his teeth.

The orc leaned forward and sniffed at the air. He turned to the dwarf and asked, "Does that smell like dog to you?"

"Oh no!" the dwarf exclaimed, pointing at the elf. "Look at his ears! They are getting all pointy like a wolf's!"

Terrified, Belac grabbed his ears. *They are! They are pointy!*

The dwarf fell to his knees laughing.

The orc had to turn and brace himself against the wall as he laughed with him. This time the orc's laughter was not silent.

Belac, his face red, jerked his hands away from his ears. His elven and always pointed ears. "That's not funny!"

The dwarf could barely speak. "Then, you don't know what funny is."

"If I do turn into a werewolf, I am going to eat you first!" Belac told the dwarf angrily. "Then I can see what funny looks like!"

The orc stopped laughing and looked at the elf. He slapped the dwarf on the shoulder and then pointed at the elf. "Look at him. He is becoming enraged." The orc's voice was somber. "It must be a full moon."

There was more laughter while Belac stood there wishing that he could turn into a werewolf and tear off their heads. Finally, the dwarf stood up and nudged the orc's arm with the back of his hand. Then the dwarf gestured for the orc to follow him, and the two began walking down the tunnel.

Without stopping, the dwarf turned to the orc and said, "You know, if he really does turn into a werewolf, we are still going to call him a gorilla-wolf-monster."

Nine

The tunnel leveled out at what Belac thought of as the bottom. He hoped it was the bottom. Shortly after, the way was blocked by a stout, wooden door set in a matching frame. To the elf, it felt more like a barrier than a door.

"Do you think it's locked?" Belac asked without enthusiasm.

"Probably not locked," the dwarf said, but continued before the elf was encouraged. "It might be barred though."

That was worse, and the elf knew it.

"Don't worry about it," the dwarf said, sensing the elf's despondency. "That door is not going to stop us. It can be locked, barred, or even nailed to the frame. All we have to do is wait for you to turn into a gorilla-wolf-monster and break it down for us."

The orc shook his head "This plan seems unwise," he warned.

"Why do you say that?" the dwarf asked.

The orc twisted around to point at the elf. "He is standing behind us." He gestured toward the door on the other side of them.

"Oh. Right." The dwarf stepped to the side. "You go first."

Belac marched past the dwarf. The elf was angry enough that he felt like he really could smash through the door. Though now, standing in front of it, he could see that the door had a simple bolt and no sign of a more complicated lock. He took hold of the bolt and jerked it to the side. He found the deep clonk that echoed down the tunnel satisfying. He shoved the door with his shoulder, expecting resistance. The heavy door swung open, banging against the inside of the tunnel wall. Belac seethed at what he saw on the other side of the doorway. It was another door. He felt like it was mocking him. He stepped forward, intent on the offending door.

"Maybe try the next one quietly," the dwarf suggested.

The orc agreed. "A much wiser plan."

Belac almost kicked the door out of spite.

The dwarf continued conversationally, "That is, unless you want something to come and kill us."

Belac suddenly remembered where he was. He remembered he could die. He remembered that he wanted to see the sun shine more than he wanted to go to war with a door. *The next one is probably locked anyway.* He walked over to the second door and gently tugged the bolt to the side. He then slowly pushed the door open. The groaning sound of unoiled hinges filled the tunnel. Never had the elf so hated a door.

The door opened into a chamber filled with an eerie, aquatic glow. Shallow pools were recessed into the floor along the walls. From the water's depths came the light, illuminating small fetishes that dangled from the ceiling. Crafted from bones, feathers, and other rubbish that Belac could not identify, the primitive things swayed slightly as the door opened fully. He stepped inside and turned in a slow circle, taking in the chamber. There was yet another door on the other side of the chamber, and a stone totem to the right. The totem stood in the center of one of the pools, the strange light displaying demonic faces carved into the stone.

"Be careful," the dwarf instructed. "Goblins like traps."

"This is goblins?" Belac asked him.

"Well, technically, this is a goblin shrine," the dwarf amended. "But yeah, this is goblins."

"Goblins?" Belac held out his hand next to his thigh. "Little guys? Ugly green faces?" He added, "With tiny knives?"

"With knives, yes," the dwarf's tone was serious.

Belac recalled what he had witnessed the dwarf do with knives. The elf shuddered.

The orc inquired, "How much trouble will this be?"

"That's a tricky question," the dwarf told him. "It's going to depend a lot on what kind of goblins they are."

"There are different kinds of goblins?" That was news to Belac. "What kind do we want?"

"The dead kind would be best," the dwarf replied dryly.

"Funny," Belac said sarcastically. "I will keep my fingers crossed."

The orc ignored the elf. "I believe it would be best if we assume some still live."

"Right," the dwarf agreed. "But the thing about goblins, is that in a lot of ways they are just like any other people. It may not be a very popular truth, but some goblins are nice enough. The problem is, most of them just want to kill you."

The orc nodded, "And this is a sacred place."

"Right." The dwarf nodded back.

Belac looked at the stone totem.

From behind, the dwarf said, "And they eat people."

The elf spun around to see if the dwarf was still serious. *He is serious.*

The orc indicated to one of the pools. "Is the water safe to drink?"

"Probably," the dwarf allowed. "But don't blame me if you die."

Belac glanced over at the pool that was closest to him. *It looks clean. It's glowing, but it looks clean.* "Are you going to drink it?" he asked.

Instead of answering, the dwarf knelt down next to one of the pools. He unslung his pack and pulled out a small metal cup. He dipped the cup in the water and brought it up to his face. He sniffed the water, paused, then took a mouthful. He swished it around in his mouth and then spat it out on the floor. He went completely still. Belac could not see him breathing. The elf could hear his own heart beating.

"I think it's fine," the dwarf said dismissively. He bent down and scooped up more of the water. "We should wash our face and hands too while we have a chance." He nodded toward the elf.

Belac raised his slender eyebrows. "You're not worried about poison?" *Because, I am.*

"Poison is a bit sophisticated for goblins," the dwarf assured him. "Besides, you don't poison something that you want to eat."

Belac sat down next to a pool, leaned over, and did as the dwarf advised. Once he cleaned himself as well as he was able, the elf scooted over to another of the pools and began to drink. As he drank, he studied a fist sized stone on the bottom of the pool. It was glowing.

The stone was, without question, one of the sources of the strange light filling the chamber. Belac reached down to take it. He stopped, thought for a moment, and then proceeded to pick up the stone. To Belac, it felt the same as any other stone. He pulled it from the water, and it stopped glowing. He dunked the stone back in the water, and the glow returned. He let the stone drop back to the bottom of the pool and then stood up. *Neat toy, but it's too heavy to carry around with me.*

Belac looked at his companions. The orc was washing his face in one of the pools and the dwarf was filling a large bladder in another. Belac was glad that the chamber had more than one pool. He followed the line of pools until he came to the totem. There was a beauty to the watery lights, something otherworldly and calling.

The totem shared none of that beauty. Its demonic carvings were crude and angry. The largest of the demonic faces was middle of the totem. The demon appeared to be screaming, its teeth surrounding a darkened nook. Belac held up the golden light he carried, peering into the dark maw. A jade light reflected from inside the stone nook. Inside was an elegantly cut gem the size of a dove's egg. Belac stared at the gem.

The orc stood and then stepped over to the totem. "Do you want it?"

"It's…" Belac struggled to find the words. "It's green."

"Yes, it's green." The orc spoke as if to a child.

"It is just…" Belac was hesitant to confide. "It's just, you can't trust the color green."

The orc stared at the elf and said nothing.

"It is untrustworthy," Belac insisted.

"The color green?"

"Yes."

"The whole color?"

"Yes."

"The color green?"

"Yes!"

The orc took a moment to stare at the elf before saying, "You're an elf."

"I know that!"

"Elves live in the forest."

"Not the smart ones! They don't!"

The orc stared at the elf. There was a slight lift in the orc's cheek. It was subtle, but Belac knew it was a smirk. The orc reached into the crevice to take the gem.

With a flash of insight, Belac knew what the orc was going to do. *He is going to make me take it! If I don't take it, he is going to chase me down, sit on me, and put that gem on my chest!* Belac did not believe that the dwarf would even attempt to save him. *That dwarf would just laugh at me!* Belac began to panic.

The stone totem bit off the orc's hand. The orc roared and pulled his arm away. With a mindless fury, the orc punched the demon face with his right fist. Now, his only fist. He stepped back, holding his left wrist below a gruesome stump. The stump was bloody, the totem was bloody, the floor was bloody, even the water held fading traces of blood. The elf, his eyes wide, stood uselessly.

Then the dwarf was there. He dropped his pack and reached inside. He pulled out a canvas bag and then dug into that. Standing, he took the orcs wrist in hand and pulled it closer to himself. The orc acted as if he were going to fight, but then relaxed and let the dwarf help him. The dwarf took a small wooden dowel dangling from a leather thong and flipped it around the orc's wrist. With quick motions, he tied the other end to the dowel and began to turn it. The bleeding did not completely stop, but they all knew the dwarf had just saved the orc's life.

The dwarf bent back down and picked up the canvas bag. The orc simply stared at the gory stump in disbelief. The dwarf slipped a pink vial from a slim wooden box and then rose.

"Give it back," the dwarf told the orc curtly.

Without arguing, the orc held his wrist out to the dwarf. The dwarf popped the stopper off the vial and splashed some of the pink fluid on the gruesome stump.

The orc relaxed immediately. "Will this heal it?" The question sounded more professional than concerned.

"It will help," the dwarf told him. "Mostly, it will ease the pain. I have something that can heal it faster, but it hurts. Kind of a lot."

"Do it." The orc was sure.

"Right," the dwarf said. "But look at that thing." He pointed at the totem.

Belac turned with the orc to look at the demon totem. The predominate demon was now smiling, its face smeared with blood.

here was a flash of light, and then the orc roared once more. The orc's stump was covered in pink flames that illuminated the surprise and pain on his face. *The dwarf just set him on fire!* The orc swung his burning stump back and forth trying to kill the flames. Finally, the orc looked down at the water in the pools.

The dwarf grabbed the damaged arm at the elbow. "You have to let it burn."

The orc looked at the dwarf through the pale flames. The orc nodded, and then the dwarf released his arm. After the pink fire faded and died, the dwarf took the remainder of what was left in the pink vial and splashed it on the stump. The orc relaxed once more.

"It's going to ich. A lot," the dwarf warned him. "Don't scratch it, and do not get it wet until it stops."

"That hurt," the orc said laughing.

"I told you it would." It sounded like the dwarf knew from experience.

Belac pointed at the orc. "And I told you not to trust the color green!"

Ten

They passed through two more doors leaving the chamber, neither of which were locked. Belac still did not understand why there were two doors to get in and then another two to get out. He did not understand anything about the chamber. *I don't understand anything about any of this!* With the return to the tunnels, the elf once more found himself watching his larger companion. The orc walked with his left arm bent and his wrist held slightly in front of his chest. However, he did not appear to be in any significant discomfort despite the position of his arm.

Belac wondered what it would be like to suffer such a fundamental loss. He tried to imagine what it would be like to live the rest of his life, missing a piece of himself. The elf's mind resisted. The thought alone was enough to make him feel sick. Watching the orc, Belac admitted a grudging respect for the orc's stoicism.

The thoughts of loss reminded Belac of what else they had lost. *I've lost my freedom, but I will have that back.* He accepted that his ruined rapier would never be returned, but then he remembered that the orc still had his poniard. *I will have that back too.* Then he thought of the people. That was loss as well. Each one of them had represented a potential that would now never be known. He tried to remember the woman's face, but his mind's eye could only see it distorted by horror and blood.

"I didn't even know her name," Belac realized. Somehow that made it worse, that not even her name could live on.

"What's that?" the dwarf asked.

"The woman," Belac explained. "I didn't even know her name."

The dwarf was less sentimental. "The one that fed herself to a gorilla-wolf-monster?"

"She was brave!" Belac scolded. *And she deserves better!*

The orc agreed. "Yes, she was."

The dwarf asked, "Did you know any of their names?"

"No." Belac shook his head. "I don't know any one's name."

"Rolan," the dwarf offered.

The word confused Belac. "What?"

"Rolan," the dwarf said again. "That is my name, Elf. Rolan."

"Oh," He tried to commit the name to memory. "I'm Belac."

"Vairug," the orc too gave his name.

"Vair-ug?" The name sounded strange to Belac.

Rolan attempted to help. "You are saying it too slow. It's Vairug." He turned to the orc. "It is Vairug, right?"

The orc agreed with a nod.

"That has got to be the most orcish name ever," Belac complained.

Vairug looked over his shoulder at the elf.

"He's an orc," Rolan reprimanded. "What did you think his name was going to be? 'Sarah?"

Vairug frowned. "You are not calling me 'Sarah." The orc was adamant.

Belac almost made a joke about how much easier 'Sarah' would be to say than 'Vairug.' He was even going to try to come up with something about how much prettier the name sounded. In the end, he decided that he did not want to find out if one hand was all the orc needed to kill him.

As long as we are on the topic of names… Belac held up his light. "What are these called?"

"What are what called?" Rolan asked.

Belac narrowed his eyes at the dwarf. "That is what I am asking you."

"You are going to need to be more specific," Rolan said dispassionately.

"These," Belac waved the light around wildly. "These light... things!"

"It is a la..." Rolan paused for a moment and then changed his answer. "It's a magic stick."

Belac did not need the orcs silent laughter to recognize the insult. "It's a magic stick?"

"That's right," the dwarf maintained.

Belac threw up a hand. "So, I can just walk into a shop, go up to the counter and say what? 'Hello. How are you doing today, fine sir? Could I please purchase a Magic Stick?!"

"Sure." Rolan laughed. "But I want to be there when you do."

Belac almost threw the 'magic stick' at the back of the dwarf's head.

"How about we call them 'light rods?" Rolan conceded.

The tunnel turned sharply right and then opened to a ravine spanned by a swaying bridge. Belac could feel a slight breeze, but it was too faint for even his elven hearing to detect. The bridge was one of ropes and planks. It was wide enough for them to all cross, though they would need to do so in single file. On the other side of the chasm was a chiseled platform with two burning braziers that did little to illuminate the bridge.

Two guards stood on the platform in front of where the path tunneled back into the rock. It was difficult for Belac to gage their size, but as best he could tell, the guards must have been at least as large as Vairug. They appeared to be armored in yellow and brown hides, and with ridiculously large helmets. Each were armed with an oddly shaped spear that they held casually at their sides. Neither of the guards were watching the bridge. Instead, they were facing each other, one gesturing to the other in conversation.

"I can't hear them," Belac said.

"It's the wind," Rolan explained softly, pulling the elf back around the corner. "That's the only reason that they didn't hear us coming."

"I don't hear any wind," Belac argued.

"That is..." Rolan waved his hand dismissively. "Don't worry about it. Just try to be more quiet."

"Why do I need to be quiet if they can't hear us?" Belac whispered.

Ignoring the question, Rolan removed his pack and held it out to the orc. "Do not lose this." He removed his light rod, held it against the wall to quell its glow, and then tucked it into a pocket.

"What are you doing," Belac wanted to know.

"I am going to take care of the sentries." Rolan peeked around the corner. "You two stay here."

"What? Why?" Belac followed the dwarf around the corner.

Rolan waved the elf back. "So, you don't die."

Rolan dropped to the ground and then crawled to the edge of the ravine. *What is he doing?* The dwarf then rolled off the edge. Belac was appalled. He did not understand what had happened or why. He did not know what he was going to do without the dwarf. *There is no way that I am ever going to make it back to the surface with nothing but a one-handed orc to help me!* He thought about surrendering himself to the guards and asking them for assistance. He was quick to decide that the guards could not be trusted. *They might work for the goblins. Or the goblins might work for them. The goblins might even be pets. What if the guards feed me to their goblins?! If I wanted to get eaten, I could just go back to the gorilla-wolf-monsters.* He thought about fangs and shuddered.

Belac turned to Vairug to ask him what they were going to do. The orc was smiling like a loon. Belac followed the orc's gaze and saw Rolan underneath the bridge. The dwarf swung hand over hand until he reached the other side. Then he transitioned from the bridge to the rock wall with a grace not rightly attributed to dwarves. *I hope that he doesn't expect me to do that.* When Rolan climbed up to the ledge and peeked over slowly, the guards were still engaged in conversation or argument, oblivious to the dwarf's crossing.

Rolan lowered himself back down and shimmied to the right, making his way around the edge to where the platform met the upper wall. The entire time, Belac fully expected one of the guards to hear the dwarf, walk over to the edge, look down, and stab him with one of their spears. However, the guards gave no indication that they were aware of the dwarf's presence. Bracing himself against the two walls, Rolan tossed something onto the other side of the platform.

"There is no way that works," Belac told the orc.

It worked. Both guards turned toward the noise and then walked over to investigate. One of them took a knee and leaned over the edge. Rolan vaulted onto the platform and then sprinted at the guards. Belac realized that the guards had to be at least twice the dwarf's size. Rolan jumped up and slammed foot first into the guard leaning over the edge. Using the collision to redirect his momentum, the dwarf sprang up toward the other guard as the first fell from the platform. Rolan's knife slashed at the remaining guard's neck as the dwarf flew past. The guard dropped his spear and covered his ruined throat. Rolan darted back in and ripped his blade through the joint of the guard's knee. The guard fell backward and then Rolan was on top of him, stabbing savagely into the guard's hands and neck.

"I think it worked," Vairug taunted.

Belac narrowed his eyes at the orc and then looked back to Rolan. Now standing next to the dead guard, the dwarf waved his companions across before turning away and entering the tunnel on the other side of the bridge. Belac shrugged. *At least I don't have to go under the bridge.*

Vairug stepped out of hiding and began to make his crossing, leaving Belac alone. *This is the side with the gorilla-wolf-monsters.* Suddenly in a rush to cross the bridge, Belac hurried to catch up with the orc. As he neared Vairug, Belac heard the ropes of the bride creaking under the orc's weight. Belac narrowed his eyes at the back of Vairug's broad shoulders. *He should have let me go first.*

The bridge began to sway more and more as they crossed, forcing Belac to refocus his attention away from the orc and back onto the task of not dying.

As the other two crossed, Rolan reemerged from the tunnel and moved to the guard that he had slaughtered. Bending over the corpse, he began tugging at the buckles of its armor. By the time that Belac finally stepped off the precarious bridge, the dwarf had already stripped the guard's heavy leather chest piece from its body.

With the bloody chest armor in hand, Rolan met his companions at the foot of the bridge. "I would have crossed one at a time."

"You did cross one at a time," Belac retorted while stepping around the dwarf.

Belac walked over to the dead guard. It was not wearing yellow and brown hides. It was another monster. One with yellowish skin and outfitted in boiled leather armor. Even with its neck shredded, the monster was frightening to behold. Its musculature was grotesque and its head far too large for its body. The face was dominated by an oversized, feline nose and a set of jutting tusks. Belac stepped away from the sour, unwashed smell of the thing. *That thing is not a goblin!*

Belac turned toward the dwarf. "That is not a goblin!"

"It's an ogre," Vairug agreed as the dwarf strapped the leather chest piece onto the orc.

Belac threw his hands out to his sides. "And do you know what an ogre is not?" He did not wait for an answer. "A goblin!" He flailed his arms around in agitation. "You said there was going to be goblins! Little guys. Crazy and vicious. But small enough for me to kick over a wall. Goblins!" He began to hop up and down. "Not ogres. Goblins! You said goblins. Ogres are evil monsters that hate everything except bone marrow and screams!"

Rolan and Vairug both stared at the elf. They said nothing.

"And they stink!" Belac added.

Rolan smiled. "At least they're not green."

Eleven

"Why does everything want to eat me?" Belac was crestfallen.

Rolan frowned at the elf. "Because you're the loudest," he admonished.

The new tunnel cut only a few paces into the wall of rock before bending sharply right and ending at a dark, spacious cavity. Stairs had been carved into the sides of the cavity, spiraling down into darkness. The steps were wide enough to accommodate an ogre.

"Are we really about to walk down into an ogre pit?" Belac hoped there was some other option.

"You can stay here and search for goblins if you want," Rolan proposed.

Belac narrowed his eyes at the dwarf.

Many things seemed unfair to the elf. One of which was that walking down stairs was more exhausting than simply walking. It just seemed wrong to him that down was not easier. He peered over the edge in an attempt to see how far they would need to travel. He could see nothing but darkness drinking the golden light he carried. Belac worried that if he were to fall, it would be forever. He moved away from the ledge, suddenly aware that there was no railing.

Belac muttered, "I think the ogres forgot to build guardrails."

"Ogres did not build this." Rolan sounded sure.

"How would you know?" Belac's tone turned teasing. "Is it because of the goooooblin shrine?"

"Yes." Rolan ignored the tone. "And because ogres don't really build anything."

"So, you think the ogres are working for the goblins?" Belac could not imagine how a goblin might possibly convince an ogre to do what it was told.

"Maybe," Rolan allowed. "It happens sometimes."

Belac did not like the uncertainty. "If the ogres are not working for the goblins, then who are they working for?"

"Now, that, is a good question," Rolan said approvingly.

"Hey!" Belac was indignant. "I can ask good questions!"

"Right." Rolan chose not to argue. "So, here is another one for you. What do you think the guards were guarding?"

Not the shrine. Belac thought to himself. *And not just some big hole in the ground.* He wondered what it could be. *It's a dragon!* It had to be. He thought back on the dungeons and the caves and the tunnel leading deeper and deeper into the rock. *They want to feed us to a dragon!*

"It's a dragon!" Belac proclaimed.

"It's not a dragon." Rolan was sure again.

"How would you know?" Belac demanded. "Do you have a crystal ball in that bag of yours that you haven't told us about?"

Rolan asked, "Why would it be a dragon?" His tone made it clear that he did not think there was a reasonable answer to his question.

"Because they want to feed us to it!" Belac explained.

"So, you think what?" Rolan was incredulous. "That a dragon, a dragon, in some elaborate scheme to have an exotic meal, enlisted ogre guards to stop the food from getting to it?"

"Maybe it's sleeping."

"The dragon?"

"Yes, the dragon!"

"I don't know if dragons need to be guarded while they sleep." Rolan laughed. "Maybe just a sign. One that says, 'BEWARE! DRAGON SLEEPING! Do not enter unless you are food."

Belac was tired of getting laughed at. "Yeah? Well, maybe ogres can't read!"

Rolan laughed at him some more. "There is no arguing with that. You are absolutely right. Ogres can't read."

Belac wondered if Vairug would stop him if he tried to push the dwarf off the stairs. Vairug gave no indication that he was sparing them any attention at all. He walked next to the edge with the tip of his new spear hanging over. The bladed head had long been neglected, but Belac expected it to be sharp enough with the orc's strength behind it. Belac thought the spear was too large for the orc, though Vairug did not seem to agree with him. Belac wondered what the orc had done with his poniard. *He better not have lost it!* Vairug still held his stump in front of his chest, but now he had taken the light rod and looped it through the leather straps on his forearm. The arrangement let Belac see that the stump had already begun to scab over.

Belac wondered how the orcish culture delt with the loss of a limb. *It must be common.* "Hey, Vairug."

"It is not a dragon." The orc guessed the wrong question.

"Fine," Belac conceded though he was still unconvinced. "What do you think it is?"

Rolan answered, "Not a dragon."

"Thanks." Belac's sarcasm was thick. "That really narrows down the possibilities for us."

"I'm glad I could help," Rolan said amiably.

"It's a door," Vairug informed them.

"How could they feed us to a door?" Belac was confused. "Do you mean, like a magic door?"

"No, Elf." Vairug pointed with his spear. "It is a door."

Belac looked out over the edge and appraised the door, finding it to be the same heavy type as the ones that they had encountered earlier at the goblin shrine. "Not magic then," he said.

Rolan kept his eyes on the door. "Let's hope not," he moderated.

The door was on the opposite side of the stairwell from where the stairs ended. The gritty floor crunched under the three escapees' steps as they walked between unlit braziers that lined the walls. The braziers troubled Belac. So many potential sources of brightness, all dead, forgotten deep underground. It felt like he was in a tomb for the light itself.

Perhaps sensing the elf's discomfort, Rolan said, "Don't worry. We will not let the door eat you."

Belac narrowed his eyes at the dwarf. *Dwarf thinks he's funny.*

Vairug readied his spear and Rolan opened the door. Belac expected to find another door on the other side. Either that, or a trap of some kind. *Rolan did say that goblins like traps.* Instead, the door opened into a short, darkened hallway.

"You know," Belac mused, "we have not really run into any traps."

Vairug looked at the elf deliberately and then held up the stump of his missing hand.

"Oh." Belac wanted to take back what he had said. "Yeah..."

One after another, the three walked into the hallway. It was cramped, but no one volunteered to stay behind. On the right side of the hallway the outlines of three doors had been chiseled into the wall. On the other, hung a discolored tarp fashioned from old hides. Rolan walked by and pushed on the center of each outline. No doorways appeared, and the wall did not move.

Vairug pointed his spear at the tarp hanging on the wall. "The smell is coming from there."

Belac sniffed at the air and then wrinkled his nose at the odd spicy smell. Rolan stepped around the elf and pulled back a corner of the tarp. He dropped the tarp and then held the butt of his rod against the wall, killing the light.

In the glow of the other's light, Rolan said, "Turn those off."

There was no confusion as to what the dwarf meant. Belac held his light rod against the wall and then turned to offer Vairug help. The orc had leaned his spear against the wall so he could use his free hand, his only hand, to put out his light.

Belac was impressed with how quickly Vairug was adjusting to the loss of his hand. The elf wondered if he himself would be able to adapt as quickly. All he could decide was that he did not want to find out.

In the absence of the golden light, Belac could see a faint glow bleeding from the edges of the tarp. Light shone off Rolan's scruffy face as the dwarf held back one side of the tarp. Belac wanted to pull back the other side of the tarp and look too, but he somehow managed to wait.

In a low voice, Rolan muttered, "It has to be gnomes." He seemed to be speaking to himself.

"Gnomes?" Belac asked. *That doesn't sound too bad.*

Rolan pulled his head back and closed the tarp. "Evil creatures," he said with casual disdain. "I might have a plan. You two stay here."

"A plan?" Belac did not want to stay and wait in the dark. "What am I supposed to do here?"

"Stay there," Rolan answered gruffly. He pulled the tarp a little to the side, dimly lighting the hallway. "See if you can figure out how to get one of those doors open." He pointed his hand at the outlines chiseled into the other wall.

Rolan slipped out of the hallway, the tarp dropping closed behind him. Belac stepped over to where the dwarf had been standing. He took hold of the tarp and discovered that there were multiple overlapping layers. He gathered them together and pushed them aside far enough to watch Rolan walk away. Belac did not try to follow the dwarf, but he wanted to see for himself what was on the other side. He felt the tarp move as Vairug made his own opening.

Belac did not know what gnomes had to do with goblins, but what he saw was clearly a goblin city. It was a squalor of short structures so packed together that many leaned against each other. They were constructed of lackluster brown rocks that must have been the same rock removed to make the tunnels. Ragged hides of various shades served as rooves and covered doorways. It was a hellish vision lit by braziers emitting thin columns of black smoke.

The smoke darkened the air, and its soot blackened the ceiling of the entire cavern. The ceiling had been cleared of stalactites and was pockmarked with ventilation shafts that were unarguably insufficient. The strange smell of spice made the elf sick to his stomach.

Belac stepped away and tugged the tarps back in place. "What is that smell? It's awful."

The hallway fell back into darkness when Vairug closed his side of the tarp. "It is what they burn for light. Did you not smell it on the fires above?"

He must mean in the braziers. Belac thought back. He must have noticed, but he did not remember doing so. He decided that he simply must have had more important things to worry about at the time. *Things like elf-eating-ogres.* It was better to concentrate on what was important: not dying, and getting out of that place while doing it. To that end, he set himself to the task of opening one of the trick doorways. He began by tracing the outlines chiseled into the stone. Working almost entirely by feel, he knocked over Vairug's spear. The elf fumbled an attempt to catch it and the spear clattered against the floor. He froze, listening for some sound of response.

When he was satisfied that nothing was coming to kill them, Belac said, "That's it. I am turning on a light."

"Before impaling yourself on my spear," Vairug suggested.

"Why would you just leave it sitting there?" Belac asked. He tapped his light rod on the wall.

Vairug gave the elf a deliberate look and held up the stump of his left wrist.

"Oh." *I forgot.* "Yeah..."

Vairug picked up the spear and set it against the other wall.

Belac went back to studying the chiseled wall. He ran the golden light over it, looking for some type of keyhole, but found nothing. He knew that Rolan had pushed on the doorways, but the elf decided to try it himself. With both hands, he pushed against each of the doorways only to slide back away from the immovable stone.

Belac took a step back, considered, and then ran his hands along the wall, searching for a hidden switch. Finally, in frustration, he kicked the center doorway. He regretted it immediately as pain shot through his foot. More light filled the hallway. Something was happening.

"I did it!" Belac exclaimed, his sore foot forgotten.

"You did what?" Rolan asked, closing the tarps behind himself.

"Oh." Belac's disappointment was evident. "I thought I figured out how to get one of the doorways open."

In the golden glow, Belac could see the dwarf doing a poor job of attempting to not smile.

Vairug turned away in silent laughter.

Twelve

Secret doors are a thing! Belac thought angrily to himself as he followed the dwarf.

"Stay close," Rolan instructed.

Belac tried to look over the hide rooves as he snuck through the goblin city.

"And stay down," Rolan ordered. He looked back at the elf and gestured with his hand.

Belac hunched back down. Walking around bent over was uncomfortable. He narrowed his eyes at the dwarf. Rolan did not have to break his back to sneak through the city. Belac glanced over at Vairug. The orc moved crouched low, obviously more accustomed to the activity. Belac was not convinced that there was any real reason to sneak around. So far, he had not seen any goblins.

"I still don't see any goblins," Belac told the dwarf. "Or gnomes, for that matter."

"Most of the goblins are up ahead," Rolan explained.

What?! "Then, why are we going this way?" Belac had liked it better when he thought that the city was empty. "Why would you want to go toward the goblins? You said they eat people! I do not want to go toward the goblins." When the dwarf did not respond quickly enough, Belac asked, "Why are we still going toward the goblins?"

"Don't worry about the goblins," Rolan told him. "It is the gnomes we need to hide from."

Don't worry about the goblins?! "Gnomes are short and look like old people. Why are we worried about gnomes?" Belac asked. "Especially when there is something else that wants to eat us. You know, goblins!"

"The goblins are probably not going to eat you," Rolan explained. "The gnomes, however, are evil, organized, and have ogres. The ogres will eat you."

Belac tried to decide if he would rather be eaten by goblins or ogres. The most he could hope for was that one of them killed him first. He needed another option. "How do you know the goblins won't eat us?" Belac had intentionally omitted the 'probably.'

"Because I told them not to," Rolan said simply.

"You told…" Belac stammered. "You talked to them? Why would you talk to them? Why would you even let them know that we're here? Do you not remember the part about how they eat people?"

"I don't like gnomes," Rolan said as if that explained everything.

"Gnomes?!" Belac lowered his voice but continued to speak forcefully. "We have been hiding from ogres, goblins, gorilla-wolf-monsters, and probably a dragon. But you are worried about gnomes? They are the only thing that does not want to eat us!"

"Again, with the dragon?" Rolan asked.

"Forget about the dragon!" Belac snapped.

"There is no dragon to forget," Rolan insisted.

"There could be a dragon!" Belac caught himself. "No. Wait. Forget about the dragon. What about the gnomes?"

"What about them," Rolan's question seemed genuine.

"Why are you so worried about them?" Belac could not understand it. "Do they shoot beams of fire out of their eyes? …or explode if you get too close? What is it?"

"No, it's nothing like that," Rolan finally began to explain. "They are evil. They are also highly intelligent, and they can pretty much live forever. And I mean crazy smart. I can't even think of anything to compare them to."

"That doesn't sound so bad." Belac thought that he must be missing something. "Not eat-you-bad."

"They are evil," Rolan said again.

Belac still did not understand. "Evil, sure. But… no fangs."

"Evil is not just hunger or rage," Rolan did his best to elucidate. "Gnomes don't have a concept of right and wrong, or good and evil. They honestly believe that those things are nothing more than insanities that affect lesser beings. They are evil."

"Okay. Evil. I got it. But… no fangs." Belac thought that he could handle evil if it was short, old, and defenseless.

"If you do not understand how dangerous something like that is," Rolan shrugged, "then lucky you. Because that is what we are facing."

Vairug added, "And ogres."

"Yes. Thank you." Rolan looked at the orc sideways. "And ogres."

Belac thought about it but could find no reason to be scared of the gnomes. They might be evil, but he was not certain that the dwarf was any better. *The ogres though…* The ogres, he could understand. He had seen them. He could still see them in his mind. He had no doubt that an ogre could tear off an elf's arms and legs. Or, for that matter, that it would if given a chance. *What is evil, if not that?*

Rolan stopped and turned to his companions. "Right. So, don't freak out."

Belac immediately readied himself to freak out.

"There are going to be some goblins around the corner," Rolan told them. "Well, actually, kind of a lot of goblins. By now, it should be most every goblin in the city. Do not freak out."

Belac did not know if he wanted to look over the top of the building to see, or scrunch down lower to avoid being seen. He scrunched down lower.

Rolan turned away from the elf. "They're friendly." Then under his breath, he muttered, "Sort of."

Belac gazed over his own shoulder and reconsidered the path that he had taken. *It's too late to go back the way I came.* Strange voices began to murmur in hushed tones, the sound growing as interest spread. *That sounds like a lot of goblins...* Belac returned his attention forward, finding that Rolan had left him behind. *I can't just keep following that crazy dwarf.*

Vairug nudged the elf's shoulder. "Move."

None of this is fair. Belac rounded the corner of the building. The sight that was waiting for him made him want to go back to the hallway with the three fake doors. He would have even gone back to his prison cell if the option had been available. *This dwarf is going to get me killed.* Rolan had brought them to a town square that was filled with goblins. *So may goblins...* Tattered rags covered unwashed bodies that were a green so dark that their skin was almost black. The goblins' twisted faces were a match to those that had been carved on the totem in the shrine; demonic, with wickedly sharp teeth. Broad noses and ears protruded aggressively from their heads. Below distended bellies hung knives. *So many knives.* Unorganized groups of anything are difficult to count, but Belac thought that there had to be hundreds of goblins in the square. *Hundreds of goblins. Hundreds of knives. Thousands of teeth.*

The whispering grew so loud, Belac had to question why they bothered to whisper at all. The elf watched, unwilling to brave the crowd as Rolan walked into the middle of the square. Surrounded by goblins, the dwarf climbed up onto a wooden box that would serve as his platform. He stood tall above the goblins and waited for the whispers to stop. There was a pregnant moment of silence, and then he spoke one sentence. It was loud, it was clear, and it was in a language that Belac did not understand.

There was another moment of silence, but just when Belac thought that the goblins would respond, Rolan continued. The language was sharp and sounded like it would be painful to speak. Despite the harsh language, the dwarf sounded confident, his voice strong.

Belac leaned in close to the orc and asked, "What is he saying?"

Vairug shrugged.

Rolan turned on his platform, addressing all of the goblins around him. He began to point his hand at them, ensuring that they were all included. The murmurings returned, this time darker. Belac could feel the change in the goblins. The dwarf pointed his hand at one of the goblins and asked a demanding question. The goblin yelled back, clearly angry. Rolan asked another question, and the goblin yelled back at him even louder. The angry murmurings of the goblins grew.

Belac took a step back. *This is going to get bad.* Many of the goblins had their hands on their knives. Some openly snarled at the dwarf. Rolan questioned more of the goblins, none of which replied agreeably. In the face of that malice, Rolan's voice only grew more resolute. He began to gesticulate aggressively as the goblins crowded closer to him. The goblins began to shout at the dwarf, not waiting to be questioned. *They are going to kill him.*

Rolan threw his fist in the air and roared something defiant in the Goblin tongue. The goblins screamed and raised their fists in the air, many holding knives. Rolan pumped his fist in the air and roared again. The goblins answered.

In horror, Belac suddenly understood. As if the psychotic dwarf had not been dangerous enough already, he now had a goblin army. Belac turned to Vairug and saw the orc with a tusked grin that was as frightening as any of the goblins' fangs. Belac looked back to Rolan in time to see the dwarf thrust his hand into the distance like an emperor and roar once more. The goblins' screams were deafening as they charged off in the direction that the dwarf had pointed.

Rolan stood like a rock in a river as the goblins rushed past him. Belac looked over the city to where the dwarf pointed, but in the haze of smoke, he could make out little more than the angular gleam of polished stone.

When the square cleared, Rolan hopped down from the box and walked over to his companions. "We need to go," he said.

"You say that like you did not just throw an army at someone," Belac complained.

Rolan shook his head. "We don't have time to stand around and talk." He turned away and began to follow after his army. "I don't know if you could tell, but those goblins are really angry."

The dwarf's walk was brisk and Belac had to run to catch up. *No elf should ever have to run to catch up to a dwarf!* Vairug ran beside him, the orc fully upright now that stealth had been abandoned.

"Yeah, about that," Belac said, matching the dwarf's pace. "Vairug wants to know how you became General Crazy Dwarf."

Vairug looked sideways at the elf as they walked.

Belac met the orc's gaze. "Well, you do, don't you?" He asked him.

Vairug shrugged and turned back to the dwarf.

Rolan explained without stopping. "Someone convinced the goblins that the gnomes were going to enslave some of them and kill the rest."

Belac did not like how flippantly the dwarf wielded an army. "Does this 'someone' happen to look like a dwarf with a bad haircut?"

Rolan stopped at the edge of the square, and a goblin stepped out from the shadows.

Belac made a less than masculine noise and hopped back.

The goblin gripped the hilt of its knife and jabbered at the elf in Goblin. The sharpened teeth scared Belac more than the knife.

Rolan said something only the goblin understood, and it took its hand off the knife. Belac was still worried about the teeth.

The goblin handed Rolan a cloth sack and then winked at Belac before darting away.

Belac asked, "What did you say?"

Rolan smiled. "That you were just intimidated by her beauty."

"I what?" Belac stammered. "Her what? That was a her?"

Rolan's smile grew. "We can take her with us if you want."

Belac shuddered. "That is not funny."

"We need to keep moving." Rolan handed the elf the cloth sack. "Carry this."

"Why do I have to carry it?" Belac did not wait for a response. "What's in it?"

"Food." Rolan started walking again. "Probably bread and bug paste."

"Bug paste? That is disgusting." Belac held the bag farther away from himself. "Bugs are not food, Rolan. Not for people anyway."

Rolan kept walking. "Feel free to starve if you don't want to eat it."

"I'm not going to eat it. I don't even want to carry it." Belac hurried after the dwarf while asking the orc, "Do you want it?"

Vairug ignored him.

Belac did not understand why the goblins would trust Rolan. *A dwarf just shows up from out of nowhere, and then, for no reason, the goblin nation wants to make him their king?* "How did you do it? How did you get an entire army to trust you?"

Rolan shrugged. "Mostly, I just told them the truth," he said as if it were simple. "Goblins are stupid. Gnomes are evil. The gnomes needed to build a prison, and they could not be bothered to do it themselves. So, they found a bunch of goblins to do it for them. The gnomes were nice to them, they fed them, they kept them safe. But now, the prison is finished, and the gnomes do not like pets."

"How could you possibly know any of that?" Belac asked disbelievingly.

"Gnomes do things like this all the time," Rolan told him. "The goblins filled in the details."

"I get it. You hate gnomes," Belac said. "But why would the goblins believe you?"

"A lot of the goblins have started to go missing," Rolan explained. "My guess, is that the gnomes have been feeding them to the ogres."

Belac was taken aback. "How…" He could not form the thought. "Why?"

"Gnomes are evil." Rolan sounded frustrated that he had to keep repeating himself. "Ogres have to eat." He held his hands apart, sweeping the city. "And I don't see any goats."

Thirteen

There was an explosion, followed by the mad laughter of a dwarf. The tree escapees had trailed the army through the goblin city to the other side of the cavern. Belac watched as smoke bellowed out of the massive tunnel ahead. The smoke, the screams, the sounds of battle, and even the elegant cobblestone path, promised a change of scenery.

Belac asked the dwarf, "Did you plan that?"

"No." Rolan was still laughing. "But I might have suggested it."

"Goblins have magic?" Belac had never heard that.

Rolan shook his head as he laughed. "They have booze."

The cobblestone path bent left and then ran straight through the gnomish complex. As far as Belac could tell, the path they followed was the complex's primary. On either side of the path, separated by its expertly crafted cobblestones, buildings had been carved into the stone walls. The stonework was of a mastery that Belac had rarely seen. The gnomes had somehow bleached the stone before polishing it to a uniformed perfection. The walls were unadorned, beveled plains, having only subtle protrusions to frame the openings and give them shape. Despite the subterranean locale, the gnomes had incorporated full-length windows of frosted, ironbound artwork.

The darkly stained wood doors had a luster that spoke of time invested not only in creation, but in maintenance and care. Above each door, hung a matching wooden plaque bearing sharp, angular lettering. *This looks like something that the dwarves might make if they were not always drunk.* The gnomish complex was beautiful. And it was on fire.

Fortunately, there was not much that could burn. The goblins, however, were trying their best all the same. Belac realized that the goblins did not seem to understand that the stone would not burn. Acrid smoke accompanied the nightmarish sight, and the elf found himself becoming overwhelmed by the pure chaos of it all.

There were corpses scattered throughout the corridor, and Belac had to step around a dead ogre surrounded by the mangled bodies of dead goblins. The elf was assaulted by an enraged roar from his right. In his haste to turn and face the hateful sound, his feet tangled with his empty scabbard, and he fell to the cobblestones. The impact with the stones hurt, but the fall saved his life. A massive, metal-banded maul swept through the space above the elf. Belac rolled onto his back and looked up at an ogre as it raised the maul above its head with both arms. A spear thudded into the ogre's chest, knocking it back. The ogre stumbled and fell away from the elf.

Belac did not even consider finishing off the ogre. He jumped to his feet and ran toward the relative safety of his companions. *I'm glad Vairug knows how to throw a spear.*

There was an explosion from inside one of the buildings that was so loud, it staggered the elf. All was madness. Fire and blood and death were everywhere Belac looked. In his shock, he lost track of his companions. Shambling around off balance, he searched for a way out. In a daze, he came to a halt and watched as a pack of goblins stabbed a little old man to death.

A hand slapped Belac's cheek so hard that the elf almost fell back down. Calloused hands grabbed his face and pulled his head down to stare into gray, dwarven eyes.

Rolan yelled, "Move!" Then he shoved the elf farther down the corridor and into madness.

Belac stumbled and Rolan grabbed him by the belt to hold him steady. Rolan kept the grip on the elf's belt and directed him forward. Belac was still struggling to think straight when they caught up to Vairug. A goblin flew through the air and then slammed into the wall in front of them, its skull crushed, neck broken.

Rolan pushed the elf toward the orc and shouted, "Take him!"

Vairug gripped Belac's vest and towed him forward. An ogre roared and smashed its maul down onto another goblin. Rolan grabbed his springer, loaded a bolt, and shot the ogre in the head. The ogre swung its maul again, this time slow and confused. Rolan reloaded and shot it again. The ogre fell to the ground and then a pack of goblins swarmed it, tiny knives stabbing viciously. Leaving the ogre to its fate, Rolan led Vairug and Belac onward. Screams, roars, and the blaze of fire chased them deeper into the complex.

Once they had moved past the worst of the noise, Rolan held up his left hand in a fist. "Hold." He went to a door and tried to force it open. When it did not open, he growled and then slammed his shoulder against it to no effect. He turned to the orc and asked, "Can you get this open?"

The orc pushed Belac against the wall and then released him. Belac could have stood on his own, but he welcomed the support of the stone. Vairug walked over to the door and kicked it. The kick was powerful, but the door held. He took a step back and kicked it again, this time with more force. When the door still did not move, he gave the dwarf a meaningful look.

Rolan growled again and stepped away from the building. "We need to see what's in there," he said, staring at a sign that hung above the door. "Wait here." Without waiting for agreement, he turned and began walking back the way that they had come.

Belac put his back to the wall and leaned against it. He took a deep breath and tried to ignore the distant screams.

Rolan returned shortly, a limp goblin slung over his shoulder. Belac had not thought that the dwarf was the kind of person who would save a goblin. Goblin or not, it seemed a noble deed to Belac.

Rolan repositioned the goblin in front of himself and then ran at the building. He smashed through the window, ripping the ironwork free and sending frosted glass flying. Inside the building, he rolled over the goblin corpse and came to his feet with a knife in hand.

Vairug and Belac looked at each other. The orc shrugged and then walked into the building through the broken window.

"One more beautiful thing destroyed," Belac said softly as he followed the orc inside.

Glass crunched under his boots as Belac stepped into the building. The inside was every bit as well-crafted as the rest of the complex. It appeared to be a shop of some type, dimly lit by only a single lamp. Strange, alien tools hung from the wall above a long workbench covered with unfinished projects. Farther back, deeper into the room, stood an armless statue. The marriage of metal and stone was elegantly intricate. Belac once more was astounded by the mastery of the gnomes' craftsmanship. *How evil could the gnomes be if they can craft a thing so majestic?*

Rolan spoke to the statue. The language he used was smooth and almost bouncy.

Belac had never heard of dwarves being able to speak with statues. At this point, he wondered if the dwarf was just making languages up. It sounded like no language that Belac had ever heard, and it certainly did not sound like something a statue would speak. The elf almost tripped over himself when the statue responded in a woman's voice.

Rolan spoke to the statue again, demanding.

The woman's voice replied again.

Rolan barked one word threateningly.

A slight figure stepped out from behind the statue. It was a little old woman dressed in what Belac could only think of as a nightgown.

The gnomish woman spoke to the dwarf once more. She stood straight with her head back in an attempt to maintain what dignity she could. However, she could not disguise the fear in her voice.

Rolan answered her with hard words, holding back deep emotion.

He is going to kill her. There was no mercy in the dwarf's stance. Belac had witnessed Rolan murder in cold blood. He had no doubt that the dwarf would do so in rage. Belac stepped between the vicious dwarf and the gnomish woman. He looked at the little old woman, terrified and alone. He could not let Rolan kill her.

Belac turned to the dwarf, held up a hand and said, "You cannot do this. I ak…"

The gnome stabbed him. The blade slid into the elf's left side and punctured a kidney. Belac shied away from the dagger and fell to a knee. He turned his head to look at the little old woman, and into her eyes. *She is going to kill me.*

In a rush, Rolan shot forward, threw the woman to the floor, penned her, and then slammed a knife into her chest three times. He held the knife ready for another blow as he stared down at her aggressively, waiting for any sign she might still fight. Belac looked away, not wanting to watch her die.

Rolan stood, looked down at the elf, and said, "That was stupid."

Rolan then walked past him and began searching the workbench on the other side of the room. Belac held his hand against the wound in his side. He was bleeding, but there was not much pain. He knew that was not necessarily a good thing.

Vairug kneeled over Belac and removed the elf's hand from the wound. The hand was covered in blood. Belac looked up past his bloody hand, past the orc trying to save his life, and saw Rolan stuffing things into his pack. The pack reminded Belac of the healing liquid that had aided the orc's bloody stump.

Though it was difficult for him to speak, Belac managed to ask, "Do you think I could get some of that pink stuff?"

Rolan turned and looked at the elf. "How bad is it?"

Vairug answered, "It is deep."

Digging into his pack, Rolan said, "I am tempted to leave you there to bleed out."

Belac narrowed his eyes at the dwarf. "You are not funny."

"I am not joking," Rolan replied.

Belac believed him.

"Here," Rolan handed a small packet to the orc. "Cram most of the paste into the wound, smear the rest around the outside, and then hold the wrapper against it until it sticks."

Vairug asked, "Should you not do it?"

"No. I need to pack this stuff up so we can get out of here." Rolan took a large leather bag and dumped it out on the floor loudly.

Belac could not believe what he was seeing. "You're looting? Now?"

"Yes." Rolan began to pack things into the bag. "I'm looting. You're bleeding out on the floor. Go on, keep talking to me like I'm the one that's stupid."

Belac really did not know what to say to that. He looked to Vairug for help, but the orc was laughing silently as he worked. Belac pulled away when Vairug pushed the paste into his wound. Exhausted by the pain, Belac tried to relax and focus on his breathing as the orc continued. He felt his entire left side get hot and then go numb as Vairug held the wrapper to the wound. After the wound had been seen to, Vairug helped the elf stand.

Belac wobbled before finding his balance. "Just a moment." He removed his belt and slipped the empty scabbards free. He tossed the longer rapier scabbard aside and then tucked the extra poniard scabbard into the leather straps of Vairug's chest armor as if it were the orc's job to carry it around for him. *How do you like it, Orc-Face?* Belac then moved his rapier to his left side, transferring more of the weight from his belt to his right hip.

Rolan dropped the leather bag that he had filled and then he extended its carry strap all the way out as far as it would allow. He held the strap out to the orc and said, "Here, carry this."

Vairug stared at the dwarf and said nothing.

Rolan dropped the strap and walked away. He pointed behind himself with his thumb. "I think you are going to want to bring that with us."

Vairug growled at the dwarf and then snatched up the strap and lifted the leather bag. He slung the strap over his head and across his chest with the bag under his injured arm. He looked around the room, then walked over to the workbench. He picked up a short, silvery axle with a ring on one end and a robust cog on the other. Holding it like a mace, he laid the cogged end across his left forearm. "I am taking this," he said as if he wanted an argument.

Fourteen

Vairug's voice echoed on water in the new chamber. "You know he dropped the food?"

"Yes," Rolan replied. "If it comes to it, we eat him first."

"Agreed." Vairug gave a single nod.

Why does everything want to eat me?

They had left the gnomish complex behind. Belac wondered if any of the gnomes would survive. He did not know if the gnomes would fight or flee. He did not know if either could save them. He had underestimated the savagery of the goblins. He wondered if the goblins would claim the complex as their own, or if they would move on to find some other life deeper in the caves. Though it may have been built by gnomes, it would no longer be a gnomish complex. He thought of the complex, empty and abandoned, the tragic union of beauty and ruin. He wondered how many other such places might litter the world; civilizations left in the wake of violence.

The cobblestone path had continued to tunnel past the chaos of the complex. On the left was now a cistern, the water held back by a raised wall too well formed to be of goblin design. The gnomes had not bleached the stone nor imposed their art, but it still somehow felt like gnomish work to Belac.

Vairug set his cogged mace against the barrier and dunked his stump into the water. Belac washed the blood from his own hands while he watched the orc. Vairug rubbed at the scabs covering his stump, and to Belac's surprise, the scabs peeled away, revealing tender flesh. The blood in the water was dark in the golden glow of their light rods.

Belac grinned at the orc. "I guess we're not drinking the water, then?"

Rolan pulled his hands from the water. "It should still be fine down on the other end."

Belac watched as the blood fanned out in the water. He thought it would be nasty to drink any of it. From the water, emerged an elongated, three-fingered hand covered in sickly pale flesh. Silently, it grabbed the side of the cistern wall. Before Belac could raise an alarm, a spherical head surged up directly in front of him in a spray of water. The head's sickly skin pulled back to reveal multiple rows of bladed teeth. *It's going to eat me!* Vairug pushed Belac back and smashed his cogged mace into the side of the creature's head. Belac fell down onto his backside and began scooting backward in horror. *What even is that?!* A strong hand grabbed his vest and dragged him farther away from the cistern.

"Get up!" Rolan commanded, pulling the elf to his feet.

Belac began to spit. "Ugh! I got it in my mouth! I got it in my mouth!" He tried to wipe the water off his tongue.

Rolan pushed the elf roughly. "Move! And stay away from the water."

You think?!

As Vairug backed away from the cistern, he asked, "What is it?"

Rolan shook his head. "I don't know, but we need to get out of here. There might be more of them."

Belac moved as fast as he was able, but his side began to pain him. "Why does everything want to eat me?!"

There was no reemergence of the creature, and no wailing screams of pursuit. As he fled, all Belac could hear was the sound of scuffling feet and his own ragged breath.

When Rolan determined that they had moved far enough from harm's way, he stopped and unholstered his springer. "Get behind me. Try to get your breathing under control. I need to hear."

"You need to hear?" Belac panted.

Rolan angled his left ear out and back in the direction that they had fled. "You are welcome to help."

Vairug held his mace ready to strike at anything that might emerge from the dark. Belac backed farther away, his hand resting on the hilt of his rapier. The three waited there in golden glow surrounded by darkness and stone. Time stretched. Nothing happened.

Rolan holstered his springer and then turned around before walking onward. "I don't think it's going to leave the water."

That did not sound very reassuring to Belac. "Are you sure?"

"No," Rolan said. "Maybe you should pay attention."

Belac narrowed his eyes at the dwarf. *I do pay attention! I pay attention to everything! It is not my fault that everything is so crazy that only a crazier crazy dwarf understands all the crazy going on!*

After a short walk, Rolan stopped again and unslung his pack. He pulled out a large bladder and took a drink before handing it to the orc. "Here," Rolan told him. "You can drink some of it, but don't put your mouth on it."

Vairug took the bladder and stared at the dwarf.

"I don't know what your saliva would do to my guts," Rolan explained impatiently.

Vairug tilted his head back and held the bladder up, pouring water into his mouth. When he tried to hand the bladder back to Rolan, the dwarf nodded toward Belac. Vairug passed the bladder over to the elf and then Belac took a drink. Belac tried not to think about what the dwarf's saliva might do to his guts.

Rolan handed each of the other two a small biscuit and then bit into one himself. Belac sniffed at the biscuit, it smelled like nothing.

Vairug bit into his biscuit. "Gauh." The orc looked like he wanted to spit it out.

Unsympathetic, Rolan said, "Just eat it."

Belac wrinkled his nose at the biscuit and then took a small bite. It was sweet and tasted of cinnamon. "This is amazing!"

"Just eat it," Rolan said again. He took the bladder back and washed down the biscuit.

Belac ate the rest of his biscuit and considered asking for another. Vairug stared at him suspiciously.

Rolan passed the bladder back to the elf. "I gave you both the same thing, Vairug. Just eat it."

Vairug gave the dwarf one more suspicious look and then crammed the rest of the biscuit into his mouth before reaching for the bladder. Belac took another swig from the bladder and then handed it over.

Belac was still considering asking for another biscuit when Rolan put the bladder away and slung his pack. Belac watched the pack sway back and forth as the dwarf walked onward. He speculated whether or not he could get one of the biscuits out of the pack without Rolan noticing. Then he remembered the last person that had tried something like that. *Rolan broke his arm and threw him off a cliff. I wonder if the poor guy just wanted a biscuit.*

Fifteen

They saw the light long before they reached its source. As Belac walked with his companions through the radiance at the end of the masterfully worked tunnel, he discovered something beyond reason. *That can't be real…* It was daylight captured in an enormous crystal-clear dome. Resting atop a formidable wall of dark gray stone, the dome sheared cleanly through the rock above, creating a smooth concavity in the ceiling of a massive cavern. *That wall is too tall for me to reach the top, even if I stood on Vairug's shoulders.* Belac knew little of stone, but it was obvious to him that the wall before him was far superior to the dull and crudely cut prison. Fit and polished much like the masonry of the gnomish complex, the stone enclosure abutted the walls of the cavern to both the left and right. In the center of the wall, a solid metal gate denied further ingress into the cavern.

The escapees stepped out of the tunnel and continued to follow the cobblestone pathway that would lead them to the gate. Belac gazed at the dome in wonderment. Completely underground, it incased the sky. Fragile traces of clouds hung in the light of midday though bereft of the sun's grace.

"It's magic," Belac said. "It has to be."

Rolan glanced at the orc. "Any idea what this is?"

Vairug answered slowly, "I do not."

"I am telling you, it's magic." *It is a giant, magic bubble.*

Vairug nodded. "It does look like magic."

"Of course, it's magic," Rolan replied irritably. "But all that means is that none of us know what it is, or how it works, or how it might try to kill us."

Belac stopped and picked up a small rock from the cavern floor. Then he threw it at the dome. The rock bounced off the dome, quietly ringing the air with a dull sound that resembled thick glass.

Rolan came to a halt and held his hands up next to his ears as if he feared his head would explode. "Do not do that." He gesticulated aggressively.

Belac did not understand the dwarf's agitation. "Why? We needed to know what would happen."

"What did you think was going to happen?!" Rolan asked. "You throw the rock, and anyone nearby hears it. You throw the rock, and it sets off some magic alarm. Or, you throw the rock, break something, and I am fairly certain someone notices the sky falling down." Rolan waved his hand at the wall. "What could you possibly have learned that would be worth announcing that we're here?"

Belac tried to think of something that might make him not sound like a fool. "No one noticed," he said defensively, and then realized that was the answer. "Now, we know no one is around."

Rolan stared at the elf stone-faced.

Belac looked to Vairug for help, but the orc shook his head.

Rolan turned away and began walking toward the gate. Following the dwarf quietly, Belac appraised the gate. He could not tell if it was solid iron, hollow, or iron backed wood, but he would have simply described it as metal. The opening it blocked was large enough for a small cart to pass through, but to Belac, it had the feel of being rarely used. The gate was closed, unmanned, and unwelcoming.

Rolan put his foot against the bottom right corner of the gate and pushed. When it did not move, he slammed his left shoulder against the gate. When that did not work, he bent down in the middle, found a handhold, and tried to lift. Unsuccessful, the dwarf stepped back and studied the unyielding barrier. Then he turned around and said, "Hey, Vairug, give me a hand."

Vairug tilted his head to the side and stared at the dwarf disapprovingly.

Rolan held up both hands in surrender, laughing. "I did not do it on purpose." He pointed above himself. "I need to get up there."

Recognizing the murder hole for what it was, Belac appreciated how fortunate they were that the gate was unmanned. Vairug bent down and put his injured wrist under his right. Rolan stepped onto the orc's hand and Vairug lifted him up. Rolan caught the edge above and wiggled himself up into the wall. Belac thought that watching a dwarf try to crawl through the ceiling might almost be worth going to prison for.

Belac watched the murder hole with Vairug as they waited for the dwarf. Belac began to worry that Rolan might not come back. Belac did not think that the dwarf would just leave them there, trapped behind the gate. *But he could.*

Belac's azure eyes moved to the orc. "Do you think something ate him?"

Vairug smiled. "What would want to eat a dwarf?"

Belac smiled with the orc. *I might actually like him.* That he enjoyed the orc's banter was rather surprising to Belac. Elves did not befriend orcs; they did not even say nice things about them.

There was a mechanical sound of large gears turning and then the gate began to move. It lifted straight up, but then stopped, creating a gap that Belac was not sure he could have fit through. He was scared to try. *I'm not getting eaten by a gate.*

Rolan's voice called from inside the wall, "Go through."

Belac looked at the orc before turning his head up toward the murder hole. "It is too low," he called out, his voice pitched to carry.

Rolan said something angrily that the elf did not comprehend, and then the mechanical sounds resumed. More daylight began to show through as the gate continued to rise.

When the gate was high enough that it looked like the orc could fit through safely, Belac shouted, "Okay, that's good." The mechanical sound did not stop, so he raised his voice. "I said that is high enough."

The noise stopped.

"Then, go through!" Rolan called angrily.

"Oh. Right." Belac nodded and then looked to the orc.

Vairug rolled under the gate. The gears began to turn again, and the gate lowered slowly. Belac did not like the idea of being under the gate as it was coming down, but he liked the idea of being stranded even less. He did not want to be trapped underground with no one for company except a horde of angry goblins. *And a… a water-zombie!* His side ached as he got down and crawled under the gate as quickly as he could. He expected the gate to slam down as soon as he was free of it, but it simply continued its slow decent as the gears turned.

Safe on the other side of the gate, Belac declared, "We are calling it a water-zombie!"

Vairug looked at the elf. "What are you talking about?"

"You know what I mean. The crazy fish monster that was all teeth." Belac put his hands in front of his mouth and used his fingers to mimic biting fangs. "The one in the water."

Vairug stared at him.

"We just saw it!" Belac insisted.

Vairug stared at him.

Belac gestured wildly. "It just tried to kill us! I know you saw it!"

Vairug shook his head. "That was not a zombie."

"It was close enough," Belac argued.

"That was also not a fish," Vairug added.

"Whatever," Belac dismissed him. "I am still calling it a water-zombie."

"It was not a zombie," Vairug said with authority.

Belac's gaze followed the cobblestone path as it continued on, lazily snaking across a vibrant field of grass to stop at the front steps of a castle. *A Castle!* The castle was more than stone and mastery, it was art and splendor. Its elegant spires and plains of white stone marbled with black and gold inspired in him thoughts of the sea, not caverns or caves. To the left was a stand of evergreens that presented a small forest which simply should not have been there. *None of this should be here.*

Rolan walked out of an opening in the wall and joined them.

Belac smiled. "It seemed like you were having trouble with the gate."

Rolan frowned at the elf. "The gate was not made for dwarves, and I didn't have an ogre handy."

Vairug stared at the dwarf.

Rolan stared right back. "You cannot get mad at me every time I use the word 'hand,' Vairug."

Right then, Belac did not care about Vairug or his missing hand. He was worried about ogres. If the gate had been designed for ogres, then there might be ogres inside the walls. The elf looked at the closed gate and felt like he was trapped in a clever cage.

Belac tried to keep the panic from his voice. "How do we get out of here?"

If Rolan noticed the elf's fear, he did not mention it. "I say we follow the wall left and circle behind those trees over there. If we can find another gate, it should have another one of those holes that we can climb down from."

Belac did not find the plan reassuring. "What if we find one and it doesn't have a murder hole?" He suddenly realized that someone might have to stay back to hold the gate. *That is not going to be me.*

Rolan shrugged gruffly. "Then, we find another way." He was obviously growing impatient. "I am not a tour guide."

"Why don't we just go to the castle?" Belac felt exposed, and he did not think anyone would let an ogre inside a castle that nice.

"We want to go past the castle," Rolan told him. "We do not want to go in the castle."

"I want to go in the castle," Belac countered.

"No. No, you don't." Rolan shook his head. "Castles have people inside. People, and defenses, and weapons, and," he waved his hands around, "magic."

"Okay. Yeah." Belac nodded and then shook his head. "I don't want to go in the castle."

"Right," Rolan agreed and then walked away.

Vairug went with the dwarf, but Belac hesitated. After a moment of indecision, he hurried to catch up with them.

Walking behind them, Belac asked, "Do you think there's a way that we could maybe…" he cleared his throat, "Not go in the forest?"

"What?" Rolan sounded confused by the question. "Why?"

Belac did not answer.

Vairug was happy to provide the information. "Belac is scared of green."

"I am not!" Belac insisted. "I just… don't trust it."

Rolan grinned. "You were serious?"

Vairug began laughing silently.

Belac narrowed his eyes at the orc. "That's right. Go ahead and laugh, Vairug," He held his hands up. "Or better yet, how about you applaud?" He clapped his hands together.

Vairug stopped laughing.

Belac asked, "Do you still trust the color green?!"

Sixteen

"But the grass is green," Rolan argued.

Belac stuck out his foot and pointed to it. "And that's why I wear boots!"

Rolan shook his head ruefully but allowed the elf his eccentricities.

As they approached the tree line, Belac narrowed his eyes at the conifers distrustfully. *Evergreens are the worst. Those things are not just green. They're a green that defies the laws of nature.* He could not have been convinced that danger did not lurk in the shadows of such sinister things. With a glance toward the distant castle, he wondered what could possibly be inside the breathtaking structure that was more perilous than a forest. Then he remembered the ogres. *Yeah, okay. We can just sneak through the forest and hope that nothing wakes up.* He tried to imagine that the trees were sleeping.

Keeping the wall of bleached stone on their left, the three escapees trekked over lush grass until they reached the edge of the tree line. *That is not a forest...* Screened by a wide ring of vibrant evergreens, a gazebo stood in the center of a small glade. Styled to match the castle, the gazebo was a large octagonal affair of white marble swirled with black and gold.

In that surreal clearing, among the pillars of the gazebo, stood a woman with flowing, blond hair that spilled across her simple gown of white linen. Her coloring so matched the gazebo, that Belac did not notice her until she turned to gaze up at the castle that loomed above the trees. On her face was a look not of longing, but of wistful acceptance. *She is gorgeous.* To Belac, she was a woman that deserved a castle, deserved a forest, deserved daylight no matter where she was. Belac stared and thought that she might be the most magical thing that he had yet to see.

A man, armored in gleaming plate mail, approached the woman from the direction of the castle. Belac was so transfixed with the mysterious woman, that he did not register the man's presence until he walked into view. *It looks like he forgot his helmet.* Belac decided that the man must have been too worried about mussing his auburn hair to don a helmet and protect his handsome face. *Stupid, handsome humans.*

The man came to a halt outside the gazebo and said, "It is time to return to the castle, Princess."

The woman threw something that bounced off the man's chest piece.

The man seemed nonplussed by the disrespect. "You must come back now, Princess. You know this to be true."

Without further dissent, the woman stepped out of the gazebo and followed the man through the trees and toward the castle. Each step she took seemed a forced act of submission.

"We have to save her," Belac declared.

"No, we don't," Rolan corrected him.

"Yes, we do," Belac argued. "Did you see her?"

"Yes. I saw her," Rolan said. "She is a princess living in a magic castle. What is there to save her from? And don't say a dragon! Don't you say a dragon!"

"There could be a dragon!" Belac did not give the dwarf a chance to argue. "Besides, did you see how that man just told her what to do? You could see that she didn't want to do it, but she had to."

"That is exactly how being a princess works," Rolan told him.

"How would you know? It's hard to picture you wearing a tiara." Belac pictured the dwarf in a pink dress wearing a tiara, then wished that he had not.

"And what is your plan?" Rolan asked. "Knock on the front door and say, 'Hello, I am here to slay the dragon and save the princess.' Is that it?"

"Well..." Belac said. "Maybe not that."

"Right." Rolan gave one strong nod. "Then, let's go back to the plan where we don't all die horribly."

As they continued on, Belac stayed next to the wall, keeping his companions between himself and the trees. He felt better knowing it was not a real forest, but he saw no reason to take any chances. If one of those trees decided to eat one of them, it was not going to be the elf.

Belac frowned at the dwarf. "Why don't you want to save the princess?"

Rolan grunted. "I don't want to save anyone."

Belac thought back to the prison cells. "You saved me." *More than once.*

"Did you just call yourself a princess?" Rolan asked slyly.

Belac did not take the bait. "You know what I mean, Rolan."

Rolan sighed. "You are a..." He searched for the right word. "An accomplice."

Belac hoped that no one in a position of authority would agree with the dwarf.

Vairug looked at the dwarf. "An accomplice?"

Rolan gave the orc a dirty look. "Saving people is work. Most anyone that cannot save themselves, is just going to get right back into a situation that they need to be saved from again. So, unless you want to spend the rest of your life saving the same people over and over again, you're just wasting your time."

"That can't be right," Belac said.

Rolan ignored him. "You can also get yourself dead trying to save people."

"Wait, wait, wait," Belac said laughing. "So, you are saying, you don't want to save the princess?"

Rolan nodded. "Right."

Belac continued, "Because we might die?"

"Right." Rolan nodded again.

"So, what you are really saying, is that you don't want to save the princess, because it might stop you from saving me?" Belac laughed some more.

"No, that's not..." Rolan stopped. "Yeah, sure. I have a save-one-princess-at-a-time policy."

Belac narrowed his eyes at the dwarf. Then he smiled and said, "Hey, Vairug. Did you hear that? Rolan just called you a princess."

Vairug looked at the elf without humor.

They continued to follow the wall past the trees, but it was obvious by that point that there would be no second gate. The wall's steady curve abutted the castle, leaving only one way for them to go. Belac was exhausted and felt like it should be getting dark soon. He looked up at the bright sky and decided that it was mocking him.

As they approached the castle, Belac began to feel disoriented. It was not until they were standing next to the side of the castle that he finally understood. The castle was of massive proportions, though scaled down to a much smaller size. It was still a building of impressive dimensions, but it had not been as far away as it had appeared. While Belac could not have thought of it as anything other than a castle, it was more of a mansion styled to look like a castle.

"It's kind of small, all things considered." Belac knew it was only small compared to his own expectations.

Rolan placed his hand upon the white stone and traced the black and gold marbling. "This castle is worth more than some kingdoms."

Maybe the castle is just dwarf sized. Belac took in the castle. It was magnificent in its own right, but it was also the only hope of escape they had left. "Are we going in?" he asked smiling.

Rolan sounded pained when he answered, "Yes. But you are going to have to be quiet."

Belac's smile grew. "So, you don't want to hear me remind you that I wanted to go to the castle as soon as we saw it?"

"No," Rolan said. "I do not."

"You don't want to hear me say that if we had done what I wanted, we could have avoided the hike through the woods?" Belac batted his eyelashes at the dwarf.

Rolan stared at the elf, waiting for him to finish.

Vairug nudged the dwarf's arm. "I bet you won't hit him."

Rolan turned his stare on the orc.

Vairug did not even try to hide his smile.

"This is going to be dangerous," Rolan told them. "We don't know what all we are going to find in there. We do know, that they have at least one heavily armed guard." He waved his hand around. "And magic. I know you think that this is a pretty castle, but we are not exactly in a friendly neighborhood."

Belac thought about where they were and what they had gone through to get there. It was hard for him to keep smiling.

Rolan finished, "So, stay close, keep quiet, and try not to touch anything."

"Do you know what this means?" Belac asked, and answered, "It means, I get to save the princess!"

Seventeen

Belac and his companions had entered the castle through a doorway that had been blocked by a large door styled to look like a drawbridge. Despite its design, the door had swung out away from the castle to allow entry. Upon seeing the door open freely, Belac had found it odd that no one had bothered to lock or bar the door. After a moment of consideration, he had concluded that there was probably not much point in locking the side door to a magic castle buried underground and protected by ogres, goblins, and monsters. Immediately after his conclusion, he had realized it was a mistake. Three escaped prisoners had just snuck inside.

The faux drawbridge had opened to a rectangular room with a low row of storage benches on the right that had been padded with scarlet, crush velvet cushions. A warm light lit the room, its glow provided by small brass torches that were affixed to the marble walls. Belac marveled at the torches. The fixtures were without heads, their flames dancing above bending brass extensions. He reminded himself that he was in a magic castle and that he had more important things to worry about.

A woman walked silently into the room, her sudden appearance startling the elf. Her chestnut hair was pulled back in a tail, she was pretty, and she was nude.

When Belac realized that it was a naked woman, his brain stopped working properly and he just stood there staring. He was startled again when the woman was pounced on by a dwarf and slung down onto the floor. Rolan turned the woman over, wrapped an arm around her neck, and began to strangle her. There was a light sound of scuffling, but the woman could not call out. *I have to stop him.* Belac moved forward, only to be held back by Vairug's left arm on his chest. Belac looked up at the orc's hard face and then down at Rolan. Calmly, the dwarf was squeezing the life out of the woman. *I can't just let them kill her.* Belac's mind raced for a way to save the helpless woman.

Rolan released his hold and allowed the woman's head to fall lifelessly to the floor.

Belac did not know what to do. "You killed her…" he uttered in disbelief.

"I didn't kill her," Rolan replied irritably. He reached into a pouch and pulled out a wooden box no bigger than his thumb. He twisted it open, and a slim vial slipped out. As the liquid inside sloshed around, it changed back and forth from blue to green.

"What is that for?" Belac asked, not entirely convinced that the woman was still alive.

Rolan put a drop of the liquid in the woman's mouth. "It is so I don't have to kill her."

The dwarfs hushed words reminded Belac that he should keep his own low. Rolan put the vial away with a practiced ease that suggested this was not the first time that he had drugged someone. Belac looked past the unconscious woman and saw that she had come from a cramped kitchen. Everything inside was well made but had a utilitarian feel. The lack of decadence made Belac think that the castle's owner did not frequent the kitchen. From the other side of the room entered another woman, brunette hair pulled back, and also completely unclothed.

Rolan tensed to move, but stopped. The woman gave no indication that she noticed them. Rolan was low, Belac was thin, but there was no way that someone could miss Vairug. When the woman picked up a knife, Belac thought that she might just be canny. However, all she did with the knife was begin preparing food.

Rolan moved into the room cautiously and snaped his fingers at the woman. Still, she gave no indication that she was aware of his presence. He moved closer and then waved a hand in front of her eyes, warry of the knife. He snapped his fingers again, this time in her face.

Quietly, Rolan said, "This is not good."

Belac disagreed. "It's better than a screaming naked woman with a knife," he argued as he joined the dwarf in the kitchen.

Rolan shook his head. "It means that there is something in here that can do that to you." He pointed at the woman.

Vairug asked softly, "Magic?"

"I don't know," Rolan said. "This seems too permanent. Also, it takes some strong magic to dominate someone this completely."

Belac held up a finger, twirled it around, and mouthed the words, "Magic. Castle."

Rolan nodded at him angrily. "Right, but I don't think someone is going to use that kind of power to make lunch."

"Then, what do you think it is?" Belac asked.

Rolan took a deep breath and then sighed. "I think it's probably a nillanan."

Belac had no idea what that was. "A nilla-what?"

"A nillanan," Rolan said again. "A mind rapist." He looked at the elf. "A faceless monster with mouths on its hands that wants to eat your brain."

Belac leaned back and looked down at the dwarf. *That can't be a real thing.* The dwarf looked serious. He also looked irritated, but he looked like that often as not.

Vairug asked the important question. "How do we kill it?"

"We don't," Rolan stated firmly. "We get ourselves out of here and hope that no one notices we were ever here until it's too late for them to do anything about it."

Leaving suited Belac just fine. He might not have known what a nillanan was, but he did not want anything to eat his brain. He followed closely as they left the kitchen and crept through a hallway. The castle had ballrooms, and dining rooms, and rooms with purposes the elf could not have guessed. One room seemed to exist solely to view the paintings that covered its walls. *Magic castle or not, this place is ridiculous.* What stood out the most about the castle was that despite the obvious wealth represented, nothing was gilded. Whoever or whatever owned the castle, cared more for the quality of things than their apparent value to others. To Belac, it made the castle feel like a home. Sneaking through a home felt different than sneaking through a castle. It was more personal, and therefore, felt like a far greater violation.

The hallway ended in a spacious foyer with banister stairs that climbed to a platform afore a grand window of stained glass. A dark mosaic of red, blue, and violet, no light shone through the window. To either side of the platform, rose more stairs leading to the upper floors. In the center of the room, standing at the foot of the stairs, were two more unclothed women. They looked so much alike, that Belac thought the women could only be sisters. Though they were svelte and more attractive, their flaxen hair was pulled back in the same fashion as the women in the kitchens.

"Yes, they're nice." Rolan's hushed voice was impatient. "But they won't fit in your pocket. So, let's go."

Belac knew that the dwarf was right, if crude in his sentiment. However, it felt wrong to just leave the women behind. He went to the one closest and looked into her hazel eyes. They were as empty and lifeless as a corpse's. Whatever had been done to her seemed to have taken her soul. Her sexual form juxtaposed with that vacant gaze left the elf disturbed. *This is wrong.*

A flash of golden movement to his left drew Belac's attention up to the second floor. *The princess!* He was running up the stairs before he realized what he was doing. He tried to formulate a plan as he went, but all he could think of was to grab the princess, hurry back to the others, and then escape before the faceless hand-monster turned the princess into one of those human dolls.

The hallway on the second floor was wider, and the openness made Belac feel lost. He did not know where to go. He tried to remember if he had heard a door close, but he did not think that he had. He raced down the hallway, hoping to find an open door. *This is taking too long.* He considered going back and getting the others, but then he passed a partially open door. He almost fell over trying to stop. The elf quickly regained his balance, pushed the door all the way open, and stepped inside.

A woman's voice complained, "You know that you are not…" before stopping midsentence.

Belac had found her. Up close, she was only more beautiful. She was younger than he had expected, but Belac did not mind. Her golden hair seemed to have a glow of its own, and her eyes could have been the sky. Her pale gown, however modest, could not hide her womanly shape. The princess stepped away, eyes wide with surprise.

Belac remembered that he was covered in blood and wearing a sword. He held up his hands and tried to give the woman a disarming smile. "I am here to rescue you."

Her face went from confusion, to disbelief, and then settled on hope. "And whom might you be?" She even sounded like a princess.

"My name is Belac." He tried to stand taller. "I am here to recue you."

"Yes, you said that bit before," the princess replied in an accent that was both noble and slightly mocking.

Belac had liked saying that he was there to rescue her, but now, she had ruined it. He tried another charming smile.

The princess did not seem to understand what the elf was waiting for. "Well, is there a plan?"

"A plan?" Belac asked.

"Yes, a plan." The princess looked at him meaningfully. "A rescue plan?"

"Yeah, that's the plan," Belac told her. "To rescue you." *Wow, humans are stupid.*

"Are you sure…" She pointed to the door. "Watch out!"

Belac twisted to look, and then fell over as he dodged away from the long, two-handed sword that would have killed him. He drew his rapier and swiped the air three times as he scrambled to his feet. The princess's guard was held back by the attacks, weak as they had been. Belac did not remember seeing a sword strapped to the guard's back. He vowed to pay closer attention the next time he was spying on a princess in a magic forest.

Belac thrust, but the man caught the rapier's blade on his cross-guard. A kick to Belac's hip put him back on the floor and he was barely able to get his rapier up in time to deflect another blow that would have killed him. The force of the two-handed swing was enough to rip the rapier from his hands and send it flying across the room. Belac looked up at the man. The guard was a professional, and he was set on killing the elf. Belac drew his poniard and threw it at him. The man held up his left arm to protect his face, but the knife bounced harmlessly against his breastplate. Belac used the throw as a distraction and rolled away, diving for his rapier. He came back to his feet with a wild backhanded swing that came nowhere close to the man.

Not wanting to give the man another chance to attack, Belac lunged. The man stepped back and swung his sword, not at the elf, but at his rapier. The rapier was hit with such force that the blade was snapped off. The shock to Belac's hand was so great that he dropped the hilt without thinking. Instinctually, he grabbed his right hand with his left and stepped backward in pain. He stumbled into a table and then found himself on the floor once more.

Belac looked up in time to see a silvery cog slam into the side of the man's head and send him sprawling sideways. Vairug stood over the man and brought the cogged mace down on his head again. *Not so handsome now, are you?*

The princess screamed.

Eighteen

"Shut that woman up!" Rolan ordered.

Belac reached for the princess, but she knocked his hand aside and began slapping him. The elf found himself retreating from a barrage of small, delicate hands. "You need to calm down, Princess!"

The princess stopped, drew herself back, and tilted her head so that she could look down her nose at the elf. She nodded her head in the direction of the orc. "I suppose he belongs to you?"

Vairug answered, "No."

The princess looked at the orc as if she were surprised that he could speak.

Vairug shook his head at the woman disapprovingly and then walked out of the room.

"Listen, Lady," Rolan said. "No more screaming if you want to go with us."

The princess turned her attention to the dwarf. "I understand," she said primly.

"I do not think you do," Rolan corrected her. "You scream like that again, and I will knock you out and leave you here."

Belac tried to calm the dwarf. "Come on, Rolan."

Rolan did not back down. "If it comes to it, you can stay with her. But I am not going to die because some princess can't keep her head."

The princess squared her shoulders. "I understand," she said again, this time with more authority.

Rolan studied her for a moment and then nodded his head, satisfied. "Right. We need to move. Do you know the way out?"

The princess furrowed her brow. "Me?"

"Yes, you." Rolan was impatient.

The princess arched an eyebrow. "Surely, you know how you found your way inside."

Still impatient, Rolan said, "You don't want to go the way we came in. Do you know another way out or not?"

"I do," the princess claimed without confidence. "But I hardly think that the guards will simply allow us to leave."

Rolan shook his head. "We are not going to give them a choice," he assured her. "Let's move."

Belac spoke up. "Wait. I have to ask something." He waited for the princess to look at him. "Serious question. Is there a dragon?"

The princess furrowed her brow again. "Why in the world would there be a dragon?"

Rolan said, "There is no dragon, Belac."

The princess regarded eth elf queerly. "And why does that seem to disappoint you so?"

Belac sighed. "Let's go," he said, walking toward the door sullenly.

Belac stopped and looked down at the dead guard. The two-handed sword lay next to him, seeming more like a fallen comrade than a dropped tool. The sword looked exactly as Belac would imagine a two-handed long-sword to look. There was a simplicity to it that he appreciated. It reminded him of the rest of the castle, an unornamented masterpiece. He bent down and picked up the sword by its black leather hilt. He was in need of a new weapon, and while heavy, the long-sword was a finer blade than the ones he had lost. He tugged the matching baldric over the guard's shoulder, smearing blood on the strap. He did not believe this was the first time the leather had been bloodied.

Belac sheathed the sword. "I was out of swords anyway." He would need to carry the scabbarded blade until he had time to adjust the baldric to fit him.

Rolan held out the elf's poniard. "Did you throw this?"

Belac took the knife and slid it into its scabbard. "It seemed like a good idea at the time."

"Right," Rolan said. "There is a lot of that going around."

Belac thought about how he had run off after the princess. "Yeah, sorry about that."

Rolan said nothing more about it and left the room.

Belac turned to the princess and smiled. "Are you ready to be rescued?"

The princess smiled, and Belac felt like every decision he had ever made had been the right one. She nodded and then they left the room together. Both Vairug and Rolan were waiting for them.

As she stepped out into the hallway, the princess said, "We will need to first descend to the lower floor." She stepped forward but seemed uneasy so close to the orc.

Belac did not blame her. He felt a little uneasy around the orc as well. "Maybe you should follow behind with me."

"Then, how will I…" the princess began to ask.

"Don't worry." Belac held up a hand. "It will work."

She did not argue. The two walked side by side as they followed together. Belac considered offering her his arm, but decided that it would be less in line with a heroic rescue. He would wait until later, when they did not have to worry about something trying to kill them. *I really hope there is a time when I don't have to worry about something trying to kill me.*

Belac soon found himself glad that he had followed behind with the princess; not only because he enjoyed her company, but because it put Rolan and Vairug between him and the horror that awaited them at the stairs. Belac halted in his tracks and stared down at the thin humanoid draped in dark robes that was standing in the center of the mid platform afore the glass mosaic.

The creature's head was pale, hairless flesh without eyes, ears, nose, or mouth. Empty, flesh covered sockets stared balefully toward those who would dare trespass in the nillanan's domain. It stood with a malicious dignity that seemed to radiate from the creature in primal warning.

On either side of the nillanan was a man armed and armored the same as the princess's guard had been. Armor gleaming, swords held out to the side, they did not stand as men waiting, but as things set aside, unmoving. The nillanan made a noise that to Belac sounded like a giant lobster clearing its throat. The men rushed up the stairs.

Rolan stepped to the right of the stairway. "Kill them," he ordered briskly.

Belac drew his sword, not knowing how to use such a long blade, but wanting to put something between himself and danger. He moved the princess behind him and attempted to look brave. *We should not have come into the castle!* Men with swords were coming to kill him, but Belac could not take his eyes away from the nillanan. *That thing is going to eat my brain!* The nillanan staggered back as a flash of silver shot through its high cheekbone, maroon blood splattering on the mosaic.

Before Belac could comprehend what had happened, the guards reached the top of the stairs. With his cogged mace, Vairug battered aside a sword and then crushed one of the men's faces. Belac thrust his sword out toward the other man, only to have it deflected down. Rolan dropped his springer and then leapt over the banister.

Belac would never have believed a dwarf could jump so far. He watched the spectacular attack as Rolan flew down the stairs with a knife held over his head and slammed into the nillanan. The dwarf buried his knife into the nillanan's neck where it met the shoulder and then drove the monster to the floor. Belac's attention was suddenly drawn back to the fight as the last man stepped inside his lowered guard and grabbed his arm. Then the cog of Vairug's mace bashed in the side of the man's head and bounced him against the wall.

Belac's heart was pounding, but he remembered how important it was to look heroic. So, he struck a pose and made a show of looking for more threats. His eyes were drawn back down to Rolan, who was hacking savagely at the nillanan's neck. The dwarf ripped the nightmarish head free from the nillanan's body and slammed it to the floor as if he thought it might try to get away. Holding it down, the dwarf stabbed his knife into the head's empty eye sockets in violent succession. Rolan then stood and kicked the head away.

Deciding that he looked sufficiently heroic, Belac sheathed his sword and turned to check on the princess. She appeared as if she might be in shock. Belac was conflicted. If she was in shock, she may not have noticed how brave he had been. However, it would also give him a chance to comfort her. *I will just have to hope that she was shocked by how brave I looked.*

Belac smiled and tried to sound strong as he comforted the woman. "Are you alright, Princess? You are safe now."

"Is he…" The princess raised her voice. "Is it dead?"

Rolan laughed. "If it's not, I bet it wishes it was."

"It is so hard to believe," the princess said. "It happened so fast. I have been here so long, and yet it died so easily."

Rolan gestured to the mess. "I don't think I would call that dying easy."

"Yes, of course," the princess conceded. "It was just so fast. And with only a knife."

Rolan began walking back up the stairs. "Right. Well, it did not look like shooting it in the face was going to get the job done."

Belac picked up the dwarf's springer and handed it to him. They all looked down at the bloody nillanan lying next to its own severed head. Dark maroon blood covered the platform and had been splattered against the glass mosaic. Some of the blood had been thrown so far that it ran down the back of one of the nude women standing at the bottom of the stairs.

Belac gazed with pity at the two women. "Will they be alright now?"

"They, who?" Rolan asked.

Belac gestured to the bottom of the stairs. "The women."

Rolan shook his head. "Those are not women."

Belac had to disagree. "I am pretty sure they are."

"No." Rolan shook his head again. "Those are not women anymore. They are not people. A nillanan strips away anything inside a person's mind that will not submit to the nillanan's will. The more someone fights, the more damage is done. It does not matter how strong they are, there will be nothing left that does not serve the nillanan."

"But the nillanan is dead," Belac argued. "There has to be some way we can fix them."

"You don't seem to understand." Rolan tried to explain. "There is nothing left to fix. The nillanan destroys whatever it is that makes a person a person. I know they look like people, but they're not. Not anymore."

The princess put her hand on the elf's arm.

"No." Belac refused to believe that there was nothing that could be done. "Then, we have to take them with us."

"We can't." Rolan was growing impatient. "Now that the nillanan is dead, there is no will to drive its slaves. Some of them have probably just stopped breathing already." He gestured toward the nude women. "Those two are going to stand there until they die."

Belac would not give up on the women so easily. "Not if we take them with us!"

"And how are you going to do that?" Rolan asked. "They will not follow you. They will not eat. They will not drink. Even if we carry them all the way back up to the surface, they will still die. Besides, what happens the first time we meet someone, and they see an orc with a naked woman tucked under his arm?"

Ooh... Yeah... Belac nodded grudgingly. "That would be bad."

"Right," Rolan said, concluding the conversation.

Belac felt the princess tighten her grip on his arm. He turned to her and suddenly knew what he had to do. He may not have been able to help the other women, but he could still save one. He could still save her. He would always remember that moment, the moment he vowed to himself that he would protect her. He would save her. He would take this light from the dark and set it free. He would do this not because it was brave or heroic, but because he had to do something to defy the evil that surrounded him.

Nineteen

Rolan was irritated. "The nillanan have all kinds of magic. Some of it, they use to stay in communication with each other. There is no way to know how far away that thing's friends are, but you had better believe it has them. It is just a matter of time before they show up here looking for him, and you are not going to want to be here when they do. We should have enough time to catch our breath and maybe find something to eat, but then we have got to get out of here."

All Belac had wanted to know was why Rolan was in such a hurry. The nillanan was dead, its slaves were harmless, and everything that wanted to kill them was on the other side of a stone wall and a magic dome. Belac wanted a nap.

However, there was no way that Belac could sleep now, not with the thought of more nillanan on the way. "I can check the kitchen."

"That's a good idea," Rolan agreed. "Take the princess. Get something for now, and more for later. Try to find something that will not rot on us."

"What are you going to do?" Belac genuinely wanted to know.

Rolan evaded the question. "I will be with Vairug in the first room on the right. The one with that big table."

Belac turned to the princess and asked, "Do you want to help me find something to eat?"

The princess looked up from the dead nillanan. "Yes. Anything to get away from this… Thing."

Waving for the princess to follow him, Belac began making his way to the kitchens. As he walked through the halls with the woman he was rescuing, Belac found that the castle felt surprisingly different to him now. The subtle press of impending doom had been replaced with a curious emptiness. It could have been because he knew that the nillanan was dead, but Belac wondered if in life, the nillanan's very will had permeated the castle.

With the confidence of someone who knew where they were going, the princess took the lead. She led the elf to the kitchens, but then stopped in the doorway. On the floor lay a nude woman, her eyes open and lifeless. *She is not breathing.* Belac shuddered at the realization that the woman's eyes looked no different than when she had still been alive and a slave to the nillanan.

In an empty voice, the princess said, "That could have been me."

Belac put his hand on her shoulder. "You are safe now, Princess."

"Am I?" the princess asked sadly.

Belac turned her to face him. There were tears in her eyes. He smiled and said, "Unless you lied to me about the dragon."

The princess laughed and then suddenly began sobbing. She put her head against the elf's chest and gripped his vest. Belac wrapped his arms around her, being careful not to hit her with his sword. He considered dropping the scabbarded blade to the floor, but decided that it would be distractingly over dramatic. He held the princess tenderly until she calmed and pulled herself away.

"You do not have to call me 'Princess." It was an intimate permission.

Belac smiled at her again. "Yeah, I kind of do."

The princess put her hand on the elf's chest where her head had been. "No. You do not."

Belac shrugged. "I don't know what else to call you." *And no one likes being called 'hey, you.'*

The princess was taken aback. "You do not know who I am?" She removed her hand from his chest.

"Well, clearly I know who you are..." Belac gestured toward her. "I just eh... don't know your name."

"No one told you my name?" The princess was confused. "And you did not think to ask before you underwent to rescue me?"

I see the problem. Belac smiled. "Yeah... About that..."

The princess stepped away from him. "Who sent you?"

Belac held up his hands as nonthreateningly as he could while holding a long-sword. "No one sent us."

The princess raised an eyebrow. "Am I to believe you simply overheard a story about a captured princess, and then elected to risk your life in an attempt to rescue her?"

"Well, no," Belac said.

"Why would you even believe such a story is true?" the princess continued. "Surely that is the kind of detail that story tellers embellish."

"I said, 'No." Belac did not like being ignored. Not by a princess anyway.

The princess stared at the elf with her eyebrow raised like she might hit him with it.

"We did not come here to rescue you," Belac admitted. "But I am going to rescue you." *If you don't kill me with that eyebrow of yours.*

The princess's face changed to one of understanding. "You are adventurers?" She took a step toward the elf. "Is that why you asked about a dragon?"

That would kind of make sense. To a princess, it would almost certainly be easier to believe that her deduction was true. Belac considered explaining everything to her, but decided that her guess was close enough to the truth to not feel like a lie.

Also, he recognized that she may not want to travel with three escaped prisoners.

So, Belac said, "I would much rather find a princess than a dragon."

The princess smiled, nodded, and then pronounced, "That would explain why you travel with a…" She held her hand out above her in an approximation of Vairug's height.

"Yes, it would," Belac agreed.

"Still." The princess put her hand on the elf's shoulder. "You do not have to call me 'Princess."

"Do you prefer, 'Hey You." Belac asked.

"No." The princess pushed him away playfully. "Emily."

Belac wanted to try the name out. "The Princess Emily."

"Just Emily," she insisted. "You do not need to call me 'Princess."

"Emily." Belac enjoyed saying her name.

Emily stepped around the counter, putting it between her and the dead woman on the floor. Whether it had been a conscious choice or not, it seemed as if she wanted to pretend that the dead woman was not there. Belac was happy to join her in that fiction. Trying to put the dead woman out of his mind, he followed the princess into another room of the kitchens.

There were currently no meals prepared, and neither of them volunteered to cook. Instead, they found an oversized plater and piled on small loaves of bread. Belac was surprised at how delicious the bread smelled. *Maybe I am just hungry.* He took one of the loaves for himself and ate it while they searched for some way to carry water back to the others. Emily found a large jug and four ceramic cups. Belac filled the jug from a small reservoir, thinking that the jug looked more like something that would be used to water a garden than to serve at a gathering. The princess did not complain, and he did not think that anyone else would care.

Though it hung loosely, Belac slipped his commandeered long-sword onto his back. *I really need to adjust this baldric.* With his hands now free, he picked up the jug of water with one hand and the four cups with his other. *I hope I don't trip over my sword and break these things.* He glanced at the princess. *I don't want to look clumsy.* Emily was attempting to balance the tray of bread as the loaves shifted on top of it. *Though, clumsy does look cute on her.*

As Belac and the princess carried their haul to the meeting room, he tried to think of something to ask. He wanted to talk with her, but he did not want to ask questions that might bring up unpleasant thoughts. *Maybe I should ask her what her favorite color is or something like that. But what if she doesn't have a favorite color? Would the question make me seem stupid? Wait! What if her favorite color is green?!* He narrowed his eyes at the woman. *She doesn't look evil...* He walked into the meeting room without asking a question.

"You ruined it," Vairug complained to the dwarf.

Rolan dismissed the orcs concern. "I will get you another one later."

Scattered across the table before them were scraps of Vairug's leather chest piece. It had been disassembled and cut into new shapes. On one side of the table sat a pile of metal surrounded by small tools.

Vairug suggested, "I want the next one to not smell like a dead ogre." Despite his complaints, he did not sound terribly upset.

Belac pushed aside what remained of the orc's leather armor, making room for the food and drink. Rolan stopped working long enough to fill one of the cups with water and grab himself a loaf of bread. Then he went back to what he had been doing with the collected scrap. Everyone ate while the dwarf worked.

Rolan picked up the leather bag that Vairug had been hauling around and set it on the table. He pulled out a silvery device of intricate design and dropped it on the table with a heavy thud. He connected leather straps to it and began to craft a strange harness using leather working tools that the dwarf was obviously familiar with.

Watching him work, Belac realized that Rolan must have once been something else. The dwarf was a craftsman. There was no doubt about it. The tools he used were his own, and he knew how to use them. When the harness was complete, Rolan went to work on the silvery metal device.

Both Emily and Belac had ceased eating, intrigued and trying to discern what the dwarf was building. Rolan stopped and pulled a slim tome from his pack. He flipped through the pages until he found what he was looking for. He read two pages and then flipped the pages back and read them again. He nodded, closed the book, and then slipped it back into his pack. He picked up the metal device and set it down in front of Vairug with another heavy thud.

Vairug looked from the device to the dwarf. "This is a vanity I do not require."

Rolan nodded absently in agreement. "Give me your stump."

Without further complaint, Vairug held out his left arm. Rolan removed the strips of gorilla-wolf-monster fur and fixed the harness to the orc. It was a complex work of leather straps and hide plates that went up to Vairug's shoulder and secured across his chest. All of which was to hold the silvery device on the end of the orc's stump where his missing hand had once been.

Uncertainly, Emily said, "That seems rather elaborate. Is that not a bit much?"

Vairug shook his head. "It's clever." He nodded to the dwarf. "He's clever."

Seeing the device now attached to the orc's stump, Belac realized that it was a fist wrought for the gnome's statue. The fist was slightly too large for the orc, and at a glance might look like something that he was wearing over a real hand. Vairug moved and flexed his arm. The straps and plates shifted as he did, keeping the fist firmly in place.

Rolan waved toward himself. "Give it back."

Vairug held out his new fist and the dwarf guided it down to the table.

Rolan made some adjustments to the fist and then said, "I'm going to need some blood."

Vairug looked at the elf.

Belac stood up and stepped away.

Rolan saved the elf. "It has to be yours, Vairug."

Vairug studied the dwarf for a moment, nodded, and then shrugged.

Rolan made a shallow cut on the orc's arm. "Just let it bleed for now." He took something out of a pocket, cupped it in his hands, and whispered into them like a crazy person. Then he opened his hands, revealing a tiny, purple stone. Taking the stone between two fingers, he dipped the stone in the orc's blood. The stone began to glow an angry purple light.

Emily joined the elf in standing.

Distractedly, Rolan said, "You can take care of the bleeding now." He set the stone in a small housing in the inside wrist of the metal fist and closed it, sealing away the light. "Put your other hand on the table."

Vairug placed his hand on the table as if he was worried the dwarf might try to cut it off.

"Turn it over, palm up. Move it closer to the other one," Rolan instructed. "Now, focus on closing both of your hands into fists."

"I only have the one hand," Vairug reminded the dwarf.

"Look down," Rolan told him. "You have two hands. Close them both."

Vairug's right hand closed.

"Now, open them," Rolan instructed.

Vairug's right hand opened.

Rolan put his hands on the orc's forearms. "I want to feel you close your hands."

Vairug's right hand closed.

Rolan shook his head. "Both of them, Vairug."

Vairug growled at him.

"Now, squeeze them as hard as you can." Rolan nodded. "Good. Now, open your hands."

Vairug's right hand opened at the same time as the metal one on his left. "No..." he said in disbelief.

Rolan released the orc. "Like I said, you have two hands."

Vairug slowly opened and closed the metal hand. "Is it magic?"

Rolan tilted his head side to side. "Sort of."

"It is a soulstone," Emily announced.

Rolan looked at her. "You are very well educated."

Belac did not understand the woman's posture. He also did not know what a soulstone was.

Emily did not argue with the dwarf. "And you are not just an adventurer."

"No one is 'just' anything, Princess." Rolan emphasized the title to make his point.

Vairug stood from the table. He stretched and flexed, the leather straps sliding across hide plates as he did. He brought his new hand up in front of his face, opening and closing the mechanical device. The hand moved slowly, though speed and control were already improving. He opened his hand and held it out to the others, palm facing them. He closed the hand in demonstration. He smiled widely, insanity in his eyes. "I am glad we brought this."

The orc had always been intimidating. Now, he was part machine and possibly insane. Belac worried that the princess was going to run. If she did, he was going to run with her.

Twenty

"You said, the nillanan have all kinds of magic," Belac argued. "Let's go up there and see what we can find. We can't just leave a magical treasure trove behind." He looked at the orc's metal hand. "We went looting when you wanted to."

Belac did not need a magic hand, but he was willing to bet that he could find something else worth taking. *There could be anything up there.* Even if all they found was a crate filled with magic hands, he could still trade them for a fortune.

Rolan was impatient again. "Do one of you have phenomenal cosmic powers that I don't know about?" He waited though no one answered. "That's what I thought. If you go up there and start meddling with things, you are either going to set off a trap, or make some other mistake because you don't know what you are playing with. You might not even make it into the room."

"Then, come with me." Belac thought about the dwarf's springer, the light rods, the potions, and the orc's magic hand. It was not until that moment that Belac realized how much magic the dwarf had used casually. "You seem to understand how this magic stuff works."

"I understand enough to know that going anywhere near that nillanan's quarters is a bad idea." Rolan shook his head. "We have already been here too long. We need to leave." He turned to the princess. "Are you ready to show us the way out?"

Emily nodded. "I am."

Belac felt a little betrayed. He knew that the princess had been living a nightmare. He understood that she must want to flee such a terrible place. Still, he had expected her to stand with him. He decided that as a princess, she simply did not comprehend how important money was.

Belac's vexation grew even more when Rolan let Emily lead from the front. Belac thought back to how they had moved through the prison. *It's not fair that she gets to walk around like she is a… a princess.* As they walked through the hallways, Vairug continued to open and close his new hand. It made a slick sound that Belac did not care for. It was like no sound that he had ever heard before, and it registered as wrong.

With most of his attention focused on his mechanical hand, Vairug asked, "How strong is it?"

Rolan understood what the orc was asking. "I don't know. You are going to have to practice with it. It should not take very long for it to get stronger, but you are not going to have as much control with it as you think you do." He looked at the orc. "So, maybe don't grab anybody you like."

The mechanical hand raised questions that Belac did not know how to answer. He did not even know how to ask the questions. It was no secret that dwarven technology existed; however, the inner workings and how they functioned were. The dwarves did not share their knowledge nor trade the complexities. They certainly did not strap one on an orc. Belac did not know how to broach the subject without insulting both Rolan and Vairug. Neither of them was someone that he wanted to insult. *At least, not if they can hear me.* He was trying to frame the question as a joke when the answer came to him. It was so obvious, it made him feel silly. The mechanical hand was not dwarven, it was gnomish. *And, "Gnomes are evil."*

The small party stepped from the hallway and directly onto a dock that accessed an underground lake. To Belac, it felt bizarre to find such a place inside a castle. He reminded himself that it was a magic castle and that nothing should surprise him any longer.

The dock was in a small cavern filled with aquamarine light that shone watery patterns against the rock. The light was the same as that of the pools in the goblin shrine. Belac knew that the bed of the lake must have been lined with the same stones. He wondered if the stones in the lake had come from the same place, or if the goblins had stolen their own from the castle. *I bet the goblins stole them.* Belac was awed by the fantastical sight and how the sophisticated architecture of the castle was grafted back into the danger of the underground.

A single craft waited unmoored next to the dock. It was an elegant vessel that appeared to be carved from a single piece of glass. It was without sails or oars, and seemed to lack any means of propulsion. Despite its elegance, it was little more than six floating benches.

Emily was unfazed by it all. "We must take the skiff."

Belac looked at the princess sadly. He wondered how long a person would have to spend in such a place for something so magical to lose its ability to impress. "The water is beautiful," he said, trying to draw her out.

"Do not touch the water!" There was fear in Emily's voice. She met the elf's eyes. "Do not touch the water."

Belac held his hands up in submission. "Don't touch the water. Got it." *Should I tell her that we drank some of it at the goblin shrine?*

The elf shrugged and then found himself having to wiggle his shoulders to readjust the baldric of his new sword. *This thing is still not adjusted quite right.* He followed Emily onto the skiff cautiously. To Belac, it did not seem like something that should be able to float. Not only did the skiff float, it did so without any perceptible shifting as he stepped into it. *Is everything here magical?* While the skiff had appeared magical at first sight, there was something different about standing on it. It made the magic feel more real.

Despite the skiff's obviously magical stability, Belac expected the boat to rock when the orc stepped in. However, the skiff remained unmoving, even when Vairug stomped his foot down three times in quick succession.

Belac winced at the orc's testing of the vessel. *Though, if it is going to sink, I guess it's better to know now.*

Belac inspected where Vairug had stomped, worried that the orc might have cracked the glass. It was then that the elf saw one of the nude women swimming under the skiff. She twisted in the water, slowly changing back and forth between translucent and opaque. She swayed lithely, floating in place under the skiff. With open interest, she stared directly at the elf. He met her eyes, and she smiled widely. The smile split her face in half, revealing long, thin fangs. Belac jumped backward away from her and almost fell out of the skiff.

"Get it away!" Belac cried, reaching for a rapier he no longer carried.

Emily walked to the front of the skiff. "The mermaids cannot harm you, so long as you do not touch the water." She looked back at the elf. "So, stay away from the water."

"Stay away from the water?! We are floating on water!" Belac searched around wildly but could no longer see the creature that had been under the skiff, pretending to be a woman. "And that is not a mermaid."

Emily tossed her silky blond hair. "Well, that is what the nillanan called them."

Belac shook his head emphatically. "No. Mermaids are beautiful women with fish for legs."

"That is absurd," Emily said disdainfully.

Belac remembered that it was his job to look brave. He readjusted his baldric and tried to stand taller.

Emily put her delicate hands on a coil of golden rope that was fixed to the front of the skiff, and pushed it off the rail. The coil glimmered as it unwound, dropping into the water below. One of the mermaids swam by and gripped the end of the rope. *Not a mermaid.* The skiff slowly began to move as she pulled them through the water. More of the lithe, nude forms joined the first, each of them taking turns pulling the rope.

Belac sat down and wondered how the goblins could have stolen rocks from the lake. He decided that he did not care. He just wanted to put the goblins and everything else behind him. He was tired. He did not know how much more he could give, both physically and emotionally. His life had never been boring, but this… this was too much.

Emily sat down on the glass bench beside the elf. Belac realized that she must feel much the same way as he did. She had been a prisoner of the underground for more time than he had. She had also been forced to face threats worse than death. Princess or not, that she could function at all was a marvel. He did not know what house she represented, but she did her people proud. He wanted to speak with her. He wanted to know more about her.

Belac cleared his throat. "So… You spoke with the nillanan?" It was not the best subject to bring up. Belac knew that as soon as he asked, but it had been the first thing that came to his mind.

It was quiet as they were pulled farther across the lake. Finally, Emily answered, "Yes."

Belac did not want to ask her more. He regretted asking her about it at all.

Emily took a deep breath. "That is why he kept me. That is why he did not turn me into one of those… things." She shuddered.

Belac wanted to put his arms around the woman. He wanted to comfort her, but he did not know what she needed. Belac would have torn out his own heart and handed it to her if he had thought it would help her.

Emily continued, "He wanted to know about the kingdom, about my people. He told me I would have to tell him if I wanted this." She tugged on her dress.

Belac did not know what to do. He did not know what to say. He had to do something. He needed to do something. He turned toward her and put his hand on her shoulder. It was the only thing he could think of, but he would have done anything for her.

Emily began to weep. She put her face against his chest, and he wrapped his arms around her. He tried to imagine what she had been through, what it must have been like. To be naked and alone, surrounded by mindless things that only looked like people. To have no one to speak to besides his own nightmarish captor. To wake every day knowing that a time would come when he was stripped of his mind and turned into one of those things around him.

Belac wanted to weep with her. Instead, he held her in his arms and said, "You are not alone anymore."

Rolan and Vairug sat silently and did not disturb them. Neither the dwarf nor the orc made a joke, and neither of them killed anyone. Belac wondered if they were sleeping.

The mermaids pulled the skiff into a tunnel that followed an underground river, the greenish blue light shining through the glass floor. Watery shapes danced against the walls to the faint echoes of their passing. It was a profound experience for the elf. It was surreal, and it was haunting. There was beauty and there was pain, while danger warred with hope. Time seemed to lose its significance. Each moment was one that might last forever. In some ways, they always would in the mind of an elf.

The second dock was not as enchanting as the castle's had been. It was far more utilitarian and cut directly into the rock. When they arrived, the skiff stopped, and the mermaids swam in a circle around the boat expectantly. Rolan and Vairug stood and walked off the skiff without saying anything. Belac paid them little mind. He stood and held Emily's hands. She rose gracefully and looked into his eyes.

Emily placed one hand on the elf's chest and said, "Thank you."

Belac had to kiss her. It was a moment so perfect, there was no allowance for thought. The water's light rippled across the princess's face and brought out the blue of her eyes. Belac leaned in to kiss her. She pushed him away with the hand on his chest.

At first, Belac did not understand. He did not know what he had done wrong. He was suddenly afraid that he may have made her feel pressured in some way. He had not been thinking about how all this might make her feel. He had simply wanted to kiss her.

Emily watched his confusion and smiled. "Belac." She did not step away. "You are a wonderful man, but..." She sounded apologetic. *You are a princess.* "You are an elf."

Twenty-One

What?! What the princess had said made absolutely no sense to the elf. *A human is lucky if they get to be with an elf!* Belac followed behind the others in an almost haphazard fashion. Polished stone walled the far side of the dock. It appeared to be the same stone as that of the defensive barrier around the castle, though Belac gave it little thought. He had more important things on his mind. Things like, why a princess would not fall in love with the charming elf that had rescued her. *The hero saves the damsel, the damsel swoons. Those are the rules.*

A guard flanked each side of an imposing, iron gate that waited ahead. The men were armored in what Belac had come to recognize as the uniform of the nillanan's guards. The meticulously maintained, full plate armor made him question why the nillanan did not provide the guards with helms. Certainly, the nillanan did not care if his slaves were comfortable. Belac reflected on how Vairug's slivery cogged mace had ended three of the castle's guards. *Maybe I should get a helmet.*

The two guards were facing inward toward each other, neither of them moving. Rolan walked up to the one on the right and shoved him. The guard fell hard, making no attempt to manage the fall.

Rolan took hold of one of the guard's legs and began to drag him out of the way. "Vairug, grab the other one," he ordered dispassionately.

Instead of pushing the guard over and dragging him, Vairug simply threw the man over his shoulder. He carried him a few steps and then tossed the guard down unceremoniously.

Rolan pulled open the iron gate. To Belac, it looked like something that would screech loudly when it was opened, but the gate groaned no more than was unavoidable due to its size. Together, the four entered the guard post and into a corridor of gray stone lit by the same brass torches that Belac had admired in the castle. He was puzzled as to why the nillanan would let such magic out of the castle. He wondered what else they might find. A little less than halfway down the corridor, they found two more guards that had once been men. One stood straight, staring at nothing. The other lay dead on the floor. As Belac walked past the guards, he could not shake how creepy it felt to walk among the dead that still drew breath. *Rolan was right. These are not people.* The guards were nothing more than the remains of the departed, waiting to rot.

Vairug broke the silence. "Do you smell that?"

Rolan grunted. It could have meant anything.

Belac sniffed at the air. He could smell something. He pulled in deeper, breathing in the smell of lavender and burned almonds. It left a nasty taste in the back of his throat.

Emily seemed to find the fragrance pleasant. "It smells sweet."

Belac decided that something was wrong with the princess. That was the only thing that explained it. She liked bad smells, and she did not want to kiss an elf. *All the time she spent as a prisoner in a magic castle must have done something to her.*

The escapees came to a four-way intersection with a guard standing mindlessly in an alcove at each corner. A new smell drifted from the left that Belac thought was even less pleasant than the last. All three of the new directions ended in a stout door a few paces past the alcoves.

Rolan turned to the princes. "Do you know where these lead?"

Emily shook her head, her golden hair shimmering in the torchlight. "I know only that the door ahead will lead us out."

Rolan nodded. "Works for me."

The dwarf walked forward and then pushed open the door. However, instead of continuing through, he stopped and waited. Belac realized that the dwarf was listening for something, and so he listened with him in building anxiety. It was quiet, but the elf had come to know that quiet was not always reassuring. Finally, Rolan walked into the room with the others following closely behind him. On the far side of a squared room was a strange contraption that rose up through a shaft in the high ceiling. To the left was a small guardhouse, and to the right, a stone table. Two guards stood lifelessly next to the contraption, and another could be seen in the guardhouse.

Walking toward the contraption, Rolan asked, "Does the lift go all the way to the surface?"

Emily shook her head though the dwarf could not see it. "It will take us to more of this." She gestured around the room.

Rolan stopped and looked at her.

Exasperated, Emily added, "And then to the surface shortly after."

Rolan went to the contraption that was promised to lift them to freedom. The dwarf pushed the guards out of his way absentmindedly and then began to inspect the workings of the machine. Belac looked at Emily in the torchlit fortress, and knew that there was no setting in which she would not be captivating. In the short time since his incarceration, Belac had experienced terror and pain that threatened to break him. Emily had been there for longer, living through things most people would not believe. He knew she had suffered more, suffered longer, and yet there she stood, regal in the fluttering light.

Rolan interrupted the elf's thoughts. "Do you know the combination, Princess?" When he called her 'princess,' it did not sound like a title.

"I am afraid not," Emily replied. "I was not aware that we would need one. We must make this work. I know of no other way out."

"I could tear it apart," Rolan said irritably. "But I don't know how long that would take." He began marching toward the guardhouse.

Belac quickly sidestepped out of the dwarf's way to avoid being run over, then he followed him to the guardhouse. Belac watched the dwarf walk over a dead guard and then push the one that was still standing out of his way. Rolan did not seem bothered in the least by the ambiguous state of the guards. He took a book from the counter and flipped through it. He tossed it over his shoulder and then reached for another. He quickly flipped through the second book as well, but then suddenly stopped and began reading intently.

Rolan looked up at the elf. "I'm going to need some time with this. It seems safe enough out there, but don't run off too far." He resumed reading without waiting for a response.

Belac tried to think of something snide to say, but decided that it was not worth the effort. He left the guardhouse and returned to the others. Emily, despite her noble bearing, was obviously uncomfortable next to the orc.

Belac pointed a thumb toward the guardhouse. "Rolan found a book. He wants us to wait while he reads it."

"What type of book?" Emily asked.

"I don't know. He found it." Belac noted that this was the first time that the princess had spoken to him since he had tried to kiss her.

"You did not ask?" Emily asked, not unkindly.

Belac did not like the question. "He cannot read the book and answer my questions at the same time."

Emily smiled as if the elf had made a joke. "Shall we have a seat then?" She moved to the table, anticipating that he would follow.

Belac followed her. He would have grumbled if he were not an elf. Vairug followed as well but stood to the side, giving them their space. The orc preoccupied himself with opening and closing his metal hand. Belac sat down across from Emily at the stone table. Begrudgingly, he looked up at her. It was hard for him to not look at a woman so beautiful.

Emily met the elf's eyes. "I am sure there will be a reward," she predicted.

Belac was caught off guard. "A reward? For killing the nillanan?" He was not sure he wanted anyone to know that he had been involved. *Rolan claims the nillanan has friends*. Belac did not want to spend the rest of his life hiding from magical monsters. That did not stop him from asking, "How much of a reward?"

"Not for slaying the nillanan." Emily's hair shimmered as she shook her head. "Though, I will allow that is worthy of reward all by itself. I meant, a reward for saving me." She smiled and the elf wanted to die. "I am a princess."

Rolan dropped the book on the table.

Belac looked at the dwarf. "That did not take long."

"I can get the lift working." Rolan did not sound happy about it.

Emily said, "Well, that is a relief."

Rolan shook his head. "Don't get too excited. We have a problem."

Belac pursed his lips. "I don't like problems."

"Right." Rolan nodded. "That's why they're called problems."

Emily did not appreciate the banter. "Is the suspense truly necessary?"

Rolan met her eyes. "We have all been poisoned." He let that sink in. "It's magic. And it's going to kill us."

"What?" Emily asked. "How?"

Vairug guessed when. "It was in the air."

Rolan nodded.

"Back in that corridor." Vairug surmised, "It was that odd smell."

Rolan nodded. "Right."

Emily did not want to believe it. "But I feel fine."

Belac did not want to believe it either.

"It's magic," Rolan repeated. "The book says you won't feel anything until it kills you."

Please, let this be another bad joke.

Emily reached over and grabbed the book from the table. She opened it and turned through the pages forcefully. "What language is this?"

"It's Gnomish." There was a hint of resignation in Rolan's voice.

Gnomes are evil. That was when Belac accepted that what the dwarf was saying was true.

Emily had not given up. "There must be some kind of antidote."

"There is." Rolan waved the orc over.

Vairug stepped closer. For the first time, Emily did not seem concerned at the orc's proximity. To Belac, it felt as if they were all now sharing a secret. Rolan tossed a handful of charms on the table. Each one was a tiny wooden rod piercing back and forth through a narrow strip of paper covered in strange writing.

Rolan picked up one of the charms. "This is the antidote." He snaped the rod. "All you have to do is break one and you don't die." He tossed the broken charm aside.

Vairug picked up one of the charms and broke it. Then, Rolan and he walked off, leaving Belac and Emily looking down at the table. There was only one charm left. Belac picked it up and held it between himself and the princess. They both stared at it. They both understood. One of them had to die.

Belac thought about the life they could have had together. The dashing hero who rescued the lovely princess. The cheers, the applause, and even the parades at their return. He could have been rewarded with a lordship, making him free to pursue her hand. They could have fallen in love and been married to the joy of a nation. They could have ruled with wisdom. They could have had children. They could have created a line that would champion the ages. They could have been a story of legend.

But that was all gone. It could never be. He looked from the charm to Emily. She could still be happy. She could still know freedom. She had endured so much, lost so much time. She was strong. She was noble. She could go on. She could return to her people. They would still applaud. There would still be parades. She could meet a handsome prince. They could fall in love and unite two kingdoms. They could have children and joy and laughter. She could still be happy. She was so beautiful.

Belac looked into eyes that could have been the sky, and he broke the charm.

Twenty-Two

Princess Emily cried out, "No!"

Belac did not know who was more surprised, the princess or himself. He had made the choice. There was no way to take it back, and he did not know if he would have. He thought that Emily was an amazing woman. He knew that she would have been amazing even if she had not been a princess. She could have represented the triumph of beauty and will over darkness and despair. It was astounding to Belac how much could be lost in so short a time. *She could have become anything.*

It was tragic, but Belac did not want to die. Despite how he felt about the princess, how she made him feel, he was not going to die for her. He began to compare her virtues to his own, easily detailing how she was no greater than himself. He dismissed the line of thought contemptibly. It did not matter. He would confront this truth. He had been the one with the choice. And he had made it. It would not have mattered if she had been the one true savior of mankind, Belac would still have broken the charm. He needed to face that.

Rolan stepped out of the guardhouse. "Would you stop it with the screaming!"

Emily wailed, "He has killed me!"

"Oh... Right." There was a trace of amusement in Rolan's voice. "Then, go ahead and feel free to scream some."

Belac did not think it was funny. He did not care how dark the dwarf's sense of humor was. "Maybe we can find another one."

Emily's eyes could not decide between hope and despair. "Can you tell me how much time I have until I die?"

Rolan shook his head. "No. But I expect it will be less than you want."

Belac's mind raced. "There were two other ways we could have gone back there. Maybe we could find another one of the charms? We can't just give up." *Maybe I can still save her.*

There was no amusement in Rolan's voice now. "And what happens if you step into another trap? If you can smell the gas, it's too late."

Belac was at a loss. He wanted to save Emily, but he did not want to die doing it. If he had wanted that, he would have just given her the charm in the first place. He realized that he should have saved the charm until after they had searched for another. It was too late now. *I have killed her again.*

"I can go first," Emily said. "Surely the gas cannot kill me twice. And if there is some other manner of trap, I will likely trigger that one as well. By magic or other means, this place can only kill me once."

I should have given her the charm.

"You will have to be quick about it," Rolan told her. "I have to rip open the controls, but it shouldn't take me long to get this working. I don't think you're going to find anything." He looked at the elf. "If you want to search while I work, go now."

Belac nodded. Emily was already moving. He followed her back to the alcoved intersection. Recoiling at the smell to his right, he pointed left suggestively. Emily nodded, resolute. She was not yet willing to surrender to fate.

Belac wondered if Emily would have made the same, selfish choice as he had. *If she had picked up that charm, would she have given it to me?* He did not think so. She was a princess, taught from birth that she was more important than other people. *She would not have sacrificed herself for some lowly adventurer that she just met.*

The thought did not make him feel any better. He would have expected it to, but it did not. The princess's lack of virtue did not excuse his own. He had still chosen to kill her so that he might live. He feared that making the choice would prove easier than living with it.

Emily opened the door without preamble and walked inside brazenly, more concerned with time than safety. Belac could understand, but he still worried for her. He waited as she inspected the interior.

Emily returned and said, "It is the barracks for the guards. We may be able to find something if we search."

Belac followed the princess into the barracks, hoping that her salvation might still be found. The room was a long rectangle, with beds on one side and foot lockers on the other. Men slept in some of the beds, but there were no personal effects in view. Belac immediately knew that they would not find any of the charms in that room. The guards were not real people. They lacked the wherewithal to hoard items or secret away one of the charms. The idea of finding anything of value there was nothing more than wishful thinking. He considered letting Emily search, of going through the motions himself. It would not have been a kindness. They would have spent time and wasted effort for no benefit.

"Emily, we are not going to find anything here." Belac could see her growing desperation, but he was not ready to give up on her yet. "Let's go check the other side. I know it smells awful, but maybe we can find something there." The princess looked like she might argue, so he added, "We can come back to this side later if we don't find one of the charms over there. Let's go look."

Emily did not say anything. Belac thought that she might not have the will left to do so. The princess walked from the room like a prisoner to the gallows. Without stopping, she crossed the intersection and opened the other door. She did not even seem to notice the smell. Belac noticed the smell. He waited for her and hoped that he would not have to get any closer to whatever it was that was making the smell.

Emily quickly returned with a disgusted look on her face. "It is the privy."

Belac was not going to search the privy. Especially one that smelled like that.

Vairug spoke from inside the doorway to the lift. "It is time to go."

Emily looked like she wanted to cry. "We are not going to find one, are we?"

Belac met the princess's eyes. He wanted to cry with her. "No." He wished it were not true. "I don't think we are."

They followed the orc into the room. Rolan stood among small pieces of metal scattered across the floor. Belac did not know what the dwarf had done to the lift, but to the elf, the contraption looked complicated enough to need all of its parts. He did not like the idea of trusting the thing in the first place. That it was now missing components did not reassure him. Rolan kicked one of the pieces out of his way as he went to the front of the lift. He looked the others over, nodded, and then stepped onto the lift. After the other three joined him, he kicked a lever to the side.

The lift began to rise, carrying the escapees upward and closer to a freedom that Belac knew would taste stale. The mechanical sound from the contraption convinced him that Rolan had taken out too many parts. Tic tock, tic tock, tic tock, tic tock, CLACK. Tic tock, tic tock, tic tock, tic tock, CLACK.

Seemingly unaware of the noise, Emily stared off into space. The sight of her broke Belac's heart. Standing there, staring away at nothing, she looked like one of the nillanan's slaves. *The nillanan did not do this to her. I did.*

No one spoke, leaving only the sound of the lift. Tic tock, tic tock, tic tock, tic tock, CLACK. The rhythm of the sound eased Belac's concerns over it. Tic tock, tic tock, tic tock, tic tock, CLACK. Every time he looked away from the princess, he worried that when he looked back, she would be gone. They still did not know how the magic would kill her, or when. Tic tock, tic tock, tic tock, tic tock, CLACK.

The sound continued over and over as they rose. Belac began to appreciate it. It was a welcome alternative to what would otherwise have been silence. Tic tock, tic tock, tic tock, tic tock, CLACK.

CLUNK CLACK. The lift shuddered, coming to a stop. They had reached the top. It was a small room with four of the nillanan's guards, one of which was dead. Belac looked on the body, knowing that Emily would soon be joining it.

Rolan held something up. "Here, Princess. Break this."

Emily looked down at the dwarf in consternation. She reached over and took the charm, holding it before herself in a daze. "How…? You…?"

Rolan walked off the lift.

Emily stared daggers at the dwarf. "Oh, you horrible little dwarf!" She broke the charm and threw it at the back of his head.

The charm was too light to travel far, and fell harmlessly to the floor. Vairug stepped off the lift, looking like a man that did not want to get caught up in someone else's drama. Belac just stood there mystified. *He must have found one while we were looking.* Belac wondered why Rolan had waited to give Emily the charm. *Probably because he is a horrible little dwarf.* Belac was happy none the less. The princess was not going to die. He had not killed her. A small, faint voice in the back of his mind insisted, *But you would have.*

Belac grabbed the princess by the shoulders and turned her to face him. "Emily! You are not going to die!"

Emily was breathing hard. "With no thanks to you!"

Belac thought that seemed a little unfair. *She looks like she is going to hit me.* Still furious, the princess stormed off. *I wonder what this is going to do to my reward…*

Twenty-Three

To Belac, traveling the corridor felt like walking through a forest of sarcophagi. Guards stood mindlessly in alcoves that lined the stone walls. The polished gray stone asserted a finality that made the elf want to look away. Rows of dark metal spikes crossed the ceiling in regular intervals. He knew that they were portcullis positioned to fall in defense, but to him, they looked like fangs waiting to close. *I want out of this place.* Belac also wanted to talk to Emily. He wanted her to know that he was sorry and that he never would have given up on her. He wanted her to understand how he felt. He wanted her to forgive him. Most of all, he wanted her to not tell her father that a selfish elf had tried to kill her.

Belac watched the princess with a sense of longing. Even from behind, the set of her shoulders was enough to let him know that she was still angry. He tried to think of some joke that he could tell to lighten the mood, but could not come up with anything that started with, 'Sorry I tried to kill you.' So, he said nothing, and followed her through the corridor.

They entered into what Belac would have thought of as a courtyard if they had not been underground. The polished gray stone had been shaped into hexagons that tiled both the floor and the high ceiling.

There were two large ballistas, one to the left and one to the right. Both of which were pointed at a massive gate of gleaming metal. More guards were stationed at the ballistas and to either side of the gate.

After taking in the defenses, Belac said, "This looks an awful lot like a place someone might keep a dragon." He looked at the princess suspiciously.

Emily spun on him. "There is no dragon! This is the main gate, you stupid elf!"

Rolan laughed.

Emily pointed at the dwarf. "And what are you laughing at?"

Rolan raised his hands up in surrender, but he was grinning so hard that it must have hurt his face. Belac speculated that the only time the dwarf did not seem irritable was when someone else was irritated instead. He wondered if Rolan was adhering to some secret dwarven quota of irritation.

"How do you think we open it?" Belac asked.

Rolan answered, "I don't know, but how about we try that little one first." His hand pointed to a door that could only be considered little when compared to the main gate.

Belac nodded. If there was a dragon behind the gate it would not be able to fit through the smaller door. *Best to not take any chances.*

Primly, Emily said, "Yes. Let's."

Walking in front of the ballistas made Belac uncomfortable, though no one else seemed to mind. He knew that the guards were too mindless to shoot the ballistas, but having that much potential energy pointed at him was concerning all the same. As he passed a ballista, he ducked down out of what he imagined the path of the missile would be. The others looked at him as if he were being silly, but he did not care. *Let them get shot in the face with a giant missile.*

Opening the smaller door proved to be a challenge. In order to slide the bolt over, Rolan had to brace his foot against the doorframe and pull. Once the door was unlocked, it took both Rolan and Vairug to force it to open.

Belac watched the princess as the other two worked. *She doesn't look like she's expecting a dragon.*

When the door opened, the light that shone through was so pure that it hurt the elf to see it. Never had Belac been so glad to know pain. Emily dashed past Rolan and Vairug. Belac could not blame her. He would relish the sun and the freedom it represented, but he knew that the princess needed it more. She deserved it more.

Belac followed Rolan and Vairug out into the light. There, Emily stood facing the sun, her eyes closed. There were tears running down her cheeks. Belac could not look away. He was finally free, but there was nothing in that freedom he would rather look at than her.

They stood on a mountainside, the sun shining on them. Belac did not know if the sun was rising or setting. In that moment, he did not care. It was the sun, it was shining, and he was free. He breathed deeply, pulling in the fresh air. He wanted to cry, and he wanted to roar in triumph. He wanted to dance, and he wanted to fall to his knees in relief. With his back to all the pain and madness that had sought to destroy him, Belac asked, "Well, now what do we do?"

Rolan laughed. "That is a remarkably human sentiment." It sounded like he was quoting someone.

Belac narrowed his eyes at the dwarf.

Emily brought her hands up to her face in an attempt to hold back her emotions. Her hands slid down her cheeks and she opened her eyes, her tears glistening in the sunlight. She clapped her hands together three times and hopped up and down giddily. "I'm free! I'm free!" She held her arms out to her sides and spun around in circle. "I'm finally free!" She tripped over a short ledge and fell down.

Vairug snuffed in amusement.

Belac narrowed his eyes at the orc. *Emily has been through enough already without having an orc laugh at her.*

Belac bent down to help the princess up. He half expected her to slap him away. He did not think that she had forgiven him yet, regardless of how happy she might be. He was certain that she would find some way to blame him for her white gown getting dirty in the fall. *Crazy woman will try and say that she fell because I'm an elf.*

Emily was not moving.

Belac put his hand on the princess's arm. "Emily?"

Emily was still.

Belac grabbed the princess's shoulder, turning her over. "Emily, are you alright?"

Emily stared up at him with lifeless, accusing eyes.

"Emily!" Belac did not know what to do. "Rolan!" He looked up, searching for the dwarf. "Rolan, Emily is hurt!"

Rolan was already there. He knelt down and swatted Belac's hands out of his way. Rolan cupped the back of the princess's neck with one hand, supporting her head while he checked the side of her head and neck with his other. Belac watched in shock, unable to move, unable to think.

Rolan shook his head. "She's dead."

"No." Belac did not believe it. They were free. He had saved her. This was not how it ended. She could not have survived captivity just to die at the threshold of freedom. There had to be something they could do. "Fix her. You have medicine in your bag, Rolan. Fix her!"

Rolan let go of the princess's neck and her head flopped down against the rocks. "I can't fix dead."

Belac fell down onto his backside. He stared at the princess. *No. No. No…*

Rolan stood and walked over to Vairug. The two began to speak in hushed voices. Belac did not hear them. They might as well have not existed. In his world, there was nothing but himself and the princess, dead at his feet. He knew he should look away. He did not want this image seared into his mind. He did not want that to be how he remembered her. Still, he did not look away. The calloused hand of a dwarf gripped the back of his collar and pulled him to his feet.

"It's time to go, Belac." There was no pity in Rolan's voice.

Belac's eyes did not leave Emily. "I can't just leave her here…"

"That is not her anymore," Rolan asserted. "That is just rotting meat that looks like her."

Belac turned on the dwarf, furious. "How can you say that?!"

Rolan had no fear of the elf's fury. "It's easy. I just open my mouth, and the truth comes out."

"Damn you, Rolan!" Belac pointed at Emily's body. "That was a person!"

"I may be damned, but I'm not wrong." Rolan seemed to stare directly into the elf's soul. "And you know it."

Belac's anger could not overcome the dwarf's stare. *I said 'that.' I said 'was.'* He knew that Rolan was right, he just did not want to know it. The elf hung his head in defeat.

Vairug put his hand on Belac's back and steered him in the right direction. Together, they followed Rolan down the mountain.

Twenty-Four

"I would have killed her," Belac confessed.

A rough road had been cut into the side of the rocky mountain. Though the nillanan had not seemed like someone who would encourage guests, the road would not have existed if it did not lead somewhere. As the three escapees traversed the mountainside, a cool breeze followed their footsteps. Forested lands awaited them below, the trees dancing in the wind. While the sun was now higher in the sky, it no longer comforted the elf. The world was dim without the princess.

"You did not kill her," Rolan contested. "The fool tripped and broke her neck."

Belac did not have the energy to yell at the dwarf. "I said, I would have." The admission hurt him.

"Are you talking about the charms?" Rolan asked.

Belac nodded. "I would have killed her."

"No." Rolan chuckled softly. "That is not how it works."

"The charms?" Belac did not see how he could have misunderstood.

"No, Belac. Not the…" Rolan shook his head. "You did not choose to kill her. You chose to not die. There's a difference."

Belac was unconvinced. "But I could have saved her."

"If you want to help people, that's great," Rolan told him. "But you have to help yourself first. Otherwise, you will spend your life a slave to other people's weakness."

"Emily was not weak," Belac argued.

Rolan shrugged. "Maybe not, but she's dead, and you're missing the point." The dwarf could be cruel.

"Is that why you waited until after the lift to give her the charm? Is that why you let us think that she was going to die?" Belac was angry again. "To prove a point?!"

Rolan shook his head. "I needed to know." He nodded to the elf. "And you needed to know."

Know that I would choose myself over the princess? "And what about Emily?" Belac asked, affronted.

Rolan shrugged.

That did not explain why the dwarf had waited until after they had taken the lift. *He could have given her the charm as soon as he found the extra one.* Belac struggled to make sense of the dwarf's actions. "You had an extra charm the entire time," he guessed as the answer came to him. *He was testing me! The evil little dwarf thought he was helping!*

Rolan had wanted the elf to face something inside himself. He had made the elf kill his own naivety. Any distress caused was of no concern to the dwarf.

Rolan spoke as if he were surprised that it had taken this long for the elf to figure it out. "Why would a fortress that size only have three antidotes to magic-death-poison? I have at least another fifty of them in my pack."

Belac wanted to strangle the dwarf. He felt the joints of his fingers begin to ache.

Rolan was not finished. "Besides, if there had only been three charms, I would not have risked you giving one to the princess. I would have broken mine, given one to Vairug, then handed you the last one and told you to break it. I would not have even explained until after the princess fell over dead."

Belac did not know what to say. He still wanted to strangle the dwarf, but… Rolan would have saved him. *He did save me. More than once.*

Belac wondered why the dwarf had cared so little for Emily. It could have been because she was royalty. Every time Rolan had called her 'princess,' it had sounded like an insult. *Leave it to a dwarf to make a royal title sound demeaning.*

Belac decided that it was his turn to test the dwarf. "What would you have done if there had only been two charms?"

Rolan did not miss a step. "I would have broken one and then let you and Vairug break the other like a wishbone."

Belac could not tell if the dwarf was joking or not. "And what if there had only been one?"

Rolan grinned. "Then, I would have had a lonely walk down the mountain."

Vairug laughed silently.

Belac wanted to hate the dwarf. It would have been easier. Rolan was a cruel, ruthless murderer. But if it were not for him, Belac would either be dead, or still in prison, waiting to die. Belac might be better off because of Rolan, but there were many others who were not. The dwarf had left a trail of death in his wake. Emily was one of those dead.

Belac wanted to hate the dwarf. "She would still be alive if it were not for us."

"Sure," Rolan agreed amiably. "Until the nillanan got tired of her and turned her into one of his braindead slaves. Think about her last moments. Not the dead body lying on the ground. Her. Finally free, her arms outstretched, dancing in the sun. That must have been the happiest moment of her life. You helped give her that."

Belac wanted to hate the dwarf, but he could not.

Vairug interrupted them. "I smell smoke."

Rolan's grunt could have been agreement or simply acknowledgement.

Belac did not see any smoke. The thought of fire should have been reassuring. Fire suggested that the road they traveled actually went somewhere of note. Once, that would have been enough to raise the elf's spirits. He would already have been dreaming of wine, women, and song. However, pessimism had infected him.

Belac did not think that they would discover a shining city waiting for them in the forest. He thought it was far more likely that they would find some gristly camp of ogres doing something awful to the last group of travelers that had journeyed down the road.

Belac sniffed the air. "I don't smell anything. Can you tell how far away it is, Vairug?

Vairug shook his head. "No. It is still faint." He took a slow, deep breath in. "I think it is more than one fire though."

Belac was impressed that the orc was capable of making such a distinction, but he did not doubt him.

Rolan asked, "Can you tell if the smoke is from wood or from coal?"

Vairug answered as best he could. "If there is coal, it is masked by the smell of wood smoke."

They continued to follow the road down and around the mountain until coming to a vista overlooking a small town in the distant valley. *It may not be a shining city, but at least it's not ogres.* The remainder of the road cut back and forth as it descended. It would cause the hike to take longer than Belac would have preferred, but he thought that if they raced the sun, they might be able to reach the town before nightfall.

Belac looked at the orc suspiciously. "I still don't smell any smoke."

Vairug shrugged. "You're an elf."

"Exactly!" Belac agreed disagreeably. "I should be able to smell better than both of you."

Vairug leaned over toward the dwarf and sniffed the air. Then he turned to the elf, leaned in close, and sniffed the air again. "Seems about the same to me."

"That is not what I meant!" Belac narrowed his eyes at the orc. *And I know that I smell better than a dwarf!* "Elves have a highly refined sense of smell."

Rolan laughed at him. "That just means that you scrunch your nose every time you smell something you don't like."

"I do not!" Belac objected.

Vairug laughed silently.

"Well, I bet I hear better than either of you," Belac said sullenly.

Rolan laughed. "Not in my experience."

"No." Belac was not having it. "Everyone knows that elves have supernatural hearing. It is one of the reasons everyone gets quiet when we're around."

Rolan said something under his breath.

Belac was not going to let the dwarf get away with it. "What was that?"

Rolan grinned. "You would know if you had supernatural hearing."

Vairug asked, "Do you want me to tell him?"

I hope you both die in a fire.

"No." Rolan had to compose himself. "When people think of elves, the first thing that comes to mind is that they have pointy ears. That makes people think that elves can hear better. But really, how would they know?" He shook his head. "If having pointed ears helped you hear better, I would have mine clipped."

As quietly as he could, Belac whispered, "I bet you can't hear this."

"I can," Vairug said.

Twenty-Five

"See?" Rolan said. "I told you that you scrunch your nose when you smell something you don't like."

Vairug nodded his head from within the hood of a splotch gray cloak that was comically too small for him.

Belac was suddenly concerned. "I don't…" He lowered his voice. "I don't wiggle my ears or anything, do I?" He touched the side of his head, his fingertips pressing against the long hair that he had lowered to cover his elven ears.

"I have never noticed," Rolan told him. "But maybe keep an eye on it."

Belac's eyes went to the side in an effort to see one of his own ears.

They had discovered that the small town in the rocky valley was little more than a mining camp. Before entering, Rolan had deemed it unnecessary to scout the edges of the town. He had, however, insisted that Vairug cover his head with the dwarf's cloak and hide his orcish face. They had passed a handful of dwarves on the way in, but most of the people in the town were human. Even now, unwashed humans walked in and out of the ugly, wooden buildings that made up the town.

Belac wondered how many of them knew what was at the other end of the road that he and his companions had walked down. *Some of these people have to know. The road only goes to one place. No one who goes up it is going to miss the giant-evil-fortress.* He reasoned that if the townspeople were aware of the giant-evil-fortress, they may not be pleased that he had escaped it. *Some of them probably worked for the nillanan. They might not be too happy if they find out that we killed their boss.*

"I don't think we should stay here any longer than we have to," Belac asserted.

"I agree with you," Rolan acknowledged. "But we need to rest. Walking through the mountains in the dark is a bad idea."

Belac's paranoia remained constant as he followed Rolan and Vairug deeper into the town. The elf's azure eyes darted from face to face as he searched the townsfolk for signs of recognition. *Can Rolan and Vairug kill all these people if they attack us?* Belac began looking into the alleys, both for hidden dangers, and for possible places that he could hide if the townspeople turned to murder. *I guess they don't need to kill them all. Just enough for me to get away.*

Doing a better job of not looking lost, Rolan led the other two to one of the town's larger buildings. The rough, wooden walls of the rickety building had never been painted. To Belac, the ugly building looked as though it might collapse at any moment. Above the front door hung a placard with a painting of a bed under a crescent moon. *People actually pay to sleep in there?* The elf was not convinced that sleeping in such a place would be preferable to sleeping outside. Rolan did not seem to share Belac's hesitation. The dwarf strolled up to the front door and opened it with a confidence that made it clear he would not be turned away.

Belac and Vairug followed Rolan into a tavern that was cramped with tables and chairs. The patrons inside were a scattering of mostly humans, though there was a small group of dwarves in one corner.

A greasy man with dark hair stood behind the counter. He froze for a moment when he saw the three who entered. Then he reached under the counter and pulled out a jar with a glowing pink light inside it. Rolan was already moving. The man opened the jar, and the pink light flew out. Rolan threw a knife at it. The knife missed and stuck into the wall next to the man behind the counter. The light dodged and then flew out the window. *That was a fairy!*

Rolan marched toward the greasy man, obviously prepared to kill anyone that got in his way. No one did.

The man held up his hands. "Peace, Master Dwarf!"

Rolan drew a knife and walked around the counter.

The man waved his hands emphatically. "Please! Peace! I only did as I was told. I only did what he told me to!"

Belac watched, unsure if Rolan would kill the man or not. Rolan had proven that he was more than willing to murder at his own discretion, but they were in the middle of a town. The dwarf could not murder everyone. *Please, don't try to murder everyone...*

Vairug stayed next to the door, guarding it as he watched the patrons. However, no one even seemed to care about the dwarf's outburst. Belac wondered if this sort of thing was common. *This might be a rougher town than I thought.*

"Who?" Rolan asked in a hard voice.

The man's relief was evident. He wanted to explain. "A man. Must have been a lord. Said his name was Serath." He did not stop there. "He gave me descriptions. He gave me the jar. He said that if you showed up, I should open it. I did not mean any harm. I swear it!"

Rolan studied the man. "What was he wearing?"

"What?" The man shook his head, confused, his fear returning.

"Tell me what he was wearing," Rolan growled. "Describe his attire. What did his clothes look like?"

The man nodded his head eagerly. "All black. With a long coat." He leaned forward. "It was finely cut." He nodded. "And clean. Despite all this." He waved his hand around. "Must have been a lord."

Rolan sheathed his knife. "We will need a room."

Belac thought that was a bad idea. He did not want to stay there. Especially not after threatening the man that was most likely the innkeeper. Not if some dark lord knew where they were. Belac could only think of one reason why someone would have their descriptions. *It must be whoever it was that put us in that prison.*

"Already paid for," the innkeeper said.

There was resignation in Rolan's voice. "Of course, it is."

The innkeeper was recovering quickly. This had not been the first time his life had been threatened. "Would you like something to eat? Or maybe an ale?"

Rolan pulled his knife from the wall and sheathed it. "We will take it in our rooms."

"Of course, Master Dwarf, of course." The greasy man had fully returned to being an innkeeper. "However, it will only be the one room."

Rolan said nothing.

"There will be plenty of beds though, I assure you, Master Dwarf," the innkeeper added quickly.

Rolan nodded. "That is probably for the best anyway."

"Of course, Master Dwarf, of course." The innkeeper stepped into the kitchen, presumably to arrange for their meals.

Rolan stood in the doorway, keeping the man in his sight. The innkeeper returned and they followed him to the stairs. The stairs groaned under Vairug's weight as they ascended to the upper level. Belac worried that the orc would fall through the floor as they walked down the hallway to their room. Fortunately, the inn was only two stories tall. Belac did not believe the building was structurally sound enough to support an addition. He was not entirely convinced that the second floor was going to hold as it was. *I would have felt safer sleeping in the nillanan's castle.*

The room that the innkeeper led them to ran along one side of the building. Though only a single door allowed access to the room, there was a window on the opposite wall that had been opened to let in fresh air. 'Fresh' was relative. *I think this room might actually smell better if that window were closed.* Seven cots were evenly spaced on the left side of the room, leaving a path that led to a table and four chairs that looked as poorly constructed as the rest of the inn. *Is this room the innkeeper's idea of revenge?*

The innkeeper swept a hand out as if proud of the squalid accommodations. "Just as I told you, Master Dwarf. There is plenty of room for you all." He put his hands together and gripped his palms. "You will have everything that you need. Everything that you need."

Rolan grunted noncommittally.

Two serving girls clothed in simple dresses of faded blue cloth walked into the room. One of the young women carried a tray that held three bowls of stew and a pile of rolls. The second serving girl carried a tray that held three large mugs. Belac narrowed his eyes at the food and drink, worried that it might be poisoned. When he saw how dirty and exhausted the girls looked, he found himself filled with pity for them. He could only imagine what other tasks might be required of the girls in such a place. *I am in no position to help them.* In his impotence, Belac felt unable to save anyone.

The innkeeper shooed the girls out of the room as soon as they set down the possibly poisoned food and drink. "All paid for. All paid for," the man said before leaving the room himself.

Belac pushed the door closed. A cursory glance was all it took for him to see that the door was without a lock. He did not find that terribly comforting. *Even if the food is not poisoned, they might send someone to kill us in our sleep.* Belac frowned at the door. *What good is this thing if I can't lock it?* Rolan shoved the elf aside and then stabbed a knife into the doorframe. With the palm of his other hand, he hammered the knife deeper into the wood. *That's kind of smart.*

The blade of the knife would prevent the door from leaving its frame. *But I bet that the innkeeper won't like that Rolan keeps stabbing the inn.*

Vairug yanked off his borrowed cloak and tossed it onto one of the cots. He set his leather bag down next to it and then walked over to the table. His cogged mace, he took with him.

Belac and Rolan joined Vairug at the table. The food smelled better than the 'fresh' air. *I really hope that the food is not poisoned.* Most of the smell was coming from the stew, but the elf would have balanced a ball on the end of his nose for one of the loaves of bread.

"It's not..." Belac's mouth watered. "You don't think it's poisoned, do you?"

"No." Rolan picked up one of the dark loaves of bread and bit off a mouthful.

Vairug took one the bowls of stew and began eating. He did not seem concerned about poison. Belac was suddenly convinced that if he waited too long, the other two were going to eat his food. He would go hungry, and they would only laugh at him.

Rolan took a bowl of stew for himself. "It would be bad for business."

There was one bowl of stew left. Belac wanted it. "What would?"

"Getting killed because he poisoned one of his guests." Rolan took a bite of the stew and spoke with this mouth full. "It is hard to make money running a business when you're dead."

That was good enough for Belac. He reached over and grabbed the last bowl of stew and one of the loaves of bread. The elf scarfed down the bread and then started on the stew.

Vairug made the elf an offer. "Trade the last of the bread for your ale?"

Belac thought about it. It was probably a good idea. He did not need the drink, and he did not think two mugs of ale would get an orc drunk. He smiled at the thought of Vairug drunk, stumbling around and falling down the steps.

He pictured Vairug crashing down through a ceiling and drunkenly roaring at some poor person that was taking a bath. Belac slid his ale over to the orc.

It did not take long for them to finish eating. Without comment, Rolan stood from the table and went over to the cot that was closest to the window. He unstrapped his pack and set it on the end of the cot. Leaning out the window, he grabbed the shutter and pulled it closed. *The shutter opens out. I wonder if he has a trick to keep it closed.* The dwarf took a handful of cordage from one of his pockets and tied one end to the inside of the shutter. He untangled the cord and tied the other end to one of the legs of his cot. Then he sat down on the edge of the cot and began removing his boots.

Vairug went to his own cot and crumpled the dwarf's cloak into a ball. He laid down, using the wadded-up cloak as a pillow.

Belac chose one of the cots for himself and sat down. "Why are we here?"

"Walls and beds," Rolan answered irritably. He laid out on the cot, resting his head on his pack.

"Yes. Thank you. I know what an inn is." Belac stopped himself from further sarcasm. "That doesn't explain why we're sleeping here. You are acting like all of this is normal. This is not normal, Rolan. We know that the guy that had us locked up in prison is coming for us. We need to get out of here."

"Serath did not have us locked up." Rolan sounded sure.

Belac did not believe him. "How do you know?"

"Because I know Serath." Rolan replied, being less forthcoming than the elf would have liked.

"That does not explain anything," Belac insisted. "How else would he know we were going to be here?"

"He just knows things." Then Rolan had the temerity to add, "It's frustrating."

Belac was tempted to let the dwarf sleep, just so he could smother him. "That still…"

"Let me sleep, Belac," Rolan interrupted. "We can talk about it in the morning."

Belac was not sure if the dwarf was actually tired, or if he was just trying to avoid the conversation. *I guess even dwarves need to sleep.* "Shouldn't someone stay awake and keep watch?"

"No need," Rolan told him. "No one is going to get in here without us knowing about it. Besides, we all need the sleep. I would not trust any of us to stay awake and keep watch anyway. It's better if we all just sleep while we can. So, go to sleep."

"But..."

"Go. To. Sleep."

Belac did not go to sleep. Not until almost dawn. He was exhausted, but there was still so much that he did not understand. He tried to piece everything together, but he knew that he was missing too much information. The only thing he could be sure of was that he was still not safe.

Twenty-Six

There are few things as truly awful as waking up to the smell of an orc's fart. Belac fell off his cot sputtering, trying to spit out the taste. "Gauh! Are you dead, Vairug?" Belac stood up and stumbled across the room toward the window. He needed air. Even the town air would be better than the smell in their room. He tripped and slammed onto the bare floor. It hurt.

Belac groaned as he rolled over and looked up at the cord tying the shuttered window to the dwarf's cot. *It's a conspiracy.*

Still lying on his cot, Rolan turned his head and opened one eye. "Your nose is scrunched up again."

"You don't smell that?" Belac asked, standing back up.

"I smell it," Rolan told him. "I just don't think it's a sign of the end times."

"Trust me," Belac said as he went to the window, "whatever heralds the end of times, it is going to smell just like this."

"Nope." Rolan rocked his head. "It will smell like soap."

Belac turned away from the window, looking back at the dwarf. "Like soap?"

"Right." Rolan sat up on his cot. "Politicians always smell like soap."

Belac laughed, coughed at the smell still in the room, and then resumed untying the cord from the shutter. With the cord free, he tossed the loose end in the dwarf's direction and pushed open the shutter. He stuck his head out the window and breathed deeply. He wished he had not. The air outside was not much better. *It's a conspiracy!*

Rolan untied the cord from his cot. "Why don't you go downstairs and order us some breakfast?" he suggested kindly. "We can let the room air out while you're gone."

Belac did not like the idea of eating in the room, but he decided to take Rolan's advice anyway. After wrenching the dwarf's knife back and forth to get it unstuck from the doorframe, he looked down at the short blade, unsure of what to do with it. *Am I supposed to just stab it into the wall somewhere?*

Rolan rose and took the knife. "Time to get up Vairug. You need to put the hood back on."

Vairug growled. He pulled the rumpled cloak out from under his head and shook it out with his real hand. Then he covered his head up with the cloak and went back to sleep.

Rolan waited for Belac to leave the room and then he swung the door open and closed, creating an air current. Belac left him to it. He retraced their steps and returned to the tavern on the lower level. The room was empty except for two men with their heads down on a table. Belac assumed they were sleeping, but he allowed that they could just as easily have been dead. If the previous day were any indication, the elf did not think that anyone would care one way or the other.

Belac walked over to the kitchen doorway. An old man in a grimy apron was staring up at the ceiling with his hands on his hips, stretching out his back. He did not seem to notice the elf. *See! Elves are quiet!*

Belac asked, "Are you the cook?"

"I am." The man did not sound happy about it.

Belac decided that trying to be friendly would be a waste of time. "We need breakfast for three."

The man sighed. "I will get to it as soon as I can."

Belac was not sure he believed the man. "And we want extra bread," he added anyway.

The man nodded. "Do you want it brought to your room?" It was a not so subtle suggestion.

"Yes, please." Belac caught himself. "Wait. Do you know where our room is?"

"One of the girls will," the man said. "You are the only elf here."

Belac started to leave but stopped. "Oh." He looked back to the man. "And no ale." *Vairug is not allowed to have any more ale.*

The old man looked at Belac like he thought the elf was crazy, but he only shrugged.

Hoping that the old man would be true to his word, Belac visited a privy and then returned to his room. When he walked in, he found Rolan and Vairug having a discussion at the table.

"The hand is causing me no trouble," Vairug said from within his hood.

"I need to take a look at your wrist," Rolan told the orc. "And you need to learn how to adjust the straps for yourself."

"You want me to unstrap all of this?" Vairug did not sound like he was going to do it.

"Not right now." Rolan reached over the table and touched the inside wrist of Vairug's metal hand. "Just remove this buckle, spin the ring underneath, and then twist off the metal fasteners."

Vairug began to fiddle with the straps on his hand. "That's clever." He took the hand off and set it on the middle of the table.

"Let me see your wrist." Rolan held out his hand.

Vairug held out his stump and the dwarf took it.

Belac said, "I don't think it's growing back."

Vairug stared at the elf from across the table.

Rolan held up a waxed paper packet that was smaller than the size of his thumb. He set it on the table and said, "Rub that on your wrist."

While the orc opened the packet one handed, Rolan continued. "You are going to have to make time every day to let your wrist breathe. You need to clean it off and let it get some air. For now, do it before and after you sleep. If a time comes that you are staying somewhere safe, you should just leave the hand off while you are sleeping."

Vairug stared at the dwarf.

"Your wrist will rot, Vairug," Rolan told him. "You could lose your whole arm."

Vairug took a deep breath and then nodded.

Belac walked over to the table and picked up the metal hand. It was a marvelous device. He would have been willing to bet that there were men who would chop off their own hand if it meant they could replace it with a magical one. *I would not. I like my hands.* The hand moved.

"Aah!" Belac threw the hand away from himself.

The hand bounced off the table and landed on the floor. Vairug looked just as surprised as the elf. He bent down and picked up the hand. The fingers opened and closed in a fist.

Vairug looked at the dwarf. "It still works."

Rolan frowned. "Then, maybe the two of you don't try to break it."

Vairug set the hand back down on the table. The hand opened and closed in a fist. He looked at the elf. Belac grinned and then reached out and flipped the hand over. Together, they watched as the hand drunkenly crawled across the table.

"You are making it do that right?" Belac wanted to make sure.

Vairug nodded.

Rolan's voice interrupted them. "Incoming."

The hand stopped moving. Vairug picked it up and set it down on the far side of the table. Two girls walked into the room carrying trays. They were the same girls as the night before and they did not look as though they had gotten much sleep. They seemed too timid to say anything.

Belac did not want to make them more uncomfortable, so he let them work in silence. He did not know if the girls were always that skittish, or if someone had warned them that last night, Rolan had thrown a knife at the innkeeper and then threatened him with another. The girls placed the trays on the table and then all but fled the room. *Maybe it just still smells too much like Vairug in here.*

Belac took one of the plates of eggs, toast, and some type of meat that he could not identify. "This will be two meals in a row that nothing has tried to kill me."

"Unless the food is poisoned," Rolan said.

Belac stopped moving with a spoonful of eggs on the way to his mouth.

Rolan smiled and then took a bite of his own eggs.

Belac went back to eating. "Not funny," he said between mouthfuls. He was not pleased about the toast. It was yesterday's bread, and he had been hoping for something fresh. *Maybe I should have been nicer to the cook.* When he finished eating, he said, "Okay, Rolan, enough is enough. No more dodging my questions."

"I am not dodging your questions," Rolan argued.

Belac was not going to be detoured. "You are very dodgy for a dwarf."

Vairug nodded.

Belac continued, "Who is this dark lord and why does he want to kill us?"

"Serath is not a 'dark lord," Rolan corrected the elf. "And he does not want to kill us."

"Then, why did he have us put in prison?" Belac wanted to know.

Rolan frowned at the elf. "He didn't."

"Then, who did?" Belac pressed.

Rolan shrugged. "I don't know."

Belac held up a finger. "Then, how do you know it was not the dark lord?"

Rolan shook his head. "I told you, Serath is not some 'dark lord.' He's a friend. If anything, he probably came here to get me out."

That did not make sense to Belac. "And how exactly was he going to get you out of that?" He pointed in what he thought was the direction of the fortress.

"I am sure that it would have been easier before we got lost in the caves," Rolan said dryly.

Belac had to agree that was a good point. The prison guards had been shamefully bad at their jobs. *But that does not explain everything.* "That does not explain how he knew we would be here. The innkeeper said, 'descriptions.' As in, more than one. Also, you are not the only disagreeable looking dwarf in town. The innkeeper went straight for that jar. He had to be looking for an elf." *I need to find a better way to hide my ears.*

Vairug looked at Belac with surprised approval. While the other two had slept, Belac had spent the night thinking. He had thought about what he knew, and he had thought about what he did not understand.

"He's a wizard," Rolan said as if that explained anything.

"The innkeeper?" Belac did not think a wizard would have let the dwarf threaten him like that.

"No, not the…" Rolan shook his head. "Serath. He's a wizard. Crazy eyes. Forbidden knowledge. Wizard."

"You are friends with a wizard?" Belac found it hard to believe that the dwarf was friends with anyone.

"That's what I said," Rolan maintained.

Belac tried to fit the new piece of information into the puzzle. *But that…* "That's cheating!"

Rolan just stared at the elf.

Belac shook his head. "Nothing has to make sense if there is a wizard involved. They don't have to follow the rules. That's what makes them a wizard!"

Rolan continued to stare at the elf and say nothing.

If Belac had been standing, he would have hopped up and down in aggravation. "You could have told me that he was a wizard before I stayed up all last night, trying to figure this out!"

Rolan continued to stare at him. "I told you to go to sleep."

Twenty-Seven

Something grabbed Belac's arm. The elf shot up from his chair and swung his arm wildly. The thing held on by the sleeve of Belac's shirt. "Get it off! Get it off!" He fell backward, tripping over his chair. He tried to fling the thing away, but it held firm. "It's going to eat me!"

A glint of silver caught Belac's eye, and he stopped flailing about. He held his arm out in front of his face and looked at the metal hand hanging from his sleeve. Vairug pounded his real hand on the table twice and laughed silently. The metal hand let go of Belac's sleeve and fell into his lap. He picked it up and chucked it in Vairug's direction. The elf was not overly concerned with breaking it in the process. *I hope it…*

The dark lord was in the room with them. He was on the other side of the room, leaning back against the wall with his arms crossed. He did not look like a wizard. His clothes were an immaculate black without adornment or symbols of power. A coat of black cloth draped down cleanly below the man's knees, and he wore black leather boots and black leather gloves. Though Belac wore some black himself, the complete blackness of the man's attire seemed excessive to him. The man's trousers and shirt were finely tailored, but no one was likely to notice with all that black. It bothered the elf more than it should have. *It's just too much black.*

Even the man's hair was black. It had a professional cut and had been combed back away from his face. He had a neat beard that looked nothing like Belac would expect from a wizard. It was short and only covered the area around the man's mouth and chin, his cheeks shaved. Belac thought it made the man look overly well groomed. The man was handsome enough that Belac could have hated him for that alone, but it was the man's eyes that Belac disliked most. They were green. *Never trust green.*

The eyes were staring directly at Belac, and he felt like they could see through him. It felt like there was nothing he could hide from those eyes. They were a green too bright for the room, and they made Belac think of fire and chains.

The man was only more handsome when he smiled. "Hello, Belac." His voice was rich and smooth.

Vairug sprang up and grabbed his mace. He had been caught unaware, but was now obviously prepared to cave in the man's skull.

The man was not concerned.

Rolan leaned back in his chair and looked up at the man. "Don't wizards know how to knock?" The dwarf sounded amused.

"I have told you before, Rolan," the man said, not unkindly. "I am not a wizard."

Rolan snorted. "Serath, you're mysterious and magical, and you know things that you are not supposed to know. That is close enough. You're a wizard." To preclude further argument, Rolan added, "Besides, I'm a dwarf, and we are speaking Dwarven. I say, you're a wizard."

The man took a moment to ponder the dwarf's words and then nodded. "So be it." He stood up straight, smiled again, and knocked on the wall. Then in a formal tone, he said, "Hello. I am the wizard Serath."

The man spoke with a strange accent that Belac could not identify. It was as if Serath spoke the same language as the rest of them, yet only he spoke it correctly. The wizard's very speech made Belac notice the flaws in his own.

Belac reminded himself that his own first language was Elven. *So, the man can speak Dwarf as well as he wants to.*

Rolan left his chair and walked over to the wizard. Then the dwarf did something that Belac would never have believed; he hugged the man. Not only did Serath seem unconcerned with having a filthy, blood crusted dwarf hug him, he put his hand on Rolan's back affectionately. Belac had not noticed how thin the man was until Rolan hugged him. It looked like the dwarf might break him.

Rolan released the wizard and stepped back. "You're late."

Serath raised an eyebrow at the dwarf.

Belac felt a pang as he was reminded of Emily. Which felt weird when he thought about it. So, he decided not to think about it.

Rolan explained, "I have already escaped."

Serath stepped past the dwarf and held his hand out to Vairug in greeting. The orc was forced to choose between rejecting the offer of friendship, or setting down his weapon. Belac thought this was yet another time that Vairug missed having two hands. Vairug looked to Rolan and then set his silvery mace on the table. He reached out and shook the wizard's hand.

Serath smiled. "It is nice to meet you, Vairug."

Belac carefully got up from the floor and stared at the man suspiciously. "How do you know who we are?"

Rolan answered for him. "Wizard."

That was not good enough for Belac. "That is not an answer."

Serath leaned back against the wall. "I am here to enlist your aid."

Belac did not know what to make of that. Rolan had claimed that the wizard was there to help them. Belac was still trying to adjust to the idea that Serath was not a dark lord come to kill them all. *Not to mention that none of us are exactly in a position to help anyone.*

"What kind of aid?" Belac asked. *You can't have any money.*

Rolan shook his head. "No, Serath."

Serath ignored the dwarf and answered, "It is a quest."

"What kind of quest?" Belac knew that the wizard was drawing him in, but the elf could not help himself.

"No, Serath," Rolan said again. "No one kills a dragon."

A dragon?

Serath smiled. "I have a plan."

Rolan stared at the man. "You always have a plan."

Serath nodded. "Wizard."

"A dragon?" Belac asked.

"Danorin," Serath said.

"No one kills a dragon, Serath," Rolan repeated.

Especially not Danorin. "The Danorin?" Belac added a 'the,' but he did not think that there was more than one. "The dragon that killed Enevic?"

Vairug asked, "Who is Enevic?"

"Enevic is a city," Belac explained. "Or it was a city, before The Danorin burned everything that wasn't stone." Belac agreed with the dwarf. *There is no way we can kill that thing.*

Vairug was no help. "Sounds like it needs to die."

"Of course, it needs to die," Rolan replied irritably. "That dragon is a menace. It burns cities to the ground and eats people. That is not the point."

"Is it not?" Vairug argued.

Belac shook his head.

Rolan glared at the orc. "If all it took was a vote, the dragon would already be dead."

Belac nodded his head in agreement.

"Still," Vairug maintained.

"We can't kill that thing the way Serath wants us to." Rolan chopped at the air. "You cannot just ride at it on a horse in shiny armor and stab it with a lance. Anyone who ever said they did was a liar. The dragon will roast and eat you."

The dwarf's phrasing tugged at Belac. "Then, you're saying that there is a way to kill the dragon."

Rolan frowned at the elf. "There is always a way to do anything."

Belac looked to the man in black. "And you know how to do it?"

Serath smiled. "Wizard."

"No, Serath," Rolan said. "Nothing has changed."

The wizard waited.

Rolan groaned. "What's changed?"

Serath smiled at a secret and pointed. "Him."

Everyone looked at Belac. He held out his arms and looked down at himself. "Me?" He looked up. The wizard had moved forward.

Serath leaned forward over the table and met the elf's eyes. "I have learned a secret." Serath stared into the elf's soul. "I have learned a spell and a ritual."

Belac could not look away.

It seemed like the world had gone silent so that it might listen to the wizard. "I can forge a weapon that will end the threat of Danorin." Serath's voice was beyond confident. "But you must wield the sword."

"Me?" Belac asked again. "Why me?"

There was magic in Serath's voice. "I can cast the spell. I can see it forged. But it must be powered by another."

That did not answer Belac's question, so he asked it again. "Why me?"

Serath continued, "Only one thing can power the sword. Only one thing."

"What?" Belac did not know what he could have.

This was the question that Serath had been waiting for. "The blood of the dragon."

"Where am I supposed to get that?" Belac decided that the wizard's plan had a serious flaw.

Serath's eyes seemed to glow brighter. "From your veins, Belac Melavar. From your veins."

Belac reeled at the mention of his full name. *He really is a wizard.* No one who was not an elf should have known Belac's full name. He still had not processed what the wizard's words had meant.

Rolan sounded troubled. "Are you sure, Serath? The blood of Danorin?"

Serath gave the dwarf a meaningful look. "It must be him."

Something warred within Rolan, but he nodded his head.

Vairug was frowning.

Belac shook his head. "I don't understand."

"The answer is hidden in what you do not know." Serath was being a wizard for all he was worth.

Belac narrowed his eyes at the man. "That is what, 'I do not understand,' means."

Serath shook his head. "We can argue that later. What I said was not meant as a riddle. The reason why you do not understand, is because you do not know who your father is."

What an awful thing to say! "Hey! Screw you, Wizard!"

What the wizard had said was true. That did not stop it from being hurtful. The Elves too cared about such things. It could be hard for someone to know who they were, if they did not know who they came from. There had been fights; fights with his mother, and fights with the other children. It was one of the reasons that Belac had left at such a young age.

"Belac," Rolan said with uncharacteristic patience. "You are not listening."

"I am so listening!" Belac snapped. "Did you hear what he just said about my father?"

"Yes, Belac, I did." Rolan took a deep breath and then let it out. "He said that your father is Danorin."

"That's crazy talk." Belac shook his head. *I'm surrounded by crazy people.* "Danorin cannot be my father. He's a dragon."

Serath offered an explanation. "A dragon can be whatever it wants to be."

"Nope." Belac shook his head again. "I'm an elf. My mother was an elf. I am an elf. My father is not a dragon!"

Serath spoke the secret plainly. "Danorin was an elf when he met your mother."

"I am an elf!" Belac was breathing heavily.

Serath nodded. "And The Danorin is your father."

Belac sat down. "I'm an elf." The fury had faded from his voice.

Serath would not relent. "The Danorin has consumed entire civilizations. He will consume more."

Unless I stop him. It was true. Deep down inside, Belac knew it was true. It was insane, but all of Belac's world had become insane. He had always wondered who his father was, what kind of elf he had been. The wizard had just told him that his father was not even a real elf. Belac believed him. Somehow, that insane truth made the insanity of his life seem more sane. He finally knew who his father was. *And they want me to kill him.* His father was a dragon. His father destroyed cities and burned people alive. *What does that make me?* It made Belac someone who was going to kill his father.

Twenty-Eight

"Do you know what this means?" Belac asked, all eyes looking to him. "I knew there was a dragon!" He jumped up out of his seat and pointed at the dwarf. "I told you so! I told you there was a dragon!"

Rolan turned to the wizard. "Are you sure about this, Serath?

Serath smiled. "Wizard."

Rolan chuckled. "You know that is going to get old, right?"

"It is your fault," Serath said, still smiling.

Rolan laughed. "Stop making me laugh, Serath. This is serious."

"As you say, Rolan." Serath nodded his head. "Wizard face." He narrowed his eyes and pursed his lips.

"Would you stop that?" Rolan shook his head, trying not to laugh. "Besides, that is not a wizard face."

"Nonsense," Serath said. "I am a wizard now. Any face I make is a wizard face."

They are friends. Belac could not deny the obvious affection. It changed the way he saw the dwarf. *Can monsters have friends?* He reflected on his time with the dwarf, trying to understand him better. Belac realized that Rolan had treated Vairug like a friend as well. *He treats me like a friend also.* Belac had simply been too terrified of the dwarf to see it. He wondered what else he might not be seeing. He was missing something. He knew he was.

Something came to Belac. "Who are you here for, Serath?"

Serath gave the elf an approving smile and then addressed his friend. "I did not know that you were in prison, Rolan. I would have come for you had I known." He gestured to the elf. "I did not even know that Belac was in prison until I came looking for him."

Belac wondered how the dwarf would take this revelation.

Rolan shrugged. "I got out anyway."

Belac felt like he should say something. "So, you came here for me?"

"I did," Serath confirmed. "Though, I am glad that my friend was with you."

It was time to ask the question. Belac took a deep breath and asked, "How much of my blood do you need?"

"All of it," Serath said.

Belac shook his head. "You can't have all of it." *Greedy wizard.*

Rolan looked at his friend. "I think he might need to keep some of it, Serath."

Belac nodded his head vigorously.

Serath smiled. "I am asking for more than merely your blood, Belac. You will need to travel the land to forge the sword. You will need to carry the blade and bear its burden. And when the time comes, you will need to face the dragon."

Belac thought about that for a moment. "Are you sure I can't just give you some of my blood? I can give you as much as you need. Just don't take it all at once."

Serath's rich voice was reassuring. "I will be with you. Even when you face the dragon, you will not do so alone." He looked at the dwarf. "I suspect our friend Rolan will be there as well."

Rolan met the wizard's gaze. "You are a bad friend." He sounded amused. "Yes, I will be there."

Serath raised his voice a little. "And what say you, Vairug? Would you have your name be legend?"

The orc had been quiet, even for Vairug. He was studying them. Deep currents turned his mind. "I care not for legends. It will be truth that binds me to this cause."

Does everyone want to be a wizard now?

Rolan said, "I think he means, 'yes."

Serath smiled. "Excellent."

I do not remember anyone asking me if I wanted to go on this absurd quest.

Rolan did not seem to see any need to ask the elf if he was going to join the quest. "So, how do we do this?"

"It will need to be done quicker than I would like," Serath confessed.

Belac narrowed his eyes. "Why is that?" *Are you afraid I'll realize that I have not agreed to any of this?*

"Timing." Serath did not sound as if he were being intentionally cryptic.

Belac complained anyway. "That is not a very helpful answer."

"Dragon slaying is not my only job." It was difficult to tell if Serath was being rude. *I think he is being rude.*

Rolan pulled them back on track. "So, time is a factor." The phrasing was suggestive.

"Indeed," Serath agreed.

"Fine," Belac allowed. "Then, how do we make the magic sword?"

"There are a few, albeit very specific requirements," Serath began.

Belac tried not to roll his eyes. He wondered if wizards even knew how to hurry.

"The first thing we will need is starmetal." Serath held up his hand to forestall argument.

Which was aggravating, because Belac really wanted to argue. Starmetal was not something that was easy to find. He had once heard of an earring made from it. That was it. It would be next to impossible to find enough to make a sword. *It would be easier to make one out of unicorn horn.*

Serath continued, "The starmetal must be forged by a giant in the fires of a live volcano. The blade will then need to be purified in the tears of the dead. After that, I can cast the spell that will create the weapon we need."

Belac's eyes grew larger with every word.

Rolan fell to the floor laughing.

Vairug said nothing.

The wizard was not smiling.

Rolan climbed to his knees. "Next, you are going to want to ask a magic tree to help us fight demons." He fell back down laughing.

Now Belac understood why the dwarf thought this was so funny. Every part of the wizard's quest was either part of a legend, or close enough to be mistaken as one. "Did you just pick the hardest part of every quest you could think of?"

Serath was not smiling. "The commonalities exist because they are all derived from a greater truth. Furthermore, the commonalities themselves lend catalyst to the reality of the event."

"...What?" Belac pointed at the wizard. "Nothing you just said makes any sense!"

Serath said, "I could go back to just answering, 'wizard."

Rolan was not laughing anymore. "Oh, no. You're serious." He stood up. "Serath, buddy..." He shook his head. "We would have a better chance with the horse and lance. How can you expect us to do any of that? We would not even be able to get the starmetal. I am not convinced that stuff even exists."

With a deep thud, Serath set a large white ingot on the table. It looked more like a bar of milk than metal. Belac could not believe it. There was nothing in the world that bar could not have bought if it was real. Some might argue that 'happiness' could not be bought, but the elf was willing to put that to the test.

Rolan picked the ingot up. "Is this real?"

Serath was smiling again. "I am going to look rather foolish if it is not."

"How did you..." Rolan held the ingot up. "Is this why no one can find starmetal?"

Serath shrugged. "Maybe they simply do not know how to find it."

"And you do?" Rolan asked.

"Wizard," Serath answered.

Belac could not help himself. "Do I get to keep the sword?"

Serath nodded. "Kill the dragon, and the sword is yours." It was an easy deal for the wizard to make.

I think I just agreed to join them. How am I going to get out of this now?

Serath held his hand out and Rolan gave him the starmetal. The wizard put the ingot in a bag strapped across his chest that hung under his coat. The bag was made from the same black cloth as the coat and seemed to almost disappear when it was shifted to the wizard's side.

Belac thought they might actually be able to do it. *We can forge the sword.* "Now, we just need a giant."

Rolan looked sideways at the wizard. "You don't happen to have one of those in your bag, do you?"

Serath grinned. "No. But I know where to find one." The wizard liked his secrets.

"How about you start with telling us where we are?" Rolan suggested.

"We are a couple of days north of Tariel." Serath smiled. "If we leave soon, that is."

Rolan thought for a moment. "Do you plan to use the pond?"

Serath nodded. "We will need to take it to Harbridge."

"Harbridge?" Rolan asked. "There are no giants in Harbridge."

"A tribe has moved into the mountains," Serath explained.

"That could mean war." Rolan said. "The Harbridgers hate giants. I think one of them ate the king or something. I misremember. It was a long time ago."

Serath shook his head. "It was his horse." He spoke as if he had been there. "Anyway, that is not what is important. The Harbridgers are currently unaware of the giants. I think it would be best if we did not correct that deficiency."

Rolan seemed to disapprove. "You know they are going to find out."

"Eventually, yes," Serath agreed. "That is one of the many reasons that we will need to hurry."

Rolan accepted what the wizard said. "Then, how are we getting to Tariel?"

"As quickly as we can manage," Serath told him.

Rolan looked surprised. "You want to walk? I thought you said we were in a hurry."

Serath looked at the dwarf without smiling. "We will purchase what horses can be found."

"That is the problem with your plans, Serath," Rolan said. "You forget too many of the details." It sounded like an old argument.

"I did not 'forget' anything," Serath asserted.

Rolan put his hands on his hips akimbo. "So, you intentionally made a plan without any way to get back to civilization?"

Serath shook his head. "You are being dramatic."

"Quickly," Rolan said, "is not a plan."

"My designs are too complex for me to micromanage every little thing, Rolan," Serath declared.

Ooh... Did he just make a dwarf joke?

Rolan did not accept the argument. "You think traveling days down a mountain through unfriendly territory is a little thing?"

Serath nodded. "In the grand scheme of things? Yes. I have every confidence that we can get down a mountain." He smiled. "Even if I have to put you in a barrel and roll you to the bottom."

"That was one time!" Rolan laughed.

"Oh?" Serath asked. "So, now you want to ride a horse?"

"No." Rolan pointed his hand at the wizard. "I want you to magic up some way to get us there."

Belac liked that idea. "Yeah. How about a magic carpet?"

Rolan nodded. "Start knitting, Wizard."

"That is not..." Serath shook his head. "You are not getting a magic carpet." He looked at Belac. "None of you are."

Belac thought about offering some kind of compromise. Something like a magic barrel. He knew what they would do though. They would tell him a normal barrel was magic, wait for him to get inside, and then they would kick him down the mountain. Belac narrowed his eyes at the dwarf. *You are going to pay for that.*

"Fine," Rolan said. "But I am not riding a horse." He started walking toward the door. "Wait here."

After the dwarf left, Belac turned to the wizard. "I don't know where he's going, but if he comes back, and I somehow happened to have a magic carpet…" He held up his hands. "It would drive him crazy." He shrugged his shoulders. "Just saying."

Twenty-Nine

Rolan returned with a bulging sack slung over his shoulder. At first glance, Belac was worried that there might be a dead body stuffed in the charcoal brown cloth. Serath was leaned back against the wall, so still that Belac wondered if wizards slept with their eyes open. Vairug sat at the table, attempting to put his metal hand back on. The elf's cot creaked as Belac rolled off of it and got to his feet.

The dwarf unceremoniously dropped his haul in the middle of the floor. The charcoal brown cloth spilled open and revealed what Rolan had been carrying. *The dwarf has been looting again.* Rolan grabbed a bunched-up wad of blue and brown cloth and tossed it at Belac.

Belac caught it easily. "This smells awful."

Rolan nodded. "It was that or something green."

"I'll take it," Belac said unhappily. He shook out the cloth and inspected his new cloak. The blue and brown striped material was heavily soiled and had a hole in it. "You want me to wear this?"

Rolan shrugged. He tossed a filled bladder on the floor in the orc's direction, then he handed a second bladder to the elf. "Don't drink that while we're in town. Wait until you can't just ask someone for water." Not waiting for a reply, he knelt down and began sorting through the pile on the floor.

Belac would not have a problem with that. He did not want to drink from the bladder at all. "What is all this?"

Rolan stopped and looked at the elf as if he were daft. "Provisions," he said dryly before returning his rummaging. He opened a copper pot and began filling it with odds and ends. He put the pot on a cream colored blanket and rolled it up. Then he took a thin rope and tied one end to each side of the bed roll, creating a strap. He held the strap up to the elf. "Here, take this."

Belac took the bedroll by the improvised strap and tested the weight. It did not seem too heavy. He had half expected the roll to fall apart, but it held.

Rolan got up and handed the elf two glass flasks with leather thongs hanging from them. "Here, loop these through your belt and try not to break them."

If you don't want something to break, you should probably not make it out of glass. Belac looked from the flasks to all the clutter still on the floor. "What is all this for?"

"We have a job." Rolan walked over to the table to get a better view of what the orc was doing. "You need to spin that ring right there. That will tighten the fasteners. Right, just like that."

"Clever." Vairug flexed his metal hand.

Rolan pointed behind himself with his thumb. "The rest of that stuff on the floor is for you."

Belac asked, "You didn't get Serath anything?"

Rolan shook his head. "He wouldn't use anything I brought him."

Vairug stood from the table and moved to the pile on the floor. The first thing that he picked up was a heavy bladed hunting knife in a leather sheath. He tucked it into the straps on his chest and pulled Belac's poniard from the sable fur wrapped around his right calf. He absently handed the scabbarded blade back to Belac and then returned to the pile.

Vairug held up a scrap of hide. "What is this for?"

"Later, I am going to use it to make soles for those socks you are calling boots," Rolan told him.

Belac asked, "Why not now?"

"I told you," Rolan said, "we have a job."

"I don't want a job," Belac complained. *I am too pretty to work.*

Serath guessed, "Merchant guards?"

"Right," Rolan confirmed. "We get to where we are going, and we get paid."

Serath nodded approvingly.

Vairug handed Rolan his splotch gray cloak and then donned the one that the dwarf had used as a sack. The charcoal brown cloak looked nicer than the one Belac had received. *I bet his smells better than mine too.*

Rolan continued, "Fortunately, the trader is a drunk. But we still need to leave now."

"Why is that fortunate?" Belac asked. "The drunk part. Not the job."

"If he weren't a drunk, he would have left earlier in the morning," Rolan explained. "We can't wait around for another trader. Besides, do you really want to sleep here another night?"

"No," Belac said. "No, I do not." *I didn't want to stay here at all.*

Vairug began stuffing things into his bag.

Belac thought to ask, "What are we guarding?" He hoped that it was not something stupid like a giant egg or a magical tiger. If he was going to have a job, he would prefer it be an easier one.

"It doesn't really matter," Rolan told him. "He said it was furs, but he could be lying."

Belac thought it mattered. "If we are smuggling something, won't we get in trouble? I think it will be hard for us to forge a magic sword in prison."

"No," Rolan assured the elf. "If the law shows up, we just stand aside. We are not getting paid to fight the Tarielan Guard."

Which, to Belac, begged the question, "Then, what are we getting paid to fight?" *Please, don't be gorilla-wolf-monsters. Please, don't be gorilla-wolf-monsters.*

Rolan shrugged. "Hopefully nothing." Then he added, "But maybe trolls."

"Trolls?!" Belac exclaimed. "Nope. That's it. I quit. Thanks for the job, but find someone else. I can walk."

Serath smiled. "You may wish to think that through a bit more, Belac. I suspect that you will change your mind."

Belac shook his head. "Not likely."

Serath's green eyes twinkled. "So, you want to walk all the way to Tariel?"

Belac nodded his head. "Yeah, I do. You can keep the trolls and the job."

Serath summed things up in an amused tone. "So, instead of receiving payment to ride on a wagon and face trolls with the aid of others, you would prefer to receive nothing and face the trolls on foot and alone. I must say Belac, that is a remarkably brave choice."

Belac felt like a cat about to be stepped on. "What was the first option again?"

Rolan answered. "That's the one where you have a job."

Belac pointed at the dwarf. "I will take that one."

"Now you want your job back?" Rolan asked.

Belac nodded his head. "Yes, please."

Rolan put his hands on his hips. "What are your qualifications?"

"What?" Belac did not understand the question.

"You want a job. Why should I hire you?" Rolan asked plainly.

So that I don't die. Belac tried to think of some other answer. "...I have a sword."

Rolan nodded. "That would be useful," he said with too much enthusiasm. "If we're lucky, one of the trolls will choke on your sword when they eat you." He pointed his hand at the elf. "You're hired!"

Belac shook his head. "I don't like this plan."

Serath turned to the dwarf. "We could try the barrel."

Rolan looked at the wizard conspiratorially. "Do you think the trolls will chase a rolling barrel?"

Serath shrugged. "They may, if there is a screaming elf inside it."

Belac continued to shake his head. "Bad plan. This is a bad plan."

Rolan asked, "What do you think, Vairug?"

Vairug shouldered his bag and then studied the elf thoughtfully. "I think we should set the barrel on fire first if we really want to make sure that he screams."

Belac's eyes went wide as he stared at the orc.

Rolan shook his head. "Bad idea."

Belac looked at the dwarf and nodded vigorously.

Rolan continued, "Trolls are scared of fire. It would just chase them off."

Belac stopped nodding.

Serath held up a finger. "That could work to our advantage."

"How is that?" Rolan asked.

Serath explained, "The elf's screams will get the troll's attention, but the fire would then cause them to flee. That could give us plenty of time to ride past. When the barrel finally stops burning, the smell of roasted elf should draw the trolls back to it, giving us even more time. Then, when one of the trolls eat the elf, it will inadvertently swallow the sword and die. It will likely be the largest of the trolls that eats him."

Rolan put his hand on his chin in thought. "You know what, Serath? I think this is the best plan that you have ever had. What do you think, Vairug?"

Vairug tilted his head to the side. "I think I am hungry now." He looked at the elf. "Do you think we have time to eat before we leave?"

Belac stepped back and pointed at the orc. "You are not eating me!" *I am not food!*

Rolan waved for the others to follow him, and then he started walking toward the door. "I told the kitchen to make us something we could take with us. They seemed happy enough to do it. I think they might want us to leave."

Belac reluctantly followed the others out of the room and down the stairs.

Serath remarked, "The plan is still missing one crucial element however."

Yeah, like how you people think you are going to get me into that barrel!

"Oh?" Rolan asked. "What is that?"

Vairug answered, "We need a barrel."

Belatedly, Belac realized that he should have pushed them all down the stairs when he had the chance.

Together, they collected a basket of food from the innkeeper and left the inn behind them. Belac decided that Rolan had been right; the staff did seem happy to see them go. Threatening to kill people tended to not inspire warm wishes. Belac wondered if he would need to become accustomed to such reception. He did not think that the dwarf was going to stop threatening to kill people. *Rolan only recently stopped actually killing people.*

As they walked through the town, both the humans and the dwarves kept their distance. Belac did not blame them. He too wanted to keep his distance from his companions. Of them all, only Serath looked to be in a presentable state, and he walked with the air of a man who would not be impeded.

They met with the trader at the edge of town. He stood up from the driver's bench of a two-horse wagon and held his arms apart dramatically in a show of displeasure. The man's brown trousers were covered by boots that went up above his knees, and his stained tunic must have been made for a man twice his size.

"I think he wants a hug," Belac said.

Rolan chuckled but said nothing.

The trader ran one hand through his dirty blond hair. In his other, he held a jug as if it were a permanent fixture. "Least one of you's big."

Belac wondered if Rolan had informed the man that Vairug was an orc. The elf grinned. Humans did not like orcs. *No one likes orcs.* Belac looked over the wagon load of cargo they would be protecting. The wagon itself was uncovered but a canvas tarp had been thrown over the lumpy cargo it carried. Belac pushed on one of the lumps. He nodded to himself. It could have been furs. *Maybe I won't get arrested.* He unstrapped his bedroll and sword, and tossed them on top of the tarp. Then he climbed up with them and easily made himself comfortable on the piles of fur.

Belac looked up at the clear sky and felt like his heart might break. He could not look at it without seeing Emily's eyes. So, he closed his own.

Thirty

"He's an orc!" someone shouted.

Belac woke up. "I am not," he muttered.

A small fire burned to the left of the wagon; night had fallen. Belac did not know if the fire was a good idea or not. Surely the trolls could see it, but Rolan had said that they feared fire. Belac was going to ask. His companions might think the question stupid, but it also might save their lives. The elf rolled off the wagon, intent on asking about fire and trolls.

A balding man in a faded red jacket had a short-sword drawn and was pointing it at Vairug. The firelight flickered around the man, giving him the appearance of an ancient oil painting that had come to life. *The trader must have brought a friend.*

On the other side of the fire, Vairug stood with his cogged mace held low and his foot on the trader's chest. Serath was next to the wagon with his hand on his forehead. Rolan was nowhere to be seen. Belac knew that if he did not do something fast, a dwarf was going to fly out of the darkness and kill the man in red.

Belac waved his hands. "Whoa, whoa, whoa. Calm down. Let's not kill anybody here." He said the last part loudly, hoping that the dwarf would hear.

The man in the red jacket gestured with his sword. "He is an orc!"

"No, he's not," Belac argued in his sleep addled state.

"Yes, he is!" The man gestured with his sword again. "I can see him standing right there."

Oh. Yeah. That. Belac did not know what to say. "Well… Ah… He just looks like an orc."

The man did not believe him. "And why is that, eh?"

Why is that? Belac held up a hand. "He's cursed."

Serath looked up at the elf but said nothing.

"What?" the man asked. "Cursed? To look like an orc?"

Sure. Why not? Belac nodded his head. "Yeah, that's right."

From the ground, the trader said, "He is lying, Bernard. Kill them!"

The trader grunted as Vairug put pressure on his chest.

Bernard pointed his sword back and forth from orc to elf. "If he is cursed, who done it?"

Belac tried to think of someone evil to blame. He said the first name that came to mind. "Danorin."

The man froze. "The Danorin?"

Belac felt some satisfaction that the man had also added 'the' to the name. He smiled. "There is only the one."

The man pointed his sword back at the orc. "And then, who is he then?"

"That," Belac tried to think of something to help sell the lie. "That, is Lord Vair…" *Can't call him Vairug.* "doe."

Vairug looked at Belac as if the elf had lost his mind, the man under his foot forgotten.

Belac shrugged.

"Lord?" The title seemed to have the desired effect on Bernard. "Lord Vairdoe?" The man ran his free hand over his balding scalp and tried to process. "So… Is he from Enevic then?"

"Sure." Belac caught himself. "I mean, sure is. Lord Vairdoe of Enevic, cursed by the dragon Danorin. See? He is totally not an orc."

Both of the men studied Vairug.

Vairug sighed. "If I were really an orc," he spoke as if it pained him a little, "don't you think that I would have already tried to kill you?"

Belac was glad that Vairug spoke Dwarven so well. It suddenly occurred to him that all of his companions spoke Dwarven better than he did. He reminded himself that he was an elf, and elves spoke Elvish. *Dwarf is a stupid language anyway.*

Bernard lowered his sword. "I am sorry Lord Vairdoe, I did not know." He tried to defend himself weakly. "How was I to guess you had been cursed?"

From the ground, the trader said, "You cannot be serious!"

Belac spoke to the man on the ground. "Do you think I would travel around with an orc? I'm an elf! I can barely tolerate the dwarf."

Vairug gave the elf a dirty look. Belac imagined that wherever Rolan was, he looked much the same.

"Hey?" Bernard asked, "Where is the little dwarf?"

"I am behind you," Rolan said in an unfriendly tone. "Waiting for 'Lord Vairdoe' over there to cave in your friend's skull before I shoot you in the back of the head."

Bernard hastily put his sword away and held up his hands. "No need for that! I said I was sorry." He looked down at the trader. "If they wanted to kill us, Richie, they would have killed us. What else makes sense?"

Vairug looked down at the trader. The man nodded grudgingly, and then Vairug took his foot off the man's chest.

"Well," Serath said. "Now that we are all friends again, how about we try to get some sleep?"

Belac asked, "Do you want me to stay up and keep watch?"

Richie sneered. "That is what we are paying you for."

Rolan walked into the light. "Do you think you can stay awake?"

Belac gestured at the camp. "I don't think I could sleep if I wanted to."

Rolan nodded and then pointed his hand up into the sky. "Wake me up when the moon gets there. Poke me with a stick or something."

Belac grinned at the idea of poking the dwarf with a stick. "Why not just sleep till dawn?"

Rolan gestured toward the orc. "I still need to fix 'Lord Vairdoe's' boots. I bet he already has holes in what he has on. That reminds me, I need to get him to take those off. I am not going to work on them while they are still strapped to his smelly, orc feet." He clapped the elf on the shoulder. "Stay awake. Stay vigilant."

Rolan went to speak with Vairug, leaving Belac to wonder why Rolan cared for the orc so much. Their friendship was an odd one to be sure. They had fought together, and they had killed together. Belac decided that there must be friendships based on less. *I guess they are my friends too, now.* Anyone that would help him fight a dragon deserved to be called a friend. It had been some time since Belac had known real friendship. He hoped these would fare better than his last ones.

Belac decided that if he was going to keep watch, it would be a good idea to get a feel for where he was. He walked the edge of the fire's light and looked out into the stony terrain that surrounded them. He tried to determine what was the most likely direction from which a troll might attack. He did this not because he was a good lookout, but because he wanted to position himself as far on the other side of the camp as he was able. *Trolls probably wouldn't just walk down the road.* As Belac moved to stand in the dirt road, the others took to their beds.

A calmness quickly settled over the camp. *This is kind of boring. But I guess being bored is better than being eaten by trolls.* When the campfire died, Belac considered relighting it. However, he did not feel like searching for wood alone in the dark, and he was still unconvinced that the trolls would not see the light. He still had the light rod that Rolan had loaned him, but the moon was bright enough that Belac did not feel he needed its glow. Also, he worried that it might show the trolls where he was.

It was not long before even the threat of trolls in the darkness was not enough to stave off the boredom of night watch. Belac decided to practice with his new sword. He had always used lighter, one-handed blades in the past, and he felt like it would be a good idea to learn how the heavier, two-handed sword balanced. He would have been offended by the accusation that he was only playing with his new sword.

As per Rolan's instructions, when the moon reached its prescribed location in the sky, Belac went to wake the dwarf. Moving quietly so as to not wake the others, he found Rolan's bed and knelt down next to it. Belac put his hand on Rolan's shoulder. Before Belac could say anything, the dwarf twisted around, grabbed the back of Belac's neck, and put a knife to his throat. The elf froze. There was an emptiness in Rolan's eyes reminiscent of the nillanan's slaves.

Awareness returned to Rolan, and then he frowned. "I thought I told you to use a stick." He took the knife away from the elf's throat and gently pushed him back.

Belac said, "Next time, I will use a stick." *A long one.*

Rolan nodded. "Or at least say something first."

I will say whatever you want, but I am still going to use a stick next time.

Rolan crawled out of his bedroll and stood up. "Do you want to try to get some sleep before morning?"

Belac shook his head.

"Right." Rolan nodded. "Then, you can keep watch while I work on these boots." He looked at the embers of the campfire. "Do you have the light rod I gave you?"

Belac worried that the dwarf might want the magical object back, but he did not think lying about it was a good idea. "Yeah."

"Strike it and hold it up while I work," Rolan instructed. "I would rather not have to do this with nothing but moonlight."

Belac was relieved. He took the rod and tapped it on the ground with a ping. He held it out casually, glad that he had an excuse to not walk around while he was on watch. He did keep watch while Rolan worked, but he paid more attention to the dwarf than the darkness.

The trolls would probably yell before they attacked anyway. Belac found that he liked watching the dwarf work. He enjoyed watching the tools transform the hide into something else. He had not spent much time watching craftsmen work, but he thought that the dwarf might be a master. He did not understand why someone who could do what Rolan could, would choose a life of blood and discomfort. *Maybe it was not a choice.*

Belac had to ask, "What were you, Rolan?"

Rolan considered the question before he answered, "I have been many things, Belac. But... I don't know that a person ever stops being something. They just become something else also."

Belac knew that the dwarf was trying to be open with him, but that did not tell him much. "Then, what are you now?"

"Right now?" Rolan took a deep breath. "I guess, I'm a dragon slayer."

Belac smiled. "You know, we have not actually killed any dragons yet."

Rolan smiled with him. "I did not say that we were any good at it."

Thirty-One

Belac woke from a nightmare in which he was being chased down a mountainside by trolls with flaming barrels for heads. He sat up and shook his head, trying to force the memory of the nightmare away. It was late in the day, but the sun had not yet set. He could see the gray wall that surrounded Tariel in the distance. Rock had been taken from the nearby mountains and stacked to protect the city and its people. *Those walls won't stop a dragon. Dragons can fly.* The towering walls had a sense of solidness to match the mountains from which they had been made. Imposing as they were, Belac was getting sick of all the gray.

Rolan sat with the trader on the driver's bench. Neither of the two seemed particularly pleased with the others company. Vairug walked the edge of the road, easily keeping pace with the wagon. His identity hidden within his charcoal brown hood, the orc appeared committed to his role as the merchant's guard. Behind the wagon, Bernard followed on the back of a chestnut mare. *He seems lost in thought. Maybe he's still trying to wrap his head around the idea of Vairug being a cursed lord.*

Belac looked to the wizard that was lounging comfortably on the bundled furs next to him. "Why didn't you wake me up?" Belac complained, though he was glad to have been allowed his sleep.

Serath smiled. "Is that a responsibility that you would like me to have?"

The question sounded friendly, but Belac could sense the trap. "I guess not."

"Nevertheless, I am glad that you are awake," Serath told him. "There is a matter that we need to discuss."

Belac thought this sounded like another trap. He wondered if the wizard had sat there all day, waiting patiently for him to wake up. He pictured Serath sitting there, watching him sleep with those green eyes. Belac shuddered. He wondered if the wizard had somehow given him nightmares so that he would wake up. *No, that is crazy.* He looked at the wizard. *Please, let that be crazy.*

"You lied," Serath said.

Belac looked around quickly to see if anyone may have heard. He gave the wizard a meaningful glare.

Serath smiled. "Everything you do has a cost, Belac. Everything." He spoke kindly, but the elf could tell that there was a seriousness in what he said. "Lying is always more expensive than it seems."

Belac did not understand what the problem was. He had lied to the humans, but in doing so, he had saved their lives. He was fairly certain that humans would rather be lied to than killed. Belac knew that he personally would prefer just about anything to being killed. He was surprised that it had worked at all, but looking back, he did not see how it could have gone better.

Belac asked, "Do you think there was another way?"

"I am a wizard," Serath reminded the elf. "I always think there is another way."

Belac accepted the reminder. He did not doubt Serath was a wizard. It was simply easy for him to forget sometimes. The man was too handsome, too young. To the elf, Serath looked more like a friendly noble than a wizard. Belac resolved himself to think about what Serath had said. *What is the point of having a wizard around, if I am not going to listen to him?*

Serath smiled at the elf fondly, and said nothing more on the matter.

The wagon reached the city gates before the sun had fully set. Belac wondered if the guards would have let them enter after dark. *If not, then we cut this trip kind of close.* He would not have wanted to spend another night outside with the trolls.

Belac looked to the wizard again. "Did you kill any trolls while I was sleeping?"

"I suspect that you would have had trouble sleeping through something like that." Serath grinned.

Belac remembered his nightmare and narrowed his eyes at the wizard.

The grand city of Tariel was notably different than the walls that kept it safe. Copper rooves topped the white plastered buildings of the interior. Domes and sweeping lines flowed across the top of the pale city in soft patina. The city made the elf uneasy. It was not the darkening alleys or the lamplit streets, it was that the entire city was covered by a layer of green copper. *These people are just asking for this city to fall on them.*

When the wagon came to a halt outside of a factorage, Belac hopped off and then retrieved his belongings. Bernard led his horse away and Richie began to unharness the horses from the wagon. Belac and his companions waited while the horses were put away, but the waiting began to take on an uncomfortable feel.

Rolan stepped into the trader's path as he returned. "You are forgetting something."

It was growing dark, and the lamplight was too dim to show Richie's face. "I don't think so." He looked around himself dramatically. "Nope, I don't think I am.

Rolan's voice was hard. "Payment."

Richie shook his head. "Nope. I paid you enough already. Now, be on your way."

Rolan did not move. "What you paid me was an advance. We agreed on twice that, once we made the city."

Belac believed him. *If Rolan had wanted to shake down the trader, he would have done it before entering the city. We could have just killed the man the last night and then brought the wagon load of goods in as our own.* In Belac's mind, if the dwarf said that they were owed more, it was true.

"I am not paying you anything." Richie obviously felt safe now that he was within the walls of the city. "I hired you all to fight trolls. No trolls, no payment. Simple as that."

Rolan walked over to Belac and yanked the flasks from the elf's belt. He then smashed both flasks against the wagon. He pulled a stone and striker from one or his pouches and faced the trader. "No, you hired us to ensure your wares arrive safely. Are you sure you don't want to pay us?"

Richie must have smelled the fumes of the liquid fuel. "You're crazy!" he exclaimed.

Serath interjected, "This is not necessary, Rolan."

Rolan shook his head. "The man is not going to cheat me."

Belac knew that the dwarf was serious. *He would burn that wagon down if he had to light himself on fire to do it.* He walked over to the trader. "You should just pay him."

Richie pointed at the dwarf. "I will call the guards!"

Rolan stared back. "Then, they can watch your wagon burn with you."

Belac could not help but smile a little. The trader had lost the moment he had acknowledged that Rolan was crazy. *A crazy person would definitely set the wagon on fire.* Belac watched as Richie tried to think through the problem. Then Belac realized something that he did not think the trader would. Rolan would set the wagon on fire. He would do it for no reason other than he had said he would. After that, Richie would have to die. There would be no other option for the dwarf. Belac could not stop him, and he did not know if the others would even try. It would be more than just the trader's cargo that burned in the wagon.

Belac tried to save the man's life again. "All he is asking, is that you be honorable." He knew that was difficult for humans.

After another moment of internal struggle, Richie pulled out a coin purse and handed it to Belac. That he had the payment already counted out confirmed Rolan was telling the truth. The dwarf put the stone and striker away.

Richie looked the elf in the eyes and said, "You're thieves."

Belac hit him. It was not something that he had intended to do. Belac had done nothing but try to help the man. *I saved his life! Twice!* For this, the man had tried to cheat him. Then the greedy trader had found the audacity to call him a thief. The hypocrite thought that he could assume moral authority. Belac wanted the man to get back up so that he could hit him again.

The trader did not get back up. He remained on the ground, but stared up at Belac with pure venom. *I should kill him.* Richie would be a problem. Belac knew it. He knew it, but he could not kill the trader.

Belac turned away. "Let's go."

Serath smiled, handsome even in the lamplight. "Everything you do."

Belac walked off. He had no idea where he was going. Vairug clapped him on the back. Serath's long legs allowed him to take the lead. Belac followed and said nothing, his emotions and thoughts were too fast to comprehend. Not far from the factorage, Rolan hurried ahead of the group and went up to a couple of men that wore blue and brown striped tabards over chainmail. The colorful striping reminded Belac of his cloak. He had forgotten it at the inn. *Whatever. It stunk anyway.*

Rolan spoke briefly with the two men, and then they rushed down the road toward the trader and his wagon. Rolan watched them run while he waited for his companions to reach him.

Serath asked him, "What was that about?"

Rolan chuckled. "It seems as if a smuggler might be preparing to burn evidence."

Serath shook his head, but he was smiling. "Rolan…"

"What?" Rolan asked. "He paid too much to move furs." He slung a hand toward the factorage. "He's going to run his mouth. He is going to be a problem. And you people are not going to let me kill him."

As they walked on, Vairug nudged the dwarf. "I would not have stopped you."

What disturbed Belac was that he did not know if he himself would have tried to stop the dwarf or not. *I wanted to kill the man myself.* Despite the city's lamps, the night darkened along with Belac's mood. Glumly, he followed his companions to an inn and the relaxation that it promised.

The elf's spirits were immediately lifted upon his first step into the inn. The smell of food and alcohol filled the air and people danced to the music of two minstrels. All human, the patrons did not dance very well. However, Belac was willing to make do. He thought that the Tarielan's sleeveless tunics seemed a strange way to dress, but the array of colors brought life to the room. On women, the tunic ended at their ankles and had a split on the sides that rose up to their thigh. Belted, they did look much like a dress. The men's tunics ended at the knees. Something Belac would have preferred to not notice when the men sat down.

Belac selected a table large enough for his party and walked over to it, enjoying the ambiance along the way. He set his bedroll to the side and unslung his baldric before taking a seat. Rolan and Vairug sat down with him while Serath spoke to the proprietor.

Belac took the coin purse that Richie had given them and slammed it down on the table. "I think we have earned this." He held his arms out to the room.

Rolan picked up the purse, tested its weight, and then put it away. "I would not mind a nice meal."

"And a drink!" Belac added cheerfully.

Rolan shook his head. "None for me. I want to get some sleep. I have been up all day."

Belac ignored the jab. He was committed to having a good time. "What about you, Vairug?"

Vairug kept his head low and covered with the hood of his cloak. "I will eat with you, but then I should stay out of sight." Wisely, he did not explain why.

Belac had not considered the persistent need for secrecy. He had become accustomed to traveling with the orc. He wanted to sit and have a drink with Vairug. *He deserves a drink as much as anyone else does.* Belac wondered what the world would look like if an elf and an orc could sit and have a drink together openly while watching the humans dance. In his mind, that world looked much the same, but with orcs in it.

Belac asked, "Do you think Serath will drink with me?"

Rolan shook his head. "No."

"What?" Belac did not want to drink alone. "Why not?"

"Serath does not drink," Rolan told him.

"Never?" Belac found that doubtful. "He never drinks?"

Rolan shrugged. "I have never seen him."

Belac shook his head. "That does not mean that he never drinks."

"Think about what he is." Rolan waited.

Wizard.

Rolan continued, "Do you really think it would be a good idea to get him drunk?"

Belac pictured the scrawny wizard on a table, barely able to stand, swaying side to side as he cast spells and did party tricks. The crowd would cheer, and the wizard's performance would grow increasingly spectacular. Spectacular and dangerous. It would not be long before there was a drunken wizard walking around town, throwing fireballs up into the air because he liked the pretty colors.

"It might not be a good idea," Belac held up a declarative finger, "but it could be hilarious."

Serath asked, "What idea is that?"

Rolan saved the elf from having to come up with something to say. "He wants you to drink with him."

"I appreciate the sentiment, Belac. I do." Serath smiled, saying 'no' without actually saying it.

Belac looked around the table and frowned. All of his friends either would not or could not drink with him. He scanned the room and picked out a particularly attractive woman with curves her tunic could not hide and hair that bounced in dark ringlets as she danced. Belac smiled once more. "I bet that she will drink with me."

Thirty-Two

When Belac awoke, all he could see was hay and faded wood. The world turned slowly around him. His head hurt and he had no idea where he was. He tried to sit up but could not. The world wobbled around him. He put a hand to his face. It was entirely possible that the elf had too much to drink the night before. His light rod hung dimly from his wrist. It hung in the wrong direction. He waved his arm out in front of himself and tried to make sense of things. The light rod hung upward. Belac groaned. He was upside down. And he was naked.

The elf hung by one foot held in a noose that had been thrown over the rafters of a barn. He tried to kick with his free leg, but his coordination was off. The world continued to turn slowly and a man in black came into view. The man was leaning back against the wall with his arms crossed, watching Belac slowly spin.

"Hey, Serath," Belac greeted him weakly.

"It looks like you had an interesting night," Serath said pleasantly.

Belac closed one eye so he could see the wizard better. That he was handsome only made the man look more smug. "I hate your face."

Serath grinned broadly.

Belac threw a punch at him. He came nowhere close to hitting the wizard, and accomplished nothing more than continuing to spin. Belac admitted to himself that he might still be a little drunk.

"Serath?"

"Yes, Belac?"

"You're a wizard, right?"

"I am."

"So, you know things?"

"I do."

"Then, do you know where my clothes are?"

The elf could hear Serath's smile. "You do not appear to have any clothes, Belac."

The wizard waited while Belac continued to watch the world slowly turn. The wizard was patient. Belac hated that.

"Serath?"

"Yes, Belac?"

"Can I get a little help here?"

"You want me to help you?"

Belac did not hear the trap. "Yes, I want you to help!"

A boot pushed into the elf's back and swung him away. Then the rope went slack and Belac crashed onto the floor. The fall hurt, but it felt good to be down. He thought he might just go back to sleep. He doubted things would be much worse when he woke back up. A rush of cold water hit him, sending a shock through his body. He tried to stand up, but his leg was still asleep and he fell back down. Another rush of cold water hit him.

Belac rolled over and faced the wizard. "Enough already!"

Serath held a bucket of water and stood next to two empty ones on the floor. He pitched the water at Belac. It hit him in the chest and splashed across the barn.

Belac sputtered water. "Are you trying to drown me?"

Serath smiled. "I am merely giving you a little help."

Belac held up a hand. "That is not helping!"

"Would you prefer to go back to hanging?" Serath inquired pleasantly.

This time, Belac did hear the trap. He reminded himself that he was dealing with a wizard. "No, thank you."

Serath tossed a pale, yellowy wad of cloth at the elf. It landed on him, covering his face. Belac climbed to his feet and shook out the tunic.

"This looks like a sundress," Belac complained.

Serath raised an eyebrow. "You can stay nude if you would prefer."

Belac narrowed his eyes at the wizard and then put on the tunic. Serath handed him a wooden comb. The elf untied his hair and began to comb it out. He had not realized how messy his long, black hair had become. Hanging upside down undoubtably had something to do with it.

Belac held up the comb. "Can I keep this?"

Serath nodded. "You never made it to your room last night, and there is no sign of your things anywhere else. Have you managed to lose everything you own?"

Belac tried to remember what he could of the night before. He thought back, hoping to recall something they might use to recover what he had lost. The last thing he could remember was the woman with the curly, black hair sitting on his lap while they drank and laughed. It was a good memory, though not particularly helpful.

Belac held up his wrist with the light rod hanging from it. "I still have this."

Serath inspected it. "That is likely the most valuable thing you owned."

Belac shrugged. "I really liked my boots." *I wonder if I can get Rolan to make me some new ones.*

"Fortunately, you have an appointment with a man who is both a cobbler and a tailor," Serath told him.

Belac agreed that he would need new clothes, but he did not know how he was going to pay for them. "Rolan still has my share from the trader, but I don't even know how much that is. I may need to find out what I can afford first."

"That is not something you need concern yourself with," Serath said dismissively.

Belac disagreed, but did not argue. *Maybe not caring about money is a wizard thing.* He trusted Serath to pay the bill. And if the bill came due, and the wizard did not pay it, Belac would just run. He needed new clothes.

Belac was glad that the wizard had thought to make the appointment. "Wait! An appointment? How long did you leave me hanging there?"

Serath smiled. "The arrangements were made before I found you. Both you and Vairug were in need of new attire."

"Do we have time to get something to eat first?" Belac was hungry and he knew it was only going to make his hangover worse. "I still want to get my pay from Rolan anyway."

"We can meet up with Vairug and get you something to eat," Serath said. "But Rolan is gone."

Rolan is gone? Belac did not know what he was going to do without him. He had begun to rely on the dwarf. Belac knew that he was going to need his help to slay the dragon. He would never have agreed to this insane quest if Rolan had not pledged to help. Rolan was useful. He was necessary. He…

"He has my money!" Belac declared. He wondered if it had been Rolan who robbed him. The light rod could have been left as a joke, a way of letting Belac know who had taken everything he had. Except, Belac did not think that Rolan would have left the light rod behind. *He would not have left me breathing.*

"You can get it from him later," Serath assured the elf.

Belac blinked. "So, he is not 'gone' gone?"

Serath shook his head. "He is off." He waved his hand. "Doing something nefarious no doubt. He said he will meet us back at the inn."

Belac followed the wizard back into the inn. They walked through the main hall and into a private dining room. They found Vairug waiting for them there, sitting alone at the table, nursing a drink. Belac stumbled over to the table and sat down across from the orc. Belac leaned back in his chair, stared up at the ceiling, and wished that the room would stop spinning.

From under his hood, Vairug said, "That is a nice dress."

"Die in a fire," Belac replied. He closed his eyes to help the room stop spinning.

"Are you going to eat that?" Vairug asked.

Belac came awake and looked around the room. He regretted doing both immediately. His hangover was increasing, and the movement made it worse. He considered going back to sleep, but the smell of food persuaded him otherwise. Servers had come and gone while he slept, but they had been professional enough to not wake him.

Belac breathed in the smell of his breakfast. "Yes." He was careful not to nod. "But if you're still hungry, Vairug, I am sure they can bring you more food." *The wizard did say to not worry about money.*

Vairug grunted.

Belac did not know what the grunt meant, so he left it alone. *I need Rolan to translate.* When Belac finished eating his breakfast, he took a drink from his mug and almost spat it out. It tasted awful. "What is this?" He looked around the room accusingly.

"It will help with your condition," Serath said. "I suggest you drink it."

Belac had forgotten that the wizard was still there. "What condition? Being alive? Not being blind?"

"It will help you feel better," Serath assured him.

Belac narrowed his eyes at the wizard. "Is it magic?"

Serath grinned. "That depends entirely on what you consider magic."

The answer confused Belac. "I don't understand."

Serath's grin grew into a smile. "Then, yes. It's magic."

Belac decided that he was in no mood for wizards. Still, he drank the vile medicine. He coughed and then asked, "When do we leave for the appointment?"

"What appointment?" Vairug asked.

Belac smirked. "We are going to get you some people-clothes."

Vairug gave the elf a disapproving look.

Serath said, "We can leave as soon as you are both ready."

"They are just waiting on us?" Belac asked.

"That is their profession," Serath replied.

Shortly after leaving the inn, Belac acknowledged that he did indeed feel better. It made him wonder what was in the potion that the wizard had given him. The drink had tasted disgusting, so he knew that it was not made from strawberries and rainbows. *I bet it was made from something nasty like eye of newt.* He resolved himself not to think about it.

As they walked through the streets, Belac paid special interest to the copper rooves. He thought Tariel could be a wonderful city if someone would just paint over all the green. *And if they found a way to stop people from getting robbed and hung upside down in a barn.*

The shop Serath led them to was advertised by a richly stained wood sign with a word scrawled onto it that was so stylized, Belac could not read it. He did not bother asking. It was not as if he were going to travel the world on a quest to slay a dragon and stop to tell the people he met along the way where he had bought his shoes.

Serath halted, not going inside. "This is the place. I have other things to see to before we can leave the city. Will you two be able to find your way back to the inn?"

Belac did not think the question was meant to be insulting, but it felt like it was a little. He turned around to reconsider the way they had come. *All I have to do is…* He really did not want to tell the wizard that he was lost.

Vairug saved him the embarrassment. "We will find our way."

Belac hoped that Vairug was not pretending to be confident. They might be in trouble if they were both trying to save their pride. He examined Vairug. If the orc was pretending, he was better at it than Belac.

Serath smiled, nodded, and then walked away.

Belac wondered if the wizard had just led them to a trap. He imagined stepping into a room where the floor fell out from beneath him and he dropped into a dark cell where he was surrounded by hungry zombies. This made him wonder why Serath had bothered to free him from the noose earlier that morning. *He could have just led the zombies to me. No. Someone would have noticed a wizard leading an army of the undead through the streets of Tariel.*

His thoughts were interrupted when Vairug went into the shop without him. Belac hurried after. There was no way he was going to let the orc use up all the best cloth. *Greedy orc.*

Thirty-Three

"This has got to be the best zombie trap ever!" Belac declared.

The inside of the shop was open, warm, and draped in various exotic cloths that hung over lush carpets. A pleasant spice filled the air and cultivated the feeling of a clean and well cared for shop.

"Why would you want to catch a zombie?" Vairug asked.

Belac shook his head. "I don't. I mean, a trap where the floor drops away and you fall into a pit of zombies."

"Would that not make it an orc trap?" Vairug gestured to the elf. "Or an elf trap?"

Belac shrugged. "Spike traps don't catch spikes."

Vairug thought about it for a moment. "Do you think the dwarves made their language confusing on purpose?"

Belac shook his head. "No, I bet humans did that to it."

Vairug stretched out his foot and tested a carpet with his toes. "I think it is safe," he said dryly.

Belac held his hands apart. "And that is exactly what you would think if this was the best zombie trap ever."

Vairug grunted.

An old man, the top of his scalp bald above curly, gray hair, stepped into the room. His velvet tunic was a shimmering beige with dark embroidery that matched his belt and sandals. "Hello."

Belac did not know what he was supposed to do or say. So, he simply repeated what he had been told. "We were told we have an appointment."

"Yes." The man nodded. "The wizard said that you would come. This way please."

They followed the old man into a fitting room with two stools waiting in the middle. Belac wondered if the room had been set up specifically for Vairug and him. He was reassured by the idea that the orc would stay close by. Vairug had saved his life more than once already. It occurred to Belac that it might be the other way around; that he might be there to reassure Vairug. The orc had never before spent time in a human city, and the customs must have been a mystery to him.

Belac hopped up onto one of the stools, showing the orc how it was done. "I am going to want trousers." He gestured to his bare legs.

The man nodded deeply. "Of course."

Belac tugged on the collar of the yellowy tunic he wore. "And something fancy." He thought of a gold and mauve silk that he had seen in the other room.

"The wizard has given us your requirements." The old man kindly told the elf, politely saying that he did not get a choice.

Belac shrugged. *Serath is paying for it.* "But not all black," he held firm. *The wizard likes too much black.*

The old man nodded again. "Of course."

Belac almost told Vairug to stand on the other stool but then realized that there was no reason to rush him. There was only one little old man, and he could not measure them both at the same time.

Stubby, worn fingers unwound a string with tiny knots tied into it at regular intervals. Belac was then tugged and positioned as the old man took his measurement. Belac smiled at the thought of how Vairug was going to respond to being measured. Without Belac there to demonstrate, Vairug may very well have murdered the tailor for measuring his inseam.

A timid young man with eyes too big for his face, slunk into the room and offered Belac a cup of something warm. The elf took the cup, held it up to his nose, and inhaled deeply. It smelled sweet and of the same spice permeating the shop. Belac sipped at the drink while the old man measured his feet.

A thought occurred to Belac. "And nothing green." He pointed his empty cup at the old man threateningly.

The old man gave a single nod but said nothing.

When the tailor was finished taking measurements, Belac hopped down from the stool and then pointed at it. "Your turn."

Vairug grunted and took a step forward. He stopped and stared at the tailor from within the dark hood of his cloak.

The old man weathered the stare professionally. "The wizard has retained our discretion along with our services."

Vairug removed the cloak and tossed it to the side.

Belac almost dropped his cup on the floor. "Well, I hope he was talking about you being an orc!"

Vairug shrugged. "What else could he have meant?"

I guess it would have been kind of stupid for Serath to not tell the tailor that one of his customers was going to be an orc. The wizard is not stupid. Belac narrowed his eyes at the orc.

The old man gestured to the stool, and Vairug stepped onto it. The orc disappointed Belac by stoically enduring the tailors measuring. *I should have made him go first.* The old man continued professionally but Vairug was not offered a drink.

Belac grinned to himself and handed the orc the empty cup. "Here, hold this."

Vairug took the cup in hand. "And what am I supposed to do with this?"

"You just hold it out to the side and then sip at it every once and a while." Belac demonstrated.

Vairug looked down into the cup. "It is empty."

"I know," Belac replied with a hint of impatience. "Just do it anyway. It's part of the process."

The skepticism was plain on Vairug's face, but he mimed drinking from the cup.

"You have to stick your pinky out," Belac told him.

Vairug lowered the cup. "This is foolish."

"Hey," Belac asked, "Do you want new clothes or not?"

Vairug growled and brought the cup up to his mouth.

"And the pinky," Belac insisted.

Vairug extended his pinky with enough force that it could have been mistaken for an obscene gesture.

The old man coughed uncomfortably. "We are done here."

Belac pointed to the orc. "Make sure he gets something in red."

The old man looked up questioningly.

Belac smiled. "It will help to hide all of the blood."

The old man fled the room with all the dignity he could muster.

Vairug looked at the elf. "Why?" It was more than a simple question.

Belac grimaced. "They did not want you to drink from their cups."

Vairug looked from the elf to the small cup. Then he shrugged and tossed it over his shoulder. The cup bounced on the carpet behind him and then clattered across the floor.

Ready to leave, Belac asked, "Do you know the way back?"

Vairug nodded.

"I don't think I believe you." Belac picked up the orc's cloak and handed it to him. "Prove it."

Vairug put on the cloak. "We could race."

Belac shook his head. "No… I ah… would not know how to run in this…" He gestured at his tunic.

"Dress," Vairug supplied.

Belac narrowed his eyes at the orc.

Together, they left the smaller room and retraced their steps through the shop. Daylight blinded them as they stepped out into the street. Belac held his hand up to block the sun.

A voice called out from the other side of the street. "Hello to you too, Elf," the man said, intentionally misinterpreting the elf's hand movement.

"Richie?" Belac asked unnecessarily.

Richie sneered, proving that his greeting had been insincere. "What? Did you think I was in jail?"

Well… Yeah. "Of course not. Why would you be in jail?" Belac forced a smile. *That was probably the wrong question to ask.*

As Belac's eyes adjusted to the light, he saw that the trader was still wearing the same filthy, ill-fitting clothes. The four rough men standing next to him holding foresting axes were new though. *How does this guy have so many friends?*

Richie pointed a drawn short-sword. "Cause of you!"

Belac leaned toward the orc and whispered, "I told you it was a trap."

Vairug shook his head slightly. "I do not see any zombies."

Belac motioned to the men standing in menace. "That looks close enough to me."

Richie swung the short-sword around as he spoke, clearly drunk. "You think you can put me in jail? You think you can steal from me?"

Belac had not done either of those things. "Of course not." He waved to the men. "So, we will just be on our way…" He took a step to the right, but a gray hand grabbed the back of his collar and prevented him from going farther. Belac stumbled as the orc pulled him back to stand closer. He narrowed his eyes at the orc.

Richie pointed his sword at the elf again. "You are going to pay, Elf." Then he pointed the sword at the orc. "That orc is going to pay." He swept the sword's point off to the side. "That cheating dwarf is going to pay. And then that liar what calls himself a wizard is going to pay."

Belac held up a finger. "Okay, that is a bad plan."

"It has to be blood," Richie said more convincingly than the elf would have expected.

Belac tried to think of something to say. He did not want to fight five men in the street. He did not want to fight them anywhere, for that matter. He held out his hands. "I am not even armed!" *Some people care about that, right?*

Vairug reached into his cloak and pulled out his hunting knife. He flipped the blade and then handed the hilt to the elf.

Belac did not thank the orc.

The trader gave no dramatic command to attack, but the men with axes moved forward together. They hefted their axes as they closed on Belac and Vairug. The man on the far left reared back to swing at the orc. Vairug stepped forward and grabbed the axe's haft with his metal hand. With his other, he broke the man's nose and then took hold of the axe, wrenching it free as the man fell backward. The man in the middle closest to Vairug, swung his axe down toward the orc. Vairug turned and swept his own axe to the side in a horizontal arc. The axe heads collided, sending the man off balance. Vairug slammed his shoulder into the man and toppled him into another of the attackers. He turned back to the first man and brought the axe down on his head in violent finality.

Belac, for his part, was barely able to dodge backward when an axe was swung his way. The wall behind him halted further retreat. He was saved when one of the other attackers crashed into the man intent on pressing the advantage. Belac looked past the tangled men to another that had suddenly lost his confidence.

The elf leapt over the two men on the ground and stabbed at the man's face. The blade tore into flesh but was deflected by the man's cheekbone. The man dropped his axe and held his hands up in defense. Belac stabbed him in the chest and they both fell to the ground together. Belac was not particularly skilled with a knife, so he stabbed the man repeatedly, not wanting to allow him the opportunity to fight.

Vairug's right hand gripped his axe below its blade and pulled it free from the dead man. The men behind him were already getting to their feet. Quickly, Vairug turned and surged at the man who was closest to him. The orc's metal fist backhanded the man in the face, caving in the side of his skull and ripping off part of his jaw. The man fell away, and Vairug stepped past him. The other man was closing on Belac as the elf stabbed the man's friend to death. Vairug crushed the man's shoulder in a metal grip and punched with the head of the axe. The tip of the blade connected with the man's temple to gruesome effect. Vairug let the man fall lifelessly to the street. Then he turned to face the trader.

Belac heard Vairug hit the man behind him. The elf turned with his knife held ready to fight. He followed Vairug's attention to the terrified trader. Belac stood, blood on the large hunting knife and splattered across his tunic. He was angry in a way that he was not prepared for. He had met plenty of unpleasant people through the years. He had even killed some of them. Never, had he wanted to kill someone so much that he could taste it. He could smell the blood in the air, and he wanted more.

Richie dropped his sword and backed away. He fell down and crawled backward as Belac strode toward him. Belac had been kind to the man. He had protected him. He had saved his life. The man in turn had gone from trying to cheat him, to trying to murder him in the street. Belac had known that the man was a problem. He had known, and he had saved him anyway. He had tried to do the right thing, tried to compensate for Rolan's cold-blooded murders.

Belac remembered the trader's words. "It has to be blood."

Richie climbed to his feet and pointed at the elf. "This is your fault!"

Belac knew that the man was right. With contempt, Belac slapped the trader's hand aside and stabbed him in the chest. He wished he could say that he mistook the trader's gesture for an attack. Or that he feared the man was reaching for a hidden blade. The truth, however, was that Belac would no longer let the man punish him for being decent.

In his mind Belac heard the wizard's words echo. *"Everything you do."*

"Drop the weapons!" A voice commanded.

Belac turned to the voice and saw that he was surrounded by armed soldiers. Neither he nor Vairug dropped their weapons. He counted four crossbows aimed at them, two on each end of the street. There were eight more armed soldiers, though some of them were busied directing onlookers away. Belac did not see any way that they could fight and survive, but he was not going to let them take Vairug. He did not know if they would execute the orc later or just kill him there in the street, but he was not going to allow it. Belac desperately searched for some way to escape, for an ally or open door. He thought they might be able to make it back to the shop, but he did not know what to do about the crossbows. Vairug was too big for them to miss.

Then Belac saw the wizard. Serath was standing behind the crowd so as to not be caught up in the scene. He held up a hand and then made a lowering gesture. The message was clear, but Belac did not want to comply with it. He shook his head at the wizard. Serath nodded and made the gesture again. Belac did not know what else to do. He dropped the knife and put a hand on Vairug's arm. Vairug looked at the elf and then tossed his axe to the side. The orc was stoic in their surrender.

Thirty-Four

"I am not crawling through the privy, Vairug," Belac said for the third time. *Especially not after you have used it.*

After being arrested, Belac and Vairug had been detained in a stately waiting room with a long table in the center that was surrounded by heavy, wooden chairs. There were two doors out of the room. They had entered through one, and the other opened to a small privy. Vairug was convinced that the elf could crawl through the privy and then find some way to open the door to the hallway. Belac wondered if Vairug would have been so set on the plan if an orc could have fit through the privy.

Vairug growled at him. "Would you rather stay in prison?"

Belac swept his hand across the room. "This is not what prison looks like, Vairug." *The table even has a tablecloth.*

"Have you checked the other door?" Vairug asked.

Belac walked around the table and pushed on the main door. There was no handle on their side. "It's locked."

"Then, this is a prison," Vairug concluded.

Stupid, smug orc.

Belac looked at the walls of their prison. The polished white was accented by tasteful copperwork and small ventilation grates.

This was not the first time that the elf had been in a castle. It was however, the first time that he had ever been escorted inside after murdering a man in full view of the authorities. "This cannot be usual. Whatever 'this' is," he told the orc.

Vairug surprised him by offering a suggestion. "It is unlikely that they encounter many orcs or elves."

"And never together." Belac thought about it for a moment and then shook his head. "No. That does not feel right. We are dealing with humans. If this was about nothing but you being an orc, they would have just killed you and then said that they were being invaded or something."

"Many of these people may not even know what an orc looks like," Vairug said.

Belac could not tell if Vairug was arguing or agreeing, so he ignored the statement. He did not want to admit it, but the orc was right. They were trapped.

Belac frowned. "Well… They didn't lock us in a room because they trust us." He did not expect a judge to believe anything they had to say.

Vairug brightened. "Then, you do want to escape."

Belac nodded his head reluctantly. "I kind of feel like we are obligated to try."

"Good." Vairug looked at the door to the privy.

"I am not crawling through the privy!" Belac said again.

The orc frowned.

Belac grabbed the back of the chair closest to him and dragged it over to the main door. He climbed onto the chair and used it to reach the ventilation grate above the door.

"You cannot fit through that," Vairug said impatiently.

"I am not crawling through the privy," Belac repeated. The grate wobbled as he pulled on it, but the elf could not get it free. "Help me with this."

The orc continued to frown as he reached up and grabbed hold of the grate. Together, they broke the grate free from the wall with a loud snap. They waited, listening for some cry of alarm, but no one came to investigate.

Vairug took the broken grate and tested its weight, swinging it to see if it might be used as a weapon.

Belac stood on the chair and looked through the hole they had created. He was relieved to not find a ring of guards with spears pointed at the door. He could not see the hallway very well, but it appeared to be empty. He thought it strange that not even a single guard had been posted. "It looks clear," the elf said in an uncertain voice.

Vairug looked up at him. "Can you reach the latch?"

Belac smiled at his own cleverness. "No. But you can." *If nothing else, seeing that confused look on Vairug's face makes it worth getting trapped in a castle.* He hopped down and stepped over to the table. He rolled the tablecloth up longways and then turned to face the orc. He held out his hand and said, "Can I get a hand?"

Vairug's confusion turned into a broad grin as he suddenly understood. He unbuckled the strap on his wrist, spun the tension ring, and then unfastened his mechanical hand. "It is starting to feel strange having it off."

Belac took the metal hand. "I know I wouldn't want to take mine off."

Belac tied one end of the tablecloth to the hand and returned to the door. He climbed back on the chair and pushed the hand through the hole above the door. The tablecloth slid through his fingers as he lowered the hand down. He could not see the latch, so he was forced to swing the hand side to side as he lowered and raised it. Working by feel, he located the latch and then swung the hand onto it.

"Grip," Belac told the orc.

The hand fell from the latch. They tried three more times before they were able to get the hand to hold. Belac could only imagine what someone passing by might think if they saw a metal hand on a rope trying to open the door. He figured it was even odds on whether they poked at it with something in curiosity or ran away screaming.

With Vairug's hand on the latch, Belac began to pull on the tablecloth. Vairug also took hold of the tablecloth and tried to help, but his angle was wrong.

"Don't help!" Belac said quickly.

Vairug let go and stepped back, holding up his wrist and open hand. The metal hand let go of the latch and Belac fell backward off the chair and spilled onto the floor. He lost his grip on the tablecloth, and it began fluttering loosely as it was pulled up and through the hole. Vairug caught the end of the tablecloth with his right hand, but knocked the chair over in his haste. The chair fell on Belac, burying him beneath it. The elf tried to kick the chair off himself, but his leg got tangled with the support. Belac stopped moving, taking a moment to collect himself.

Vairug looked down at the elf tied in a knot with a chair. "Do you still want me to not help?"

"Die in a fire," Belac huffed but could not get a full breath tangled as he was.

Vairug kicked the chair, and the elf rolled over with it. "I can now someday tell the story of how I aided the heroic dragon slayer in his struggle..." Vairug had to stop himself from laughing. "With a chair."

Belac pushed the chair away and climbed to his feet. He narrowed his eyes at Vairug and then kicked the chair. The elf was barefooted, so it stubbed his toe. He hopped away and then leaned on the table.

Belac pointed at the toppled chair. "That's it! We are using a different chair."

True to his word, Belac selected a more agreeable chair and dragged it over to the door. He took the tablecloth from Vairug, and they repeated the process of gripping the latch. It took them five tries before they got a firm hold, and then another seven to disengage the lock. Belac and Vairug grinned at each other like children when the door cracked open. Belac let go of the tablecloth and hopped off the chair. Vairug moved the chair out of the way and then Belac pushed the door open.

On the other side of the hallway stood a man in black, leaning against the wall with his arms crossed. Belac wanted to slap the handsome off his face.

Serath smiled. "I must ask. What exactly was the next part of your plan?"

Belac did not have an answer, so instead he accused the wizard. "You were there the whole time?" He knew that was not possible. Belac had checked earlier, and there had been no wizards in the hallway.

Vairug bent over and snatched up his metal hand. Belac thought that he might throw it at the wizard. Vairug untied the tablecloth, pulled it the rest of the way through the hole, and then tossed it back into the room.

Serath bent down and picked up two bundles of off-white cloth tied with twine. "I brought you both a change of clothes." He walked over and offered them the bundles.

Belac accepted his bundle but asked, "You want us to go back inside?" He pointed into the waiting room that had been their prison.

"You can change in the hallway if you would prefer," Serath replied amiably.

Vairug went back into the room without saying anything.

Belac pointed at the wizard. "I almost crawled through the privy!"

Serath did not try to hide his amusement. "That sounds like a rather elaborate plan."

"No, that's…" Belac narrowed his eyes at the wizard.

Serath raised a questioning eyebrow.

The elf turned and went back into the waiting room, mumbling under his breath, "You better hope I don't turn into a gorilla-wolf-monster."

Serath shut the door behind the elf.

Belac closed his eyes and tried not to explode. "Do you think we can kill him?" he asked.

Vairug did not seem to understand that the question was a joke. "Rolan would not like it."

Belac dropped his bundle on the table and untied the twine. The cloth covering was a short cloak that he opened and left on the table. Inside, he found the promised change of clothes and a pair of boots. Belac shook out his new undergarments. The clothes had been made with haste and the stitching showed it. He shrugged. *Sometimes, good now is better than best later.* The elf removed his bloodied tunic and hurriedly dressed. He tucked black trousers into black boots and then a fluffy white shirt into the trousers. The clothes fit, but it was obvious to Belac that the tailor was unfamiliar with their style. He looked down at the discarded tunic and decided to leave it where it lay.

Vairug held up a crimson sash, "What is this for?"

"It's a sash. It goes around your waist." Belac took the sash and tied it around the orc. "Like this."

Belac stepped back and appraised the orc. With the knee-high boots, dark trousers, and sleeveless white shirt, the crimson sash made Vairug look like a swashbuckler. The orc put on a voluminous white cloak and hid his gray face and short tusks with the hood.

Belac shook his head. "No. They already know that you're an orc." He pushed back the orc's hood and adjusted the cloak to cover his left side and the metal hand. "Now you're ready."

Vairug gathered up all of his old clothes and piled them on his dark cloak. He rolled it up and tied the ends with twine. He then hid the improvised pack under his new cloak. "Now, I am ready." He frowned at the door. "If the wizard opens the door this time."

Belac balled up a fist and slammed it against the door loudly. The door opened freely under the force of the blow, and he lost his balance. He tripped over the broken grate on the floor and fell into the hallway. He looked up at the wizard leaning against the wall.

Serath looked down at the elf and waited patiently while he got to his feet. "Much better," Serath said with a nod. He looked the orc over and then nodded again. "Much better. However, I do suggest that you pull the hood back up before you leave the castle."

Belac asked, "Who are we meeting?"

Serath grinned and tilted his head to the side.

Belac was getting tired of people being surprised when he figured something out. "We were being held in a castle's waiting room instead of rotting in a cell." He held up a finger. "And no one has tried to torture us yet."

Vairug looked at the elf. "Yet?"

Belac ignored him. "Someone wants to meet us."

Serath stepped away from the wall. "Indeed." He began to walk down the hallway, forcing the other two to follow. "There is someone who would like to meet The Dragon Slayer and Lord Vairdoe of Enevic."

Belac backhanded the orc's arm. "You hear that? You're Lord Vairdoe again."

Vairug shrugged. "It is better than being called 'Sarah."

Thirty-Five

The throne room was less ostentatious than Belac had expected it to be. Looking at it, he felt a growing understanding of Tariel itself. Strong, understated architecture allowed the people to bring color and life to the city. There was less to distract from what was truly important to them; each other. There were few nobles present, far fewer than the expansive chamber could have held. They wore the same long and short tunics as their people, but of embroidered velvets. The gleam of precious gems flickered as they moved. *These nobles are more decorated than the whole castle.* The king stood afore the throne on a raised dais, his arms held wide in greeting. His velvet was indigo, the embroidery gold. The only jewelry the man wore was the golden crown of leaves resting on his curls of jet black hair.

"Serath!" The king called out, sounding genuinely glad to see the wizard.

Belac watched in disbelief as Serath walked up the steps of the dais and embraced the king. Belac looked around, wondering why no guards had challenged the wizard. He found guards aplenty, though all of them appeared to be more concerned with the orc in the throne room.

Serath released the king and moved to stand beside him. He put one arm around the king's shoulders, gesturing with the other toward the elf and orc. "Alvin, I present you with the illustrious heroes that you wished to meet." He cupped his mouth as if whispering a secret, and loudly said, "Don't chop off their heads."

The king smiled and the nobles laughed. Belac was having a hard time processing any of it. He wondered if Vairug was as confused as he was. Belac looked over at the orc, but Vairug was as stoic as ever. *Maybe he is too ignorant of humans to understand how bizarre this all is.*

As quietly as he could, Belac said, "Do not move." He did not want the orc to get skewered for trying to hug the king.

Vairug gave a slight nod.

King Alvin looked down at the elf and orc. "So, this is who will slay The Danorin."

Serath took his arm off the king's shoulders. "That is the plan."

Belac held up a hand in greeting and smiled. He felt stupid as soon as he did it.

Though King Alvin did not wave back, he said, "We welcome you to Tariel," his tone bordering between formal and friendly. "Tell me, were you truly captured and brought here by a nillanan?"

Belac worried what the stoic orc might say, so he answered himself. "Yes… my lord… your lord… your lordship… your highness… my majesty?"

King Alvin laughed. "In this instance, you would say, 'Your Majesty.' Though, fear not my elven friend, there are many of my own people who would not know the proper address."

"Thank you." Belac replied and then added, "Your Majesty." He did not like having to thank someone for telling him to call them 'majesty.' *But I really do not want my head chopped off.*

"From what I have been told, it seems as if I should be thanking you," King Alvin countered. "Tell me. Is it true that you slew the nillanan? To do so after being captured is remarkable."

"We did, Your Majesty," Belac corrected the king subtlety. He hoped, so subtlety that no one noticed.

"Then, I do thank you for ridding us of the foul creature," King Alvin said grandly. "On behalf of all Tariel."

Belac thought it was kind of lazy for one man to thank him on behalf of an entire kingdom. If Belac slept with every wife in Tariel, he did not think that he could apologize to just one man and have them all forgive him.

King Alvin's voice became somber. "And Lord Vairdoe. What befell Enevic is tragic. Tell me, are the rumors true? Will nought but the death of Danorin free you from your curse?"

Vairug said nothing.

Belac elbowed him.

Vairug frowned at the elf and then addressed the king. "The events of Enevic are difficult to speak of, Your Majesty." Only someone who knew the orc would have noticed his smirk. "But I will walk this world as an orc until the dragon Danorin is slain."

King Alvin stepped down from the dais, leaving the wizard next to the empty throne. He came to a halt in front of the orc and looked him in the eye. "The demands of my kingship are many," he held out his open hand, "but I would shake your hand before you go."

Belac almost laughed at how the guards must have felt. Vairug took the king's hand and nodded to him in respect. *Good thing Vairug lost his left hand.* Belac imagined Vairug crushing the king's hand in a metal grip. Then he wondered if the king would have even shaken hands with such a thing.

King Alvin returned the nod and released the orc. Then he took a sidestep and offered his hand to the elf. As they shook hands, the king said, "You do your people proud."

Belac had not considered that before. He was not doing this for the Elves. Also, he did not think that the Elves would appreciate him representing them. *If an orc can represent a kingdom of dead humans, I guess I can represent the Elves.* Had Belac thought deeper, he would have realized that he would rather have stood for the dead.

When the king returned to the dais, Serath clapped him on the shoulder and said, "I will see them out."

King Alvin nodded and then signaled to an attendant. Serath left the throne behind, taking Belac and Vairug by the arm, and turning them toward the doors. The nobles chattered among themselves as the three passed by. Belac smiled and waved to a particularly pretty woman in pink. He did not feel stupid this time, but he would have preferred to have not been dragged away by the wizard.

Two guards stepped in front of the doors that exited the throne room. Belac thought someone might have come to their senses and decided to kill the three of them after all. He tensed, ready to fight long enough to flee, but Serath marched them on. The guards opened the doors, and the elf restrained an almost overwhelming urge to stick out his tongue as he walked past them.

Belac waited until they were away from the guards to ask, "What just happened?"

Serath released the elf's and orc's arms, but continued to lead them down the hallway. "You have been legitimized."

"I don't know what that means," Belac told the wizard.

"It means that King Alvin," Serath pointed back toward the doors to the throne room, "the king of all Tariel, has personally indorsed you and blessed our quest."

Belac nodded in agreement. "Right. I get all that. But you are saying it like it means something more than what you are saying. Is this a human thing, or are you just being all wizardy on purpose?"

Vairug grunted.

Serath did not seem offended. "It means, that you will not go to prison for murdering five men in the street, and that the city watch will disturb us no further. Also, they will be opening the pond early for us tomorrow. As long as you are in the Kingdom of Tariel, you will be treated as royalty."

Belac thought about that for a moment. "Then, are we really sure we want to leave tomorrow? Why not stay for a week… or two? We can always kill the dragon a week later. Or a month… or two."

Serath shook his head. "As I have previously explained, this quest relies quite a bit on timing. I have prepared much in advance. However, there is still a considerable amount that must be seen to."

Belac felt reasonably certain that the wizard had in fact, not explained. "But still…"

Serath stopped and faced the elf. "Belac, I understand why you would want to stay and be treated like a hero. But while you did, the dragon would still be free. And the world would still burn." He put his hands on the elf's shoulders. "And all that time, Belac, we could have been struggling to be worthy of that heroic treatment."

Belac could not meet the wizard's eyes. Serath had not called him a coward, only reminded him that he could be brave. The idea of slaying a dragon was so implausible that Belac could easily forget how serious the others were. *They actually believe that they can kill a dragon. No. They believe that I can kill a dragon.*

Serath squeezed the elf's shoulders and then released him. "Through that door is a courtyard. If you leave through the main gate and follow the street, you should be able to find your way back to the inn. Rolan might already be there waiting for you two. You can tell him that he missed getting to meet the king."

Belac did not understand why the wizard could not show them the way. "What about you?"

"I still have things to see to here." Serath smiled. "Like helping Alvin explain to people why he is letting an orc run loose in his city." He nodded to the orc and then walked away.

Belac turned to the orc. "Sorry, Lord Vairdoe, but it is time to cover up." He straitened the orc's cloak and then pulled up the hood.

Vairug gestured to the elf. "Where is yours?"

Belac stepped back. "My what?"

Vairug held out the edge of his cloak. "This."

My cloak! "I left it back there in the waiting room." Belac considered going back for it but decided that it was not worth the effort. He had not much cared for the cloak anyway. "Maybe someone else can use it to escape."

Vairug was frowning inside his hood.

"What's wrong?" Belac asked him.

Vairug pinched his sleeveless shirt and pulled it away from himself. "I am starting to understand why humans wear things like this." He was unhappy with the confession.

Belac grinned ear to ear. "These are nothing! Just wait until we get somewhere where they know how to make real clothes."

"You do not like them?" Vairug sounded a little surprised.

"They don't fit right." Belac squirmed. "And mine ich." That may have been because his last bath had been on the floor of a barn.

There was doubt in Vairug's voice. "I do not know if I should get use to this."

"Nonsense." Belac dismissed the orc's concerns without understanding them. "You are Lord Vairdoe of Enevic. You could be rich if we play this right. After we kill the dragon, all we have to do is a little research, and we could set you up as a real lord. You might be able to rule all of Enevic!"

"After we kill the dragon?" Vairug smiled.

Belac nodded. "I don't think that Serath will let us get away with this if we don't."

"After the dragon is dead, Lord Vairdoe is supposed to turn back into a human," Vairug pointed out. "I think people will notice when I do not."

Belac shook his head and held up a finger. "I have that figured out. We keep telling people that you have to kill Danorin to break the curse. Then, when I, The Dragon Slayer, kill him, Lord Vairdoe gets trapped as an orc." He held his hands apart and waited for Vairug to see his genius. "Lord Vairdoe can't kill the dragon if I kill it first!"

"Even if we could convince the world that Lord Vairdoe should rule Enevic," Vairug's voice became mournful, "there would be no one to rule."

Once again, Belac did not understand the orc. "Exactly! There would be no one to argue or question your claim."

"No." Vairug shook his head and made a decision. "When we kill the dragon, Lord Vairdoe dies with it."

Thirty-Six

"Maybe we should go around," Belac suggested.

Vairug nodded in agreement.

The street ahead was congested with a gathering crowd of people, all standing outside the same building. Some pointed at the building in excitement while others appeared distraught. Belac looked down an alleyway and wondered how lost Vairug and he were about to get. Looking back at the crowd, he thought that it might be better to instead push through.

One of the buildings upper windows shattered, and a man flew out of it backward. The man crashed into the ground and the crowd backed away from the broken body. Something monstrous had torn out the man's throat. A woman screamed, and men cried out in alarm. In the shattered frame above, stood a dwarf that was scanning the crowd. Fire roared behind him.

Belac cupped his hands in front of his mouth. "Rolan!"

Rolan did not bother with pleasant greetings. He yelled, "There is a man downstairs! Get him out!" Then he disappeared, lost among shadows and flame.

There was an explosion and more fire. *We cannot take that dwarf anywhere.* Belac looked to Vairug, but the orc was already moving. Belac followed after him, the orc pushing bystanders out of his way.

The people were disoriented. They wanted to help, but did not know how; they wanted to flee, but could not stop watching the fire. Belac wished that the people would do a better job of blocking the way. He did not want to run into a burning building.

Vairug ran up and kicked in a wooden door. Belac expected fire to come rushing out of the building though none did. Vairug charged through the doorway, but Belac hesitated. They were not braving a fire to save Rolan. They were being asked to save someone else, someone who Belac had never met. The elf did not know if he was willing to burn alive in the attempt.

An explosion rocked Belac. He could not leave Vairug inside alone. The orc would be expecting his aid. Vairug dying without his help would only be slightly worse than Vairug surviving without his help. Belac took a deep breath and forced himself through the doorway.

The ceiling was in flames, but what little could burn on the lower floor had yet to be ingulfed. *The fire must have started on one of the levels above.* There was a stairway to the left and a caged counter in the back of the room. On the floor behind the cage lay an overweight man with blood covering his bald scalp. Vairug rattled the door to the cage to no avail.

Belac would have left the man. He did not know the man, and he did not know anything about him. Belac could not think of any reason that he and his friends should burn to death trying to save the man. He looked at Vairug and knew that the orc would not leave. *That stupid orc is going to stay there and fight with that cage door until the burning building falls down on his head.*

Belac growled and ran for the stairs. He climbed them on his hands and knees. His plan had been to crawl across the upper floors, but the spreading flames convinced him that speed was more important than clean air. He raced through the upper hallway, leaping over patches of fire and debris. He coughed and hacked as he ran. Smoke burned his eyes and fire roared around him.

The elf stumbled into a room, hoping that it was the right one. A second door was open, and the room was aflame. He held his hands up before him, trying in vain to hold back the heat. He looked through the smoke, searching for something that he could use. A locked chest that was almost as big as he was caught his eye. Committed to action, he picked up the chest and then jumped into the fire roaring in the corner. *I hope this works as well as a dead goblin!*

Belac landed on the chest and then fell through the burning floor. Fire and the bars of a cage flashed in the elf's vision as he rode the chest down into the lower level. The chest crashed onto the building's first floor and then burning debris fell onto the elf's back. He rolled off the chest, his body moving stiffly. Air circulated up into the new hole above, and embers fell from the ceiling. *This might have been a bad plan…*

Vairug stared at the elf through the bars of the cage, his eyes wide with disbelief. On his hands and knees, Belac looked up at the door to the cage, hoping to find a simple latch that he could throw. The door needed a key. He rolled onto his posterior and began searching for where the key might be. Tears ran down his cheeks, creating muddy rivers in the soot that covered them.

Vairug shouted. "On his belt!"

Belac returned to his hands and knees and began crawling to the unconscious man on the floor. *Why is this guy even in here? Who tries to hide from a fire by getting in a cage?!* Belac rested his forehead on the man's chest as he fumbled to remove the keys. *What? Did he run down the stairs, look at the front door, and say, "I don't want the fire to follow me outside. Maybe I should just hide in that cage instead."?*

With the keys finally in hand, the elf crawled to the cage's door. Vairug had knelt low to escape the thickening smoke. He grabbed Belac's arm through the bars and steadied him while the elf found the correct key. After trying three keys, Belac found the one that would turn the lock. When the cage door opened, Vairug released Belac's arm, and the elf fell backward. The ceiling in the larger room collapsed. Burning furniture crashed down, blocking the way out.

As Vairug opened the cage door, Belac waved him toward the unconscious man. The elf began coughing on the thick smoke violently. *We need to get out of here!*

Vairug clutched the man under the arms and dragged him out of the cage. Belac rolled to his hands and knees. It was too hot. He felt like the heat alone might kill him before the fire took them. The elf crawled, keeping his head down. He coughed and cried, knowing he would not survive this.

Vairug dropped the man and grasped the edge of a burning desk with his metal hand. He attempted to lift the desk, but it ripped apart in a shower of sparks. The orc kicked the burning pieces out of their path and then turned back around. He looked up past the unconscious man and to Belac, prepared to abandon the man and save the elf if he must.

Belac waved the orc on. *Just get that man out of my way!* The smoke was too thick. Belac did not try to speak, he could hardly breathe. The fire roared so loud that it muted the sound of his own coughing. He focused on crawling after the man as Vairug dragged the unconscious form to the exit.

Leaving the fire behind, Belac continued to crawl through the street until he reached the building on the opposite side. He rolled over and leaned against the wall, continuing to cough as he tried to catch his breath. The elf looked down at his hands, expecting to see blood. They were covered in soot and his shirt would never again be white, but there was no blood to be found. He leaned his head back against the wall and closed his eyes. He tried to not think of the fire. In his mind he could still see the flames; still feel their heat and their hunger to consume him. *And dragons breathe that stuff.*

"Hey, you!" an authoritative voice called out. "What is going on here?"

Vairug coughed, spat, and then replied, "This man requires aid."

Belac opened his eyes. They watered, the air stinging so much that he almost closed them again. He blinked hard in an effort to clear the residue of the smoke. If he wanted to see, he would have to do so in pain.

Two of the city watch had come to investigate the explosions. One turned to the other and said, "You stay here. I will go fetch a healer."

The other held out his hands angrily. "What am I supposed to do here?"

"Keep people back," the first called back as he walked away. "Find out what happened."

Belac tried to speak but coughed instead.

Vairug looked down at the elf. "What's wrong?"

Belac tried to speak again. "Rolan," he croaked.

Together, they looked at the burning building. Neither of them wanted to return to that hell. One of the widows on the top floor shattered and a chair flew out into the air. The chair crashed into the street, almost hitting the people crowded below. Rolan jumped through the broken frame, twisted in mid-air and swung back toward the building. The dwarf hung from a rope that appeared to be fashioned from curtains or bed sheets. *He might have just tied together the tunics of all the people that he murdered up there.*

The dwarf descended the makeshift rope as far as it would allow, then he pushed away from the wall. He released the rope, twisted around, and then rolled when he hit the ground. The bystanders backed farther away from the dwarf than they had from the falling chair. There was another explosion and then the roof of the building caved in.

The man from the city watch pointed at Rolan. "Stop right there, Dwarf! You have some explaining to do!"

Rolan ignored the watchman and walked past him. The dwarf considered his friends and then nodded to the man they had rescued. "That's the wrong guy."

"What?!" Belac went into a fit of coughing.

Rolan laughed. "I'm just kidding. Good job." He pointed his hand at the orc's left leg. No longer laughing, he said, "You are on fire."

Vairug looked down at his smoldering cloak. He ripped it off and threw it away from himself. Agape, Belac stared at the orc. Vairug was exposed. Surrounded on the streets of Tariel, he stood in his buccaneer costume, his metal hand gleaming in the afternoon light. Gray skin is what the people saw.

"It's an orc!"

"Look!"

"What?"

"No."

"That's him."

"Cursed…"

"The Lord."

"Lord Weirdo or something."

"Can't be right…"

"…orc…"

The man from the city watch had a hand at his waist, gripping the truncheon he carried there.

"Donny, no!" The watchman's partner had returned. He ran over and put a hand on the frightened man's shoulder. "That is Lord Vairdoe." He emphasized the title.

The watchman's words were all the conformation that the crowd required.

"It is him!"

"An orc?"

"…cursed."

"Dragon ate his hand."

"Faced Danorin."

"Lord Vairdoe?"

"…saved that man."

"Foreign lord saving us…"

"…hero."

"Fought a dragon!"

"…fight it again."

"…break curse"

"Hero for sure…"

"…Lord Vairdoe."

A man in the crown began to cheer, "Vair-doe! Vair-doe! Vair-doe!"

Without hesitation, the crowd took up the cheer. "Vair-doe! Vair-doe! Vair-doe!" The intensity of the crowd grew with each repetition. "Vair-doe! Vair-doe! Vair-doe!"

It hurt, but Belac laughed anyway. *Maybe Lord Vairdoe will not die after all.*

Thirty-Seven

Belac did not know where Rolan got the little pink beads, or if they were medicine or magic, but they were amazing. As Belac lay in the copper tub, relaxing in the warm water with the tiny bubbles floating up, he was exceedingly pleased that the dwarf had not died in a fire.

Belac took a deep breath, inhaling the fumes. They made him feel a little lightheaded, but at least he could breathe naturally again. Truth be told, he did not mind the lightheadedness. His skin tingled and it had been healed of the heat burns that had increased in discomfort as he returned to the inn.

Cheers had followed the three heroes their entire way back to the inn. By now, all of Tariel must have known of Lord Vairdoe and The Dragon Slayer's quest to rid the world of The Danorin. Belac had lain on the floor in his room, listening to the cheers as a bath had been prepared for him. Rolan had dropped the small pouch of beads on the elf's chest and told him to pour them in the bath. Belac had been so sore that he almost did not get in the tub.

The cheering had stopped, but every now and again there would be a collective cry of "Vairdoe!"

Belac opened his eyes without pain for the first time since the fire. His room was well furnished, and he regretted not being able to sleep in it the night before. He slapped the water in the tub, disappointed that the bubbles had stopped. *I guess there's no reason to just sit here in this dirty water.*

The elf stood and stepped out of the copper bathtub. He looked for a towel and found one folded on the bed. It sat next to a white cloth bundle tied up exactly like the one that Serath had brought to him in the castle. Belac dried off with the towel and then tossed it over by the tub. He unwrapped the white cloth and inspected the clothes inside. They had been made from the same cloth as the ones now ruined by the fire. However, the stitching was noticeably better. Serath must have ordered two sets; one made quickly, and another made well.

Belac dressed and went downstairs, intent on finding something to eat. His hunger was one thing the bath had not cured. The scene that awaited him would have been beyond belief only a day before. Belac would have laughed if he had been told at breakfast, that at dinner, he would walk down and see Vairug drinking openly without fear of discovery.

Vairug sat in clean clothes, and with a new cloak draped over the back of a nearby chair. He held his mug up, saluting the elf. "Belac!" The orc was clearly dunk.

Belac waved to the orc politely and then said to the dwarf, "Thanks for the beads. Those things were great." He sat down at the table with them. "Where is Serath?

Rolan gestured noncommittally.

"He is hiding!" Vairug accused happily.

Belac smiled. "Hiding from all the fun, hu?"

Vairug nodded seriously.

A man in an orange tunic walked up to the table and timidly said, "Lord Vairdoe?"

Vairug turned his whole body to face the man.

"Can I buy you a drink?" the man asked. "I would like to be able to say that I did."

"I will make you a deal," Vairug said. "I will let you buy me a drink if, and only if… you let me dink it!"

The man laughed and yelled, "Vairdoe!"

A chorus of voices replied loudly, "Vairdoe!"

Vairug slammed his hand down on the table and laughed. He gestured around the room. "They do that every time!"

Belac looked at the tusks sticking out of the orc's smile and could not help himself. He raised his fist in the air and yelled, "Vairdoe!"

The room erupted, "Vairdoe!"

Vairug nodded his head happily, smiling so big that it must have hurt. He stopped and wiped the smile off of his face. He pointed at the elf. "I think you were right." He held his arms out wide. "I think we should stay."

Belac laughed with the orc. When the elf had imagined being able to drink with his friend, it had been nothing like this. The people not only tolerated the orc, they cheered him. Food forgotten, Belac felt the need to drink. He scanned the room, looking for a server. He saw a familiar face.

The dark-haired woman from the previous evening stood in the main entrance, silhouetted by the night. With an enchanting smile, her gaze drifted in Belac's direction. Her eyes suddenly widened and then she fled the inn, the door slamming closed behind her. Belac could only think of one reason that she would flee at the sight of him. *She must have seen Vairug. What woman would not be afraid of an orc?* He decided to go after her. He could explain and then introduce her to Vairug. She might even offer to dance with the orc after she learned that he was a lord.

Belac stood from the table. "Hold that thought," he told the orc.

Rolan muttered, "I would not count on it."

Before the door had slammed, the woman had turned right. Belac left the inn and chased after her. He could smell traces of her perfume. Belac did not know if it was a side effect of the beads, or if the woman simply wore too much perfume. The smell faded and he stopped. The elf backtracked to an alley he had passed and then grinned to himself. *Vairug would be proud.*

Belac followed the smell of perfume down the alley to a stable yard. He found the woman with three men in matching red tunics standing next to a streetlamp.

The woman looked back at the elf's approach. "Oh, no! He followed me." She moved to stand behind the men.

"No problem sweetheart," one of the men said. "We can just rob him again."

As the men laughed at him, Belac allowed that there may indeed be another reason that the woman had fled at the sight of him. *So… maybe Vairug is not going to be proud after all.* Belac would have run if he had thought he could get away. The men were too close, and they would have been on him as soon as he turned.

The men began to fan out, preparing to surround the elf. Belac considered letting them do it. Standing there stoic and strong, he might have been able to make them reconsider the threat he posed. The problem was, he did not think that it would work. He was too scared to be intimidating, and he did not think the street thugs would back down in front of the woman. *I need to strike first.* The stable yard was open, but there was a wall to his right. If Belac could keep his back to the wall, he might still have a chance. He moved as fast as he could and slammed into the thug on his right, shoving the man away. Surprised by the attack, the man fell backward and hit the ground hard.

The thug on the left grabbed Belac's hair and pulled him to the side. The elf twisted and punched the man below the belt. The man let go of Belac's hair and staggered away. The last thug barreled in, pushing Belac toward the wall. The elf's arm swept up, brushing the man's hands aside. Belac took hold of the man's head and tried to smash it through the plastered wall. The wall held, so Belac maintained the pressure and dragged the man's face against the rough texture. The man cried out in agony, leaving behind a smear of blood and flesh.

Arms wrapped around Belac from behind. The first thug had regained his feet. The man pulled him back and the two fell onto the open yard with Belac on top. The elf attempted to elbow the man, but could not get a solid shot in.

The woman ran up and kicked Belac in the ribs. Without thinking, he kicked her back. The heal of his boot connected with her knee and broke her leg. She screamed as she fell to the ground.

The thug that had pulled the elf's hair stood hunched over, staring bloody murder at him. The man pulled out a knife. "Guess where I am going to cut you first."

Belac twisted and kicked, trying to free himself.

A new voice joined the mayhem. "What is all this!" asked a patrolman holding a lantern.

Belac shouted, "They are trying to kill me!"

A second patrolman pointed a truncheon at the crying woman. "What happened to her?"

"Trying to kill me!" Belac shouted again.

With a roar, the thug with the ruined face charged at the patrolmen. The second patrolman backhanded the thug with his truncheon. The truncheon caught the man on the side of the head and sent him sprawling. Then the patrolman stepped over to the thug and clubbed him in the head again for good measure. At the sound of a lantern hitting the ground, the armed patrolman turned to look at his partner. The thug with the knife had one arm wrapped around the other patrolman's head, holding him up as he sank his blade into the man's side repeatedly.

"No!" The armed patrolman rushed to help his partner but was too late.

The thug reached around and slit his victim's throat. The armed patrolman brought his truncheon down on the thug's wrist with a sickening crack, causing the bloodied knife to clatter away against the stone of the yard. The thug cried out in pain, but the patrolman was not finished. Pressing the attack, the patrolman clubbed the thug in the head. The thug stumbled backward, blood pouring from his scalp, but he did not fall. The patrolman hit him again. There was no elegance in the patrolman's blows. The thug fell limply to the ground and then the patrolman hit him in the head again and again and again.

The thug holding Belac released him and wiggled out from under him. Belac twisted around and grabbed the thug's ankles as he attempted to flee. The thug fell face down onto the ground.

Belac called out to the patrolman, "He is trying to get away!"

The thug attempted to rise, but the patrolman brought the truncheon down on his skull. Grunting with effort, the patrolman continued to beat the thug to death. Belac had many times seen patrolmen and guards carrying truncheons. He had always thought of them as nothing more than tools used to help subdue drunks and the like. Watching the patrolman's brutality, Belac would never again make that mistake.

Belac rolled away from the dead man and got to his feet shakenly. He looked at the death around him. *Maybe I just don't tell Vairug about this.*

The patrolman pointed his bloody truncheon at the woman sobbing on the ground. "Were they trying to take the woman?"

Belac shook his head. "No. She was in on it. They use her to lure men out."

The patrolman did not look away from the woman. "Then, you had best be on your way."

Belac was forced to make a choice. He did not make a heroic one. He turned and walked away.

As he returned to the inn, Belac rubbed at his sore ribs. After everything that had happened down that alley, the kick to his side had been the only real hurt he had received. It served as a reminder of who had given it to him, and it followed him relentlessly.

Entering the inn, the elf saw that Rolan and Vairug sat at a full table. Rolan had his hand on his forehead, and Vairug was laughing boisterously. Belac used the table being full as an excuse to sit alone. He ordered bread and soup, both of which tasted stale. He tried to not think about the woman. When that did not work, he tried to tell himself that he did not know what was going to happen to her. When that did not work, he tried to tell himself that he did not care. When that did not work, he drank.

Thirty-Eight

The grass Belac slept on was so soft that he would not have cared if it had been green. The elf opened his eyes to a world that was too vibrant to be real. He was surrounded by white, willowy trees with shimmering, amethyst leaves. His gaze traveled past the trees to a sky of perfect black. Understandably disoriented, his head lulled to the side. A breeze he did not feel stirred the grass, causing it to shift from a shade of violet to that of royal blue. There was no light, and yet he could see more clearly than in the midday sun. The silence was complete. He could not even hear himself breathe.

"That's it," Belac said. "No more drinking."

"You are awake!" announced a young woman's voice happily.

Belac looked at the tiny, naked woman standing on his chest. "No. No, I don't think I am."

The woman was a beautiful interpretation of the female form. Her platinum hair and powdery white skin seemed to hold more life than the color would allow. Her dark eyes had a depth that pulled on Belac's soul. She was a sight that he would have relished waking to in other circumstances. Those circumstances, however, would have included the woman not being small enough to fit on the palm of his hand.

She put her hands on her hips. "You are awake." She leaned forward. "How else would you be speaking with me?" Her youthful voice did not have the high squeaky sound that the elf would have expected from a person so small.

"I have been awake," Belac told her. "This is not it."

The tiny woman dropped her hands, exasperated. "You are awake in dreams, silly."

That's crazy talk. Belac considered poking the woman to see if she was real, but he worried that she might bite him. "What are you?"

The woman stamped a foot on the elf's chest and pointed at his nose. "That's rude!"

Belac almost laughed at her. "Then… Who are you?"

She crossed her arms under her breast and turned her head away. "That is rude too. Though, for very different reasons."

Belac simply did not know what to make of the adorable little woman. *She is probably not even real.* He smiled as an idea came to him. "Hello. My name is Belac, and I'm an elf. I think you are a stunningly beautiful woman, and I am very pleased to meet you."

The tiny woman danced on the elf's chest, her knees lifting high in excitement. "Oh Belac, I am so glad to finally meet you! You are so… You are so pretty!"

This time, Belac did laugh. He marveled at that beautiful, magical creature calling him 'pretty.' He wondered if there was a way to make her bigger. "Whose dream is this?"

The woman stopped dancing and looked around frightened. She held a finger up to her lips and then shook it side to side at him. She then stood still for a moment, waiting. Nothing happened. Belac was not even sure she breathed.

Suddenly, the woman smiled, brightening the world. "I have so much to tell you, Belac." Her voice turned serious. "You do not know how much danger you are in."

Belac disagreed with her. *I know how much danger I am in. A wizard has me on a quest to slay a dragon. A dragon!*

The world darkened and the grass turned to snakes. The trees shook violently, and the silence changed into a deep brassy note of terror. The sound intensified until it broke into a deafening roar. Behind and inside that roar rose the snarling hate of demons. Trees were ripped free and thrown into the dark.

Silvery translucent wings appeared on the woman's back and she flew from Belac's chest. She hovered above him, trying to look in every direction at once.

Belac got to his feet and stood facing her. "What is this?"

"You have to go!" The woman pushed his chest.

Belac fell backward into a pool that he knew had not been there before. He continued to fall into the pool, losing his sense of direction. He was drowning. He could not breathe. He could not see. He tried to cry out but could not make a sound. He fought with the water, desperate and wild.

Belac woke in a fight with his bed sheets. He threw them to the side and laid back, trying to catch his breath. His heart raced so fast that he feared it might tear itself apart. He stared at the ceiling of his room, trying to breathe in the reality of it. *Okay. Now, I am awake.*

The door opened and Rolan stepped inside the room. The dwarf was barefoot but fully dressed. He looked at the kitchen knife that had been hammered into the doorframe. The door opened outward. "Is there something in here trying to kill you, or do you just need another bed pan?"

"Rolan?" Belac asked.

"I think that is obvious." Rolan's voice was dry.

Belac ignored the dwarf's attempts at humor. "If you are ever a magical being capable of transcending the bounds of reality, intent on delivering a message of dire importance at the risk of sudden destruction… Please, for the love of all that is good and true in the world, just deliver the message. Skip the hellos. Say it plainly. And say it quickly."

"Deal," Rolan agreed. "Now, go back to sleep." He looked at the kitchen knife again, shook his head, and then left the room. The door clicked shut behind him.

"And don't waste time telling them how pretty you think they are!" Belac yelled at the door.

The elf wondered if his dream had been real. *As real as a magical dream can be…* In stories, when someone was given a magical message, they were also given some proof that the message was real. They would return with a wound or trinket of some kind that would leave no question as to whether or not it had been simply imagined. He looked down at his chest, expecting to find tiny footprints. The moonlight shining through his window was bright enough to show him that there were no marks. He felt around the bed, searching for a silvery wing, a platinum hair, or even a purple snake. He found nothing.

Belac wondered if he should go back to sleep. He might be able to return to the dream. If he could find the woman again, she could explain. He remembered the sound that had drained the light. He did not want to go back there.

It was a dream, Belac told himself. *How dangerous could it be?* Then he worried that it might have been his soul that had traveled when he dreamed. He worried what would happen if that malevolent force that had come, came for his soul.

Belac did not sleep. He did not try to sleep.

Thirty-Nine

"You look miserable," Rolan said, sitting down at one of the tables in the tavern. He sounded pleased by the observation.

Belac looked up at the dwarf but said nothing. He continued to sip at his drink. The server had claimed that it would wake him up and calm his nerves at the same time. *This stuff tastes vile.* He wondered if Serath had made the server offer it to him.

"Did you get robbed again last night?" Rolan asked.

"Almost," Belac admitted.

Rolan laughed. "You have nothing. Why would someone try to rob you again?"

"It seemed like spite mostly," Belac told the dwarf. "Speaking of which, I need money."

"What for?" Rolan asked.

"To buy things," Belac replied irritably. "It's money. What do you think it's for?"

Rolan shrugged. "Some people just throw it into wells."

"Well… Well… I am too tired to think of a joke with wells. Just give me the money." Belac took a sip of his drink. "I still haven't been paid for the job protecting the trader."

Rolan laughed again. "Didn't you stab him to death?"

Belac pointed at the dwarf. "That was after he paid us!"

"Is that what you are going to tell the next person that wants to hire us?" Rolan laughed more.

"Die in a fire." Belac thought about the day before. *Maybe I should stop saying that.*

A leather purse landed on the table with a heavy thud. Belac picked it up and tucked it into his shirt. He knew better than to count it out in the open.

Vairug dropped his bag next to the table and sat down beside Rolan. The orc put his arms on the table and then rested his head on his right hand.

Belac smiled. "You look miserable."

Rolan leaned closer to the orc. "Vairdoe!" he called out.

There were few people in the main room, but they replied loudly, "Vairdoe!"

Vairug covered his head with his hands. He said something that sounded like, "Bawragawl."

Belac did not know if it was Orcish or if Vairug had just vomited in his own mouth.

Serath set a tumbler down in front of the orc. "This will help."

Vairug looked at the drink as if he might slap it off the table. Then he looked up at the wizard suspiciously.

Serath lifted an eyebrow and grinned.

Vairug growled but proceeded to drink the wizard's foul concoction. When Vairug finished the drink, he made a disgusted face and looked back to the wizard with no less suspicion. "Did you just poison me?"

"You poisoned yourself," Serath told the orc. "What I gave you was an antidote of sorts."

"Why are you complaining?" Rolan asked dismissively. "You drank it, and I feel fine."

Vairug rolled his head to look at the dwarf. "That is a bad joke."

Rolan shrugged. "They can't all be good. You'll get spoiled."

Three little girls in pigtails brought out plates of eggs and toast. After setting the plates on the table, one of the girls shouted, "Vairdoe!"

There were more people in the room now and they all yelled, "Vairdoe!"

Vairug growled.

The youngest of the girls walked over and poked the orc. She squealed and then ran back into the kitchen. Smiling, the other two girls beamed up at the orc. One of the girls was missing a tooth.

Vairug looked down at the girls and something inside him melted. He held his hands up beside his head and playfully went, "Rawr, rawr, rawr, rawr, rawr."

The two girls squealed happily and ran into the kitchen with the younger one.

There was a contentedness to the orc as he ate his breakfast with Belac and Rolan. After they had finished eating, Belac noticed the three girls peaking over a counter to watch Vairug. He nudged the orc and pointed with his chin toward the little girls. Belac could not help but smile at the orc and his admirers.

Vairug quickly turned toward the girls with his hands held up beside his head and went, "Rawr, rawr, rawr, rawr, rawr."

The girls squealed in unison and popped down behind the counter.

When Vairug turned back to the table, his contentment was gone. "It is a shame we cannot stay."

Serath put his hand on the orc's shoulder. "And we should leave now. As I said, they are opening the pond early for us. It may already be open."

They stood from the table and collected what gear they had. Belac had nothing extra to carry other than a spare pair of boots. They were not even particularly well-made boots. He had considered taking the kitchen knife with him, but he did not want to steal from the inn.

When they stepped outside, Belac was blinded by the morning sun. He saw the crowd as his eyes adjusted. People lined both sides of the street. Some of them had children sitting on their shoulders. All the varying colors of the people's tunics reminded Belac of field of wildflowers.

Someone shouted, "Vair-doe!"

A cheer was taken up, "Vair-doe! Vair-doe! Vair-doe!"

Belac took in the raw energy of the crowd. "Is this really warranted?" he asked the wizard.

Serath leaned close to be more easily heard over the crowd. "People love stories. They love heroes. These people get to say that they saw a true hero. A man that fought a dragon and survived. A man that lost his hand, lost his humanity, lost his country. And despite it all, was determined to fight the dragon once more. A man that would fight to see his people avenged and his humanity restored."

Belac felt himself getting caught up in the wizard's words.

"Vair-doe! Vair-doe! Vair-doe!"

Serath continued, "A day will come, Belac, when it is your name called out in the streets. And it will be the stories of The Dragon Slayer that people tell their children."

There was a rush of sound unlike anything Belac had ever heard, and then a deafening explosion as an enormous boulder of jagged gray stone crashed down in the middle of the city. Buildings toppled and the ground shook in thunderous protest.

Belac looked up from where he had fallen in the street. Only the wizard still stood. Belac followed Serath's gaze up and over to the city wall. A mountain in the shape of a man peered over the massive wall like an angry neighbor. Half of its face was vaguely feminine, the rest rough and ill-formed. It was a being of stone and rage, and it was staring down at Belac. *It's here for me.* The elf could feel the thing's hate.

Vairug grabbed the elf and pulled him to his feet. "Get up!"

The air thundered as the colossus broke off a chunk of the wall. Rubble rained down from the fistful of stone.

Serath yelled, "Run!" and then took off at a sprint.

Belac, Rolan, and Vairug chased after the wizard. The crowd scattered in chaos. Children screamed as families tried to find each other. The colossus threw its handful of broken stone into the city. The elf's terror rose as they ran toward the oncoming stone. Serath had not changed course and Belac was not going to run off on his own. *Why is a giant-rock-monster coming to kill me?!* The stone flew overhead and crashed into the city behind them, demolishing the inn and surrounding buildings.

Belac was shoved from behind and thrown forward. The ground slapped him in the face, and he bounced before stopping. He climbed to his knees, moaning. He touched his left cheek, and his hand came away bloody. He looked around him at the floating dust and debris. He looked back at the blood on his hand, confused.

Once again, Belac was dragged to his feet by the orc. Vairug pushed him forward and Belac stumbled, almost falling back down. Vairug gripped the elf's shirt to steady him.

Serath stood in the street, his eyes closed and one hand outstretched. The hand slowly moved from one side to the other before the wizard opened his eyes. "This way!" He began to run.

There was more thunder of breaking stone as the others followed the wizard down the street. Belac tried to look up at the giant-rock-monster and almost tripped. He focused on the wizard and ran.

Serath came to a halt and spun around, his hands held out. "Stop!"

The three stumbled to a halt. This time Belac saw the stone hit the city. It crashed down, ripping through buildings like they were made of paper. A wall of dust and sound rose up and rushed toward them. It hit the wizard in the back, whipping out his coat as it passed. Belac was thrown backward and rolled down the street. *These people just haaaaad to cover their city in green!*

Serath bent down and helped Belac up. Vairug rested on one knee, but Rolan was already on his feet. Belac tried to blink the dust from his eyes. He coughed, sneezed, and could barely stand. Vairug stood and spat to the side.

"There is still a way," Serath said and then led them down an alley.

The giant-rock-monster began to hammer its fists into the city wall with an insistent repetition of thunder. It smashed stone away, strewing more destruction into the city. The giant-rock-monster was coming for them. *Nothing can stop that thing!*

A building on their left collapsed and Belac found himself on the ground once more. He knew that he had to keep moving, even though there was no way to outrun what was coming; knew he had to get away, even though there was nowhere they could hide. So, he crawled.

Vairug pulled the elf to his feet and supported him as they stumbled onward. They followed the wizard, trusting him to find some way for them to survive. The giant-rock-monster was inside the walls. It smashed through buildings, sending debris and devastation across the city. The elf could feel its baleful attention on him.

Serath shouted "Down here!" his voice barely heard over the sounds of destruction. Then he disappeared down a flight of stairs.

Belac fell as he raced down the stairs, but Rolan caught him. Together, they descended into the darkness, fleeing the sounds of the giant-rock-monster.

Forty

In a stone chamber below the city streets, the four adventurers paused to catch their breaths and take stock. Serath alone seemed unwinded. The heavy breathing of the others echoed faintly into a tunnel that connected to the chamber. Dust floated in the diffuse light that shone down through the stairwell. The thundering sounds of the giant-rock-monster had ceased, but a high pitched humming had lingered in Belac's ears.

"You lost your boots," Rolan commented.

Belac looked down at his feet. His boots were still there. He wondered if he had misunderstood the dwarf.

"The other ones," Rolan told him.

"Aww." Belac had lost his spare boots along the way, "I liked those boots." Frantically the elf patted down his shirt. "The purse! I lost the money!"

Rolan chuckled.

Belac narrowed his eyes at the dwarf. "You think this is funny?"

Rolan shrugged. "It was only coppers."

"You gave me a purse filled with coppers?!" *I knew that I should have counted it.*

Rolan held out his palms. "I thought you would just lose it."

"That is no excuse!" Belac argued. "You didn't know that I was going to lose anything."

Rolan smiled. "Hey, Belac, where is your purse?"

"Die in a fire," Belac replied.

Rolan shook his head. "That is probably not going to happen down here."

Belac asked, "Why is that?"

"This is the city cistern," Rolan explained. "It's where they keep all the water."

"I know what a cistern is!" Belac had not known what a cistern was. *I don't see any water.*

Vairug asked, "Why has it stopped?"

Belac knew what 'it' the orc referred to; they all did.

Serath pointed a finger up and twirled it around. "All this stone confuses it."

Vairug followed up, "And what is that thing?"

"It is a colossus," Serath told them. "It is a vessel of power and emotion, leashed to the will of its creator. It has been a very long time since such a thing has walked our world."

"Why?" If Belac knew how to make one, he would have made many. *The first thing I would do with them is send them to kill the one that is trying to kill me.*

"The creation requires an immense amount of power and skill," Serath explained. "That colossus represents an investment of effort and time far in excess of its size."

And it is the size of a mountain! "Then, why is it here now?" Belac asked without considering the question.

Serath shook his head sadly. "You thought you could tell the world that you intend to kill one of the oldest, darkest, and most powerful things alive… and nothing would happen?"

I did this? Belac thought of the devastation to the city and the dead in the streets. He thought of how the inn had been obliterated with the people still inside. He thought of the three little girls and wanted to cry. He wondered how many other children had died, how many people. The lives not lost would still be destroyed. He remembered the wizard's words. *"Everything you do."*

Rolan spoke into the silence, "We cannot hide down here forever."

"You are right," Serath agreed. "We need to travel through the cistern. We can exit closer to the Temple of the Ancient. With any luck, we can make it to the pond before it is shut off."

Rolan sighed. "Serath, your plans are great and all, but I was hoping for something a little less dependent on luck."

"If we waste time developing a more reassuring plan, the pond will close," Serath predicted. "This plan will work. But we need to go now."

Rolan nodded. Dust fell from his hair, and he sneezed.

Something about the dust piqued Belac's curiosity. He looked from Rolan to Vairug and then to himself. All of them were covered in white, powdery dust. Only the wizard was clean, his black somehow pristine. Belac shook out his hair with one hand while catching the dust in the palm of his other. He walked over to Serath and threw the handful of dust at his chest. The dust hit the wizard and then slid down his front without leaving a trace.

Serath shook his head and smiled ruefully. "Wizard."

"That is just not fair," Belac complained.

"Wizard." Serath stepped past the elf and continued farther into the cistern.

Belac followed in line behind the dwarf. "Hey, Serath. Can you… I don't know, wiggle your fingers at me or something and make it so that I don't get dirty?"

Serath shook his head. "No."

Belac did not give up. "Come on. I will say, 'Thank you,' like… seven times."

"No."

"Fine. What about eleven times?"

"No."

"Why not?"

"It does not work that way."

"What does not work that way?"

Serath threw up his hands. "Reality."

"I don't understand."

"That is exactly what I am attempting to tell you."

Vairug clapped the elf on the shoulder. "Just be dirty."

"But I don't want to be dirty," Belac complained.

Rolan called back, "It's good for you."

"No, it is not!" Belac shook his head. "It makes you smell."

"Women like that," Vairug asserted.

Belac could not believe this. "I can assure you, they do not."

Vairug laughed silently. "I think Belac wore a dress too long. Now, he thinks that he knows what women want."

"It was not a dress!" Belac insisted.

"Do you hear that Rolan? Belac thinks that he knows what women want," Vairug smiled at the elf, "but he does not even know what a dress looks like."

"Die in a fire," Belac told him.

Vairug continued to laugh silently.

Rolan called over his shoulder, "Vairug, come help me with this gate."

The orc stepped around Belac to help the dwarf. Metal screeched as Rolan pulled on the gate, his foot braced against the wall. Vairug slid his cogged mace from a loop on his belt and wedged it between the gate and the wall. The orc heaved and the gate opened with a loud snap that echoed down the passageway. They walked through the gateway with Serath following close behind.

Belac hurried to join them, worried that the gate might close and lock itself, sealing him away from the protection of his friends. He passed through the gate and discovered what a cistern was. 'Cistern' was too ugly a word to describe the magnificence of the chamber. Shafts of light fell down onto dark water of unknown depths. The stone pathway continued out over the water between rows of pillars that must have held up half of the city. Belac could not believe the beauty of the craftsmanship. He did not understand why the people of Tariel would create such a place, only to leave it forgotten beneath them.

Belac muttered, "I guess I found all the water."

Vairug turned to respond. A dark green monster erupted from the waters below, its mouth open and its teeth exposed.

The orc was fast enough to grab the monster's lower jaw with his metal hand and push the thing aside. The wedged shaped mouth bit down on the orc's hand.

Belac stumbled backward and almost fell into the dark water on the other side of the walkway. He looked on in horror as Vairug struggled to swing his cogged mace. The monster rolled, yanking the orc with it back into the water.

Rolan drew a knife in each fist and leapt out over the water with his arms held out to his sides like bladed wings. He plunged the knives into the monster and was rolled under the water. Using one knife as a hand hold, he stabbed the other into the monster repeatedly. When the monster stopped rolling, the dwarf did not stop stabbing.

Vairug splashed his way back to the walkway. His left hand did not work, and Belac had to help pull him back up. Long shapes glided through the water.

Belac yelled, "Rolan!"

Serath ran out across the water, his feat never sinking below the surface. He reached down and gripped Rolan's pack. The dwarf splashed wildly as Serath pulled him through the water and back onto the stone walkway. Rolan got to his hands and knees and spat out water.

Serath helped the dwarf stand. "We cannot stay here!"

More of the monsters emerged and began to tear apart the dead one floating in the water. Belac did not want that to happen to him. He crawled away, getting to his feet as he fled. Vairug snatched up his dropped mace and chased after. Belac ran as far as he could, but the cistern was too large, and he was too tired. He began to slow and stumble more than run.

Vairug raised his voice, "Serath."

Serath stopped running and looked back. He stepped to the side and said, "Go!" waving the others ahead forcefully.

They continued through the cistern walking. Serath stayed in the rear, facing behind them and walking backward. Belac worried that Serath might accidentally step into the water, but then he remembered that evidently, the wizard could walk on water.

Forty-One

Arms crossed, Serath leaned his back against one of the stone walls. "We can rest here, but not for long."

Belac was glad for the rest, but even more so to be out of the cistern. He looked at the stairs leading up and remembered what awaited them above. *I wonder how long I could just stay here.*

"Did you see that?" Rolan asked. "I just killed a dragon!"

Belac shook his head. "That was not a dragon."

"It looked like a dragon to me," Rolan argued. "I think you just want to be the only dragon slayer."

"That was not a dragon," Belac said again. "It was too small."

"Baby dragons are still dragons," Rolan insisted.

"It did not even have wings!" Belac pointed out.

Rolan shrugged. "Maybe dragons are born without wings. Did you think of that? Maybe it just takes a while for them to grow."

Belac threw up his hands. "Dragons breathe fire!"

Rolan shook his head. "Not the dead ones. They don't."

"This is ridiculous." Belac crossed his arms and looked away. The orc sat quietly staring at his damaged hand. "Vairug, you have got some seriously bad luck when it comes to hands."

Vairug looked up at the elf. "That was never a problem before."

Belac shook his head. "Do not blame me. None of that was my fault." He held up a finger. "You know what both of those times had in common?"

Vairug closed his eyes. "Don't say it."

"Green!" Belac said.

Vairug growled.

Serath stepped away from the wall. "We have delayed as long as we can. We will go up these stairs and then strait through the alleyway. When we reach the main street, we will turn right and continue on to the Temple of the Ancient." He waited for everyone to nod. "When we get to the pond, do not wait. Go through. I will make sure that you all get there."

Looking at the steps, Belac suddenly understood how men facing execution must feel. He was being asked to step forward, knowing that what waited was almost certain death. It was awful. His body did not want to obey him. His legs became stiff, and his hands shook. He took a deep breath and closed his eyes. *I can do this. All I have to do is run.* The thought did not make him feel like the hero he was believed to be. His breath was shaky when he let it out.

Vairug nudged the elf. "Do you still want to race?"

Belac shook his head. "What?"

"I asked if you wanted to race," Vairug said. "Back at the tailor, you wanted to race. I bet I can get to this 'pond' before you can."

Belac remembered the conversation. "That was you! You wanted to race!"

Vairug shook his head. "It is too late to back out now, Belac. I do not care if you did lose your good boots."

"No, I didn't. I lost the other ones." Belac held out his foot. "These are much better than those."

Vairug nodded. "Good. Then, we can race."

"Wait! What?" Belac shook his head.

"Yes! What?" Vairug agreed. "What should we wager?"

"I don't want to wager anything," Belac told him.

Rolan grumbled, "You don't have anything to wager."

Vairug pointed at the elf's feet. "He still has his good boots."

"You cannot have my boots!" Belac took a step away.

Rolan chuckled. "He knows he's going to lose."

"Die in a fire." Belac would show them. Wager or no wager, they could eat his dust while they got ground to paste by the colossus. He had learned long ago that if he really wanted to win, the best strategy was to cheat. He sprinted up the stairs, stealing a head start.

As Belac exited the stairwell, the brightness of the sun blinded him, and he almost crashed into a wall. He held up a hand to shade his eyes as he stumbled away from the wall, and then he ran through the alleyway. After the short stretch of alleyway, he turned right onto the street as the wizard had instructed. The ground began to shake and buildings behind him collapsed. Belac ran faster.

Patinaed rooftops and trailing debris scattered across the city as the colossus swatted buildings out of its way. Belac could feel its hate getting closer. The sapphire marble walls of the Temple of the Ancient should have promised sanctuary. They may have, if the massive bronze gate had not stood closed in denial.

Through the ornate bars of the gate, Belac could see the majesty of the temple. It was a fortress of stone and bronze inlay, the two interweaving masterfully in the tracery of its windows. The graceful buttresses and spires created a foreboding presence, but it was the pond that offered true safety. Magenta runes glowed inside the translucent crystal arch that spanned the courtyard. Beneath the arch, the world distorted in gentle waves resembling the waters that gave the pond its name. Harbridge waited on the other side. Harbridge and safety.

Belac shook the gate in frustration and fear. Topped with bladed spikes, the tall bars would be perilous to climb. He looked to the walls, but the severe vertical groves carved into the stone offered no purchase. The air itself quaked and Belac cringed away from the sound.

From behind the elf, Serath explained, "The colossus has fallen into the cistern. We must hurry."

Did the wizard plan that? The sound of the colossus's rage only intensified as it began to tear apart the street in its effort to climb from the cistern. Serath reached into his bag and pulled out an ornate bronze key. He inserted it into the gate, unlocking it with a series of mechanical clicks. The gate swung open, and the wizard waved the others through. Once the others were in the courtyard and running toward the pond, Serath followed suit. The plastered side of a building slammed into the gate behind them, ripping it away in a shriek of twisted metal before crashing onto the ground. The colossus was free.

Shying away from the explosive sound, Belac fell and slid across bronze symbols set into the sapphire marble of the courtyard. *I'm so close!* Vairug came to a halt and turned around, obviously intent on helping the elf.

Serath pointed and yelled, "Go!"

Vairug hesitated and then ran, catching up to the dwarf easily. Vairug matched his pace, and together they ran through the arch of the pond.

Belac scampered to his feet and ran after them, Serath on his heels. People on the other side of the pond pointed at them from Harbridge. The ground shook and Belac fell again. Serath pulled him up and then held him by the shoulders, facing him. The undulating surface of the pond was close enough for them to touch.

Serath yelled, "Go through the pond. Wait for me at the Lucky Duck."

The Lucky Duck? The world shook at the coming of the colossus. Belac met the wizard's eyes. "You want your final words to be, 'lucky duck?"

There was no fear in the green depths of Serath's eyes. "No words are final." He pushed the elf through the arch.

Belac fell backward through the pond, landing in Harbridge. The sky was dark with clouds. The corner of a roof flew past him, the copper gleaming where it had been severed by the pond's closing. He looked up at the crystal arch. Tariel was no longer on the other side.

"No words are final." Tariel had been destroyed and the wizard lost, but all Belac could think was, *Those were really good last words.*

Epilogue

She fled through dreams, knowing there was no escape. What pursued her could not be stopped. There was nowhere to hide and no one to save her. Not even her own people would protect her from what was coming. She could feel it getting closer, feel the darkening of dreams as it followed. This would be a time of nightmares and despair.

She had understood the gravity of her choice, and yet, she could not let that dark thing have him. It had for too long gone unchallenged. Someone needed to oppose. Someone needed to end that menacing creature. Now, the world's salvation would cost her everything she was.

In the darkness of a shallow mind, it caught her. Her wings burned and she fell. She could flee no farther. Her wings had been more than physical, a part of her soul had burned away with them. She sobbed in the darkness. Something darker still approached. There would be no bargaining, just as there had been no escape. The flames took her, and the Fairy queen's screams echoed through dreams.

PART TWO

Prologue

His steps echoed on water and stone as he strode from the Temple of the Deep. It had been a productive night. His disciples were growing. Every pledge increased their power, and every voice, their reach. The world could still have salvation.

He knew that it would not be he himself who championed the light. He would do all that he could to prepare, but it would be another to right the world. The forces set against him were too great. He could not hope to conquer that darkness alone.

Eleron lowered himself into a shallow boat and allowed his acolytes to row him out of the secluded cave. As they followed the coast toward the sprawling docks of Harbridge, he stared out into the ocean. In all his years, he had never found anything to compete with the beauty of moonlight on black waves. The ocean was part of him, and he could almost feel the moon's caress.

With an effort of will, he pulled himself away. He could not afford to lose himself, not now. He had too much to do. For too long, the world had withered in darkness under a shadow of threatening malice. And now, finally, someone had come that could stand against that ancient creature. A champion had come to bring the world salvation.

Though Eleron's power came with many restrictions, he believed that he had found a way. He had brought the people knowledge of the Deep. These esoteric secrets would give them a weapon against something that for too long had wrought destruction with impunity. Still, he knew that the Followers of the Deep would not be sufficient alone. They would need to be there for the one who was to come. They would need to support and aid their champion of the light. And, as had so often been required of heroes facing great evil, they would need to sacrifice.

Eleron prayed to the Deep that the loss would be bearable. It pained him how tragic it was that some must die so that others might be free. He hated how the good must suffer in the opposition of evil. Most of all, he raged at the fact that he could not simply pay the price himself.

When they arrived at the docks, he climbed from the modest craft. There was still so much to do. He would need…

Something broke his wards. Eleron knew what it must be. With a gesture, he sent his acolytes away. They could only die if they remained with him, and every voice was needed. He would stand alone. He would not, however, stand defenseless. Eleron drew on the ocean, pulling in power and life. He had known he would not be the one to stop this creature, but he would never surrender. He too would demand a price. He would show this dark thing what it was to suffer. He would herald the light to come. And so, Eleron stood alone.

He felt the darkness of its approach. He reached out into the water and fed to it his will. An enormous hand of shaped water rose from the ocean beside him. The hand picked up a nearby fishing boat and ripped it from its moorings. With a tremendous force backed by the weight of the ocean, Eleron threw the boat.

The boat was swept aside in a spray of shattered wood and twisted iron. Eleron was prepared for the flames that answered. He angled the watery hand between himself and the oncoming storm. Steam filled the air as the hand pulled water from the ocean in his defense. He needed another attack.

Eleron reached out into the steam and focused it in a torrent of scalding water. He showed his teeth in defiance as he returned the fire's heat. And then, the fires took him. Eleron's screams of defiance pierced the night. However, defiance could not stop the flames.

One

"I hate prison!" Belac rattled the cell door.

"I do not believe that you are intended to like it," Vairug replied, his voice infuriatingly calm.

"Die in a fire!" Belac kicked the bars of his cell.

In an amused tone, Vairug asked, "How is any of this my fault?"

With no reason readily apparent, Belac answered, "Pick a reason!"

After a moment of silence, Vairug said, "Because, I am so handsome."

"What?" Belac looked in the orc's direction even though there were multiple walls of stone between them.

Vairug patiently explained his joke. "You told me to pick a reason."

Belac narrowed his eyes at the wall. *Orcs are not handsome.* It was hard to be handsome with gray skin and tusks.

When the elf did not respond, Vairug continued, "So, I chose…"

"I get it, Vairug!" Belac scanned his cell, searching for some way to escape. Steel bars caged him within the shadows of his stone prison with nothing but a wooden bucket. He did not think that the wooden bucket would be of any help, so he kicked it into the back of the cell.

The bucket broke in half against the stone wall. Now, he did not even have a bucket. Belac growled.

When the two of them had been brought to their cells, one of the guards had carried a lantern. The light had filtered through the bars and moved along the dirty off-white stone walls. The guards had put Belac in the cell on the far left, and Vairug in the one on the far right, leaving two empty cells between them. Then, the guards had taken the light with them, leaving the cells in a grim grayness. The only light now was the dim glow spilling down the corridor to their cells.

Belac gazed over to the open corridor. *Only one single way toward freedom and light.* He disliked how familiar the situation was. "We need to escape."

"Is there a privy on your side?" Vairug asked.

"I am not crawling through the privy, Vairug!" Despite his words, if there had been a privy, Belac would have crawled through it.

Disgruntled, Vairug said, "Then, unless you turn into a gorilla-wolf-monster and rip out the bars, I do not think we are getting free any time soon."

Belac narrowed his eyes at the wall. Then he turned his back to it and sat down on the cold stone floor. He leaned back against the wall in frustrated surrender. The wall moved. It was almost imperceptible, but the wall moved.

The elf jumped to his feet and turned to study the wall. Belac grinned. He did not know much about stone, but he was fairly sure that walls made from it were not supposed to move. He began placing his hands on the wall in different locations and applying pressure. It did not take him long to determine where the wall was weakest. Low and center, he could just barely see the wall move when he pressed.

Belac brushed a lock of stray hair out of his face, tucking it behind his pointed ears. "Sing something."

"What?" Vairug asked.

"I don't care. Just do it." Belac told the orc.

"Do, what?" Vairug was obviously confused.

Oh. Belac stepped over to the bars of his cell. "I need you to sing something."

"What?" Vairug asked again.

Belac growled and then raised his voice. "I need you to sing something!"

"I heard you," Vairug said. "What do you want me to sing?"

Oh. Belac shook his head. "It doesn't matter. I just need the noise."

"Why?" Vairug asked. "What are you doing over there?"

Belac looked at the wall. "Ah… Maybe killing us."

"I would prefer it if you did not," Vairug said flatly.

Belac frowned. "Just sing something, Vairug."

The orc began to sing. It was awful. Belac did not know if Vairug was one of the worst singers that he had ever heard, or if it was simply impossible to make Orcish sound pleasing. Whatever the reason, the singing was sure to obscure any noise Belac made. He got down on the floor and laid on his back with his knees bent and his feet on the wall. He pushed as hard as he could, but all that happened was that he slid away from the wall. The elf scooted closer and began to stomp on the wall with both feet. Little by little, the wall moved more and more.

When his boots punched through the wall, Belac twisted to his side and curled up in a ball. He did not know how much of the wall was going to fall on him, but he covered his head and hoped for the best. It took him a moment to realize that he was not dead, and that he had not been buried under an avalanche of stone.

Belac rolled onto his back and returned to kicking the wall, expanding the hole. Still worried that the wall might fall on him, he was careful where he kicked. He only kicked around the edges of the hole, and he stopped as soon as it was large enough for him to fit through.

Belac sat up and began moving the loose stones out of his way. "I made it through the wall!"

Vairug stopped singing. "What?"

"I said, I made it through the wall." Belac wriggled through the hole he had made.

"Then, why are you still here?" Vairug asked.

Belac stood and brushed his hands against his thighs. His black trousers were too filthy to clean his hands, but he was able to remove the grit. "I am in one of the other cells."

Sounding disappointed, Vairug asked, "Does it have a privy?"

Stupid orc. Belac opened the door to the cell and stepped out. He walked over to Vairug's cell and looked at him through the bars. The orc still wore his dark boots and trousers with the sleeveless white tunic; however, they were dirty and torn. The guards had taken his metal hand. Belac remembered how contemptibly they had cut the leather straps and tossed the prosthetic aside. They had not even let the orc keep his scarlet sash.

"I am not crawling through the privy, Vairug," Belac said through the bars.

Vairug looked up in surprise. "It was unlocked?"

"Why would they lock an empty cell?" Belac asked.

Vairug shrugged and then nodded his head. "Get me out of here."

Belac held up his empty hands. "What do you want me to do? Chew through the bars?"

Vairug looked the elf dead in the eyes. "Yes."

Belac frowned. "Try to find a weak spot in the wall. I will see if I can find something that will help."

The elf went to the corridor, but then stopped. No one had ever taught him how to sneak. He wanted to move quietly, but he did not know how to go about doing it. He thought about hunching over and walking on his tip toes, but that seemed silly to him. Finally, he decided to simply walk slowly and be careful where he stepped.

The corridor was relatively long, though there was only a single door along the way. Belac tested the door, but it was locked. He ran his fingers across the keyhole and wondered what was inside. The sound of laughter pulled his attention away. He continued down the corridor until it opened up to a larger room lit by lamplight.

A stone stairway led up on the other side, promising freedom. An empty cot covered with a beige blanket had been pushed into the corner on the right side of the room, looking forgotten. On the other side of the room, two guards sat at a square table, drinking and playing dice. If it were not for their brown tabards with a red stripe across the breast, Belac would not have been sure that they were guards. On the wall behind them, hung a set of keys.

Belac did not see how he could get the keys without alarming the guards. He also did not think that he could have made it to the stairs and escaped alone. Even if he could have, he would not have abandoned the orc. *I need to go check on Vairug. I could really use his help.* He backed away as quietly as he could and retreated down the corridor. He paid special attention to the door as he passed it, worried someone might walk through at any moment.

When Belac returned to Vairug's cell, the orc was rubbing his shoulder.

Vairug heard the elf approach. "This wall is not moving, Belac."

Belac frowned. *What would Rolan do?* The elf thought for a moment. *He would probably just kill everybody.* Belac did not want to kill anyone, but he did have an idea. "Wait here," he told the orc.

Vairug gave the elf an irritated look.

Belac ignored him and returned to the open cell. He picked up a stone in each hand and then walked back through the corridor. *I am going to get myself killed.* He considered going back to his cell and waiting like he knew he was supposed to. He shook his head. They might eventually let him out, but he did not think they would do the same for Vairug. *Sometimes, risk is all there is.*

Belac tossed one of the stones toward the empty cot. The stone struck the hard floor and rolled under the edge of the hanging blanket. Both of the guards leapt up from their chairs and reached for the truncheons at their waists. They looked from the cot, to each other, and then back to the cot.

Belac stood absolutely still, hiding around the corner. When Rolan had used this trick, it had been used on ogres. *Humans are smarter than ogres. Not by much, but still…* They might not eat him, but he had witnessed what an angry human could do with one of those clubs.

"What was that, then?" one of the guards asked.

The other shook his head and drew his truncheon. The first drew his truncheon as well, and then they walked over to the cot. Belac almost laughed. *Yeah, not by much.* One of the guards gripped the coarse blanket covering the cot and flipped it back, his truncheon ready to strike.

Belac surged across the room toward the closer of the two guards and slammed his stone into the side of the man's head. The man fell to his knees, but Belac lost his grip on the stone. Unarmed, the elf jumped onto the back of the other guard. Belac tried to remember how Rolan had strangled the nude woman back at the magic castle. The guard, however, was not as cooperative as the mindless woman had been. He twisted around and crashed backward on to the edge of the cot. Belac took the force of the fall on the back of his shoulder but managed to hold on. The guard swung his truncheon up and hit Belac in the head. The blow hurt, but still the elf held on. The guard hit him again, though there was little strength behind it this time. The guard dropped his truncheon and went limp in Belac's arms. Belac continued to hold on to the guard until he was certain that the man was unconscious. *Humans can be sneaky.*

Belac let go of the guard and stood, breathing hard. He remembered the other guard and turned, anticipating an attack. The guard was on his knees, sitting on his heels, staring at the wall confused. Cautiously, Belac stepped around him and ran over to grab the keys from the peg on the wall. He then returned to the unconscious guard and gripped the man's ankles.

Belac hurriedly began to drag the guard back to the cells, but the man was heavy. Just past the locked door, the guard started to thrash around as he regained consciousness.

Belac released the guard's ankles and jumped on him. He tried to get his arms around the guard's neck but caught an elbow to the face. He fell from the guard and banged his head on the stone floor.

Belac forgot where he was. He looked up at the rough walls and ceiling. *Funny how even when the walls are white, they can still look gray.* A kick to his side focused his attention. He rolled away from the pain, but the guard kicked him again. Belac was ready for the next kick. He took the blow in his midsection and wrapped his arms around the guard's foot. The guard pulled away and fell back as his boot came off.

Belac scrambled to his feet and clubbed the guard in the face with his own boot. The guard rolled to the side and then climbed to his feet using the wall for support. Belac threw the boot at the back of the guard's head. The heel of the boot connected with the base of the guard's skull, and he stumbled into the wall. Belac jumped onto the guard's back, wrapping his arms around the man's neck.

The guard refused to go down. He staggered through the corridor as he tried to sling the elf off his back. Similarly committed, Belac refused to let go. Together, they crashed into the bars of the cells. The guard slammed Belac into the bars while the elf fought to secure his hold.

From within his cell, Vairug instructed, "Put your right hand inside your left elbow."

Belac shouted, "I know how to strangle someone, Vairug!"

"Then, stop playing with the man, and do it," Vairug countered.

Belac did as the orc had instructed. The guard went limp, and Belac rode him to the floor. The elf maintained the hold longer this time. Partly to ensure that the guard remained unconscious, but largely out of spite. Belac was not happy with the man.

Two

"You lost the keys?" Vairug complained.

Belac called back, "Shut up, Vairug. Or I will leave you in that cage." He scanned the dim corridor, searching for the lost keys.

"No, you won't," Vairug said confidently.

"Yes, I will!" Belac snatched the keys off the floor and returned to the cells.

"No. I do not think you will," Vairug insisted.

Belac locked the cell with an unconscious guard inside it, and then he stepped over to the orc's. "Oh? Why do you think that?" he asked, looking at the orc through the bars of his cell.

Vairug stood a little taller and grinned. "Because, I know a secret."

Belac tilted his head to the side. "And what's that?"

Vairug looked at the door to his cell significantly.

Belac narrowed his eyes at the orc, but he unlocked the cell.

Vairug stepped out of the cell and nodded his thanks.

"Well?" Belac asked.

"Well, what?" Vairug asked in turn.

Belac narrowed his eyes at the orc. "What's the secret?"

"Belac." Vairug shook his head. "It is a secret."

"Die in a fire," Belac said, smiling.

Vairug started down the corridor. "Let's leave this place."

Belac walked with him. "We still need to lock up the other guard before we go."

"There were two of them?" Vairug sounded surprised.

Belac was too offended to be proud. "Yes, there were two of them!"

When they passed the locked door, Belac considered stopping to open it, but decided that they should see to the other guard first. *I hope he is still there!* The elf began to walk faster. If the guard had recovered his senses, he may already have gone for help. An alarm could be sounded at any moment.

Belac quickly discovered his concerns were unwarranted. The guard still sat on his heels, staring aimlessly. The elf let out a sigh of relief.

"What did you do to him?" Vairug asked.

Belac shrugged. "I hit him with a rock."

Vairug gestured to the guard. "I think you may have broken him."

"He might get better," Belac said defensively.

Vairug looked at the elf sideways. "Do you want him to get better?"

Belac kneeled in front of the guard. "I don't want to kill anyone we don't need to."

"I agree," Vairug said. "But we need to kill everyone that would seek to imprison us."

"You sound like Rolan." Belac unbuckled the guard's belt and set it aside.

Vairug grinned. "Then, my throat must be dry."

Belac ignored the orc's attempt at humor, and continued to focus on the task at hand. The guard offered no resistance, yet it was a chore to remove his tabard. When Belac finally got it off, he slid the tabard over his own head and donned it himself. He picked up the discarded belt and buckled it around his own waist.

Belac nodded to the guard. "Help me get him into a cell."

Vairug reached down and hauled the guard up.

Belac got under one of the man's arms and then Vairug released him. The guard offered no resistance as Belac directed their shambling through the corridor. Belac laid the man down in Vairug's cell and then locked him inside.

Vairug said, "I do not think he is going anywhere."

"He could get better," Belac insisted.

When they left the cells behind, the guard that Belac had strangled was still unconscious. The elf tried not to think about it. *They could both be fine.* He went to the mysterious door, intent on finally unlocking it.

Vairug shook his head. "We do not have time for this, Belac." He sounded as if he knew that he would be ignored.

"There could be anything in there," Belac argued, selecting a key. "It could be a super-secret escape tunnel for all we know."

"In the prison?" Vairug asked skeptically.

Belac nodded. "Humans are sneaky." The key did not fit. He kicked the door. The keys were too large for the lock. Belac turned to the orc. "Okay, you win. We can just forget the door." He started down the corridor. "But only because you asked."

Vairug grunted at him.

"Just remember this the next time I want something," Belac told the orc.

Vairug did not even bother grunting.

A woman walked down the stairs ahead of them. She wore a simple, chocolatey brown dress and carried a tray of food. Her dark hair shimmered in the lamplight and shadows played across her pale skin. The woman turned toward the guard's table, giving no indication that she had noticed Belac and Vairug.

The elf froze. He did not know what to do. There was nowhere in the corridor to hide. They could try running back to the cells, but the woman might hear them. Also, one of the guards could regain their senses at any moment. She would be sure to hear that. *Maybe she will just leave.*

"Hello?" the woman called out.

Belac groaned.

The woman walked over to the corridor and was silhouetted by the room's lamplight. It was too late for them to run. Belac may have passed for a guard in the darkness, but there was no mistaking Vairug. The woman's hands covered her mouth in a moment of fright. *I have to stop her now.*

Belac rushed at the woman. She spun around and fled. He tackled her before she reached the stairs, and together they rolled across the floor. She twisted out of his grip and began to slap at him in a fury of blows. He tried to fend her off, but the woman was relentless.

"A little help here!" Belac called to the orc.

"You just killed two guards," Vairug said. "Now you're having trouble with a woman?" He walked over to the table and picked up an apple.

Belac looked over at the orc. "I did not kill them!" *They could still get better.*

Vairug stared back at the elf and said nothing. He took a bite out of his apple.

The woman kicked Belac between the legs. It was a glancing blow, but it hurt. He suddenly had far less patience for the woman. He grabbed her wrists and shook her.

"Listen, Woman!" Belac growled.

She went ridged in affront.

Without letting go of her wrist, Belac pointed a finger at her. "You need to calm down!"

"I will not!" she said.

Belac laughed angrily, trying to control his temper. "Woman…"

She attempted to pull free. "Let me go!"

Belac almost fell over as he struggled with her. "Stop it!"

The woman stopped and glared at him. "I will scream!" she threatened.

"And if you do, I will feed you to the orc!" Belac told her.

The woman looked at Vairug. He took another bite out of his apple. She looked back to Belac, eyes wide. The elf would have felt sorry for her if he had not still been in pain.

In a frightened voice, the woman asked, "What do you want?"

Belac had to think about that. He had mostly just wanted her to stop hitting him. They could not take her with them, and they could not let her go. He looked around the room for something that he could use to tie her up. *Maybe if we shred that blanket…*

Vairug tossed his apple core down on the table. "We can put her in the last cell."

That's right! We can just lock her in my cell. "Of course, we are going to put her in the cell," Belac told the orc. He then addressed the frightened woman, saying, "We are going to lock you up next to the guards. We're not going to hurt you, but you need to stop fighting us."

"She was fighting you," Vairug corrected him.

Belac narrowed his eyes at the orc.

Seeking reassurance, the woman asked, "And you won't hurt me?"

Belac released her and stood. "That is what I said." He held a hand out toward the cells in what he felt was a polite invitation given the circumstances.

The woman stood and straitened her dress. She walked into the corridor sideways, keeping her captors in view. Vairug took the lantern from the table, and they followed her back to the cells. The guards were both unconscious.

The woman halted at the sight of the men. "What did you do to them?" Her frightened tone was accusing.

Vairug grunted. "He thinks they will get better."

Belac narrowed his eyes at the orc, and then he turned back to the woman. "That is your cell there." He pointed to a cell.

She stepped into the cell, closing the door behind herself as if the bars were there to keep the other two out.

As Belac locked the cell, an idea came to him. *This is genius!* He wriggled out of the guard's tabard that he had stolen, and then he pushed it through the bars. "Take your dress off and put this on."

The woman backed farther into the cell. "You said you wouldn't hurt me."

"I am not going to hurt you," Belac told her. "I just need your dress."

She crossed her arms. "I will not!"

"You can cover up with the tabard." Belac turned around. "Look. We won't even watch." He motioned for the orc to turn around.

Vairug gave the elf an exasperated look, but then turned away.

The woman was defiant. "No!"

Belac looked over his shoulder at her. "You can take the dress off," he pointed at the orc, "or he can take the dress off. What's it going to be?"

The woman stared bloody murder at the elf and then made an impatient shooing motion. "Well, turn around!"

Belac turned around and listened as she changed. The rustling of cloth was quick and angry.

The woman held her dress out between the bars. "Here."

Belac turned back around and took the dress. With a smile, he said, "That tabard looks nice on you."

It was dark in the cell, but Belac could have sworn that he saw the woman blush.

Three

Belac stepped away from the orc. "Are you ready to go, Sarah?"

Vairug looked like he wanted to kill the elf. "This is not going to work."

Belac smiled. "Sure it will." *This is genius!*

Vairug held out his arms. "No one is going to believe this, Belac."

Belac had taken the pillow from the cot and removed its cover. He had set the cover aside and then twisted the pillow in the middle, making two large lumps. He had then stuffed that into Vairug's tunic and wrapped him with the beige blanket. While it hid the orc's face, it only came down to his knees, and it looked nothing like a dress. It was a thoroughly unconvincing disguise.

"People see what they expect to see," Belac told the orc. "Besides, everyone is going to be looking at me." He twirled, and the hem of his dress lifted up.

"We look ridiculous," Vairug complained.

Belac covered his own head with the folded pillowcase and tied it under his chin, hiding his elven ears. "All we have to do is make it out of the prison. Then we can drop the act."

"Fine," Vairug conceded. "But do not call me 'Sarah."

They left the lantern behind and crawled up the stairs. The plan was to leave the same way that they had been brought in. They knew it might be necessary to make a detour along the way, but at least they had a fair idea of where they were going. *And if Vairug knocks down a wall, we are not going through it!*

Hiding in the stairwell, Belac peeked into the room above. The first thing he noticed was the guard sitting at a large desk to the right. Belac did not know if the guard was a sergeant, a commander, or a secretary, but he was sure that the man could raise an alarm. The guard was reading through papers that Belac assumed were reports of some kind. There was a door next to the desk and two more on the far side of the room. However, it was the heavy door on the left that interested the elf. *That is our way out.*

One of the doors on the far side opened, and a guard walked into the room. The guard left the door open and went to speak with the man behind the desk. Belac did not give them any attention. He was too preoccupied staring through the open door. On the other side were rows and rows of cots, many of them with lumps that could only be sleeping guards. The doors had been closed when Vairug and he passed by on the way in. Belac had preferred it that way.

The guard walked back into the room filled with sleeping men and closed the door behind himself. Belac let out a sigh of relief. He looked to the guard behind the desk. The man had already returned to reading his papers. *If we are going to do this, it has to be now.*

Belac motioned for Vairug to follow him, and then he walked up the stairs. His heart raced, but he tried to walk as casually as he could. Too slow and they would look like they were sneaking, too fast and they would draw attention. Their pace needed to be natural. *Nothing to see here but two human-serving-women.*

They made it through the double doors and into an empty courtyard. Belac's fear transformed into elation. *This is going to work!* If they could make it through the checkpoint on the left, they would be free. Even if they were discovered, they might still be able to escape by simply running.

Belac did not think that it would be easy to run in a dress, but he was willing to try. It was more important that Vairug get free anyway. The humans were less likely to kill an elf. *As long as Vairug gets away, I can just blame him for what happened to the guards.*

Vairug started walking toward the gate on the right. "We need to go this way."

"No!" Belac hissed. "We came in through there." He gestured to the check point on the left.

Vairug continued walking the other way.

Belac considered letting the orc go get himself killed. Then he groaned and hurried to catch up with him. "This is the wrong way!"

Vairug ignored the elf.

"We need to go back," Belac pressed. "We are almost free." *You big, stupid orc!*

Vairug said nothing. He looked like a dog following a scent.

They passed through the gate into a stable yard. A cobblestone path followed the outer wall on the left and the stables hugged the base of the castle on the right. While the stables were rather plain, the castle was something special. An imposing fortress of grandeur and might, its hard utilitarian design was softened by the chalky off-white stone of its construction. It was a place of beauty; but one prepared to weather the storm.

"Hey, You!" a man called.

Belac pretended he did not know that the man was talking to them. He walked faster, pulling Vairug with him. It was too late to turn back now.

"Wait a moment!" the man called.

Belac maintained their pace. They were committed now. Their only hope was that the man would not think that troubling two women was worth the effort of chasing them down.

"I said wait!" The man was getting angry.

Another stablehand moved into the path ahead, ready to stop them. The man held out a hand, his face growing confused as they approached. Belac closed his eyes hard, trying to contrive some way out of his predicament. They were trapped. He opened his eyes and kept walking, not knowing what else to do. Vairug walked straight up to the man that was blocking their way. Realization donned on the man's face right before Vairug punched it.

"Tommy, fetch the guard!" the other man called out.

Belac ran for the doors ahead. He did not know what was on the other side, but he knew that they could not stay where they were. If they survived the army of vengeful guards, he would spend the rest of his life in prison.

A stablehand slammed into the elf, tackling him. Belac landed on his back with the man's shoulder in his gut. Belac drove his elbow down into the back of the man's head and neck repeatedly until the man went limp. Then he shoved the man off of him and stood. He looked down at the man and then kicked him in the head.

Another stablehand came into view. Belac took a swing at him without thinking. The man blocked the attack like someone who knew how to fight. Belac got tangled in the hem of his dress and fell face first onto the cobblestones.

The man laughed. "Crazy woman thinks she can fight."

Belac rolled over and kicked out low. His heel connected with the man's ankle with a sickening pop. The man collapsed to the ground, his face twisted in paralyzing pain.

Belac stood. His head bobbed as he shouted at the man. "Who's the crazy woman now?!" *Wait. That doesn't make any sense.*

Vairug grabbed the elf's arm. Guards were coming, their boots sounding like a stampede on the cobblestones. Belac tossed his hair back and out of his face, then ran for the door that was closest to him. *This is all Vairug's fault! All he had to do was turn left!* He opened the door and then followed Vairug inside.

There was a heavy timber that could be used to bar the door, but there was more than one door and there was not enough time to bar them all. They were in an empty room with one hallway exiting to the right. Belac did not like the idea of going farther into the castle, but they did not have a choice. They ran down the hallway, passing closed doors on their left. There was no time to explore. They needed to get as far away from the guards as they could if they were to have any chance of escape.

The doors to the stable yard slammed open behind them. The guards were gaining fast. *I wonder if I can convince them that I really am a woman, and that Vairug abducted me.*

The hallway led to an open room with a long table in the center. Around the table sat hard looking men in chainmail. Belac and Vairug came to a halt. There was nowhere else for them to run. The men at the table stood, displaying a black anchor emblazoned across each of their tabards. Some of them drew swords. These men were not city guards.

Belac stepped away from the orc and pointed at him. "Do you know who this is?"

No one answered.

Belac continued, "This is Lord Vairdoe of Enevic, the only man to face the dragon Danorin and survive!"

Vairug stood taller, thrusting out his pillow stuffed chest.

Belac groaned.

Four

"Explain to me how this is not your fault!" Belac stood behind the bars, wearing nothing but a faded blue bedsheet tied over one shoulder.

Vairug glared at the elf from behind the bars of his cell on the other side of the room. He too wore nothing but a faded blue bedsheet, though his was tired around his waist like a skirt. "I told you they were not going to believe us!" he shouted at the elf.

Another voice joined the conversation. "Apologies, Lord Vairdoe." The voice was rough but well trained. "But you are here precisely because they do believe you."

There were five cells arranged in an octagonal pattern, the exit flanked by two bare walls. The only light was what crept in from under the iron bound door. Their new prison was larger and had a considerably more substantial feel. The bars were thicker, the walls were thicker, and judging from the descent into the prison, the ceiling was thicker as well.

Belac's gaze traveled across the other cells, but he could not see the man who had spoken. "And who are you?"

A disheveled man stepped up to the bars of the center cell. He was bearded and thin in a way that promised the misery of Belac's future. *At least elves don't have to grow all that ugly fur on their face.* Belac's face itched just looking at the man.

"I am Lord Ecard von Leaos of Enevic, General of the Ninth," the man said proudly.

That might be a problem. "I thought everyone from Enevic was dead," Belac replied.

The man's voice turned solemn. "So did I."

A lord would have a family. The man must have lost everyone he ever knew.

Ecard continued, trying to push past his despondency. "Until I learned of you, Lord Vairdoe. We may be the last, but at least we are not alone."

Belac did not give the orc a chance to respond. "How do you know about Lord Vairdoe?" *Especially if you really are a prisoner.*

"I am interrogated often," Ecard explained, "and soldiers are gossips."

Vairug asked, "And do you know me?"

Belac would have thrown something at the orc if there had been anything to throw. *How would he know you? You are not really a lord! Stupid orc.*

Ecard's answer was unsure. "I believe we may have met once at a banquet. It was long ago. Please, do not take offence, but I was young, and I had little time for local lords."

Belac could not tell if the man was lying or not. *Lords are good at that.* Obviously, the man had never met Lord Vairdoe. There was no Lord Vairdoe. However, even if Ecard was lying, he could be doing so simply to be polite. Most humans actually thought it was kind to lie to each other.

Belac decided to probe the man's story. "How long have you been here?"

Ecard accepted the question as genuine. "I am afraid that this is my only measure." He gestured to his unruly beard.

Vairug asked a better question. "How did you survive Enevic?"

"I was not there," Ecard confessed. His voice was filled with sorrow and regret.

Belac believed him. Lords were liars and humans were sneaky, but that pain was real. It was something so profound and honest, it made the elf ashamed of his own lies. *"Everything you do."*

Vairug seemed unmoved. "And why were you not there?"

Belac thought the question harsh.

Ecard held his hands out to the walls of his cell. The gesture was one of both demonstration and submission. "I was captured; my men slaughtered." He gripped the bars of his cell and rested his forehead against them. "We were ambushed on the border." He ground his forehead into the bars and then looked up in the orc's direction. "They want Enevic, Lord Vairdoe. They wanted it before the dragon came." His voice lost its strength. "And now, I fear they will have it."

Belac nodded to himself. "That's why they captured Vairu… Lord Vairdoe," he inferred.

"Indeed, it must be so," Ecard agreed.

Belac looked over at the fallen lord. The man might still be useful, but Belac would need to find some way to motivate him. "That just means that they are going to be extra angry when we escape and take you with us."

Ecard's smile was patronizing. "You think you can escape?"

Sure," Belac said confidently. "We are great at breaking out of prisons."

Ecard seemed surprised by his own laughter. "Do you break out of prisons often?"

Belac nodded. "We just broke out of one earlier today."

"My apologies, but I fear you are mistaken. I believe you were being held in a jail. Though to be fair, you were to be moved here anyway."

"What's the difference?" Belac agreed with the orc's thoughts on prisons. *If I can't get out, it's a prison.*

Ecard explained, "I believe that a jail is meant to be more temporary. They tend to have less security as a result. I fear you may find escaping a prison to be a bit more challenging."

Belac narrowed his eyes at the man. *Stupid, Dwarven language.* "It doesn't matter. That was not the first prison that we broke out of."

Vairug interjected, "He just told you it was not a prison."

Belac turned his glare on the orc. "Was your door locked?"

Vairug smiled. "Then, this is a prison," he quoted himself.

Ecard began to recite an ancient poem. "Locked doors do not a prison make. Only the mind must freedom forsake. When boundary…"

"Pretty words," Belac interrupted. *Prison is bad enough without having to listen to your awful poetry.* "But whatever you want to call it, we are breaking out of here." *Hopefully before you start spouting poetry again.*

"That sounds wonderful, my elven friend," Ecard said sadly. "But I fear that is not the case."

"Belac," the elf supplied.

"What's that?" Ecard asked.

"That is my name," Belac told him.

Smiling mischievously, Vairug added, "The Dragon Slayer."

Ecard was taken aback. "You have slain a dragon?"

Belac frowned at the orc. "I am new at it."

The door groaned and light spilled into the cells, forcing Ecard to shield his eyes. The light emphasized how filthy the man was. His feet were bare, and his once noble attire tattered and torn. The clothes hung loosely from his withered form in wretched testimony.

Two men entered the room. The light behind them was too bright for Belac to see their chest, but he knew they would bear a red stripe across them.

One of the guards bent at the knees and leaned forward. "Hey, Lordy, Lordy." He spoke as if speaking to a dog. "Are you ready to have some fun?"

Ecard instinctually cringed. Something deep inside the man shifted. He got to his hands and knees, placing his head on the stone floor. Belac could hear him whine.

"Aw," the guard said in mock sympathy. "Does Lordy want to stay in his cage?" Laughing, he stood up straight.

Ecard did not answer.

The guard swept his gaze across the other cells in the room before returning his attention to the man whimpering on the floor. "Does Lordy like his new friends? Do you want to stay with your new friends?"

Belac could not comprehend what he was witnessing. The change in Ecard was simply too extreme to seem real.

The guard walked over and put his foot between the bars of Ecard's cell. The guard wiggled his foot a little and whistled. "Come on, Lordy. Show your friends who's a good lord."

On his hands and knees, Ecard crawled over to the bars of his cell and began to lick the guard's boot. Laughter came from the other guard standing by the doorway.

Satisfied that his boot was sufficiently clean, the first guard pulled his foot back. "That's a good lord." He unlocked the cell and dropped a leather collar on the floor. "Put it on." His voice had turned serious.

Ecard picked up the collar and held it in his hand.

He stared down at the thing for a moment in hopeless indecision. Everything that the man was warred inside himself as he railed against what he knew he was about to do. It was not about saving face. It was pure dread at where they were going to take him and what would be done there. The scene terrified Belac. The elf knew his turn would come.

Ecard sat back on his heels and buckled on the collar. He returned to his hands and knees, looking down at floor.

The guard laughed. "Now look at that," the guard said. He looked down, once more speaking to a dog. "Come on, Lordy. Come on." The guard clapped his hands. "Lordy gets to go for a walk."

There were few things that could be as vile as a human. It was their empathy. They knew what it was to hurt. They understood degradation. It was easy to see how such a thing could be abused. However, Belac did not understand why some of them enjoyed it so much.

The guard attached a leash to the collar. Ecard's eyes never left the floor as he was led from the room on his hands and knees. The guards shut the door, leaving behind an oppressive silence.

"We need to get out of here, Vairug," Belac said seriously.

"Yes," Vairug agreed. "But how?" He did not seem as troubled as the elf.

"I don't care." Belac pointed at the closed door. "But they are not turning me into that."

Vairug shook his head. "They cannot."

"You think he was faking?" It had not looked like the man was faking to Belac.

"No," Vairug said. "He is broken."

Belac felt the panic creeping into his own voice. "They did that! And we are next! They are going to starve us. They are going to torture us. They are..."

Vairug interrupted him forcefully. "There is pain in life, Belac. It can only show you who you are."

Belac focused on the orc. "You think the man was just weak?"

"I think the man chose to be." Vairug stared into the elf's eyes as if there were no bars between them. "What will you choose, Belac?"

Not that. Belac realized that they had been put in the cells with Ecard to show them what would happen to them if they did not submit. *Maybe the truth is something different. Maybe that is what will happen to us if we do submit.*

Belac met the orc's stare. "They want to scare us into giving them something they can't take."

Vairug nodded, determination hardening his face. "I say we give them something else."

Five

"I told them," Ecard sobbed.

The guards had dragged the man into the cell by his feet, his limp form leaving behind a trail of blood as flesh scraped over stone. The man's ruined shirt hung in tatters around his waist, and his back was covered in blood and grit. In the dim of the prison, Belac had not known if the man was still alive.

When Ecard had regained consciousness, he sobbed; at first uncontrollably, and then in quiet shame. Belac could not look at him. He did not want to look at him. However, he could not block out the sound of the man's sobs, nor the smell of his blood.

"I told them!" Ecard cried again. "I'm sorry. I told them."

Belac gripped the bars of his cell. "You told them what?"

Ecard continued to sob, repeating, "I'm sorry. I'm sorry. I'm sorry."

Belac could not take much more of it. "Burn your eyes, Ecard! You told them what?"

Ecard tried unsuccessfully to hold back his tears. "Everything! I told them everything."

Belac looked to the orc. "What could he have told them?"

It was dark, but Vairug may have shrugged.

Belac turned back to the man on the floor. "You are going to have to do better than that, Ecard."

"I'm sorry. I'm sorry. I'm sorry," Ecard sobbed.

"I don't care if you're sorry, Ecard!" Belac shouted. "I just want to know what you told them."

"Everything!" the man wailed. "I told them you were the Dragon Slayer. I told them he was Lord Vairdoe. I told them you were going to escape."

Belac laughed in relief. "Ecard," the elf shook his head, "they already know who we are. We told them. Remember?"

Ecard looked up at the elf. "But I…"

Belac continued, "And everyone that is in prison, wants to escape prison. That's how you know it's a prison."

Ecard quit sobbing as he listened to the elf intently.

"Besides," Belac said, "we just escaped from one of their prisons. They have to know that we are going to try again."

Vairug corrected him. "That was jail."

Belac pointed at the orc threateningly.

Vairug held up his hand and wrist.

There was desperation in Ecard's voice. "So, I have not betrayed you?"

Belac shook his head. "Nope."

"Yes, he did," Vairug denounced.

Belac turned his attention back to the orc. "He didn't tell them anything that they did not already know, Vairug."

"He would have," contended Vairug.

Belac tried to think of an argument, but he knew that the orc was right. "At least now, we know not to tell him anything."

Belac knew that what he had said would hurt Ecard's feelings. *It will also cover any holes in our story.* While the Harbridgers were keeping Vairug in prison because they thought he was Lord Vairdoe, it would be worse if they learned the truth. They would kill him. There would be no reason to keep a one-handed orc alive.

Vairug nodded grudgingly.

Belac did not know if the orc actually understood or not. *At least he didn't argue.* "Now, we just need to figure out how we are going to get out of here."

Vairug pointed his wrist toward the center cell. "And how are we going to do that with him listening?"

Once again, Belac wanted to argue but could not think of anything to say. *Maybe we can use him. If we make fake plans while Ecard is listening, then what he tells the guards when he is interrogated will just mislead them. There might even be a way to get the guards to do something in response to a fake plan that would help us escape.* Belac began to contemplate how he might trick the guards. *The real plan would have to be complicated.*

The sound of cloth tearing interrupted Belac's musings. He tried to locate the sound. He thought it was coming from the center cell, but he could not see anything. *Ecard is not there.* The man must have moved to the back of his cell.

"Ecard?" Belac called.

The tearing of cloth continued.

Belac looked over to the orc's cell.

Vairug held up his hand and shook his head in confusion.

Rustling in Ecard's cell drew their attention. The man limped resolutely to the bars of his cell holding a rope fashioned from his torn bedsheet. He tied one end to the top of the bars. The other was looped around his neck.

"What are you doing, Ecard?" Belac asked though the answer was obvious.

Ecard turned away from them, facing the back of his cell. "I'm sorry," he said in true contrition, and then leaned forward.

Belac watched in horror as the man strangled himself. There was nothing he could do. *That stupid human just insists on ruining my plans!*

Ecard was bathed in light as the door groaned open. The man began to twitch against the rope. Belac turned to see if the guards would help. He was sure they would save him if they could. *If they wanted him dead, he would be dead.*

Belac shouted into the light. "Cut him down!"

Someone far too short to be a guard ran into the room and drew a knife. Metal scraped against metal, and Ecard fell to the floor. The man twitched some more, and then began to breathe heavily.

"Rolan?" Belac thought he might be imagining the dwarf.

With his darkly stained wooden springer held in his off hand, Rolan sheathed his knife and then walked over to Belac's cell. The dwarf looked him up and down through the bars.

After a moment, Rolan grinned. "You are going to need shoes."

"Ha!" Belac laughed. *I don't have to be a prison dog!*

Rolan unlocked the elf's cell and then tossed him the keys. "Go get Vairug out."

The dwarf moved to stand next to the exit with his springer held low and ready, his splotchy gray outfit blending in with the shadowed stone. *Anyone that comes down that corridor is going to die before they know that they're in a fight.* Belac did not care in the least that the dwarf had no sense of fair play. No one could work in a place like that and not know what they were supporting. Belac opened Vairug's cell, hoping that Rolan would get the opportunity to kill some of the guards while he did.

"Let's leave this place," Vairug said, stepping out of his cell.

Belac nodded toward the center cell. "We still need to get him out."

Vairug frowned. "The man is wrong."

"Why? Because he smells funny?" Belac remembered the last person that the orc had called 'wrong.' "He has been locked in a prison, Vairug."

Belac hurried to Ecard's cell and unlocked it. The man had not moved from where he had fallen to the floor. Belac nudged the man with his foot. Ecard shied away and curled into a ball.

"Get up, Ecard," Belac ordered.

When the man did not comply, Belac grabbed one of Ecard's scrawny arms and yanked him to a sitting position. The man did not resist, but nor did he respond.

Belac slapped the man. "Get on your feet and walk out of this cell, or stay here and know that you deserve everything that comes next." There was no time for pity.

The elf had lost his patience. He was about to push Ecard away and leave him there to suffer and die. However, in the instant before he did, the man looked up at him. While what Belac saw was not resolve, it was at least a willingness to try. He released Ecard's arm and stood. He did not help the man stand. If Ecard lacked the will to leave the prison cell, Belac would abandon him. *I will not die for a man too weak to live.*

Six

The corridor was short. It led from their cells to a hexagonal room with three closed doors and two other corridors. In the center of the room stood an immense glass lamp that trickled smoke up into a channel in the domed ceiling. The off-white stone structure of the prison matched the aesthetics of the castle perfectly. *This has to be the nicest prison I have ever been in.*

Strewn across the floor lay four dead guards. It appeared as if Rolan had shot them all. *That would explain why we did not hear any screaming.* Belac took dark pleasure in the fact that he recognized one of them. That man being dead seemed to make the world a better place.

Belac nodded toward the dead guard. "Does that make you as happy as it does me?"

Ecard grinned despite his obvious pain. "More, I would imagine."

Belac hefted the man, repositioning Ecard to make it easier to support him. Rolan marched off to the left. Belac was glad that the dwarf knew where he was going, but he could not help but wonder what was to the right. *Who else might be trapped in this nightmare?*

Belac raised his voice. "What's that way?"

Rolan did not look back. "What's, what way?"

Belac pointed. "That way!"

"You are going to need to be more specific," Rolan said without looking.

Belac would have hopped up and down if he had not been supporting someone. "You know what I mean, Rolan! It's the only other way to go!"

Rolan glanced toward the other corridor but did not stop walking. "I don't know, but it doesn't matter."

"How can you know it doesn't matter, if you don't even know what's down there?" Belac argued, following the dwarf out of the room.

"Because the exit is this way," Rolan told him.

"But there could be more prisoners," Belac pressed. "Maybe they could help."

"It does not matter." Rolan looked back at the elf and the man that he all but carried. "We cannot take anyone else with us."

"But maybe they could help," Belac tried one last time.

"We don't need help. What we need, is to hurry," Rolan said, ending the debate.

Belac still wanted to go check, but there was no way that he was going to go running off by himself wearing nothing but a bedsheet. *Even if I had a magic suit of armor that made me fly, I would still not go back there alone.* Belac thought about how much fun such a suit might be. *I take it back. I would totally be willing to go back there alone if someone would give me a magic suit of armor that let me fly.* Belac considered some more. *I would be willing to do it for a magic carpet and some clean trousers.* He would have been willing to forgo the trousers.

The corridor ended at a junction that led left and right. Rolan turned right without hesitation.

Vairug stopped. "We need to go this way."

Rolan disagreed. "No, we don't."

Vairug did not move. He appeared to be struggling with something. "It's my hand, Rolan."

Rolan stopped and looked back at the orc. "I can make you a new one. There is no way we can find it in all of this." He gestured negligently.

Vairug gave the dwarf a look that was almost pleading. "I can feel it, Rolan."

"That is probably not good." Rolan sounded as if he were understating.

Vairug looked down the other corridor. "It is not far."

Rolan's gaze traveled over Belac and Ecard, then he said, "We will have to be quick about it. There are people waiting on us."

Belac asked, "Do we have to return this way?"

Rolan nodded.

Belac lowered Ecard to the floor. He was willing to take the man with them when they escaped. He was even willing to help him walk. However, he was not willing to carry him deeper into the prison and risk getting himself or his friends killed. *He can just rest here. Maybe he will get some of his strength back.*

Belac stood. "Stay here and we will get you on the way back," he told the man.

Rolan stepped past them. "If someone else shows up, just close your eyes and keep looking like you're dead."

Belac wiped his hands on his bedsheet. He followed after Rolan and Vairug, not wanting to be left behind. He was worried Ecard might die or disappear while they were gone, but there was only so much that he could do for the man. *I am not going to just stay there and die with him.*

The first stretch of the corridor was clear. However, after a sharp turn to the left, they ran into more guards. Luckily, the guards were not prepared for escaped prisoners. Had they been, they still would not have been prepared for Rolan. *Who could possibly be prepared for that crazy little dwarf?*

There were two guards facing each other, speaking in hushed voices. Rolan quickly stepped around Vairug and shot the one on the right. The man's head snapped to the side as the steel dart passed through. The other guard stepped back in confusion. Before the man could process what was happening, Rolan had another bolt loaded and the springer aimed. The guard searched for threats in the corridor, but he looked the wrong way. Rolan's bolt took the man in the back of the head.

The sound of the two guards falling to the floor drew the attention of another in a nearby room. The man walked out into the corridor and was promptly shot in the head. Belac marveled at how fast Rolan could reload. The dwarf's hands moved with a practiced ease, seeming to operate without his direct attention. *He doesn't even look at the thing when he loads it.*

Rolan stepped into the doorway of the room that the guard had exited. His springer thracked twice more in rapid succession. There was a cry of alarm from inside and then another shot.

Rolan stepped back into the corridor, another bolt already loaded into his springer. A guard entered the corridor from a room on the other side and swung a truncheon at the dwarf. Rolan leaned away and low, the truncheon sweeping past where his head had been. He pulled a knife free and then leaned back in, burying the blade in the man's thigh. The guard fell to his opposite knee, stopping the fall with an open hand. The springer thracked and a bolt pinged off the stone ceiling after passing through the underside of the man's jaw and out the top of his head. Rolan reloaded the springer while sidestepping to the wall on his left. Another guard stepped into the corridor and Rolan shot him in the face. The sound of Rolan reloading was followed by an anticipatory silence.

Belac and Vairug looked at each other and then back to the dwarf. *Anyone who says that dwarves don't know how to make arrows right is just wrong.*

Rolan crept to the door, knelt down, and peeked into the room, scanning for threats. After determining that the room was safe, he continued down the corridor.

"Wait," Vairug said. "I think it is in there." He pointed a truncheon at the room that the dwarf had just cleared.

Rolan halted where he was, his springer held ready. Vairug hurried into the room, Belac following close behind. It was a small office dominated by an ornate desk.

Vairug walked around the desk and went straight to a small table in the back corner. He tossed the truncheon aside and picked up his metal hand with the remains of its leather harness dangling from it. He tucked the hand under his left arm and grabbed his silvery cogged mace. Evidently, the guards had considered them a matched set. Vairug was grinning broadly when he turned around.

The sight of the orc's tusks jutting out of his happy grin almost made Belac laugh. He smiled with the orc, unable to do anything less. *Now, we just have to escape.* He turned around to leave but stopped. A scabbarded sword hung on the wall next to the door. The two-handed long-sword had a black leather wrapped hilt with a black anchor enameled on the center of its polished steel cross-guard. A long, black leather scabbard with steel accents concealed the blade, but the sword appeared to be a fine weapon.

Belac reached up and took the sword off the wall. *It's pretty, but it wouldn't matter if it was made out of rust and horse leather. I need a weapon. And I know how to use a sword.*

There were shouts from the corridor followed by Rolan's commanding voice. "We need to move!"

The springer thracked as Belac stepped from the office. He almost tripped over the dead man on the floor. Belac noticed that the man's tabard bore the black anchor.

Vairug followed the elf out into the corridor. "I have it," he announced, signaling that they could leave.

Belac and Vairug hurried back down the corridor. Rolan turned and chased after them, pausing only to retrieve his knife from one of the dead guards. When they reached the corner, the dwarf turned around and used it for cover as he sent another bolt flying.

Rolan stepped back behind the corner. "Run ahead and get your friend moving," he instructed as he reloaded. "Just follow the hallway. I will catch up." He dug into one of his pouches and pulled out a small brass orb. He struck it on the wall and smoke began to spray out. Then he reached around the corner and threw the orb. "I said go!"

Belac hiked up his bedsheet and ran as fast as he could without tripping over the folds. When he saw Ecard, he thought that the man might be dead. Ecard lay on his side motionless, giving no indication that he was aware of Belac's return.

"Time to go, Ecard," Belac said, lifting the man up from under his arm.

Ecard came awake with a start. "What?" The man did not seem to know where he was.

"We have to go," Belac told him.

Ecard did not resist, but he was of little help, confused as he was. "Where?"

"Away from all the people coming to kill us, Ecard." Belac began to drag the man down the corridor.

Vairug's feet pattered on the stone as he joined the elf. "We need to move faster, Belac."

He wants me to leave Ecard behind. "How much faster?" Belac asked.

Vairug glanced back the way they had come. "There are many guards coming, Belac."

Belac looked back as well. Rolan was running down the corridor toward them. Belac thought Rolan ran well for a dwarf.

Rolan slowed when he reached the others. "We need to move faster." He turned around and began walking backward.

He is not even breathing hard.

"That is what I told him," Vairug said.

Rolan took the orc's metal hand. "Carry him."

Vairug growled, but bent down and hoisted Ecard over his left shoulder.

Rolan handed the metal hand to the elf. "Get moving."

Seven

They moved quickly, all things considered. Still, Belac could hear the guards charging through the corridor behind them. He did not understand how Rolan thought they were going to escape. The guards would catch them soon.

Belac looked to the dwarf. "I thought you stopped them with your gas ball thingy."

Rolan shook his head. "That was just smoke. It's not going to slow them down much now that they know it won't hurt them."

"Then, how are we supposed to get away?" Belac was trying not to panic, but the guards were getting louder.

"Next door on the right," Rolan told him.

Belac did not trust how easily the answer had come to the dwarf. "Unless it's a magic door that leads to an enchanted forest, I don't think that is going to be good enough, Rolan."

Vairug ran past the door.

Belac stopped and called after him, "Vairug!"

The orc looked back, and then almost dropped Ecard while changing course. Vairug was tired. Much like anyone in prison, life had not been going their way of late.

Belac stepped through the doorway. He did not find himself in an enchanted forest. Rolan had led them to a loosely packed storage room that appeared to be used primarily to house lamp oil.

Ecard's head bounced off the doorframe as Vairug rushed into the room. The man was either unconscious or too exhausted to complain.

Rolan shot a bolt down the corridor and then joined them inside. "Back of the room." He waved them on.

That seemed like a tactical mistake to Belac, but he trusted in the dwarf's expertise. *It's not like I have a lot of options right now anyway.* Navigating around the crates of lamp oil as quickly as he could, the elf hurried further into the cluttered room. At the back of the room, two large crates had been pulled away from the wall to expose a crudely chiseled passage. *Someone dug a hole into the prison!*

Belac took one look at the hole in the stone wall and stopped. "No. No. Nope. Nu uh. No more caves, Rolan."

Rolan had no patience for the elf's reluctance. "It's just a tunnel. Now move!"

Vairug did not stop and wait for them to come to agreement. He collided with the elf and pushed him toward the hole. Belac stumbled into the stone tunnel. Behind him, he heard guards knocking over crates in their pursuit. Even with the tunnel taken into consideration, Belac did not see how he and the others were going to escape. *I bet the guards know how to use a tunnel every bit as well as we do.* The cramped tunnel would be easier to defend, but that would only buy them so much time. The guards were sure to overwhelm them before they could escape.

Rolan's voice called from the entrance to the tunnel. "Keep moving!"

Belac looked back over his shoulder as he fled. "I didn't plan on stopping!"

An explosion threw Belac to the ground. Lying on his back, the elf tried to remember where he was. He looked at all the stone. *Am I in prison again?*

"Iaezadon," Belac mumbled. He could not hear his own voice. He wondered what device his torturers were using to create the loud ringing noise that was boring into his brain.

Rolan helped the elf sit up. "Your plan to not stop is not going very well."

Belac could barely hear the dwarf. *He's not making any sense.* He shook his head and almost toppled over.

"Easy there." Rolan put his hand on the elf's shoulder to steady him. "Follow my finger." He moved his finger back and forth in front of the elf's face.

Belac tried to swat the dwarf's hand away and missed. "Lamawits!" he said unintelligibly. Belac did not even know what he was trying to say.

Rolan turned his head away from the elf. "You two, keep moving down the tunnel. There are people expecting you. Don't kill them."

Why isn't he making any sense? "Crasadal," Belac muttered.

Rolan put a small vial up to the elf's lips. "Here, drink this." He poured liquid into the elf's mouth.

Belac tried to spit it out. "Galawadal!"

Rolan grabbed the elf's jaw forcefully and wrenched his head against the dwarf's chest. "We do not have time for this." He poured the rest of the vial between the elf's lips and then covered his mouth with a callused hand.

Belac fought as the dwarf forced him to choak down the bitter liquid. When Rolan was satisfied that the elf had swallowed the potion, he released him. Belac's world spun. He could smell the color of the rocks and taste the insides of his own eyelids. *Everything is so bright!* Then the world faded to shadow. The off-white tunnel walls lost their magic, and the elf could not taste anything at all. A dim light came from farther down the tunnel. *I should go that way.*

Rolan put a hand on the elf's shoulder to stop him from getting up. "Give it a moment."

As Belac regained his senses, the ringing in his ears abated. "What did you do to me?"

Rolan was suddenly impatient. "I rescued you from prison."

Belac got to his feet. "I am not rescued yet."

"Do you want to wait here and prove me wrong?" Rolan asked.

Belac looked to the light at the end of the tunnel. "Ah… No."

"Right." Rolan marched off down the tunnel.

Belac bent down and picked up his new sword and Vairug's shiny hand. *If I left Vairug's hand here, he would probably make us come back and 'rescue' it.* Belac did not understand why the metal hand was so important to the orc. It was broken. *I get why he would want a magic hand. I do. But a pile of twisted metal someone else has to carry around for him? Not so much.*

The tunnel led to a wide opening in the side of a cliff. Belac was met with the sight of ocean and sun. It was in that moment that the elf finally felt rescued. He took a deep breath, expecting to smell the sea. *That's strange.*

"I don't smell anything," Belac said confused.

Rolan was dismissive. "You probably won't for a while."

"What?" Belac asked. "Why not?"

Rolan shrugged. "It happens sometimes if you drink too much of the potion I gave you."

Belac's head snaped toward the dwarf. "You say that like it's my fault!"

Rolan did not argue. "You were not cooperating."

Belac almost threw the orc's metal hand down on the rocks. "So, you poisoned me?!"

Rolan waved a hand absently. "You will be fine." Then he softly muttered, "Probably."

Belac held out Vairug's metal hand with the ruined harness hanging from it. He flipped the loose leather straps around the hand and then offered it to the orc. Vairug took the hand with a nod of thanks. Behind him stood two men at the edge of the cliff. Even if they had not been dressed as sailors, it would have been obvious from how they handled the rigging piled at their feet. *If they are working with Rolan, they are probably pirates.*

Belac scanned the small cave again. "Where is Ecard?"

Vairug nodded toward the edge. "He is already headed down."

Belac did not know how they were going to get down, but he suspected that he would need his hands. He adjusted the baldric of his new sword and then slipped it over his head and onto his shoulder.

When he saw Vairug trying to juggle his mace and metal hand, Belac decided that the orc would need to be adjusted as well. He took the metal hand back and unwrapped the leather straps. He tied the two longest straps together and then hung the device on Vairug's shoulder with the straps crossing his chest and back.

Belac took a step back to get a better look at the orc. "That should work," he muttered to himself. An idea came to him. "Wait." He took one of the other straps and tied it in a small loop. "See if that will hold your mace."

Vairug wiggled the mace into the loop and then nodded.

"Belac." Rolan waved the elf over to the edge of the cliff.

"How did you find this place?" Belac asked as he joined the dwarf. *There is no way he had time to make this himself.*

"The only difference between a well kept secret and a poorly kept one is how much it cost," Rolan explained while securing a wide leather belt around the elf's waist. He looked up and met the elf's eyes. "You owe me a boat."

"What?" Belac asked. *I don't have a boat!*

Vairug spoke up. "He still owes me a knife."

Belac looked at the orc. "I do not."

"You lost mine," Vairug insisted. "Back at the tailor in Tariel."

The guards took it! Belac shook his head. "That doesn't count."

Vairug held out his open hand, palm up. "Give me my knife back."

"I don't have your knife!" Belac told him.

Vairug nodded, lowering his hand. "Then, you owe me a knife."

"And a pair of boots," Rolan added.

Belac pointed at the dwarf. "Now, wait there. I did not take your boots!" *They wouldn't even fit.*

Vairug nodded. "You lost them in the bet."

"What?!" Belac shook his head. *Who makes a bet with a dwarf's boots?*

"In the race," Vairug reminded him. "You bet your boots."

"The good ones," Rolan added.

Belac remembered. He had explicitly refused to bet with his boots. "Lies and slander."

Rolan looked at the elf sideways. "Are you saying that you didn't lose the race?"

Belac had lost the race. *Technically.*

Rolan saw the look on the elf's face and nodded. "Right."

"No. Not right!" Belac had not bet his boots.

Vairug's cheek twitched as he suppressed a grin. "That is how a race works, Belac."

Belac shook his head. "No. I never bet my boots."

Rolan held up a hand. "Everyone that thinks Belac owes us a boat and a pair of boots, raise your hand."

Vairug raised his hand. "And a knife."

Rolan nodded. "And a knife."

Belac looked back and forth at them. *This is crazy!*

Rolan lowered his hand. "Now, everyone that thinks Belac does not owe us anything, raise your hand."

Vairug dropped his hand quickly.

Belac's hand shot up like he thought his vote would matter.

Rolan pushed him off the cliff.

Belac screamed something unkind as he fell.

Eight

Belac almost lost his new sword when the rope tightened. Had the fall stopped more abruptly, he would have. However, somehow, the sailors above applied resistance to the rope tied to the ring of Belac's waist harness. The elf was safe, but he still would have kicked Rolan in the face if he could.

Once it became apparent that Belac was not going to fall to his death, he came to enjoy the decent. The sky above and the ocean below were about as contrasting with prison as he could imagine. Hanging suspended between the two offered both peace and promise. A two-masted ship waited below, ready to smuggle him to freedom. A breeze whipped through the elf's hair and caused his bedsheet to flutter to the side. He wiggled his toes in the air. *I am going to need shoes.*

Belac had expected them to simply lower him into the sea, but a man on the ship reached out with a long crook and hooked the line. The elf was swung over to the ship and lowered onto the deck. The sailor unfastened the rope from Belac's leather waist harness and then tugged on the rope three times. He waited a moment before tugging on the rope again, and then the sailor tossed the rope overboard, trusting the men above to understand his message.

The sailor turned and smiled, showing off his missing teeth. "Best get below deck with the other."

Belac saw no reason why he could not wait in the fresh air, but he did not argue. He went below deck, past a small kitchen area, and found the main hold. Ecard sat on a coil of thick rope, staring at his hands. At first, Belac did not think that the man realized he was there.

Then Ecard spoke. "I did not believe you."

The gravity of the man's confession set off a warning in the elf. Belac' left hand moved to his scabbard, securing it for a faster draw. He had wanted to save the man, but Belac was prepared to cut him down if he proved to be a threat. *I will need to be careful with the sword in here. It is a tight space, and I don't want the blade to get caught on anything. A short swipe, and then a thrust.*

Ecard looked up from his hands. "How could you be so sure?"

Belac relaxed a little, but he did not remove his hand from the scabbard. "Sure, about what?"

"That you would escape!" Ecard was untethering.

Belac was perplexed. "We did escape."

Ecard shook his head, his wild hair whipping about violently. "But how did you know?!" His voice quivered as if he were close to tears. "How did you know to not give up?!"

Belac had not really thought about it. *I was not really there for very long.* Still, Belac did not think that he ever would have given up. "I would have just kept trying."

"You think it is just that easy?" There was accusation in Ecard's question.

Belac shrugged. "I did not say that it would have been easy." *Though, it kind of was.*

Ecard laughed mirthlessly and went back to staring at his hands. "And what if you had died?" His voice was soft and sounded lost. "What if you had died in that place without ever getting free?"

Belac did not see much point in the question. "Then, I would have never known I failed?" *Because, I would be dead. That's how being dead works.*

"To never know failure…" Ecard accepted the answer as if it were something profound.

A thump came from the deck above. Belac decided to leave Ecard to his own thoughts. He retraced his steps and returned topside, curious who had come down from the cliff. When he saw that it was Vairug, he considered pushing him off the ship.

Belac leaned out over the railing and looked down at the water. "Do you think you could swim with only one hand?"

Vairug frowned at the elf.

"Maybe we should take a vote," Belac suggested.

The sailor stepped away from the orc and tugged on the rope before throwing it overboard.

Belac raised his hand. "Everyone that wants to find out if Vairug can swim, raise their hand."

Vairug tilted his head to the side and stared dangerously at the elf.

The sailor looked like he wanted to be anywhere else.

Belac lowered his hand. "Now, everyone that wants to watch the orc drown in the ocean," he began to shout, "because he threw me off a cliff!" Then he spoke calmly, "Raise your hand." Belac raised his hand back up dramatically.

Vairug straitened his head and looked down at the elf. "Rolan pushed you."

Belac pointed a finger at the orc, trying to think of an argument. "Your right."

"You know…" Vairug looked up toward the ascending rope. "Rolan is coming down next…" he said slyly.

Belac's grin hurt his face. He gazed up the cliff face, ringing his hand villainously as he waited for the dwarf to be lowered. He felt like a lion, waiting in its pit to be fed.

When Rolan was finally within reach, the sailor hooked the line. Belac silently took the crook from the man before he could pull Rolan aboard. The elf began to work the crook in a tight circle, causing the dwarf to swing wide.

Rolan's short legs kicked frantically as he tried to maintain his balance. "Stop it, Belac!"

Belac leaned out toward the dwarf. "Maybe we should take a vote!"

"Sodding ingrate!" Rolan shouted.

The rope slipped out of the crook and Belac stumbled, almost dropping it overboard. Rolan quickly regained control of his momentum and began to climb the rope as it continued to lower him toward the water. The dwarf began to swing back and forth, bringing himself closer to the ship. Belac looked around for help. Vairug was below deck, peeking up from the steps. Belac handed the crook to the sailor and ran.

Rolan landed on the deck with a thud. He untied the rope and then chased after the elf. *There is nowhere to go!* Belac did not want to jump into the ocean, but he knew he would be trapped if he fled below deck. He ran to the main mast and began to climb. The elf no longer felt like a lion. He felt like a treed house cat fleeing an angry badger.

"Dwarves can't climb trees!" Belac knew what he said made no sense.

Belac climbed up to the crow's nest and looked down expecting to see Rolan climbing up with a knife in his teeth. The dwarf stood at the base of mast, looking up. Belac knew what he was thinking. Rolan was trying to decide between cutting down the mast or setting it on fire.

Belac looked to the smaller mast, wondering if he could make the jump. *Nope. That would kill me.* He looked back down. Rolan was gone. It did not make the elf feel safer. He looked around, but Rolan was nowhere to be seen.

Belac watched from the crow's nest as one of the sailors was lowered from above. *How is the last one going to get down? There is no one left up there to lower him.* Instead of tossing the end of the rope overboard to be pulled back up, the sailors on deck tied another rope to it. One of them held the first rope while the other wrapped the new rope around the ship's rail before binding the two ropes together. They tugged on the newly bound rope and braced themselves. When it tightened, they let out the rope hand over hand. It twisted around the railing to slowly rise up the cliff, lowering the last sailor down. *Pirates are clever.*

When the last sailor landed on the deck, the others wasted no time untying him. They immediately began to set sail while he untied himself and pulled the other end of the rope back down. The men were professionals, and it showed. Watching them work, Belac had forgotten about the homicidal dwarf hunting him. Remembering with a start, the elf spun around in the crow's nest, scared Rolan might be behind him. The crow's nest was mercifully free of dwarves. Belac breathed a sigh of relief. He scanned the deck of the ship, searching for Rolan, but the dwarf was still nowhere to be found. Belac sat down in the crow's nest. He did not think for a moment that Rolan had forgotten about him. *A dwarf might forget how much they have had to drink, but they will never forget a grudge.*

As the ship pulled away from the cliffs, the full grandeur of Harborage came into view. High above the rocky cliffs were mansions of matching stone. While each was unique, they shared a design similar to that of the castle proper. What distinguished them most were the vibrant colors of their elaborate rooves. Each was painted an exotic color of which Belac had never seen before. Basking in the light of the sun, the homes of the aristocracy were a declaration of life and prosperity.

Above them all, towered the castle that Belac had recently escaped. He looked away from the fortress, his eyes following the coast. Farther away, the cliffs became lower and lower until they reached a city of nautical artisanship that stretched out along the shore. It was an assemblage of wooden buildings that could only have been shaped by the same masters that were responsible for the ships that filled the harbor. The harbor itself was an extension of the city, following the coast and causing Harbridge to seem like a city spilling into the sea.

It was a place unlike any other in the world, yet Belac was glad to leave Harbridge behind. He remained in the crow's nest as they continued out to sea, resigned to sitting up there until they reached whatever port they stopped at next. However, a port is not where they stopped.

With Harbridge still in sight, if barely so, they met another ship. Belac counted three masts on the larger vessel. At first, he worried that it was there to arrest them. He dismissed the idea quickly. *Rolan would not have stopped for them if they were here to arrest us. He would have just blown them up or something.* The sails were dropped, and then lines were thrown between the ships so that they could be brought closer together.

Now, Belac had a dilemma. He looked down from the crow's nest to find Rolan staring back up at him. The dwarf knew that Belac could not stay up there. So did Belac.

Belac looked from one ship to the other. "Maybe you should wait for me over there," he called down to the dwarf.

"Thanks," Rolan called back up in a friendly voice that was obviously false. "But I don't mind waiting for you here. Come on down."

"Promise you will not throw me in the ocean," Belac replied.

After a moment, Rolan loudly said, "No." His voice was no longer friendly.

I am not going down there. Belac looked to the other ship. *I really need to get a magic carpet.* His attention returned to the ship that he was trapped on. Rigging ran from the top of the mast to the end of the boom. *If I can get to that wooden arm thing, I can jump over to the other ship.*

Belac swung out and wrapped a leg around a rope. His plan had been to slide down, but the feel of the rope against his bare leg changed his mind. He moved his hands to the rope and then let his legs hang below him. Shifting his weight, he swung from hand to hand as he lowered himself down the rope. The angle made the maneuver awkward, and he found himself having to move faster the farther he went. Unable to keep up, his hands slipped.

The elf fell backward with a shout. His shoulder clipped something hard and then he fell into the ocean. The water felt like a slap to the face.

Disoriented, Belac flailed below the surface. He could not distinguish up from down. *The ocean is trying to eat me!* The black anchor on his new sword suddenly felt like more than a decoration. As the sword pulled against him, it felt like an anchor in truth. *If the sword is pulling me down…* Belac struggled against the weight of the sword, realizing up must be the other way.

He broke the surface of the water, trying to breathe and spit out sea water at the same time. He splashed loudly as he fought to stay above the water. He would have lost his bedsheet if it had not been held down by the baldric of his sword and the thick leather belt he still wore.

"Help!" Belac shouted up between the ships.

A rope was tossed down from the larger ship. Belac grabbed the rope and allowed it to take his weight as he waited to be pulled up. After he caught his breath, the elf frowned. No one was pulling him up. He tugged on the rope three times. He waited while no one pulled him back up. He tugged on the rope again. *They are not going to pull me up.*

Belac swished around in the water, placing his bare feet against the hull of the ship. "If I get a splinter…" he grumbled as he used the rope to walk up the side of the ship.

When Belac neared the railing, he was forced to stop and consider. He needed to change the way he was climbing and was unsure how to go about it. Rolan leaned out over the rail. The dwarf smiled and waved before the line went slack.

Belac screamed something unkind as he fell.

Nine

"Why are we going back to Harbridge?" Belac asked of no one in particular. *I do not want to go back to Harbridge.*

"We are not headed back to Harbridge," an unfamiliar voice said from behind the elf. "At least, not at the moment."

It sure looks like we are headed to Harbridge to me. Belac turned away from the bow of the ship. He recognized the bald man immediately. "Hey! It's you. From the fire in Tariel." He pointed at the man. "I saved your life!"

The man tapped his nose and then nodded agreeably, spreading his arms wide. A pale blue tunic covered his rotund midsection in the style of Tariel. "And now, I have saved yours." His voice was slightly higher than was common among men.

Belac appreciated that the man had the sense to wear trousers under his tunic. "You saved me?" *I do not remember seeing you in the prison.*

The man lowered his arms and leaned forward. "I contributed," he said conspiratorially.

Belac took him at his word. "Thanks. It makes me extra glad you're not dead."

The man laughed. "Yes, well, I always pay my debts."

"Wait." Belac realized that something did not add up. "How are you not dead."

"From what I understand, I have you to thank for that," the man replied. "You and your large friend."

Belac shook his head. "I'm not talking about the fire. How did you survive Tariel? The colossus destroyed everything."

"Ah," the man said nodding. "I see your confusion." He furrowed his brow. "I doubt this 'colossus' destroyed everything. Also, there would have been many who fled the city. Tariel is likely to have survivors that outnumber the dead."

Belac had no way of knowing what the colossus had done after the pond closed. It could have laid waste to the entire city in frustration and rage. He did not see how anyone left behind could have survived. "How did you escape? Is the pond working again? Did anyone else come through with you? What happened to the colossus?"

The man held up his hand, halting the elf's questions. "When I left Tariel, all was well. If someone other than Rolan Brightstone had told me of what transpired in my absence, I would have doubted the account."

Brightstone? Belac pushed the thought away. *I have more important concerns than Rolan's name.* "Then how are you even here?"

"Well, I used the pond," the man said as if the answer should have been evident.

How? Belac tried to make sense of things. "You knew it would be opened early?"

Rolan interjected, "There's a reason people call him 'Daikon Knowit."

The dwarf's sudden appearance startled Belac. He was still worried that Rolan was going to throw him back into the ocean. Belac had just started to get dry, and he was in no mood for another swim.

Daikon turned to look at the dwarf. "They call me 'Daikon Knowit' because that is my name, Rolan," the man said unconvincingly.

"Sure, it is," Rolan sounded like he knew a secret.

Belac did not really care what the man's name was. "If we are not going to Harbridge, why does it look like we are going to Harbridge?"

Daikon seemed pleased to answer the question. "We plan to follow the coastline past the city. From what I understand, Rolan has arranged further transportation."

Belac assumed that the wind had something to do with their heading, but it still looked like they were headed to Harbridge to him. "Then, where are we going?"

"Be careful asking Daikon too many questions," Rolan warned. "He keeps a tally in his head."

"Rolan…" Daikon said in mock affront.

Rolan stepped to the side and pointed with his hand to an open hatch. "Vairug has a change of clothes for you. He should be easy enough to find below deck."

Belac worried it might be a trap. He narrowed his eyes at the hatch.

"Or you can stay up here in a bedsheet," Rolan added irritably.

Belac turned toward the dwarf. "How did you know we would need clothes?"

"Both you and Vairug got pretty torn up escaping Tariel." Rolan shrugged. "And you lose stuff."

"I do not!" Belac argued.

"You are wearing a bedsheet," Rolan said dryly.

"I…" Belac stopped. *Okay, maybe I lose stuff.*

"Right." Rolan nodded.

Belac turned away and bumped into a sailor. "Oh! Sorry."

The sailor nodded absently, returning to his work. "The Deep be with you."

Belac took an indirect path to the hatch. There were more sailors on deck, and he did not want to distract them. He was worried that he would cause one of them to make a mistake, and the ship would crash into Harbridge. *I do not want to go back to Harbridge.* He climbed down through the hatch, having to kick his bedsheet out of the way to keep from stepping on it.

The climb down was short, but it made Belac question why any woman would tolerate a dress. *I hope Rolan got me trousers.*

The ship was larger than the last; however, it was still easy to locate Vairug. *The orc is usually quiet, but he is not exactly small.* Belac found him in a cramped compartment doing his best to pretend that Ecard was not sitting in the room with him. Sitting on crates, Vairug was leaned back, staring at the ceiling, while Ecard stared at the floor. *It is probably better if they don't talk to each other too much anyway.*

Belac stepped into the stuffy compartment, finding it an uncomfortably close space. "Hey um… Lord Vairdoe," he tried to remind the orc who he was supposed to be. "Rolan said you have some clothes for me."

Vairug leaned forward, reached down, and picked up a leather bag with its strap cinched tight. Without saying anything, he tossed the bag to Belac. The elf hoped that the clothes inside were nicer than what Vairug had on. *That is too much brown.* The orc's short boots and long trousers were slightly different shades of dark brown. His wool shirt was of a lighter color, yet it too was brown.

"We need to get you another red sash," Belac said. He thought the crimson sash had looked nice on the orc. *It somehow made him look a little more sophisticated. Sure, he still looked like something that might rip your head off, but the sash helped.*

Vairug leaned back and returned to staring at the ceiling. "I do not think that is a high priority at the moment."

Belac uncinched the strap on the leather bag and then dumped its contents on the floor. "Nonsense," he said as he began to change clothes. "It is not enough to save the world. You have to look good doing it."

"Is that so?" Vairug asked though it was obvious he disagreed.

"Why would you just save the world?" Belac asked, "When you could save the world and inspire people at the same time?" *And be famous.*

Vairug tilted his head to the side so that he could look at the elf.

Belac knew that he was on to something. He tried to figure out how to explain as he spoke. "Saving the world is hard work." He had never thought about it, but it felt like he was explaining something that he had unconsciously understood. "But if you look the part, you can inspire other people while you're at it. If you can do that, they won't just help you, they will go off on their own and keep trying to make the world a better place." *Hopefully, a better place for us.* "What is the cost of a sash when compared to that?" *Besides, there has got to be some way to make money being a famous hero.*

Ecard looked up from the floor. "The elves are wise."

Vairug laughed silently at the man.

Belac narrowed his eyes at the orc.

Ten

"I am not wearing this, Rolan." Belac held out the crumpled cloth as if it might bite him.

Rolan did not take the cloak. "Then, you can freeze to death."

Belac narrowed his eyes at the dwarf. *He did this on purpose!* "It's green!"

Rolan did a poor job of trying to hide his grin. "Is it?"

"You know it is!" Just holding the cloak made Belac uncomfortable. He thought about throwing it into the ocean. Then he thought about throwing the dwarf.

"What do you know?" Rolan asked disingenuously. "It is green."

With the exception of the cloak, all of Belac's new clothes matched the browns that Vairug now wore. Rolan must have made a special effort to find the richly dyed green cloak. *I bet he paid extra for it!* Belac wanted to wrap the cloak around a rock and beat the dwarf to death with it.

Vairug reached out and took the cloak without saying anything. When Belac turned to thank him, Vairug stuffed the cloak into the leather bag at the elf side. Vairug smiled, his tusks jutting out.

Belac did not thank him.

Rolan gestured. "Now get in the boat."

Belac turned back toward the dwarf and held out his hands. "I am in the boat." *Stupid dwarf.*

"No," Rolan corrected him. "You are on a ship." He pointed his hand out over the rear of the ship. "Get in the boat."

Belac leaned out over the rail. Two sailors waited in a rowboat suspended below deck level. The men looked thoroughly untrustworthy. "Maybe we should lower Ecard down first."

"He is not going with us," Rolan replied.

What? "Why not?" Belac asked.

Vairug answered, "He is useless."

Belac narrowed his eyes at the orc.

Rolan tried to preempt an argument. "Vairug is right."

Belac argued. "We can't just abandon the man."

"Sure, we can," Rolan said dismissively.

Vairug nodded.

Rolan continued before the elf could speak. "Daikon will see him safe, and then the man can make his own way." He cut his hand through the air. "Ecard would be nothing but a problem for us if we took him."

Belac nodded grudgingly. *We can't give him the opportunity to question 'Lord Vairdoe.'*

Vairug gestured down to the main deck. "Does he know that he's not coming with us?"

Clad in Belac's old bedsheet, Ecard was a wretched sight to behold. *Now that I am looking at him, I am kind of glad we can't take him with us.* The man looked lost until he located them on the stern deck. As Ecard made his way up the steps, Belac noticed that the man was already moving around better. *I wonder how much of him will recover.*

Ecard looked from the orc to the elf. "You are leaving."

Belac did not know if the man had overheard something or if he was simply guessing. "We still have a dragon to kill."

Rolan made it clear that the man would not be coming with them. "Daikon will see you safe."

Ecard's gaze returned to the orc. "And you, Lord Vairdoe, do you have any advice for me?"

Vairug was quiet for a moment before answering, "Do not forget to keep your pinky up when you drink." He held up his pinky as he had at the tailor in Tariel.

Ecard shook his head slowly. "You are the wisest men I have ever known."

Rolan coughed and turned away.

Belac grinned and stepped up onto the rail of the ship. "Be sure to remember that when you tell the story." He hopped down into the dinghy waiting below. *Having my sword strapped to my back definitely has some advantages.* If he had attempted the jump with a sword at his hip, it likely would have caught on something.

Vairug was more careful getting down. As the orc climbed into the boat with the use of only one functioning hand, Belac considered trying to help. *I would probably just get in his way. With my luck, he would end up pushing me overboard.* Vairug sat down on the bench in the middle of the dinghy, repositioning the mace sticking out of his bag.

Rolan vaulted over the railing and landed in the boat with them. *It is amazing that backpack never throws him off balance.* The dwarf stomped his foot twice and called back up, "Lower us down."

The rowboat lurched and then began to descend. Belac lost his footing and had to grab the side of the boat. He quickly lowered himself to the bottom and braced his feet against the other side. His scabbarded sword pressed into his back uncomfortably. *Worth it.*

Rolan stood firm as the dinghy shimmied in the air. After the boat settled into the water, the sailors unhooked the rigging and extended the oars. One of them began to whistle a jaunty tune while the other rowed them toward shore. The dwarf put his hands on his hips and stared off into the inland.

Belac relaxed and then sat up to better see where they were headed. He held up a hand to shade his eyes. *It is almost like the sun moves through the sky just so it can blind me no matter which way I am facing.* On the other side of a rocky shore, were rolling hills of dry grass.

More golden than green, the grass stirred in a cool breeze that Belac could feel already. They had passed beyond the busy docks of Harbridge, and the country that awaited them felt empty in comparison. Mountains in the distance crowded the shore and marked the southern border of Enevic.

The dinghy beached on the rocky shore, and the whistling stopped. The sailor at the bow hopped over the side and stabilized the boat. Then Rolan marched off the dinghy and continued inland.

Belac used the side of the boat to get to his feet and then hurried after the dwarf. "Thanks for the ride," he said to the sailor holding the boat.

"May The Deep be with you," the sailor replied.

Maybe they are not pirates after all. They seem nice enough. Belac thought for a moment. *And not one of them had on a red sash.*

After Vairug jumped down next to Belac, the sailor began to push the dinghy back into the sea. Together, Belac and the orc trudged across the rocks to catch up with Rolan.

"You are kind of in a hurry," Belac noted.

Rolan did not slow his pace. "It's getting late."

Belac had more questions. "Where are we going?" he asked as they walked up a grassy rise.

"There is a wagon waiting for us on the other side of the next hill," Rolan told him.

"What? Why?" Belac asked. *You better not be taking us back to Harbridge.*

Rolan answered the why. "Because I told them to."

Belac frowned at the dwarf. "Fine. But how do you know that they are there?"

"I could see them from the ship," Rolan explained. "Why else do you think we stopped here?" He held out his hands, encompassing the countryside.

"I don't know," Belac said, getting a little irritated. "That's why I'm asking you."

Rolan sighed. "I hired a wagon and a team to move it. They are waiting for us up ahead by the road. We need to meet up with them and then they can take us to our camp for the night." He looked over at the elf. "I would rather get there before it's dark."

Belac nodded. *That all makes sense.* "Then what?"

"Then, we sleep." Rolan sounded like he needed sleep.

Grumpy dwarf. Belac was about to press Rolan for more answers, but Vairug stepped between them.

"Will there be food at this camp?" Vairug asked.

"There had better be." Rolan shook his head. "If there's not, I might end up eating one of the horses."

When the wagon came into view, Belac was surprised by its size. He had expected it to be a modest flatbed with a canvas covering. What Rolan had arranged was a long wooden enclosure that looked more like a small house on wheels.

"I don't see any horses," Belac said. *Maybe they already ate them.* "I am not pulling that wagon, Rolan."

Vairug nodded. "Agreed."

Rolan pointed his hand off to the right. "Do you see the way those two hills come together there?" He moved his hand a little to the left. "There is probably a brook that runs through over there. If I had to guess, I would say the horses are on the other side of that hill, getting watered."

"Guess all you want," Belac said. "I am still not pulling the wagon."

As they approached the wagon, a man with dirty blond hair and a smile hopped down from the driver's bench, shouting, "Rolan!"

"I see you," Rolan grumbled.

The man was dressed plainly, with a cream colored blouse tucked into brown trousers. A long-sword hung from his back, and he moved as if he were accustomed to its weight. "Rolan! It is so good to see you!" he said louder than Belac thought was necessary.

Men began to exit the rear of the wagon. Belac counted six. All of them carried a weapon of some type.

"That is more men than I paid for," Rolan said in a conversational tone.

The men spread out to either side of the man who had issued the greeting. The formation made it clear that he was the one who led them. Belac took a couple of steps to the side, instinctually wanting to prevent the men from getting too far to his right.

The leader held his arms out to his sides, still smiling. "I do not think payment is going to be a problem."

If the man is trying to put me at ease, he is bad at his job. Belac looked at the other men again. The weapons they carried were not sheathed or put away; they were held in their hands, ready for use.

Eleven

"You are making a mistake, Larry." Rolan did not seem overly concerned by it.

The man took offence. "My name is not Larry!"

Rolan turned to the orc. "I thought his name was Larry."

Not-Larry pointed at the dwarf. "You know my name!"

Rolan returned his attention to the man. "Are you sure it's not Larry?"

"I know my name!" Not-Larry shouted at the dwarf.

Rolan held out his hands. "I thought you said, I knew it?"

"What?" Not-Larry was having trouble keeping up with the dwarf's banter.

Rolan loosened the straps of his backpack. "Here," he said removing the pack.

Not-Larry stared at the dwarf in confusion. Rolan walked forward and tossed the pack to him. Not-Larry caught the pack and Rolan buried a knife high on the inside of the man's thigh. Before the other men could respond, Rolan darted toward the ones on his left.

Vairug responded immediately. Holding his leather bag down with his left forearm, he attempted to pull free his cogged mace. He let out a growl of pain when an arrow punched into the left side of his chest.

Belac tried to draw his sword as he moved farther to the right and away from the violence. The sword was too long for the blade to clear the scabbard. Frantically, he slipped his head out of the baldric and drew the long-sword, dropping the scabbard as soon as it was free.

A man came at Belac with a rapier. Having years of experience using such a slim blade, Belac knew to expect the lunge. He did not engage the blade, instead waiting for the man to commit before stepping to the side with a backhanded sweep of his long-sword. The blade slashed through the man's bicep, rendering the arm useless. Belac reversed the swing, and the tip of his blade cut into the side of the man's neck. Belac continued to follow the blade's momentum, turning to face the wagon. *I have to stop the archer.* He did not know if the man with the rapier was dead, but Belac could not stop to finish him. Rolan would be a challenging target for the bowman. *The dwarf is fast, and short, and he moves like a crazy person.* Vairug, however, would be hard to miss.

Belac sprinted through the chaos, his attention locked on the wagon. *Please, don't shoot me!* He leapt up onto the driver's bench and swung his long-sword in a horizontal arch over the top of the cabin. The blade hacked through the back of the bowman's left ankle. The man cried out in pain and alarm before falling backward off the side of the wagon. *You really should have shot me.*

From his elevated position, Belac looked back to see if Vairug still lived. The orc grappled with one man while another with an axe attempted to circle around them. Vairug ripped the barbed arrow out of his own chest and stabbed his opponent in the neck. The man fell to his knees, pulling Vairug down with him. The man with the axe positioned himself to attack the exposed orc.

With a cry of fury, Belac jumped from the wagon, his sword held high above his head. Using the force of his fall and the strength of both arms, he brought the blade down in a savage blow. The sharpened steel landed above the man's shoulder and tore through his torso at an angle.

Blood splattered onto the ground, and the two halves of the man fell next to a startled Vairug.

Belac looked over the man that he had just cut in half, past the orc on the ground, and to the dwarf standing among the bodies of the fallen. From behind the wagon, a man with a short-sword charged at Rolan. The dwarf's back was to the man, and Belac did not know if Rolan could turn in time to save himself.

Without further thought, Belac threw his sword, shouting, "Rolan!"

Rolan dove forward as Belac's sword flew end over end. The blade intercepted the man, spinning him around after sinking into his chest. Rolan rolled over one of the corpses before coming to his feet at the same time as the man hit the ground. *I can't believe that worked.* Belac had only been attempting to disrupt the man's charge. The elf looked down, breathing hard. The dirt under his boots had turned into a bloody sludge. *I'm glad I still can't smell anything.* Vairug rose, growling at the pain in his chest.

A pathetic moan came from the man with Belac's sword sticking out of him. Rolan walked over and kicked the man in the head. The man recoiled, but was too hurt to fight back. Rolan put a foot on the man's chest and took hold of the sword's leather wrapped hilt. The steel scraped on something as Rolan pulled the blade free.

The man groaned in torment and then began to sob, "No. No. No..."

Rolan plunged the sword back into the man, ending his pleas. The dwarf jerked the blade back out and then stepped over the dead man. He held the sword up. "You know, you are not supposed to throw these."

Now, who's the ingrate? Belac spread his arms wide. "It looks like it worked to me."

"But now what are you going to do about him?" Rolan pointed with his other hand.

Belac spun around to see who was behind him. He fell backward, landing on his backside. Scooting away, he searched for the threat though there was no one behind him other than Vairug.

A black anchor came into view on Belac's right. He turned his head and found Rolan holding out the long-sword for him to take. Both the dwarf and the sword were smeared with blood. When Belac reached for the hilt, he saw that he too had blood on his hands.

"Die in a fire," Belac said, taking the sword.

Rolan said nothing. Obviously, he felt as if he had made his point. *Oh, I get the point. Next time, let the dwarf die!*

Rolan stepped around the dead and picked up his pack. Instead of returning it to his back, he opened the top and rummaged around inside while he walked to the orc. *I hope he has something that can fix Vairug.*

The faint sound of something dragging over dirt caught the elf's attention. Belac turned to his left, looking under the wagon. The bowman was crawling across the road, dragging his bloody stump behind him. Belac scampered under the wagon, chasing after the man. *I should have just walked around.* On the other side of the wagon, Belac stood and then approached the man cautiously.

The bowman rolled onto his back and stared up at the elf. Belac looked down at him without pity. The man had used his own belt as a tourniquet, but his face was blanched white and waxy.

The man held his hand out feebly. All he could manage to say was, "Peace."

Belac shrugged. "Sure," he said, and then stabbed the man in the chest. After pulling the blade free, he held up the sword and considered the blood. *I need to find something I can use to clean this off.*

Belac walked around the front of the wagon toward the first of the men he had killed in the fight. The man had died on his knees with his face pressed to the ground. Using the back of the man's shirt, Belac cleaned his sword as best he could. He then retrieved his discarded scabbard and slid the blade home.

Belac looked over the field of dead. *I don't feel anything.* He did not care that he had just helped kill nine men. He did not feel the need to rationalize it or explain it away. His foes were dead. Belac's thoughts would have troubled him if he had taken the time to analyze them. Instead, he kicked the kneeling dead man, knocking the body over. He tugged off the man's boots and drew a small knife from a sheath on the man's hip. Then Belac joined his friends at the front of the wagon. Vairug was sitting on the side step to the driver's bench while Rolan bandaged the wound in his chest. Belac dropped the pair of boots in the orc's lap.

Vairug looked at the elf, confused. "What do you want me to do with these?"

Belac stabbed the small knife into the side of the wagon next to the orc. "Eat them."

Rolan laughed as the elf walked away. "You still owe me a boat!"

Belac had decided that he wanted a knife for himself. *There has to be something worth taking in all this mess.* He began to search the dead but was mostly disappointed with what he found. Finally, on one of the men that Rolan had killed, he found a dagger that appeared serviceable. He took the sheath as well, but the man's belt had been slashed in the conflict. On another of the men, he found a belt that he thought would work. *Nope. This thing is already starting to crack.* The belt had been used to carry a small, leather pouch. Inside the pouch was a stone and striker and coiled bit of twine. He kept the pouch but tossed the belt aside.

The elf returned to the corpse of the man who had wielded a rapier. *I know he has one.* Belac unbuckled the man's belt and stripped off the rapier scabbard and the crude, leather knife sheath. *Good enough.* He slid both the small pouch and his new dagger onto the belt before buckling it on below the waist harness that he still wore around his midsection. His eyes drifted to the crude rapier lying on the ground. *Pitted and dull.* He briefly considered taking the rapier but decided against it. *A rapier is great if I'm in a duel or I just want to poke holes in drunks, but that is not really my life right now.* He thought about what he had faced recently. *Monsters, small armies, small armies of monsters…* He did not think that his life was going to get easier any time soon.

Belac walked to Not-Larry's corpse and removed the man's long-sword. He did not take the time to inspect the quality of the blade, but the undyed leather that covered the scabbard and wrapped the hilt was well worn. *Long-swords are probably better for fighting monsters.* He returned to the front of the wagon and placed the sword on the driver's bench.

Vairug asked, "Are you taking trophies now?"

Belac shrugged. "Sometimes, I lose stuff."

Rolan chuckled and clapped the elf on the shoulder.

Belac did not understand the approval, but he recognized it for what it was. He nodded toward the orc. "Is he going to die?"

"Eventually," Rolan said in a dry tone.

Vairug showed his tusks with a smile. "Would you care to make a wager on that?"

Rolan chortled. "Might as well make it for three wishes."

Belac smiled with them. *That is a safer bet than the one I made.* He narrowed his eyes at the orc. *But I never bet my boots!*

Twelve

"Are you sure the horses are over there?" Belac asked.

"No," Rolan said. "But I don't think they pulled that wagon all the way out here with humans." He gestured back to the men they had just killed.

Belac nodded. "That makes sense."

"That is why I said it," Rolan replied shortly.

Belac narrowed his eyes at the dwarf.

A horse whinnied on the other side of the hill. Belac increased his pace, hoping to avoid an 'I told you so' from the dwarf. The sun hit his eyes as he crested the rise. Looking down, Belac continued to walk toward the sound of the horses.

"Hey!" called the voice of a young man.

Belac looked up at the man. *Of course. They left a guard.* He was glad that he only saw one. *This guy is not much more than a boy.* Not-Larry must have left the youngest of them to watch the horses.

Thrack. The man's head snapped back, and he fell into the brook. He appeared even younger in the motionlessness of death.

Belac growled angrily.

"What?" Rolan asked impatiently.

Belac pointed at the dead man. "Do you know how many dead bodies I had to search to find a belt?" The man's belt looked so new, it could have been made that morning. "I'm taking it." The elf walked over to the dead man and straddled the brook.

"You just said that you already found one," Rolan pointed out.

"I don't care," Belac replied peevishly. "I am taking it." The belt slid easily off the young man's corpse. "I will just take them all." Belac swept his arm out across the world, the belt flopping around in his grip. "All the belts!" He stepped away from the brook. "And then, I can build a castle out of them. And when people walk by, they can point at it, and they can say, 'Oh, no. Don't go over there. That is where the crazy elf lives that will kill you and Steal! Your! Belt!"

Rolan laughed.

One of the horses snorted.

Belac narrowed his eyes at the horse. He thought it might be laughing at him too. There were four horses, and he thought that they could stand to lose one.

"Hey," Rolan said laughing. "It's not the horse's fault your crazy."

"I'm crazy?!" Belac's eyes went wide.

Rolan nodded merrily. "A little bit."

Belac threw the belt. It flew over the dwarf's head and landed in the grass behind him.

Rolan was unperturbed. "There goes your evil, belt empire."

One of the horses whinnied.

Belac turned his ire on them, trying to ascertain the offender. "I can always make more belts out of horse hide!"

"Not unless you want to pull the wagon," Rolan told him.

Belac narrowed his eyes at the horses. "I can wait."

"Glad to hear it," Rolan said dismissively. "Grab two of the leads, and let's get out of here."

The horses all looked the same to Belac. Their dark brown coats with long black manes, tails, and furry feet often referred to as feathers, were simply too uniform for him to tell them apart. "They sure are big."

Rolan took two of the horses' leads. "They are Enevician."

I guess they are kind of pretty. Belac gathered up the other two horses, taking a lead in each hand. "Maybe I won't turn you into belts."

The elf had calmed down by the time they returned to the wagon. Vairug was waiting for them and appeared to be recovering quickly. *Rolan must have crammed some of that pink pasty stuff into the wound.*

Vairug inspected the horses admiringly. "These are beautiful creatures."

Belac offered him the leads. "You can have them."

Rolan protested. "You cannot give away my horses, Belac."

Belac shrugged. "Fine." He nodded to the orc. "You can only have my two."

"They are all mine," Rolan insisted.

"All horses?" Belac asked.

Vairug shook his head. "You cannot claim all horses."

Rolan frowned at them. "Just these particular horses."

Belac held up a finger. "You said these horses were Enevician."

"That's right," Rolan agreed impatiently.

Belac pointed at the orc. "That means, they are his."

"What?" Rolan stepped around the horse that he had just harnessed to the wagon. "How?"

Belac held out both of his hands toward the orc in an introductory manor. "Lord Vairdoe of Enevic."

Vairug stood up straighter and tilted his head back with an exaggerated air of nobility.

Rolan shook his head. "Give me a break."

"You ask for clemency?" Belac nodded his head. "I may be able to negotiate on behalf of His Majesty Lord Vairdoe."

"His Majesty?" Rolan asked unmoved.

Vairug stood there and attempted to look more noble.

Belac answered as if the question had been respectful. "I may be able to convince him to rent them to you." He tapped the side of his nose. "Once we have negotiated suitable compensation."

Rolan took another one of the horses and positioned it in front of the wagon. "Lords don't tap their noses like that."

Belac did not argue. "That is why His Majesty has me."

Rolan harnessed the horse and then looked at the orc. "And you want to rent me my own horses?"

Belac interjected, "Once we have negotiated suitable compensation."

Rolan grunted. "Maybe you are lords." He took the lead of another horse. Harnessing the horse, he said, "How about we deduct the tariff from your transportation fees?"

"What?" Belac did not like the sound of that. "No."

"Yeah," Rolan said agreeably. "It would be a good start toward paying what you already owe." He took the lead to the last horse and moved it into position. "The cost of hiring the two ships was considerable." He began to harness the horse. "The interest alone is enough to bury you."

Belac raised his voice. "You were rescuing us!"

Rolan nodded while he worked. "And I am prepared to temporarily wave that fee."

Vairug deflated and looked at the elf disapprovingly. "You are a bad negotiator."

"Wait," Belac said. "What if we reward you with the horses?" He searched for the correct phrasing. "For services rendered."

"Deal," Rolan agreed, stepping away from the horses.

Belac smiled happily and nudged Vairug.

Rolan continued, "Now, we just need to discuss the cost of your further transportation."

Belac pointed at the dwarf. "Now, wait right there!"

"No." Rolan shook his head. "Can't wait here. All this death is going to draw the ghouls soon. I plan on being well away from here before that sun finishes setting."

He is just trying to scare me. "Ghouls?" Belac asked uncertainly.

Rolan nodded and then walked to the back of the wagon.

"Um," Belac said, following after the dwarf. "Maybe we can work something out."

"Right." Rolan opened the door to the wagon. "Now, get inside."

"You don't want one of us to ride outside with you?" Belac did not want to leave the dwarf alone if there really were ghouls coming.

Rolan shook his head. "There are going to be people searching for you two. Anyone that sees us will remember an elf or an orc. We are probably not going to run into anyone else out here, but if we do, no one is going to think twice about a dwarf driving a wagon toward the old Enevician mines."

"But..." Belac began.

"We don't have time for this," Rolan said, interrupting the elf. "It's getting dark. We need to move. Get in the wagon."

Belac frowned at the dwarf but then climbed into the wagon. Inside the cabin, there were long benches along either side that looked about as comfortable as a prison cell. In the front of the cabin, wooden barrels and boxes had been stacked and lashed to the wall. *This place is definitely unfit for a lord.* Belac chose the bench on his left and took a seat. Vairug climbed into the cabin behind him. The orc's size made the space feel even more confined. He sat on the bench across from Belac and then Rolan closed the door. The inside of the cabin was left darkened, lit only by the faint traces of light that crept through the closed door and side panels.

Belac's eyes adjusted as they waited for Rolan to get the wagon moving. *I wonder how far we can get before night comes.* The stacked boxes rattled as the wagon bounced them around. Belac could already tell this was not going to be a comfortable trip.

In an accusatory tone, Vairug said, "You gave away my horses."

Belac narrowed his eyes at the orc but did not argue.

They rode without speaking while Belac tried to organize his thoughts. The inside of the cabin grew dimmer as they were jostled around. Vairug seemed content with the relative quiet.

Finally, Belac confessed, "I thought he left us."

After arriving at the Temple of the Ancient in Harbridge, Belac and Vairug had immediately been arrested. Rolan had backed away from them, blending in with the excited crowd. While there had been nothing the dwarf could have done to help them, Belac had felt abandoned. He had never expected Rolan to come rescue them.

"He did leave us," Vairug said matter-of-factly.

"I know," Belac struggled to explain, "But he came back."

"He did that too," Vairug allowed. "You are not wrong that he left. But you are wrong, if you think he did it because he is a coward. Rolan is not a coward."

"No, that's not it." The idea that the dwarf might be a coward had never even occurred to Belac. "I just didn't think he was going to come back."

Vairug grunted, but said nothing more.

Belac thought that the only reason Rolan was able to continue as far into the night as he did was that the moon replaced the sun. After the wagon was brought to a halt and the cabin door opened, the dwarf stood bathed in moonlight.

Rolan pointed his hand to a cloth sack on the floor of the cabin. "Toss me that bag."

Belac picked up the sack, but instead of throwing it, he handed it to the dwarf. "What's in it?"

"Hoods for the horses," Rolan told him.

Belac followed the dwarf out of the wagon. "So they won't run off?"

The wagon had been stopped in the grass on the side of the road just before its course veered off to the left. The horses were still harnessed and Belac got the impression that Rolan was going to leave them that way for the night.

Belac felt like the horses deserved some relief after pulling the wagon. "Shouldn't we at least take off the harnesses?"

"No," Rolan said in a tone that would allow no argument. "It would be dangerous for them if we did." He began to put the hoods over the horses' heads. "Also, there is a chance we will need to run tonight. They need to be ready to go if we do."

The night seemed peaceful to Belac. "Why would we need to run?"

"I was not joking about the ghouls," Rolan told him.

"Then, why are we stopping at all?" Belac asked incredulously.

Rolan finished hooding the last horse. "It is not safe to continue at night."

Belac gestured to the road. "We got this far all right."

Rolan stepped away from the horses and waved the elf to the back of the wagon. "That was using the road. This is as far as we are taking the road."

Belac moved as the dwarf directed, but asked, "So you want to sleep while there's ghouls running around?"

"In the wagon. Yes." Rolan took hold of the door.

Belac crawled inside the cabin, feeling like bait in a trap. "How are we all going to fit in here?"

Rolan followed the elf inside, closing the door behind himself. "You and I each take a bench, Vairug sleeps on the floor."

Vairug made a grunt that only the dwarf could interpret.

"You can sleep on the bench if you want to Vairug, but you are not going to fit," Rolan replied impatiently.

Vairug grunted again.

This time, Belac thought he understood. *It sounds like "Fine. But don't expect me to like it."* The elf felt much the same way.

As they laid out for the night, Rolan said, "You are going to have to be quiet, Belac."

"What?" Belac felt a little insulted.

"I'm serious, Belac." Rolan's tone matched his claim. "The ghouls won't care about the horses, but you have to be quiet."

"Why don't they care about the horses?" Belac asked.

"Because they do not smell like people, and they are not dead," Rolan explained. "The ghouls should have plenty to eat without bothering us, but you have to be quiet."

Belac's curiosity was not satisfied. "But what..."

Vairug spoke over the elf. "Should we gag him?"

Rolan answered, "It might be better to just stake him down in the middle of the road."

Belac decided that curiosity would be easier to ignore than hungry ghouls.

Thirteen

Sleep was not something the elf found that night. In undismissible fear, he had strained his hearing in an effort to discern what might be coming to kill them. The only sound he could be sure of was that of the sharp wind that howled as it blew past the wagon. However, Belac could have sworn that masked beneath the wind, he could hear the sounds of pattering feet and the gnashing of teeth. All the while, strange shapes had created fluttering shadows in the moonlight that crept into the cabin.

When Rolan sat up suddenly on the bench across from him, Belac almost screamed.

"Are the zombies here?" Belac asked in fright.

"Ghouls are not zombies," Rolan replied.

"Whatever." Belac looked around in the dark wagon. "Are they here to eat us?"

Rolan rubbed the sleep out of his eyes. "They should be gone by now. Why don't you go check?"

Belac did not want to be the one to stick his head out the door just to see if something bit it off. "...It's still dark out."

"No," Rolan corrected the elf. "It is dark in here. It's early dawn out there. You should be able to see."

That means they can see me! Belac knew the argument would not add up with his last one, so instead he suggested, "Maybe we should wait a little longer." *Like until one of you two go first.*

Rolan moved to the front of the cabin and began to rearrange boxes. "Sure. But try not to think about waterfalls while you wait."

What do waterfalls...? "Die in a fire," Belac said sourly.

"Not if I stay close enough to hear the waterfall." Rolan slammed a box down on the bench.

Vairug growled at him from the floor.

Belac looked toward the door in the back of the cabin. *No choice now... Evil little dwarf.* He got up and stepped around Vairug as he made his way to the door. He cracked the door open and looked outside. Rolan had been right. Belac could see outside, if not well.

Vairug grabbed the elf's ankle and went, "Rarrr!"

Belac threw the door open in his haste to get away. He tried to turn while jumping away and fell backward out of the wagon.

Lying on his back in the trodden grass, Belac stared up at the dim sky while the orc laughed at him. *I don't have my sword.* He wanted to be mad at Vairug, but was too angry with himself. *What if there had been zombies, or ghouls, or whatever? What if there had been something out here waiting to kill me? I did not even remember to bring a sword. What was I going to do? Face monsters with nothing but a dagger and a belly full of fear?*

Belac climbed to his feet and then reached over the orc to take his long-sword with the black anchor. He did not say anything to Vairug. Belac was not mad at the orc, but he was not going to thank him for the reminder either. He looked around the outside of the wagon, searching first for present threats, and then for signs that any may have been there previously. He expected to find trails of footprints surrounding the wagon, but there was nothing in the vicinity that suggested anything had stalked them in the night. *Did Rolan make up the story about the ghouls?* He considered why the dwarf might do that. *Maybe he thought it would be funny.* Belac frowned. *Or he just wanted me to be quiet so he could sleep.*

Whether or not there had ever been ghouls in the night, there was nothing the elf could see that worried him at the moment. He slipped the baldric over his head and hung the sword on his back. His hair got caught under the strap, so he took the time to straighten it as best he could without a comb. He ran his fingers through the long, black mess until he got out the worst of the tangles, before tying it in a knot behind his head. *I am going to need to make a comb or something.*

Remembering waterfalls, Belac scanned the landscape for a convenient tree. Finding nothing suitable, he returned to the back of the wagon. Vairug had not moved, but Rolan was already preparing for the journey ahead. The dwarf slid steel darts into his leather pouches, replacing what he had shot with ammunition he pulled from a box on the bench inside the cabin.

"Hey, Rolan…" Belac coughed. "There are no trees."

Rolan waved his hand dismissively. "Then use the side of a hill."

Belac shrugged and then did as the dwarf had instructed. When he returned to the wagon, Rolan was busy rearranging boxes once more.

"What now?" Belac asked the dwarf.

Rolan stepped around the orc and hopped out of the cabin. He handed the elf a waterskin and a waxed paper package. "You take this and climb up on top of the wagon. Go ahead and eat, but keep an eye out while you do. Watch down the road the way we came. If you see any movement or dust in the air, call out." He knocked on the side of the wagon. "Time to get up Vairug. I need you to give me a hand."

Vairug sat up. "That is not funny, Rolan."

Rolan shook his head. "I've told you, Vairug. I am not changing the way I speak every time one of you two get something chopped off."

Belac's eyes went wide. *I don't want anything chopped off!*

Vairug frowned at the dwarf.

"Now get up," Rolan continued. "Harnessing the horses was simple enough, but we need to brush them down, and you can reach the top of their backs easier than I can."

Vairug growled, but he got up and stepped out of the cabin.

Belac went around to the front of the wagon and used the driver's bench to climb up on top. He sat cross-legged, facing the rear so he could watch the road while he ate. The sun had begun to rise over the ocean on his left, but he saw no evidence that anyone from Harbridge was coming to kill them.

The trail rations that Rolan had provided tasted like nothing. Belac realized it was not the rations. *I still can't taste anything.* He sniffed the air. *Nothing.* He thought about the night he had spent trapped in the cabin with Rolan and Vairug. *Maybe I should be glad that I can't smell or taste anything.*

After Belac finished his breakfast, he continued to watch the road while Rolan and Vairug prepared themselves, the horses, and the wagon to move. They worked quickly and were ready to go before the sun was fully above the horizon.

Belac called down from the top of the wagon, "Shouldn't we feed and water the horses or something?"

Rolan climbed up onto the driver's bench to better speak with the elf. "We will. But first, I want to get to that river up ahead."

"I don't see a river," Belac said.

Rolan pointed towards the mountains with his hand. "Do you see those trees?"

Belac looked in the direction that the dwarf had indicated. "No, I don't see anything but those bushes there." He pointed.

Rolan lowered his hand. "They're not bushes. What you are seeing is the tops of trees on the other side of a hill."

Belac nodded his understanding.

Rolan continued, "We can't stay on the road, so I am going to have you walk out in front of the horses and look for holes we might fall into or rocks we might hit. Keep us moving toward that stand of trees, but pay attention."

"What do we do if there is a hole or something?" Belac asked.

"Lead us around it if you can," Rolan explained. "If you can't, we will need to pull out the planks under the wagon."

Belac thought that sounded easy. *Not as easy as riding on a wagon.* "Why do I have to walk?"

"You and Vairug are going to take turns," Rolan gestured toward the orc. "He still needs to eat. So, you go first."

Belac noticed the dwarf did not mention himself. "What about you?"

"I am driving the wagon," Rolan told him. It was a statement of fact. "Just lead us to the trees. Then we can feed and water the horses, and Vairug can take over while you ride up here with me."

Belac frowned. "Fine. But if a monster-killer-rabbit or something jumps out of a hole and bites off my leg, and then I bleed out and die, I am going to blame you."

Rolan gave a short nod. "I can live with that."

Belac climbed down from the wagon and positioned himself in front of the horses. He made sure he was far enough out that Rolan would have time to change course, but not so far that he could not yell at the dwarf if he wanted to. Once they began to move, Belac found that he enjoyed the walk. There were only a few times that he redirected the wagon. One of which was simply to see how it would work when he did. The other times may or may not have been necessary, but the elf chose to error on the side of caution.

"Better an extra step than a broken foot," Belac quoted the old saying to himself. He was just about to congratulate himself on how good a job he was doing, when something occurred to him. *I still don't know where we are going.*

Fourteen

"Where are we going?" Belac asked.

Seated next to him on the wagon, Rolan pointed with his hand toward the mountains ahead. "That way."

"No, Rolan." Belac did not even bother looking where the dwarf had pointed. "We took care of the horses, we crossed the river, no one is trying to kill us." He swept his hands in an X in front of himself. "No more excuses." He spoke as forcefully as he could. "Where are we going?"

Rolan looked at the elf sideways. "No, really. That way."

Belac pointed toward the immense gray mountain range. "That way?"

Rolan nodded. "Right."

"Toward the mountains?" Belac pressed irritably.

Rolan nodded again. "Right."

"Why?" Belac shouted. "What's in the mountains?" *And if he says, 'rocks,' I am going to…*

"Giants," Rolan said simply.

Belac looked at the mountains. "…Giants?" He remembered the colossus in Tariel. He remembered the destruction and the sheer unstoppable size of the thing.

Rolan reminded the elf of something else. "We need one to forge the sword."

Belac turned his head toward the dwarf, but his eyes did not want to leave the mountains. "How do you even know they are there?" *I don't see any giants.*

"Serath says they're there," Rolan answered. "If Serath says they're there, they are there." He sounded sure.

"You spoke to Serath?" Belac asked, relieved. "How did he make it out of Tariel? Where is he?"

Rolan shook his head. "No, I have not seen him since we took the pond. I don't know where he is now."

Belac's relief evaporated. "Then, maybe we should wait on him." *And if he never shows, I never have to face a giant. ...or a dragon.*

"No," Rolan replied, but he did not sound as if he thought that the idea was necessarily a bad one. "Serath said that time was an issue. We can't just wait. I'm sure that the colossus in Tariel is going to interfere with his plans some, but we can do this. If we can find the giants and convince a smith to come with us, we will be ready to head to the volcano when Serath finds us."

Belac's eyes had finally focused on the dwarf. "You say that like you are ordering a sandwich!" He lowered the pitch of his voice mockingly. "If we just order Serath something to eat now, he can join us when its ready. That way, we can save time and ignore the fact that Serath might be dead."

Rolan frowned at the elf. "I don't sound like that."

Belac spread his arms. "Sorry, I didn't have any gravel to gargle first."

Rolan shook his head. "And, Serath is not dead."

"How could you possibly know that?" Belac thought the dwarf was kidding himself.

Rolan's confidence did not waver. "I know Serath. He's not dead."

Belac recognized that the dwarf was too stubborn to have a proper discussion about it. "Fine," he allowed. "But how are we even going to find the giants without him?" He regretted the question as soon as he asked it. *They are giants.*

"Serath told me where they are," Rolan explained. "It should not be too hard to find them."

"Serath told you?" Belac asked. "When?"

"We don't all spend our time drinking, sleeping, or getting into trouble," Rolan replied.

Belac nodded. "I know. You people are boring."

Rolan snorted.

Vairug called out, "Go around!" waving his hand to the side.

Rolan steered the horses around a depression that would have gotten the wagon stuck.

Belac waited until the dwarf had them back on course before asking more questions. "So, let's say we find the giants." He emphasized, "And they don't eat us." He paused for effect. "How do you plan on convincing one of them to come with us?"

"Right..." Rolan said. "About that..."

"You don't know!" Belac pointed at the dwarf, happy to see him uncertain about something.

"We will figure something out," Rolan asserted irritably. "We will just need to talk to them and find out what they want."

Belac could not believe how bad this plan was. "What could a giant possibly want from us?" He emphasized, "Other than to eat us."

Rolan shrugged. "I don't know. They are probably going to want us to plunder some ancient ancestral tomb or something. It could be anything. We just have to talk to them first." A thought came to him. "Maybe I can offer to broker a peace agreement between them and Harbridge."

Belac gestured back the way they had come. "Harbridge wants to kill us!"

Rolan looked at the elf sideways. "Maybe we don't tell the giants that."

I should have stayed on the ship with the pirates. Belac wondered if pirates had to take an oath.

"Don't worry about it," Rolan continued. "I am sure we can find some way to convince them."

"And then what?" Belac asked in a doomed voice.

Rolan shrugged. "And then we head back to Harbridge and wait for Serath."

"I don't want to go back to Harbridge." Belac was starting to think the dwarf's plan was intentionally bad. "Harbridge wants to kill us!"

Rolan waved his hand dismissively. "Don't worry about it. I have a place we can hide."

Belac threw up his hands. "How are you going to hide a giant?!"

Rolan looked at the elf. "I don't understand the question."

"It's a giant!" Belac yelled so loud that Vairug looked back to check on them.

Rolan grinned like he knew something the elf did not. "What do you think a giant is?"

Now, Belac did not understand the question. "…A giant. Like the colossus, but with a beard."

Rolan chuckled. "No."

"What do you mean, 'no?" Belac asked. "That is what the word 'giant' means!"

Rolan shook his head. "They are not that big."

Belac did not believe him. "Then, why are they called 'giants?"

Rolan thought for a moment. "They might be a little bigger than an ogre, but not by much."

Belac remembered the ogres. "That does not seem very… giant."

"That is what happens when people talk about things they don't really understand." Rolan shrugged. "Some of them have beards, if that makes you feel better."

Belac frowned at the dwarf. "Then, why are people so scared of giants if they are not… I don't know… giant?"

"You mean, other than the whole 'people not understanding things' thing?" Rolan took a deep breath and then let it out slowly. "If you ask Serath, it is because they are better than other people."

Belac did not try to hide his disbelief. "How?"

"In just about every way there is." Rolan did not sound pleased by the admission. "They are bigger, stronger, smarter, and more resilient than anything else you would still think of as people."

Belac shook his head. "Then, why don't giants rule the world?"

"That is where things get kind of complicated," Rolan said. "Serath says it has to do with ingenuity."

Belac smiled. "The giants have too much ingenuity?"

Rolan shook his head. "No, not enough."

Belac did not think that was a very good argument. "Then, how can you say they are better?"

"Serath says something like, and I'm quoting here, probably poorly, that ingenuity is 'the compensative response to inadequacy or the perception there of.' The man is a wizard, so don't expect him to be easy to understand." Rolan took another breath. "I think what he is saying, is that because giants are better than everyone else, they don't need to make as many things." He turned to the elf. "Things' make a big difference in a power struggle."

Belac was unconvinced. "You are saying, people only make things because they are weak?"

Rolan shook his head. "No." He gestured above the elf's shoulder to the hilt of the long-sword strapped to his back. "But would you carry that around with you, if you could kill people with nothing but the power of your mind?"

Belac realized that the argument did make a strange sort of sense. *I really don't like that it makes sense.* "Wait!" He focused on the dwarf's face. "Are you saying a giant can kill me with just its mind?"

Rolan chuckled. "No. I am just making a point."

Belac let out a sigh of relief. "What do you think?"

"I think Serath has some strange ideas." Rolan shrugged. "That does not make them wrong."

Belac asked a more pointed question. "Do you think the giants are better than us?"

"I think 'better' is subjective," Rolan told him.

Now, that was something Belac could agree with. He grinned. "You know, that is just a clever way of not answering my question."

Rolan returned the grin with a sly one of his own. "Thanks."

Fifteen

"But, what if the ghouls eat him?" Belac asked

"He will be fine," Rolan said dismissively before standing up and walking away with the waterskin that he had just filled from a babbling creek.

Vairug stopped brushing the horse that he was caring for and turned around to face the elf. "I will be fine."

Belac was becoming more and more convinced that the ghouls were fictitious. "Is that because there are no ghouls?"

Rolan walked past the elf. "They probably won't come this far from the road. Besides, he can sleep in the wagon. Even if they do come out this far, the ghouls won't bother him if he sleeps in there."

Vairug tried to reassure the elf. "Don't worry, Belac. The ghouls are not going to eat me."

"That's right," Rolan agreed. "If something eats him, it probably won't be the ghouls."

Belac looked around nervously. The scraggly trees that lined the creek did not offer many places for something to hide, but he was not ready to trust even the trees.

Vairug turned toward the dwarf. "Nothing is going to eat me, Rolan." He sounded a little offended.

Belac was still concerned. "It just feels wrong to leave you behind."

Vairug stepped away from the horses. "Are you coming back?"

Belac looked up at the massive formation of rock that the dwarf wanted them to climb. "I hope so."

Vairug nodded. "Then, focus on that. I will be fine."

Rolan called from behind the wagon. "We are not leaving until tomorrow morning. You can say your goodbyes then."

Belac shrugged. *Yeah, okay.* He pointed at the horse brush in the orc's hand. "Let me see that."

Vairug tossed him the brush and then put his hand on one of the horses. "Be careful with this one. It will bite you."

Why does everything want to eat me? Belac reached back and untied his hair. "It's not for the horses."

Vairug frowned. "That is exactly what that brush is for."

"Not right now, it's not," Belac said brushing the tangles out of his long black hair.

"You should just braid it," Vairug told the elf. He held up his own thick braid of long, black hair.

Belac dismissed the suggestion. "I like it tied back in a knot. It stays out of my way and does not get caught on anything." *And it's pretty when I let it down.*

Rolan walked over to join them. "I could just cut it off for you," he offered.

Belac looked at the dwarf's butchered hair. "No." He pointed the brush at him. "Bad dwarf!"

Rolan snorted and walked off to prepare for the night.

Belac handed the brush back to the orc. "I need something to eat."

"There are some trail rations in the wagon." Vairug nodded toward the dwarf. "Rolan says we should not start a fire."

Rolan called out, "No fires!"

Belac did not care if the food was fresh or not. *I still can't taste anything anyway.* He ate trail rations and then readied himself for the night as the sun set in the distance. In the fading light, he crawled into the back of the wagon and laid out on his side of the cabin. After staying awake the night before, sleep came easily. If he dreamed, he did not remember; and if things moved in the night, he did not notice.

A box slamming down on the opposite bench brought Belac awake.

Vairug growled from the floor.

Belac looked at the dwarf sleepily. "There are nicer ways to wake people up."

Rolan shrugged. "There are less nice ones too."

Belac was too groggy to argue with the dwarf. He sat up and took his black scabbarded long-sword in hand. Being careful not to step on Vairug, the elf made his way to the door. As Belac stumbled out of the cabin, he felt a small amount of pride in remembering to bring the sword with him.

Rolan spoke from within the cabin. "You can't keep sleeping in your boots, Belac."

"What?" Belac shook his head. *It is too early for this.*

"Your feet are going to rot," Rolan explained. "Whenever you can, you need to take your boots off while you are sleeping. You need to air your feet, your boots too."

Belac knew that the dwarf was right. *With my luck, I will survive all the monsters, just to die of foot rot.* Belac nodded. "Your right," he said and then set off to greet the morning.

The elf walked around the camp, such as it was, and searched for signs that anything had been there in the night. Finding nothing, he strapped his sword to his back and continued to move around the camp, stretching and preparing for the climb ahead. Belac preferred to sleep through the morning, but he had to admit that they could be peaceful. *Though, sleep is peaceful too.* The morning had a quiet promise to it that was simply not present at any other time of the day.

Belac stopped next to the creek and watched the water flow from the mountains. The gentle sounds of the water made him thirsty, so he knelt down to drink. Something shot at the elf from his right. He rolled to his left and then came to his feet gripping the hilt of his sword. The squirrel stopped short and barked at the elf before turning and running up a tree.

From behind the elf, Rolan said, "At least we know you're awake."

Belac had not heard the dwarf approach. "We need to get you a bell or something."

"Sure." Rolan nodded. "I can ring it when I need you to go fetch something for me."

Belac frowned, but then noticed the two waxed paper packages that the dwarf was holding. "Is that breakfast?"

Rolan handed him both packages. "Stuff one of them in your bag. You can eat the other one now, but be quick about it. We need to get moving." He pulled the strap of a waterskin off his shoulder and offered it to the elf. "Here. Take this."

Belac took the waterskin, trying to balance the packages in his other hand, but dropped one of them on the ground. He narrowed his eyes at the package. *Just for that, I am going to eat you first.*

"Try to get in the habit of drinking from the skin and then refilling it in the stream," Rolan advised.

Belac lowered the waterskin to the ground and then stuffed the package he held into the leather bag he wore at his side. "Why bother? It's easier to just drink from the stream."

"It will cycle fresh water into the skin," Rolan explained. "Also, it makes it easier to spot killer squirrels."

Belac nodded. He did not think that the dwarf was really talking about squirrels. *It sounds like a hassle, but it might be worth the extra effort if it helps me not die.* He sat on the ground and picked up the dropped package. *You thought you could escape.* He pealed open the waxed paper and began to eat his tasteless breakfast. "Where is Vairug?" he asked between bites.

"He is still in the wagon," Rolan said irritably. He turned his head to the wagon and raised his voice. "He can sleep the whole time we are gone if he wants. But if something happens to the horses, he is pulling the wagon back to Harbridge!"

Belac grinned at the thought of Vairug trying to pull the heavy wagon by himself. *I wonder if I could get Rolan to make me a bull whip.*

"Are you through eating?" Rolan asked.

Belac shook his head and took another bite. "See? Still eating," he said with his mouthful. He started to choke on the dry food and had to wash it down with a drink from the waterskin. The water was warmer than he would have liked, but he was more concerned with not choking to death.

"Don't forget to fill that back up," Rolan said, gazing off toward the mountains.

Belac finished eating, drank from the waterskin, and then refilled it in the creek. After getting to his feet, he asked, "Are you sure Vairug is going to be okay here by himself?"

"No," Rolan replied unapologetically. "But someone needs to stay with the horses. Lorance was supposed to stay here with two other men, but you saw how that turned out."

"Lorance?" Belac did not recognize the name. "You mean Larry?"

Rolan chuckled. "Yeah. His name was Lorance."

Belac was confused. "You said his name was 'Larry.' I don't think 'Larry' is short for 'Lorance."

"It's not," Rolan agreed. "I just wanted him off balance."

"Maybe that explains why he wanted to kill you," Belac said ruefully.

Rolan shook his head. "He must have figured he could make more killing me than helping me."

"Why?" Belac did not think that the dwarf would have told the men he hired that they were involved in a prison break.

Rolan looked at the elf sideways. "Not everyone likes me."

Sixteen

"So, we are not climbing the mountains?" Belac was fairly certain that the dwarf had pointed to the mountains.

Rolan shook his head. "Why would we climb the mountains?" Gray rock shifted under his boots, but the dwarf never seemed to lose his footing.

Belac looked up at the massive mountains on either side of them. "To get to the giants?"

"What would giants be doing on the top of a mountain?" Rolan asked.

"I don't know," Belac said. *I don't know what giants do.* "Eating goats?"

Rolan chuckled.

"Fine!" Belac said irritably. "Then, where are we going?"

Rolan gestured to the mountains around them.

Belac narrowed his eyes at the dwarf. The elf's foot slipped on a loose rock, and he had to grab the dwarf's shoulder to keep from falling. Despite Rolan's claims they would not be climbing a mountain, the route they took brought them higher with every step. Belac could already feel the cold beginning to slow his reflexes. The elf looked down at the leather bag that he carried on his side.

"Just put it on," Rolan told him and then resumed his march into the mountains.

Belac groaned. He knew that the dwarf was right. He pulled the cloak from his bag, careful not to lose the waxed paper package inside. "You did this on purpose!"

Rolan called over his shoulder. "If I did, don't you think I would know that?"

"What?" Belac looked away from the cloak and toward the dwarf. "What are you talking about?"

Rolan stopped and turned around. "Never mind." He pointed his hand at the cloak that the elf held. "Just put it on."

Belac removed his sword and then used the baldric to lower it to the ground with the top of the scabbard resting on his foot. He shook out the thick, green, winter cloak and draped it over his shoulders. The thing made his skin crawl. He fashioned the cloak in place though what he really wanted to do was rip it off and throw it in Rolan's face.

Belac kicked the sword up into his hands and then slipped the baldric over his head. "Don't blame me when something terrible happens!"

Rolan shook his head but said nothing. Instead, he turned to resume moving onward. The dwarf froze.

Farther ahead, at the top of the rise, stood a masculine silhouette of pure white. Wild, white hair and pale skin, the giant stood naked in the cold. Its muscles rippled as the giant raised a two-handed great-hammer forged from solid steel. Then the giant charged, roaring in murderous challenge. His thunderous voice echoed through the mountains and seeped into Belac's bones.

The elf stepped back, only to slip on the loose rocks underfoot and fall backward. He tried to scoot away but got tangled with his cloak and long-sword. Belac could not take his eyes off the giant's bulging muscles and unbridled rage.

Rolan reached for his springer and pulled it free. The dwarf gave no indication that he would give ground to the giant.

The giant suddenly fell from view, dropping into an unseen hole in the pathway. His roar changed from one of rage to that of surprise. The abruptness made Belac question if what he had seen had been real. He looked away from the empty path ahead and fixed his gaze on Rolan, searching the dwarf for evidence of the truth. Neither of them moved in the silence that followed.

A voice called up from the hole.

Belac could not make out what it said, but Rolan walked over to the edge of the hole and looked down cautiously. Belac scrambled to his feet and hurried to join the dwarf.

Rolan called down into the hole in a language the elf did not understand.

After a moment, a deep voice replied, "Yes." The giant sounded resigned.

Rolan sat down next to the edge of the hole, smiling. "You seem to have gotten yourself into some trouble."

The giant yelled something angrily in the language Belac did not understand.

Rolan's smile only broadened. "I guess we could just leave, if that's what you want."

After another moment of silence, the giant called up, "What do you want, Dwarf?" He spoke in a way that suggested Dwarven was too soft a language for him to speak properly.

"Me?" Rolan asked in mock surprise. "What I want, is to help you get out of that hole."

"I would be willing to assist you in that." The giant's deep voice was guarded.

Belac leaned over the edge to see the giant. The drop was dangerously far, even for a giant. Inside was a rounded cave with dark tunnels too small for the giant to have crawled through. Dust filled the air and created a visible shaft of light that angled down into the darkness. Rocks had fallen on the giant, and his leg was bent in the wrong direction. The giant gazed up from behind a bushy white beard, no longer frightening in his vulnerability.

Belac called down, "We are looking for a smith."

Rolan frowned at the elf but said nothing.

"I am a smith," the giant claimed.

Rolan snorted.

Belac agreed with the dwarf. "That seems rather convenient," he said sarcastically.

"This does not seem convenient to me, Dwarf!" the giant replied angrily.

"Hey!" Belac said, offended. "I am not a dwarf!"

This appeared to confuse the giant. "Then, what are you?"

Rolan spoke up. "Someone that is going to leave you to die in that hole if you don't be nice!"

"I'm an elf," Belac told the giant.

"An elf?" The giant was more confused. "What are you doing here?"

"I told you," Belac explained again, "we are looking for a smith."

"You have found one." Either the giant understood, or he no longer cared. "Now, get me out of this cave."

Belac was not ready to do that just yet. "How do I know you won't try to eat me?"

Rolan put a palm to his face and shook his head.

The giant's response was unfriendly. "Why would I want to eat you?"

Belac looked around. "I don't see any goats!"

Rolan laughed.

The giant said nothing for a moment and then called up, "I want to talk to the dwarf again."

Belac bristled. "Too bad! You're the one stuck in a hole! So, if you want out, you are going to have to talk to me!"

The giant mulled that over quietly before replying. "Very well. Go find my brother Morkan. He will help you get me out of this cave, and then we can discuss why you need a smith."

Belac narrowed his eyes at the giant. "How do I know he won't try to eat me?"

The giant sighed. "Tell him Ghoram sent you, and that I need his help. He will not eat you."

Belac looked at the dwarf.

Rolan shrugged.

Belac leaned back over the edge. "How do we find him?"

"Continue to follow the path until it splits," the giant instructed. "When you get there, take the path to the right. Be sure to make yourself known."

Belac stepped away from the edge. "Do you think we can trust him?"

Rolan shook his head. "It doesn't matter. We came to speak with the giants. No matter how this works out, helping him helps us."

Belac nodded. *And if he is a smith, we can't just let him die.* "We have to help him."

Rolan stood up and walked around the hole.

"Wait." Belac pointed to the dark opening. "What if there are more of these caves under the path ahead?"

Rolan knelt down and touched the edge of the hole. "Do you see these? They're tool marks. That means something made this deliberately."

Belac did not find that reassuring. "It also means that there could be more of these things. I do not want to get trapped in a hole, waiting for unlikely travelers to find us."

Rolan stood up again. "There might be more of them, but they probably won't fall in on us."

"Why not?" Belac was not convinced.

Rolan kicked at the edge of the trap. "This had to be made for a giant. Both of us are a lot lighter than he is." He nodded toward the hole. "If we don't walk right next to each other, and we pay attention to where we step, we should be fine."

Belac did not like that the dwarf's plan to avoid a trap was to walk into the trap. "That does not sound safe, Rolan."

Rolan shrugged. "If it makes you feel better, the giant made it all the way out here before he fell into one of these."

That did actually make Belac feel better. "Why are you so sure this was made for a giant?"

"What else could it be for?" Rolan asked. "If the trap had been made for something other than a giant, the giants would have made it."

Belac grinned. "Do you think he could have fallen into his own trap?"

Rolan shook his head and sighed. "I hope not."

Belac lost his grin. "Why?"

Rolan stared at the elf, stonefaced. "I really don't like having to ask stupid people for help."

Seventeen

"There are too many rocks," Belac complained.

Rolan responded irritably, "You can't not step on the rocks, Belac."

"Watch me!" Belac replied. *I am not falling in a hole!*

The elf walked along the edge of the path, careful to only step on solid ground. *The crazy dwarf can wade through the loose rocks if he wants, but when he falls in a hole, I am going to point at him and laugh.* He thought for a moment. *And then get out of the way before he shoots me.*

"I should have left you with the horses," Rolan grumbled.

Belac looked up. *That is a good idea! Why didn't I think of that? I could be with the horses, sleeping in the wagon while Vairug freezes in the mountains and worries about falling in a hole.* "Why did you bring me?"

"Because, you are The Dragon Slayer," Rolan replied shortly.

Belac nodded. *That does kind of make sense.* "But…"

Rolan held up a hand. "Quiet."

Belac stopped speaking. He stopped moving. The elf listened searchingly but could hear nothing other than the hollow sound of the wind sweeping through the mountains.

The path split a short way ahead. From the right, a giant strolled toward them. His exact size was difficult to make out at a distance, but he carried a two-handed great-hammer resting on his shoulder and walked as if he were in no hurry.

"Hello!" Belac called out loudly.

Rolan turned and looked at the elf furiously.

Belac held his hands out to his sides. "He said to make ourselves known."

Rolan frowned and turned back toward the giant.

The giant had stopped where the path split. He stood with the heavy, metal head of his great-hammer planted on the ground in front of his feet. His hands rested on the shaft in a way that suggested patience, if not peace. Swollen muscle and pale skin, the giant blocked their path as surely as a mountain.

I think I would rather try to climb a mountain. Belac tip-toed around the dwarf, being careful where he stepped. He waved to the giant. "Hello there."

The giant said nothing until the elf approached. "Are you here to fight?" His deep voice sounded older than that of the other giant's.

Belac shook his head quickly. "No!" He stared at the giant wide eyed, worried that he had made a mistake.

The giant was huge. He leaned over the great-hammer glaring down at the elf. The top of Belac's head only came to the bottom of the giant's chest. Unquestionably male, the giant wore nothing except a thick leather strap wrapped tightly around his left forearm. His white hair and complexion matched his brothers, but this was the first time that Belac had looked into a giant's eyes. Washed of color, the irises were a ring of white inside another of black. The effect made the giant appear insane.

"Why not?" the giant asked.

Because I don't want you to kill me! Belac shook his head some more.

"We should fight," the giant rumbled.

Belac continued to shake his head, trying to think of something to say. He pointed at the giant. "You are not allowed to eat me!"

The giant leaned back. "I will enjoy your death."

Belac stepped away. "Gordan said you wouldn't eat me!"

"Gordan?" the giant asked. "Do you mean Ghoram?"

Belac held up a finger. "Yeah! That's the one!"

The giant shook his head slowly. "Ghoram would not say that."

"He did!" Belac assured him. "Your Morgan, right?"

"Morkan!" the giant growled.

Belac took another step back, nodding. "Morkan, right." He held up his hands. "Ghoram needs your help."

This seemed to sober the giant. "He would not send you."

Belac made a conscience decision that he was not going to take another step back. "Your brother is stuck in a cave."

Morkan said nothing. He simply stood there, staring at the elf with his insane eyes.

"He fell into a hole and broke his leg," Belac continued. "He told us to find his brother," he gestured to the giant and was careful to say his name correctly, "Morkan." Belac decided that if the giant moved aggressively, he was going to rush forward and try to bury his dagger in its kneecap. *And then I am going to run.*

Morkan tilted his head to the side and grinned, the combination making him look more insane. "Did he threaten to eat you?"

Belac shook his head. "No. I… I just kind of assumed."

The giant laughed, and Belac almost took another step back despite himself.

"Take me to my brother." Morkan hefted his great-hammer to grip it beneath the heavy head.

Belac held up a hand to forestall the giant. "You are going to need a rope."

Morkan made a rumbling sound deep in his throat. "Wait here." He turned and ran back up the path that he had been guarding.

"That could have gone worse," Rolan said, not quite approvingly.

Belac jumped at the sound of the dwarf's voice. He put a hand to his chest, over his racing heart. "Why didn't you say something?"

Rolan shrugged. "He didn't want to fight me."

"He could have killed me!" Belac said accusingly.

Rolan raised his eyebrows and nodded as if to say, 'I know.'

Belac narrowed his eyes at the dwarf.

Rolan grinned.

Belac turned his attention to the path that the giant had taken. "Do you think he is getting a rope?"

"What else?" Rolan asked.

"I don't know," Belac shrugged. "Maybe he went to get a giant army." *I don't think that sounds right.* "An army of giants?"

"Giants don't have armies," Rolan said dismissively.

"Whatever." Belac did not care what the dwarf called them. "A giant angry mob of giants that wants to kill us."

"No." Rolan did not sound concerned. "He believed you."

Belac looked back to the dwarf. "You think?"

Rolan shrugged. "You're not dead."

"That's..." Belac nodded. "That's a good point." *The giant would not have needed an army to kill me.*

Rolan grunted in agreement.

"Hey, Rolan." Belac sounded a little uncomfortable.

Rolan responded, "What?"

"Um..." Belac coughed. "Why are they naked?"

"That is a bad question," Rolan told him.

Belac did not think it was a bad question. *People are supposed to wear clothes.* "Why? Is it rude to ask?"

"No." Rolan shook his head. "But you don't need a reason to not do something. Well... not unless you have another reason to do it, but that is sort of my point."

"What?" Belac felt like the dwarf was trying to be confusing.

"They don't have any reason to wear clothes," Rolan said more concisely.

Belac thought this might be part of the argument that the giants were better than everyone else. "They don't get cold?"

"Did he look cold to you?" Rolan asked.

Belac coughed. "No. No, he did not."

Eighteen

"Stop staring at me, and show me where my brother is." Morkan's deep voice was not winded despite his run. He had returned without his great-hammer, carrying instead a heavy coil of leather rope.

Belac coughed. "Um… Yeah." He turned and started walking back the way they had come. "But be careful, or you might fall into another one of the traps."

Morkan followed after the elf. "Did you make these traps?"

Belac shook his head. "Of course not!"

Rolan added, "We cannot even be sure that there are more traps."

Morkan seemed to believe them. "I will be careful."

As they retraced their steps, Rolan asked, "Do you know who might be trying to trap you?"

"It might be you," Morkan said.

Belac shook his head. "It's not us."

The giant offered no sign of agreement.

"You know?" Belac said a little perturbed. "You are not very friendly."

Rolan chuckled.

Morkan's frown could be heard when he spoke. "I will consider being friendly when I know my brother is safe."

Belac pointed. "He is in that hole over there."

"I see it." Morkan confirmed. He stepped around the elf and hurried toward his brother, his long gait moving him ahead quickly.

"Be careful!" Belac called after him and then grumbled, "Stupid giant."

Morkan leaned over the edge of the cave opening and called down to his brother in a language that Belac assumed was Giant. *What would that be called? Giantese?* The giant's deep voice did not sound concerned. It sounded like the giant was mocking his brother.

Ghoram yelled something back. He too did not sound concerned with his brother's safety.

Morkan laughed and began to ready the leather rope.

Belac leaned over the edge of the hole. "Did you miss us?"

Ghoram said something in Giant that made Rolan and Morkan laugh.

Something moved in the cave. A small shape emerged from one of the dark tunnels that surrounded the trapped giant. It began to take form as it moved closer to the light. It was shaped vaguely like a person and was dressed in hides, but its flesh was covered in pale blue scales, and it had a thick tail. Black, soulless eyes gleamed as the light illuminated its reptilian face.

Belac pointed. "What is that?!"

Morkan shouted something to his brother.

Ghoram turned and threw a rock at the creature. It dodged fluidly and then let out a hissing bark. It carried a primitive spear, and its malicious intent was obvious.

I can't let it kill the smith. Without a smith, there could be no magic sword. The quest would be over. There would be no way to stop the dragon. *There would be no Dragon Slayer.*

Belac grabbed the end of the leather rope and slid it through the ring on his waist harness. "Hold the rope!" Gripping the rope in one hand, he jumped into the cave.

The rope tightened and Belac swung inside the cave instead of crashing against the rock floor. His green cloak fanned out under his sword as the elf was spun around. He released the rope and fell the rest of the way into the cave. The distance of the fall was short enough for him to land safely, but he felt the shock ran up into his shins.

Remembering the last time he had tried to draw his sword, Belac lifted the scabbard over his head before pulling the blade free. He faced the creature with the sword in his right hand and the scabbard in his left. *What is that thing? It's like a… creepy, blue, lizard goblin.* The creature was no taller than Rolan, yet it attacked Belac without hesitation. It hissed at the elf and began to thrust wildly with its spear.

Belac was able to fend off the thrusts, but they were too fast for him to counter. Movement on his right warned him that he was being flanked. *I do not have time to dance with this thing.* He knocked the spear aside with his scabbard and thrust with his long-sword. The blade sank deep into the creature's chest and the tip of the sword was pulled down when it fell. Belac put his foot on the creature's chest and pulled his sword free just in time to swing the blade in a wide arc toward another of the creatures as it leapt at him. The blade caught the creature in midair, hacking through its arm and into its chest as it flew past.

Belac pointed his sword at the injured giant and called up to the opening of the cave. "Get him out!" *And then get me out!*

More of the creatures were coming. The elf had no way of knowing how many there would be. *If I am too defensive, I could be overwhelmed.* He looked at his sword. *I will need to rely on the blade's reach.*

Guttural hissing echoed from the dark tunnels around the elf. While fear could make their numbers sound larger than they were, Belac knew that there were too many of them for him to face alone. *I don't need to kill them all.* He took a deep breath. *Just enough to survive.*

One of the creatures rushed out of a tunnel on Belac's left. He pivoted and brought the end of his sword down on the scaly head. He controlled the momentum of the blade with a figure eight pattern and hacked into another reptilian face that was approaching on his right. *I cannot wait for them to attack first.* He took a step forward and swung the sword down at another of the creatures. Tiny, wicked teeth glistened as the creature hissed in defiance. It attempted to block with a spear, but the force of Belac's swing was too great and the elf's blade tore into the creature's torso.

More of the guttural hissing filled the rocky cave. Belac spun to face the danger behind him. Ghoram had tied the leather rope under his arms and was being slowly lifted toward the light above. Barely off the ground, he dangled like bait on a hook. Blue scales and vicious teeth moved in the shadows on the other side of the giant.

I have to stop them. Belac sprinted at an angle to his left. He ran up the wall of the cave and then kicked off, turning to his right. With a backhanded swing, he brought his sword down in a diagonal sweep that cleaved into the back of a reptilian skull. He continued to move forward, swinging his long-sword at another of the creatures. The creature screamed something that Belac did not understand before the blade bit into its face.

The remaining creatures turned from the giant and surged at the elf. Belac stepped away from the rising giant in hope that he would draw them away. With an awkward motion he deflected a thrusting spear to his right and then slammed his empty scabbard into the side of a reptilian head. He brought the scabbard back to the left, deflecting another spear while he stabbed at the staggered creature. The blade sank deep, but the elf was quick to jerk the sword free before it could be pulled down.

A spear's tip gouged into Belac's left side. He shied away from the pain and swung his sword up in a diagonal back cut that slashed open his attacker's chest. More of the creatures poured into the cave from the dark tunnels. Hissing barks and flashing teeth promised the elf more pain.

Small rocks fell from above as Ghoram was pulled out of the cave. *One less thing to worry about.* While Belac would no longer be distracted with protecting the giant, the creatures too were now of singular purpose. Soulless eyes tracked the elf as the creatures moved to surround him.

Belac raised his sword high into the air and shouted in the Elven tongue, "I am not food!" His azure blue eyes were alit with madness as he charged into battle.

Before Belac reached the first creature, a silvery bolt shot through its skull. The shot had come from above and to the left, so the elf moved left. With an aggressive forward back cut, he slashed at blue scales as he passed by. Another bolt shot down into the pack.

Belac pressed forward as the creatures tripped over their own dead. He brought the sword down in a diagonal backhand that cut one of the creatures in half. A silvery flash shot down from above. Belac stepped past the creature that he had cut in half and swung his sword into another. The blade hacked into flesh but was slowed by the hides the creature wore. The sword's edge was beginning to dull, and Belac was beginning to tire.

A clawed hand covered in blue scales gripped the elf's left arm. He tried to shake himself free, but the claws tore into him, drawing blood. Rolan continued to shoot down from the edge above, but the creatures were crawling over the corpses of their dead to get to Belac. The elf slammed the cross-guard of his sword into the reptilian head of the creature that held his arm. The cross-guard punctured the creature's skull, and Belac's arm was suddenly released. He ripped his sword free and slashed to his right. The blade cut into a creature's chest but caught on its spine. Belac's sword was wrenched from his hand as the creature was shoved aside by another. The oncoming creature took a bolt to the head and fell limply.

Rolan's strong voice ordered, "Grab the rope!"

Belac transferred his empty scabbard to his right hand and swung it like a club. The polished steel chape of the scabbard smashed into a scaly blue face.

Belac wrapped his left arm around the leather rope and then tugged on it three times in quick succession. The rope tightened, and he began to rise toward the opening above. He used the scabbard to knock away an overextended thrust of a spear, the motion causing him to spin gracelessly. The elf kicked in the air, trying to regain what control he could. He flailed with his scabbard, deflecting the thrusts of spears as he was lifted higher.

A sharp pain in the back of his left thigh informed Belac that he had missed one of the spears. He swung his scabbard behind him blindly. The attack connected with something, but it was too chaotic for him to know what he had hit. *I hope I took out one of its eyes!*

Once the elf had been lifted beyond their reach, one of the creatures threw its spear. Belac swatted the spear away with his scabbard, but he knew more would soon follow. The creatures hissed their fury at the prey that might escape them.

Belac's left hand dragged on chiseled rock. He twisted around to face the lip and pushed away with the scabbard clenched in his right fist. A spear flew past his boots as he swung backward. He whipped his feet up to brace himself against the crudely shaped rim of the opening. Another spear flew past behind him as he was pulled the rest of the way from the cave. Belac stumbled away from the hole before turning around to glare at it. He kicked a loose rock and sent it tumbling into the cave. *I am not food!*

Nineteen

"Your battle cry is, 'I am not food?" Rolan laughed.

"Die in a fire," Belac replied.

Rolan continued to laugh as he treated the elf's wounds.

"It sounds better in Elven!" Belac argued defensively.

Rolan stopped laughing long enough to say, "That is only because no one is going to understand what you are saying!"

Morkan spoke over the dwarf's laughter. "We cannot remain here." Despite his assertion, the giant did not sound frightened.

Rolan agreed with the giant. "Can you move your brother?"

"I can move myself!" Ghoram told the dwarf angrily.

Morkan ignored his brother's outburst. "His leg is too injured to walk on, but with my assistance, I believe we can manage."

Ghoram said something irritably in Giant.

"Right," Rolan responded. "Which means that we should not have to listen to you complain along the way."

Morkan laughed.

Belac felt exhausted. "Just give me a moment."

Rolan shook his head. "You have had a moment."

Ghoram said something in Giant that sounded snide.

Rolan nodded toward the giant. "He's right. The scalics will know a way around. They might take the time to organize before they come for us, but they will come for us. We need to move."

"Scalics?" Belac asked. "The creepy-blue-lizard-goblins?"

Rolan shook his head. "We are not calling them that."

"I don't care what we call them," Belac said. "Scalic' works for me." *It takes less time to say anyway.*

The loose rocks underfoot shifted as Morkan helped his brother to stand on his uninjured foot.

Ghoram said something in Giant that sounded remarkably unappreciative.

Belac spoke in Elven, "Do giants speak Elven?"

"Probably not," Rolan replied without bothering to speak in Elven.

In Elven, Belac suggested, "Maybe I should speak nothing but Elven until they realize I don't speak Giant."

Rolan replied in passable Elven, "Do you think that is a good way to make friends?"

Belac frowned. *He's right. We are here to ask for help. I am just being petty.* He stood and turned toward the giants. "You should let us go first and check for more traps."

"Good idea," Rolan said in response to both conversations.

Belac and Rolan began walking up the path, leaving Ghoram and Morkan to shuffle up behind them. Belac could tell that Rolan did not expect them to find another cave trap. *This still gives us the opportunity to seem more useful than we actually are.* Despite Rolan's apparent lack of concern, Belac was careful where he stepped. *We need to show the giants that we are doing more than just walking up the path. …Also, I really don't want to fall in another hole.*

"Hold up," Rolan said when they reached the split in the path.

Belac stopped and turned around to check on the trailing giants. They had not fallen into any traps, but Belac understood why Rolan wanted to wait for them.

"You still think the scalics are going to attack," Belac surmised.

"Oh, they are going to attack," Rolan assured him.

Belac looked at the dwarf. "Why are you so certain?"

"Scalics are extremely territorial," Rolan explained. "The giants started a war when they moved into this part of the mountains."

"Do you think the giants knew?" Belac asked.

Rolan shrugged. "They had to know it would come from somewhere. If not the scalics, then the Harbridgers, or something else."

Belac did not understand the dwarf's assertion. "Who expects to be hunted by creepy-blue-lizard-goblins that live under the rocks?"

"We are not calling them that," Rolan said reflexively.

"Fine." Belac saw no reason to argue about it. "Scalic. Whatever."

"If it was not scalics, it would be something else," Rolan explained. "Nothing likes living around giants."

"Why?" The giants did not seem too bad to Belac. *If they would just put on clothes…*

Rolan shrugged. "They're giants."

Once upon a time, the answer may have been enough for Belac. That was before his best friend happened to be an orc. *If you think the world is simple, it's not. You are.* He looked at the dwarf, another friend. "You don't have a beard."

Rolan looked at the elf sideways. "So?"

Belac shrugged. "Everyone knows that dwarves have beards." He hoped the dwarf would understand his point.

Rolan frowned in thought for a moment. "A wise man once said, 'Extremism is the intellectual inability to distinguish nuance."

Belac thought that the dwarf was agreeing with him. He smiled. "It was Serath, right?"

Rolan turned and started up the path to the right.

Belac caught up to the dwarf and circled around to face him. "I'm right! It was Serath!"

Rolan grumbled, "It was Serath."

Belac nodded. "That sounds like something a wizard would say."

Something splattered on the elf's left shoulder. Without thinking, Belac reached up to his shoulder to investigate. His hand smeared white paste across the green of his cloak. Disgusted, he pulled his hand away and looked to the sky in search of the perpetrator. A bird that he thought may have been an eagle flew high in the sky.

Belac looked at the white mess on his hand and then held it away from himself, unsure what to do about it. *Ugh. I want this off.* He tried to sling it off his hand to no avail. Finally, he simply wiped his hand on the side of his cloak.

Rolan grinned. "That is supposed to be lucky."

Belac narrowed his eyes at the dwarf. "Bad luck is still luck."

Rolan chuckled. "You think you have bad luck?"

Belac shook his head. "No. I think this stupid cloak that you're making me wear has bad luck!" He pointed a mostly clean finger at the dwarf. "And you know why!"

"It's green?" Rolan asked in mock speculation.

"It's green!" Belac confirmed angrily.

With Ghoram's arm over Morkan's shoulders for support, the giants had continued their approach and were now close enough to join the conversation.

Morkan questioned them in a tone without inflection. "Why are you arguing?"

Rolan nodded toward the elf. "He thinks it's my fault a bird marked him."

Belac shook his head. "It did not 'mark' me, Rolan. It..."

Morkan cut the elf off. "How could that be his fault?" He looked at the dwarf. "Do you command the raptor?"

Belac narrowed his eyes at the dwarf. *He had better not!*

Rolan shook his head, smiling. "I did not even see the bird."

Ghoram said something in Giant.

Rolan looked at the elf. "Do you want to tell them?"

Belac suddenly felt exposed. "What I want, is for us to get moving." He pointed behind himself with his thumb. "We need to stop standing around here, and get somewhere safe."

Rolan nodded, frowning happily. "You heard The Dragon Slayer. Let's get moving." He marched off past the elf.

Belac turned and followed the dwarf up the path, eager to leave the conversation behind.

In obvious disbelief, Morkan asked, "You claim the elf is a dragon slayer?"

"The Dragon Slayer," Rolan corrected the giant.

Morkan laughed, almost dropping the other giant.

Ghoram spoke, this time in Dwarven. "Do not laugh brother. I have witnessed." The phrase seemed to have a deeper meaning. "The elf is fierce."

It did not go unnoticed that the giant had spoken in Dwarven. *He wanted me to hear that. He wanted me to understand.* Still, Belac felt as if he were missing something. He stopped and faced the giants. "Then, will you help me?"

Morkan's insane looking eyes widened. "To kill a dragon?"

Despite how similar Ghoram's eyes were to his brother's, they looked more tired than insane. "Not even a giant could kill a dragon."

"I don't need you to kill it," Belac told him. "I just need you to make me a sword."

"The lands of man have many swords," Ghoram replied cryptically.

Belac's clear blue eyes met the giant's insane rings. "I need a special one."

Ghoram did not look away. "One forged by a giant."

Joining them, Rolan said, "That's why we're here."

Morkan gazed intently at the elf. "You wish to be legend."

Rolan answered for the elf. "Maybe a giant can't kill a dragon. But a legend can."

Ghoram's attention never left the elf. "Then, you will have your sword."

Twenty

Belac looked back at the giants that followed a short way behind them. "Do you think they are really going to make the sword for me?" he asked the dwarf.

"That is what they said," Rolan replied.

Belac turned his attention to the dwarf. "People can say anything they want. That does not make it true."

Rolan chuckled.

Belac narrowed his eyes at the dwarf. "What is so funny?"

"You. Accusing other people of lying." Rolan laughed. "I watched you convince three countries that an orc was the long lost king of Enevic."

Belac frowned. "I never said he was the king."

Rolan laughed some more.

It bothered the elf that Rolan thought of him as a liar. When Belac thought about Rolan, he felt like he could trust him. *He has always been honest with me. Even when I did not like it.* Belac regretted that he had not made the dwarf feel the same way about him. He felt as if he had lost something and did not know how to get it back. In his mind, he heard the wizard's words. *"Everything you do."* He thought that he might finally be starting to understand what the wizard had meant when he said that everything had a cost.

Belac dismissed the unpleasant thoughts. "I asked what you thought. Not, what they said."

Rolan nodded. "I think they said that they would forge the sword for you."

Belac imagined the dwarf falling into a trap and getting eaten by creepy-blue-lizard-goblins. "And, what do you think about what they said?"

Rolan shrugged. "I think that's the most we can hope for right now. We asked for help. They said, 'yes.' Were you expecting a signed contract?"

Belac wondered how long it would take him to dig one of those cave traps by himself. *It would only need to be big enough for a dwarf.*

Rolan clapped the elf on the shoulder. "Don't worry about it so much. When we get to the giants' camp, I will sit down with them and work out all the details."

Belac thought he understood what the dwarf was telling him. "You want me to let you do the talking."

"I want you to let me negotiate," Rolan corrected him. "After that, you can talk as much as you want to."

Belac considered arguing, but decided to trust the dwarf. "Is there anything I should not say?"

Rolan nodded. "There is a lot you should not say."

Belac frowned and repeated something the dwarf had said often. "You are going to need to be more specific."

Rolan chuckled. "Maybe don't tell them that you keep getting thrown in prison."

As they continued on, the mountains began to crowd closer until there were steep cliffs rising to either side of the path. There was plenty of space for the giants to walk, but the undeniable size of the mountains made Belac feel small. They reminded him that there were things in the world far greater than he was. *I don't like it.*

The faint sound of hammering began to echo through the pass. *We must be getting close.* Belac wondered how Rolan and he would be received by the other giants. He thought back on how they had met Ghoram and Morkan. *Hopefully, better than that.*

As it turned out, the giants did not have a camp. What they had were giant walls of steel that lined a portion of the cliff face on both sides of the mountain pass. Oversized doors and shutters of gleaming metal made it obvious that the giants did not welcome visitors. While all the doors on the left were shut tight, a set of sliding double doors stood open farther ahead on the right. Orange light and the sound of hammering came from the open doors. It was impossible for Belac to know how far into the side of the mountain the complex encroached; however, he felt it was safe to assume that it would be sized for giants.

Belac glanced at the dwarf. "This is more than a camp, Rolan."

Rolan nodded. "Your right. This is not something temporary. The giants plan on staying."

Belac looked back to the dwarf. "Is that a problem?"

Rolan shook his head. "Not for us." He shrugged. "It's just not what I was expecting."

That sounded like a problem to Belac. "What were you expecting?"

"Leather hides and caves," Rolan said.

Belac pointed to the open doors leading into the metal wall on the right. "That is sort of a cave." *A cave with a metal wall in front of it is still a cave.*

"It is the permanence," Rolan tried to explain. "That is what's important here."

"Why?" Belac asked. "You said the mountains belong to Enevic, and they are all dead." *Well, except Ecard. But that man is not any threat to the giants.*

Rolan shook his head. "The mountains might technically belong to Enevic, but the giants are not supposed to be this far south. If the Harbridgers find out the giants are here, they will have to do something about it. The giants know that." He gestured to the metal walls. "And they are preparing to stay anyway."

"War," Belac predicted.

Rolan nodded gravely.

It occurred to Belac that the dwarf might be overlooking something. "They may not let us leave."

Rolan tilted his head to the side and frowned as if he had tasted something sour. "That's possible, but I don't think we have to worry about that."

"Because we helped them?" Belac guessed.

Rolan shook his head. "We are not humans." He gestured to himself. "That means we are not Harbridgers. I can probably convince them to let us go."

Belac did not find that very reassuring.

Rolan continued, "Besides, they agreed to forge the sword for you. They can't do that and keep us here."

Belac looked at Ghoram and Morkan as they approached. *I hope giants are honorable.*

Rolan nudged the elf. "I am going to help them inside and then see what I can work out. You can rest here for a bit, but I expect they will want to talk to you too."

Rolan went to help the giants, but there was nothing for him to do other than holding open one of the steel doors on the left. He followed the two giants inside, leaving Belac alone in the shadowed mountain pass.

The elf waited patiently for all of a dozen heartbeats, before walking over to the open double doors to investigate. The hammering sounded like a smithy to Belac. *Maybe they have more than one smith.* If given the choice, he would have preferred a giant smith without a broken leg.

As expected, Belac found that the doorway led to a smithy. A cave had been cut into the rock of the mountain side and then smoothed into a large chamber. The smithy was sweltering hot despite the ventilation shafts cut into the high ceiling above. A giant stood on the other side of a glowing forge, shaping steel. Belac watched as the giant hammered the glowing metal, but could not discern what was being forged. The giant set down its hammer and tongs and then stepped away from the forge. It removed a heavy leather apron and set it aside. The giant stared down at the elf inquisitively.

Belac had meant to say, 'hello.' Truly, he had. However, standing before the unclothed giantess, he forgot how to formulate thought. He stared at her unimaginably perfect proportions and realized that her size only made them easier to appreciate.

"You have come a long way to stare at me," the giantess said.

It took every bit of self-control Belac possessed to move his gaze up to the giantess's face. Her long white hair had been pulled back and it drew his attention to the insane rings in her eyes. *Even those are beautiful.* He could not remember how to speak.

"How are you here?" the giantess asked.

Belac did not understand the question. He may have been able to explain 'why' he was there, but even that would have been difficult at the moment. His eyes began to travel down.

The giantess seemed unconcerned by his attention. "Speak, Elf."

"Belac," he managed to say.

"Belac?" the giantess repeated. "It that the Elven word for..."

"Nope," Belac interrupted her. "That's me. That's my name. Belac. I'm an elf." *Stop talking.* He looked back up at her face and smiled.

"I am Breana." There was a depth to her voice, though it was no less feminine for having it. "Why are you here, Belac the elf?"

Belac almost said that it was to see her, but stopped himself. "I came to ask the giants to make me a sword."

Breana's high cheekbones seemed to harden. "The giants are not for hire."

Belac shook his head. "Ghoram already said he would help."

"Ghoram?" Breana looked like she had been slapped. "Ghoram told you that he would forge a sword for you?"

Belac nodded. "I need it to kill a dragon."

Breana laughed.

Belac would have been willing to brave the mountains just to hear that laugh.

Breana's smile was a lovely thing to behold. "I did not know that elves were funny." She shook her head. "No one kills a dragon."

Twenty-One

Belac attempted to stand taller. "Well, I'm killing one anyway," he told the giantess.

Breana gestured to the elf. "You think you are going to kill a dragon?" She laughed again.

Belac had to force himself to keep his eyes on the giantess's face. *It is a beautiful face.* He nodded. "Yes."

She stopped laughing but continued to smile. "How are 'You' going to kill a dragon?"

Belac had been ready for the question. "With the sword Ghoram said he would make for me," he explained. "That's why we are here." *Though, I would have come just to stare at you.*

Breana shook her head. "You will need more than a sword to kill a dragon. Ghoram is not a wizard." She laughed at the idea.

"Not a problem," Belac told the giantess. "I already have one of those." *Well… sort of. …maybe. …I hope Serath is not dead.*

Breana appraised the elf as if she thought this might be another joke. "You have a wizard?" She tilted her head in disbelief. "A wizard?"

Belac chose not to be offended. "How else am I going to make a magic sword?" He held his hands out to his sides. "I need a giant to make the sword, and I need a wizard to make it magic."

"You're insane," said the giantess with insane looking eyes. "Ghoram would never agree to this."

Belac dropped his hands and frowned. "He already has." The elf smiled. "He said he witnessed my bravery, and now he is going to help me become a legend." *I may have left out some of the conversation.*

Breana was no longer smiling. "Ghoram said he witnessed you?"

Belac nodded agreeably. "After I saved him from the creepy-blue-lizard-goblins."

"You are insane." Breana shook her head. "How did you get here?"

Belac thought the question odd. *Maybe it is because I told her I have a wizard? Maybe she thinks I have a magic carpet or something.* "I walked." *I really need to get a magic carpet.*

Breana was unsatisfied with the answer. "How did you find us?"

"Oh!" Belac nodded. "Serath told us where to look. That's the wizard." He gestured back to the open doors. "And then Ghoram told us how to get here."

Breana shook her head. "Ghoram would not tell you that."

"He needed us to find Morkan," Belac explained. "Ghoram fell into a cave and broke his leg. We needed help to get him out."

Breana attempted to restrain a grin. "Ghoram fell into a cave?"

Belac nodded. "It was a trap. The scalics made it." He realized he had not told her what a scalic was. "Those are the creepy-blue-lizard-goblins."

"The things you say you saved Ghoram from?" Breana sounded unconvinced.

Belac decided that the giantess was too pretty for him to be mad at. "I jumped into the cave and fought them while Ghoram was pulled to safety." There was more than a trace of pride in his voice.

"You fought creepy-blue-lizard-goblins with your bare hands?" Breana asked as if she were pointing out a hole in his story.

Belac removed his empty scabbard and showed it to her. "I had a sword."

"You had a sword?" Breana asked, still not believing the elf.

"I lost it fighting the scalics." Belac returned the empty scabbard to his back. He pulled aside his cloak and pointed to the bloody tear in the side of his shirt. "They poked me a few times too."

Breana leaned down to inspect the wound. "Why would you fight to save Ghoram?"

It sounds like she is starting to believe me. Belac considered saying something to make himself seem braver than he was. *"Everything you do."* The elf decided to tell her the truth. "He said he was a smith."

Breana leaned back and looked down at the elf. "All giants are 'smiths." She said the word 'smith' as if it were a pejorative. She gestured to the empty scabbard on his back. "You already had a sword. Why would you risk your life to get another one?"

Once again, Belac considered bravado. He could have told the giantess that he had been unafraid. He could have claimed that he was someone who would imperil his life for a stranger. He could have even suggested that he enjoyed the thrill of combat. Instead, he told her the truth. "The sword I need has to be made in a special place, and it has to be made by a giant."

While she may not have believed the elf, Breana seemed intrigued. "Why must this sword be forged by a giant?"

Belac shrugged. "Serath says that the sword has to be made by a giant for the ritual to work. Serath is the wizard," he reminded her. "It also has to be made out of starmetal."

Breana laughed again. She turned and rested one hand on a workbench as if she needed the support to keep from falling over.

Belac enjoyed watching her laugh. *I would be willing to watch her do just about anything.*

Breana looked at the elf with a tear in her eye. "I think I might keep you. Are you always this funny?"

If anyone was going to keep Belac, he would have wanted it to be the giantess. *The problem is, she sounds like she thinks I'm a pet.* He was flattered, offended, and disconcerted all at once. Not knowing what to say, he simply continued to watch her laugh.

From behind the elf, Morkan said, "I see that you have met Breana."

Belac turned toward the voice. Next to Morkan, stood Rolan. The dwarf stared stupidly at the giantess as she laughed. *I can't say I blame him.* Belac suddenly felt like he himself had been caught doing something he shouldn't.

"Morkan!" Breana began to speak to the other giant in their own language. She sounded like she was telling him a joke.

Morkan waited patiently.

Breana paused, and then spoke as if she were explaining the joke.

When the giantess stopped, Morkan replied in Dwarven, "What the elf says is true."

Breana looked at the elf and spoke in Giant incredulously.

Morkan looked at the elf as well, though he spoke in Dwarven. "No. We cannot help them. Ghoram is too injured to travel, and I must remain in case of conflict."

Belac felt lied to. "You agreed to help me." *So much for the honor of giants.*

Breana said something angrily in Giant.

Morkan said, "I am willing to forge a sword, but I cannot leave our home." It was uncertain whom he was speaking to.

Breana gestured vaguely to her right and shouted in Giant.

Morkan replied in Giant, his tone no longer patient.

Breana pointed at the giant and began to berate him. Belac did not understand what she was saying, but her scorn was unmistakable.

Rolan evidently agreed with her. "I think that is a wonderful idea."

Belac had forgotten that the dwarf was there. *Not my fault. That woman is distracting.*

Breana looked at the dwarf as if she had not noticed him before. "Who are you?"

Rolan walked over to the giantess and looked up into her eyes. He was tall for a dwarf, but he stood no taller than her hips. "My name is Rolan. And I think you are absolutely right."

Breana's smile seemed to brighten the room. She nodded and then turned away.

Morkan said something in Giant. He did not sound pleased.

Breana ignored him. She took a large hide satchel from one of the workbenches and began stuffing tools into it.

Still speaking in Giant, Morkan said something that sounded like a threat.

Rolan's response was not friendly.

Belac was beginning to think that Giant was not a friendly language.

Breana turned to look at the dwarf but said nothing.

Rolan was staring at Morkan as if he were about to climb up there and cut out the giant's eyes. Belac did not know what would happen if they fought, but he was sure that he would not have bet against Rolan.

Morkan threw up his hands, shouted in Giant, and then stormed out of the smithy.

Rolan continued to stare at the doorway until they heard another metal door slam shut. He turned around and said, "We need to leave now."

Belac did not understand how everything had gone wrong so fast. "We can't just leave, Rolan. We need a smith. We have to convince one of them to come with us."

"We have a smith," Rolan stated plainly.

Belac was confused for a moment. *He thinks he can make the sword himself!* Belac shook his head. "It has to be a giant."

Rolan gestured behind the elf. "We have one."

Belac turned around, still confused. Breana slung her satchel over her head and ran the strap across her chest between her breasts. Belac remembered her words. *"All giants are smiths."*

Breana picked up a long leather cord and began to wrap it around her left forearm. "If the men are too weak to bear our honor, then I will."

Twenty-Two

Belac followed behind Rolan and Breana as they journeyed through the mountains. And while the view was pleasant, Belac really wanted someone to explain what had just happened. Rolan and Breana had continued to speak with each other after leaving the giants' stronghold. *The problem is I don't speak Giant.* Belac thought for a moment. *No. The problem is that they refuse to speak a proper language!*

Belac decided to say something. "Do one of you want to tell me what just happened back there?"

"No," Rolan said without turning.

Breana nudged the dwarf but laughed. She turned to look back at the elf, smiling. "What do you not understand, Belac?"

Belac knew that the giantess was trying to be nice, but he thought she might not comprehend what 'not understanding' was. "How about we start with why Morkan suddenly wants to kill us!"

Rolan grumbled, "I think Morkan probably always wanted to kill us."

Breana frowned at the dwarf in a way that seemed more like a smile. "Morkan did not wish for me to leave." She glanced back toward the elf. "So then, he behaved like a fool."

"Yeah, I got that part," Belac said irritably.

Breana frowned at the elf. It did not resemble a smile in the least. "Then, what do you not understand?"

Belac threw up his hands. "Why are you coming with us?!"

Rolan answered. "We need a smith," he said in a matter-of-fact tone that made the elf want to kick him in the back of the head.

"I know we need a smith, Rolan!" Belac gestured back toward the giants' stronghold. "Surely, we could have found another giant to come with us that was a…"

Breana stopped and glared at the elf. "A what?"

Belac halted at the challenge in that glare. He almost turned around and ran away. "A…" He coughed. *Do not say 'a man.'* "A… A less important person."

Rolan laughed.

Belac narrowed his eyes at the dwarf.

Rolan stood with his arms crossed in a posture that clearly relayed that the elf was on his own.

"Oh?" Breana asked in complete disbelief. "You would rather have your sword forged by someone that is less important?"

Belac held up his hands in surrender. "I mean, someone less important to Morkan. If he did not want you to go with us, he could have just sent a different giant instead."

Breana's glare became a look of suspicion. "There is no one else to send. Lamana and Helana are away." She shook her head and leaned forward. "Even if they were here, they would not go with you."

There are no other giants? Belac tried to make sense of what he was being told. "Then, why are you coming with us?"

Rolan grumbled, "We need a smith," but to the elf it sounded like, *"Shut up before you change her mind."*

Breana answered for herself. "Ghoram promised to forge your sword in payment for saving his life." She pointed at the elf aggressively. "I will not be the daughter of an oath breaker!"

The daughter? Belac grinned. "I saved your father!"

Breana said something irritably in Giant before turning around and continuing down the path.

Belac waited until the giantess was far enough away that he did not think she would hear him. "Are we really going to let her make the sword for us?" he asked the dwarf.

Rolan stopped smiling but kept his arms crossed. "That woman is stronger than any human man that has ever existed. She is older, wiser, and more experienced in the forging of metal than any human smith. We are not only going to let her make the sword, we are going to thank her for doing it." The dwarf turned and walked off after the giantess.

Belac's concern was not that Breana was a woman. *The problem is that she is just too pretty.* Weapons and war were ugly things to the elf. He felt that their creation was better left to ugly people. If Belac was going to face a dragon with nothing but a sword in hand, he wanted it forged by the ugliest and meanest person he could imagine. He felt like Breana was simply too good to create the weapon he needed.

Nothing seemed right to Belac. Serath was supposed to be there. Vairug was supposed to be there. And Breana was supposed to be an insane, terrifying giant of war. Something was wrong. Something was responsible for all this. And Belac had a definite idea what that was. *It is this stupid green cloak!* He knew it to his bones. *When I get out of these mountains, I am going to set this thing on fire!* In discontented silence, the elf began a determined march out of the mountains. He had a cloak to burn.

Belac caught up to Rolan and Breana at the opening to the cave trap. The giantess was staring down into the hole studying something while the dwarf waited patiently.

Breana turned at the elf's approach. "You jumped in there?" Her tone did not suggest it had been bravery.

Belac pulled back his cloak and gestured to his harnessing belt. "I sort of swung halfway down and then fell the rest of the way. There was not a lot of time to plan."

Searching for conformation, Breana looked from the elf to the dwarf. *She thinks I am a liar too!*

Rolan nodded. "He jumped."

Breana returned her attention to the darkened hole. "And then you fought in there?"

Belac nodded though he knew the giantess could not see him. He did not think she really wanted an answer anyway. He joined her next to the hole and looked down into the darkening cave. The bodies of the dead scalics were no longer there. Whatever had taken the corpses away had also taken his sword. The cave had grown dark in the fading of day, but Belac knew that the rock below would be stained with blood long after he had quit the mountains.

"What are you smiling at?" Breana asked the elf.

Belac had not realized that he was smiling. In Elven, he said, "I am not food."

Rolan chuckled. "Let's hope they remember that." He walked around the hole to continue down the path.

Breana followed after the dwarf. "What did he say?"

She could have just asked me. I am standing right here!

Rolan answered with amusement. "The resolving battle cry of the Elven house of Melavar."

"Hey!" Belac shouted. "Who said you could go around telling people my name?" Then he added, "Rolan Brightstone."

Rolan looked back and frowned at the elf. "You wanted to be a famous dragon slayer but not have anyone know your name?"

"I…" Belac had not considered that. *What I want, is for no one to come and try to kill Belac Melavar!*

Breana smiled at the dwarf. "Your name is 'Brightstone?' That is a beautiful name."

Rolan grumbled. "That is not my name. It's my family's name. I am not allowed to use it."

That seemed strange to Belac. "Why not?" *Even I can use my family's name if I want to.*

Rolan shrugged dismissively. "Dwarven culture is complicated. We use a caste system. That makes names a bit more significant than they are for other people."

Breana was careful with her question. "Did they find you unworthy?"

Rolan shook his head. "It is more complicated than that. Every system, every culture, will have those that suffer for it. It would be great if that suffering were limited to the people that deserved it, but that is just not how it works."

How can he be so calm? While Belac could not have articulated the thought, what bothered him was the idea that an entire civilization was willing to collectively decide to deny the truth of who a person was. "Why are you not more upset?"

Rolan shrugged again. "It was a long time ago, Belac." Amusement bled into his voice. "I was not always so... understanding."

Belac had never thought of the dwarf as someone who would be 'understanding' if wronged. "What changed?"

Rolan sighed. "I traveled the world. And I found that there was more to it, than my own misfortune."

Twenty-Three

Rolan growled.

Even though Belac walked three paces behind, he worried that the dwarf might turn around and bite him. He considered diminutive murderer warily. *I am not food!*

Breana did not seem worried that she would get bitten. She looked around at the gray mountains that surrounded them. "Are you mad at the rocks?" she asked playfully.

"I smell a fire," Rolan said irritably.

Breana sniffed at the air with her perfectly shaped nose. "I smell it too."

Rolan nodded. "So does everything else around." He increased the speed of his stride. "I said, no fires."

As Belac hurried after the dwarf, he was suddenly worried about the absent orc. *Dragons breathe fire.* "Do you think Vairug got eaten by the dragon?"

On reflex, Rolan said, "There is no dragon, Belac."

Easily matching his pace, Breana looked down at the dwarf. "If there is no dragon, then why do you need a magic sword that can kill a dragon?"

Rolan frowned up at the giantess. "Fine. There is a dragon. There is just not a dragon right here, right now." He pointed down the path with his whole hand. "What there is, is a reckless orc, doing something stupid."

Breana smiled down at the dwarf's frown. "You travel with an orc?" she asked with an amused surprise.

Rolan returned his attention down the rocky path. "It's complicated," he said dismissively.

"No, it's not," Belac disagreed without thinking. "Vairug is our friend, and he wants to help us kill Danorin."

"Danorin?" Breana asked with less amusement in her voice.

Belac nodded. "That's the dragon."

Breana did not need the explanation. "I know what The Danorin is." She shook her head. "I hope you die bravely."

I don't! Belac decided that they needed to get another giant. He did not want one that expected him to die. He wanted one that would let him ride on its shoulders while they charged into battle screaming in defiance. *Wait a moment... That sounds an awful lot like dying bravely.* "Well, I hope we come up with a better plan than that."

When they finally reached the base of the mountain, Vairug was nowhere to be seen. Belac looked out over the rolling hills of golden grass. *Where would he go?* Belac revisited the idea that the orc may have been eaten. *I guess something other than a dragon could have eaten him.*

Vairug stepped away from the wagon and walked over to join them. *Oh, yeah. The wagon.* The orc stopped a short distance away and stared openly at the unclothed giantess. Rolan glared at him, but Vairug did not seem to notice. *Completely understandable.*

Belac gestured to the orc. "Breana, this is Vairug. He's an orc." Belac then gestured to the giantess. "Vairug, this is Breana. She is a giant."

Vairug did not look away from the giantess. "The giants are very pretty," he said by way of introduction.

Rolan grumbled, "Not all of them." He marched past the orc. "We got lucky."

Breana looked at the orc like he was a puppy that had just done a backflip. "Hello, Vairug."

Rolan kicked dirt at the remains of a small fire. "I said no fires, Vairug."

Vairug turned calmly to face the dwarf. "I kept it small. It is daytime; no one saw it. And the smoke will not travel to the road."

"I could smell it," Rolan argued irritably.

"The wind is blowing toward the mountains." Vairug shrugged. "I caught a squirrel and wanted to cook it."

Belac pointed at the orc dramatically. "You ate my squirrel!"

Vairug looked back at the elf as if he thought he was crazy. "Then, put your name on the next one."

He ate my squirrel! Belac did not understand why it bothered him so much. He thought about it for a moment. *I guess I can forgive him. The squirrel was kind of rude anyway.*

Breana walked toward the dark Enevician horses. "Those are beautiful."

"Don't eat them!" Belac said, remembering the story of the giant that had eaten the king's horse.

Breana gave the elf a perturbed look. "Why would I eat them?" She ran her fingers through one of the horses' black manes. "They are such beautiful creatures."

"Yes," Vairug said. "Beautiful."

Belac did not think that the orc was referring to the horses. *Am I the only one that wanted an ugly giant?*

Rolan waved negligently toward the setting sun. "We need to bed down for the night. I want to have this wagon ready to move before dawn. And that means waking up early."

Belac gestured to the wagon. "I don't think we can all fit in there, Rolan. Where is everyone going to sleep?"

Rolan nodded toward the giantess. "Breana is going to keep watch and make sure that we wake up early enough to get this wagon moving on time."

Belac considered the giantess. "Don't giants need to sleep too?"

"She can sleep in the wagon tomorrow on the way to Harbridge," Rolan stipulated. "But if her uncle shows up in the night looking for her, I want her awake."

Her uncle? Belac was confused for a moment. *Morkan!* He felt like he really should have put that together sooner. *If Morkan is Ghoram's brother, and Ghoram is Breana's father, then that makes Morkan Breana's uncle.* Morkan's behavior suddenly made more sense to the elf. *He did not want his niece to go running off with two strange men that she had just met.* Belac almost laughed.

Rolan frowned at the elf. "You are not going to think it's funny if you wake up to an angry giant."

Belac recalled the threatening, insane look of the giant's eyes, but he did not think that Morkan would try to kill them in their sleep. The elf kept his smile and walked past Rolan to where Breana stood with the horses. Belac removed his baldric and then unbuckled his cloak. He held the heavy green cloth out to the giantess.

Breana took the cloak with a questioning look.

Belac nodded to the cloak. "You can lay it out and have something to sit on."

Breana's smile had a slight touch of surprise in it. "Thank you, Belac."

The elf shrugged and tried not to blush. *I just want to get rid of the thing.* He glanced at the remnants of Vairug's small campfire. *And I don't think Rolan is going to let me burn it.* Belac smiled shyly and nodded to the giantess before turning and walking over to the back of the wagon. He tossed his empty scabbard inside the cabin and then sat down in the doorway. He dug into the bag at his side and pulled out the wrapped ration. *I should have eaten this earlier.*

Belac still could not taste anything. He sniffed at the food. *Maybe that is a good thing.* He could not smell the rations, but he did not think that they would have smelled appealing if he could. *I just hope my taste comes back in time to have a real meal.*

Rolan walked up to the elf and stared at him for a moment. "You are in the way."

Belac's back straitened. *That is kind of a hurtful thing to say.*

Rolan waved impatiently. "Move."

"Oh!" Belac scooted to the side so that the dwarf could step past him.

Rolan went inside the cabin and began to arrange things for the night. The sound of the boxes being moved around was loud in the closed space, but Belac did his best to ignore it. He finished eating and then crawled into the wagon.

Taking a seat on one of the benches, Belac asked, "Do you know where my other sword is?"

"The one you stole from Lorance?" Rolan questioned in response.

"I did not steal it," Belac argued. "He was already dead when I took it."

Rolan chuckled. "So, if a couple of guys kill you and then take your coin purse, you would not call it stealing?"

"I would not call it anything," Belac replied. "I would be dead."

"Right." Rolan nodded. "But that is still a seriously big loophole."

"Fine." Belac changed tact. "I am just borrowing it. If Lorance wants his sword back, all he has to do is let me know."

Rolan held up a hand to stop the elf. "So, if a rotting corpse walks up to you and says," he held out his arms and spoke in a slow, deep voice, "Give. Me. My. Sword." He dropped his arms and laughed. "You are going to just hand it over to him?"

Belac laughed with the dwarf. "I never agreed to give it to him hilt first."

Twenty-Four

That night, Belac dreamed of Emily. He was with the princess once more in the nillanan's domain. This time, they were alone. This time, things were different.

The world felt washed away and nothing seemed true except Emily. The princess stared back at him from across a stone table, complete trust in her eyes. Golden hair framed the noble features of her face, and Belac wanted nothing more than to reach out and touch the delicate skin of the cheek beneath. She was an icon of innocence too lovely to behold. He looked away.

Instead, Belac studied the magic charm in his hand. It was a thing without form or substance; however, its power was undeniably real. He held the power of life and death itself. Life for one, and death for another. He had chosen life; life for himself. And in so doing, he had chosen death for another. He had chosen death for Emily. *I killed her.*

Belac's lost gaze returned to the princess. They were now on the mechanical lift, rising slowly to the freedom above. Emily was dead in his arms. Her lifeless eyes stared back at him. *A blue that could have been the sky…* He wept, and tears rained down on her face.

Never had the elf known such sorrow. Even when he had held her in his arms last, he had escaped the depth of his emotion. Now, he drowned. There was nothing but sorrow. *Soon, there will be nothing left of me.* Belac clung to the memory of Emily as if he clung to himself.

The world rocked, and strange noise pressed in. Belac felt like his heart was being washed away with the dream.

"...Attack!" a woman's strong voice cried out.

The dream was shaken away as a gruff voice ordered, "Get up!"

Belac's eyes opened to darkness and confusion. He could hear scuffling outside the wagon. Rolan turned away, put his hand on Vairug's shoulder, and vaulted feet first over the orc. He landed in front of the door and threw it open before flying out into the night.

Moonlight lit the inside of the cabin and brought with it a sense of reality. Vairug rose from the floor, his cogged mace glinting as he charged out of the wagon.

Belac's heart was racing, but his thoughts were still slow. *I need to move faster.* Whatever was happening, he did not want his friends to have to face it without him. He grabbed his boots and began to tug them on as fast as he could. The sounds of battle and guttural hissing informed the elf what awaited him outside. *It's the creepy-blue-lizard-goblins!* The horses screamed and then Belac heard the sound of something heavy hitting the ground.

Remembering to take his new sword with him, Belac scampered out of the cabin. The moon was so bright, the elf almost needed to shield his eyes. He had stepped into yet another surreal world; one of black and white contrast that left the colors of life forgotten. Belac drew his sword and then tossed the empty scabbard back into the cabin. He felt the uneven leather that wrapped the hilt of the sword digging into his palm. *I hope this sword works as well as the last one.* He immediately changed his mind. *Better! I hope it works better!*

Rolan's voice called out in the night. "Vairug! Get the horses!"

Belac did not know how Vairug was going to do that with only one hand while also carrying a mace. *Can orcs juggle? Who would not want to see an orc juggle?* The scalics that attacked Belac afforded him no time to consider it further. The suddenness of their attack reminded the elf that he needed to pay more attention to not dying. Had they not hissed at him, Belac may have died unaware, thinking about an orcish carnival.

Belac swung his sword up and to his left, the back of the blade cutting into a hissing face. Black blood sprayed from pale scales bleached by the moonlight. Taking the hilt in both hands, Belac turned the swords momentum in the air above him and brought the blade down and through the torso of another scalic. He lifted the sword back up above him and then twisted sideways as he dodged a spear thrust toward his midsection. Swinging the sword down, he hacked into the back of the attacking scalic's neck, severing its reptilian head.

Wanting to finish the last of his attackers quickly, Belac thrust his long blade at the remaining scalic's chest. A crude spear pushed the sword away; however, Belac continued to press forward. He slammed his hip into the scalic, knocking it off balance before sweeping the blade of his sword up and clipping the side of the creature's head. The blow was awkward, but the blade bit into the scalic's skull with a wet crunching sound as it tore away a slab of bone and brain.

Belac spun around in a circle, searching for more threats. He could hear the sounds of fighting, but the only other person he could see was Vairug. *The others must be on the other side of the wagon.* The orc held the lead of a frightened horse and was directing it toward the front of the wagon. Another horse lay dead on the ground next to more slain scalics, a spear jutting from the animal's side. *Rolan must be harnessing the other two.*

Guttural hissing came from the other side of the wagon, angry and insistent. *That leaves Breana to fight alone!* Belac raced to the left side of the wagon, running toward Vairug and the last horse. The sparce trees lining the creek made the approach feel less exposed. He wanted to help Breana, but he did not want to die doing it. *I can't be much help dead.* More guttural hissing on his left warned Belac of another attack. Rising from the creek bed, four scalics surged out, their fangs gleaming in the night. *I have to stop them from getting to Vairug!* Belac changed course and rushed at the scalics.

Belac's first swing was wild, and the scalic that he had intended to kill dodged easily. The creature twisted and countered with a thrust of its spear. Belac was able to swat the crude thing aside, but he knew focusing on defense would only get him killed. He stepped in dangerously close to the scalic and wrenched his sword down into where its neck met shoulder. The blade cut deep into the creature and caught on rib and spine. Blood gushed across Belac's front and splattered against his teeth. He put his shoulder into the dying scalic and threw it bodily toward two of the others as he pulled his blade free. As Belac turned with the throw, he saw that a scalic had gotten behind him. He let the momentum of the turn flow up into the sword and then brought it down on the scalic. The blade cleaved through the creature, the thick hides it wore doing little to slow the steel.

Belac's commitment to the swing left him bent forward with his sword held out behind him. He looked back past the blade and saw the oncoming scalics. Leaping away, the elf rolled over the upper half of the scalic that he had cleaved in two. He came to his feet swinging his sword in a wide arch as he turned to face the vicious things. The blade swept through the air between him and the scalics, halting their advance. Belac stepped into the momentum he had created and swung his sword overhead in a one-handed grip. It felt like his shoulder was being torn from its socket, but the extra reach allowed his blade to slice through another reptilian face.

The remaining scalic let out an enraged hiss and lunged at the elf. Belac's left hand joined his right on the sword's hilt in an underhanded grip. He used the sword to guide the spear aside and then drove his blade into the scalic's chest. He pinned the creature to the ground and then stomped a booted foot down on its slim, scaly neck. Holding the scalic down with his foot, Belac jerked his sword free. *I hope Breana saw all that.* His attention snaped toward the front of the wagon. *Breana!* He remembered his need to save her.

It was then that Belac witnessed the giantess. Ahead of the wagon, farther into the night, Breana was surrounded by scalics. Most of the creatures were dead, their broken bodies scattered around her. She fought naked, with nothing but the leather cord wrapped tightly around her left forearm, and a blacksmith's hammer gripped firmly in her right fist. Her hair had come undone, allowing the white strands to gleam silver as she moved in the moonlight. Where she moved, scalics died. Her hammer tore through the creatures, ripping away gory chunks of flesh and bone. With every strike, one of the scalics fell. Though they were fearless in their assault, they could not stop her swings. The giantess had already killed more of the creatures than Belac had; and yet still, she faced more.

As Belac stared transfixed, he realized that Breana was not slowing down. He saw no sign of fatigue or faulter. *How can she…* The rhythm of her swings only increased. While another would tire from such extreme exertion, she seemed to breathe in the death, and feed it to her rage.

Belac did not care what she looked like. Breana was a terrifying giant of war.

Twenty-Five

"Why are the mountains on fire?" Belac pointed toward the mountains with his sword. He glanced at the giantess before quickly looking away.

Breana's white skin was painted with blood and gore like a canvas depicting the horrors of war. The insane rings in her eyes shown with an excitement the night could not hide. It was the first time that Belac did not want to look at her.

Breana's voice was far too calm for a woman who had slaughtered so many. "It is more of these scalic things." She swept her arm out to the dead around her.

I know that! Belac glanced at the giantess again and decided that he should keep his thoughts to himself. *That is not a woman I should argue with.* He felt safer looking at the army coming to kill them. The mountains were alight with countless flames of ember orange that had lit in a wave across the rocky prominence. *Every one of those flames is a creepy-blue-lizard-goblin that wants to kill me.*

Breana's smile could be heard in her words. "Think of it as dragon slaying practice."

I would really rather start with wooden cutouts. Or maybe a padded leather dummy on puppet strings. Belac took a deep breath to steady himself. "If I die before I kill a dragon, will people still call me 'The Dragon Slayer?"

There was no fear in Breana's voice. "Survive this, and your name will be sung in legend."

"No deal." Belac shook his head. "For this, I deserve a song even if I die."

Breana's laugh was almost enough to make the elf forget his terror of her.

The dots of fire began to pour down the mountainside. The scalics moved quietly, but their numbers were too great for them to be silent. *Even had they come without the torches, we still would have heard them.* Belac considered the torches. *The moon must be bright enough for the scalics to see without them. The torches are to frighten us.* That the scalics wanted him frightened changed things for the elf. True predators did not want their prey frightened. It made the scalics seem less monstrous to Belac. *Monstrous or not, they still want me dead.*

Rolan shouted from behind the elf, "Belac! Get on the wagon!"

Belac and Breana turned to see the dwarf standing on the driver's bench with Vairug seated next to him. *Yes, please.* Belac decided that he really did not want a song. He ran to the wagon, not caring how cowardly he looked.

Belac tossed his sword on top of the wagon's cabin where it landed with a clangor. He followed after it, scrambling past Rolan on the driver's bench. Belac snatched up his sword and then wedged his foot under a luggage rail. He looked at the fiery scalic horde in the distance. *Why is the wagon not moving?*

Rolan pointed his hand away from the mountains commandingly. "Breana, lead us to the road. Follow our tracks as best you can, but watch out for anything that will break a wheel. We need to move fast."

Yes. Fast. Belac nodded emphatically. *Why is the wagon still not moving?* He looked from side to side, though no one else was there. *Am I the only one who realizes that the wagon needs to be moving?!* He slammed his hand down on the roof of the cabin. "Let's go!"

Rolan plopped down on the driver's bench and flicked the reins. The wagon lurched forward and began to turn to the right. The motion jostled Belac, and his face bounced against the roof of the cabin. He yanked his foot free and rolled over before lodging it back under the luggage rail on the opposite side. Sitting up, the elf expected his fear to abate as they fled. It did not.

The closest of the scalics broke away from the main horde and sped toward the wagon. Belac did not know if they were an advance force, or simply the warriors too eager to wait, too blood thirsty to allow their enemy to escape. *Whatever they are, those will be some of their most dangerous.*

Belac swept a fallen lock of his long black hair behind his pointed ear. "They are still coming, Rolan!"

Will three horses be fast enough? The elf glanced behind himself toward the surviving horses. Breana loped ahead, leading them away and to safety. Belac looked back to the flaming army of scalics racing toward him. He decided that he would prefer to have the giantess on the other side of the wagon. *I want her between me and those things!*

The scalics were faster than the horses. Using their thick tails for balance, the reptilian creatures ran bent forward. *It looks like they are slithering through the air.* Each of the scalics brought with them a crude spear in one hand and a blazing torch in the other, the open flames giving their pale blue scales an orange hue in the night.

Staring at the hellish sight, Belac realized something. *The fight is not over.* Safety was not something he would be given freely. Escape would require more combat. Leather creaked as he tightened his grip on the hilt of his sword. *Lizards and fire.* He looked up, his azure eyes cutting through the moonlight. *Dragon slaying practice.*

Belac pulled his foot free from the railing once more and rolled forward onto his knees. He made his stance as wide as he could, using both his feet and knees for balance.

The wagon shook beneath him, but Belac was determined to fight. If a song were to be sung, it would not be of an elf that had cowered in the night.

A burning torch flew up and landed on the wagon. Belac picked the torch up and threw it back down at one of the scalics. The fiery head of the torch slammed into the unfortunate scalic's skull. Its hiss of pain was joined by others of threatening malice.

A spear flew past Belac. *I should try to dodge those.* He heard claws dig into wood on his right. Turning toward the sound of the climbing scalic, Belac held his sword out to his left in preparation to swing. When the scaly head popped up, his blade hacked through it.

This time, Belac saw the scalic that threw its spear. It twisted while running and hurled the weapon with an alien grace. Belac dropped onto his back, the spear flying through the air where his chest had just been. Behind him, claws dug into the wagon. Rolling onto his stomach, Belac swung his sword at the climbing scalic. The swing was weak, but it was enough to dissuade the creature. The blade cut into its jaw and sent it spinning away from the wagon.

Following the swing, Belac rolled onto his back. A spear thudded into the side of the wagon. *We are not going to escape if we don't move faster.* He sat up and got his legs under himself. He looked back toward the pursuing horde. Discarded torches had set the grass on fire. The spreading patches of flame might slow the larger force, but it would not stop the wagon from being boarded.

All around him, Belac heard claws digging into wood. Relentless in their chase, the scalics had set the world on fire for the chance to taste elven blood. *I am not food!* Belac knew he could not wait for them to all come at him at once. He leaned over the side to see if he could stop one there. A scalic clinging to the side of the wagon hissed up at the elf and thrust a spear toward his face. Belac turned away from the spear and swung his sword at the scalic blindly. The steel shuddered in his hand as his blade cut through scales and skull.

Another scalic rose from the back of the wagon, thrusting its spear without hesitation. Belac slapped the spear aside with his left hand and then buried the length of his blade in the scalic's bony chest. Blood spattered across Belac's face as the creature attempted to hiss.

Two more of the scalics climbed onto the wagon's roof. Expecting their attack to be immediate, Belac wrenched the impaled scalic between himself and its kin. The elf's back slammed onto the top of the wagon as their weight pressed down onto the dying scalic. Struggling to hold back their reaching claws, Belac braced his feet on the impaled scalic and kicked the tangled mass of frenzied reptiles away from him. His sword slid wetly from the scalic's chest as the creatures were thrown over the side. However, the force of the shove pushed Belac back and he rolled off the rear of the wagon.

With luck born of desperation, Belac grabbed the end of the luggage rail. Holding on almost broke his wrist, but he slammed into the back of the wagon instead of the ground speeding past below. A scalic ran toward him, preparing to thrust with its spear. Belac's sword swept out in a wild backhanded swing that hacked into its reptilian snout. The scalic was sent off balance and it tripped, tumbling to a motionless stop.

Hanging twisted from the back of the wagon, Belac stared at the burning hills. Hazy smoke and spreading flames had joined the scalic's cause. It was as if the night itself were angry. Fire and fury hungered for the elf. *I need a new job.*

Twenty-Six

Belac spun around to face the wagon. *Why do I want to be a dragon slayer anyway?* He tossed his sword up onto the wagon's roof. *That has got to be the worse career choice in the history of the world.* He reached up and grabbed the end of the luggage rail with his now free hand. *I might as well have chosen to be a…* He paused, trying to think of something more dangerous than a dragon slayer. *…A nothing! Nothing is more dangerous than being a dragon slayer!*

Belac whipped his body and then braced his feet against the back of the wagon. He pushed off with his legs and pulled with his arms, vaulting himself onto the top of the cabin. The wagon lurched and he had to grab the luggage rail again to keep from falling over. Bent forward on one knee, holding onto the railing for support, he looked up to find a reptilian warrior holding a sword.

Hey! That's mine! Staring at the scalic, Belac decided that if a lizard could smile, that is what it would look like. "Stupid, thieving lizard!"

Rolan reached back with a knife and stabbed the scalic in the side of its rib cage. The scalic pulled away from the blow and then collapsed to its knees. Belac rushed at it and grabbed the hilt of his sword. He pried the weapon loose and then shoved the scalic off the wagon.

Belac shouted at the dwarf, "Where have you been?!"

Rolan gestured irritably ahead of the wagon. "I've been keeping the scalics from killing the horses." He held up his springer as evidence.

"Well, that's! ..." Belac stopped shouting. "Okay, that was probably a good idea."

Rolan growled and then leapt onto the cabin with the elf. He stood on the center of the roof, his short legs easily balancing him despite the wagon's jostling. With a professional focus, he proceeded to load and shoot his springer at the trailing scalics.

If he had done this from the beginning, maybe I would not have almost died six times! Belac did not know how many times he had almost died, but he was sure that it was at least six. *Wait. If I am busy almost dying, and Rolan is shooting at the scalics, who is driving the wagon?* A quick glance showed Belac that Vairug held the reins. *Oh great. I'm riding on the back of a wagon while a one-handed orc races it through the hills at night!* Belac looked back toward the horde of scalics chasing them. *And the hills are on fire!* He wanted to hop up and down in agitation.

Instead, Belac took a deep breath and watched Rolan kill scalics. *Even if we somehow manage to get away, the scalics could just follow the trail of their dead and find us.* Belac decided that if the only way he could find someone was to follow a trail of corpses that looked exactly like himself, he would need to reconsider his priorities.

Rolan turned away from the fiery death following them and put his hand on Belac's shoulder. He then used the elf to steady himself as he climbed down onto the driver's bench.

Belac glanced back toward the scalics. "I don't think they are giving up, Rolan."

Rolan holstered his springer. "If that fire does not stop them, the road might."

"The road?" Belac did not believe him. "Why would the road stop them?" He thought it sounded like the start of a bad joke.

"It is what it represents," Rolan began to explain.

"And what is that?" Belac asked.

Rolan frowned at the interruption. "Civilization," he answered and then continued his explanation. "The scalics are primitive, but they are not stupid. They understand how dangerous civilization is." He looked back at the elf. "And they know better than to wake sleeping dragons."

"I don't know why you are looking at me?" Belac said defensively. "If Danorin is asleep when it's time to kill him, I am not going to wake him up before I do it!"

Rolan grinned grudgingly. Leaning over to the other side of the bench, he nudged the orc. "Slow us down."

Belac understood that racing a wagon off road was perilous. *It's amazing that we haven't broken a wheel already.* He speculated that somewhere amongst the chaos, his hated green cloak must have been set on fire. *That is the only thing that could explain our luck.* Still, when the wagon began to slow, Belac almost panicked.

"Why are we slowing down?!" Belac's attention bounced back and forth between the slowing horses and the fires behind them.

Rolan answered calmly. "Not even Enevician horses can keep that pace up all night. We need to let them catch their breath. Besides, the scalics have fallen too far behind. They are not going to catch us." He looked back at the elf. "Not unless we run the horses to death."

"What?!" Belac asked. *That is not how a chase works! You keep running until you're safe!* "What if there is another group without torches?"

Vairug answered, "Then, we kill them."

Belac narrowed his eyes at the orc.

Rolan did not allow for argument. "When we make the road, we can pick up the pace. That will put the most distance between us and the scalics."

Belac appreciated the goal, if not the plan. "Why are they so determined to kill us?"

Rolan began to count on his fingers. "You interfered in a war. You aided their enemy. You killed kind of a lot of them." He gestured toward the fires still burning. "And you set their home on fire."

Belac pointed to the fire and smoke behind them. "I did not set that!"

Rolan nodded. "Feel free to go tell them that." He pointed with his thumb.

In a helpful tone, Vairug said, "I can stop the wagon if you want to get off and go back."

Belac narrowed his eyes at the orc again. "Did you know that they tell stories about how funny orcs are?"

Vairug shook his head. "No." He sounded a little surprised.

Belac shouted, "That's because they are not!"

Vairug laughed. "Is that why I never hear about wise elves?"

Belac sputtered. "That..."

Rolan issued a sharp laugh. "Look at his face!"

Vairug turned in his seat to see the elf.

Belac let go of the luggage rail and gestured forcefully toward the horses. "Watch where you are going!"

Vairug made a show of peering ahead at the rolling hills of grass rippling in the moonlight. "Do you think I'm going to hit a tree?" His gaze lingered on the giantess. "Though, if you insist..."

Rolan chuckled deeply. "Be careful, Vairug. That woman will rip off your other hand."

Vairug snorted. "As long as it is only my hand." He shrugged. "You can make me another one of those."

Rolan laughed at the idea, but Belac did not think it was funny. He could see it now. As they continued their quest, Vairug would have more and more of himself replaced until he was more machine than orc. *Maybe that is what will let him survive the dragon. Maybe he will be the only one that survives.* Belac thought of Vairug, more metal than flesh, standing alone among charred ruins. Belac could feel the tragedy of it. *Mostly because I would be dead.*

The elf sat quietly while his friends laughed. *We can't keep this up. One of us is going to die.* The thought of Rolan or Vairug being lost was no more preferable than being crippled himself. *How much can a person lose before there is no longer a reason to go on?*

Breana's voice drew the elf from his dark thoughts. "There is a river ahead!"

Rolan stood up and shouted over the horses, "We can cross it. It's more shallow than it looks."

Belac slapped the orc on the shoulder and pointed ahead. "Look. Trees."

Vairug growled, "I see them."

Elated that they would escape the scalics, Belac turned to the dwarf. "This means that we're almost to the road!"

Rolan nodded. "The river should also stop the fire if the wind changes."

Belac looked back. The fires still raged, but he could not actually see any of the scalics. He had not considered the direction of the wind. *If it had been blowing the other way, we could have been burned to death.* That settled things for the elf. *No doubt about it. That green cloak is ash.*

Twenty-Seven

"How many scalics do you think I killed with that fire?" Belac asked over the rumbling of the wagon.

True to his word, Rolan had increased their speed once they were on the road. While the horses could have run faster, their pace was quick enough that Belac felt safer every moment that passed.

Rolan answered inquisitively, "Now, you want credit for the fire?"

Belac shrugged. "Fire or steel, a dead scalic is still dead."

Jogging beside the wagon, Breana asked, "You started the fire?"

Belac did not think she sounded happy about it. "Only the first one." Then he added, "Sort of."

Breana harrumphed, but said nothing.

Belac noted that after all she had done, the giantess was not winded. She had fought what amounted to a small army and then ran ahead of the horses. However, when given the option to ride on the wagon, she had chosen to run alongside it instead. *Maybe giants really are just better.*

Something slammed into the lead horse. It was thrown violently off the road, pulling the other two horses with it. The animals fell in a tangled heap, and the wagon was wrenched to the side. The wheels snapped and the wagon toppled into the road with a crash of broken wood.

Belac was launched from the roof to fly backward into the night. He yelled unintelligibly as he flew, his arms and legs flailing for balance. His yell ended abruptly when he collided with the road. He hit with his upper shoulders, and his feet were thrown over his head. He bounced and rolled gracelessly until he lay face down in the middle of the road.

There was a moment of nothingness, and then Belac woke to a world of pain. He did not know how many of his bones had been broken, but his body refused to move. *No.* It was a thought that denied all others. *No.* He did not understand what had happened, but he would not accept this new reality. He would move again.

"No." Belac's voice was a painful croak. His hand twitched and his shoulder spasmed. With the force of pure will, he pushed away from the road and rolled himself onto his back. For a moment, there was nothing in the world except him and his pain. *If it hurts, then I can still feel. If I can feel, I can move.* True or not, the thought gave him strength.

The horses were screaming, but they sounded too far away. Belac focused on lifting his other hand. It hurt to move, but the arm responded. He held his hand in front of his face and stared at the blood and grit smeared across his palm. The horses had stopped screaming.

The thing that attacked him was gray in the moonlight. Black eyes and bladed teeth rushed into Belac's view. Terrified into the present, he held the thing back with both hands, his pain forgotten. Dull fingertips dug into the elf's arms, and the teeth moved closer in. Warm drool leaked down onto Belac's cheek as he turned his face away. The teeth continued to move closer until they were held back by nothing but Belac's left forearm against the monster's neck. Snarling, gargling sounds came from the thing as it bit at the air between them.

With frantic determination, Belac forced the numb fingers of his right hand to grip the hilt of his dagger. He jerked the blade free from its sheath and stabbed the monster in its naked chest. The monster continued to bite at the air, each snap of its jaw bringing teeth closer to the elf's face. As the monster bit, Belac stabbed, seeking to pierce its heart.

When the monster stopped biting, Belac did not stop stabbing. He rolled over on top of the vile thing and began to hammer his dagger into its chest repeatedly. The elf was snarling as he bared teeth of his own. He would have been horrified had he somehow saw how closely he resembled the monster in that moment.

Belac stood and stumbled away from the gruesome work. He only vaguely realized that he could stand. He stared down at the thing that had tried to kill him. *It has to be a ghoul.* Waxy gray skin covered a sexless humanoid form. Though masculine in bone structure, Belac would not have thought of the thing as a man even if it had not been absent of genitalia.

There will be more. Belac spun around, unsteady on his feet. The toppled wagon had been swarmed by ghouls and still more poured in from the hills to his left. The nightmarish things ran on their hands and feet with an unnatural gait, their gray, hairless skin gleaming in the moonlight. *Where did my sword go?*

Already up and fighting, Rolan stabbed a ghoul under its jaw while standing over the corpse of another. The dwarf leaned in with his shoulders and flipped the ghoul over his back using the knife as a handle. Not satisfied that it was dead, Rolan then stomped on the ghoul's skull.

Vairug was lying next to the wagon, struggling to lift the broken mass off his long, braided hair. With his wrist together, he pushed against the grip of his single hand. The wagon, however, was simply too heavy for the orc to move.

Where is Breana?! A gray body flew over the wagon and landed limply in the road. Its chest had been caved in and it was missing an arm. Belac looked past the top of the wagon and saw a glimpse of something white. *And that would be her.*

Rolan ran to the struggling orc and knelt down next to him. He reached out with his knife and cut through Vairug's braid with a quick motion.

"Get up," Rolan ordered briskly before standing and then vaulting over a dead horse.

Vairug sat up, clutching the remains of his severed braid. He appeared more shocked than when he had lost his hand. A ghoul leapt onto the back corner of the wagon, black eyes directed at the distraught orc. Thin lips peeled away from the ghoul's bladed teeth.

Belac was running before he could think. He caught the ghoul in mid-air as it attempted to pounce on Vairug. Belac slammed the ghoul against the wagon and then drove his dagger into its chest. Convinced that a single thrust would prove insufficient, he stabbed the monster repeatedly. When the ghoul stopped fighting and Belac was sure that it was dead, the elf stepped back and let the bloody carcass fall to the ground.

Belac turned to the startled orc. "Stop playing with your hair, and get up!"

Vairug's eyes hardened at the words, but he began to climb to his feet. Belac helped the orc stand and then he rounded the front of the wagon, circling dead ghouls and mangled horses as he made his way to Rolan.

The dwarf had moved ahead of Breana, tearing into the oncoming ghouls like a fish swimming upstream. The giantess followed in his wake, swinging her hammer over and around the dwarf. One misstep, and they would have killed each other. *I am staying over here.* Belac was willing to fight, but he was not walking into that. Vairug bumped into him when he stopped, causing the elf to stumble and trip over a dead ghoul. Belac fell into the road, smearing something awful on his shoulders and back. He rolled away from the muddy mix of bodily fluids and glared up at the orc angrily.

"Hold them back!" Rolan ordered and then stepped aside for the giantess.

Without bothering to answer, Breana pressed into the fray. Hammer and fury rebuked the monsters' hunger. Though her advance was halted, the ghouls continued to die around her.

Vairug bent down and hooked his left wrist under Belac's arm, helping him to stand. Rolan ran past them, both hands digging into pouches on either side of his belt. He pulled a slim vial from each pouch and threw them at the wagon, first one and then the other. When the second vial broke against the liquid from the first, fire engulfed the wagon.

Rolan turned away from the flames, ready to continue the fight. However, the ghouls immediately shrank back as the night was burned away. They cried in strange gargling voices and retreated beyond the fire's glow.

Rolan called out, "We have to move!" his commanding tone drawing the others attention to him and the fire raging behind.

Breana walked backward, away from the ghouls. "How? Where can we go?"

Belac agreed with her. If the fire held back the ghouls, he wanted to stay there until the sun came up. *The sun counts as fire, right?*

Rolan was not interested in consension. "East." He removed his pack and set it down in front of himself. With quick movements, he pulled out a long wooden box and set it to the side. "We have to make it to the ocean." He slung his pack and picked up the box before standing. "We have to move now."

With more hope than belief, Belac asked, "Ghouls can't swim?"

Rolan ignored him. "Breana, you hold the rear, but don't stop to fight the ghouls. If someone goes down, pick them up and carry them to the front."

Breana nodded.

Vairug spoke proudly, "I will not need to be carried."

Rolan scowled at the orc. "If you don't want to be carried, then don't stop running."

Twenty-Eight

"Do you people have to set everything on fire?!" Breana asked as they fled through the night.

The flames had spread from the wagon to the dry grass behind them. And while the fire separated them from the ghouls, they would be no less dead if they were caught. Belac glanced back at the blaze and thought about the monsters on the other side. *I really do not want to get eaten alive by ghouls.* He never before would have believed that being burned to death was a preferable alternative to anything.

Vairug answered the giantess, "I have set nothing on fire."

Belac swiveled and then pointed at the orc as they ran. "Liar! You ate my squirrel!"

"Enough!" Rolan called back over his shoulder. "You can argue when we are safe."

As far as Belac could tell, they were never going to be safe. *The dwarf thinks he's clever.* He narrowed his eyes at the back of Roland's head. *You are not going to trick me with reason!*

Belac asked, "And you think that the ocean is safe?" Drinking in taverns, he had listened to many sailors' stories. *The ocean is no safer than land.* Sea monsters, pirates, curses, and demons disguised as men were but the beginning of the dangers that the ocean had to offer. *The ocean even has its own dragons!*

Rolan gestured into the air aimlessly with one hand. "Safe…er"

"Oh?" Belac's tone was sarcastic. "Because that is what people wish for before they sleep. Children everywhere close their eyes and say, 'I hope everyone I love is safe," he yelled the last part, "Er!"

Rolan's answer was amused. "The smart ones do."

Belac looked around for something to throw at the dwarf. Grass and shadows were the only things readily available. He considered throwing one of his boots, but he did not think Rolan would give it back to him. *At least, not nicely.*

They crested a hill, and Belac saw the ocean waiting for them on the other side of a rocky shore. Moonlight danced on the surface of waters too great to be tamed. *It just looks like one more thing that wants to kill me.*

Rolan maintained their pace, neither slowing at the reassurance of safety, nor speeding into its embrace. Belac felt like this was the time that something would happen. He did not know what it would be, but he felt like they were too close to safety to reach it unimpeded. He expected the ghouls to head them off, or scalics to flank from the side. *Or a giant fiery ball of fire to fall from the sky and set us all on fire.*

When nothing bad happened, Belac decided that the only reason nothing had was that he had known it was coming. In his mind, the catastrophe was simply holding back until he was unprepared. *It is just trying to make me doubt myself.* He narrowed his eyes at nothing. *Stupid, sneaky …badness!*

Rolan stopped at the ocean's edge. He took the wooden box he carried in both hands and twisted the top free. He tossed the smaller piece aside and slid a glass bottle from the open container. Inside the bottle nestled a miniature boat with a single sail. Rolan gripped the bottle by the neck and smashed it on a nearby rock. In a shower of shattered glass, the toy boat fell to the shore with its mast broken. Rolan dropped the empty box, then picked up the broken boat and threw it into the ocean.

As the miniature boat flew through the air, it began to grow in size. When it landed in the water a short way from the rocks of the shore, the boat was large enough to carry them all. The simple fishing boat was small, but it could no longer be called miniature.

Breana gasped in amazement.

Belac pointed and said, "Your boat is broken."

Rolan growled at the elf, "Get in." He waded out into the ocean without waiting.

Breana followed, happy to investigate the magical boat. Belac thought she might offer to help the dwarf, but Rolan lifted himself up and over the side before Breana reached him.

Vairug nudged the elf on the shoulder with his forearm then pointed with his wrist. "That does look safer."

Belac mumbled, "That is only because we have not set it on fire yet."

Vairug walked backward into the ocean. "That sounds like an agreement to me."

Belac decided that some sort of argument was necessary. "It's broken! What are we going to do? Sit in it and just float around all night?"

From aboard, Rolan said, "It has oars, Belac. Now, get in the boat."

Vairug added, "Or you can stay and wait for the ghouls."

Belac rushed past Vairug in his hurry to get to the boat. He climbed inside and stood staring back toward the shore. The glow of both fires could still be seen in the distance.

From behind him, Rolan said, "Hey, Belac."

Belac turned around and Rolan pushed him in the chest. The side of the boat pressed into the back of Belac's calves, and then he fell out of the boat backward. The elf crashed into the ocean and sank into the dark water before he understood what had just happened. *Sneaky dwarf!*

Belac splashed above the surface, trying to breathe and spit out sea water at the same time. He looked up to see Rolan staring down at him. The dwarf had one foot on the side of the boat and was resting his weight on the raised knee with his arms crossed.

Rolan only smiled, but the elf could hear its meaning. *"Are you ready to stop playing this game yet?"*

Belac sputtered out sea water. "Hate you!"

Rolan's smile only broadened. "You needed a wash anyway."

While in the prosses of climbing into the boat, Vairug began to laugh so hard that he lost his balance and fell into the water with Belac. Unlike the elf, Vairug came back to the surface still laughing. Belac splashed at the orc, but Vairug only laughed harder. Though he laughed quietly, it looked like the effort might kill him.

Belac splashed at the orc again. "That's right, laugh yourself to death!"

An oar slid into the water behind the elf. In a conversational tone, Breana said, "I assume we are following the coastline to Harbridge?" She began to row the boat to sea.

Belac ducked away from the oar that glided toward his head. The boat accelerated sluggishly, but it was obvious to the elf that Breana meant to leave him behind. He grabbed the side of the boat and scrambled aboard as quickly as he could.

Vairug, having only one hand, found it more challenging to climb into the moving vessel. Belac reached over the side and helped the orc up. When Vairug was safely aboard, Belac rolled over and leaned against the inside of the hull, too exhausted to bother taking a seat.

Vairug stood, wobbled on his feet, and then sat down on a bench to keep from falling back into the ocean. The orc took a deep breath and looked up tiredly. His black hair had come undone, and it hung wetly against the sides of his face. Bathed in the light of the moon, he appeared remarkably human.

I wonder if I could talk him into filing down those tusks? Belac closed his eyes and relaxed, finally feeling safe. *I am still not telling Rolan he was right.*

In an irritated voice, Rolan asked, "What is it, Vairug?"

Vairug was ready with his response. "You cut off my hair!"

Belac opened his eyes, curious how this would be resolved. He did not think that Vairug would fare very well if they fought on the boat. The dwarf's short legs would give Rolan an advantage in stability, and he had twice as many hands. *Still… Vairug is really strong.*

Rolan frowned. "I saved your life." He gestured dismissively at the orc. "Besides, all that hair made you look like a girl."

Breana stopped rowing and covered her mouth with both hands. Belac thought it was adorable that the giantess was completely nude, but she felt like it was her smile that needed to be covered up.

Vairug looked like his eyes might pop out of his head. It was obvious that he had no idea how to respond to such an accusation. He glanced to Belac, presumably for some offering of support. The elf was not even trying to hide his smile. *Now, I have to call him 'Sarah.'*

Vairug pointed his empty hand at the elf. "What about him?"

What about me?

Rolan shrugged. "He's an elf. He looks like a girl anyway."

"I do not!" Belac moved a lock of his hair away from his face with a delicate finger.

Breana's hands were now covering her entire face, and her body was rigid in an effort to not laugh. Belac almost told her to get back to rowing, but managed to constrain his own stupidity. *I do not want to swim all the way back to Harbridge.*

Rolan continued, "You wore your hair pulled back anyway. Just tie it in a knot on top of your head or something and let's move on." When the orc did not answer, Rolan said, "Besides, hair grows back." He absently reached up and tugged on a longer tuft of his choppy hair, muttering, "It's annoying like that."

Breana resumed rowing while doing a poor job at not smiling.

Now that they were moving again, Belac had to ask, "Why didn't we stay at the wagon? The ghouls were scared of the fire. We could have just waited for daybreak." He looked sideways at the giantess while he spoke to the dwarf. "Did you just want to show off your fancy boat?"

Rolan shook his head, unoffended. "Ghouls don't like fire, but it's not magic. Once their eyes adjusted to the light, they would have rushed us again. Only this time, we would have had to fight with a burning wagon behind us."

Vairug mumble glumly, "And you set it on fire."

Rolan looked at the orc. "What?"

"My hair!" Vairug growled. "You cut it off. And then you set it on fire!"

Twenty-Nine

Breana was adamant. "I am not wearing that."

Standing across from her, Rolan replied with forced patience, "Yes, you are." He had cut the sail from the broken mast, and he wanted the giantess to wear it as a cloak.

Breana stood and picked up an oar like she was preparing to hit him with it. "I disagree."

"Woman..." Rolan took a deep breath, angled his head down, and turned it to the side in self-restraint. "It is not dawn yet. If someone sees us sneaking in through the harbor, they may not notice that you're a giant. Distance plays tricks on people. But if anyone sees this," he gestured up and down at the nude giantess, "they are definitely going to notice."

Belac nodded but said nothing. The movement drew Breana's attention, and she glared down at the elf. He offered her a smile of exaggerated friendliness and hoped that she would not hit him.

Breana returned her stare to the dwarf, the insane rings in her eyes more threatening than the oar she held. "Let them notice!"

Rolan pinched the bridge of his nose. "That would defeat the entire purpose of sneaking."

Breana gestured with the oar. "You just don't want anyone else to look at me!"

"Exactly!" Rolan agreed with exasperation. "Anyone that looks at you is going to want to talk to you, or they are going to want to talk about you."

"Let them talk!" Breana leaned forward to glare at the dwarf more forcefully.

Rolan closed his eyes and repeated, "That would defeat the entire purpose of sneaking."

Breana threw the oar down. "Then, why don't you wear it!"

Rolan shouted, "Because I'm not a giant, naked woman!"

Breana stared at the dwarf as if he had just insulted her. Her silence was louder than his shout.

Rolan took another deep breath. "When we get to the storehouse, I will wear whatever you want, and you can dance naked in the loading bay. But unless you want to start a war with the whole city," he held up the canvas sail, "you are going to put this on."

Belac turned to Vairug and widened his eyes. The orc smiled and shrugged. Not wanting to miss anything, Belac quickly looked back to the giantess. She seemed to be thinking. *Not good.* Belac smiled. *Not good for Rolan, anyway.*

Breana stepped over the bench between her and the dwarf. She took the sail, draped it over her head, and then wrapped the sides around her shoulders. She sat down, saying, "Someone else will need to row." There was a calmness to her voice that sounded dangerous.

Rolan ignored her tone. "You heard the woman, Belac." He pointed his hand toward the oars. "Get rowing."

Belac stood. "Why do I have to row?" he asked while shuffling to the stern of the boat.

Rolan sat down across from the giantess. "My hope is that you get too exhausted to complain."

Belac sat down and began to position the oars. "And what happens when I don't stop complaining?"

Rolan chuckled. "Then, the three of us will get off at Harbridge, and you can keep on rowing."

Breana stifled a laugh and then kicked the dwarf for making her do it.

Belac glanced over his shoulder toward the sprawling docks of Harbridge in the distance. Though notably absent a lighthouse, the piers were lit with the flickering light of hanging lanterns. As he rowed, he wondered if they would be able to actually sneak into the city unchallenged. *I guess the sail Breana has on might work as a kind of camouflage in the harbor.*

The corner of the harbor they docked at was darker than the rest. Belac suspected that they were not the only people who preferred to travel unnoticed. The pier was in disrepair and appeared to have been damaged in some kind of fire. *What were the smugglers moving that could burn through so much of the docks?* He considered the rocky shores they had passed and wondered how many smuggler's caches had been hidden in the shadows.

Rolan took hold of a dock mooring and held the boat steady while Breana climbed out. Vairug followed the giantess onto the pier with the hood of his charcoal brown cloak pulled low to hide his face. Looking at the two standing in the open with their identities so thoroughly concealed, Belac decided to do what he could to hide his own lineage. He reached back and untied his long hair, allowing it to cover his elven ears. It was an unsophisticated disguise, but he could think of nothing else that might help.

Rolan hopped onto the pier, and Belac hurried after him before the boat could waft away. The elf turned around and considered the boat as it bobbed in the dark water.

Belac pointed at the abandoned vessel. "Don't you want to tie it up or something?"

Rolan shook his head. "It is not worth the effort. It's better if it floats off or someone takes it."

Belac looked at the dwarf askew. "You want to throw away a magic boat?"

Rolan shrugged. "You cannot get it back in the bottle."

Belac remembered the shards of broken glass. "That seems like a pretty obvious design flaw."

Rolan disagreed. "Not if you want to sell more magic bottles."

The idea of someone with magic behaving so cynically bothered Belac. *Why be greedy if you have magic?*

Rolan waved the elf to follow him. "Come on. You can frown while we walk."

Belac scratched at the side of his head as he followed Rolan through the docks. The elf's hair tickled the tips of his ears more than he thought it should have. *I hope we get to wherever we are going soon.* While the few people that walked the docks were wise enough to avoid the darkened piers, Belac knew that it was safer to keep his elven ears hidden. The physical sensation was tolerable, but there was something upsetting about being forced to be uncomfortable. *I can't believe that I have to hide what I am just because of a bunch of stupid humans.* With a start, Belac realized that he might understand a little of what Breana felt. *I wonder if there is something I can do to make her feel more comfortable.*

The storehouse that Rolan led them to was close to where they had docked. Like the rest of the buildings in lower Harbridge, it resembled an oversized ship that had been flipped upside down. The timbers were aged but the wood retained a luster that spoke to the caretaker's pride.

As Belac was beginning to find customary, Rolan barged inside like he owned the place. The door swung in and struck a hanging bell that rang throughout the small office. A lamp burned brightly, illuminating the tall man that stood up from behind a counter.

The man's eyes went wide with shock. "Rolan…"

Rolan walked around the counter and casually stabbed the man in the chest. The man fell to his knees and stared at the dwarf confused. Rolan shook his head disapprovingly and pushed the man away. Turning his back on the dying man, Rolan walked through an open doorway.

Belac glanced at Vairug, unsure what they should do. The orc held out his arms and shook his head, obviously at a loss. Belac looked back to the empty doorway, wondering if he should go help. There was the sound of scuffling and a heavy chair hitting the floor, and then silence.

Rolan came back through the doorway, blood dripping from his knife. He pointed his open hand at the door they had entered. "Lock that door," he said calmly as he walked to a large sliding door on the opposite side of the room.

Breana hastily shut the door, causing the bell to ring again. Vairug reached in front of her and pulled the bolt in place. *Are we keeping people out, or are we stopping them from getting away from Rolan?*

Wheels rolled in their track loudly as Rolan pushed the larger door to the side. He stepped into the open storeroom and navigated past shelves filled with boxes of merchandise. Rolan seemed to know where he was going, and he moved with a sense of purpose. Not knowing what else to do, Belac hurried after the dwarf. *Is he just going to kill everybody?*

A muscular man with a shaved head took one look at Rolan and froze. He dropped the crate he was carrying and held up his hands. "I didn't know, Rolan." He shook his head and looked down at the floor. "They did not tell me until I came in this morning."

Rolan studied the man without offering any reassurance. He scratched at the stubble on his cheek and then pointed his hand at the man. "Stay there."

Belac watched as Rolan walked over to a shelf and began to rummage through the boxes. Belac thought that the man may have had a chance at escape if he had chosen to run. The man was clearly terrified, but he waited obediently instead of running or attempting to fight.

Rolan walked back to the man and handed him a small, multifaceted glass bottle with a dark brown liquid inside. "This is going to tell me if you are telling the truth. Drink it, and then tell me again how you did not know." He took a step back and held his knife ready to strike. "Try to tell a lie, and you'll die for it."

The man nodded eagerly and downed the contents of the bottle. "I swear I didn't know, Rolan. I would have done something."

Rolan lowered his knife and nodded. "Go find two more men you know we can trust, and bring them back here."

The man nodded deeply. "Absolutely. I know just who to get." He turned away to go but then stopped and looked back. "I am really glad that you're not dead, Boss."

Rolan nodded impatiently and then the man ran to do as he was bidden.

Belac leaned forward and turned his head to the side so that he could see the dwarf's face. "You have truth potions?"

Rolan shrugged. "It was rum."

Thirty

Rolan led his three companions through the cluttered maze of inventory and to a wall on the far side of the storeroom. He took hold of one of the tall shelving units and pulled. Both the shelves and a section of the wall swung smoothly into the aisle, revealing a hidden room on the other side. Belac waited with Breana and Vairug as Rolan walked inside and lit a brass lamp. The dwarf left the lamp sitting on an old, well-worn table in the middle of the room. He turned to face the others still waiting outside and then he waved them into the room impatiently.

Rolan pointed his hand to his left. "The privy is through there." He then pointed his other hand to his right. "The beds are over there." He dropped his hands and nodded to his companions. "Go to sleep."

Vairug looked at the row of bunk beds lining the wall and then back to the dwarf. "It will be daylight any moment now."

Rolan nodded. "Exactly.' He pointed his hand toward the others as a collective. "None of you people can be seen. Hide here. Get some sleep. And then, you can move around in the storehouse tonight."

Belac yawned. He was so tired that he almost did not argue. "Look at us, Rolan. We are filthy."

Rolan shook his head and nodded at the same time. "The sheets can be washed." Under his breath he added, "Or thrown away." Sensing that the elf was not through arguing, Rolan raised his voice and continued, "I will have a tub brought in and you can bathe when you wake up."

Belac wanted to argue, but he looked at the beds and decided that he wanted to sleep more. "Fine. But I get the top bunk."

Sounding exhausted as well, Vairug said, "There are six beds, Belac."

It took Belac a moment to come up with a response. "And you can't have them all!"

Vairug opened his mouth to say something, but sighed instead. He walked away from the elf and sat down on the lower bunk of a set of beds in the far corner of the room. *I don't think I have ever seen him look so tired.*

Belac walked over and took another look at the orc. When he was satisfied that Vairug was not dying, Belac climbed up onto the bed above him.

"What are you doing, Belac?" Vairug asked tiredly. "There are plenty of other beds to choose from."

Yeah. But if something comes in here and tries to kill me, I want you in the way. Belac smiled. "I can't protect you from the other side of the room."

Vairug laughed softly at the idea, but said nothing.

Breana laid down on the floor between the table and a wall of shelves filled with dried food. She closed her eyes and her breathing immediately took on the slow rhythm of slumber. *I am going to have to remember to not step on her if I need to go to the privy.*

From the doorway, Rolan said, "And take off your boots." Without waiting for argument, he shut the secret door and left the others hidden inside.

Belac kicked off his boots, letting each one fall to the floor with a clomp. *I would have forgotten to take those off.* The elf wondered how Rolan stayed so mindful. *He always seems to know what to do next.*

Belac pinched at the gray wool blanket covering his bed. The fibers were coarse but strong. *It is all I can do to just deal with what is happening to me in the moment.* He stretched out on the bed and closed his eyes, unaware of the seed that he had just planted in his own mind.

Belac's bed shook.

"Wake up," Rolan said.

Belac opened his eyes. He shook his head and muttered, "I will do it later." He closed his eyes and tried to go back to sleep.

Rolan took the elf's toe and squeezed it with his thumb. Belac shot up in bed, jerking his foot away from the pain. For a moment, he thought that something might have bitten him. *I am not food!* Belac narrowed his eyes and peered over the side of the bed, searching for the dwarf. Even in the dim room, Belac's azure eyes were alight with cold intensity. *Evil little…*

Rolan was completely nude. Without the loose, splotchy clothes that usually hid his shape, the dwarf was nothing but muscle and hair.

Belac fell out of bed in his haste to withdraw from the sight. He clutched at the mattress clumsily and managed to get his feet under himself before he hit the floor. He tilted his head backward and looked down, trying to keep only the dwarf's head and shoulders in view.

"Good. You're awake." Rolan said as if nothing had happened.

Belac did not know what to say. "Um… You're…"

Rolan pointed his hand at the bottom bunk of the set of beds next to him, drawing the elf's gaze lower. "Take that change of clothes and go wash up." He pointed to the open doorway with his thumb. "There is a tub in the storeroom next to the loading bay. Everything is already set up for you."

Belac glanced down at the pile of folded brown clothes before returning his focus to the dwarf's face. "Are you… ah… sure that you don't need them?"

Rolan frowned. "It was either this, or listen to her call me an oath breaker."

From the table, Breana called out, "You are still not dancing!" Her smile was brighter than the room.

Rolan turned around. "I said, you could dance," he told the giantess gruffly. "I am not dancing."

Please, don't make the dwarf dance.

Breana, nude again herself, turned toward the dwarf. "Well, I think you should dance."

Belac closed his eyes. *She is going to make the dwarf dance.*

"Tough," Rolan told the giantess. "I am not dancing."

Belac wanted to leave the room. *The problem is that there is a naked dwarf in my way.* He averted his eyes and crawled in between the beds of the bunk next to him. Careful to not look too far to his left, Belac reached over and took the folded pile of clothes. He stared at the flickering light in the open doorway as if it were salvation itself.

Though the elf attempted stealth, his exaggerated movements only made his exit more conspicuous. Despite this, Belac was able to flee the room without further trouble. *Don't see me. Don't see me. Don't see me.* He considered closing the secret door behind himself, but he did not want to chance drawing any attention. The storeroom was lit by a series of small glass lamps that led him to a large, copper bathtub waiting next to the closed doors of the loading bay.

Belac looked from the tub to a wooden chair with a towel draped over its back. He turned around slowly, scanning the shadowed storeroom suspiciously. *This is not very private.* He looked back to the copper tub and the steam rising from the water. *It looks like a trap.* Belac narrowed his eyes at the tub. Lamplight flickered against the polished copper. *I am missing something.* The elf set his change of clothes down on the chair and proceeded to walk around the metal bathtub. *I don't see anything green…* He kicked the tub and then hopped backward away from it. He drew his dagger and waited for something to happen.

The copper tub reverberated with a soft depth, but appeared to be nothing more than a bathtub filled with steaming water. Belac thought the water looked a little too inviting. He took a step closer and cautiously leaned over the top to look down into the water. He quickly stabbed the water with his dagger and then hopped away.

Belac waited, ready for anything. He thought that he could almost hear the flickering of the lamplight around him. After a moment, he allowed his guard to lower a little. *I think it is entirely possible that this is just a bathtub.* He stared at the steam rising from the water. *I am just going to have to risk it.*

Belac set his dagger on top of his change of clothes while he undressed and then, still unconvinced of his safety, took the dagger in hand once more. The elf climbed into the tub, his sore muscles relaxing as he sank into the heated water. With his dagger held clutched to his chest, Belac laid back in the tub, and for a moment, thought that the relief might be something worth getting eaten for. He imagined the copper bathtub growing fangs as it came to life, chomped shut, and swallowed him whole. *I take it back!* The elf shot up with a splash to stand dripping wet in the middle of the bathtub staring down at the water with his dagger held ready to stab the metal monster.

I think I might be going crazy. He lowered the dagger and stood up strait. *Is crazy contagious?* He thought that in some ways it must be. Belac dropped his dagger to the floor beside the copper tub. If it were his own insanity he was fighting, the dagger would be of little use.

The elf lowered himself back down into the water and repositioned more comfortably in the tub. He closed his eyes and allowed the warmth of the water to seep into him. As he inhaled and exhaled, he focused on the fact that it was he who willed the breath.

It's all too much. The thought was shallow. Belac focused on the thought, trying to isolate the feeling. *I am going to die.* He suddenly wanted to reject what he felt. He wanted to think about something else. He wanted to feel something else. His mind began to turn to food, to sex, to drink, to anything that would avoid that awful thought.

Belac took another deep breath. And then, lying comfortably in a bathtub, he did the single bravest thing that he had ever done. He faced the truth. *I am not enough.* The thought was not shallow.

Thirty-One

Becoming 'more' was a lofty goal. Belac considered how he was going to go about achieving this, but he could come up with no easy answers. By the time he had finished bathing and changing into his new clothes, he had just about decided that there may not actually be an easy answer to be found. *I think there should always be an easy answer.*

Belac knew that he did not want to die. He did not think this made him weak. *It makes me not stupid.* He also knew that as he was, he would get himself killed long before he ever slayed a dragon. *I guess I could just… not try to slay a dragon.* Belac shook his head. *The dragon needs to die.* The Danorin was not only a menace to the world, it was a threat that Belac did not believe would ever leave him in peace. And if he were being honest with himself, the elf did not want to let down Rolan and Vairug. He felt that it would be worse than merely disappointing his friends, it would be a betrayal. *No. The dragon has to die.* He nodded to himself. *Now… How do I be someone that can do that?*

When Belac entered the secret room, he completely forgot what he had been thinking about. He was so stunned by what he saw, that for a moment, he could not think at all. Breana, naked as she preferred, was sitting on her knees next to the table while Rolan, also naked, braided her long, white hair into two buns on top of her head.

Vairug sat on the other side of the cluttered table eating small, flat noodles from a bowl, seeming oblivious to the bizarre scene. *This can't be real.*

Breana touched the finished bun on the right side of her head and smiled happily. "Look how pretty it is!"

"Stop moving," Rolan said as he worked to braid the other side.

Breana held up a silvered hand mirror and inspected the complexly braided bun. "Why doesn't everyone wear their hair like this?"

Rolan shrugged. "Most dwarven women do."

Breana looked at the dwarf slyly. "Do the dwarven men braid their hair for them?"

Rolan huffed in amusement. "No," he said seriously.

The giantess's teeth gleamed in her smile. She looked so happy that Belac thought she might start bouncing up and down at any moment. *How long did I sleep?*

Vairug stopped shoveling noodles into his mouth long enough to say, "You should eat."

No. I should go back to sleep and hope that the world makes more sense when I wake up again. Belac tossed his dirty clothes to the side. "What is it?"

Vairug swallowed and then answered, "Food."

Belac frowned at the orc, but sat down in the chair next to him. "You did not ask what it was before you started eating it?"

Rolan spoke absently, "It's Salber."

Belac picked up a spoon and poked at the creamy, gray noodles in the serving bowl. The flat noodles were smothered in a sauce thick with tiny bits of mushroom and shredded meat. *This actually looks alright.* He scooped some of the noodles into a smaller bowl and brought the dish up to his face.

Belac sniffed at the noodles and then growled, "Rolan!"

"What?" Rolan replied irritably.

Belac glared at the dwarf. "I still can't smell anything!"

"Lucky you," Rolan said dismissively.

Belac slammed his bowl of noodles on the table. "How is that lucky?"

Rolan pointed his hand towards the elf's discarded boots. "It does not smell great in here. Why do you think we have the secret door to our secret room wide open?"

Belac glanced at the open door. *I did not think about that.*

Rolan asked," You know what 'secret' means, right?"

Belac narrowed his eyes at the dwarf.

Vairug nudged the elf. "I know what it means."

Belac gave the orc a curious look.

Vairug's cheek twitched. "But I can't tell you."

Breana shook her head and laughed. "That's a bad joke."

Vairug shrugged and went back to eating.

"Stop moving," Rolan told the giantess again.

Breana tried to look at the dwarf without moving her head. "How long until it's finished?"

"I am doing the same thing to both sides," Rolan told her. "You were here when I did the other one."

Breana twisted her shoulders without moving her head and swatted the dwarf's legs.

Rolan turned to the side to ensure that nothing important was hit. "Stop moving."

Breana crossed her arms under her breast. "Well, hurry up!" She uncrossed her arms and picked up the hand mirror from the table. "I want to see what it looks like when you are finished." She angled the mirror to the right side of her head.

"You know what would make this go faster?" Rolan smiled. "If you would stop moving."

Breana swatted the dwarf again, though there was little effort in it this time.

Belac closed his eyes and shook his head slowly. *Do I even remember a time when things made sense?*

Vairug asked, "Are you going to eat that?"

Belac picked up his bowl of noodles and moved it away from the orc protectively. "Of course, I'm eating it!"

Vairug frowned. "Then, you are doing it wrong." He scooped up a spoonful of his own noodles and held them up. "You have to put them in your mouth." He demonstrated, putting the noodles in his mouth and chewing dramatically.

And now, I am taking dining advice from an orc. Belac smiled with sudden inspiration. He reached over with his spoon and scooped up noodles from Vairug's bowl. Belac crammed the noodles into his own mouth, almost spitting them back out laughing.

Speaking while he chewed, Belac said, "You're right. That is how to do it."

Vairug glowered at the elf.

Belac's spoon darted out as he attempted to steal more of Vairug's food. The orc intercepted Belac with a spoon of his own. The tiny metal shovels clashed and then Belac and Vairug stared at each other over their locked spoons. With a fury of short movements, the two began to battle each other with the spoons. The dull, muted clatter of spoons filled the room until Vairug leaned away, disengaging. Belac angled his spoon at the orc in a mockery of a fencing stance. Vairug's hand shot out and his spoon rapped the elf's knuckles.

"Aeiow!" Belac dropped his spoon and tried to shake the pain out of his hand.

Vairug reached over with his spoon and took a scoop of noodles from Belac's bowl. With a tusked grin, Vairug ate the noodles. He seemed too pleased by his victory to be upset with the elf.

From across the table, Breana said, "I feel like it would be best if we left that fight out of the song."

Rolan chuckled. "You don't want to sing about The Battle of the Spoons?"

Breana shook her head primly.

With obviously disingenuous affront, Vairug accused, "You would deny my glorious triumph?"

Breana laughed at the orc.

Belac said, "You can tell the story." He flexed his sore hand. "Just leave out the part about the spoons."

Rolan's chuckle was so deep that it sounded like a cough. "You think you are going to look better in that story," he emphasized, "without the spoons?"

Breana giggled. "I could sing of how the daring elf and the fearsome orc wiggled their fingers at each other."

Rolan laughed. "Until the elf screamed like a cat that just had its tail stepped on."

Belac narrowed his eyes at the dwarf.

Vairug nudged the elf and nodded toward the giantess. "She thinks I'm fearsome." He grinned proudly.

Belac shook his head. "Fine," he said exasperated. "You can just say we used swords." He mimed fencing with the orc.

Breana laughed fully. "You want me to sing a story about you getting into a sword fight with an orc over a bowl of noodles?"

Rolan put his hand on the giantess's shoulder for support as he laughed. "And losing!"

Belac narrowed his eyes again. *Stupid, naked dwarf!*

Breana began to sing,

"And they fought for the bowl in the hidden room.
When the elf stole what would the orc consume.
And they fought for noodles with swords in gloom.
Till the elf lost with a cat scream of doom."

Her song had been meant in jest. However, her voice was simply too beautiful to be funny. A stunned silence followed that quickly began to feel confusingly awkward.

Breana's voice sounded as irritated as any dwarf's. "You are allowed to laugh."

Rolan did. Then he patted the giantess on her shoulder and said, "It's finished."

Breana put a hand to the left side of her head and used the silvered mirror to inspect the braided bun. Her smile was as wonderful as her song.

Belac scowled. "Can't you make us fight over something better than noodles?" *If I am going to die in a song, I don't want it to be over noodles.*

Vairug nodded, his tusks jutting playfully from his smile. "The elf can be fighting to avenge his pet squirrel."

Thirty-Two

Belac crossed his arms and stared at the dwarf seated on the other side of the table from him. "I need new clothes, Rolan."

Rolan swallowed his food before answering, "You have new clothes." He gestured to the elf. "You're wearing them."

Belac ignored the retort. "And a sword."

Still seated comfortably on the floor, Breana lowered her hand mirror and said, "I thought that forging you a sword was the first part of our quest."

Rolan pointed at the giantess and nodded as he chewed.

Belac shook his head. "I can't wait for the magic one." *Too many things want to kill me.* "I need one now." He thought for a moment. "And a new bag. And another cloak." He pointed at the dwarf. "One that is not green!"

Rolan quit eating and stared at the elf.

Belac continued, "And a …"

"Stop," Rolan said, resigned. He pushed his bowl of noodles away and stood. "Come on." He waved for the elf to follow. "Let's go get you something to write on."

Belac liked this idea. *If I make a list, Rolan can't try to tell me he forgot something.* He hopped out of his chair and followed the dwarf out into the storeroom. *And I am going to write, 'NOT GREEN!' next to every single thing on the list!*

In the storeroom, two roughly dressed men were in the process of carrying the copper tub out into the loading bay. Belac grabbed the hilt of his dagger. *They are stealing the bathtub!*

"Calm down," Rolan told him. "They work for me." He looked sideways at the elf. "So, don't kill them."

Me?! I am not the one who goes around killing everybody! Belac narrowed his eyes at the dwarf.

As he led the elf past the men, Rolan asked, "Where did you think the bath came from?"

I did not really think about it. Belac shrugged though the dwarf could not see it.

Rolan continued, "Everyone else is clean. That means everyone else took a bath before you. Where did you think the fresh water came from?"

This time, Belac's shrug was more aggressive. *What do I care where the water came from?* "It was a bath, Rolan. I bathed."

Rolan shook his head and kept walking.

Belac felt offended by the dwarf's apparent disapproval. "What? Do you ask where the water came from every time you take a bath?"

Rolan halted outside the sliding door to the front room. He took a deep breath and said, "I am not saying that you should ask, Belac. I am saying that you should think."

Wheels rolled in their track as Rolan slid the door open. Belac wanted to argue with the dwarf but there was something in his words that almost seemed compassionate. *Is this what dwarves are like when they are being nice?* Belac shook his head and followed Rolan into the front room. *No wonder they don't bother doing it very often.*

The first thing Belac noticed in the room was the obvious lack of dead bodies. Belac was sure that he had seen the dwarf kill someone in there. "What happened to the dead guy?" *Maybe they just piled him in the corner of the office with the rest of the people Rolan killed today.*

"Fish food," Rolan answered with a professional tone.

Belac grimaced. "I don't think I'm going to be able to eat fish for a while."

Heading into the office, Rolan asked, "What do you think you were eating earlier?"

Belac's eyes went wide. "You fed me dead guy?"

"No." Rolan chuckled. "Fish."

"Oh." Belac shook his head. "Well, that's okay." He followed the dwarf into the office. "Don't feed me people."

"Sure," Rolan agreed absently. He walked to the other side of a large desk, pulled out a drawer, and took out a crisp sheet of paper. He slapped the paper on the desk before reaching back into the desk drawer.

"Wait," Belac said. "Is this your office?" He looked around the room. It was well appointed, with dark wooden cabinetry polished to a satin sheen. Nothing appeared to be out of place. *...No dead bodies...*

Rolan set a writing implement down on the desk. "It's one of them."

Belac pointed to the doorway with his thumb. "Then, why did you come in and start killing everybody?"

Rolan frowned. "Evidently, I am in a disagreement with another distributor." He waved his hand dismissively. "Don't worry about it."

Belac decided to worry about it. "What is the disagreement about?"

Rolan walked back around the desk. "Whether or not I should keep breathing."

Belac looked at the dwarf curiously. "That sounds like something worth worrying about."

Rolan shook his head dispassionately. "I will take care of it."

Belac did not need to ask how the dwarf would do that. He knew Rolan well enough to know that people would die and something would be set on fire.

Rolan clapped the elf on the arm. "Make your list. I am going to go finish eating."

As Rolan exited the office, Belac wondered how the dwarf could be so confident while walking around in the nude. *Maybe he just knows that no one is going to want to look at him unless they have to.*

While naked dwarves were not a regular occurrence in Belac's life, he had encountered enough clothed ones to expect a hefty midsection. However, Rolan's physique was clearly defined. *That dwarf can't even get fat right.*

Belac walked around the large desk and took a seat in the highbacked, leather chair on the other side. The chair was surprisingly comfortable. *I wonder how often Rolan actually sits here.* It was hard for Belac to imagine the dwarf working in an office day in and day out.

Belac picked up the uncut grease pencil resting next to the sheet of paper. *What is this thing?* Obviously Rolan had intended for him to write with it somehow. *Why else would he have left it on the desk for me?* At the end of the slender black rod, hung a thin string. Belac tugged gently on the string, but nothing happened. *Maybe the string is not supposed to be there. I guess I could cut it off...* He unintentionally pulled the string at an angle and the string cut through the paper wrapping. At first, the elf feared that he had damaged it, but as the loose paper unraveled, it exposed a waxy, black core.

"That's genius!" Belac said aloud. He wondered how the dwarves had come up with such a thing. *There is no way humans would be smart enough to think of something like this.* He hoped that he would be allowed to keep the marvelous instrument.

Belac began to make a list of everything that he thought he would need for his quest. He was careful to include only the details he felt were most important. *If I am too specific, Rolan might just tell me that he could not find what I wanted.* He tapped the grease pencil on the page in thought and then added a final request. *I probably should have put that at the top of the list.*

The elf stood and took his list from the desk. Before leaving, he appraised the room one last time. *It is a nice office, but Rolan does not belong here.* He thought that Rolan should be out exploring ancient ruins, or leading armies of the damned in some righteous crusade, or almost anything other than sitting in an office counting coins.

Belac retraced his steps through the storeroom. The loading bay doors were closed and the only sign there had been a bath set up next to them was a slightly damp floor. The workers, or whatever they were to Rolan, were nowhere to be seen.

Belac took a moment to consider the bath. *I guess… If someone saw the bathtub, they might question who it was for.* He nodded thoughtfully. *A secret room is a lot easier to keep secret if no one is looking for it.* Belac grinned, pleased with himself. He followed the glass lamps back to the secret room. *I don't know… Is it still a secret room if the door is wide open and there is a trail of lights leading to it?*

Rolan and Vairug sat at the table, facing each other while Breana lounged on the floor. Her double braided bun made the giantess appear more youthful, and to Belac, she seemed more energetic despite how she lounged. He found it difficult to not stare at her.

Belac forced himself to look at Rolan. The elf suddenly smiled so broadly that it hurt his face. He could hardly believe what he saw.

Rolan frowned as the elf laughed.

Belac pointed with the grease pencil. "Your hair!"

Rolan shook his head dismissively. "Shut up, Belac."

The dwarf's stubble had been shaved close, and his hair had been cut even. Without his jagged, haphazard tufts of hair, Rolan looked even more naked than before.

Breana sat up and held her hand mirror out so that the dwarf could see himself. "Doesn't it look nice!"

Rolan growled, but he was gentle as he pushed the mirror away. "Give me the list." He held out his hand.

Smiling, Belac handed him the sheet of paper. *I bet she makes you wash your clothes next!*

Rolan scanned the list. "This is ridiculous." He held up the sheet of paper and looked at the elf scornfully.

Belac shook his head, disagreeing. "We are not mercenaries, Rolan. We are heroes. What we are trying to do is heroic." He held out his hands. "We need to look heroic."

Vairug spoke up. "I think you should listen to him, Rolan."

Rolan looked at the orc and pointed to the last item on the list. "He wants a giant bag of gold."

Vairug grinned. "How much does he want?"

Rolan handed him the list. "He doesn't specify. It just says, 'not green.'"

Vairug accepted the list and began to look it over. *Vairug can read?* Scholarly was not something typically associated with orcs.

Vairug lowered the sheet of paper. "How would you even carry a silk pavilion?"

Belac pointed. "Next thing on the list."

Vairug shook his head and flattened the sheet of paper on the table. He took the grease pencil from the elf and then, frowning like a disappointed professor, he proceeded to draw lines through Belac's desires.

Thirty-Three

Absent distraction, it does not take long for an elf to get bored. Belac, despite his parentage, was very much an elf. He spent some time exploring the storehouse, but Rolan had warned against opening any of the containers. While the dwarf had insisted it could be dangerous, Belac was convinced that Rolan simply did not want him to find the liquor.

Still, Belac was not willing to risk having his face blown off. So, he paced around the storeroom until it began to feel like a prison. *It is not the size of the cell that makes something a prison.* He decided to return to the secret room and annoy people until someone found him something to drink.

Vairug was in the back corner of the room, laid out on a bed. Belac chose to let him rest. He did not know if the orc was asleep or not, but Belac remembered how tired Vairug had seemed before. *He is not going to know where the booze are anyway.*

The heavy table had been pushed to the side of the room, making space for Rolan to sit on the floor next to Breana. Adorned in nothing but the flickering of lamplight, the two spoke to each other in hushed voices.

Breana asked, "But, how would you…"

With a devilish smile, Rolan gave an answer that the elf could not quite distinguish.

Breana replied with a surprised, "Oh!" and then said, "Oh..." her smile becoming wicked as well.

Nope. Belac turned on his heels. *I do not want anything to do with whatever that is.* He walked back into the storeroom, trying in vain to not think about what he had just witnessed. *He's a dwarf! She is a giant!* Belac shook his head, attempting to banish the image of Breana's wicked smile.

The elf was in the front room of the storehouse before he knew where he was going. *I need fresh air.* He crossed the room and unlocked the front entrance. Remembering how noisy the hanging bell had been, he reached up and held it out of the way as he opened the door. *I don't want the others to think someone is breaking in. The last thing I need is for a naked dwarf to come flying out of the dark with a knife.*

Closing the door without ringing the bell required some awkward maneuvering, but Belac managed to do it. *Getting back in is going to be more difficult.* The elf shrugged. *I'll worry about it later.* He covered his ears with his hair. Despite his bath earlier, the long strands were a mess. *I bet Breana has a brush or a comb I could borrow.* Belac had put both a brush and a comb on his list of wants, but he did not know when Rolan would acquire them. *After all the lines Vairug drew on my list, I don't even know if I will get one of them at all.*

Belac walked away from the storehouse with no real direction in mind. Hanging lanterns illuminated many of the docks along the sprawling harbor, though there was a disorderly feel to their spacing. The elf took a deep breath but found himself unsatisfied by it. The air was too thick to feel fresh. And while he still could not smell anything, he was convinced that the air would stink. He turned at the next cobbled street and headed farther into the city in hope of finding fresher air.

Unlike the fringes of the harbor, the remainder of the city was left to rely on the dim moonlight that filtered through the clouds above. As he walked the streets, Belac began to realize that Harbridge felt alive in a way unlike any other city he had ever visited.

While some cities seemed to die when the night settled in, others developed an energy that promised unknown excitement. In Harbridge however, it felt like the buildings themselves were slumbering. The timber hulls seemed to breathe in the darkness, groaning faintly with the breezes that blew gently through the city. There was a quiet peace that offered the wholesomeness of a hamlet, irrespective of the city's size. What Belac appreciated most was that this all made it remarkably easy to locate the nearest tavern.

Light and sound poured lazily from the open doors of an establishment under a sign that read, 'The Drunken Mermaid.' *Ha!* Belac laughed to himself. *No one that has ever actually seen a mermaid would want to drink with one.* His mind summoned an image of the ethereal beings that had swam in the underground lake. *I don't care how beautiful a woman is, fangs are a deal breaker.*

Regardless of the tavern's name, Belac would have gone inside had he the coin to buy a drink. He was fairly confident that he could convince someone to pay for his company. Though, not without drawing attention to himself. He was not as noticeable as a giant or a one-handed orc, but he could not hazard the chance of someone mentioning the elf they had met. *It was a lot more fun being a hero than it is being a fugitive.*

"Hello there, Friend," said a man's voice in a mocking tone.

Belac spun to his left to face a group of four men. Even standing in the light provided by the tavern, the men's dark clothes blended with the wooden city. *I guess Harbridgers just really like brown.* Two of the men stepped closer, offering insincere smiles.

The one on the elf's left asked, "Are you looking for a drink?" His voice was as fake as the first's.

Belac said nothing. He did not know what the men wanted, but he was sure that it was not to buy him a drink. *This is not an accidental encounter.*

"Why don't you come with us," the man on the right said. It did not sound like a suggestion.

The man on the left nodded agreeably. "We can get you a drink… We can all have a seat… We can all get to know each other…"

Belac did not like the way the men spoke to him. It was obvious that they were trying to intimidate him. That is not what they were doing. The elf shifted his stance so that none of the men would be able to get behind him easily. The men misinterpreted the movement, believing it to be in response to the mention of alcohol.

The man on the left smiled in truth. "You can have as much to drink as you want. Our treat."

The man on the right finally told the elf what this was about. "And then, if you want to talk to us a little about your boss…" The man grinned in a way that only a fool would trust. "You could walk away with a purse heavy enough to buy your own drinks."

"See," the man on the left added, "we're friends."

A moment passed and Belac said nothing. *I am going to have to kill them.* He knew these men were not going to let him walk away.

The man on the left leaned to the side and presented his hip, displaying the short-sword that hung there. "We're friends, right?" he said in an unfriendly tone.

Now. Belac grabbed the hilt of the man's sword with his right hand. With his left, he drew his own dagger and stabbed the man in the chest. Pushing the man away using the dagger still buried in his chest, Belac pulled the short-sword from its sheath.

Belac let the man fall from his dagger as he pivoted toward the man on the right. With a quick thrust, Belac plunged the tip of the sword into the other man's chest. Instead of running the man through, Belac jerked the short-sword back after piercing his heart.

Belac stepped toward the man who had stood behind the one on his left. The man held up his hands, wide eyed and confused. Belac swung the short blade down into where the man's neck met his shoulder. The steel caught in the man's ribcage and Belac released the hilt, allowing the sword to fall with the man.

The last man turned to flee, but Belac grabbed a fistful of his hair with his free hand and stabbed the man in the side of the neck. Belac stabbed the man twice more before they fell to the street together. Straddling the man's back, Belac brought his dagger down three more times, ravaging the man's neck.

A man shouted, and a woman screamed.

Belac stood, feeling a little lightheaded. Another shout followed the first. *I should probably get out of here now.* More shouts came from the tavern and then someone blew a whistle. *That secret room is seeming really nice right about now.*

Belac stepped away from the bloody bodies in the street and began to jog toward the docks. Farther ahead, two men with a red stripe across their chests dashed into the street carrying lanterns. They stopped and then one of them blew another whistle. The shrill sound was more than loud enough to announce their location to any other watchman nearby. *Not good.*

Belac turned and began to run back up the street. *I can sneak back to the storehouse once I get away.* Another whistle answered from the direction of the tavern. Realizing that he was trapped, Belac ran between two of the buildings on his right.

It was then that it started to rain. What started as a mild sprinkle, quickly became a steady downpour. Belac felt like the world itself was trying to drown him. *It's a conspiracy!*

On the other side of the buildings, the elf was faced with a choice. He could turn right and head for the docks, or he could turn left and move deeper into the city. If he tried for the docks and could get around the watchmen, he would find safety in the storehouse. However, that would also risk leading the city watch back to his friends. After only the slightest hesitation, Belac turned left.

Rain ran down the sides of the nautical buildings and flowed into the street. Belac's boots splashed as he sprinted through the water and deeper into the city. A whistle blew behind him. *I made the right choice.* A lantern appeared in the street ahead of him and another whistle pierced the night. *Maybe not.*

Belac turned and ran between two more buildings. The way was blocked with crates, but he thought that he would be able to climb over them. *This could work to my advantage.* Without slowing, the elf leapt into the air and planted his foot against the center of the crates. Instead of vaulting over as he had intended, the crates collapsed, and he crashed into a paved stable yard on the other side. He rolled over the crates, and his back hit the stones with a splash.

"It's a conspiracy," Belac muttered aloud.

Whistles spurred the elf to action. He stood, realizing that he had dropped his dagger in the fall. He scanned the stable yard, frantically searching for a way to flee, but the stable and the gates were all closed. Watchmen climbed over the broken crates, their whistles blowing shrilly into the rain.

Belac spun around, looking for his dagger. *I can't let them take me.* He did not believe that Harbridge would allow him to escape imprisonment a third time. More watchmen entered the stable yard, lanterns emblazoning the red stripe across each of their chests. Accepting his dagger as lost, Belac stepped away from the men of the city watch.

Belac's clothes were soaked through, and his long hair was plastered to the sides of his face, exposing his elven ears. He pointed at the guards. "Okay!" He hopped up and down as he yelled, "Which one of you is wearing green?!"

Thirty-Four

Two of the watchmen looked at each other in confusion before returning their attention to the irate, rain-soaked elf. Everyone in the stable yard was drenched and the deluge showed no sign of ceasing soon. One of the other watchmen blew his whistle. To Belac, the whistle sounded different than the others, though no one else seemed to notice.

One of the watchmen stepped forward and declared, "You are under arrest!"

Belac disagreed firmly. "No. I'm not."

The watchmen shifted uneasily in the rain, some of them pulling out truncheons. The odd whistle blew again. Belac stood his ground, ready to fight the next man that took another step toward him.

The first watchman to have spoken pointed his truncheon at the elf. "Put down your weapon!"

What? Are you afraid I am going to stab you with my ears? Belac held his empty hands out to his sides.

The gate to the stable yard shook loudly and then was forced open. Both Belac and the watchmen looked toward the breached gate. *More watchmen? Or a way out?*

A sandy haired man wearing a loose vest and short legged trousers stepped into the stable yard. He turned back and shouted into the night, "Over here!" He waved an arm above his head, beckoning. "This way!"

And here come the angry peasants with pitchforks. Belac considered trying to hide behind the guards. *Maybe I can sneak away while everyone is distracted with each other.*

A small army of men armed with short-swords and cutlasses surged into the stable yard. There was no questioning their violent intent. Belac turned to the watchmen, suddenly more than willing to be arrested. A watchman lurking in the rear brought his truncheon down on another watchman's head. The traitorous watchman did not stop there, but instead continued to hammer into his comrades from behind as they were focused on the charging mob.

Belac began to slowly walk backward away from the furious cries of battle. *Don't see me. Don't see me. Don't see me.*

The watchmen faced the armed men valiantly, but were quickly cut down. Belac watched with increasing concern as the army of men drove their blades into the bodies of the fallen to assure that none survived.

The lone watchman still standing clasped hands with the man who had opened the gate. They exchanged quiet words that the rain disguised, though the watchman's allegiance was clear. The two men nodded to each other before releasing their grips and then the watchman turned away. The traitor stepped past scattered crates and the bodies of the dead alike as he marched off into the night.

Belac realized that all the other men were staring at him. *I think they see me.* The elf's eyes searched the yard again. *I could really use that dagger…*

The man who appeared to lead the others pushed through the crowd. He halted a respectful distance from the elf and then asked, "You are the foreign elf?"

Belac pointed at one of his own ears. He did not think Harbridge had any local elves.

The man nodded. "We are of The Deep. You must come with us." He tilted his head earnestly. "There will be more of the unborn."

Belac did not like the sound of that. "The unborn?"

The man gestured to the dead watchmen. "Those who have yet to know The Deep."

"So… More watchmen?" Belac asked for clarification.

The man nodded. "Yes. Among others."

Something about 'The Deep' tugged at Belac's memory. This was not the first time that he had heard it spoken of. *The sailors that helped me escape from prison mentioned something about it.* At the time, he had simply not considered it. *It just sounded like something a sailor would say.*

Belac shook his head. "Sure." *What else am I going to do?*

The man nodded. "Follow close. We will see you away to safety."

Belac motioned for the man to lead on. *No reason to just stand around here.* He glanced at the slain bodies of the city watch. *And a lot of reasons not to.*

The man led Belac out of the stable yard through the open gate. The mob of armed men trailed along behind them protectively. Belac did not think that it was a particularly sneaky way of escaping, but it worked well enough. *I am not dead, and I'm not in prison. So, I should probably not complain.*

They crossed streets and navigated back alleys until Belac was thoroughly lost. The darkness and the rain only added to his sense of dependency. *What is safety that comes from another?* To Belac, it seemed more like a form of submission. And while the relief offered by both could be comforting, they were not the same thing.

Whistles began to sound in the distance. *We are not moving fast enough.* Belac grabbed the arm of the man he was following, bringing him to a halt. *I should probably ask his name.* The man turned, a question on his face.

Belac gestured to the mob following them. "This is too many people. It makes us too easy to track."

The leader of the mob nodded and then stepped around the elf. He leaned close to one of the other men and spoke into his ear. Belac could not make out what was said, but the man nodded in acknowledgement. The leader turned back to the elf while the other man relayed his orders.

The mob's leader leaned in closer to the elf and gestured to the men behind them. "They are going to lead the unborn away."

Belac nodded. He was still uncomfortable with the term 'unborn,' but he thought the plan was a good one. "What is your name?"

"I am Gelb," the man told him.

"Well, Gelb, let's get out of here." Belac turned and resumed walking in the direction that they had previously been headed.

Gelb hurriedly moved ahead of the elf and then proceeded to lead him further into the city. Four men from the mob stayed with them, silently trailing in a loose formation.

"Where are we going?" Belac asked over the rain.

"To a safehouse." Though Gelb answered readily, the details were of little use to the elf. "It is a building across the street from The Pelican's Perch."

Upon hearing the answer, Belac felt like his question may have been a rather stupid one. *I don't know where The Pelican's Perch is.* He wanted to hop up and down in frustration. *I don't know where anything in this cursed city is!*

"It is not far from where we are now," Gelb continued. "Once we get there, we have a plan to take you safely away."

Whistles were blown in seeming random directions as the arrant members of the mob went about their work misdirecting the city watch. The shrill sounds of the watchmen's whistles reminded Belac what the alternative was. *I guess I get to find out what The Pelican's Perch is.* He did not think it could be a worse place than prison.

Leading him away from a back alley, Gelb indicated to a modestly sized building. "This is the safehouse. We will have you safely away soon."

Belac found himself a little disappointed that he did not get to discover what The Pelican's Perch was. The safehouse itself was even more of a disappointment. When Gelb had described it as a 'building,' Belac had imagined that it would be something larger than a tool shed. Obviously crafted by the same masterful shipwrights that had shaped the rest of the city, there was nothing about the safehouse other than its size to distinguish it from the other structures. *It might even be a good place to hide.* Belac glanced back at the men following him. *If there were not six of us.*

"It's kind of small," Belac complained. *Though, it will be nice to get out of the rain.*

Gelb attempted to reassure the elf. "We will not be here long."

Without an eave to hide under, Belac was forced to stand miserably in the rain while Gelb unlocked the door to the safehouse. The man stood on his toes and reached up above the doorframe. He took hold of a hidden ring connected to a thin cable that ran into the wall. He pulled firmly, and the door opened with a metallic click. With his other hand, he pushed the door inward.

Belac followed Gelb into the safehouse and then stepped aside as the four other men crowded inside with them. The interior was dark, and the men stumbled into each other as they found a place to stand.

Belac's eyes adjusted as Gelb moved through the single room. The walls were bare and the furniture simple. Bed, wardrobe, dresser, table, and a short stool; nothing about the room seemed lived in. To Belac, it all made the inside of the safehouse look like an unused guestroom.

Gelb opened a dresser drawer and pulled out a folded towel. He offered the towel to the elf, saying, "You should dry yourself off."

Belac took the towel, shook it out, and began to dry himself, starting with his hair. His clothes were too soaked for the towel to dry, but he did the best he could. Holding the damp towel out to his side, he realized that none of the others were drying themselves. *I hope I was not supposed to share the towel.*

Belac tossed the towel onto the table. "What about you?"

"We have to go back outside into the rain," Gelb explained. "We would only get wet again."

Belac looked around the room. "And you want me to stay here?"

The shake of Gelb's head could barely be made out in the darkness. "No. It would not be safe for you to remain here." He stepped to the other side of the room and opened the narrow wardrobe that stood there. The inside was empty, and the walls were lined with a padded leather. "We will move you the rest of the way with this." He gestured to the inside of the wardrobe. "This way, you will not only be hidden, but out of the rain as well."

Belac glanced at the open wardrobe. *Rain or no rain, I am not getting in there.* He looked back to the man who wanted him to crawl inside. "I am not getting in a box."

Gelb held his hands out toward the wardrobe. "This is the only way to move you safely." He touched the padded leather inside. "It is well padded." He pointed to a series of baffled slits. "And there are vents." He turned back to the elf. "You will be safe inside."

Belac stared at the man and said nothing. *I am not getting in the box, Gelb.*

"You will be comfortable, I assure you," Gelb persisted.

Belac maintained his stare. "That is not the point, Gelb."

Gelb tilted his head. "I do not understand."

Belac tilted his own head to match the man's. "You don't understand why I don't want to climb into a coffin?"

Gelb was silent for a moment. "You do not trust us?"

Belac said nothing.

"You are alone in a room with five armed men," Gelb told the elf. "Just this night, you witnessed us slaughter many of the city watch."

Belac's hand drifted to his hip, searching for the hilt of a dagger that was no longer there.

Gelb continued, "If we wanted to harm you, we could." He gestured to the door. "But you can leave if that is what you want." He dropped his hand. "We offer you only aid."

Belac growled. He hated how convincing the argument was.

Thirty-Five

The waxed canvas tarp covering the cart was thrown aside, exposing the wardrobe. Rain beat against the wood, the sound muted by the padded leather inside. Lying on his back, Belac braced himself against the inside walls as his dark sanctuary was dragged from the cart. The wardrobe tilted into an upright position, shaking the elf's small world.

"Are we there?" Belac asked with premature optimism.

Gelb hushed him, saying, "Be quiet."

Belac was silent for a moment. *He would not need me to be quiet if we were already there.* Whispering loudly, Belac asked, "Where are we going?" *I probably should have asked that before I climbed into the box.*

The wardrobe tilted to the side, and the bottom rose up as the men positioned it for carry. Belac's weight shifted inside, and he found himself resting uncomfortably on his shoulder. He wiggled around in search of a more tolerable arrangement.

One of the men carrying the wardrobe said, "You need to stop moving around in there."

Belac narrowed his eyes at the padded wall, knowing that the man was on the other side. "Then, stop bouncing me around."

The man only grumbled in reply.

When nothing else was said, Belac asked again, "Where are we going?"

Gelb's answer was an obvious attempt to quiet the elf. "We are taking you to the temple."

Belac shook his head. *Bad idea.* "Last time I was there, things did not go very well."

Genuinely surprised, Gelb asked, "You have been to the temple?"

"They threw me in prison!" Belac explained. He did his best to sound like a grumpy dwarf and said, "How did you think I got to Harbridge?"

Gelb's tone became one of understanding. "You speak of the Temple of the Ancient." He spat audibly. "We would not take you there."

"Then, where are you taking me?" Belac asked, confused.

"You will be taken to the Temple of the Deep." Gelb's voice was solemn. "There, you will be given the honor to judge... and be judged."

Belac did not like the sound of that last part. "Ah... You know what, Gelb? That sounds like an awful lot of trouble for you to go through. I, ah... You... You have already done so much to help me. I just... Ah... I would not want you to have to go through all that trouble."

There was no response.

Belac continued, "I have an idea. Why don't you just let me out here, and I can sneak off on my own?" The rain pattered on the wardrobe as he waited for a reply.

"You will be taken to the Temple of the Deep. You will judge. And you will be judged." There was finality in Gelb's voice.

You see, Belac?! The elf was furious with himself. *This is why you don't let strangers lock you in a box!* He pushed against the doors of the wardrobe, attempting to force them open. Try as he might, the doors would not budge. Whoever had built the box had never intended for it to be used as a wardrobe.

Belac kicked at the doors. "Let me out!"

"Calm yourself," Gelb admonished the elf. "All will be well."

Belac kicked the doors again, but accepted that he was not going to be able to break out of the box on his own. "Hey, Gelb, buddy." The elf smiled, hoping his captors could hear it in his voice. "Why don't you let me out of the box?"

The suggestion was ignored.

Belac clenched his jaw and gritted his teeth in an effort to keep smiling. "Come on, Gelb. Just let me out of the box." *And maybe I won't have to kill you!*

The wardrobe began to sway; moderately at first and then more drastically. The foot of the wardrobe crashed down and then the back was gently lowered. The swaying was replaced with a rocking motion that Belac recognized as the movement of a boat. His eyes darted to the vents in the wardrobe. *Water could get in as easily as air.* The Temple of the Deep suddenly had a much more ominous implication.

Gelb spoke to his men. "I will see him on from here. You have all done well this night. May the Deep be with you."

In disjointed harmony, each of the men replied, "May the Deep be with you."

The sound of oars slapping into the ocean could barely be heard over the thick pattering of the rain. The oars swooshed through the water as Gelb began to row them away. With each of his rhythmic strokes, the oars creaked against the side of the boat.

Belac wiggled around in the wardrobe, repositioning himself in an unsuccessful attempt to see through the vents. "Gelb."

Gelb ignored him.

"Hey, Gelb."

There was no response.

"Gelb?"

Nothing.

"Geeeeelllllb…"

Still nothing.

Belac shouted, "Gelb!"

"What?!" Gelb replied angrily.

"Are you going to drown me?" Belac asked disapprovingly.

"What?" Gelb did not attempt to hide his confusion. "What are you talking about? Why would I drown you?"

"The Temple of the Deep," Belac clarified. "Do I have to drown to get there?" *I really hope that I'm not giving this guy ideas.*

"Of course not." Gelb's voice sounded offended. "The temple is a place of light and truth." After a moment of silence he added, "You have some peculiar thoughts about the world."

Did he just call me crazy? Belac yelled, "Did you just call me crazy?!" He hammered his fist against the inside of the wardrobe. "You locked me in a box!" He kicked the doors. "Now, you're rowing me out to sea! Which one of us is acting like a crazy person?!"

"All will be well," Gelb said simply.

Belac's sarcastic reply had a slightly hysterical edge to it. "No… That doesn't sound crazy at all!" He yelled the last part so loud it hurt his throat.

"All will be well," Gelb repeated.

Belac crossed his arms and wished for all he was worth that he could turn into a gorilla-wolf-monster. *I would bust out of this box and rip Gelb's stupid head off his stupid shoulders.* The elf proceeded to spend an unhealthy amount of time thinking of all the ways that he wanted to kill Gelb.

The rain suddenly stopped beating down on the wardrobe, bringing Belac immediately alert. Water still fell into the ocean, its sound echoing around them. *We are in some kind of cave.* The boat bumped into something with a deep thunk. Muffled voices approached the craft as its forward motion was arrested.

A man's cold voice spoke calmly above the others. "Is this him? Is this the foreign elf?"

Gelb answered, "I believe so. The commandments leave little doubt."

"Then, The Deep shines upon us." There was praise in the man's cold voice.

Gelb agreed, "We were lucky." Then he added, "Though, many of the unborn were not."

"A pity," the man said dismissively. "All will be well."

"All will be well," Gelb repeated.

Belac groaned. *Crazy zealots. All is most certainly not going to be well.*

Boots thudded on the inside of the boat's hull and then the wardrobe was lifted into the air again. Belac braced himself against the sides, still worried that he would be cast into the water. The elf's world wobbled as the wardrobe was transferred from the boat. He considered crying out and asking the new people for help, but it was fairly obvious that they knew he was in the box and that it was where they wanted him to stay.

Belac attempted to speculate on where they might be taking him, but his mind kept returning to the image of a pit with a huge snake the size of a large tree. *I know they are going to try to feed me to something.*

After being carried further into the temple, the wardrobe was laid down flat on a stone floor. Belac twisted around in the box to lie face down. *I need to be able to get to my feet as soon as these doors open.* His ears strained for any sounds that could inform him of what was happening outside the wardrobe.

Boots echoed on stone as more men joined the others. Time seemed to stretch. Muffled sounds drifted into the box, though they did nothing to illustrate what transpired without. *I cannot even tell how many men are out there.*

The man with the cold voice spoke. "Prepare him for the Eye."

When the doors of the wardrobe opened, Belac shot to his feet. He lashed out, striking the first person he saw. The punch connected with an old man's nose, knocking him back as he tripped over his own robes. Someone grabbed the elf from behind, pulling him away from the wardrobe. Belac swung a wild backhand that hit no one.

"Hold him!" one of the men called out.

More hands took hold of the elf, trapping his arms. Belac kicked at another robed man, aiming between his legs. "You are not feeding me to a snake!" He kicked his heal at the men behind him. His boot snaped one of the men's knees with a satisfying pop.

Belac was wrenched backward, the motion lifting him off his feet. The men grabbed his legs and held him outstretched as he thrashed in the air. Facing the roughly cut dome ceiling, Belac continued to struggle as ropes were tied to his ankles and wrists.

"He needs to be facing downward," the cold voice decreed.

Using the ropes, the men twisted Belac around to face the floor. His head jerked side to side as he appraised the stone chamber. Discolored tallow candles burned from within shallow recesses in the walls, giving life to shadows. Men in hooded robes of midnight blue stood around the elf. None of them looked on him kindly. Their angry stares and restrained aggression did nothing to calm Belac's fears. He struggled against the ropes but could find no leverage stretched out as he was.

"Position him over the Eye," the cold voice commanded.

The men holding Belac strung between them moved toward the center of the chamber. They arranged themselves over a large iris shutter that covered the middle of the stone floor. The elf hung horizontally, facing the dark metal as the men backed away, his ropes sliding through the men's grips as they increased the length between them.

"I'm poisoned!" Belac told his captors. "Whatever you feed me to is going to get sick and die!"

The men ignored his lies.

Strange mechanical sounds issued from beneath the metal shutter, and its blades began to rotate away like the dilatating of an eye. A perfectly round pool of water waited in the dark below. The blades of the shutter retracted into the stone, leaving Belac suspended in mid-air above a fall that he was certain would kill him. He stopped fighting with the ropes.

The men not holding Belac aloft began to walk around the edge of the opening. One at a time, they took up a hushed chant until they spoke the gnostic words in unison. The waters below began to churn in the opposite direction, and the air hummed with visceral effect. The robed men chanted louder and continued to circle the elf. White light surged up from the water's impossible depths.

Belac closed his eyes and tried to turn away, but the light burned through his eyelids. He could feel the light shining through him. He could feel it seeping into the marrow of his bones. The light shifted in color, becoming a vibrant red. It persisted for only a moment, and then the light was gone. Breathing heavily, Belac opened his eyes. *I'm not dead!*

The chanting stopped, and the robed men stood facing toward the elf. The strange mechanical sounds resumed, and the shutter's dark blades began to close.

One of the men asked, "What does this mean?" The voice belonged to Gelb.

A cold voice answered, "He must be taken to The Deep."

Thirty-Six

Getting Belac back in the box proved easier than the elf would have liked to admit. With his ankles and wrist already secured with ropes, the robed men had little trouble binding his feet together and his hands behind his back. Once he was trussed, it was nothing for them to dump him back in the wardrobe and slam the doors.

Belac thrashed about, but with his hands tied, he was even less likely to escape than before. When the wardrobe was lifted, he did not make it easy for those who would carry it. Belac rammed his shoulders against the walls inside, hoping that he could cause one of the men to lose their grip. *If I can get one of them to drop the box, maybe it will break open.* He stopped moving. *And then what? I wiggle away?*

Recognizing that freeing himself from his bonds should be his first priority, Belac abandoned his previous plan. As the men carried the elf from the temple, he contorted himself in the wardrobe until he was able to get his hands on the ropes that bound his ankles. Though he fumbled blindly, it soon became apparent that whoever had tied the ropes had known what they were doing.

The cold voice issued orders. "Take him directly to the Sea Spice. The captain will obey. The foreign elf must reach The Deep. There can be no delays. There can be no mistakes."

The voice of Gelb replied, "I do not understand why there is such a need for haste."

"It is not for you to understand why," the cold voice explained dispassionately. "You too must obey. All will be well."

"Could he..." Gelb began to ask but was cut off.

"He is a foreign elf and must be taken to The Deep," the cold voice overrode.

Submissively, Gelb acceded, "All will be well."

"May The Deep be with you," the cold voice intoned.

Gelb replied, "May The Deep be with you," accepting that the conversation was over.

After the wardrobe was lowered into the boat, Belac went back to worrying at his ropes. The discussion had distracted him despite offering no information that he thought was particularly helpful. *It seems like Gelb has some of the same questions I do...*

Someone climbed into the boat and took up the oars. Belac assumed that it was Gelb. As the boat was rowed from the cave, Belac noticed that the strokes were rougher than before. Even when the rain began to beat on the wardrobe once more, the slap of the oars against the water punctuated every stroke. For a moment, Belac thought that someone else must have taken up the task. *No, that's not it.* He smiled to himself. *Gelb is angry.*

"Hey, Gelb." Belac knew that the man would hear the smile in his voice.

The forceful jerking motion of the oars continued, but the rower did not reply.

"Gelb?" Belac knew it was him.

There was no answer.

Belac laughed. "Geeeeelllllb."

"What?" Gelb answered unhappily.

"Do you want to talk about it?" Belac asked.

Gelb continued his angry rowing. "Talk about what?"

Belac took the opportunity to ask the question that he thought was the most important. "Where are we going?"

"We are headed back to Harbridge," Gelb said in an obvious attempt to avoid answering the real question.

"Right," Belac acknowledged. "But it is not like when we get there, you are going to open the box and say, 'Go! Be free little elf!" Belac's irritation began to show through. "You are going to put me on another boat, Gelb. The Sea Spice. That's the ship that is going to take us wherever it is you are taking me."

"Yes," Gelb confirmed needlessly.

"Where are you taking me, Gelb?" Belac asked again.

Gelb continued to row angrily in the rain without answering.

Belac slammed his head against the inside of the wardrobe. "Where are you taking me, Gelb?!"

Gelb answered with resignation, "You will be taken to The Deep."

"And what does that mean?" Belac was becoming increasingly frustrated by all the religious overtones.

"It means…" Gelb searched for the words. "I believe it means that we will all be judged for what we do next."

They are going to feed me to the ocean! Belac shouted, "I knew you were going to drown me!"

Gelb ignored the elf's accusations. Belac allowed him to, focusing instead on his own growing need to be free of his restraints. He picked determinedly at the rope around his ankles, trying to somehow loosen the knots. As Gelb continued to row, the elf tried not to think about how each stroke brought him closer to ritual sacrifice.

Belac almost cried out in triumph when the first loop in the knot pulled loose. He was by no means an expert in the art of tying knots, but he understood enough to know that the first one would be the most difficult. The remainder of the knot loosened quickly and then all but fell apart in the elf's hands. *Now, I can at least kick one of them in the face.*

Belac rolled around in the wardrobe, straitening himself back out. *Now, I just need to get my hands free… And get out of this box… And kill Gelb… And somehow escape an army of crazy zealots that want to feed me to the ocean…* Once he thought about it, his achievement lost much of its value.

Heavy ropes fell limply onto the wardrobe. Gelb had not bothered to dock the rowboat. *He just rowed us strait to the ship.* Hands slid down the ropes, and boots landed in the boat. How Gelb communicated with the men was a mystery to Belac. *Please, let them be using hand signals or something.* He hoped it was not more magic.

Belac was jostled about as the sailors secured their ropes to the wardrobe. The thick cording of the ropes rubbed against the railing above, vibrating inside the wardrobe's small confines as it was lifted from the rowboat. The elf lay as still as he could, afraid his prison might slip and crash into the sea. The wardrobe collided gently with the hull of the ship and then was dragged up and over the side.

Once more, Belac considered screaming for help. *It wouldn't do any good. They would just laugh at me, ignore me, or shake the box to shut me up.*

A raspy voice asked, "What have you brought me, priest?"

Gelb's voice disclosed none of his reservations. "We have found the foreign elf. It will be your task to carry him to The Deep."

"You have him in there?" The raspy voice sounded surprised.

Gelb continued as if the question had been rhetorical. "Have him taken below. We must depart immediately."

"Immediately?" The rasped question was dissenting. "Many of the crew are on liberty."

"Immediately," Gelb reasserted. "The foreign elf must be taken to The Deep. He must be taken now."

Belac silently hoped that the raspy voice would continue to argue. *Come on man. Be a pirate! Tell that Gelb to go suck eggs!*

Gelb concluded, "All will be well."

The raspy voice replied, "All will be well." The supplication in the man's voice was complete.

The elf was disgusted by the exchange. *Humans really need to find a religion based on truth and reason.*

Belac's thoughts were disrupted when the wardrobe was lifted and then lowered down into the ships hold. He braced his legs against the inside of the wardrobe, though he was less worried about falling into the belly of a ship than he had been about plunging into the ocean.

Once the wardrobe was safely lowered, the heavy ropes dropped down on top of it and a hatch above slammed shut. Alone in the dark, Belac returned to the dilemma of his bondage. The elf twisted and struggled until his shoulders were sore and his body exhausted. But try as he might, he could not so much as reach the knots securing his wrist.

Lying face down with his forehead against the padded leather, Belac breathed deeply. *I can't give up.* He knew that no one would be coming to save him this time. There was no way his friends could even know where he was. *The zealots of The Deep moved me too fast; too quietly.* His time was limited. *Once they get me to The Deep, that's it. No more Belac.*

The elf ground his forehead into the leather beneath him. *If only I still had my dagger.* Belac smiled suddenly. *I still have something else!* He wiggled around and tugged on his belt until he could reach his small hip-pouch. His delicate fingers unfastened the buckle and then dug inside. *That striker might be small, but its metal. I can use it to cut through the ropes and…* He thought for a moment. *…And then figure out some way to get out of this box!*

Belac took the steel striker and began to rub its edge against the rope that secured his wrist behind him. His shoulders were sore, and his forearms tired quickly, but the elf was determined to persist. *And when I get out of here, I am going to use what's left of these ropes to strangle Gelb!* A hatch opened and Belac froze, listening intently.

Gelb spoke conversationally. "You may sit with us, but you must remain silent. What happens next will be sacred. You must not interfere."

A youthful voice answered, "I understand, it's just…"

"All will be well," Gelb interrupted kindly.

Belac resumed sawing at the rope with a vengeance. *I have to hurry!* Even if he could not find a way out of the wardrobe, he wanted his hands free when they opened the doors.

The youthful voice asked, "Is there anything I can do to help?"

Gelb's answer could have been that of an uncle to a nephew. "You can observe and learn." His smile could be heard as he continued, "If you can do it silently."

Belac ran one of his fingers along the rope, inspecting his progress. *It's not working!* The striker had not so much as frayed the rope. Whatever the rope had been made from, the striker was not going to be able to cut through it. *I can't give up. If I do, I'm dead. These people are going to toss me in the ocean and watch me drown.*

The elf fought back his despair. *There must be a way.* He wondered what his friends would do if it were one of them trapped in the wardrobe. *Vairug would just slip the rope off the stump of his missing hand, smash the box apart, and then use one of the broken pieces to club everyone to death.* Never before had Belac thought it might be better to be a one-handed orc.

Belac considered his other friend. *Rolan might not be as strong as Vairug, but there is no way that dwarf would stay trapped in this box.* The elf's mind hardened, his resolve focusing. He knew how to free himself. *Someone is going to pay for this.*

Thirty-Seven

Belac used the metal striker to peel up the edge of the padded leather inside the wardrobe. Whoever had constructed his prison had possessed the foresight to affix it with glue rather than nails. Nails would have provided the elf with another option. *There is no other way. I do this, or I die.*

Belac had to shuffle around inside the wardrobe, but once he had stripped the padded leather free, he began to separate the padding from the leather. He did not know what the fibrous material was, but he had to trust that it would work well enough for his plan. He piled the loose padding on one side of the wardrobe and then stuffed the leather between his back and hands. It was difficult work with his arms behind his back, but Belac was committed.

With his steel striker in one hand and his stone in the other, the elf began to throw sparks at the pile of padding. Light flashed in the wardrobe as Belac struggled to start a fire. He could not see if the sparks were catching behind him, so he fanned at the padding with his hands sporadically.

When the fire caught, its heat was immediately noticeable. Light filled the wardrobe, and dark smoke began to drift toward the vents. *I don't have much time now. I have to be quick, before they open the doors and stop me.* He tucked the striker between the back of his left wrist and the rope he could not cut. The elf scooted closer to the fire, and then he held his wrist to the flames.

The striker provided less protection than Belac had hoped, and his flesh began to sear. He focused on his breathing as he suffered the pain. *There is no other way.* His breathing deepened as the pain intensified. *I will burn my whole bloody hand off if that is what it takes to be free!*

"Look..." the youthful voice said in wonder. "It's light!"

Gelb responded commandingly, "Help me!"

The youthful voice asked, "Could he..."

"Shut up and help me!" Gelb ordered hastily.

The rope around Belac's wrist snapped. He rolled away from the flames and braced his right hand against the back of the wardrobe. He coughed at the smoke as he waited in his burning prison. When the doors opened behind him, the elf surged out of the wardrobe. He grabbed the head of a young man with curly brown hair and slammed it into the closest wall. Maddened by pain, Belac slammed the man's head against the wall until he felt the skull fracture in his hands.

Belac pressed his left shoulder into the man's chest, holding him up against the wall as he drew the man's cutlass with his right hand. The elf turned away, leaving the lifeless body to collapse behind him. Belac stood with his left hand clutched in front of his chest. The skin was swollen and wet, with black soot where blisters had yet to peel.

"I'm not happy with you, Gelb." Belac stated flatly.

Gelb dropped the cloak that he had been using to smother the fire. He turned to the elf, saying, "You do not understand!"

Belac thrust horizontally with the cutlas. The blade slid between Gelb's ribs and pierced his heart. The man's eyes held nothing but startled disbelief.

Belac looked on the man without pity. "You're just lucky that I can't turn into a gorilla-wolf-monster."

Belac jerked the blade free and then flexed his left hand in pain. *I don't know what these water worshiping freaks want with me, but I am going to demonstrate the severity of their mistake.*

Belac leaned the cutlass against the wall and used his teeth to untie the burned rope that hung from his wrist. Finally free of the ropes, he took the short, slightly curved sword in hand once more. He scanned the shadows around him, examining the ships hold. The dark, treated timbers were made visible by a single lantern hanging next to a steep set of stairs. The light dimly displayed cargo strapped in place, but the only thing in that cramped room that Belac cared about was the closed hatch waiting above the stairs.

He flexed his left hand again. The pain was torturous, but he could not afford to let the hand get stiff. He climbed the stairs and then used his left shoulder to push the hatch open. Rain beat down on the elf as he stepped onto the deck. Each drop of water that hit his wrist felt like fire.

The ship was modest in size. However, at that moment, Belac was not interested in the logistics of the Sea Spice. There were five men at the helm of the ship that he needed to kill. Four stood next to the wheel, while another lazed against the stern railing, staring back toward Harbridge. The sailors seemed largely unconcerned with the rain, and only one of them had opted to don a hat and coat. *That must be the captain.*

Keeping his injured wrist close to his chest, Belac began to walk toward the ship's helm. He flexed his hand, associating the pain with the masters of the ship. Snarling, the elf fixed his attention on the man in the hat. *I am starting with him.* He approached the captain from behind. Without announcing himself, Belac slashed at the left side of the man's neck. The blade sliced through tender flesh and grated against the captain's spine as Belac stepped past.

The elf brought the cutlass back across and down, hacking into a startled sailor's neck and upper chest. The man closest to Belac took a step back while another drew a knife and lunged. Belac pivoted away to his right and swept his cutlass in a tight circle, severing the hand that held the knife. The man cried out in anguish, gripping his gory wrist as he fell to his knees.

Belac naturally transitioned from the move to a stance that positioned the blade of his cutlass horizontally in front of him with its hilt held close to his right shoulder. With a fully committed lunge of his own, he thrust the blade into a frightened sailor fumbling to unsheathe a sword. Belac pulled his blade free and stepped away as the man fell.

The last sailor still standing did so motionlessly, the rain flattening his sandy blond hair against his boyish face. One of the fallen men sobbed weakly as he bled out on the deck of the ship. Belac looked away from the terrified sailor and drove his blade down into the dying man's back, ending the sobs.

Returning his attention to the young sailor, Belac pointed the bloody cutlass at him. "Turn this ship around."

The sailor held up his hands, shaking his head.

Belac thought that the man might try to jump off the ship. He took a step forward and shouted, "Now!"

The sailor moved his hands to protect his face. "I can't sail the ship by myself!"

Belac gestured aggressively with the cutlass. "I don't want you to sail it! I want you to point it back at the city!"

"But..." the sailor began to argue.

"Do it!" Belac hopped up and down as he shouted, "Or I am going to chop off your head and use it to float my way back!"

The sailor nodded and then sidestepped around the elf. "I need to get to the wheel."

Belac waved negligently with the cutlass. "Do what you need to. Just get us headed back to Harbridge." He stepped aside and let the man work.

It took longer than Belac liked, but the lone sailor was able to steer the ship back toward the docks of Harbridge. The elf stared off into the distance, watching the rain fall on the dimly lit harbor. *I should probably find out what this guy knows about The Deep.* He turned to interrogate his captive.

The sailor thrust a short-sword at Belac's chest. The elf parried reflexively and stepped to his left, away from the sailor. As Belac pivoted to face his attacker, he brought his cutlass up over his own head and then slashed at the side of the man's neck. The sailor dropped his sword and put a hand against the cut in his neck. Blood pulsed out between his fingers as he stared at the elf in horror. The sailor's legs gave out, and he collapsed to the deck.

Belac watched as the sailor bled out much the same as had his captain. *Stupid zealots!* "I wasn't going to kill you!" he told the dying man irritably.

Belac looked back toward Harbridge. *At least I am headed the right way now.* He frowned. *That harbor is getting close kind of fast...* He glanced at the lines that manipulated the ship. *This could be a problem.* He considered trying to drop the anchor, but he did not know how to go about doing that. *It would probably just rip free anyway.*

"New plan," Belac said to himself. He turned left and went to the port side of the ship. He tossed the stolen cutlass aside and took hold of the railing. *Well, at least this way, Rolan gets the boat I owe him.* He watched as the docks drew closer, and then leapt from the side of the ship.

The elf splashed into the ocean shoulder first. When the saltwater hit his injured wrist, it felt like the flesh was being scoured away with burning needles. Despite the pain, he clawed his way to the surface. The ship crashed into the docks with the thunder of cracking wood. Belac began to swim away, worried someone might see him near the wreck. *I don't think that this is going to make anyone want to throw me in prison less.*

He selected a pier that had fewer lanterns than the others. Swimming to it, he could feel the pain of his burned wrist all the way down to his elbow. *I am free. The hand still works. Focus on getting away.* He found a narrow ladder and took hold of one of its lower rungs with his right hand. Resting his forehead against the back of his knuckles, he spent a moment getting his breathing under control.

Belac reached up for the next rung with his left hand. His grip was weak, but he refused to stop using the hand. He pulled himself up the ladder, gritting his teeth as he endured the pain that seemed to have seeped into the bones of his fingers. He crawled over the edge and then rolled onto his back. His left arm trembled against his chest as he closed his eyes and tried to will away the pain.

"Well, what do we have here?" a jovial voice asked over the rain.

Belac's eyes snaped open. He rolled to his left, pressing his right palm against the pier in an effort to rise. Then something heavy slapped him in the back of the head, and his struggle ended.

Thirty-Eight

"Why is he not wearing a hood?" a man admonished.

Belac could almost recognize the voice. Whoever it was, if they did not want him to see, Belac was going to look. He opened his eyes and took in the familiar face. The man's scarlet tunic and its embroidered gold flowers seemed appropriate, but his voice was wrong. The man that Belac knew spoke at least two octaves higher.

"Daikon?" Belac asked, confused.

The portly man sighed. He gave one of the men holding Belac an unhappy look.

The previously jovial voice said, "Sorry, Boss." He sounded like he meant it.

Daikon lowered his gaze to the barely conscious elf. "It would have been better had you not seen me." He glanced at his underling and gave another disapproving look.

The men holding Belac shifted uncomfortably.

Daikon sighed again. "Bring him to my office. I might as well find out what else he knows." He turned around and strode through the dimly lit hallway.

The tips of Belac's boots slid across the hardwood floor as the men dragged him between them. Dim, flickering lamplight gave the stained wood panel walls a sinister aspect as he passed through the hallway. *Why would Daikon do this?*

While Daikon's office was larger than the hallway, it offered a no more reassuring atmosphere. To the left lay an oversized desk afore an array of doored cabinets. Clean and inviting in a professional manner, the space was starkly contrasted by a partitioning wall of steel bars on the right. The men dragged Belac into the holding cell and dropped him unceremoniously onto the floor.

"Use the smaller manacles," Daikon instructed offhandedly. *What is wrong with his voice?*

Belac groaned as his arms were wrenched behind his back, and then cried out when his wrists were shackled. Loose skin peeled from the elf's wounded wrist as the irons were twisted into place. *Why…*

With an apathetic tone, in a voice still lower than it should be, Daikon said, "Go ahead and shackle his feet as well."

Belac tried to understand what was happening, but pain and confusion thwarted him. He did not even consider resisting as they bound his ankles in chains.

"Is this what you hit him with?" Daikon asked one of his men.

The no longer jovial voice answered, "Yes."

There was a thud of something dropped on the desk, then Daikon said, "Here. Give him this."

Belac was rolled onto his back, the manacles digging into his wrist painfully. The pain was nothing compared to what came next. One of the men held Belac's mouth open while the other poured a cold liquid down his throat. The agony that followed was overwhelming. Acidic fire burned through the elf, the sensation more intense than any he had ever experienced. He screamed, but the pain drowned out his ability to hear it.

The pain seemed to bleed out of his left foot, leaving Belac numb inside. Breathing deeply, he almost gagged on the smell of burning lamp oil. He staired up at the steel bars crossing the ceiling of his cell. Without thinking, Belac said, "I like Rolan's healing potions better." It was exactly the wrong thing to say.

With an emotionless voice, Daikon said, "Beat him."

The first kick dislodged the elf's jaw. The second broke a rib. Belac rolled to the side, bringing his knees up in a feeble attempt to protect himself. A boot stomped down on the back of his head, smashing his brow into the floor. Another stomp broke another one of his ribs. The men took turns kicking the shackled elf, their blows controlled but brutal. Worse than the pain of being beaten, was the feeling of complete helplessness. Belac could not fight back, he could not defend, and he could not stop what was being done to him.

"That's enough," Daikon finally decided.

A hand grabbed Belac's hair and forced him to sit up before jerking his head back at an angle. He tried to open his eyes, but only one would do so. Daikon stared back at him from the other side of the bars where he stood impassively.

Acidic fire burned through Belac again, the sensation no easier to suffer than before. He could feel his bones mend and his jaw relocate. Flesh knitted back together, and bruises faded. Only the memory of pain lingered.

"Now," Daikon said conversationally. "Let's discuss what you know."

Belac glared at the man. "I know that I should have let you burn!"

Daikon grinned and tapped the side of his nose. "But then, you," he pointed at the elf, "would still be in prison."

Belac craned his neck forward, pulling against the hand that held his hair. "I am in prison!" *Stupid human.*

Daikon carried a small three-legged stool into the cell and sat down in front of the elf. "No, Belac," he said smiling. "You are in my office."

Belac did not care how much it would hurt. "I think Rolan's is nicer."

Daikon slapped Belac with something heavy. The force of the blow knocked the elf back to the floor. Daikon came from his seat and stood over him. Then the man proceeded to slap Belac in the face repeatedly with vicious efficiency.

The bones in Belac's face broke under the assault and he could feel pieces of shattered teeth on his tongue. Unconsciousness saved him from the worst of the beating, but the relief was short lived. Acidic fire brought the elf awake with a scream. He felt the bones in his face shift back into place and his teeth grow back.

A leg against his back, and a fist gripping his hair kept Belac seated upright. Daikon was once more seated on his small stool in front of the elf. The man slapped a leather blackjack against his own palm suggestively.

Daikon's dark eyes met the elf's azure. "Do not upset me again."

The man's calm voice made his words no less threatening in the wake of Belac's pain. The elf waited silently, wondering if Daikon would actually kill him. *If he is willing to do this to me, he is willing to kill me.*

Daikon nodded. "Now," he said again, "Let's discuss what you know."

Belac glared at the man, but said nothing.

"Why do the Followers of The Deep want you?" Daikon asked.

Belac frowned. "They want to drown me."

Daikon tilted his head forward and regarded the elf suspiciously. "They are willing to pay a rather large sum to simply drown you."

Belac shrugged as best he could with his arms shackled behind his back. "I killed a bunch of them. They are probably mad at me."

"You want me to believe that you have been killing the Followers of The Deep?" Daikon asked.

Belac shook his head. "No. What I want is for you to let me go." *So that I can kill you.*

Daikon smiled at the elf's answer. "Why would you kill Followers of The Deep?"

"They're crazy!" Belac told him.

"Of that, there can be no doubt," Daikon agreed. "Have you taken it upon yourself to go around and kill all of the world's crazy people?"

Belac thought for a moment. "Not all of them."

Daikon grinned, asking, "And is your reticence due to sloth or hypocrisy?"

Belac did not understand the man's joke. "Is what due to what?"

Daikon waved the issue aside. "Tell me how Rolan found the castle."

Belac did not understand the question any more than he had the joke. "I don't know what you are talking about."

Daikon glanced up at the man behind the elf. "Cocklan, reach back there and break a couple of his fingers."

"No." Belac shook his head, pulling against the hand that held his hair. "Wait, wait! Wait, wait, wait, wait!" He tried to shy away from the man behind him. "I don't know what you are talking about! I don't know!"

Daikon held up an empty hand, bringing the looming torture to a halt. "The nillanan's castle. How did he find the nillanan's castle?"

Belac shrugged again, confused by the question. "We just found it."

"You 'just found' a magic castle?" Daikon asked disbelievingly.

"It's not like it was very well hidden," Belac explained. "There was a road that led up to it and everything."

"No," Daikon disputed. "There is a forbidden road in an unknown mining camp that leads to an uninfiltrateable fortress that was guarded vigilantly by heavily armed men."

"Yeah." Belac nodded slightly. "That is not how you keep something secret."

One of the men behind Belac stifled a laugh.

Daikon glanced at the man and sighed before returning his attention to the elf. "Well, it seems as if this discussion has simplified things a great deal."

Belac looked at the man curiously. *...Are you going to let me go now?*

"If you don't know anything useful," Daikon continued, "And, the Followers of The Deep are simply going to kill you," he smiled, "then, it is of no concern that you have seen me."

Belac attempted to stand, but was held down by the man behind him. "You are going to give me to the crazy cult people?!"

Daikon stood and picked up his stool. "No, Belac," he said as he walked out of the cell. "I am going to sell you to them."

Thirty-Nine

Belac tried to convince himself that all was not lost. He was alone in a dark prison cell, shackled and condemned. *But at least no one is about to drown me.* He tested his chains. *And my wrist is healed.* He looked at the locked door to his cell. *This is just another prison. And I am a prison-escaping professional.* He glanced at the metal links between his ankles. *Though… I am probably not burning those off.* He wiggled around, bringing his feet up behind himself. *There has got to be some way to get these off.* He ran his fingers over the manacles and discovered that there was in fact a way to get them off. With a key.

Belac looked through the bars of his cell and stared at the light shining under the solid wood door to the hallway. "Okay, Rolan," the elf said aloud. "Feel free to break down that door and come rescue me any time now." *Being rescued still counts as an escape.*

When no psychotic, killer dwarves came charging through the door, Belac dropped his head to the floor. *I am going to need a new plan.* He closed his eyes, attempting to devise some means of escape.

Belac woke up when the office door opened and light flooded into the room. *Rescue?* Daikon entered the office and Belac frowned. *I don't think Daikon is here to rescue me.*

The man's face was lit by a small brass lamp that he carried into the room with him. He had changed clothes and now wore a tunic of crimson velvet with golden fish embroidered across his ample midsection. He appeared well rested and in good spirits. *However long I slept, it was too long.*

Daikon took a moment to consider the elf. "You smell terrible, Belac."

Belac narrowed his eyes at the man. "Set me free and I will go find a bath." *Right after I kill you.* Belac was well aware that he stunk. *I think it might have been better when I could not smell anything at all.*

Daikon set the brass lamp on the edge of his oversized desk. "I have a better idea."

The man walked over to one of the cabinets on the far side of the room and opened the panel door. He removed something and then shut the cabinet door without showing the elf what else was inside. He returned to his desk and set down a cylindrical object of multifaceted, blue glass. Picking up the small lamp once more, Daikon touched its flame to the top of the cylinder. Fire crawled across the top and continued to burn without smoke. The man then busied himself with filling and lighting the other two larger lamps in the room.

A strange smell drifted down to Belac. He could not identify the sent, but he knew it smelled better than he did. *Whatever that thing is, it's magic.* "You're the distributer that's trying to kill Rolan," Belac guessed.

Daikon blew out the small lamp and set it on his desk. "No, Belac. It is important that a man not be seen as someone who would betray a friend."

Be seen. Belac was ashamed of how quickly he could reconstruct the man's plans. "You convinced someone else to kill him."

Daikon smile became one of mild surprise.

Belac continued, "This way, once your 'friend' is dead, you get to avenge him."

Daikon was no longer smiling.

"Why get rid of one competitor," Belac asked rhetorically, "when you could get rid of two and look like the hero at the same time."

Daikon tapped the side of his nose. "It is fortunate that the Followers of The Deep want you dead."

Belac flopped around until he was in a seated position. "If you want us dead, why did you help me escape from prison?" He shook his head. "It would have been easier to just have us killed."

Daikon grinned. "It is important for a man to pay his debts."

And he arranged for us to be killed as soon as we were out of his care. Belac thought about it for a moment and then smiled. The elf started to laugh quietly to himself.

"You think that's amusing?" Daikon asked dangerously.

Belac shook his head. "I figured it out."

"Yes," Daikon agreed. "And soon you will be dead."

Belac laughed harder. "If I figured it out," he met the man's eyes, "then, Rolan figured it out."

Daikon frowned at the elf disapprovingly. "I do not believe that is likely."

Belac laughed at the man. "You are gonna die…" his laughter took over.

Daikon shook his head in reproach. "Believe what you will, fool."

Someone knocked on the inside of the doorframe and then two men with sandy blond hair walked into the room. "Hey, Boss," said the man who must have been Cocklan. "Everything is set up."

The two men in shades of brown stood facing the one in velvet red. Both men were powerfully built, but their deference to Daikon was unquestionable.

Daikon nodded. "Go ahead and take him to the carriage. I will be with you shortly." He looked at his men. "And this time, put a hood on him."

"Sure thing, Boss," Cocklan affirmed, nodding.

Daikon pulled a key from his pocket and held it out. Cocklan stepped over to the desk and took the key. With a glance at the imprisoned elf, he moved to the bars of the cell. The man unlocked the door and then swung it open, leaving the key in its lock.

Belac did not expect it to accomplish anything useful, but he kicked at the man when Cocklan entered the cell. Obviously accustomed to dealing with prisoners, Cocklan kicked the elf's feet away and dropped a knee down onto his gut. The man reached back, preparing to throw a punch.

Daikon stopped the man, saying, "Don't damage his face. He will need to be recognizable."

Cocklan frowned down at the elf. Instead of striking him, the man pointed a finger at the elf's face and warned, "Behave."

Belac glared at the man, but did not struggle as he was pulled to his feet. Once they were standing, Belac tried to headbutt him. Cocklan leaned away from the attack and then punched the elf in his stomach. Belac bent over double and would have fallen if not for the man's hand holding onto the back of his shirt.

"Behave," Cocklan said again.

Cocklan pulled Belac upright and the other man put a hood over his head. The dense weave of the fabric blocked any light that did not creep in under the bottom. One of the men punched Belac in the stomach again and he almost threw up in the hood.

Cocklan asked, "What was that for?" His question sounded like professional curiosity.

The other man said, "It's just a reminder."

Don't worry. Belac straitened himself and glared into the darkness of his hood. *I won't forget to kill you too.*

Cocklan turned the elf away from the other man. Then he picked Belac up and threw him over a shoulder. With one arm wrapped around the back of the elf's legs, Cocklan carried him out of the cell.

Belac bounced uncomfortably as he was carried from the office to the carriage. *I have to find some way out of this.* The problem was that he could not conceive of a plan that did not require him to wait for an opportunity to present itself. Not only did Belac loath waiting, he was not convinced that such an opportunity would develop without some form of intervention. *I wonder if just paying attention counts as doing something.*

The door to the carriage opened and Belac was thrown inside. With his arms and legs chained and a hood over his head, he was unable to control his flight. He crashed backward onto a bench and then fell to the floor. Belac rubbed his head against the floorboards, attempting to remove the hood. *Anything I can see is information I might need.* In a time when he possessed so little, the value of information had never seemed so great.

One of the men entered the carriage and moved Belac bodily to the bench. Once the elf was seated upright, his hood was adjusted back into place. Obviously, his captors too had some understanding of the value of information. Belac groaned. *It's not fair. Big humans are supposed to be stupid.*

"Hey, Cocklan," the other man said as he climbed into the carriage. "When we are finished with this business, do you want to go get something to eat at the Lucky Duck?"

The Lucky Duck! Belac's eyes went wide in the shadows of his hood.

"Sure," Cocklan agreed. "As long as the boss doesn't need us for something else."

The Lucky Duck! Belac's mind reeled. *How did I forget about the Lucky Duck?! That is where we were supposed to be waiting for Serath. Not some shady warehouse in the docks. And certainly not out in the mountains with giants, ghouls, and creepy-blue-lizard-goblins!* He had simply been too caught up in events. He had never stopped to consider that there might be an alternative. *Did I even tell the others about the Lucky Duck?*

Someone else climbed into the carriage and then the door slammed shut. A fist pounded up against the cabins ceiling, informing the driver that the occupants were ready to travel. The sound of horses' hooves on stone carried into the cabin as the carriage began to move.

Could Serath be there? Would he just sit there; eating duck or whatever it is they serve there? What if his wizardness made the man so patient that he just sat there while we all died? The elf was suddenly angry at Serath. *Lazy Wizard! The stupid human is just sitting around stuffing his handsome face with duck while the rest of us suffer and die! What's the point in having a wizard, if he is not going to follow us around and throw magic at everything?!*

Forty

"You know that I'm trying to kill a dragon, right?" Belac complained more than inquired.

The man seated next to Belac laughed.

Seated across from the elf, Daikon responded, "No one kills a dragon, Belac."

"Well, I am going to," Belac argued.

"I do not believe that is likely," Daikon said without feeling.

"The Danorin," Belac expounded. "I am going to kill it."

The unnamed man laughed more. "I would pay in gold just to watch you try."

"I am not interested in your delusions." Daikon's tone suited his words. "No one kills a dragon."

"Wait," the unnamed man said, still laughing. "I have got to hear this. How…"

"Enough, Ester," Daikon cut the man off. "Do your job. Pay attention."

Ester said nothing more. There was an emptiness left in the absence of his laughter.

Belac decided to answer the man anyway. "A wizard has promised me a magic sword."

No one answered. No one laughed.

Belac knew they were still listening to him. "Daikon knows it's true."

The quiet that lingered now felt like an ally to the elf. *Let them worry about wizards and magic. Let them worry about a sword that can slay dragons. Let them worry about the vengeance my friends will bring.* Belac smiled in the darkness of his hood.

The elf's smile faded when the carriage came to a halt. Any retaliation his friends might bring would not stop him from being drowned and sent to The Deep. *They can't avenge me if I'm not dead.* The two other men exited the cabin, leaving Ester to manage Belac.

Ester nudged the elf's shoulder. "Really? A magic sword?"

Belac smiled in his hood. "I am sure you will see it soon."

Ester scoffed. Then he grabbed the elf and threw him out of the cabin head first. Before Belac could cry out, he was caught by Cocklan. The large man set the elf's feet on the ground, and then picked him back up. He threw the elf over his shoulder and began to follow Daikon. Faint moonlight edged its way under the hem of Belac's hood, revealing nothing other than that it was night. Ester's boots clomped onto the cobblestones, and then the door to the carriage slammed shut. *Okay, opportunity. You can show up any time now.*

The walk to the place of the meeting was a short one. Despite how uncomfortable it was to be carried hanging over someone's shoulder, Belac would have preferred for the walk to last all night. Instead, the elf was set down on his feet and left to stand in the dark unknown.

After a moment of silent anticipation, Belac's hood was ripped off his head. Stray strands of hair were pulled from his scalp, and what remained was a tangled mess. He stood in a darkened alley between two buildings that resembled upside down ships. Pale lunar light shone over the peaks of the buildings as the moon began its rise.

Daikon tossed the hood aside and turned away from the elf. Cocklan and Ester each stood off to either side, waiting protectively without obtruding. A dozen paces down the alley stood a tall figure in hooded robes of midnight blue.

"Here is your purchase," Daikon said, speaking in his higher voice. "I will now accept the artifact."

From within the voluminous robes, a hand rose out. In its grip, a severed head hung from a tangle of long, sandy blond hair. Without preamble, the head was flung into the empty space between Daikon and the robed figure. Everyone watched in silence as the head landed on the cobblestones and rolled toward Daikon.

Belac looked up from the gristly head in confusion. The robed figure threw something to the side. Glass shattered, and fire erupted. Flames sped out in a line, creating a fiery ring around them all. Crossbow bolts shot through the flames from the darkness beyond. Both Cocklan and Ester were struck multiple times, though many of the missiles flew wide. Daikon stood stoically in the blazing light, not even so much as glancing at his men as they died.

The robed figure reached up and threw back his hood. The robe fell to the ground, revealing a malevolent dwarf standing on a wooden cask. The fire's light danced angrily against his hardened face. Rolan hopped off the cask and drew two knives in underhanded grips. The dwarf said nothing as he marched forward.

Smiling happily, Belac turned to gloat at Daikon. *I told you, you were going to die.* The man drew a dagger from his sleeve and stabbed Belac in the chest. Daikon, his face devoid of emotion, turned away from the elf. Belac collapsed to the ground, coughing blood as he struggled to breathe.

Blood smeared on his dagger, Daikon slashed at Rolan's eyes. The dwarf ducked low and cut into the man's midsection. Bright white stuffing flew from the wound as the knife rent through crimson fabric. With a left jab, the man punched Rolan in the face and then followed up with another slash of his dagger. Rolan spun away from the attack, coming around with both knives held up in a fighter's stance.

Daikon turned his left side away from the dwarf and placed his left hand against his own chest, presenting the dagger with his right. Belac stared up at the gaping wound in the man's artificial belly. *He's not even fat? How fake can one man be?!*

Daikon focused intently on the dwarf. "He is dying, Rolan." His voice had returned to its lower register.

Rolan said nothing. Instead, he threw his left knife at the man and then went in fast with his right.

Daikon pivoted back and to his right, slapping Rolan's thrown knife out of the air with his left hand. He took another step back with his left foot, pivoting away from the dwarf's attempt to cut his thigh. Daikon's dagger swept up and across as he slashed at the dwarf again.

Rolan dropped away, his left hand on the cobblestones supporting his weight as he rotated under the sweeping blade. When Daikon's dagger reached its zenith, the man pirouetted around to face the dwarf once more. With a fluid grace, the man bent at the knees, sinking into a balanced stance.

Rolan grabbed the back of the man's left calve with his free hand, and then stabbed at Daikon's thigh. Daikon's left hand chopped down inside the dwarf's right forearm, stopping the knife. Daikon slid his right foot forward while thrusting his dagger at the dwarf's chest. Rolan released the man's leg and deflected the thrust upward and away with the back of his left hand. As soon as Daikon's left leg was free, the man twisted and kneed Rolan in the face with his right. The dwarf staggered back, while Daikon settled back into his balanced stance.

Before Rolan could recover, Daikon pressed the attack. Rolan reversed the grip on his knife as the man moved toward him. With a strait throw, Rolan buried his knife in the top of the man's right boot. Daikon stumbled forward, gritting his teeth in pain. Committed by the momentum of his advance, the man thrust his dagger artlessly at the dwarf's neck.

Rolan stepped in, sweeping the man's right arm up and away with his left. The dwarf's arm continued to circle around Daikon's, trapping both the dagger and the arm. Rolan then threw a devastating, side elbow that fractured Daikon's jaw and knocked the man over backward. Keeping Daikon's arm trapped, Rolan's right wrist joined his left behind the man's elbow. Wrenching backward, Rolan broke the man's arm.

Involuntarily, Daikon cried out and dropped his dagger. Rolan released the man and then kicked the dagger away. The steel clattered across the cobblestones as it passed through the wall of flames.

With his left hand, Daikon ripped the knife out of his own foot and rolled toward Rolan. The dwarf took a step back as Daikon raked at the air wildly with the knife. There was now emotion in the man's face. Flames mirrored in his dark eyes as he stared at the dwarf with virulent hate.

Rolan unbuckled one of his pouches and pulled out a metal flask. He spun the top off, and then flicked the lid contemptuously at Daikon. Careful to stay out of the knife's range, Rolan circled the man on the ground. Daikon's hateful glare never faltered as the dwarf splashed the liquid contents of the flask onto him. Casually, Rolan held the flask out to the wall of flames and lit its mouth on fire. Then, without looking away from the man, he tossed the burning flask at Daikon's feet.

Daikon cried out in torment as the flames engulfed him. Dropping the knife, he rolled and swatted at the flames as he was burned alive. Rolan stood by and watched as the man struggled in vain to smother the fire. When Daikon's attempts ended and his cries finally stopped, Rolan turned away from the man and went to check on Belac.

Rolan knelt and supported the elf's head with a hand on the back of his neck. Snapping his fingers in the elf's face, Rolan asked, "Are you still with me?"

Belac coughed blood and willed all of his effort into saying, "…Meet Serath…Lucky Duck…"

Lucky Duck? As Belac's world faded away, all he could think was, Please, d*on't let those be my last words.*

Epilogue

When she fell, she had been so happy that she had not cared. Freedom had for so long been denied her, that the sensation of falling was something she had embraced. Years lost underground, attended by mindless servants, her prison had been a thing of beauty. When she had finally seen the sun, it had redefined what beauty was to her.

Laughing, crying, twirling in the sunlight, she had opened her arms to the world. Then she had fallen, and freedom was taken from her. Lying on her back, she had not been able to move. She had not been able to speak. She had not even been able to breathe. As the morning sun faded to black, someone had spoken her name.

The darkness that had followed could have lasted for an eternity. Instead, it had been interrupted by a voice. The voice had seared her mind and echoed in nothingness. As painful as it had been, she had welcomed the sound in her desperate solitude.

"Has your will been lost?" The voice had been all that there was.

She had not been able to speak. Still, she had willed her words into existence. "Where am I?"

The voice had answered, "In a place before death."

As her own sorrow almost washed her away, she had reached out to the voice. "Can you save me?"

"There will be a cost," the voice had warned.

She would have paid anything to once again be free. "Would I have my freedom?"

"No," the voice had told her. "You would have duty, obligation, and service. But you would also have life. More life than you could have ever had before."

Life itself was a promise. To her, it had been an opportunity to someday regain her stolen freedom. She had not cared how much it would cost her; she had wanted to survive. "I accept."

"So be it," had been the voice's final words to her.

Time was beyond measure in that place. Alone in the void, she contemplated hope. She considered what her life had once been, and she wondered what it might yet become. She awoke naked and alone in a spacious dodecagonal chamber of polished obsidian stone. Darkness climbed endlessly above her. Lying on her back, she was supported by a monolithic protrusion in the center of a seamless floor.

She opened her eyes, and breathed in the sweetness of life. She was surrounded by a thick white mist that filled the bottom of the chamber. Small pink and purple lights flashed in the mist like lightning in a storm cloud. She did not yet understand the nature of her new life, and she could never have imagined what it would cost.

PART THREE

Prologue

He knew there was a better way. He believed the designs outlined were insufficient and that their efforts would be squandered. He knew that there must be another way. However, Sanderan had been set to task. Prodigious commitments had been established, and escalation was no longer avoidable. A man of ethics, Sanderan had found himself obligated to the completion of works not his own.

Though Sanderan had never appreciated the implacable temperament of the sea, there he was. One of five men being rowed to the place of ritual, he alone faced reservations. Black water parted as the boats glid under the stary night. Without the glittering beacons on the floating platforms ahead, Sanderan may have eschewed his duty.

As they neared the ritual sight, the rowboats drifted away from each other, each transporting a man to one of five small platforms. Chained together and bound to the bed of the sea, the platforms bobbed gently on the calm waters. Though more than a ship's length apart from each other, the anchored staging created a single place of power.

Careful to keep his midnight blue robes out of the water, Sanderan moved from the boat to one of the platforms. The raft shifted precariously under his feet, but he had little difficulty positioning himself.

He waited for the others to arrange themselves, and then he began to chant. The voices of his collaborators were too far away for him to hear, but he could feel their strength as they joined him. Chanting into the encircled darkness, Sanderan began to open the ancient gateway below.

As his voice reached out through the watery realm, Sanderan felt the world darken. Though he had known something would come to stop them, he had hoped they would have more time. Fire lit the night as flames consumed the ship that had carried him to The Deep. He continued to chant.

Despair shot through Sanderan as he felt death ripple across the water. He knew what dark thing had come for him. He could feel it coming closer. Still, he continued to chant.

One of the voices stopped chanting. Sanderan put more of himself into the ritual. Another voice ended. Struggling to maintain the forces they had called, Sanderan felt yet another voice silenced. He knew what he would have to sacrifice, but still, he continued to chant.

When the last of his supporters died, Sanderan gave himself to the ritual. Fueling the chant with his very essence, he opened the gateway below him. Unable to hold such exertion for long, he prayed that salvation would come. His chant became a scream as fire engulfed him. Despite the torment, Sanderan took satisfaction in the knowledge that his task had been accomplished.

One

Belac gripped the bars and shook the door to his cell. "Let me out!"

He had awoke laid out on a cot, naked under a stained blanket. The deeply treated timber room had swayed gently around him, informing him that he was once more at sea. It was not until he had rose and tied the blanket around his waist, that the elf realized he was in a prison. *I hate prison!*

Belac glared through the bars at his captor on the other side. Dressed in a splotchy gray uniform, the dwarf appeared unphased by the elf's ire.

"I mean it, Rolan!" Belac shook the bars again. "Let me out of here!"

Gray eyes as hard as stone stared back at the elf.

Belac thrashed his head and shouted, "I want out!"

Rolan's grin twisted his stubbled cheek.

Belac narrowed his azure eyes at the dwarf. "We are on a ship," Belac stated the obvious. "We are at sea. Where am I going to go?"

Rolan chuckled. "Nowhere, if you stay in there."

Belac grabbed for the dwarf's face. With his arm stretched out between the bars, Belac raked at the air while Rolan laughed at him. The blanket slipped free from the elf's slender waist and fell to the floor.

Belac quickly retracted his arm and bent to reach for the blanket. He slammed his forehead into the bars of the door and staggered backward. His feet tangled in the blanket, and he spilled onto the floor.

Rolan continued to laugh.

"Die in a fire," Belac said as he stood and gathered the blanket back around himself. He glared at the dwarf. "Why am I in prison, Rolan?"

Rolan shook his head. "You're not."

Belac surveyed the small confines of his cell and the iron bars blocking his exit. "This looks like a prison to me." *And I would know.*

Rolan shook his head again, smiling. "It's a brig."

Belac narrowed his eyes at the dwarf. "And do you know what a brig is?" he asked and answered, "A prison!" The blanket almost fell back down as he shouted, "It's just a prison on a boat!"

Rolan nodded, laughing. "I guess it is."

Belac ground his teeth and wished that the dwarf was not such a good judge of distance. *If I could just get my hands around his neck…* He took a deep breath. "Rolan, why am I in the brig?"

Rolan nodded amiably. "That is a good question."

Belac wanted to chew through the bars. "I know it's a good question, Rolan. That's why I asked it!"

"We could not wait for you to wake up," Rolan explained. "The brig was just a convenient place to put you." He smiled. "It turns out that it has all kinds of benefits."

Belac frowned. "Sleeping?"

Rolan nodded.

Belac tried to recall the last thing he could remember from before he woke up. *I was bleeding to death in a back alley…* "How long?" he asked. "How long was I sleeping?"

"You were out for a couple of weeks," Rolan told him. "The knife was poisoned."

Belac's fingers traced the scar on his chest.

"Magic poison," Rolan continued. "You almost died."

A rich voice spoke from the side. "I think it would be safe enough to let him out."

Rolan shrugged. "The door is unlocked," he said offhandedly.

Belac's attention jerked toward the man who had spoken. "Serath?"

Still clothed in immaculate black, the wizard was leaning against the far wall with his arms crossed. Belac was certain that the man had not been there before. *But that is really him!*

"Serath!" Belac was happier to see the wizard than he would have expected. "You're not dead!"

Rolan scowled. "Of course, he's not dead."

Belac ignored the dwarf. "How are you not dead?" he asked the wizard.

Serath simply smiled.

Rolan answered for the wizard. "The man is too stubborn to die." He sounded proud.

"Right..." Belac said. "But, what about the giant rock monster? You know. The one that was tearing apart the city?"

"The colossus?" Serath's question was a subtle correction. "Its hate was unable to sustain it after you left." The wizard shook his head ruefully. "Alvin wanted to have the remains broken down and used to rebuild the city walls."

Rolan chuckled. "That is probably a bad idea," he said, though approval colored his words.

Serath's green eyes twinkled in the dim lighting. "That is what I told him."

Belac remembered the colossus. He remembered the unbelievable size and power of the thing. "It just... died?"

Serath shook his head. "It was never really alive in any biological sense. Hate is a powerful force, but it can burn itself out in the absence of direction."

Belac pushed away the memory of families screaming in terror. He closed his eyes and tried not to see the faces of children now dead. *For Tariel alone, I would kill that dragon.* The elf's eyes opened with renewed determination. "Did anyone see the dragon?"

"No," Serath said, shaking his head. "I doubt that the dragon was there long, if he was there at all. The Danorin is remarkably canny. And he is not working alone."

"Why would anyone work with that thing?" Belac asked, though he already knew the answer. *Some people are just evil.*

Serath's shrug was one of enduring acceptance. "The same reason why people follow evil kings or corrupt politicians. They believe their interests are aligned. One of the many failings of man is that of priority."

Belac found no comfort in the wizard's words. "Then, after I kill the dragon, I will be happy to help them follow."

Serath's handsome face brightened into a smile. "Well then," he ran a gloved thumb and forefinger around the sides of his mouth, flattening his trim beard, "we should prepare." He took his weight off the wall and walked from the room.

Rolan followed the wizard without saying anything. Belac moved to follow as well, but bumped into the door of his cell. The elf glowered at the bars, then reached through and pulled the bolt free on the other side.

Pushing the door open, Belac called out, "Where are we going?"

Rolan replied without stopping. "Cavasca."

Belac kicked the hem of his blanket out of his way as he hurried after the other two. "What's in Cavasca?"

"A volcano," Rolan replied, still not stopping.

"We are going to make the sword!" Belac guessed happily.

Rolan couched his response. "Only if Serath is right about Agadon."

Serath glanced back to look at the dwarf disapprovingly. "I can assure you, I am."

Confused, Belac asked, "Who is Agadon?"

"That's the name of the volcano," Rolan explained.

Serath shook his head. "That is not entirely accurate."

Rolan looked up at the wizard irritably. "That's all superstitious nonsense, and you know it."

"I know many things," Serath replied with smug crypticness.

Obviously, the man can't let anyone forget that he's a wizard. Belac shook his head. "Right about what?" he asked, trying to steer the conversation back to something he thought might be useful.

Rolan answered as they climbed a short set of stairs. "He says Agadon is going to wake up soon."

"And it will," Serath assured the dwarf.

Stepping onto the main deck, Belac asked, "How does a volcano wake up?" He narrowed his eyes at the wizard. "What is Agadon really?"

Rolan sighed.

Serath seemed pleased to answer. "The people of Cavasca believe that deep beneath what others might call a dormant volcano, lies Agadon… The Sleeping Dragon."

Two

Belac followed in a stunned silence. *A dragon? …How are we going to make a sword with an angry dragon trying to kill us?* He did not think the dragon would be happy when it woke up. *What if it blames us for waking it up?* Belac's eyes shot toward Serath. *What if that crazy wizard plans on waking it up?!*

Belac followed Rolan and Serath into the captain's quarters. The trepid elf found the cabin's walls to be surprisingly comforting. *At least the dragon can't see me in here.* Belac frowned. *That does not make any sense. The dragon would still be sleeping.* He narrowed his eyes at the wizard. *If there even is a dragon.*

"But, it's not a dragon," Belac asserted unsurely. "Right?"

Serath turned and smiled. "I do not believe so. No."

Rolan shook his head irritably. "It's not a dragon."

Serath shrugged noncommittally.

Rolan growled at him.

Serath smiled impishly in return.

Belac wanted more confirmation. "So, Agadon is just a volcano?"

Rolan scoffed, "Just a volcano…"

"That is not entirely accurate," Serath repeated himself patiently. "While true that Agadon is a volcano," he held up a gloved hand to forestall interruption, "it is not 'just' a volcano." He lowered his hand and then gestured in a revealing manner. "Agadon is a legend. It is a belief held so long, that even those who doubt, do so without conviction."

Rolan grumbled, "I have plenty of conviction."

Serath ignored the dwarf, and spoke conspiratorially. "Though, I suspect that this legend will not harm your own."

Belac suddenly felt like it was easier to breathe. "I am just glad it's not a dragon."

Rolan mumbled, "Says The Dragon Slayer."

Belac narrowed his eyes at the dwarf.

Rolan dropped a black canvas duffle bag at the elf's feet. "Get dressed."

Belac pointed to the large bag. "Is that mine?!" He wondered how much of what he had asked for was actually in the bag. *They did not show me the list after Vairug got finished drawing lines all over it.*

"It is now," Rolan told him. "So, maybe try not to lose it."

Belac frowned at the bag. "It is supposed to be leather."

Rolan looked at the elf irritably. "You get canvas."

Belac considered the waxed canvas and then shrugged. *At least it's not green.* He bent down to open the bag. "Whatever you got me, it has to fit better than an old blanket."

Serath's response was encouraging. "We still have your measurements from when you visited the tailor in Tariel."

Grumpy as a dwarf, Rolan added, "And you have not changed much."

Belac glanced up and gave the dwarf a perturbed look. "I have changed lots of times. You are the one still running around wearing the same filthy clothes."

Despite Belac's words, the dwarf's clothes appeared clean. In fact, Rolan's recent haircut made him a contender for the most well groomed dwarf that Belac had ever seen. *Doesn't count.* Belac refused to retract his statement. *His clothes are all splotchy.*

Rolan scowled at the elf. "I was not talking about your clothes, Belac."

"You are being unfair, Rolan." Serath offered the admonishment kindly. "I believe our friend has grown more than your estimations would allow."

"See?" Belac quipped. "The wizard is on my side."

Serath smiled and placed a gloved hand on the elf's shoulder. "Always, Belac." Then the wizard walked out of the cabin.

The room feels emptier without him. Belac had not realized how much he had missed the wizard. It was a comfort to be supported by someone who understood reality so well that they could bend it to their will. *Having Serath with us might be more important than having the sword. There would be no quest without him.*

Belac looked past the scowling dwarf, and surveyed the captain's quarters. Fading light shined through tall windows, illuminating a large navigation table in the back of the room. To its right, a bed and cabinets had been crafted into the wall. The plush bed was a luxury that represented the privilege of position. On the other side of the room stood a privacy screen next to a collection of closed chests. Belac picked up his duffle bag and moved behind the standing screen so that he could get dressed with some degree of modesty.

Rolan spoke from the other side of the screen. "I don't think there is anyone on the ship that has not seen you naked, Belac."

Belac attempted to throw his voice over the top of the screen. "That is not the point."

Rolan grumbled something that the elf could not make out through the screen.

Belac continued to argue anyway. "It is not about whether people have seen you or not. It is about being able to change without feeling like people are staring at you."

Belac unlaced the end of the duffle bag and began to dump its contents onto the floor. There was less inside than he had asked for, but that was to be expected. *Maybe if I had asked for twice as much, I might have gotten half of what I wanted.*

"No one is staring at you," Rolan said dismissively.

Belac gestured to the screen. "I know that. I am behind the screen." *Stupid dwarf.* "That is why I am back here."

Rolan offered no counter.

Belac picked through the pile of clothes and began to dress himself. Despite the wizard's assurances, Belac was surprised at how well the clothes fit him. *It is nice to finally have some proper clothes.* He noticed that some of what he had asked for was not quite right, but decided that he could complain about it later. He had half expected the entire bag to be filled with nothing but green cloaks.

Belac tucked a pale blue blouse into black trousers and then stomped his feet into soft black leather boots. He crammed the remainder of the clothes back into his duffle bag and then held the blanket up over the screen. "What do you want me to do with this?"

"Hold on to it," Rolan told him. "It has been getting cool in the evening."

Belac rolled the blanket up and then stuffed it under one of the duffle bag's straps. He left the bag where it was and stepped out from behind the screen. "I still need a sword."

Rolan nodded and then walked over to one of the closed chests. He flipped open the lid and pulled out a sword and dagger, their scabbarded blades wrapped together with wide leather straps. The polished steel buckles and accents gleamed against the blackened leather as he set the bundle on the navigation table. "This should do until we get you the magic one."

Belac walked over to the navigation table and frowned down at the sword. "That's not funny, Rolan."

Rolan set a black leather belt pouch down next to the scabbarded blades. "What's not funny?" he asked innocently.

Belac looked at the dwarf. "That is not a long-sword."

"The sword looks long to me," Rolan said with mock sincerity.

Belac narrowed his eyes at the dwarf. "You know what kind of sword that is, Rolan."

Rolan nodded agreeably. "The man who sold it to me called it a 'hand-and-a-half." A smile flickered across the dwarf's face.

Belac gestured aggressively at the broad blade that had been fixed into a disproportionately long hilt. "And do you know what else it's called?"

Rolan choked down a laugh.

"A bastard-sword!" Belac shouted.

Laughter began to escape the dwarf. "I wonder why they call it that," Rolan said as he struggled to maintain a straight face.

"Because the blade is too short for the stupid handle!" Belac glared at the dwarf. "But that is not the point, and you know it!"

Rolan coughed as he tried to hold back his laughter. "I'm sure that the sword has a point, Belac."

Belac snarled at the dwarf. "It's a bastard-sword!"

Rolan laughed openly now. "It seemed…"

Belac pointed at the dwarf and shouted, "Don't you say, 'appropriate!"

Rolan took a step back, laughing. He held his hands up in surrender. "Like a good idea at the time."

Belac continued to glare at the dwarf. *We will see if you still think that sword is funny after I use it to chop off your head!*

Rolan got his laughter under control and then leaned forward as if he were sharing a secret. "At least it's not green."

Three

Belac stormed out of the captain's quarters, leaving behind both the sword and dagger. He did not even remember to take his duffle bag. *Stupid dwarf thinks he's funny.*

"Glad you're not dead," said a familiar voice.

Belac turned to his right and glared at Vairug. The orc looked like a hero from a swashbuckling novel. Above black trousers and turn-down boots, a crimson sash held a white sleeveless shirt tight around the orc's waist. A leather harness covered his left shoulder and ran down a muscular arm, the straps securing a gleaming metal hand to his wrist.

Vairug raised the silvery prosthetic and gripped its fingers in the air in a playful greeting.

Belac pointed at the orc. "Did you know about the sword?!"

Vairug lowered his mechanical hand. Small tusk jutted from his confused grin. "Yes." He tilted his head to the side as he considered the elf. "And so did you."

"I did not!" Belac argued. "How would I know?"

"You are not making any sense, Belac." Vairug's tone became concerned. "What's wrong? Is there some reason we cannot forge the sword?"

"What?" Now, Belac was confused. *He thinks I am talking about the magic sword.* Belac shook his head. "Not that one."

Vairug's response was a questioning silence.

He did not know. Belac nodded toward the captain's quarters. "Rolan got me a bastard-sword."

Vairug's cheek twitched.

Belac narrowed his eyes at the orc. "It's not funny."

Vairug did not argue. He stood tall and stoic, waiting for the elf to say something reasonable.

The setting sun reflected off the ocean and flashed in the orc's eyes, causing them to take on a deep blue hue. With his thick black hair tied high behind his head, Vairug looked as much like a lord as any man Belac had ever seen. *I can almost believe it... I know that it's not true, but I can almost believe it anyway.* Belac could almost believe he was standing before Lord Vairdoe of Enevic.

"You look like you want to kiss me," Vairug complained.

Belac bristled. "I do not!"

Vairug did not argue.

Belac turned away from the orc and looked out across the long deck of the three-masted ship. A giantess sat cross-legged at the bow of the ship, gazing out into the horizon. Belac smiled. *Now her, I would be willing to kiss.* While Belac was surprised to see Breana above deck, he was not surprised to see that she was nude. Belac glanced at the men sailing the ship. *I wonder if anyone is going to believe them when the sailors tell their tail.* Belac frowned. None of the men were staring at the unclothed giantess; they would not so much as look in Breana's direction.

Belac gestured to the giantess. "What is going on there?"

Vairug turned toward the bow. "At first, the men were pleased to have her aboard."

Belac laughed. "I bet."

Vairug smiled. "And then one of them thought he could touch her."

Belac winced.

Vairug looked at the elf. "She tore the man's arm off and threw him over the side."

Belac rolled his shoulders uncomfortably.

Vairug continued, "The man bled out before his friends could get him back on board the ship."

Belac felt a little sorry for the nameless man. "Maybe someone should have warned them."

Vairug grunted. "They were warned."

Belac nodded to himself. *It's because she's so beautiful. I can see how it would be hard for them to believe that she could be dangerous.* "Is Rolan mad at her?"

"No." Vairug laughed silently. "He used the severed arm to beat one of the men when they suggested throwing her off the ship."

Horrifying as the claim was, Belac believed it. "Has there been any sign of mutiny?"

Vairug looked at the elf askance. "They are on a ship with a giant, an orc, a wizard, and a dragon slayer." He laughed. "Not even humans are stupid enough to attempt a mutiny."

Belac grinned at the reminder that he was The Dragon Slayer. "You left out the psychotic dwarf."

Vairug nodded deeply. "You're right. Few men would be brave enough to mutiny against Captain Brightstone."

Belac's grin split into a smile. "Captain Brightstone?"

"He hates to be called that," Vairug said happily.

"Rolan is the captain?" Belac laughed. "Do you think he would rather be called 'Captain Crazy Dwarf?"

Vairug's tusks jutted from his grin. "I think we should find out."

A gnarled old woman walked up and poked Belac in his chest. Disheveled, gray hair and cragged face, she carried with her a determined attitude. *Where did she come from?*

"You take yourself back to bed right this instant!" the old woman ordered in a hard voice.

Belac took an uncertain step back. "Who are you?"

"Ezela," Vairug answered as if the woman's name left a bad taste in his mouth. "Rolan hired her to care for you while you slept. She..."

"And I did not watch over you all day and night so that you could catch your death wondering around on a ship!" Ezela declared, speaking over the orc.

Belac looked back and forth from the woman to the orc. "Rolan got me a nanny?!"

Ezela tsked angrily. "Someone had to take care of you." She gave the orc a venomous glare. "And this fancy lord was not going to do it."

Vairug scowled at the woman.

She thinks he's a lord. Belac grinned. *The woman hates him for being a lord instead of fearing him because he's an orc.* Belac shook his head. *Vairug can't win for losing.*

Ezela poked the orc in the chest with a bony finger. "Don't you look at me like that!"

Vairug growled at her.

Ezela pointed her finger up at the orc's face. "Don't you think I won't bend you over my knee."

Hoping no one noticed him grinning, Belac took a slow step to the side. *I think I will just let Vairug handle this.*

Ezela wheeled on the elf. "And where do you think you are going?"

Belac held up his hands reflexively. "Nowhere."

Ezela took an aggressive step toward the elf. "You are going back to bed. That is where you are going."

Belac shook his head. "I don't wanna."

Ezela reached up and tried to grab one of the elf's pointed ears.

Belac swatted her hand away with both of his own. "Hey, stop that!" he said, backing away from the old woman.

"Don't you tell me what to do, young man!" Ezela pointed at the elf threateningly. "I will have none of that!"

Belac tried to look to Vairug for help, but the orc was no longer there. *Coward orc.*

Ezela advanced toward the elf. "You are meant to stay in bed until we reach Cavasca."

"Listen, lady." Belac pointed at her. "Unless you want to go for a swim, you leave my ears alone."

Ezela stopped and stared at the elf in affront. "Breana!" she shouted as if summoning an angry spirit.

The giantess stood and began to walk across the deck of the ship. The setting sun bathed her alabaster skin in golden light, and made her double braided bun appear almost blond. Despite her alluring figure, every sailor on the ship looked away as she passed by. Belac attempted to keep his focus on her face, but he lacked the sailor's will to look away.

Breana halted next to the old woman and asked, "What's wrong, Ezela?"

Ezela indicated toward the elf with her chin. "He said that he is going to throw me in the ocean." She looked up at the giantess. "He wants to watch me drown!"

Breana crossed her arms under her breast and stared at the elf accusingly.

Belac pointed. "That crazy old woman is trying to pull my ears!"

"Belac!" Breana said reproachfully.

Continuing to play the victim, Ezela said, "I was only trying to care for the boy."

The black and white rings of Breana's eyes bore into the elf as she scolded him. "Belac, this woman has been seeing to your every need for days!"

Belac leaned forward cautiously and addressed the old woman. "Thank you. But your services are no longer required." He quickly leaned back away so that the woman could not grab his ears. He then took a step back and to the side, putting the giantess between himself and the old woman.

The scorn in Ezela's voice was unfettered. "What a heartless thing to say!"

Breana turned her back to the elf and placed a hand on the old woman's shoulder. "Come with me, Ezela." She twisted around to glare down at the elf. "Belac can go take care of himself."

Well, that's rude. Belac narrowed his eyes at the giantess. *She kills a man for touching her; but I stop someone from ripping off one of my ears, and suddenly I'm the bad guy?* He shook his head. Out of the corner of his eye, he noticed an orc's head sticking up out of an open hatch. Belac's attention snapped toward the orc. Vairug's head dropped back down as soon as he realized that he had been detected.

Belac shouted, "That's right, coward! Hide!"

Breana stopped and turned around. "What did you just say to me?" she asked, her question sounding like a threat.

Belac's eyes went wide. He held up his hands and shook them side to side. "No, no, no, no, no!"

Four

"I probably needed a bath anyway," Belac muttered to himself as the sailors helped him back onto the ship. He climbed over the rail and stood, dripping sea water onto the ship's deck.

Vairug's gray face twisted into a smile. "At least she did not tear off your arm."

One of the sailors stared at the orc's metal hand speculatively.

Belac had to laugh. "It was actually kind of fun."

"Do you always scream like a girl when you are having fun?" Vairug asked.

Belac grinned. "It depends on how much fun I am having."

One of the sailors exclaimed, "She could have killed you!"

"Nah." Belac began to squeeze water out of his long black hair. "She likes me."

The sailor shook his head and then walked away mumbling. "… kill us all."

Belac disregarded the potentially mutinous sailor. *It was fun flying through the air like that.* "I wonder if I can get her to throw me again." *Maybe if I sneak up, tap her on the shoulder, and then hide…*

"Are you really willing to risk losing one of your arms?" Vairug asked.

Belac looked at the orc. "You don't think she would actually hurt me, do you?"

"I do not think that she would have thrown you off the ship and into the hazards of the ocean, if she wanted to keep you safe," Vairug replied dryly.

Belac turned toward the bow of the ship and studied the giantess. His elven face scrunched up and then he said, "Maybe I am looking at this wrong."

"I would be willing to bet your boots that you are," Vairug told him.

Belac turned and narrowed his eyes at the orc. "I never bet my boots."

Vairug's shrug was mocking.

Belac grabbed one of the sailors' arms and began to whisper into his ear.

The sailor listened intently and then voiced his only concern. "The captain won't like it."

Belac knew what the sailor wanted to hear. "You can tell him I did it."

The sailor nodded and then ran to do as he had been instructed.

Vairug spoke as if he knew his words would go unheeded. "This is unwise."

"Maybe," Belac admitted. "But, either we are friends, and this is all a game," his attention returned to the bow of the ship, "or that giant just accosted me and put my life in danger."

Vairug said nothing.

Belac continued to study the giantess. *I really hope that we're friends.*

A man that Belac did not recognize walked over and offered him a small pouch of dried rice. The first sailor had obviously conscripted others into their cause. Belac accepted the small pouch and gave the man a commanding nod of gratitude. The man issued a casual salute before running off to join the other conspirators.

Vairug said, "I think I have seen those signs of mutiny you were asking about."

Belac frowned at the orc. "It's not mutiny."

Vairug ignored the elf's denial. "Are you planning to have the men call you 'Captain Crazy Elf?"

"It's not mutiny," Belac muttered.

Vairug pointed to an open hatch. "I think I will have a better view from over there."

Belac nodded. "I've got this." *Now, when people ask me how I became The Dragon Slayer, I can tell them that I practiced on giants.*

The sailors worked quickly. Belac did not think that the wind alone would be enough for what he had planned, so he had to wait while the sailors hoisted some of the heavier cargo. The elf tossed his pouch of rice up and then snatched it out of the air. *Now, it's time for some dragon slaying practice.*

Belac walked slowly to the foremast, positioning himself so that the thick spar was between him and the giantess. His slender fingers pulled open the mouth of the small pouch and then removed a single grain of rice. He threw the grain at Breana, but it was so tiny that he did not even see where it went. *There is a problem with the plan...* Belac took a pinch of rice and threw it as hard as he could. The wind blew the rice away, preventing it from reaching the giantess. *The rice is just too light.*

Belac sighed. *Fine.* He closed the pouch. *If this does not work, I will just have to find something else to throw.* He stepped away from his concealment and threw the pouch at Breana. The pouch flew through the air and smacked into the back of her head.

Belac's azure eyes went wide. *Probably should not have hit her in the head.* He hopped behind the foremast, but his shoulder stuck out conspicuously.

"Belac!" Breana shouted furiously.

Belac ran. "Mistakes were made!" he called back as he fled.

Breana gave chase, her heavy footfalls thundering against the ship's deck.

Belac ran behind the larger mainmast. He popped his head around the side and asked, "We are still friends, right?"

The insane rings in Breana's eyes did not look friendly. She slowed but continued to close on the elf.

Belac backed away, knowing the foremast would not be enough to protect him. When Belac reached the ship's railing, it became apparent that he was running out of space to flee. He continued to back away toward the stern of the ship with his hands held up nonthreateningly.

Breana glared down at the elf. "I hope a shark eats you this time, Belac."

Belac met the giantess's eyes. "Not this time." He grabbed a rope tied to the railing, and pulled the slipknot loose.

Heavy crates dropped down and pulled ropes through the ship's tackle. Wind caught in the mainsail as the ship's massive boom arm swung with building speed toward the angry giantess. Breana ducked slightly and looked up as the boom swung overhead, but it came nowhere close to hitting her. Her gaze fell onto the elf, her vexed disbelief unconcealed. It was as if she were offended by how pathetic the trap had been.

Belac smiled, frightened and with nowhere left to run. *I really really hope we are friends.*

Then a rope tightened around Breana's ankle and yanked the giantess off her feet. She was slung across the deck and off the side of the ship. As she swung out over the ocean, one of the sailors cut the rope, and Breana flew out into the air like a stone flung from a trebuchet.

"Which one of your arms do you think she is going to tear off?" Vairug asked.

Belac jumped away from the orc and then turned to glare at him. *Sneaky orc.* "She is not going to tear off my arms."

"I would not be so certain," Vairug told him.

Belac stood on his tip toes and tried to locate the giantess in the ocean, but he had not even seen where she splashed. "She can't kill me."

Vairug disagreed. "I am confident that she can."

Belac shook his head. "Her honor won't let her. She still needs to make the sword for me."

Vairug snorted. "People are buried with their swords all the time, Belac."

The elf suddenly felt like he had fallen off a cliff. *I really should have thought of that…* Belac shook his head again. "It doesn't matter. We're friends."

Vairug pointed toward where the giantess had been thrown from the ship. "That may have changed things."

Belac frowned at the orc and then began to make his way to the bridge. *The cards have been delt. There is nothing left to do but play out the hand.* He walked up the stairs to the bridge deck and approached the sailor at the wheel.

"Okay," Belac pointed with his thumb, "now we need to turn around and go get her."

The helmsman did not try to hide his confusion. "Why for anything would you want to do that?"

Belac laughed. He could empathize with the man's concerns. "She went back for me." He hoped the answer was a reason that the helmsman could respect.

The helmsman nodded gloomily and began to turn the ship. He called out orders and the men hurried about the labor of sailing the ship. Changing the course of so large a vessel was no simple task. However, the sailors were more than proficient. The ship turned and the quest to rescue the drowning giantess commenced.

Rolan stepped onto the bridge, asking, "Why are we turning around again?"

The helmsman hunched down slightly in an attempt to make himself seem smaller.

Belac knew he should be the one to answer. "I… ah…" He hoped the dwarf would not be mad at him. "I kind of threw Breana off the ship."

Rolan gave a single short bark of laughter. "Good luck with that," he said before turning away and walking back down the steps.

Belac glanced at the helmsman. "She is not going to kill me." The assurance sounded weak.

When it was time to haul Breana back onto the ship, Belac made sure he was the first person on the rope that would pull her abord. *Maybe she will be less likely to kill me if she sees that I helped her back up.* Breana, however, was not willing to wait for the men to pull her up. As soon as she took hold of the line, she began to climb up the side of the ship. Belac and the men were forced to shuffle as they readjusted their grips on the rope.

When Breana climbed over the rail, Belac's face was the first she saw. One of the giantess's braids had come undone, and sea water dripped from the limply hanging tangle of hair. The black and white rings of her insane eyes locked onto the elf. Belac met the stare and tried to stand taller as the giantess stomped toward him.

Breana halted in front of the elf and bore down on him like a storm cloud. It was as if the sun broke when she smiled. "That was well done, little elf."

Belac's smile split his face. "It was fun, right?"

Five

Lying comfortably in a hammock below deck, Vairug asked, "How did you know Breana would respond the way that she did?"

Belac twisted around in his own hammock, trying to situate himself. "Her uncle."

"Explain," Vairug prompted the elf.

Belac jerked his body left and right as he strove to match the orc's comfort. The hammock began to swing precariously, and he stopped struggling. "When I met Morkan, that's her uncle, the first thing he did was ask me if I wanted to fight." He began to cautiously wiggle in the hammock. "I thought he was threatening to kill me, but Rolan didn't say anything."

Vairug reflected silently for a moment before saying, "I do not understand."

Belac scootched up in the hammock, hoping a different angle might help. "If Rolan thought Morkan was going to kill me, he would have done something."

"What does this have to do with Breana?" Vairug asked.

Belac began to thrash about in the hammock again. He growled in frustration and then waited for the hammock to stop swinging. "I think that it has to be some kind of giant thing. Maybe it's like an informal greeting." He wiggled testingly. "Or maybe more like an initiation of sorts."

Vairug was quiet for a moment. "It sounds like you did not know anything."

"I knew it was something," Belac retorted. He bounced in the hammock tentatively. "Besides, I can't just let her treat me like that. No one is going to believe in a dragon slayer that lets himself be tyrannized."

Vairug grunted noncommittally.

The elf rolled out of the hammock and then kicked it. The cloth flopped up into the air but came down undamaged. Belac turned and looked at the orc. "Have you ever heard the story about the cowardly hero?"

Vairug frowned, shook his head, and then said, "No." He sounded interested.

"That's because there isn't one," Belac told him.

The orc's smile was lost in the darkness.

Belac looked around the room at the other shapes resting comfortably in hammocks. None of the sailors seemed to have a problem sleeping on the hanging cloth. *I hate these things! Only humans would be stupid enough to make a bed like this.* The elf glared in Vairug's direction. *Or maybe it was the orcs. Maybe these hammock things are really just orcish torture devises, and humans are too stupid to realize it.*

Belac untied his hammock and laid it out on the floor. "Don't let anyone step on me," he told the orc.

"Why not go sleep in your room?" Vairug asked.

Belac sniffed at the floor. "Gak." He shook his head. "I am not sleeping in prison."

"It is not a prison," Vairug argued. "It is where you have been sleeping for days."

Belac frowned into the darkness. "Someone could lock the door."

"Take the keys in with you," Vairug suggested.

I can do that? Belac was no longer frowning. "How do I get the keys?" *Maybe I need to sneak into the captain's quarters. I wonder if Rolan sleeps with them tied around his neck or something.*

Vairug's plan was simpler. "They should be hanging on the wall. All you need to do is pick them up and take them in with you."

Belac smiled. "Vairug, you are the smartest orc I know."

Vairug grunted.

Belac hopped up, leaving the loathsome hammock on the floor. He exited the crew's quarters, careful as he passed by the men hanging in their beds. The sailors gave no indication that any of them were still awake, but Belac was sure that some of them must have been listening to his conversation with Vairug.

Moving around the ship at night kind of feels like being a spy or an assassin. As he slipped through the darkness, the elf began to contemplate the appeal of skullduggery. *I wonder how those people get so sneaky. Is it just special shoes or something? Maybe they have to take a class.* Belac imagined a small child sneaking through a dark room while grown men threw tomatoes at it. *Hardly seems worth it.* He looked down at his feet and tried to think of some way to convince Rolan to make him 'sneaky-boots.'

"Hello, Belac," a rich voice said pleasantly.

The elf's heart skipped a beat. Belac's attention snapped up toward the figure waiting ahead of him. He narrowed his eyes at the wizard. Leaning against the wall with his arms crossed, the man in black seemed part of the shadows.

"Stop sneaking up on me!" Belac hissed at the wizard.

Serath's deep green eyes seemed to glow faintly in the darkness. "Are you having trouble sleeping?"

As kind as the wizard was, the man's eyes terrified Belac. Usually, he could let himself forget that they were green; however, in the darkness, they were all the elf could see. Belac's mind was pulled back to a time of death and despair.

Serath interrupted the elf's thoughts. "Perhaps the night air will help."

Belac tore himself away from the wizard's eyes. "Sure…" He shook his head. "It has to smell better than a room full of sailors."

Uncrossing his arms, Serath stepped over to a set of stairs that would take him above deck. He began to ascend without waiting for the elf. Belac moved to follow the wizard up the stairs. *It's not his fault that his eyes are green.*

A sliver of the moon lit the night sky above. As the elf stepped onto the main deck, he marveled at how the light filled the emptiness around them. Belac stopped and took a deep breath of sea air. While he did not care for the salty taste, it was better than what was below deck. He glanced over at the captain's quarters. The door was shut, but light shown at the edges and out the back of the ship.

"Is Rolan still awake" Belac asked, turning back to the wizard.

Serath's teeth gleamed in the night. "I would advise you not disturb him."

Belac shrugged. *Whatever.* He looked at the wizard curiously. "So, what are you doing?" *There can't be much for a wizard to do on a ship.*

"I am checking on you," Serath answered directly. "You were quite ill, Belac."

"Oh." Belac was caught off guard. *Rolan said the poison was magic.* He nodded to himself. *It might have taken a wizard to save me.* "Did you cure the poison?"

Serath nodded. "I believe so."

"And that's why you are checking on me," Belac concluded.

Serath smiled agreeably.

"I guess it's a good thing to have a wizard around," Belac said in gratitude. "Wait. How are you here? Is the pond working again?"

"It is," Serath confirmed. "Though it did take some time to restore its function."

Belac thought the Harbridgers were fortunate that the wizard had stayed behind. "Did you fix it?"

"Sadly, the creation of such devises is beyond me," Serath confessed. "I worry that a day will come when the ponds are lost to us entirely."

I guess wizards can't just fix everything. Belac thought for a moment. "A lot would change without the ponds."

"That is an understatement," Serath replied.

Something occurred to Belac. "It would change the balance of power. Port cities like Harbridge would become mercantile juggernauts."

Serath nodded approvingly. "Much would be needed to avoid open warfare."

Belac tried to imagine what the human lands would be like without the ponds. "People would starve." *Not all of them, and not everywhere, but too many still.* The elf had never before considered something so internationally complex.

"Troubling as the possibility is," Serath said, redirecting the elf's thoughts, "The Danorin is a significantly more pressing matter."

Belac nodded. "I will be ready." *I just need the sword.*

There was pride in Serath's smile. "As you chase your destiny, remember: you cannot save the world only once."

Belac gazed out into the ocean. Beyond the black waves waited the rest of the world. *Save the world?* He had before joked about saving the world. *But is that what I am? Someone who can save the world?*

Belac turned back to question the wizard further, but Serath was not there. *I guess he got tired of staring at the side of my head.* The elf rubbed his arms. *It is getting kind of cold. I wonder how long I have been out here.*

Belac made his way back down to the brig. *I can worry about saving the world after I get some sleep.* Despite the dark, he found the keys hanging on the wall just as Vairug had said he would. *I guess they need the keys to be easy to get to if they have to lock someone in one of the cells.* As he walked toward his cell, he heard the faint sounds of someone stirring.

At first, he thought that someone might be waiting to ambush him inside. However, even in the dim lighting, he was able to see that the cell was empty. When the sounds came again, he realized they were coming from the other cell next to his own. He stepped over to the cell and peeked inside cautiously. *The ambusher might have just picked the wrong room.*

Ezela slept on a cot in the cell, her fragile form wrapped tightly in a blanket. The sight of the old woman tugged at Belac's emotions. *She must have been sleeping here next to me the whole time.* He watched over her for a short time, and then quietly shut the door for her.

Six

Belac awoke to the sound of an old woman screaming. He smiled as he looked up at the ceiling. *Today is going to be a great day.*

Ezela shook the door to her cell. "Let me out of here!"

Belac sat up in his cot and swung his legs off the side. He put his bare feet on the floor, but if the cot had sat higher, he would have kicked them in the air gleefully.

"Help!" Ezela called out. "Someone has locked me in!"

Savoring the old woman's distress, Belac calmly put on his boots. The door to the other cell rattled violently. *The old woman might actually break the door down if she keeps that up.* Belac flipped the keys in his hand and walked out of his cell.

"Belac?" Ezela asked, confused.

"Good morning, Ezela," Belac replied cheerfully as he made a show of hanging the keys back on the wall.

No longer confused, Ezela ordered, "Belac Melavar, you open this door this instant!"

Belac frowned at the use of his full name. *I wonder who told her that.*

Impatient to be free, Ezela warned, "Don't you make me tell you again, young man!"

Belac's smile returned. "And if I open the door for you, what then?" he asked. "Are you going to be nice?"

Ezela stared bloody murder at the elf.

Belac held up a finger. "That does not look like you are being nice."

While Ezela's glare remained steady, she said, "I'll be nice." The words sounded like they tasted bitter.

Belac crossed his arms. "Do you promise not to sic any giants on me?"

Ezela answered through clinched teeth. "I promise."

Belac pointed his finger at her. "And no more trying to pull on my ears!"

Ezela gave a single angry nod.

Belac leaned forward. "You can still grab Vairug's ears if you want to." *She might not know that name.* "I mean Lord Vairdoe."

Ezela continued to glare at the elf, but said nothing.

"Right," Belac said nodding. He stepped over to the closed cell door and slid the bolt aside without needing to unlock it.

Ezela's mouth dropped open as the door swung out. Belac winked at her and then walked away. He left the old woman alone in the brig and made his way above deck. *Now, it's time to get something to eat.* He hoped that he could find something better than the hard biscuits they had fed him the night before.

Belac took a deep breath of salty sea air and speculated on how to best locate the galley. He noticed that the door to the captain's quarters was open, so he decided to make a detour. *Rolan might have some secret captainy food stashed somewhere.* As he walked past the men going about the business of sailing the ship, he waved and pretended that he understood what they were doing. When Belac stepped off the main deck and into the disagreement taking place in the captain's quarters, he worried that he may have made a mistake.

Serath stood in the middle of the room shaking his head rejectingly.

Sitting on the edge of the bed, Breana argued with the wizard. "It has to be cast."

Serath turned toward the dwarf standing next to the navigation table.

Arms crossed, Rolan said nothing.

Serath turned back toward the giantess. "It cannot be cast. It…"

"That is the only way that it can be done," Breana said, interrupting the wizard.

Serath shook his head again. "The sword must be 'forged' in a live volcano," he insisted. "Forged. Not, cast."

Rolan added, "By a giant." It was unclear whose side he was championing.

Serath gave the dwarf a perturbed look. "Yes, Rolan. By a giant. Thank you."

Rolan smiled at his friend's aggravation.

"The problem is not the giant," Breana said testily. "It is the volcano that is the problem. The live volcano."

Serath waved a gloved hand dismissively. "The volcano can be managed."

Breana would not be dismissed. "You do not understand." It was a dangerous thing to say to a wizard. "Forging requires repeated heating and cooling of the metal. It takes days to forge a sword properly."

Serath opened his mouth to speak but the giantess spoke over him.

"Forging starmetal is only going to make this more difficult," Breana continued. "I have never seen anything like it before. We do not know how long it will take to heat. We do not know how long it will stay workable. We do not know anything about starmetal at all." She glared at the wizard. "Not anything except that I am supposed to figure everything out myself while I try to forge it!"

Serath waited patiently for the giantess to finish speaking. Then he waited a moment more to ensure she knew that he had been choosing to wait. "I believe I can help with that."

Breana purposely directed her gaze at the wizard's scrawny arms. "You do not look like a smith to me."

Rolan smiled but remained quiet.

Serath neither defended nor explained himself, instead asking, "If the temperature of the metal were to remain almost perfect, would you then be able to forge the sword?"

Uncomfortable with the hypothetical, Breana stipulated, "It would still take me hours."

Serath nodded. "I can manage hours."

"You can do that?" Breana asked with a trace of doubt.

Belac decided that it was now safe to join the conversation. "Wizard," he stated in answer to the giantess's question.

The bed creaked as Breana shifted her attention toward the elf. "You just want your sword."

While the words were phrased as an accusation, Belac could detect no trap. He shrugged. "Dragons are too hard to kill with my bear hands."

Soft laughter carried from the dwarf on the other side of the room.

Breana shook her head and smiled despite herself. "Fine. You win, Wizard."

Serath met the giantess's eyes. "Victory is something that we will all share," he told her.

Breana's smile brightened and she nodded her head in agreeance.

She is so cute. Breana's long white hair had been rebraided into the twin buns that sat on either side of the top of her head. While the giantess was undeniably a woman, Belac had always thought that the braided buns made her look more youthful. *She looks like she is about to stick her tongue out at someone.*

Belac remembered how her hair had looked the evening prior. "Your hair looks nice, Breana."

Breana touched one of the buns and said, "Thank you." She blushed. "Rolan fixed it last night."

Rolan returned the discussion to the forging of the sword. "Will we still need to set up the magma tap?"

"We will," Serath said, nodding. "My assistance will be limited."

Belac knew that at some point, the wizard would need his blood. "Is there anything you need me to do?" *Please, say, 'no.'*

Serath did not ask for the elf's blood. "We should all be present at the time of the forging. Until then, it would be best if you aided the people of Cavasca. They will…"

Vairug barreled into the room. He pushed Belac out of his way and then turned around and slammed the door to the captain's quarters. The orc put his back against the door and looked at the others with the eyes of the hunted.

Vairug pointed at the elf and demanded to know, "Did you tell that woman, I locked her in the brig?"

Belac laughed, shook his head, and said, "No," all at once. *But I can guess what woman you mean.*

Vairug's finger jerked toward the dwarf still standing next to the navigation table. "Why did you have to bring that horrible creature on board this ship with us?"

Rolan smiled as he said, "You are going to need to be more specific."

Vairug growled. "You know who I mean, Rolan!" The orc looked like he wanted to spit. "Ezela! That nasty old woman that has been taking care of Belac."

Rolan snorted. "It sounds like you just answered your own question."

Breana frowned at the orc. "I think Ezela is delightful."

Vairug ignored the giantess. "You could have hired someone else."

Rolan shrugged. "Technically, I did not hire her."

Vairug dropped his hand and looked at the wizard. "You brought that old crone on board?"

Serath arched an eyebrow.

Rolan explained, "She has a younger sister in Cavasca. In exchange for looking after Belac, she gets to ride with us."

Vairug gestured to the elf. "And now that he is awake, does that mean I can send her off the ship?"

Breana answered, "Not unless you want to swim in after her."

Vairug was quiet for a moment. "How far from shore are we?"

Belac immediately recognized the orc's plan. "You are willing to try swimming all the way to shore?" he asked, laughing.

Breana raised her voice admonishingly. "Vairug!"

Vairug glanced at the door and then looked back to the others. "I'm thinking!"

Seven

Belac adjusted the wide strap holding his new sword in place on his back. The baldric had been designed so that the sword could be worn on either the hip or back. He already had a dagger and pouch belted around his waist, so he decided to carry the sword behind him. *I think it stays out of the way better like this anyway.*

Rolan pointed his hand at the black canvas duffle bag on the floor. "And don't forget your bag this time."

Belac thought that the bag should be safe where it was. "Are we not sleeping on the ship?"

Rolan shouldered his rucksack and sinched the straps. "Serath has other plans. He wants us to talk to people, let them know that we are serious about the volcano."

The dwarf's rucksack looked more comfortable to carry than the canvas duffle bag. *I should have asked for a backpack.* Belac wondered if it was too late to ask for something better.

Rolan continued, "That is going to be up to you mostly. The rest of us are going to be busy setting up the smithy for Breana."

Belac had never visited Cavasca before. "Why would any of those people listen to me?"

Rolan gestured at the elf. "You're The Dragon Slayer."

Belac stood a little taller. "Does that make you my herald?" he asked smiling.

Rolan chuckled. "Serath will vouch for you. The man is a convincing advocate. As long as you remember who you are, you should be fine."

Belac did not understand. "Remember who I am?"

Rolan's stony gray eyes met the elf's. "The Dragon Slayer." He emphasized 'The.' "You said you wanted to be a hero. You said that you want to be a legend and stand defiant for all." He made a fist in the air. "Remember that."

Belac did not remember the part about defiance. *I think people should be defiant for themselves.* Still, he thought he understood what the dwarf meant. "You want me to stay out of trouble."

Rolan nodded. "That would help."

That sounded more like the dwarf to Belac. "What about Vairug? Is he Lord Vairdoe here?"

"He has to be," Rolan affirmed. "Cavasca is more disconnected than some other cities, but the story of Lord Vairdoe will reach these people eventually. It may have already for all we know."

Belac wondered how far his lie would spread. "Where is Cavasca? Is it an island?"

Rolan shook his head. "It's not an island. We're on a peninsula south of Harbridge. The people here would have a real problem if this were an island."

"A volcano is not a real problem?" Belac asked without thinking.

"Not if they evacuate," Rolan answered as if it should be obvious. "Everyone can just load up wagons and carts and whatnot. Worst case scenario, some people will have to walk with whatever they can carry. There is a road that leads all the way around the gulf and up to Harbridge."

Belac nodded. "And there would be no way to get everyone to safety if this were an island."

"Right," Rolan confirmed. "No city has enough ships to transport everyone that lives in it."

Belac held out a questioning hand. "How do we know these people are even going to believe us?"

Rolan shrugged. "A lot of them won't. But when that volcano erupts, and death starts raining down on their heads, I suspect they will change their minds."

Belac frowned thoughtfully. "That could be too late."

Rolan nodded. "It will be for some of them."

That is why it's so important that we find some way to convince them. Belac wanted to help. "What do I need to do?"

Rolan clapped the elf on the shoulder. "Go with Serath. Listen to what he says. Try to look heroic." He pointed his hand at the black canvas duffle bag on the floor. "And don't forget your bag this time."

Belac bent down and grabbed his loosely packed duffle bag. He tugged the blanket out from under a strap and tossed it aside. He extended the strap and then slung the bag over his shoulder. It pressed his sword into his back, but the discomfort was tolerable. *If Serath would just make me that flying carpet, I would not have problems like this.*

Rolan waited for the elf to exit the room before following him out onto the main deck and shutting the door behind them. Belac turned and gazed into the distance. The volcano was close enough that they could have walked to it. Its dark rock stood in stark contrast to the vibrancy of life that surrounded it. Looming high as if it were merely another mountain, Agadon slumbered still.

Cavasca spread out from the base of the volcano, covering the land below all the way to the ocean's shore. Red clay tile rooves blanketed the city, sheltering the short one and two-story buildings of tan and reddish brown rock. Though far smaller than a capital, the city seemed to be flourishing surprisingly well despite the absence of a pond. People bustled along cobblestone streets of light brown stone that wound throughout the city, unaware of the disaster to come.

It's beautiful, but it is going to be destroyed. It seemed like such a waste to Belac. "Why would anyone build a city here?"

"They mine the volcano," Rolan explained. "There are other mines all over the region, but the ones in Agadon are the most lucrative."

"But that doesn't mean that they have to live next to the thing," Belac argued. "What if we had not come to warn them?"

"They probably don't think about it," Rolan answered dismissively. "Humans don't live as long as we do. Entire generations have come and gone without there being any sign that the volcano is going to erupt. It is hard for a person to be scared of something that has been with them every day of their life and has never caused any problems. At this point, they don't really see the volcano as a threat. Most of these people don't really believe that it is ever going to erupt. To them, it is just some unlikely event that someone else might have to worry about at some other time that might not ever happen."

Belac thought he understood. "Because Agadon is just a legend."

Rolan did not argue with the assessment. "Humans can convince themselves of all sorts of things if it suits them."

How do I persuade people that are like that? They need to know what is coming. Visions of Tariel assaulted the elf. He heard the cries of children as he remembered the devastation. Belac could not stand by and do nothing as another city was destroyed. *I have to help these people.*

"If they will not believe the truth," Belac thought out loud, "maybe they will believe a lie."

"What do you mean?" Rolan asked.

Belac turned his head slightly toward the dwarf, though his eyes continued to study the city. "What if we tell them that Agadon is real?" His eyes moved to the dwarf's face. "What if we tell them that Agadon really is a dragon and that he is about to wake up?"

Rolan met the elf's eyes. "How is that any better than what we are telling them already?"

"Maybe we can use the legend," Belac proposed. "It might be easier for them to believe that a dragon is finally waking up than it is for them to believe that a mountain is suddenly going to explode for no reason."

Rolan shook his head. "Anyone that actually believes in the dragon will make that connection for themselves. If you go around telling everyone that you think Agadon is really a dragon, all you are going to do is make everyone else think you're a crazy person. Next to no one will believe us then."

Belac frowned thoughtfully. He did not like it, but he knew that the dwarf was correct. *Why does Rolan always get to be right?*

"Besides," Rolan continued, "the truth has the added benefit of being... you know, the truth."

Belac did not care about the truth; he cared about stopping people from being consumed by fire and death. "There has to be some way."

Rolan nodded. "There is. Trust Serath. He has a plan. You can't save everyone, but if you help him, you will save the most you can."

Belac sighed. "Yeah. Okay."

Rolan led Belac off the ship and down the gangplank to where Vairug and Serath waited on the pier below. The orc stood hidden beneath a voluminous white cloak though his posture was proud and unafraid.

Serath appraised the elf before saying, "You should put on your jacket."

"What? Why?" Belac asked. The humid air was already uncomfortably warm.

Serath explained as if it were a courtesy. "The jacket will make you more presentable. The way in which you appear now will affect how you are viewed in the future."

Belac pointed up at the midday sun. "It's kind of hot."

Serath smiled patiently. "That is of no great concern."

I guess if he can walk around all day in that big black coat, I can put on a jacket. Belac set his duffle bag down on the pier.

Rolan said, "It's a good thing you did not forget your bag this time."

Belac narrowed his eyes at the dwarf before returning to the task at hand. He opened the duffle bag and dug around inside until he found his new jacket. He fought with the other clothes as he tugged the thin jacket out of the bag. Not wanting to set the clean garment on the pier, he tucked it under his arm while he closed the canvas bag.

Belac stood and shook out the jacket. The silky blue cloth shimmered like the waters of a deep lake. *It's nice to have proper clothes again.* His slender thumb traced some of the silver scrawling embroidered across the dark blue fabric.

Impatient as ever, Rolan asked, "Are you going to ask it for a dance, or put it on?"

Belac frowned at the dwarf and then handed him the jacket. "Here. Hold it for a moment."

Rolan took the jacket without further comment.

Belac removed his bastard-sword and set it down on top of his duffle bag. Then he unbuckled his belt and dropped it on top of the pile as well. *With my luck, one of these people we came to save is going to sneak over here and try to steal my stuff.* He narrowed his eyes and scanned the harbor as he reached for his jacket.

Belac did not know what the thin jacket was made from, but it was light weight and comfortable despite the heat. *This thing definitely looks nicer than a plain blue shirt.* He rearmed himself and then reached for his black duffle bag.

Serath stopped the elf. "A moment," he said, stepping closer.

The wizard brushed his gloved hands across Belac's shoulders and then down the front of his jacket. Where the man's hands passed, wrinkles disappeared from the cloth. *Now it looks even better!*

"Is the jacket magic now?" Belac asked expectantly.

Serath's handsome face smiled. "No. However, you are considerably more presentable."

Belac frowned. "I would rather have the magic."

Eight

"You're not going with us?" Belac asked, a little disappointed.

Rolan shook his head. "I have arrangements to make. The bureaucrats will just get in my way."

"Rolan," Serath said with a lighthearted disapproval.

Rolan faced the wizard. "Listen, Serath. I am not saying that they don't have their uses. But if you want that equipment to make it up to the volcano in time, we cannot depend on politicians."

Serath smiled. "That is why I am depending on you."

"Right," Rolan said with a nod. "Then, you three go look fancy, and I will get the work done."

Belac laughed. "Now, this plan, I like."

Serath waved Belac and Vairug to follow. Together, they left the dwarf behind at the docks. As they traveled the cobblestone streets, the three drew the attention of those they passed. Belac found himself feeling like the honor guard of an exotic lord. *That is probably what these people see when they look at us. The way Serath walks, he might as well be a king come calling.* Belac wanted to ask Serath how he knew where he was going, but the wizard moved with a sense of purpose.

Though Belac felt pressured by the pace, Serath showed no indication of slowing. People instinctually moved out of the wizard's path, creating a wake of pedestrians. Intrigued murmuring began to rise above the sounds of the city, and anxious opinions spread like a contagion.

It was not until they reached the city's center, that Serath stopped afore a grand fountain of stone and artistry. Carvings of scaled fish swimming in exaggerated currents held back a tranquil pool of still water. At first, Belac thought the wizard was going to walk onto the water's surface in demonstration of his power. *He needs to let them know that he's a wizard if he wants them to listen to him.* Serath employed an alternative.

"You should both cover your ears," Serath instructed as he reached a gloved hand out over the water.

Belac dropped his duffle bag onto the cobblestones and covered his pointed ears. He glanced in Vairug's direction. The orc had one hand over an ear and his left forearm over the other.

Serath limned a design across the water and then turned away. When the wizard spoke, his voice was deafening. "Gentle people of Cavasca."

Belac's hands were not enough to protect him from the sound. Frightened people staggered away from the fountain, covering their ears in pain. Belac took a step away from the fountain and pressed his hands tighter to the sides of his head.

Serath continued to address the city at large. "I have come with Belac Melavar, The Dragon Slayer." He paused, and the city was silent. "We have come to you in a time of peril foretold."

The man sure as death sounds like a wizard. Belac took another step back.

Serath's voice was the only one in the city. "In three days hence, the dreaded Agadon will awaken. Fire will rain from the sky. Molten rock will pour down the mountain. And your homes will be devoured as those who remain beg for deliverance that will not come."

Cavasca answered with silence as terror gripped the hearts of its people. Of the entire city, only a single child was brave enough to cry.

When Serath spoke again, there was kindness to his words despite their dire warning. "Cavasca must be abandoned. You must gather your strength and organize for your collective exodos. For those who remain will perish in the fury of Agadon." The wizard allowed his words to weigh on the people's souls before adding, "In three days hence."

Belac realized that he had closed his eyes in an attempt to shut out the intensity of the wizard's voice. He opened his eyes and took in the sight of people cowering in the street. *They may not thank us, but none of them will be able to say they were not warned.*

Serath waved his hand and then spoke with a voice no longer projected by magic. "You can lower your hands now."

Belac could barely hear what the wizard said, but he lowered his hands. He glared at the wizard through lingering pain. "You could have warned us!"

Serath raised an eyebrow. "I did warn you."

Vairug stood with the elf. "Belac is right, Serath. That was too loud."

Serath studied them both for a moment and then bowed. "My apologies. I will be more considerate in the future."

Belac blinked. He had not expected the wizard to apologize. He was not really sure how to respond to the apology, so he simply shrugged uncomfortably.

Vairug grunted.

Belac picked his duffle bag back up and shouldered it. "So… what now?"

"Now," Serath said with a smile. "We must attend the audience that the council is almost certainly convening as we speak."

Still not completely pleased with the wizard, Vairug asked, "Would they not have preferred you spoke to them before…" he gestured to the fountain, "that?"

Serath chuckled smoothly. "I am sure that they absolutely would have preferred to be consulted."

Belac guessed at the wizard's reasoning. "This way, they don't get a choice."

Serath's tone took on a hard edge. "They never had a choice."

Vairug frowned from within his hood. "Do you think that the council might not believe you?"

Serath traced his beard while formulating his answer. "I think that Rolan does not despise politicians without cause."

Belac laughed. *I think that is the meanest thing I have ever heard Serath say.*

Vairug did not join in the laughter. "Will the council send men to arrest us?"

Serath shook his head. "They would call it an escort."

Belac did not think the orc would recognize the distinction. "Is there anyway we can avoid that?"

Serath smiled at the elf. "There is indeed. We simply continue on as planned, and deny them the opportunity."

Without waiting for further comment, the wizard turned away from the fountain. Belac and Vairug hurried after him, neither of them willing to be left behind to the mercy of their forthcoming escorts. *There is no guarantee that they would even take us to the council. They could just as easily 'escort' us to a prison cell.*

While the city was now louder than before, hushed silence traveled with the wizard. As Belac and Vairug followed Serath down the middle of the street, people stepped aside and stared in quiet apprehension. Belac considered smiling and waving in an attempt to assuage the people's fears. However, he decided that the people of Cavasca were better off afraid. *We need them to be scared, or they will convince themselves that it is safe to stay here.*

The march to the council estate was shorter than the one that had taken them to the fountain. The walled complex was decorated with superfluous pillars of stone that added an air of gravity though they appeared to support nothing at all. The gates stood open and unguarded, allowing for entry unchallenged. Belac and Vairug followed the wizard across an empty courtyard and directly to the steps of a tall state building.

As they climbed the wide steps, an uncertain voice called out from behind them, "Hey, You! Who are you?"

They ignored the voice and entered the state building. Belac was surprised by the spaciousness of the interior. The open foyer was absent of clutter and the ceiling reached so high that it left no room for a second floor. Polished plaster panels overlapped along the walls, creating geometric patterns that broke up the sounds that would otherwise echo throughout the building.

Two men dressed in stately attire stood arguing in the foyer. *I bet I can guess what they are talking about.* The men stopped speaking as soon as they saw the wizard and his companions.

As Serath walked past the speechless men, he said, "Inform the council I will see them now."

Belac and Vairug stayed close to the wizard as they proceeded into the main corridor and continued on. At the end of the corridor, they came to a set of closed double doors. Without stopping, Serath pushed both of the doors open and strode into the next room.

Belac glanced backward, expecting someone to run up and tackle them at any moment. "Hey, Serath. I know you are friends with King Alvin and everything, but I don't think these people answer to Tariel."

Vairug confirmed the assessment as he entered the room. "These lands belong to Harbridge."

Nine

Tiered pews climbed the walls on either side of the room, angled so as to face a raised stage. Clinging to the back wall, the stage held in display five ornate desks. On the floor below, stood a small platform surrounded by a waist high wooden railing. Serath leaned against the railing, waiting patiently for the council to arrive.

Belac glared at the wizard. "Why didn't you tell me that we were still in Harbridge?" *I hate Harbridge!*

Serath raised an eyebrow. "Harbridge is a rather large place, Belac."

Belac narrowed his eyes at the wizard. "Rolan said we were south of Harbridge."

Serath nodded. "We are south of the capital."

Belac understood the confusion now. *Stupid humans.* "Why would they use the same name for the city that they do for the whole country?"

Serath answered as if the question had not been rhetorical. "Because the capital cities existed long before their boundaries were drawn."

Belac frowned. *That kind of makes sense. It is not like somebody sat down, drew a map, and said, "You people live here. You people live there."*

Belac shook his head. "They could still change one of the names," he said, maintaining his complaint. "It's confusing for no reason."

Serath grinned at the elf. "The humans who reside here do not appear to suffer your confusion."

Vairug laughed silently, the movement catching the elf's attention.

Belac turned toward the orc. "You think this is funny?"

Vairug nodded from within his hood.

Belac spread his arms. "Harbridge wants to kill me!"

Serath dismissed the elf's excitement. "Harbridge does not want to kill you."

Belac pointed at the wizard. "I almost died like nine times!" *It had to be at least nine.*

Serath crossed his arms and sighed at the elf. "There may be people in Harbridge that want to kill you. However, as of yet, none would know where you are. You are as safe here as you would be anywhere else."

Though intent on arguing, Belac was distracted by the doors opening behind him. He turned to face the four men who entered the room. Looking past them, Belac paid special interest to the two guards that remained outside in the corridor. The only armor the men wore were strange metal hats, but they had swords on their hips and murder in their eyes.

When the doors closed, Belac directed his full attention to the four men that had entered unannounced. One of them seemed too young to be a councilman, but Belac felt certain that was what the men must be. All dressed in finely tailored clothing, the men approached as if they were prepared for a debate.

As the men made their way down the aisle, Belac noted, "One of them is missing."

Under his breath, Vairug asked, "How do you know that?"

Belac pointed behind himself with his thumb. "There are five seats on that dais."

With an attitude of put-upon regency, the youngest of the councilmen asked, "What is the meaning of this?" His voice sounded more mature than the man looked.

Belac thought the question was a particularly stupid one. *Serath just shouted at them with magic. There is no way they don't know why we are here.* He reconsidered. *Unless...* "Do you read lips?" he asked.

Perplexed, the youngest of the councilmen replied, "What relevance could such a thing possibly have?"

Belac brought his hand up to his own face and held it hovering in front of his mouth. "We need to know if you can hear us or not."

The youngest of the councilmen straitened his spine and tilted his head so as to look down his nose at the elf.

Belac dropped his hand and smiled. "Good. You can hear us." *And that means you know why we are here.*

With more patience than his fellow councilman, a thin man with curly hair stated, "You will need to explain yourselves."

Instead of explaining, Serath asked, "Is there one among you named Logan Celles?"

The oldest of the councilmen ran a hand through his thinning, gray hair. "That would be me."

Without taking his weight off the railing, Serath held out a document sealed with bright red wax. He offered no other explanation.

Councilman Celles stepped forward and took the document. As he stepped back to stand with the other councilmen, he appraised Serath openly. There was a shrewdness to Logan Celles that would not be intimidated by a wizard. Without taking his eyes off the wizard, the councilman waved the document casually and then sniffed at the wax seal.

Belac thought the action rather odd, but said nothing.

The youngest of the councilmen was less diplomatic. "Well, what does it say?"

Paying the youngest councilman no mind, Celles broke the seal and unfolded the document. All emotion drained from the man's face as he read what was written within. He looked up from the creased page, staring at the wizard as if seeing him for the first time. Silently, Celles held the opened document out to his right, offering it to another councilman.

A heavy-set man took the hanging page and read over it quickly. "This is preposterous," he declared, holding the document disdainfully. "This cannot be true."

"It is authentic," Councilman Celles said with certainty.

The youngest of the councilmen asked again, "What does it say?"

The curly haired councilman took the document and began to read it for himself.

Scowling, the heavy-set councilman asked, "What makes you so sure, Celles?"

Councilman Celles answered with authority, "It's coded."

The other three councilmen turned to stare at Celles. There was a moment of complete silence as the significance of the man's words sank in. *I am guessing Serath knew this guy's name for a reason.*

The youngest of the councilmen pointed. "You're a spy!" he accused angrily.

"I am a patriot!" Councilman Celles barked proudly in response.

The curly haired councilman asked quietly, "How long, Logan?"

Councilman Celles took a deep breath and faced the friend he had betrayed. "For longer than you have known me."

The heavy-set councilman adapted to the news quicker than the other two. "So, that means it's true after all."

The youngest of the councilmen reached for the document. "But what does it say?"

The curly haired councilman handed over the document, though he continued to stare at the man who had once been his friend.

Councilman Celles looked away. "What now?" he asked in resignation.

Serath answered as if the drama had never taken place. "Let us begin with introductions." He then waited for the other man to speak.

Councilman Celles indicated to the heavy-set man standing beside him. "This is Councilman Pocman." Next was the man with curly hair. "Councilman Francis." Last was the youngest of the councilmen. "And Councilman Archer."

Councilman Archer stood staring down at the document he held in his hands, reading it over and over as if he hoped that the words might change if he read them enough times.

Councilman Celles turned back to the wizard. "What would you have of us?"

Serath's handsome face smiled pleasantly. He took his weight off the railing and gestured to the elf. "This is Belac Melavar, The Dragon Slayer."

Belac tried to stand taller. He was still uncomfortable with the wizard telling people his full name, but he did not complain. *It is probably too late to keep it a secret anyway.*

Councilman Francis looked at the hooded orc and asked skeptically, "And, is he a dragon slayer as well?"

Serath's smile broadened. "Have you not heard of Lord Vairdoe of Enevic? His legend reaches farther than that of Agadon."

Councilman Pocman did not mask his interest. "Lord Vairdoe?" he asked, emphasizing the title.

Belac almost laughed. *They thought they were all important until a real lord showed up. Well... not a real lord. But they don't know that.*

Councilman Francis misunderstood the orc's purpose. "Surely you do not intend to appoint an Enevician lord."

Serath explained, "Lord Vairdoe has pledged himself to The Dragon Slayer's cause. Together, they have ventured far in their quest. However, Cavasca is but one step they must take. Your people are fortunate to have them here."

Councilman Pocman spoke bluntly, "We are not so removed from the world that we are unaware of what befell the country of Enevic." His tone became mocking as he said, "Dragon slayers?"

Belac felt a sudden irrational urge to defend Lord Vairdoe and the honor of the Enevician dead. Councilman Celles noticed the change in the elf. He shifted his stance, ready to intervene if Belac attacked the other councilman.

Serath answered the mocking tone with somber dignity. "In what greater tragedy could such a man be forged."

Councilman Celles attempted to redirect the conversation. "And have you brought your dragon slayers to Cavasca with designs of slaying Agadon?"

"Agadon is no dragon," Councilman Pocman stated forcefully.

Serath allowed the conversation to return to the present. "We are here to warn you. We are here to assist you. And we are here to forge a sword in the fires of Agadon."

Councilman Francis recognized that some element was missing. "There are less arduous ways by which to acquire a sword."

Serath politely disagreed. "Not the one we seek."

Councilman Francis was not satisfied by the reply. "That strikes me as an awful lot of trouble to go through for a sword."

Belac spoke up. "I need it to kill Danorin."

The dragon's name brought Councilman Archer back into the conversation. "The Danorin?"

Serath's rich voice drew the councilmen's attention back to him. "It is believed that only with the death of the dragon Danorin will Lord Vairdoe's curse be lifted, and his humanity restored."

Vairug stepped forward and reached for his hood with both hands, one of gray flesh and the other gleaming metal. He pulled back his hood, revealing his tusks and orcish complexion. Dark eyes regarded the councilmen without fear. "The people of Enevic will be avenged."

Ten

Lounging atop the lush covers of his bed, Belac hoped that he never forgot the looks on the councilmen's faces. *None of them wanted to argue anymore once they found out they were standing next to an orc.* He thought Councilman Pocman's expression had been the best. If Belac had been an artist, he would have drawn a picture of the man's face and kept it with him always.

The suite Belac had been shown to was one of the nicest places he had ever stayed. Flowing, satin cloth draped the windows with crimson folds, and embroidered pillows cushioned gilded furniture. *I wonder if I could get Serath to stuff this place in a bottle for me. It seems like such a waste to leave it for the volcano.*

The elf hopped off the opulent bed and began to stretch. *I need something to do.* He amended his thoughts. *Or drink.* He nodded to himself. *I should investigate the apartment.* He walked from the bedroom into a large den. *I should find out what all is in here with me. It is the only responsible thing to do.*

A wall of cabinets waited on the other side of the room, separated from the elf by two armchairs, a sofa, and a collection of small end tables. Staying close to the white plastered walls, Belac walked around a furry, red and gold rug as he made his way to the other side of the room. Once there, he began to open and close cabinet doors at random in his search for alcohol.

In the lower cabinets, Belac found racks with more bottles of wine than one person could possibly drink in the time he planned to stay in Cavasca. He grabbed one of the bottles without considering vintage. *Better it go to me than to the volcano.*

With his bottle of wine in hand, Belac walked over to the nearest armchair and sat down. He shifted around in the chair as he adjusted the sheathed dagger at his hip and then kicked off his boots. He curled his toes on the fuzzy rug and relaxed before lifting the bottle of wine up for better inspection. Dark and red, he expected it to taste bitter. *I don't care what it tastes like as long as there's booze in it.* He wrapped his slender fingers around the corked stopper and wiggled it free. Then he tossed the stopper over his shoulder and drank straight from the bottle. The wine was sweet and robust with notes of charred wood.

Belac looked at the bottle again. "Wow!" he said aloud. "I would drink this even if it didn't have booze in it."

He took another drink of the wine. *New mission.* The elf decided with resolve. *I have to rescue the wine.* He nodded to himself. *They might not let me take it with me when I leave, so I am going to need to smuggle it out in my stomach.* He took another drink. *Only way to keep it safe.*

As he sat drinking wine and enjoying the tribute held in trust for people of position, Belac wondered if the humans would let him be a politician. *They can't all be born politicians. I can learn how to stand around and tell other people what to do.*

Belac pointed his free hand at the sofa and shouted in a commanding voice, "Reposition that seating apparatus three breaths to the left!"

He laughed at his own joke and then resumed drinking the wine. *Ooh! I bet Vairug can make me a politician once he is king! Enevic is not going to be a very nice place until it gets more people living there again, but maybe he can send me off somewhere as an ambassador.* Belac liked that idea. *People are super nice to ambassadors.*

The elf held his empty bottle up high and looked at it with one eye closed. *I should have brought another bottle with me. Two hands, two bottles. Why else would people have two hands?* He set the empty bottle on the table next to him and stood up. Suddenly lightheaded, he stumbled and laughed. *I think I need to use the chamber pot first.* He walked away from the wine rack and back into the bedroom.

After using the chamber pot, Belac turned to leave the room. The gleam of steel accents pulled his attention to the bastard-sword at the foot of the bed. The elf narrowed his eyes at the sword. *Stupid dwarf.* Belac walked over to the bed and picked up the scabbarded sword. *Rolan thinks he is so funny…* He drew the sword and dropped the scabbard on the bed. Despite its name and design, Belac thought it felt good to hold a sword once more. When monsters and men had come for him, often it had been a blade that stopped them.

In Elven, Belac intoned, "I am not food."

He decided that if he was going to keep the sword, he should practice with it. *It is the only responsible thing to do.* He whipped the sword over his head and swung it in an arc over the bed. Following the blade, he turned and swept it through the middle of the room with a flourish. Belac then proceeded to run through the suite, his sword slashing the air as he cut down imaginary foes. Its relatively short blade allowed him to swing the sword indoors, but still he needed to be careful not to hit the walls.

Belac leapt over a table, twisting in the air to slash at the imaginary monster pouncing at him from behind. Continuing to swing the sword in increasingly complex patterns, the elf tripped over his own boots and fell toward the floor. Agilely controlling the fall, he rolled across his shoulders and came to his feet with an upward slash directed at the opponent that, in his mind, must have pushed him down. His sword cut through the empty air and struck the ceiling above him. A shower of plaster and dust fell down onto his head as the blade clanked off.

Belac sneezed and waved one arm wildly in defense of this unforeseen attack. He swung his sword blindly and stepped backward. His bare foot came down on the discarded wine stoper, causing his leg to recoil in pain. He fell backward, landing flat on the rug.

Belac groaned, and then laughed as he stared up at the ceiling. "It's a conspiracy!" he proclaimed between laughs.

The elf rolled over and climbed to his feet using one of the armchairs. *Okay. If I am going to do this, I should go outside before I kill myself.* Sword held low, he walked to the door of his suite. *Only responsible thing to do.* He threw the door open wide and exited his suite without closing the door behind himself.

Belac walked out into the empty square that connected the dignitary suites. While not as spacious as the courtyard, the square was wide enough for him to swing his sword without hitting anything. He stopped in the center of the square, his bare feet planted on the time worn stone beneath him. He held the sword out in front of himself in a defensive stance. He had never liked the balance of broader bladed one-handed swords. He shifted his stance and brought his left hand forward to grip the sword's hilt below his right. His hands felt cramped, but it was still more comfortable to support the sword with both hands.

With a quick motion, he took a controlled swing. The blade arced tightly through the air in front of him as he stepped to the side. *There is just not enough space on the hilt for my wrist to move naturally.* He released his left hand from the hilt and performed the maneuver again one-handed. The arc of the blade was noticeably wider, but the swing felt much more natural. Returning to a defensive stance, he gripped the hilt with both hands. Belac grinned. *Okay. I think I see how this works.*

The elf began to dance in the square, his sword's blade sweeping in wide arcs as he altered his grip. It quickly occurred to him that he could just as easily transition to a left-handed swing as he could a right. By bringing his hands together between swings, he could transfer the hilt from one hand to the other while maintaining a secure grip. *That is the real advantage of the extended hilt.*

Belac's grin could have understandably been mistaken for a snarl as he continued his inebriated elven ballet, his movements every bit as graceful as they were appallingly dangerous. Finally, he stopped in the middle of the square, once more in a defensive stance. Breathing hard and sweating, he gazed at the sword in his hands. *Okay. So, maybe I don't hate it.*

From the open doorway of another suite, Vairug asked, "Are you preparing to fight ghost?"

Smiling, Belac looked at his orcish friend and tried to think of something clever to say. The elf's smile turned into a confused frown when he saw the leather duffle bag at Vairug's side.

Belac pointed his sword at the orc. "Where are you going?"

Vairug stepped into the square. "Serath says that they have pools of water here that are forever hot."

Belac lowered his sword. "These people have magic pools?"

Vairug shook his head. "He says that it is not magic."

Belac frowned. "It sounds like magic to me." He pointed his sword at the orc again. "Wait here. I want to go too."

Belac turned and ran into his suite. He tossed his sword on the sofa and went straight for the open wine racks. He took a bottle of wine in each hand, holding the bottles by their necks. Then he half ran, half frolicked, back out into the square.

Holding the bottles up high, Belac declared, "Two hands, two bottles!"

Vairug scowled at the elf and said nothing.

Remembering that the orc only had one real hand, Belac smiled. "I guess that means you get one."

Eleven

Tall, freestanding lamps cast flickering light against dim stone walls, creating an intimate atmosphere. Vairug set his leather duffle bag down on a stone bench that ran along the back wall of the chamber.

Belac gestured at the bag with one of his bottles of wine. "Why do you get a leather one?" he complained, his words echoing.

"A leather bag?" Vairug asked for clarification.

Belac nodded sloppily. "The one I got is made out of cloth."

Vairug shrugged and then unbuckled the belt that held his cogged mace in a ring. "It could be, because Rolan does not think I will lose mine."

"I am not going to lose my bag," Belac argued.

Vairug untied his sash and tossed it next to his duffle bag. "I never said that you would."

Belac harrumphed.

Vairug removed his shirt and added it to the pile. "Belac," he waited for the elf to look at him, "where is your bag?"

"Die in a fire," Belac told the orc. "It is in my room." *...I think.*

Vairug began unbuckling the harness that secured his mechanical prosthetic. "Are you going to get in the pool like that? You will get your pretty jacket wet."

Belac set his wine bottles down on the stone bench. "Don't act like you don't like nice clothes too, Vairug." He pointed at the orc's crimson sash. "Or is that fancy strip of cloth a super secret back up weapon?"

Vairug grunted. "I could strangle you with it if you want."

Belac laughed and began to undress himself. As he did, he studied the pool. Square and shallow, steam blanketed the water with a faint haze. Fluted pillars surrounded the pool and supported the domed ceiling above. The attendant had claimed that the pool was a private one, but Belac thought that it was large enough for a party of six.

Belac picked up one of the bottles of wine by the neck and pointed its base at the other. "That one is yours," he told the orc before walking over to the edge of the pool.

Belac dipped his toe in the water. It was pleasantly warm, but the water gave off a peculiar mineral smell that the elf did not trust. He had been assured that the pool was not magic. Evidently, the ingenuitous people of Cavasca had somehow engineered a means of piping in spring water that had been heated by the volcano. *That seems a little too smart for humans.*

Vairug stepped into the pool and sat down in one of the corners. The orc tucked his bottle of wine under his left arm and yanked the stopper out with his right hand. He set the stopper aside and drank deeply from the bottle. "Gauch," he said, looking down at the bottle disdainfully. He frowned and then took another drink. "At least it is strong."

Belac glanced down at his own bottle. *I hope I just gave him a bad one.* He wanted to open his own bottle and find out how it tasted, but he decided that he should get in the pool first. Without further thought, the elf hopped into the water and sat down in the corner to Vairug's left. Belac wiggled the stopper out of his bottle and set it to the side so that he could keep an eye on it. *Sneaky little wine stopper is not going to trip me again.* He took a tentative drink and was pleased to discover that his wine tasted sweet.

Belac came to trust the pool more and more with every drink of his wine. Finally, he declared, "This. Explains. Everything."

"And what is it that you think needs to be explained?" Vairug inquired humorously.

Belac pointed emphatically at the water in the pool. "This!" He swept the room with his bottle of wine. "This is why you build a city next to a volcano." He took a drink from the bottle. "Do you think they have volcanos in Enevic?"

Vairug sighed. "I have told you, Belac. I cannot rule Enevic."

Belac shook his head with exaggerated movement. "Sure, you can. We can explain why you're an orc." He thought for a moment. "It would probably be more convincing if you married a human woman though." He shrugged. "But, it can't be that hard to find a woman that wants to be a queen."

Vairug frowned. "I do not really like human women."

Belac shifted in the pool so that he could look at the orc more easily. "Why not?" *How does anyone not like human women?* "I know they don't live very long, but they are really soft."

Vairug nodded. "I know." His voice took on an uncharacteristically timid tone. "I have always worried that I would break one."

Belac laughed at the orc.

Vairug pointed his stump at the elf. "Orcish women are different!" he proclaimed defensively.

Belac took a drink from his dwindling bottle of wine and then asked, "Different, how?"

Vairug rolled his shoulders before answering, "Orcish women only desire men that are strong enough to take what they want."

"Ooh. Yeah…" Belac nodded. "I don't think human women would like that very much."

Vairug shrugged and nodded in agreeance.

Belac continued, "Usually, they want you to kind of trick them into it."

"They want you to trick them?" Vairug asked, disbelieving.

Belac shook his head. "It is more like they want you, to let them, pretend that they are being tricked."

"That seems rather complicated," Vairug commented, still unconvinced.

"Or bribes!" Belac added. "They like bribes."

Vairug set his wine bottle aside and asked, "You bribe women to sleep with you?"

Belac shook his head. "You are not allowed to call it a bribe." He took another drink of wine. "It is one of those human things where they think that if they use a different word, it will magically change reality."

Vairug grinned on one side of his face. "And what word do they use to describe this arrangement?"

Belac held up a finger. "Romance."

Vairug laughed silently. "I believe I will stick to orcish women."

Belac leaned back and rested his arms on the sides of the pool. *How are we going to get an orcish woman all the way to Enevic?* He decided that they would have to find a way to use the ponds. *We will need to come up with a story for her. Maybe something about a magic spell that went wrong.* He thought that would work. *We could say that she was trying to change the man she loved back into a human, but instead, she got turned into an orc.* It was a tragic story that would tug at people's hearts. *Now, I just need to convince Vairug to be King.*

Without looking at the orc, Belac asked, "Do you like being Lord Vairdoe?"

Vairug was silent for a moment before answering, "There is a problem with your question, Belac."

Belac turned his head to look at the orc. "What do you mean?"

"I cannot be Lord Vairdoe," Vairug explained. "I can only pretend to be." He laughed silently. "Maybe things would be different if I were human."

Belac smiled at the irony.

Vairug cut the air with his stump. "I will not live my life pretending to be someone or something that I am not. To do so, weakens a person. What is worse, is that it denies the world what it has created."

Belac thought that was a strange way of looking at things, but he said nothing and waited for the orc to continue.

"What if the world needs an orc," Vairug questioned, "and I am busy pretending to be a human?" He looked at the elf. "What if the world needs a hero, and you are busy acting like a fool?"

Belac replied drunkenly, "I can be both."

Vairug ignored the bluster. "Has it not occurred to you, that you could just as easily be a hero acting like a fool, as a fool pretending to be a hero?"

Belac leaned away from the orc, but Vairug's gaze seemed to follow him.

"What are you, Belac Melavar?" There was a depth of emotion to Vairug's words that the elf had not expected. "Are you some fool, wondering around the world aimlessly? Or are you a hero, trying to set it right?"

Belac could not look away. He took a breath and then confessed to his friend, "I am someone who is less than I would like to be."

Vairug broke eye contact and slowly sank lower into the pool. "That was not a foolish answer."

Twelve

Belac awoke resting against the closed door to his suite. He did not remember how he had arrived there, but he assumed that the door had simply proven too complex for him to operate. Through heavy eyelids, he looked out into the empty square and wondered if any of the servants had seen him sleeping in the doorway. *Does anyone even still work here?* If Belac knew everything was going to be destroyed in a couple of days, he would not have gone to work.

Groaning, he reached up and took hold of the door handle. He used it to pull himself up with another groan that verged on a whimper. He pressed his forehead against the door and closed his eyes. He focused on breathing, though he found the effort exhausting. When he finally gathered the will to move on, he slid the bolt to the side and pushed the door open.

Belac managed to take all of two steps into the unlit suite before tripping over his duffle bag. He spilled onto the floor, landing on his knee and then shoulder. His head bounced off the rug, its padding the only thing that saved him from a concussion. With more groaning, he rolled over and kicked the duffle bag. Muffled glass clanked inside, but the bag stayed where it was.

"That's right…" Belac muttered to himself. "I have to save the wine." He closed his eyes and decided that he could worry about it later.

A shadowy presence brought the elf awake. He opened his eyes to see Serath standing in the doorway, blocking the morning light. The wizard held a metal tankard in one hand and a small plate in the other. Belac could smell the sweetness of whatever was on the plate. His awareness sharpened. *What is that?*

Though Serath's face was shadowed, his smile could be heard in his words. "It seems as if you have had another eventful night."

Belac rolled over onto his hands and knees. He breathed in the sweet smell. *I don't know what that is, but I want it.* He got his feet under himself and stood, his nose following the smell. On the small plate lay a large pastry that had been drizzled with white frosting. *It barely fits on the plate!* Belac licked his lips.

Serath turned, simultaneously moving the plate away while offering out the tankard. "Here. Drink this first."

Belac did not think he was fast enough to snatch the pastry away from the wizard, so he accepted the tankard instead. He intended to drink it all in one go, but the concoction was simply too vile. Halfway through, he stopped and held the tankard away from himself, his face twisted in revulsion.

Belac looked to the wizard. "I think these are getting worse."

Serath was close enough that his smile could be seen despite the shadows. "Is that so?"

Belac narrowed his eyes at the wizard.

Serath looked down at the pastry and then over at the tankard the elf still held.

Belac scowled and then drank what remained of the wizard's vile medicine. He held the empty tankard out. "Here. Give me the food now."

Serath took the empty tankard and then handed the plate to the elf. "You will enjoy it more if you can wait for the potion to take effect."

Belac frowned at the pastry. "I really kind of want to eat it now."

Serath shrugged. "It is your choice."

Belac sighed and set the plate on an end table.

Serath nodded approvingly. "The council has decreed that the people of Cavasca will begin preparations to evacuate the city and its surrounding areas. Tomorrow, the bulk of the population will set out on their journeys north."

Belac was relieved by the news. *That means most of them should survive.*

Serath continued, "Today, I would like you to walk the streets and offer encouragement where you can. Let the people know who you are. Give them inspiration. Show them that there is hope for the future."

Belac did not know how he was supposed to do all that. "Do you want me to tell people I am here to fight Agadon?"

Serath shook his head. "No, Belac. Lies are not free. Everything you do has a cost. Everything you do," he repeated for emphasis. "That lie would only hurt our cause."

Belac had expected the answer, but it led him to another question. "What about Vairug?"

"Lord Vairdoe," Serath corrected the elf, "is a distraction that would be better off avoided."

I guess he thinks that lie is already paid for. Belac frowned. *Or maybe it is just too late to take it back.* Belac suddenly worried that the price of his lie might fall on Vairug.

"There is no need for concern," Serath assured the elf. "Lord Vairdoe will accompany me as I see to our own preparation. It is unlikely he will be troubled."

Belac tucked a lock of his long, black hair behind one of his ears. "You want me to face those people all by myself?"

Serath's reply was less than helpful. "Your question implies a conflict that need not exist."

"But, what if they blame me for the volcano?" Belac pressed. *Humans love blaming other people for stuff.*

"Tell them the truth," Serath instructed. "I believe you will find people more receptive to it than you might expect."

"Fine," Belac said. "But if I get stripped naked and hung upside down, this time, it is your fault."

"I accept your terms," Serath agreed, smiling. Then he turned and left the suite.

Belac went about the business of preparing for the day, and then he sat down to eat his pastry. It tasted as sweet as it smelled and had tiny pieces of nuts that the elf thought were delicious. *I don't know if it is any better than it would have been before, but this was definitely worth waiting for.*

He licked the frosting off his thumbs and forefingers and then used his pinkies to move his hair out of his face. *I have to do something about my hair.* He stood and then wiped his hands on his trousers as he walked into the bedroom. Using his dagger, he cut a thin strip of cloth from his pale gray bedsheets. *This is all going to be ruined by the volcano anyway.* He tied his long hair back with the ribbon, thinking that the color would match nicely with the silver scrawling on his silky jacket.

Belac then returned to the sofa and picked up his bastard-sword. He slung the baldric over his head, positioning the sword on his back. Careful to step over his duffle bag on the way out, he exited the suite. Still not seeing any servants, he wondered what they would think if one of them came to tidy his suite. *Why would they even bother? Everyone that works here is probably just running around, stuffing shiny things into their pockets.* He hoped that no one would steal his wine while he was gone.

What Belac witnessed when he reached the courtyard suggested that he had guessed correctly. People moved through the courtyard carrying chest and furniture in a chaos that resembled looting more than anything else. *At least no one looks like they plan on staying.* The elf navigated past the hustling people, leaving the council estate behind.

The city proper was no less chaotic than the courtyard had been. The people of Cavasca went about their preparations with an alacrity that Belac found surprising. *They believe us!* As he made his way through the city, it quickly became apparent that there was nothing for him to do.

When last he had walked the streets with Serath, everyone had stopped and stared. Now, they paid him no mind. *How am I supposed to inspire people if they don't give me any attention? What am I supposed to do? Stop them from working so that I can tell them that they should be working?*

The elf wondered through the city desultorily, unconcerned that he might get lost. *It's hard to get lost when I have a landmark the size of a volcano.* Eventually, Belac came upon an old woman struggling in the street. When he saw her, he almost turned and walked away. Straining to load a heavy rocking chair into the back of a wagon, the woman was clearly insufficient for the task. *It is not like anybody really needs a rocking chair anyway.*

Convinced that he was making a mistake, Belac walked over and took hold of one side of the chair. Ezela stared at the elf for a moment, and then they lifted the chair without saying anything. Once the rocking chair was loaded into the wagon, she studied the elf silently again.

Belac stubbornly refused to speak first.

Ezela tilted her head and pointed with her chin, indicating that the elf should follow her.

Belac narrowed his eyes at the old woman, but followed her into a small building. The interior was obviously a home despite its state of disarray. Countless yellow flowers had been painted on the walls, and hanging vines clung to the wooden trim. Another woman waited inside, packing clothes into a cedar chest. Though of a similar age to Ezela, the woman seemed to have lived a happier life. *That must be Ezela's sister.* The woman smiled brightly at seeing Belac enter.

"And who do we have here?" the woman asked before looking to her sister.

Ezela answered sullenly, "Marry, this is Belac."

The other woman's voice was as sweet as her sister's was sour. "Meredith," she amended. "Only Ezela calls me Marry."

Belac grinned. "Hello, Meredith. It is nice to meet you." He meant it.

Ezela smiled cruelly. "Belac is here to load the wagon for us."

Thirteen

Dripping sweat, Belac decided that if slaying dragons turned out to be as much work as moving furniture, he was going to quit. Ezela had wanted the elf to pack everything himself while she and her sister stood to the side and clucked orders at him. Instead, Belac had offered to help move the heaviest of the furniture before he left. The implication had been clear that he would be leaving either way. *I should have just left without helping at all.*

As he loaded furniture onto the wagon, he envisioned ways he could have gotten out of work. However, the best plan he could come up with was to point, tell them to look over there, and then run. *There is no way those old women could catch me.*

After he had loaded everything that he thought the women would not be able to handle themselves, Belac went back inside to say his goodbyes. *I feel like I should get some kind of reward for this. Maybe cookies or something.* Inside, the home somehow seemed more cluttered despite the portions that had been packed away. He stood facing Meredith, though he addressed Ezela as well.

Belac held his hands out to his sides. "Well, Ladies, it is time for me to go." He lowered his hands. "I think you two can get everything else, and there are still a lot of other people that might need my help." *But I hope not.*

Meredith smiled and kissed the elf on his cheek while her sister glowered. "Thank you, Belac," Meredith said, "I am sure we can see to the rest."

Belac blushed a little and then bowed before leaving. While the kiss had not been a cookie, it made him happy to have helped. *Now, I need to find something to do that does not require any actual work.* The sun had risen high above the city, and Belac wanted out of the heat.

The Birdsong Tavern provided the elf with an excuse he could not pass up. Belac looked up at the hanging sign with the image of two plump birds burned into the wood above the tavern's name. *This is perfect. I can go inside, have a drink, and tell anyone that's in there that they need to get back to work.* The door stood propped open, causing the tavern to seem inviting despite its dimly lit interior.

Belac walked into the tavern and breathed deeply, anticipating the strange smells of local cuisine. He frowned at detecting nothing but the sour smell of spilled wine. The interior of the tavern had not been plastered or painted. Instead, the exposed wood had been oiled to a deep luster that added to the tavern's inviting character. While faint noises came from the doorway to the kitchen, Belac was alone in the main room.

"I don't hear any birds singing," Belac muttered to himself as he appraised the Birdsong Tavern. *No singing. No people. No food… I wonder if they even still have booze.*

A curvy woman with sandy blond hair stepped out of the kitchen. Belac smiled. *Now, there is a woman that looks like she knows how to have fun.* The elf cleared his throat to get her attention.

The woman wiped her hands on the sides of her modestly cut, blue dress. "I am sorry, Sir. But we are not serving anyone until…" she began to explain but stopped. She focused on the elf through the dim lighting. "It's you!"

Uh-oh. Belac wondered what the chances were that he had met that particular barmaid somewhere else before. *…This would be a great time for a bribe.*

The woman pointed. "You're him!" she said, smiling broadly. "You're the one! You came here to save us!"

Belac's grin was mostly one of relief. *I just hope she doesn't think I am Vairug.* He held out his arms to his sides. "Belac Melavar. At your service." *Please, don't ask for service.*

The woman covered her mouth with both hands and hopped in excitement. She then pointed at the elf again. "You're The Dragon Slayer!"

Now, Belac's grin was one of genuine optimism. *I wonder if I can get her to bounce up and down like that some more.*

"Why are you in here?" she asked and then added playfully, "We don't have any dragons in here."

Belac walked up to the bar. "I was hoping I could get a drink."

Her smile fell. "Oh, I'm sorry. We are not allowed to serve anything to anyone until the celebration."

Belac frowned. *That sounds like a stupid rule.* "What celebration?" he asked. *Wait… Am I getting a celebration?* He felt like he should have been told. *Is today Belac-Day?*

"The farewell celebration," the woman told him. "Once everyone has packed and provisioned, the entire city is going to have a celebration as a way of saying goodbye to Cavasca." She smiled suggestively. "It is going to be a wild night."

Belac liked this plan. "So, the faster the work gets done, the sooner the fun can begin?" He was now certain that the woman would know how to have fun. "What can I do to help?"

"You want to help?" the woman asked, surprised. "You want to help us pack?"

"Sure." Belac smiled as charmingly as he could. "How could I say, 'no,' to someone as lovely as you?"

The woman snorted.

The snort was not very lady like, but Belac thought it was cute. "What do you want me to do?" The tavern's soft shadows could not hide the interest in his azure eyes.

The woman smiled, her expression open and wide. She covered her mouth with a hand, but her dark eyes met the elf's. After a brief moment, she lowered her hand and said, "Come with me," before turning and walking back into the kitchen.

Belac vaulted over the bar to follow her. *We're skipping to the fun part!* He followed the woman through the empty kitchen and into a small back room that the tavern used to store small casks of wine.

The woman gestured to the casks. "This is where we keep the special selections." She turned and smiled at the elf mischievously. Then she stepped past him and pointed down the hallway outside. "If you take them through there, you will find the loading bay. These go in the last wagon."

"Wait… What?" Belac stammered.

Still smiling, the woman tilted her head as if sharing a secret. "Now, we can tell the customers that this wine was saved by The Dragon Slayer himself."

"I… You… What?" Belac's brain had still not caught up with what was happening.

The woman left the storage room, but halted on the other side of the doorway. She turned around and placed a hand against the doorframe. "I am Debra, by the way," she said before continuing on.

Belac shook his head and laughed as he realized that he had been defeated. *I knew that woman would be fun.* He picked up one of the casks of wine. Though considerably smaller than a barrel, Belac still found the casks difficult to carry. By the time he got it to the loading bay, he had already decided that he needed to find some other way to help.

The bay doors on both sides of the loading area had been braced open, allowing fresh air to circulate inside. Sunlight spilled in through the open doors and provided the only illumination for those working to load the wagons. Eager to set down the cask, Belac walked past a group of men loading large barrels onto one of the four unhitched wagons. The looks the men gave him were far less admiring than Debra's had been, but they said nothing as the elf passed by.

Belac loaded the wine cask onto the last wagon and then stretched his back. He had not bothered to count how many casks were in the storeroom, but he knew that he did not want to be the one to move them all. He headed back to the storeroom, wondering how he was going to get himself out of his predicament. *I guess I could just sneak off. I could spend the rest of the day thinking up an excuse and then come back for Debra during the celebration.* When a little girl stepped out in front of him, Belac almost walked over her.

Her light brown hair in pigtails, the little girl was no taller than the elf's waist. Staring up at him, she declared, "You're Belac."

Belac looked down at the little girl curiously. Hemmed just below her knees, her brown sundress was even lighter than her hair. At first, Belac wondered how she knew his name, but then remembered that Serath had shouted it at everyone with magic.

The little girl put her hands on her hips. "Debra says it's my job to make sure you behave."

"What?" Belac was once more caught off guard. "Who are you?"

The little girl stood firm and announced, "I'm Gwen. And I'm your boss now."

"Yeah, okay," Belac said and then stepped around the girl. *You're not the boss of me.* Having not yet planned a route for escape, he returned to the storeroom.

The soles of little sandals pattered on the stone floor as Gwen followed the elf into the storeroom. She pointed at the cask he was in the process of picking up and said, "Take that one."

Belac narrowed his eyes at the little girl, but continued to carry the wine cask out of the storeroom.

Marching along behind the elf, Gwen said, "Now, you need to take it to the wagon."

Belac seriously considered dropping the cask and just walking away. He glanced back at the little girl that thought she could boss him around. *...I guess she is kind of adorable...*

When they reached the loading bay, Gwen hurried ahead of the elf and pointed toward the last wagon. "You have to put it on that one there."

Belac grinned despite himself. "Yes. Thank you."

This time, the men loading barrels pointed and laughed as the elf walked past them. Trailing after the little girl, Belac could not bring himself to take offence. *I would laugh at me too.* He loaded the cask onto the wagon and then stretched his back again.

Belac looked down at the little girl. "I think you should carry the next one."

Gwen smiled, displaying that she was missing her four lower front teeth. She shook her head vigorously, causing her pigtails to whip from side to side. "No. That's your job!"

Belac grinned at the cuspids that jutted from the little girl's mouth like tusks. "You look like an orc I know."

"I do not!" Gwen said, laughing.

"Sure, you do," Belac insisted playfully.

Gwen shook her head again. "No, Silly. I'm a girl, not an orc!"

Belac shrugged. "Orcs can be girls."

Surprised, Gwen asked, "Really?"

Belac shrugged again. "Sure."

Their conversation was interrupted when Debra walked over to them and asked, "Belac, would you be willing to deliver a letter to my brother for me?"

Yes, please. Belac would happily take any excuse to get out of loading the rest of the casks.

Gwen tugged on the older woman's dress. "Debra, Debra! Belac says I can be an orc!" She let go of the woman's dress and went, "Rawr!"

Debra glanced down at the little girl and then looked at the elf questioningly.

Belac shook his head. "I did not tell her that," he said hastily.

"Did too!" Gwen insisted. "Rawr!"

Belac glared at the adorable little girl.

Fourteen

The directions Debra gave Belac seemed simple enough to follow. All he had to do was travel the road out of the city and then continue on until he came to an old dairy farm on his left. *'First farm on the left,' are pretty easy directions in a city.* Wanting to avoid any more manual labor, the elf had wasted no time before setting off to find Debra's brother.

Belac had originally planned to make his errand last all day, but the sun was still high in the sky when he left the limits of the city behind. Just as Debra had promised him, the dairy farm proved no challenge to locate. Frowning, Belac realized that he would need to fabricate some new excuse to not immediately return to the tavern. *Maybe I will get lucky, and her brother will be out searching for a lost cow or something.*

Belac surveyed the property as he approached. A pair of long, stone walled barns and a matching farmhouse waited in the pastoral clearing ahead. Creeping vines clung to the buildings' brown and reddish stones below rooves of the same red clay tiles that covered the city. While unremarkable in size, the dairy farm had a sense of enduring to it. *This farm could be as old as Cavasca itself.*

A small boy in brown clothing came out of the farmhouse. When he saw Belac, the boy turned and ran across the front yard toward the nearest of the barns. The boy stumbled as he ran, but recovered and then darted into the barn. Belac altered his course and began walking toward the barn. *I still don't see any cows, but I guess I know where the people are.* Before he reached the barn, two men came out and hailed the elf.

"Hello!" one of the men called out with a strong voice.

Belac waved, but did not otherwise reply until he was close enough to do so without shouting. "Hello." He pointed to the older of the two men. "Are you Henry?"

Both men were dressed in plain, brown clothing that would have been just as fashionable in Harbridge Capital as it seemed to be in Cavasca. The younger of the men was barely old enough to be considered a man, but Belac chose to be generous with his estimation. With similar facial features and sandy blond hair, the men were obviously father and son.

"I am," Henry said, confirming who he was. "And who are you?"

I guess Serath's magic wizard voice did not reach this far out. Belac waved again. "I'm Belac." He held out the letter he had been entrusted with. "I have a message from your sister."

While Henry's face looked as strong as his voice sounded, neither could hide his concern. "Is she alright?" he asked, reaching for the letter.

"Oh? Yeah!" Belac shook his head and nodded at the same time. "Debra is fine." *Or at least she was when I left.*

Henry opened the letter and began reading, his concern fading away with each word. He looked up from the page relieved, but then his face hardened. "Gwyneth!" He pointed at the ground next to himself. "Get over here right now!" He glanced over at the elf. "You brought Gwen with you?"

Belac held up his hands and shook his head. "Nope."

Gwen walked over to them with her head lowered sheepishly.

Henry cupped the little girl's chin and gently lifted her face so that she would look at him. "Why are you here Gwen?"

Gwen stamped one of her small feet. "I want to be an orc!" she declared miserably.

Belac covered his eyes with a hand.

Henry let the little girl pull away from him. Unsure he had heard her correctly, he asked, "You want to be an orc?"

"Belac says people can be orcs," Gwen explained petulantly. "It's true! I checked! He is friends with a weirdo."

Henry looked at the elf, obviously wanting a better explanation.

Belac held up his hand. "I travel with a man named Lord Vairdoe. He was cursed, and now he has to live as an orc." Belac looked at the little girl. "You do not want to be an orc."

"Do too!" Gwen insisted. "Rawr!"

Henry shook his head ruefully. "Scot, take Gwen and have her help your brothers."

Scot put his hands on the little girl's shoulders, and steered her toward the barn. "Come on. Let's go, you little orc."

Henry pointed toward the house with his thumb. "If you want to come inside, you can have something to drink while I write a reply. Debra needs to know that Gwen is here."

Belac nodded. "Sure." *No stupid, city celebration rules out here.*

Though he would appreciate the drink, Belac did not like that he would have to go straight back to the tavern. *Debra is probably already worried about Gwen.* He began to speculate on how he might deliver the message without falling into the trap of employment. The thoughts were interrupted when he realized that there was no walkway to the house. *I have to walk on the grass…* While Belac could not have distinguished one type of grass from another, what he stepped onto was far too green for his liking. As he walked across the yard, the grass made his feet itch through his boots. *If that lazy wizard would just make me a flying carpet…*

Belac's feet continued to itch even after he stepped over the home's threshold and onto the hardwood floor inside. He knew that he would have to walk across the green again when he left. "About that drink," he reminded his host.

Henry nodded and walked into the kitchen area without saying anything.

The inside of the farmhouse and its simple furniture were a collection of varying shades of wood. Though nothing was polished and nothing gleamed, the aged woods had the feel of things well cared for. Belac realized that for this farmer, leaving his home would be much like abandoning a family member. *I wonder how many generations lived here.*

Henry returned to the main room and offered the elf a wooden tankard. "This should not take long, but you are welcome to sit down and have a rest."

Belac accepted the refreshment. "Thank you." He looked down into the tankard and frowned. *That's not wine.* He sniffed at the milk. *I guess some people put booze in milk.* He could detect no smell of alcohol.

Belac lifted his head and narrowed his eyes at Henry, but the man had already moved to a desk on the other side of the room. Deciding that it was a waste of effort to stare at the man's back, Belac walked over to a wooden rocking chair and sat down. He took a drink from the tankard. *That's not bad.* He downed the rest of the milk and then set the empty tankard on the floor next to the chair.

Belac pitched his voice to be heard across the room. "Your cows make tasty milk."

"Goats," Henry replied distractedly.

"Goats?" Belac asked. "Why would you milk goats?"

Henry stopped writing, and glanced over his shoulder. "That is how you get goat's milk."

Belac frowned.

Henry returned to his writing. "Goats are better than cows," he explained without looking back.

Belac was not sure if he liked Henry or not. He felt like the man should be more appreciative. *Maybe he doesn't realize that I am only doing this because I like his sister.* Belac decided to give the man the benefit of a doubt. *He does have kind of a lot going on in his life right now.* The elf was a little proud of his own charitable nature.

Henry stood, his chair squealing as it dragged across the hard wood floor. He turned and held up a folded sheet of paper. "This should explain well enough."

Belac pushed himself up out of the rocking chair though he was in no hurry to leave.

Henry lowered his hand and tapped the note against his thigh as he stared at the elf. "So. You're him?"

Belac suddenly worried that he had fallen for some type of trap.

Henry clarified, "You're The Dragon Slayer?" He did not sound impressed.

Despite the man's tone, Belac was relieved. He held his hands out to his sides. "That's me."

"Are you here to fight Agadon?" Henry asked.

Belac laughed at the idea. "I don't fight volcanos."

Henry grinned. "Then..."

The front door slammed against the inside wall as someone barged into the house. Belac grabbed the hilt of his sword with one hand and the lower scabbard with his other as he spun to face the sound.

Distraught, Scot shouted, "Dad! There gone! I think they ran off!"

"Slow down, Son," Henry said, tossing the folded letter on top of the desk. "You think you lost some of the heard?"

Belac let his hands slide away from his sword as he studied the young man. *He would not be that worried about goats.*

Scot shook his head. "Brandon, Frank, and Gwen. I think they went into the forest!"

"You were supposed to watch them!" Henry shouted furiously and then rushed over to a tall cabinet.

Scot tried to defend himself. "Gwen was pretending to be an orc, and chasing the boys around. Someone needed to get the work done."

Henry threw open the cabinet doors and pulled out a broad sword. He slid the sword into an undyed leather sheath and tossed it across the room to his son. Reaching back into the cabinet, Henry retrieved another sword and sheath. "We have to hurry," he ordered, driving the sword into its sheath.

Belac was forced to step aside as Henry rushed past him. Whatever had the men so concerned, they did not plan on stopping to explain it to Belac. Not understanding the men's fears, he followed them outside.

Hopping as he tried to run gingerly across the grass, Belac called out, "Why is this such a problem?"

Henry yelled back, "There are hobbs in the forest!"

"Hobbs?" Belac did not know what that was.

Henry glanced back. "Hobbs, hobgoblins, and all kinds of other monsters!"

Belac ran faster. *It is almost like these people look for dangerous things to live near!*

Fifteen

Belac did not know what a hobb or a hobgoblin was, but he did not want anything to eat Gwen. The elf ran toward the forest, more concerned about the little girl than he was about the green of the lush vegetation ahead. He had transferred his scabbarded sword from his back to his left hand, ready to use it on anything that tried to hurt that little girl.

Henry brought them to a halt at the edge of the forest. He turned around, gesturing left and right with his sheathed sword. "Spread out!" he ordered, "But not so far that you cannot hear the others call!" He then turned and ran headlong into the forest.

Scot ran to the left, leaving Belac to go right. The elf sprinted along the fringe of the forest before turning and plunging into the shadows and green. Thick with undergrowth, the forest would have been unnavigable without the deer trails that crossed back and forth throughout. Relying on the volcano in the distance to maintain his sense of direction, Belac ran deeper into the forest using the twisting trails. He considered calling out to Gwen, but Belac did not want the two men searching with him to think that he had found her. *If they are not calling out to the children, they probably have a reason.* He remained silent, not wanting his own ignorance and fear to endanger the lost children further.

"Dad!" Scot yelled, though his voice was so faint, the elf could barely hear it. "Over here! It's the hobbs! It's the hobbs!"

Belac ran toward the man's voice, leaping over a tangle of vines when the trail he was on did not lead in the direction that he needed to go. Distant cries of terror and pain spurred him to run faster. He no longer saw the green around him. As the shapes of the forest filtered past him, all his mind's eye could see was the face of a little girl with tusks and pigtails.

Belac burst from the trees into an open glade of weeds and grass. Scot lay motionless on the ground, his body mangled and bloody. Henry stood over his son, swinging his sword wildly at the creatures that surrounded them. Squat, round bodies draped in tattered, vermilion cloth, the creatures jabbered in high pitched, guttural voices. Though small in stature, the hobbs were many in number. Every one of the vicious creatures wielded a weapon in each hand. Long squarish clubs with a single dagger-like iron spike, the crude war-picks raked at the weeping father.

Belac drew his sword without slowing as he rushed to aid the man. One of the hobbs swung a war-pick into Henry's back. The spike sank into the man's upper shoulder, and then he was pulled backward. Another war-pick bit into Henry's hip, and the man was pulled to the ground next to his mutilated son. Crowding in, the hobbs hammered their war-picks down onto the man. All before Belac could reach them.

The elf issued no war cry, focusing instead on the killing to come. In an angled arc he brought his sword down on one of the jabbering creatures. The hobb's hooded, vermilion rags offered scant protection against the sharpened steel. The blade tore through the back of the creature, sending it sprawling to the side. Belac swept the blade up and then brought it down in a diagonal slash to his right, cutting into another hobb. The hobb fared no better than the first, falling to the ground with a gaping cleft in its torso.

Belac took a step toward another of the hobbs as it turned to face him in surprise. Sunlight shone into the hobb's vermilion hood as it angled its neckless head. Black eyes bulged sickeningly from the dark orange flesh of its face. The hobb's squashed features pulled back to reveal a hateful smile of fanged teeth as it screeched maliciously at the elf. Then Belac's blade cleaved through the demonic face.

Belac absently noticed that his blade cut too easily. The hobbs bloated bodies were soft and their bones unnaturally malleable. He instinctually recognized that while his sword could tear through them, the creatures could possess some unforeseen resilience.

As one of the hobbs backed away, Belac advanced on it. He led with an awkward thrust of his sword that the hobb batted away with one of its war-picks. Belac accepted the transfer of force and brought his blade around in a tight circle that hacked into the side of the creature's head. Spinning to his left, Belac reached out with a wide back cut that ripped through the shoulder of another hobb that had been attempting to flank him.

Knowing that he could not let them surround him, Belac hopped backward. His left heel clipped one of the fallen hobbs, and his graceful maneuver turned into a stumbling retreat. He parried a war-pick to his right with his sword and then lashed out with his scabbard. The long wooden handle of another war-pick knocked his scabbard aside, but Belac thrust his sword down into the hobbs squat face. Belac moved forward with the rotund body as it fell backward, stepping away from the other oncoming hobbs. He ripped his sword free as he spun to his right, slinging blood from the blade as it traveled over his head in a vertical arc. Bringing his empty scabbard up in front of himself, he settled into a defensive stance.

Belac only had an instant before the jabbering creatures would close on him again, but he used it to gauge their numbers. *That is a lot of bug-eyed monsters.* He had slain fewer than half of the vicious things, and done nothing to lessen their ire.

Belac rushed at the hobb to his far left. With an underhanded thrust of his scabbard, he slammed its steel chape into the hobb's forehead. The hobb reeled, allowing Belac to slash his sword through its torso as he ran past.

One of the hobbs closed from Belac's right, while another circled around him ahead. The elf leapt into the air and spun to his left, throwing his scabbard at the hobb that would have attacked from his right as he whirled completely around. Not looking to see what effect his scabbard had on the creature, Belac focused on the flanker. Following the fluid motion of the spin, he reached out with a wide back cut that slashed into the back of the hobb's head. The force of his swing brought the elf around to face the opposite direction, his boots digging into the rich soil as he redirected his charge. Belac surged forward, determined to punish the hobbs' resolve.

Screeching with mindless abandon, a hobb swung both of its war-picks down at Belac's chest. Belac brought his sword across and swept the war-picks aside, bringing his blade down on top of them. Continuing his charge, he dragged the back of his sword's edge into the creature's twisted, orange face. The blade dug deep into the hobb's skull before ripping a gory section free. Belac whipped his sword up over his head and brought it down on another hobb. The hobb attempted to block the attack with one of its war-picks, but the sword drove down with enough force to bury its blade in the hobb's chest. Belac's right foot rose and then slammed into the hobb's face, shoving the pudgy thing off the end of his blade.

Belac stepped back and then moved to his left, trying to position the bodies of the dead between himself and the relentless hobbs. Despite their stubby appendages, the hobbs were able to dart around their fallen with seemingly less effort than Belac. One of the hobbs swung a war-pick low at the elf's knees. Unprepared for the hobb's quickness, Belac hastily kicked out to stop the attack. The sole of his boot connected with the war-pick's long wooden handle, and the weapon bounced away.

As Belac's foot came back to the ground he thrust downward with his sword. The steel scraped wetly against fangs as the blade slid into the hobb's open mouth.

Belac yanked his sword free and stumbled two steps backward. He dodged left, barely able to avoid the spike of a war-pick that would have stabbed into his shoulder. He swung his sword out wide, slashing into the side of his attacker. Stumbling back another step, Belac knew that he was faltering. Screeching on his left warned Belac that he would be attacked before he could recover. He dove to his right, tucking into a controlled roll. His blade cut through the air as he came to his feet, ensuring him the space that he needed. *These evil things will not have me!*

Belac stepped back in toward the hobb that had attacked him, sweeping his sword up in a back cut that slipped between the creature's guard. The blade rent through the hobb's chest and then hung in the air above the elf. Belac gripped his hilt with both hands as he spun around, and then he swung the sword low with his left hand. The blade cut into a hobb's jaw and severed the top portion of its head. Belac's right hand returned to the hilt in an underhanded grip as he redirected his momentum. He thrust the sword's tip to his right, moving his left palm behind the hilt's pommel.

Belac looked down the length of his blade and into the black eyes of the hobb impaled on his sword. He watched impassively as the life faded from the last of the hobbs, and then he let it slide from the end of his sword. Breathing deeply, Belac searched the tree line for more threats. The air was thick with the smell of rotten fruit. An anguished groan informed him that at least one of the men was not dead. He hurried to where the two men lay, and then he knelt down beside them. Scot was already dead.

Henry gestured feebly with a trembling hand that was covered in blood. "...hobbs... ...took them..." was all he could manage to say.

Belac was surprised that the man could speak at all. It was not merely the blood and stab wounds; pieces of the man had been torn away. Belac did not know how he could help the man. He did not even know if the man could be helped. What Belac did know, was that there was a little girl that needed him. He stood, retrieved his scabbard, and then ran in the direction the that dying man had pointed.

Sixteen

More than once, Belac had needed to run for his life. However, before that moment, never had he run so fast. The glade stretched long and bent toward the volcano, ending at the edge of a dry riverbed. It was there that Belac found the hobbs. While they were fewer in number than the other pack he had faced, Belac knew that there were still too many of them for him to fight without first catching his breath.

Belac slowed and moved closer to the trees for what little cover they might provide. Their green leaves made his skin crawl, but he ignored the sensation. Surprise had helped him survive the last fight, and he was not yet willing to surrender that advantage. He stalked closer to the hobbs, having to balance speed with his need for respite.

Belac was prepared to follow the hobbs all the way back to their lair. There, he could find the children and then devise some means of escape. He discarded his plan when he saw the three large, vermilion sacks being dragged behind the hobbs. The coarse walls of the sacks budged erratically as small bodies thrashed inside. *I can't let them make it back to their camp.* He did not know how many hobbs would be waiting at such a camp, but he recognized that the children would become no easier to rescue.

Dragging the squirming children behind them like stolen goods, the hobbs moved into the trees and toward the volcano in the distance. Short bodies and stubby legs, it was the hobbs that now advanced in concealment.

Belac cursed in Elven and hurried to catch up with the hobbs. He ran to where they had left the glade, and discovered a wide trail that could not have been made by nature. *They will be able to move too fast on this. I have to find some way to slow them.* He had gained on the hobbs enough to hear them jabbering ahead of him, but Belac knew that he needed to risk getting closer still.

The elf moved as quickly as he could while remaining sure of his footing. The forest trail wound through the trees and thick underbrush, obscuring his vision. Belac focused on the hobbs' abrasive voices, using the ugly sounds to keep track of the creatures as he hurried to catch them. His left hand tightened its grip on the scabbard of his sword. He knew that he would soon need the blade.

The sounds of the hobbs' voices became muted, and then stone thundered as it grated against stone. Belac abandoned caution and ran up the trail in haste. The sound led him to a massive, moss blanketed stone slab that was sliding out to cover the opening to a ramped stone corridor. Angled down into the ground, the shadowed corridor was the only way that the hobbs could have gone. Belac could feel the children slipping away from him as the opening became smaller and smaller.

The elf's run changed into a full sprint. *You cannot have them!* The opening was already too small for him to run through, so he rolled into the narrowing gap. Due to both his speed and the angle of the ramp, he rolled more times than he had intended. Regaining his footing halfway down the ramp, he came to his feet dizzy but determined. He drew his sword and charged down the ramp, a dark silhouette as the sun was shut away behind him.

Strange violet light lit the corridor at the bottom of the ramp. Standing in the light, a lone hobb looked up in startlement. The hobb held at its side a tall wooden crook with a crude lantern hanging from it. The violet light shone from the lantern, contrasting with the vibrancy of the hobb's vermilion rags. Apon seeing the elf, the hobb lifted its crook and thrust the lantern out defensively.

Belac knocked the crook aside with his empty scabbard and then ran his blade into the hobb's chest. The lantern crashed to the stone floor and violet fire spread out across the smooth tiles. Belac ripped his sword free from the hobb's chest, and quickly stepped away. He stared over the pool of fire into the corridor ahead and at the hobbs awash in violet light.

Belac snarled and then leaped into the flames, willing to burn if that is what it took to save the children. The fire's heat reached up for him as if yearning to be fed. Violet light illuminated the elf like the vengeful incarnation he had become. His feet cleared the blazing stones, and his momentum carried him forward.

The hobbs fled. Jabbering in terror, three of the hobbs dragged vermilion sacks through an open doorway at the end of the corridor ahead. No braver than their kin, the other hobbs bolted down the corridor in desperation to join them. Belac, however, would allow them no safety.

Hounding the vile creatures, Belac cut them down as they fled. The stone corridor was wide enough for him to swing his sword, but he needed to keep close to one wall to prevent his blade from striking the other. Moving from side to side as he ran, Belac's sword painted the walls with trails of dark blood.

The hobbs frightened screeching was suddenly drowned out by the grating of stone against stone. The shadowed doorway ahead began to narrow as vertical stone slabs closed in from both sides. The hobbs beyond had chosen to abandon the majority of their pack. Those that remained behind would be a sacrifice the others made to slow the righteousness that pursued them.

Belac intensified his speed, his swings becoming frantic. *No!* The hobbs began to crowd the narrowing doorway as their escape became a struggle with each other. Belac hacked into the hobbs between himself and the stone slabs that were threatening to close him away from the children. *You cannot have them!*

The slabs thundered when they closed, their denial echoing through the corridor. The last of the hobbs turned to face the elf, knowing they had nowhere else to go. Belac cut one down as it turned, but the other three attacked.

Belac thrust his scabbard at the hobb on his far left, the steel chape slamming into a dark orange cheek. The hobb's fangs tore into its own flesh as they ripped through the side of its mouth. Belac pushed away from the hobb while thrusting his sword into another one on his right. He deflected a war-pick with his scabbard and then spun right, pulling his sword free. Continuing the spin, he slashed down into the hobb that had almost struck him. Darting left, he thrust his scabbard's chape again at the hobb he had pushed away. Not caring where he hit the hobb, Belac thrust the end of his scabbard down twice more, each blow harder than the one before. With the hobb staggered against the wall, Belac reared back and then brought his sword down on the hobb. The steel of his blade scraped against the stone wall as he cut the hobb in two.

Stepping over the fallen, Belac's boots left bloody prints on the stone. He slammed his shoulder against the stone slabs that blocked his passage, but they might as well have been a solid wall. He punched the stone with his sword's cross-guard and screamed at the door. Rage flew from his mouth in a shower of spittle. The violet light was beginning to fade behind him. Soon, Belac would be alone in the dark with the putrid smell of rotting fruit and the taste of his own failure. He stepped away from the door and took a deep breath, grimacing at the smell of the dead hobbs. *I have not failed until I quit.* Belac was not going to quit. He would not let those children pay for his failure.

Belac slung his empty scabbard over his shoulder and then turned towards the dying light. To either side of the flickering violet flames, an open doorway drank the light. He listened for a moment, searching for any sounds of threat. He scanned the bodies of the savaged hobbs but none of the fallen still lived. Belac reached down and yanked off one of the hobbs' vermilion hoods. Standing, he used the cloth to wipe his sword before tossing the bloody rag aside. He removed his scabbard, slid his sword home, and then returned them to his back.

His slim fingers undid the buckles on his hip pouch and then began to dig around inside. Once he found what he was searching for, he pulled it free by its looped leather thong. *I am really glad that Rolan got me one of these.* After losing the first light rod, Belac had not expected the dwarf to trust him with another. He closed his hip pouch and then tapped the small rod against the wall. The rod pinged against the stone, and golden light filled his side of the corridor.

Belac flipped the leather thong around his left wrist, then tucked the rod through the loop. Tightening the thong, he made sure he could use both of his hands without losing the light rod. As the rod dangled from his wrist, he saw that something somewhere had ripped the sleeve of his jacket. Not wanting to risk the sleeve catching on something, he used his dagger to cut off the lower half. He tucked the silky scrap of cloth into his belt as he returned to the door.

Small angular characters had been chiseled into the door's pale gray stone in five concentric circles. The elf held his light rod closer to the stone slabs so that he could inspect their oddly familiar markings. He traced the lettering, but he could not read the language. Whatever instruction they might impart, Belac would not be able to decipher it. He balled up his fist and pressed his knuckles against the door. *I cannot just wait here. Every moment I do, the hobbs take the children farther away.* He pushed himself away from the door and turned around.

The violet light had been replaced with the faint smell of burnt blood. Two darkened doorways waited for the elf on the other side of the congested dead. *I will not be stopped here.* Belac's boots stepped into thick blood as he walked through the corridor of dead hobbs. The corridor through the doorway to his left was passable, but parts of the ceiling had collapsed, and black rock filled portions of what lie beyond. The corridor to his right was obstructed by nothing but darkness. Remembering what had happened the last time he trusted a cave in, he turned right and carried golden light into the darkness.

Seventeen

The corridor turned sharply right. The change in direction encouraged the elf so much that he did not bother checking around the corner for traps or an ambush. It was all he could do to stop himself from running. The corridor was long, and Belac needed to find the children before they were lost forever.

Running is not going to help me save those children. He did not know where he was, or where he was going; only that he was unwelcome. If he were not careful, he could fall into a trap or set off an alarm. *I really should have checked the corner back there.* What concerned him more than the immediate danger, was that he might miss something of importance. *I need an advantage. I need information. I need… I need help.* Belac was alone. He was also the only chance the children had.

Golden light pushed back the darkness as Belac advanced, but it was unable to penetrate far. When he finally came to a stone door at the end of the corridor, Belac feared he might need to go back and try the other way. *No, wait… That looks like it's cracked open.* Moving closer, he saw that he was correct. The door was different than the one that had stopped him before. It was different than any door he had ever seen. The pale stone door was a tall oval set into the center of a matching stone frame that completely surrounded it. There was no visible handle or latch. *It is not meant to be opened from this side.*

Two rows of large block lettering had been chiseled into the stone door. While Belac could not read the words, they felt like a warning.

Belac reached out and placed his palm on the door. *There is nothing this could say that would stop me.* Belac was surprised when the door, so imposing in its solidity, moved silently away from the pressure of his hand. Continuing to push the door open, he marveled at how effortlessly it swung out. What he found on the other side made him forget about the door.

The polished stone walls of the corridor ahead had been bleached white. On the left side, eight shadowed doorways stood open. Fragments of splintered wood were scattered throughout the corridor. The violence done to the ruined doors was punctuated by the dark splatterings of dried blood. It was not the gore that frightened the elf; it was the white. He knew of only one thing that could have built such a place. *Gnomes.*

Rolan's voice spoke in Belac's mind. "*Gnomes are evil.*" The elf's side pained sympathetically at the memory of being stabbed. *Gnomes are evil.* Belac thought back to the long corridor. *Did I smell anything?* The only smell he could remember was that of the slaughtered hobbs. *That rotting fruit smell could have masked poisoned air.* He realized that he might already be dead.

I could search for one of those magic antidote charms… Belac shook his head. *No.* Every moment he spent searching for a charm would be one when he was not searching for the children. *If I am poisoned, I'm poisoned. I can have Rolan and Serath take a look at me after I save the children.* He stepped through the doorway. And then the gore began to scare him.

Blood had been splattered and spattered from the ceiling to the floor of the corridor. *What could have done this?* Though the blood had long since dried, something sinister could still be waiting inside the complex. *Something more evil than gnomes…* Belac slipped his sword over his head, pulled it out of its scabbard, and then returned the scabbard to his back. He wanted to keep a hand free, but he was not walking into that bloody corridor without a weapon drawn.

Belac tip toed to the first doorway, cautious to avoid the chunks of broken wood. The silence in the complex was so complete that he could feel his pointed ears straining for sound. He held his left hand out into the first room, allowing the light rod to fill the small chamber with its golden glow. A toppled chair lay in the middle of the floor between a cluttered desk and a closed cabinet. The miniature furniture made the gnomish office look like a child's study room. More blood decorated the room, but Belac found no one inside. His gaze was pulled to the desk. Open notebooks and loose sheets of paper had been splashed with blood, forever defacing what had once been written. *I would not be able to read it anyway.*

Assured that there was nothing in the room that would attack him from behind, Belac moved to check the other offices. He was quick but quiet, worried that each doorway would reveal the thing that had caused the carnage. *There are no bodies…* Despite all the blood, there were no corpses, no torn pieces of flesh, and no offal remains. Under the horror of blood, there was a sterility to the complex that Belac found even more unsettling.

Of all the offices, only two were absent of blood. Doors hanging open neglectedly, the two rooms appeared to have been passed by. Belac did not believe the occupants had been spared.

After the offices, a trail of smeared blood led around a corner to the left and into a junctional corridor. A short distance past the new corridor, a gleaming metal wheel protruded from the back of another tall oval stone door. Belac hurried past the bloody corridor, and went for the closed door instead. *The gnome-killing-psycho-monster can just stay here and have the place to itself.*

Belac gripped the metal wheel with his left hand and attempted to turn it to the left. When the wheel did not budge, he tried the other direction. There was no play in the wheel. He bent down and placed his sword on the top of his right foot. Then he straightened and gripped the wheel with both hands. He attempted to wrench the wheel to the left and right repeatedly, but still, it would not move.

Belac frowned at the wheel. *Broken piece of...* He noticed a small hole in the center of the wheel. *Wait. Is that a keyhole?* He ran his thumb over the perfectly drilled hole. *I don't have time for this!* He growled. *I have no more time to search for a key than I do for one of those magic charms.*

The elf kicked his sword up into his hand. His grip tightened on the hilt as he turned around. *I have to find another way.* He looked toward the bloody corridor now on his right. *All that blood has to lead somewhere.* Belac knew that it might soon be his blood that covered the walls; but he was needed, and fear would not be enough to stop him.

He moved to the other corridor and peered around the corner. The blood smeared on the floor continued a short distance down the corridor before leading into the first of four cased doorways on the right. Past the widely spaced doorways, another metal wheel gleamed at the end of the corridor. The last half of the corridor appeared mostly free of blood. It served as an example of what the gnomish architecture would look like without its profane decoration. To Belac, it made the blood all the more horrific.

He crept around the corner and approached the first cased doorway. He tried to pay attention to all of his surroundings, but his eyes kept getting drawn back down to the blood smeared on the stone floor. He found himself increasingly more frightened to look up; each time, afraid that a monstrous face would be waiting for him. Belac's mind began to conjure images of drool pouring from jagged teeth.

Belac forced himself to look away from the bloody floor and into the room through the doorway. He saw a disheveled man with pointed ears outlined in his golden light. Belac raised his sword with its tip forward, ready to thrust at the other elf. At the exact same time, the other elf raised his sword as well. *Come and die!* Belac's heart pounded in his chest as he prepared to be attacked. The other elf waited with indomitable patience. Heart still beating fast, Belac lowered his sword and scowled at his own reflection.

The entire back wall of the room was a single pane of solid glass. Dark shadowy shapes danced on the other side of the glass, obscured by the reflection of the light rod's faint glow. Broken glass crunched under Belac's boots as he stepped into the room. To his left, miniature desks sat afore a short partitioning wall. Dried blood and broken glass, the partition had obviously failed. *What were they keeping in there?*

More glass crunched as Belac walked toward the breached partition. Abutting the wall on his left, another wheeled door provided the only intended access to the other side. A strange table with straps and hinged rails sat in the center of the partitioned cell. On the other side of the table, a row of short stone counters ran along the back of the wall. Alien tools with purposes Belac could only have guessed at lay scattered across the tabletops. To the right, a full quarter of the space was nothing but a pool of dark water.

Belac backed away from the partition. *What is this place?* He looked toward the glass wall on his right. As he moved, he thought he saw a tiny glint on the other side of the glass. Captured in the thralls of his own curiosity, he walked up to the glass. He held his light rod closer to the glass, hoping it might allow him to see beyond. A river of dark water flowed past at level with the floor.

With a flick of his arm, Belac brought the light rod up into his hand. He pressed the end of the rod against the center of his sword's cross-guard, and the inside of the room went black. As Belac's eyes adjusted, he began to make out what had drawn his attention. The tiny glint was light shining from an open door on the other side of the underground river. Looking closer, he saw that the light gleamed faintly off a silvery walkway that bridged the two sides. *That is what is on the other side of the locked door in the corridor.*

Belac stepped away from the glass. *I still need to check that other door.* He struck his light rod against the cross-guard of his sword and light returned to the room. The sound of the rod's ping was odd and its light dull, so Belac tapped the light rod against the stone wall as he exited the room. The rod pinged cleanly, and its light brightened. As Belac continued farther down the corridor, he realized that he had just announced himself to anything nearby.

Eighteen

Belac's grip tightened on the hilt of his sword. *Maybe it left…* The elf crept farther down the corridor. *Why would a gnome-killing-psycho-monster stay here anyway?* He looked at the blood on the walls. *The gnomes have got to be dead.* He glanced over his shoulder toward the corridor that led back to the gnome's offices that he had passed earlier. He redirected his attention back to the cased doorway ahead. *What if I just tell it that I'm not a gnome?*

Belac stepped halfway into the room with his light raised high and his sword pulled back, ready to thrust. *What if it only speaks Gnomish?* Golden light revealed another partitioned room. However, unlike the first, the partitioning glass remained unbroken. There was no blood on the walls, and no sign of struggle.

I don't know how to say, "I'm not a gnome. Don't eat me!" in Gnomish. Belac stepped back out into the corridor. *That really seems like something I should learn how to say.* He continued down the corridor. *I should learn how to say, "I'm an elf. Don't eat me!" in every language there is.* The walls had progressively less blood on them as he moved toward the next room. *There can't be that many languages I would have to learn…* The little blood left on the walls appeared to have been flung far. *Wait!* Belac froze. *I bet there are things that like to eat elves especially…* He shook his head. *I will need to think of something else to say.*

He stepped into the next room, again with his light high and his sword prepared to thrust. *What about, "I'm poisoned! Don't eat me!"?* The room was no different than the previous one. *That's better, but I still don't know how to say it in Gnomish.* He stepped back into the corridor and then turned toward the final doorway. *I wonder if I can get Rolan to make me a little book? He knows a lot of languages…* The lack of blood in the corridor ahead was not comforting enough to overcome the knowledge that if the gnome-killing-psycho-monster was still in that part of the complex, it would be in the final room.

Belac took a deep breath and then walked toward the last of the cased doorways. He realized another problem as he approached the shadowed opening. *If I speak in gnomish when I tell the gnome-killing-psycho-monster that I am not a gnome, it might not believe me.* He narrowed his eyes at the doorway. *Stupid gnome-killing-psycho-monster.*

Belac stepped into the room, once more with his light rod raised high and his sword ready to attack. Another room with its partition intact, no monsters waited inside for the elf. Belac lowered the light rod and relaxed, allowing some of the tension in his shoulders to ease. *I still need to find a way out of here. I might be safe, but those children are not.* He backed out of the room and then made his way to the wheeled door at the end of the corridor. *Please, be unlocked.* Belac felt like the complex had slowed his progress too much already. He needed to move on. He needed to find the children before the hobbs did something awful to them. He needed the door to be unlocked.

Belac gripped the silvery wheel and tried to turn it. When it would not move one way, he tried the other. Angrily, Belac jerked side to side, attempting to force the metal wheel. He wanted to rip it free and use it to bash a hole in the stone door. He kicked the door and then took a step back. His toe hurt.

Belac pushed his frustration aside, and turned away from the door. He had another plan; he just did not like it very much. He marched back into the gore and returned to the first of the cased doorways. He went inside the room, armed with the belief that he was alone.

Glass crunched under his feet as he turned in a small circle. He scanned the walls again, hoping that he would find a set of keys hidden under all the blood. When he found no hidden keys, the elf accepted that he only had one option.

He slipped the strap of his scabbard over his head, sheathed his sword, and then slung his scabbarded sword back behind him. The movements were becoming so natural that he barely needed to think about what he was doing. Belac stepped onto one of the miniature desks, scattering tiny pieces of broken glass as he hopped over the short partitioning wall.

The other side of the partition made Belac feel trapped and vulnerable. He wanted out, but he knew that there was only one way he could go. He stepped over to the pool of dark water, and stared down into its black depths. The surface wavered gently, constantly disturbed by unseen currents. *This has got to be connected to the river on the other side of the wall.*

Belac put his right hand on the edge of the pool, and hopped into the water. The cool rush was unpleasant, but the water was not so cold that Belac was concerned by it. He could not stand around avoiding discomfort. He was needed elsewhere. And he was needed now.

The elf took a deep breath, held it, and pushed himself below the pool's surface. The sound of turbulent water roared in Belac's ears. He raised his knees and placed both feet against the inside wall of the pool. Kicking away from the wall, he twisted into a spiral as he shot through the water. He had expected to find bars or a removable grate under the glass wall. Instead, he passed through a wide opening and was caught by the rivers current.

Belac lost sense of up and down. His arms and legs flailed as he struggled to right himself. He came to the surface splashing wildly, saved by luck and instinct. The oppressive sound of roaring water filled the cavern. Gasping for breath, Belac fought to regain control. He wanted to raise his light rod high and cast back the cavern's darkness, but he needed his hand to swim.

The back left side of Belac's head clonked against the underside of the metal bridge that spanned the river. The force of the impact sent his head down into the water. Twisting away, Belac reached up with his right hand. He grabbed one of the supports under the bridge and held on for dear life. The rivers current brought him around to face the underside of the bridge as he was whisked up from behind.

Pale, golden light lit the underside of the bridge as Belac's left hand grabbed another of the metal supports. He pulled himself up closer to the bridge and breathed through the walkway's grating. *The river is trying to eat me!* He began to climb out from under the bridge, pulling himself against the river's current. *You are not going to eat me, you stupid river!*

Once Belac reached the edge of the decking, he scooched his hands left until he came to one of the bridges support piers. Using the metal pier to help him fight the rivers flow, he climbed up and over the side of the bridge. Rising unsteadily to his feet, he turned and faced the oncoming river.

Belac spit water out of his mouth and then pointed down at the river. "I am not food!" The sound of the water rushing through the cavern drowned out the elf's words.

He took a step backward and looked up, taking in a deep breath. *I don't have time to stand here yelling at a river. I need to keep moving.* Belac reached back and untied the gray ribbon holding his long hair. He squeezed most of the water out of his hair before pulling it back tight and retying the ribbon. Rolling his shoulders, he focused on his need to move forward.

The light rod had dimmed significantly, so Belac knelt down and struck it against the bridges silvery grating. He did not think that there was any reason to worry about the sound of the rod pinging against the bridge. The river was loud enough to prevent anything from hearing the light rod come to life, no matter what might be waiting ahead.

Knelt down, with his right hand on the grating, Belac felt the bridge shudder. Concerned, he looked to his right. At the edge of the golden glow, between him and the open door beyond, a monstrous form stood hunched on all fours. The grotesque thing's torso was of the same dimensions as its legs, all long and no thicker than a man's wrist. Its spherical head was too large for its elongated body, and was faceless except for a deep horizontal crease across the center. Sickly pale flesh glistened wetly though the thing was absolutely still.

Belac knew what the thing was. *It's a crazy-fish-monster-water-zombie!* He shot to his feet and stared at the monster. Even on all fours, the thing stood taller than the elf. Belac could feel the monster studying him despite it having no eyes. *That thing wants to eat me.*

Though the monster remained perfectly still, Belac felt the bridge shudder under his feet. He glanced behind himself toward the other side of the bridge. Two more of the monsters waited in the darkness that the golden glow struggled to hold back. Startled, Belac stepped away, turning to face the monsters. They did not move, but the bridge shuddered again.

Belac's attention snaped back to the first monster. Motionless, the thing had moved closer into the light. Its pale skin looked droukit and dead. The bridge shuddered again. Belac backed away from the monster, glancing over his left shoulder in growing panic. The other two monsters had moved closer.

Belac backed up to the edge of the bridge, his heals hanging off the side. Moving his head quickly left to right repeatedly, he tried to keep all the monsters in view. The monsters did not move; patiently, they waited for their prey to falter. *I can't keep this up forever.* Eventually, the monsters would have him.

I have to fight. If he could cut his way through the single monster, he might be able to reach the open door before the other two caught him. Belac began to breathe deeply as he attempted to control his heartbeat. Careful not to make any sudden motions that might incite the monsters, he reached back and removed his scabbarded sword.

Belac could feel his senses reaching down into the bridge in anticipation of another shudder. His eyes darted side to side as he continued to turn his head slightly left and right. The monsters remained unmoving. Slowly, Belac drew his sword. The naked blade made him feel less alone. Though still, he was outnumbered.

The water's roar was louder than his words, but Belac resolutely spoke in elven, "I am not food."

He charged right, his boots hammering against the grating. The solitary monster did not move, but Belac knew that the other two already pursued him. *I will not be stopped!* Water erupted to Belac's left as another monster surged out of the river. Its spherical head split open to present multiple rows of long, pointed teeth.

Belac turned as he ran, thrusting his sword into the fanged maw. The monster slammed into the elf, throwing him off the side of the bridge. Belac hit the river with the weight of the impaled monster still on top of him. They plunged deeper into the dark water in a tangled mass of flailing limbs. Belac lost hold of his sword as he fought both the monster and the river's current. There was no up, no down; only the dull, watery illumination of the nightmarish thing that Belac struggled against.

Then the water's pressure disappeared, and Belac was falling through air.

Nineteen

Belac awoke to something tugging on his right foot. He opened his eyes to see what it was, only to find himself in blackness. He tasted vomit in his mouth, though he did not understand why. Lying on his back, he was dizzy. Head and shoulder supported by rock, his right side was dry, but his left felt like it was floating on water. Nothing made sense to the elf.

The sound of a waterfall carried from far in the distance, echoing through the rocky cavern. *Any moment now, a man in black is going to show up and tell me I had another eventful night.* The tugging on his foot brought Belac's thoughts into focus. He kicked irritably at whatever was tugging on his foot, and then rolled away from the water. His scabbard splashed water across him as it was pulled from the river.

Lying on his right side, Belac untangled the scabbard's strap from his wrist. He tossed the scabbard aside and then rolled onto his knees and elbows. He rested his forehead against the cool rock of the floor and tried to breathe naturally, but he began to cough and spit up water. Even when the coughing ceased, his breathing continued to tremble.

Belac pushed himself up onto his hands. It felt like he was holding back the world. He raised his left arm and swung his light rod into his hand. He let his arm swing down, and the light rod struck the cavern floor.

The light rod pinged, its golden light pushing back the darkness. Supporting his upper body with one arm, Belac stared down at the stony floor. Thick swirls of black and brown, it was as if the rock's colors had been dancing with each other before being frozen in time. He closed his eyes and leaned back to sit on his ankles. *Not even Cavascan wine would be worth this headache.* When he opened his eyes, he was staring at the twisted form of a monster. *A crazy-fish-monster-water-zombie!*

Belac threw himself away from the monster. He fell on his backside and began to scoot away. Motionless, with its mouth fully open, the monster lay dead on the stone riverbank. The hilt of Belac's sword protruded from the gruesome mouth. Halted only by the steel cross-guard, the sword's blade had pierced the skull and ran back into the monster's narrow torso.

Something moved on Belac's left. He turned toward the movement and shoved himself away in an effort to escape whatever it was that wanted to kill him. He toppled backward into the river, splashing wildly as he sank below the water. His feet found the bottom of the river, and he stood up, his hair slinging water as his shoulders broke the surface. Somewhere he had lost his ribbon, but that was not what concerned him. The elf's left hand shot out of the water, holding his light rod high. A bright red scaled creature with a long, bushy tail barked at Belac. The body of the reptile was not much bigger than a house cat, but the thick, furry tail doubled its size. *It's a giant, red lizard-squirrel!*

Belac pointed at the lizard-squirrel. "I am not food!"

The lizard-squirrel sat back on its haunches with its front legs held to its chest like little arms. Seemingly content to maintain its quasi-standing posture, the lizard-squirrel tilted its head as it regarded the elf.

Okay. Belac could not help but grin. *It might still try to eat me, but that has got to be one of the cutest things I have ever seen.* He pointed at the reptile again. "Stay."

The lizard-squirrel watched Belac curiously as the elf climbed out of the river. Remaining close to the river's edge, Belac stood dripping water onto the cavern floor. The lizard-squirrel merely continued to stare at the elf.

Belac nodded approvingly at the reptile. "Good, Squirrel."

Belac squeezed water out of his hair and then began to press what he could out of his clothes. As he did, he noticed that a part of his right boot was missing above his pinky toe. Upon further inspection, he found that the sole had small bite marks in it. *If I had slept longer, I might not have a foot.* He amended his thinking. *I guess I might still have 'a' foot. I would just not have two feet.*

Belac pointed at the reptile. "I need two feet!"

The lizard-squirrel barked, but stayed where it was.

Keeping the lizard-squirrel in view, Belac walked over to the dead crazy-fish-monster-water-zombie. *This thing needs a shorter name.* He looked down at the hideous rows of teeth. *It's definitely a fish-monster.* He kicked the monster's head to make sure that it was not still alive despite having his sword ran through it. *If it's a fish-monster, I guess I don't need to call it a water-something…*

Still not trusting that the monster was dead, Belac sat down and put each of his feet on either side of the open jaws. Then he reached forward and took hold of his sword's hilt. He pushed with his feet as he pulled his sword free from the dead monster's mouth.

The lizard-squirrel hopped away and barked at the elf's sudden movement.

Belac got to his feet and said, "Don't worry, little buddy. I am not going to eat you." *Even if you did try to eat me first.*

Belac looked down at the monster that he was now sure was dead. *I know Vairug says it's not a zombie, but that looks like zombie flesh to me.* Belac swung his sword and hacked off one of the monsters three fingered hands. He picked the severed hand up and then tossed it toward the lizard-squirrel.

"There," Belac told the skittish reptile. "You can eat that. It's zombie-fish-monster."

Cautiously, the lizard-squirrel approached the gristly offering. It sniffed at the blood seeping from the cut meat, and then backed away. Still focused on the severed hand, the lizard-squirrel barked angrily.

Belac bent down and picked up his scabbard. "Yeah. I would not eat it either." He poured the water out of the scabbard and then sent his sword home.

The lizard-squirrel moved farther away from the severed hand and then looked up at Belac expectantly. Belac slipped his baldric over his head and positioned the scabbarded sword on his back. He drew his dagger and cut a piece of leather from the end of the baldric. *The strap does not need to be that long anyway.*

"Here." Belac tossed the scrap of leather to the waiting reptile. "That has got to be as good as boot leather."

The lizard-squirrel ran over and snatched up the scrap of leather. It sat back on its haunches and held the scrap up to its mouth with scaly, four fingered hands. With quick motions, the lizard-squirrel began to gnaw at the leather. *Definitely one of the cutest things I have ever seen.*

Belac turned away from the feeding reptile, and gazed out at the dark water that had carried him there. The cavern had widened, and the river split. Belac had washed up on the far right side of the fork. The water on the left flowed faster, and the elf was not certain that he would have survived it. *But I did survive. And now, I need to make sure that the children do as well.*

Belac turned back to the lizard-squirrel. "You don't happen to know how to get out of here do you?"

Finished eating, the bushy tailed reptile ran around in a tight circle and then looked up at the elf expectantly.

Belac shook his head. "You want more food, you show me the way out."

The lizard-squirrel tilted its head to the side.

"Out." Belac held up a hand and wiggled two of his fingers like they were tiny legs. "Take me," he gestured up at nothing, "out."

The lizard-squirrel continued to stare at the elf.

"You should have a staring contest with Vairug," Belac told the hungry reptile.

Belac considered his options. He could go back and try to swim up a waterfall, fight three more zombie-fish-monsters, and then hope that the other side of the gnomish complex would lead to the children. Or, he could go forward, follow the river, and hope that he found another way. If he could have been sure that the complex above would lead him to the children, Belac would have braved the monsters.

The elf sighed. It was easy to get turned around underground, but he thought the river flowed in the general direction that he needed to go. *Besides, the river has to go somewhere.* Even if he could not find the children, the river might lead him out. *I could get help and then come back.* He almost dismissed the idea outright. He did not want to leave the children behind. *It does not matter what I want. I need to do whatever will give them the best chance.*

Belac gestured down river. "I am going that way," he told the lizard-squirrel. "If you help me find the children I'm looking for, I will make sure you get fed." He turned and began to walk along the side of the river.

As Belac moved away, the lizard-squirrel trailed behind him, staying within the glow of the light rod.

After reconsidering what he had said, Belac glanced down at the reptile. "You are not allowed to eat the children."

Twenty

The lizard-squirrel bumped into the side of Belac's calf as it ran past him. Belac did not know if the strange reptile understood where he wanted to go, or if it was simply waiting for him to trip and die so that it could eat his boots.

"Find the children, and you can have all the boots you want," Belac called after the lizard-squirrel. "I will organize an old boot collection drive for you."

The bright red scaled lizard-squirrel barked and then ran off into the shadows on the right. Stopping outside of a large, round opening in the rockface, the lizard-squirrel turned around and barked. It ran around in a tight circle, chasing its long, bushy tail. Then it stopped again and sat back on its haunches.

Belac would have liked to believe that he would have seen the opening without the reptile's aid. However, the opening was dark, and he had been more focused on the river. There had been no new signs of zombie-fish-monsters, but Belac did not want to be caught unaware. *Having an extra set of senses is going to be useful.*

Belac drew his dagger and cut off another piece of his baldric's strap. He tossed the scrap of leather to the reptile, asking, "Who's a good squirrel?"

The lizard-squirrel snatched up its treat and began to gnaw on it, holding the leather in both of its scaly fingered hands.

Belac looked back toward the river. He was not thirsty, but he did not know how long it would be until he found water again. *If the river is not safe to drink, I am already in trouble.* He walked over to the edge and knelt down. *I wonder how much of this I drank when I was drowning.* He scooped water into his hand and then brought it up to his mouth. *It tastes better than the water in some cities that I've been to.* Trying not to think about the things swimming in the river upstream, he drank more of the water.

Belac was almost shoved into the river as the lizard-squirrel brushed past him. The reptile lowered its head to the water and began to drink. There was a comradery to the act that Belac felt was endearing. Slowly, he reached out and touched the reptile's bushy tail. He had expected it to be hard and coarse, but the tail was as soft as any fur Belac had ever felt.

The lizard-squirrel stopped drinking. It lifted its head from the water and looked back at Belac's hand on its tail. It looked up at Belac's face for a moment, and then returned to drinking from the river.

Belac ran his fingers through the reptile's soft, red hair and then stood. *I hope squirrel-face here knows where it's going.* He turned and faced the opening in the rocky cavern wall. *I can't tell if that is natural or not…* A round tunnel, too tall for him to reach the top standing on Vairug's shoulders, its circular shape seemed out of place to the elf. *Not-natural might be a good thing. Not-natural would mean that it goes somewhere.*

Belac was beginning to worry that he might have chosen the wrong direction. *If I don't find something soon, I may need to go back to the gnome enclave.* The weight of his choices scared him. His mistakes would be paid for with the lives of children.

Belac hardened his resolve, and marched onward. *Indulging my own fear will not save those children.* He moved into the tunnel, believing that any decision was better than indecision. The tunnel's round walls were smooth, but so uneven that they almost looked ribbed. A slight draft blew through the tunnel as if pulling Belac into it. Stretching long and bending left, the tunnel seemed to lead only to darkness.

The black and brown swirls of the rock created a mildly dizzying effect as Belac's light rod swung from his wrist. Tiny claws skittered on the stone as the lizard-squirrel ran past the elf's legs. The reptile moved ahead, but remained well within the bounds of the bobbing light.

"You had better not be leading me to a giant pack of lizard-squirrels," Belac said threateningly. "Just think of all the old boots you will miss out on if you try to eat me."

Belac imagined the lizard-squirrel eating piles of old boots until it got so big that they needed to hold towns hostage for their used footwear. *I wonder what the town people will think when I show up riding a giant, red lizard-squirrel and say, "It's your old boots, or your life!"*

Farther ahead, another tunnel intersected with the one that Belac traveled through. *I hope my new friend here knows which way to go.* The lizard-squirrel walked into the intersection confidently, continuing straight without giving any sign that it would be altering its course. *It sure seems like it knows where it's going.* A dusky maroon colored hand reached out from the dark tunnel on the right and grabbed the lizard-squirrel. The reptile barked in panic as bony fingers tightened around its body and pulled it into the darkness.

Belac rushed forward without thinking. He made it to the intersection in time to witness massive, block teeth bite down on the lizard-squirrel's head. Fat, scarlet lips smacked wetly as powerful jaws rippled a blubberous face. Eyes too wide under a shock of wispy black hair, the monstrous thing was a mockery of the human form. *Is that a troll?!* Its naked, maroon colored skin was covered with patches of cracked scabs. Bloated and legless, its pear-shaped body filled the tunnel.

When the troll saw Belac, it crammed the remainder of the lizard-squirrel into its mouth and began to chew determinedly. Belac backed away from the thing. He did not remember drawing his blade, but he held his sword in one hand and his scabbard in the other.

The troll let out a deep bellowing moan and began to move forward using its long arms to swing its weighty lower body in a lumbering gait. It followed Belac through the intersection and into the tunnel on the other side. Sound boomed through the tunnels as the troll moaned louder. Belac could now smell the rank musk of the troll's unwashed flesh. He knew the thing coming for him was too much for him to fight.

The troll's arm swung out as it grabbed for the elf. Belac dodged back, rolling away from the reaching hand. As he came to his feet, the elf was backhanded into the wall. Belac dropped his scabbard, but managed to keep hold of his sword. Half leaning, half lying against the circular wall of the tunnel, he looked up to see the troll reaching for him with its other hand.

Belac thrust his sword into the center of the maroon hand as it grabbed him. The troll roared at the pain, but its bony fingers wrapped around the elf's shoulders in a crushing grip. Arms pinned, Belac thrashed as the troll lifted him up and brought him to its mouth. He looked into the troll's dark, gluttonous eyes as its fat lips pulled away from its open mouth.

I am not food! Belac swung his knees up and braced his feet on the troll's lower jaw. Gripping the hilt of his sword with both hands, he pushed back with the strength of his legs. He slipped down into the troll's grip as steel cut through the lower half of the monstrous hand. Belac and the troll roared together as he fell away from it in a spray of dark blood.

Belac slammed onto the tunnel floor with his left shoulder and then rolled away. Fueled by adrenaline, the elf surged to his feet and turned toward the troll. Sword gripped tightly in his right hand, Belac wiped blood from his face with his left.

The troll's ruined hand held close to its body, it roared at the elf in rage.

Belac screamed in irrational fury, "You ate my squirrel!" and charged at the troll.

The troll brought its undamaged fist down like a hammer. Belac evaded by running up the left side of the tunnel as he rushed forward. Leaping off the wall, he thrust his sword into the troll's naked chest. The blade penetrated all the way to its cross-guard, and then Belac collided with the troll. Together, they crashed down onto the ramped section of the tunnel's stone floor.

Belac slid off the side of the troll, but was able to maintain his grip on his sword. Using the hilt, he pulled himself up on top of the troll. *I am not done with you yet.* He ripped his sword free and then hopped away. Not waiting for the troll to react, Belac brought his blade down on its exposed neck. The sword's edge sank deep; but despite the elf's fury, it took him another five swings before the troll's head was completely severed.

Belac pointed his bloody sword at the troll's head. "Now, I'm done with you."

Belac staggered away from the decapitated troll and then sat down. He was suddenly so exhausted, he thought he might pass out. His heart hurt and his hands were trembling. He set his sword down next to him and focused on continuing to breathe. His headache was back, and he thought that he might throw up. He looked up toward the rounded ceiling and closed his eyes. As soon as his breathing steadied, he felt his anger beginning to return. *I don't have time for this!* Anything could be happening to the children. Belac did not have time to be weak. *I need to get on my feet. I need to take my sword. And I need to kill everything that would stop me from saving those children!* The elf took hold of his sword and stood. *So, that is what I am going to do.*

Twenty-One

Belac decided to trust his dead friend. After retrieving his scabbard, he returned to the intersection and continued down the tunnel that the lizard-squirrel had shown him. He slung the scabbard onto his back, but he kept his sword in hand. Unknown dangers waited ahead, and Belac was not going to allow any of them to stop him. *Anything that does not hold its hands up and say, "Don't eat me," is getting killed.*

Belac had attempted to wipe the blood from his sword using the rag looped through his belt, but the silky fabric was not absorbent enough to be of much help. He had wiped off as much as he could and then accepted that the blade was simply going to be a little bloody. There was still more blood on the elf than there had been on his sword. *Maybe the blood will help camouflage me.* His skin began to itch as the blood dried. He scratched at his neck. *I hope troll blood is not poisonous.* The jerky motions caused his long hair to fall forward into his face. He growled at the hair, but it refused to go back in place on its own. Halting, he placed his sword on his foot and then tied his hair back behind his head. He would have preferred to use another ribbon, but he did not have one. He needed his hair to stay out of his way and an Elven knot was tried and true.

Belac kicked his sword up into his hand and continued down the tunnel. *I should just start carrying a bag filled with ribbons.* He nodded to himself. *There has got to be all sorts of useful things that I could do with a bag of ribbons.* He strived to conceive what grand purpose a bag filled with ribbons might have. *I could use them to tie my hair. I could mark trails with them. I could… tie other things with them.* He frowned. *Okay. So, mostly I would just tie stuff with them.* A thought came to him. *Ooh! Maybe I could learn how to fight with them! No one would expect that!* He imagined snapping ribbons into people's eyes and then tying their fingers together. *I wonder if there is a way to throw flaming ribbons at people…*

Belac could hear the faint sound of trickling water ahead. *Did I go the wrong way?* He shook his head. *No. The tunnel must run between two rivers.* He reconsidered. *I guess it could be the same river.* He wondered if the tunnel was a short cut, or if the lizard-squirrel had been leading him around something.

Belac missed the lizard-squirrel. It was not merely that he had lost his guide; it was also the reptile's friendly nature. Now alone as he explored the darkness of the underground, he was without the comfort of the lizard-squirrel's presence. The elf growled at himself. *I am not here for comfort. I am here to save those children!*

Belac exited the tunnel into a winding cavern split by a single river of flowing water. He did not know if the dark water came from the same place as the other river, but he felt sure they must be connected in some way. Far to the right, where the cavern turned with a bank in the river, pale light bled around the wall. Hidden behind rock and perspective, the mystery of what waited beyond called to the elf. The pale light indicated that something other than endless passages would be found ahead. It offered affirmation that his choices had been the right ones. And it represented the possibility that he might still rescue the children. *Maybe I can find something that will lead me back to the hobbs.* Belac lowered his expectations. *Or at least something that will help me track them.* He began following the river toward the light.

As Belac got closer, the light's strangeness became more and more apparent. It seemed to wash away the brown coloring from the rock, leaving behind only pale violet to swirl with the black. Belac knew the light was not natural. *That is the hobbs' fire.* He remembered how the violet light had lit the corridor as he had slaughtered the last pack of hobbs. *I will cut through as many of those things as I need to. I will save those children!*

On the darker side of the bank, the pale violet light reflected off a large, silvery net that blocked the elf's progress. Anchored into the rock, cords of shimmering metal hung from the ceiling and walls like a giant spider's web. Belac did not know what the net was meant for, but its holes were too small for even a child to crawl through.

Belac studied the net, searching for the best place to try to cut it. Then he noticed that despite the net being anchored into either side of the river, its lines did not touch the water. *I guess they are not trying to catch zombie-fish-monsters.* Belac looked at his sword. Even if it could cut through the net's silvery metal cords, his blade would be damaged. He returned his sword to his back and then knelt down next to the river.

Hopping into the water feet first, Belac tried to splash as little as possible. He did not know how far the noise would travel, or if it would even be detectable over the river's steady flow, but he did not think it was worth finding out. *I need to be able to kill as many of them as I can before they know that I'm here.* His feet found the riverbed with the dark water barely chest high. He flicked his light rod into his hand and pressed the end against the rock of the rivers shore. The golden light died, leaving the one of unhealthy violet to sparkle over the dark water unchallenged.

Deciding not to disturb the netting, Belac ducked down into the water and swam with the current. *If I touch the net, it might set off an alarm.* The river guided Belac under the netting and continued to pull at him after he resurfaced. Keeping his head above water, Belac took long bouncing strides as he allowed the current to carry him around the river's long bend.

Traveling into the perverse light, the elf marveled at what he discovered hidden behind the wall of rock to his right. Open pastures and fields of crop stretched out into a section of the cavern that was astonishingly vast. To the right, against the wall closest to the river's bend, an entire hamlet had been erected underground. Small, wooden cottages and long barns, the hamlet was bathed in the pale violet light. High above the buildings, suspended by thick chains of black metal, a huge, glass cauldron burned like a profane substitution of the sun. Bright violet flames rose from the cauldron, illuminating a ceiling of jagged rock ornamented with rows of black rings. The rings guided the heavy chains over the hamlet and down along the cavern's wall. Larger than any of the cottages below, the glass cauldron burned bright enough to light the whole of the hidden world. *How does that thing not pull the ceiling down?*

Hobbs walked in the violet light like vile impersonations of villagers. Tall, sinewy forms moved among them. Canid heads and curved spines, the nightmarish things walked upright with a predatorial grace. Belac did not recognize the creatures, but he could guess what they were. *Those have to be the hobgoblins.*

As Belac floated past the hamlet, he searched for signs of the abducted children. While he saw no indications that they were there, the children could have been locked inside any of the wooden cottages. *I can't search all that without getting caught.* Belac's mind began to analyze the hamlet with a different objective. He needed information. If he wanted a plan with a chance of success, he needed to understand what he was dealing with. So, he took in every detail he could as he bobbed down the river.

The surreal cavern was only made more unsettling by the hamlet's resemblance to the familiar. It was an agricultural civilization that spoke to an intelligent design. Belac did not know if it was another remnant of the gnomes, or if the hobbs and hobgoblins had created the hamlet on their own. *They even have pigs running around.* Belac's stomach suddenly felt like he was falling. *I never saw what was in the sacks…*

The elf's feet settled on the riverbed. He stood staring at the livestock. *Anything could have been in those sacks.* He recalled the sight of the bulging, vermilion cloth. *I never saw what was inside.* The dairy farm had used goats. *The hobbs could have just been stealing the farmer's goats.* Belac began to despair. *Did I come all the way to this evil place to rescue goats?* Belac shook his head, refusing to believe it. *No. Scot said that the hobbs took the children.* He thought back to the exchange. *Henry believed him.* He nodded to himself. *Three missing children, three squirming sacks.* He gazed out into the pastures. *And I don't see any goats.*

Belac relaxed and allowed himself to slowly float downstream as he considered how to proceed. *I have to find some way to search that crazy village.* He decided that he would need to disguise himself. *I can't make myself taller, but I can squat down and waddle. If I cover up with something, I might be able to pass for a hobb.* He glanced up at the fiery cauldron. *I wonder if that thing ever stops burning.* Darkness would help his disguise.

If I am going to do this, I have to find something to disguise myself with. Small sheds dotted the farmland around a larger barn. *I can search those. It has got to be easier to sneak around a barn than a village full of monsters.* While he saw few hobbs working the fields, Belac would still need to be careful to avoid being seen. If one of the hobbs or hobgoblins discovered him, he could soon find himself having to deal with them all.

Belac climbed out of the river, keeping low in a crouch. He removed his sword, drew it, and then returned the scabbard to his back. Bent forward, he moved as quickly as he could while staying close to the ground. He hoped that if something saw him, the unnatural light would cause him to be dismissed as just another hobb in the distance. He skulked to the nearest of the small buildings but was disappointed by what he found. It was nothing more than an extension of a pig pen. It appeared as if the shed were intended to offer the pigs shelter from weather that the cavern would almost certainly never have.

The pigs seemed completely unconcerned by the elf's trespass. Belac narrowed his eyes at the pigs. He felt that the pigs were too content in their captivity under the violet, alchemical sun. *Traitors.* He left the pigs behind, and began moving toward another of the smaller buildings. *Stupid pigs. I did not want to have to rescue you anyway.*

The second building presented no more opportunity than the first. A shed for crude farming implements, there was nothing inside that Belac thought he could use as a disguise. He sighed and gazed out at the largest of the buildings. *I am going to have to check that barn if I want to find something. I am just wasting my time with the sheds.*

As Belac approached the barn, he searched for anything nearby that might want to kill him. Far in the distance, he saw hobbs that would surely qualify. Preoccupied tilling soil, the hobbs gave no indication that they had noticed the elf. Beyond the hobbs, four hobgoblins lounged in a pasture like they had stopped for a picnic. There was a wrongness to the casual behavior that the violet light seemed to feed.

Then Belac heard a sound that gave him hope even as it broke his heart. He heard the sound of a child crying.

Twenty-Two

Though he only heard the sound of a single child crying, Belac allowed himself the hope that he would find all three. He approached the rear of the barn, his every movement cautious. A rough, wooden door hung open. *Wide enough for a hobb, high enough for a hobgoblin.* He did not expect to find the children alone.

Hiding behind the left side of the doorway, Belac peered into the barn's dusky interior. Pale violet light shone through cracks in the walls and ceiling. To the right side, the children huddled together in a pen built for small animals. There was a hobb for each of the three children, and one hobgoblin towering over them all.

Standing in the center of the barn, the hobgoblin was an insult to creation. Thrice as tall as the hobbs, its sinewy body was clothed only in a long skirt of vermilion rags, leaving its bony chest and arms exposed. Yellowy tan skin covered its twisted frame and stretched tightly over its fanged face. A mane of wild, black hair stirred as the hobgoblin turned toward the children. Dark, soulless eyes set deeply in its canid skull, the hobgoblin glared balefully at the crying child.

It was the younger of the two boys that cried. Gwen had her face buried against the older boy's chest, and the older boy had his eyes closed. The crying child could not look away from the monster. Held in place by a hobb, the boy could not escape his terror.

The hobgoblin lifted a wicked hand with long, needle-like fingertips, and pointed at the crying boy. The hobb holding the small boy began to drag him from the pen. The boy attempted to resist but was too terrified to think. The hobb brought the boy before the hobgoblin, and then grabbed the back of the boy's sandy hair.

The hobgoblin reached out with one of its long, pointed fingers, and traced the side of the boy's face. With a disturbingly dainty manner, the hobgoblin pulled its finger away from the terrified child. The boy wept uncontrollably as he stared up at the hobgoblin. It tilted its canid head to the side as it stared down into the boy's wide eyes. Then the hobgoblin's finger shot out and stabbed into the boy's eye socket. The long, needle tipped finger pierced deep into the boy's brain, instantly ending his sobs.

The boy's small body trembled where he stood. It was as if his body wanted to collapse, but it no longer knew how. The hobgoblin continued to study the child emotionlessly as it pulled its finger back. The long tip slid out cleanly, and then the boy collapsed. The hobb holding the boy jabbered happily as it guided the child to the ground.

Belac was moving before he understood what he was doing. Bent on murder and vengeance, the elf charged at the hobgoblin. Its doglike face turned toward him as it raised one of its wicked hands. Pointing a needle tipped finger at the elf, the hobgoblin made a wet sound in its throat.

Belac severed the hand that had hurt the child. The savagery of his follow up swing cut through the hobgoblin's neck and lower jaw. His rage unsated, Belac brought his blade down on the closest hobb's head. He then turned to face the other two.

The darkness in the monster's eyes was nothing compared to the hate in Belac's blue. *These things will die!* One of the hobbs cowered, the other tried to flee; neither was saved his wrath.

Belac cut down the hobb that attempted to flee, and then he advanced on the other. The last hobb had retreated to the back of the pen and faced away with its hands pressed to the sides of its head. Belac did not think about what the children saw. It would not have mattered if he had. His sword hacked into the cowering hobb, and then he snarled at the corpse.

In a moment of enraged madness, Belac considered marching out of the barn and waging war on the nearby hamlet. He wanted to kill everything that lived under that chained, violet sun. *What I want is not what is important.* He turned toward the children that he had come to rescue. *Only what they need.*

The older boy looked up at Belac with fear and confusion. Clutching Gwen to his chest protectively, the boy shied away. His sandy hair fell into his eyes, but he did not look away from the elf. *Both boys look so much like their father…*

Belac nodded to the boy. "Keep an eye on her." He then stepped past the two children holding each other.

The younger boy lay flat on his back, staring up at the ceiling blankly. Belac knelt down and snapped his fingers in front of the boy's face. There was no response from the boy; no indication that he was even aware.

Gwen spoke from behind the elf. "Belac?"

Belac turned his head to look at the little girl. She stood one small step away from the older boy. Even the evil, violet light could not distort the innocence in her eyes.

Belac offered her an exhausted grin. "Hello, Gwen."

The little girl rushed at him. She wrapped her small arms around the elf's waist as she knocked him over. Belac hastily set his sword out of the way, not wanting either of them to be cut.

Her face pressed against the elf's ribs, Gwen began to sob. "I'm sorry. I'm sorry. I'm sorry. I'm sorry."

Belac put his hand on the girl's head and almost started crying with her. Instead, he took a deep breath. *She does not need more tears.* The smell of rotten fruit reminded Belac where he was. *These children are not safe yet.* He put his hands on the little girl's shoulders and gently pushed her away.

Looking into her watery eyes, Belac said, "We can't stay here, Gwen."

The little girl wiped snot from her face and nodded. Belac helped her to stand and then did so himself. He looked from the little girl to the older boy, and then to the younger boy on the floor. Belac had a problem. *I have no idea how I am going to get these children out of here.*

Gwen, her voice timid, asked, "Is Brandon going to be okay?"

Belac assumed she meant the injured boy. "I don't know, Gwen." He tried to balance honesty with optimism. "But we are going to take him with us, and then we can find someone to help him."

Gwen nodded, looking as if she were about to cry.

I have to do something. Wasting time would not only be unsafe, it would encourage the children to fall into despondence. *I need to give them something to do also.*

Belac nodded toward the older boy. "What's your name?"

"I'm…" The boy struggled with his emotions. "I'm Frank."

"Alright, Frank," Belac pointed his hand at the boy on the floor, "I need you to help Gwen move Brandon over by the back door." He pointed his hand toward the door that he had entered through. "You got that?"

Frank nodded, but did not move.

Belac clapped his hands together. "Well! Let's go."

Both Frank and Gwen hopped at the sound of Belac's hands slapping together. Suddenly focused on their task, they hurried toward Brandon.

Belac bent down and grabbed one of the stubby legs of the hobb that had not died in the pen. He considered his options as he dragged the bloody corpse into the pen with the others. *I can't take the children back the way I came in. Even if I could find some way to get them up the waterfall, the zombie-fish-monsters would tear them apart.* He walked out of the pen.

Frank had his forearms under Brandon's armpits. Gwen, for her part, was trying to take hold of the boy's ankles. Belac let them struggle with their task while he walked over to deal with the hobgoblin. *I can't take them back the way they came in.* Belac grabbed both of the headless hobgoblin's ankles. *I don't know where the doors are, and I wouldn't know how to open them if I found them.* With lurching steps backward, Belac dragged the dead hobgoblin into the pen. *There is only one way to go.* He dropped the hobgoblin's legs and then walked out of the pen.

Frank and Gwen had managed to move Brandon to the door, and were now attempting to lower him back down without dropping him. Belac kicked the hobgoblin's severed hand into the pen. *We have to keep following the river.* He reached down and grabbed a fistful of the hobgoblin's black mane. *I don't know if that way is safe, but I know the other ones are not.* He tossed the severed head into the pen. *The river has to lead somewhere. If it does not let out above ground, maybe we can find some other way.* He kicked the hobgoblin's lower jaw into the pen. *Even if all we find is just someplace to hide, we would be better off than we are now.*

Belac glanced to where Frank and Gwen stood over Brandon. The boys' brown trousers and tunic did not look like they would offer much more protection than Gwen's dress. *At least they all have shoes.* It was clear that the children were waiting to be told what to do next. Belac took a deep breath. *They are not going to be able to carry him.* Part of the reason he had asked them to move the injured boy was to see how well they could do it.

Belac bent down, picked up his sword, and then went through the quick motions of returning it to his back. He walked over to the children. "Gwen, I need you to hold Frank's hand and make sure that he doesn't get too far from me."

The little girl nodded seriously, but Frank argued, "But, I am older than her!"

Belac winked at the boy. "That's why she is in charge."

Frank was confused for a moment, but then said, "Oh!" He nodded. "Right."

Belac looked down at the youngest of the three children. *I am going to have to carry him.* Such a small thing, the boy would be easy to carry. What worried Belac was what would happen if he needed to fight. If something tried to stop them, he would have to drop the boy. The other two children would not be able to outrun monsters, and Belac could not protect them while carrying Brandon in his arms. Once the boy had been dropped, there would be decisions that needed to be made. Belac pushed the thoughts aside. *Focus on what needs to be done now.* The elf knelt down and scooped Brandon into his arms, holding the boy as he would a sleeping child.

Belac looked at the other two children. "Stay close. Stay quiet."

Belac waited for both of the children to nod before he stood and walked out of the barn. Out in the pasture, between him and where he needed to go, dozens of hobgoblins danced in celebration.

Twenty-Three

The dance of the hobgoblins would have been beautiful had it not been performed by the twisted creatures that gave it life. Flowing movements and leaping strides, the hobgoblins were unworthy of such effortless grace. As they danced in the pale violet light, they threw each other into the air. Their layered skirts of vermilion cloth twirled as they spun, arms open wide and unfettered. The hedonistic expression of joy was a primal testament to the cruelty of the world.

Belac did not know what had gathered the hobgoblins, but he felt certain that the celebration must have something to do with the children. It simply would have been too much of a coincidence otherwise. Whatever their reasons for being there, the hobgoblins were effectively guarding Belac's route of escape. Even as he watched them dance, four of the hobgoblins broke away from the others and jumped into the river. Monsters at play, the hobgoblins danced in the dark water.

Belac moved to the other side of the barn, using it to hide from the hobgoblins. The children came with him, though their eyes tracked the dancing monsters. Belac considered his options, realizing that he would have fewer of them every moment that passed. He could risk taking the children deeper into the farmland, but he worried that the hobbs would find them there.

Not only would the hobbs have the advantage, but they were also sure to summon the hobgoblins. *There is no way to get these children out of here.* Belac growled. *Then, I will make a way.*

"Belac?" Gwen's voice sounded scared.

Belac turned away from the barn, gesturing with his nose. "Let's go."

Belac led Frank and Gwen away from the dancing hobgoblins at a brisk pace. There was no safe direction that he could take them, but he knew waiting would only increase the danger. He scanned ahead between glances back at the children that followed him. Every time he looked at the children, he hated how the violet light touched them. It reminded him of how the hobgoblin had caressed Brandon's face.

Belac had decided to take the children to the pig pen. They could hide in the shed, and with any luck, the swine would help mask their scent. He narrowed his eyes at the pigs. He did not trust the round, fleshy things, but their movement and sound would provide even more cover for the children. *Stupid pigs would probably turn us in if they could.*

Belac nodded toward the short gate. "Open that for me."

Frank moved forward and opened the gate while Gwen clutched at Belac's pant leg.

"Don't let the pigs out," Belac said as he hurried into the pen.

The pigs showed no interest in escape, but a hobb would want to return a loose pig. Belac needed time. Nowhere in that cavern would be safe for long. Once the hobgoblins learned that the children were missing, a search would be inevitable. Belac knew that the monsters would find them if they stayed in the cavern. However, remaining in the cavern had never been an option. *I just need more time.*

Belac knelt and laid Brandon down in the shed. Then he swiveled and waved the other children close. *This next part is going to be tough.* Belac's plan would require the children's cooperation. He knew they would not want to do what they were told.

Belac looked into the eyes of the scared little girl. "I need you to stay here."

Immediately, she began to shake her head, terror building within her. Gwen's eyes watered and her voice quivered. "No... No. I'm sorry. I'll be good." She grabbed at the elf's sleeve. "I promise. I'll be good." She began to cry.

Belac wrapped his arms around the little girl and kissed the top of her head.

Frank, scared and confused by the perceived abandonment, asked, "You want to leave us with the pigs?"

Belac looked up from the precious thing in his arms. "I need you to hide here."

Gwen shook her head 'no' against the elf's chest.

Frank's fear began to dominate his confusion. "And you are going to just leave us here?!"

Belac met the boy's eyes and vowed, "I will be back."

Gwen gripped the elf tighter.

Wanting to cry, Belac took hold of the little girl's arms and peeled them away from him. "I need you to stay here." Gently, he pushed the little girl toward the older boy. "You need to make sure she stays here."

Frank wrapped his arms around Gwen. She did not fight the embrace, but neither did she seem comforted by it. Belac did not have time to worry about the children's comfort. He recalled an ancient Elven quote. *"Time has no soul to suffer at the tears of the innocent."* He knew that he had taken too long already. *I need to go.*

Belac stood. "I'm serious, Frank. I do not care what you have to do; make sure she stays here. Sit on her if you need to."

Belac still worried that Gwen would try to follow him. She had done so before. He briefly considered what he might say to her, and what arguments he could make. However, he decided that if he did not hurry, it would not matter what he said. So, he vaulted over the fence and began moving toward the hamlet.

Belac removed his sword and carried it in its scabbard. It was easier to run without the sword riding on his back, and his need for urgency felt greater than that of stealth. If he were seen, he could lead the hobgoblins away from the children. It would cause him to change his plan, but if he did not hurry, his plan was not going to work anyway. Committing to action, Belac ran toward the hamlet at an angle. He wanted to approach from the river's side, but he worried that the hobgoblins would see him if he got too close to the water too soon. He felt dangerously exposed as it was. The violet light he ran though seemed to resent his intrusion; shining brightly so that others might witness the transgression.

Belac slowed as he neared the hamlet. Despite his haste, Belac knew that running directly into the settlement would be suicide. He really hoped his plan would not require suicide. He crouched down and changed direction. Moving straight toward the river, he felt like he would be discovered at any moment.

When Belac reached the river, he slipped his baldric over his head and hopped into the dark water. Staying close to the shore, he used the rockface to help him push his way upstream. He felt safer in the water. The hobgoblins were far downstream, and Belac did not think that any of the hobbs in the hamlet would notice his head bobbing in the dark water. He continued against the current until he was on the other side of the hamlet. There, he crawled out of the river with slow, controlled movements.

Belac slipped his scabbarded sword off his back and then began to sneak toward the hamlet. He stayed low and moved cautiously as he followed the cavern wall. *Don't see me. Don't see me. Don't see me.* The distance from the river to the first of the cottages was little more than a stone's throw away. However, Belac knew that in this open space was where he was most likely to be seen.

When the elf stepped into the shadows cast by the cottages, he was able to breathe easier, but his heart continued to pound in his chest. He began to move faster, relying on the shadows and rock to hide him. Hurrying farther into the hamlet, the deep sound of the cauldron's flames grew louder.

As Belac slunk through the shadows, he felt like he was hiding from the sick, violet light as much as he was from the monsters that lived in the homes beneath it. *I think I'm going to add purple to the list of colors I don't like.*

Belac stopped and studied a building of obviously unique design and purpose. Similar in size to the neighboring cottages, the building had large, cased doorways on either end that exposed its open interior. Inside, two hobbs stood next to the massive mechanical contraption that the building had been constructed to house. Facing the opening opposite the elf, the hobbs gestured and jabbered incoherently.

Belac drew his sword and then slung the scabbard onto his back. Creeping forward, he drew his dagger in an underhanded grip. He entered the building quietly, approaching the hobbs with his naked blades held ready. Once he was as close as he thought he could get undetected, Belac rushed at the hobb on the right and ran his sword into its back. As the other hobb turned, Belac plunged his dagger down into the top of its head. He jerked his dagger free as the hobb collapsed, and then he buried the short blade into the other hobb's skull.

Using his dagger for leverage, Belac ripped his sword out of the hobb that he held impaled. As the hobb fell, Belac jerked his dagger free again. Absently, he wiped his dagger on his thigh before returning it to its sheath. His attention had already shifted to the contraption he had come to find.

A mass of metal wheels and cogs, the contraption was supported by riveted bars that sank deep into the rock. Its workings confounded the elf. Though three thick, black chains rose up through the roof, he could identify only two control wheels. With one wheel on either side of the contraption, he did not know how the middle chain could be manipulated. *I guess it doesn't matter.* He stepped over to the wheel on the left. *I only need to release one of the chains. That should make the cauldron tip over and pour fire down on the village.* He nodded to himself. *I don't think the hobgoblins will want to keep dancing when their homes are on fire.*

A hobgoblin walked into the building through the doorway on Belac's left. The elf spun to his right while stepping toward the hobgoblin. His sword arced out in a sweeping backhanded cut that slashed through the hobgoblin's knee. His blade swinging up behind him, Belac took a quick step around the hobgoblin as it crashed forward onto its forearms. Belac raised his arms above his head and gripped the hilt of his sword with both hands. Focusing on the back of the hobgoblin's neck, he attacked with all the force he could bring to bear. The edge of the steel swung over the elf's head and then bit deeply into a wooden support beam on the ceiling.

The hobgoblin raked with its hardened fingertips, the long needle points clawing through the air as they sped toward Belac's midsection. Belac was quick enough to catch the hobgoblin's bony forearm, but its bestial strength knocked him off his feet. The hobgoblin's twisted form rose up over Belac, opening its canid jaws wide. Belac looked up at glistening fangs as he breathed in the smell of rotting meat.

Maintaining his hold on the hobgoblins forearm with his left hand, Belac drew his dagger with his right. As the hobgoblin lunged for him, he thrust the dagger upward under its jaw. Dark blood poured down Belac's arm as he forced the jaws closed. Eyes wide with more anger than fear, Belac pulled the dagger closer. The blade ripped through the underside of the hobgoblin's jaw and hooked behind the inside of its chin. *I am not food!* Belac stared into the hobgoblins black soulless eye, and snarled.

The hobgoblin fought to get away. It thrashed wildly until it broke the grip on its arm. The elf, unable to match the hobgoblin's strength, lost control of it. Belac pulled his knees up and rocked back onto his upper shoulders. He put his feet under the hobgoblin's canid head and kicked out. There was a wet crunching noise and then the hobgoblin went completely still. Belac rolled out from under the hobgoblin with his dagger ready to attack. The hilt of Belac's sword was imbedded in the top of the hobgoblin's skull. The sword, still stuck in the ceiling, held the lifeless corpse in place.

"I totally meant to do that," Belac said though there was no one there to hear his lie.

Belac used the pommel of his dagger to hammer the hobgoblin's skull off his sword's hilt. The body crumpled to the floor, and Belac backed away. Blood dripped from the hilt of the sword onto the dead hobgoblin beneath it. *It is going to be hard to get a good grip on that.* Belac bent down and ripped off one of the hobb's vermilion hoods. He used it to wipe off his dagger, then slid the blade back into its sheath. Stepping around the dead bodies, Belac returned to his sword and used the rag to wipe off the worst of the blood. Then he tossed the bloody rag aside and took hold of his sword's hilt.

Wood squeaked loudly as Belac pushed the hilt away from himself. Moving to stand over the dead hobgoblin, he worked the sword back and forth until the blade came free. *Now, I just need to release one of those chains, and I can get out of here.* He stepped away from the dead hobgoblin and took hold of the wheel on the left side of the contraption. He attempted to turn the wheel first one way and then the other, but he could not get it to move more than a finger's width.

Belac stepped to the side and investigated the contraption's inner workings. He did not know what he was looking at; but if he was right, all he needed to do was knock one small metal plate loose and the chain should be released. *If hobbs and hobgoblins can figure this out, then so can I.* With one hand, he moved the wheel as far as he could. Then he aimed his sword and slammed its pommel against the side of the plate.

When the metal plate did not slide free as expected, Belac growled and then proceeded to strike it repeatedly. He began to worry that another hobgoblin might hear him, but he had no other plan. If he could not cause a distraction, all would be hopeless. So, he hammered in frustration, not knowing what else to do. Finally, the metal plate broke free. Nothing happened.

Belac took a step back. *Why didn't that work?* Something snapped on the other side of the contraption. All three of the chains began to move upward as the mechanisms inside screeched and hummed. The speed of the chains continued to increase as gears ground louder and louder. Belac took another step back. *Uhm… I might have made a mistake.*

The ensuing explosion was so violent, its sonic shock knocked Belac unconscious.

Twenty-Four

Belac awoke to a world of dusk and haze. Angry, violet light flared in the doorway, illuminating the particles of dust that filled the air. The sounds of a storm raged in the cavern outside. Belac rolled onto his hands and knees with a groan. He spat blood onto the floor. The blood concerned him less than the feeling of not being able to catch his breath.

Belac did not yet comprehend what he had done, but he was fairly certain that it would qualify as a distraction. He ignored the blood and looked for his sword. He found it lying among the corpses of the monsters he had slain. He crawled to the sword on his hands and knees, grabbed the hilt, and then staggered to his feet. *I have to get back to the children.*

Belac stumbled out of the doorway, and witnessed the devastation he had wrought. The buildings in the middle of the hamlet had been demolished. Burning piles of stone and timber, they were consumed by violet flames that blazed high above the wreckage. The fire had spread to the nearby homes, becoming bright orange and wrathful. As Belac stared at the pair of swirling infernos, he felt like he was watching two elemental forces war over the ruins of the hidden civilization. Fighting for dominion, the fires roared at each other in avarice demand.

Hobbs and hobgoblins scurried at the edges of the fire beneath clouds of dark smoke. The pale violet flames that had once given light to their lives now strived to consume them. The black chains no longer held the glass cauldron blazing aloft. The chains had fallen. The cauldron had fallen. And the flames had been set free.

Unsteady on his feet, the elf moved into the ragged shadows. *Let the monsters burn. I have children to save.* The farther he got from the fire, the easier it became to breathe. By the time he reached the river, Belac thought that he might be able to swim without drowning himself. He removed his scabbard, sheathed his sword, and returned it to his back. Then he tripped and fell into the river.

After coming to the surface, Belac closed his eyes and allowed the current to carry him downstream. A cool breeze blew over the river as air was pulled into the cavern to feed the growing flames. *I don't have time to relax. The children are waiting for me. I need to get them out of here before the hobbs and hobgoblins start looking for us.* He began to swim with the current.

Belac swam until he neared the pig pen, and then he climbed out of the river. Dripping wet, he scanned for hobbs and hobgoblins as he returned to where he had left the children. *If that little girl ran off, I am going to find her, and then I am going to find one of those hobb sacks, and then I'm going to stuff her in it.* When he reached the shed, he found all three of the children hiding inside. Gwen was covered in mud with one of her pigtails plastered to the side of her head. She had a piglet tucked under one arm, and a splintered piece of wood held like a sword in her other.

Gwen raised her toy sword up defensively when she saw the elf vault over the fence, but then lowered it when she realized who he was. "Belac!"

The piglet squealed.

Belac waved a hand. "Get rid of that."

Gwen dropped the piece of wood but continued to hold the filthy piglet close.

Belac frowned. "The pig, Gwen. You can't keep the pig."

Gwen wrapped her other arm around the piglet. "But it's scared! It needs me to protect it!"

The piglet squirmed in her arms.

Belac looked at the older boy suspiciously. "Did you tell her that?"

Frank held out his arms. "You told me to do whatever it took!"

Belac looked back at the muddy little girl with her piglet. *We don't have time to argue about this.* "Fine. Keep the pig." He narrowed his eyes at the piglet. "But don't trust it. It might be a spy."

Gwen squished her tiny face in confusion, but did not say anything.

Wasting no more time, Belac picked up the limp form of the injured child. "Frank, get the gate."

Frank rushed to the gate and held it open as Belac carried Brandon through. Gwen, her piglet in her arms, hurried after the elf. Then Frank followed them out and began to close the gate behind himself.

"Leave it open," Belac told him.

"But the pigs will get out," Frank replied.

Belac nodded as he continued on. "Good. Anything that adds to the chaos is only going to help us escape."

Leaving the gate open, Frank ran to catch up with the elf. "So… That was you? Did you do the," he touched the tips of his fingers together and mimed an explosion with his hands.

Belac answered without looking at the boy, "Yeah. But it is only going to buy us so much time."

"How much time?" Frank asked.

Belac shook his head. "I don't know. That's why we need to hurry."

The arable land was darker without the fiery cauldron burning high above it. The flames of the ruined hamlet still lit the cavern, but now the shadows stretched out long and fluttered. To Belac, it felt as if the darkness was reaching out for the children. *It does not want to let them go.*

Belac led the children to the river at an angle, continuing to follow the dark water downstream. He knew that the children would have difficulty maintaining the pace he set. He pressed on anyway, also knowing that he needed to get them away. *We can slow down a bit once we get out of this cave.* The hobgoblins were no longer dancing in the field, but Belac knew it was only a matter of time before they returned. *When those things come back, they are not going to be dancing in joy. They are going to hunt us down. And they are going to try to eat us.*

As they neared the dark narrowing of the cavern and the escape that the elf hoped to find, Belac noticed the glimmer of silver lines. *It's another net.* He began to consider how he was going to get all three of the children to the other side. He could not think of a way that would not require multiple trips under the net. Though it would be relatively brief, he did not like the idea of leaving the children separated and vulnerable.

A bright, violet explosion on the elf's right startled him so much that he almost dropped the boy he carried. Turning toward the explosion, Belac found a hobgoblin sprinting at him with malicious commitment. A patch of violet fire burned on the cavern floor, the pale flames blanching the hobgoblin's dog-like skull. A fiery, violet trail arced over the hobgoblin and landed with another explosion of light. The hobgoblin charged past the patches of fire while two hobbs began loading glass orbs into large vermilion slings.

Belac half lowered, half dropped Brandon to the ground. It was time for decisions to be made. Belac removed his scabbarded sword and drew the blade as he marched forward. *I will just kill everything.* He thrust his sword upward at an angle toward the hobgoblin's fanged maw. The hobgoblin twisted away from the blade, so Belac followed the thrust with two cross patterned slashes. The hobgoblin danced away from the steel, though its black eyes stayed locked on the elf like a predator stalking its prey.

Another violet light exploded on Belac's left, throwing a jagged rock up into the side of his face. *The hobbs are getting closer.* Knowing he needed to press the attack, Belac moved forward with a downward diagonal slash. The hobgoblin ducked under the sweeping blade and clawed at the elf's side. The needle-like tips of the hobgoblin's long fingers ripped through Belac's silk jacket and tore into the skin covering his ribcage.

The hobgoblin stepped away, holding up the bloodied tips of its fingers. It tilted its head to the side as it gloated at the elf.

Blood covering half of his face, and more seeping from the wound to his ribs, Belac lowered his guard. He spoke contemptuously in Elven, "I am not food."

The change in the hobgoblin was immediate. Though it could only have understood the elf's tone, that was enough to enrage it. Fanged jaws open wide, the hobgoblin lunged for the elf.

Belac stepped away with his right foot while swinging his scabbard straight up. The scabbard struck against the underside of the hobgoblin's lower jaw, knocking its head back. Belac pivoted on his left foot, stepping forward with his right while swinging his sword up and over his head. The steel's edge hacked through the hobgoblin's neck and then Belac's shoulder slammed into its chest. The hobgoblin's body fell away to Belac's right, while its canid head rolled over the elf's shoulders and fell to his left.

Belac straitened, standing tall over the decapitated hobgoblin. He looked toward the hobbs. *You're next.* One of the hobbs launched a glass orb from its sling. As a fiery, violet trail established the missile's trajectory through the air, Belac realized that it was flying too high to hit him. It had been aimed to hit the children.

Belac leapt into the air, swinging his sword at the flaming orb. Violet light exploded when his steel shattered the glass. Liquid fire rained down on the elf's arm and shoulder. As soon as his feet touched the ground, Belac dropped his scabbard and put his left hand between his head and the violet flames clinging to his arm. Running, he dove into the river headfirst.

Belac reached out and slapped his left palm on the bottom of the river. Twisting in the dark water, he put his feet against the riverbed and surged upward. Left hand finding the rock of the shore, he vaulted out of the river, screaming. His sword broke the surface of the water, held ready to attack, but the hobbs were not yet within reach. Swinging his feet under himself, Belac rushed forward.

The hobbs backed away from the charging elf. One of them tripped backward while the other turned to flee. Belac's sword hacked into the hobb on the ground as he ran past it. The other hobb did not make it much farther before Belac's blade cut through the back of its spine.

As he came to a halt, Belac stumbled two steps to his left. Blood pounding in his ears, he scanned the distance, looking for something else to kill. *I will show these things what happens when they take children!* The thought of children tugged at Belac's mind. *The children…* He shook his head and turned away from the burning hamlet. Frank and Gwen still stood next to Brandon. Both of the children stared back in shock. *At least they didn't run off.* Belac stepped around the patches of flame and retrieved his scabbard. He sheathed his sword and moved it to his back.

The piglet squirmed out of Gwen's arms and ran away from her. "Piggy-Pig!" She called after the piglet, proving that there was someone worse at naming things than Belac.

The little girl chased after the piglet. Belac moved forward, snatching Gwen up with an arm around her waist. Not slowing to argue or explain, Belac jumped into the river.

Gwen thrashed as she was carried downriver. "Piggy-Pig!"

Belac grabbed the little girl's tiny nose and covered her mouth with one hand. "Hold your breath," he told her before ducking under the silver net.

Once they resurfaced on the other side, Belac lifted the little girl up and set her on the shore.

Gwen curled into a ball and sobbed, "Piggy-Pig."

Belac dipped back down into the water and returned to the other side of the net. The little girl's distress pained him, but he did not have time to indulge her. *More things will be coming to kill us. Not just the hobbs and hobgoblins, but whatever is waiting for us ahead.* He climbed out of the river and hurried to the two boys.

Frank pointed back toward the barn. "Do you want me to go catch the pig?"

"No, I don't want you to go catch the pig!" Belac told him shortly.

Not waiting for further instruction, Frank ran past the elf and dove into the river. He grabbed the silver net as he swam under, and then he used the metal cords to climb up on the other side.

Belac took one final look at the burning hamlet. The violet and orange fires still warred in the dark smoke, but the orange flames were beginning to win. Belac scanned the river and fields, searching for pursuers. Finding nothing, he knelt down and collected the last of the children.

Twenty-Five

Belac's light rod pinged against rock. Golden light shone on all three of the children's faces. The wonder and surprise of two was outweighed by the emptiness of the third. Looking down at Brandon's closed eyes and relaxed features, Belac did not know if the boy would ever wake again. The torn flesh over Belac's ribs hurt him less than the sight of the injured child. He resituated the boy in his arms, and then stood.

Resuming their slow escape, Belac kept his right arm pressed against the side of his wounded ribs. It made carrying the child awkward, but Belac thought it was better than bleeding out. He had used the silky scrap of cloth cut from his sleeve as an improvised bandage, but he worried that it would not be enough.

Frank made no attempt to hide his amazement. "What is that?"

Belac continued to follow the river through the stretching cavern. "It's a magic stick."

"Really?" Frank asked. "Can it do other things?" He hopped forward and mimed pointing a magic wand at the darkness ahead of them. "Like shoot fireballs? Or call down lightning? Or turn people into stone? Or make things fly around with your mind?" He waved his hand around and made nonsensical sound effects.

Belac shook his head tiredly. "No."

Frank seemed to not hear the answer. "Is that how you made the giant purple fire thing fall on the hobbs?"

Belac sighed. "No. I used my sword for that." *I should have just told him it was a light rod.*

There was a trace of disbelief in Frank's response. "You did that with a sword?"

Belac chuckled despite the pain. "How is me using a sword harder to believe than me using a magic stick?"

"Because... It's magic?" Frank answered as if it should be obvious.

Belac narrowed his eyes at the boy. *Little human thinks he's smart.* He frowned. *Still... The kid does kind of have a point.* "All the magic stick does is make light."

Frank furrowed his brow. "That does not seem very magical."

Belac grinned, dry blood cracking on his cheek. "Hold up your finger."

Frank did as he was instructed, though he looked at the elf skeptically.

Belac nodded. "Now, make it glow."

Frank dropped his hand. "I can't do that," he said with exasperation.

Belac smiled. "It would be magical if you could."

Frank went quiet in thought.

Belac glanced back at Gwen to make sure that she was still following. *She is still angry at me.* She had not wanted to get up and walk. Harsh words had been necessary. *If she is still mad at me, it means she is still alive.* He decided to focus on the way forward.

Another of the round tunnels bore into the rockface ahead and to the right. Belac remembered what had happened in the last one. *I can't take the children in there. We need to find a way that looks more like something people made.* He did not know that a gnomish complex would be any safer than one of the tunnels, but he recalled something that Rolan had once told him.

"Caves and tunnels do not go where you want them to, just because you want them to."

Frank broke his silence. "Mr. Bell."

Belac glanced at the boy. "It's Belac."

"Oh! Sorry," Frank apologized quickly.

I don't think I actually introduced myself. Belac shrugged. The motion sent pain lacing through his side.

"Uhm…" Frank continued, "How did you learn how to do all that?"

Belac shook his head. "Do all what?"

"Uhm…" Frank seemed hesitant. "Fight monsters with a sword."

Belac considered whether or not that was something he should talk to a child about. He decided that if the child in question had witnessed him chop a monster into pieces, it was probably okay to have a discussion about it. "I have some…" he searched for the proper Dwarven phrasing, "formal education." He nodded. "But it is not as useful as you might expect."

"What?" Frank asked, confused. "Why not?"

Belac grimaced. "I was taught how to fight people. Monsters don't really behave like people. They don't move the same way. They don't think the same way."

"They're scary," Frank added in a small voice.

Belac nodded. "You are right about that."

Frank's voice became defiant. "My dad is not scared of them. I bet he comes down here and kills all of them for what they did to Brandon!"

It was not until that moment that Belac realized how much Frank had lost. He had lost his father. He had lost his older brother. He may have already lost his younger brother. And he would soon lose his home. *I can't tell him what is waiting for him up there.* Belac could not risk the boy giving into grief. *I already have one upset child to deal with.* He glanced back at Gwen again. She was glaring at him.

Let her glare. Belac returned his attention to what lay ahead. He noticed that the brown swirls in the rock had become a darker reddish shade. More and more, the walls were pockmarked with rough recesses that must have been created by air pockets trapped when the ancient stone was formed. To Belac, the change made the cavern seem as if it were growing angry with his encroachment. *This place is not meant for elves.*

Gwen finally decided to speak. "You killed Piggy-Pig!"

Belac looked back at the little girl and frowned. "I did not."

"You might as well have," Gwen pouted.

Belac shook his head. "I can't keep you safe if you are running around chasing after a pig." *Besides, it was probably a spy anyway.*

Gwen sounded on the verge of tears. "He would have behaved!"

Belac did not bother to argue with her.

Frank, however, was less reticent. "It was just a stupid pig, Gwen."

Gwen shouted, "Piggy-Pig is smart!"

"Good!" Frank countered, "Then, that means it doesn't need you!"

Gwen screamed, "You're a stupid pig!" and kicked the older boy in the leg.

Belac stopped walking. He wanted to yell at the children. He wanted to tell them that they were not safe. He wanted to tell them that they could die. He wanted them to understand that their behavior had consequences. Belac took a deep breath, refusing to allow his aches to make him act rashly. He knew yelling would achieve nothing positive. *They are not just humans; they are children.* He could think of only one thing to do.

Frank and Gwen were silent. They knew the elf was unhappy with them. And they knew it was their fault. Neither of them wanted to draw attention to themselves.

Gently, Belac laid Brandon down on the cavern floor. He took a moment to study the boy's calm face before standing slowly. Lifting his right arm, Belac inspected the wound across the side of his ribs. Blood still seeped, but he did not think that he was going to bleed out. He took another deep breath as he endured the pain. Then, without saying anything, he walked away.

The elf had taken less than a dozen steps before Frank pleaded, "What about Brandon? Are you just going to leave him here?"

Belac answered without looking back. "You carry him." He continued on, taking the light with him.

"Get his feet!" Frank demanded.

Gwen did not argue with him. Together, they hurried to lift Brandon as the light dimmed around them. United by purpose, they raced against the growing darkness.

Belac stopped with the children barely beyond the brightness of the golden light. He knelt down next to the river and began scooping water up to his mouth. As he drank, he watched the children out of the corner of his eye. *I would rather have them be scared than dead.* Carrying Brandon would be difficult for Frank and Gwen. Belac hoped that they would be too tired and distracted to continue fighting with each other.

Gwen walked backward into the light, holding Brandon's feet. Frank followed, supporting Brandon's upper body with his arms wrapped around the injured boy's chest. Though their progress would be slowed moving this way, Belac could not think of a better plan. He tapped his light rod against the shore and then stood. Holding his right arm tucked tightly to his side, he turned away from the children and continued to follow the river.

"Don't fall too far behind," Belac warned. However, he was careful to set a pace that was slow enough for the children to keep up with him.

Twenty-Six

Belac sat by the edge of an underground lake, staring out into its churning, dark waters. Four rivers fed the lake, including the one that he had followed. Flowing currents became low, choppy waves as they converged in the lake. *All that water has to go somewhere.* He shook his head sadly. *It's just not somewhere I can take the children.* Wherever the dark water flowed, it could only have done so through channels hidden below the dark turbulent surface.

Surrounded by rough, pockmarked, reddish rock, Belac felt like he was trapped in the throat of the world. *How am I going to save these children?* The river's terminus left him no clear path forward. He considered following one of the other rivers upstream, but they all went in directions that would take them farther under the volcano. It was as if their hopes had ended with the river.

He briefly considered backtracking to the burning cavern but was quick to rule out the idea. Belac had left a trail of dead behind him. He worried that the hobbs and hobgoblins would already be on their way to find him. He growled. *If they were smart, they would just let me go.* He stood and turned toward the children that he had come to save.

Frank and Gwen were obviously exhausted. They sat next to Brandon, both of them breathing deeply and staring at nothing. Belac appreciated that they were too tired to argue or ask questions, but he was concerned that he was pushing them too hard. Behind them and to the left, was another of the large, round tunnels. Belac knew that the tunnels were dangerous. However, every option he could see was dangerous. *If there was a safe path, I would take it.* At least the tunnel seemed to go in a direction away from the volcano. *Whichever way I choose, I need to make the decision now. We can't just wait here.*

Belac waved the children toward himself. "You two, come over here and get a drink from the lake."

Frank and Gwen moved to do as they were told, though they did so lethargically. Belac walked past them and stopped at the opening to the tunnel. While it was as large and round as the other tunnels, the pockmarked rock presented cavities that the children could fall into. *They won't be able to carry Brandon through there.* He suspected that was just as well. Though the wound to his side hurt, Belac knew that Frank and Gwen needed a rest from carrying the injured boy.

Belac continued to study the tunnel. He did not think the cavities would be a problem as long as he and the children were cautious. While it would not excessively hamper their escape, the hazardous passage might slow pursuit. *That decides it.* He nodded. *We need to keep moving. I think this is the best chance we have.*

Belac stepped away from the tunnel and went to check on Brandon. Frank and Gwen sat at the lake's edge much the same as had the elf. Belac wondered if they too realized that his plans were not working as well as he had wanted. *Do they know that I am just choosing the lesser of the bad options?* He did not think so. *They are children. They trust me. It has probably not even occurred to them that I might not know what I'm doing.*

Belac knelt over Brandon and palmed the side of the boy's face. Brandon's jaw was slack and Belac thought that his breathing was getting more shallow. *Crying is not going to help any of these children.* Belac cradled the injured boy in his arms and stood.

Belac focused on keeping the emotion out of his voice. "Frank, Gwen, get up. It's time to go."

The two children got to their feet quickly, suddenly worried that the elf would leave them behind.

Belac tried to sound as confident as he could. "We are going into the tunnel. Watch where you step." He made sure to emphasize, "Do. Not. Get. In front of me."

Belac waited for both of the children to nod before turning around and leading them to the tunnel. He considered letting one of them carry the light rod, but he needed them to be concentrated on following him. The light gave them both a tether and a focal point. He did not think the children would get lost in a tunnel, but he wanted them to stay close all the same. *Besides, if something does come to eat us, the light might attract it.*

They moved through the tunnel faster than Belac had expected they would. The cavities proved less troublesome than they might have been, but they were also deeper than he had anticipated. As they continued on, the cavities became larger and larger though fewer in number. The tunnel itself seemed to bend slightly up and down as well as left and right. The persistent change in direction made it difficult for Belac to determine with certainty, but he thought that the tunnel was gradually leading them upward. Aware that desire could create a powerful bias, he refused to succumb to optimism.

Something changed. At first, Belac did not understand what it was. He knew it was not merely paranoia; the change was something physical. *The pressure in the air is different…* A slight breeze began to stir the elf's hair. Belac stopped moving. His pointed ears tingled as they strained for information.

The children were silent. Though they may not have been able to feel the change in the air, they could tell that something was wrong by just looking at the elf. The tunnel suddenly felt less like a passage, and more like a trap.

Belac heard the sound before the children did. A deep muted dragging of leather over stone, something was in the tunnel behind them. Belac turned slowly toward the sound and stared into the darkness. The air itself was shaking, the vibration intensifying as the sound grew closer. There was movement beyond the light.

A wall of wrinkled, gray flesh pushed its way into the golden glow. The center peeled open as the thing exposed its sphinctered mouth. Long, horn-like fangs rimmed the mouth, each moving independently around a single, massive, amber eye that shone like polished glass. The teeth clattered against the tunnel's walls as the mouth moved toward Belac and the children.

"Run!" Belac yelled before turning away from the moving wall of death.

Belac ran. Carrying Brandon, he could not wait for the other two children. If Frank and Gwen did not run when he told them to, then there was nothing else he could do for them. The thing that followed was too big. There was no way for him to get around it; no way for him to attack it without running headfirst into its clawing mouth.

Still, Belac looked back. The children were running, but the mouth was moving faster. They would not be able to escape. Belac's mind raced. *Need a new plan. Need a new plan.* There was nowhere to run. The tunnel stretched ahead, but the thing behind them was getting closer. *We can't run.* Belac stopped. He turned toward the wall of teeth and looked into its amber eye. Belac had out paced the children, but not by much. When they halted in front of him, they continued to move like skittish horses.

Belac gesture forcibly with his head and yelled, "Get in!"

The terrified children looked down at the cavity in the tunnel wall with consternation.

"Get in!" Belac screamed in rage.

Frank grabbed Gwen and dragged her down into the cavity with him. Belac threw Brandon down on top of them. There was no more room for the elf. Belac glanced over at the hungry mouth. It was too close; he could feel the warm moist air of its breath.

"Stay down!" Belac ordered, backing away from the mouth. The clattering of teeth on stone had grown so loud that Belac did not even know if the children heard him. He turned away, desperately hoping that they would know what to do.

Belac ran, faster now that he was unburdened. However, he knew that he would faulter long before the horrific mouth surrendered its meal. *I am not food.* Belac focused on the thought as he ran. *I am not food. I am not food. I am not food.* The light rod swung violently as he pumped his arms. Golden light threw shadows wildly, but Belac saw what he was looking for ahead. He ran halfway up the wall on his left at an angle, and then ran back down and up the other side. He grabbed the edge of a cavity and pulled himself up into the ceiling.

A horn shaped fang swept into the cavity and ripped a chunk of rock free as the mouth moved past the opening. Gray, leathery skin rippled below Belac as the great worm pushed its way through the tunnel. Sound rumbled loudly in the stone pocket. The elf's arms trembled from the effort of holding himself in place. Blood dripped from his side down onto the gray, undulating flesh. As frightening as the sight was, Belac knew that it would be worse for the children he had forced into the dark.

Once the great worm had passed, Belac dropped down into the tunnel. He watched as the worm's long, gray tail was dragged from the light. He did not believe for a moment that the danger was truly over. Belac pressed his arm tightly to his side and rushed back to the children. He found them huddled together with their eyes closed. Brandon had a gouge in his shoulder where one of the worm's fangs had ripped into him.

Belac crouched down. "Quick, hand me Brandon."

Neither of the children moved.

"Frank!" Belac shouted angrily.

Frank's eyes popped open, but he still did not move. He stared up as if he feared the elf might strike him.

Belac did not apologize for the harshness of his voice. He held out a hand. "Brandon is hurt. Help me get him out of there."

Frank pushed Brandon up while Belac pulled the younger boy out. Belac moved the injured boy away from the cavity and then drew his dagger. He cut the boy's sleeve off and inspected the wound. Brandon was bleeding, but not very fast. Belac worried that it was due to how slow the boy's heart was beating. Belac cut Brandon's sleeve into a bandage and used it to dress the boy's wound as best he could.

Standing in the tunnel, staring down at his younger brother, Frank asked, "Is he going to be all right?"

Belac did not answer the boy. "Gwen, get out of the hole. We need to go."

Gwen's voice came up from the shadowed cavity. "What if it comes back?"

Belac shook his head. "I don't think it can turn around. If we hurry, we can follow it and use it to make sure that there is nothing else in the tunnel ahead of us."

"I want to go home," Gwen said miserably.

Belac tried to be patient. "That is where we are headed, Gwen. But you have to get out of the hole."

Gwen's head rose up from the cavity. "I…" Her voice became even more timid. "I need to pee."

"Yeah, uhm…" Belac did not know what to tell her. "You should do that before you come out of the hole."

Twenty-Seven

They plodded through the tunnel until the rock became black and brittle. It was not the color that concerned Belac, but the absence of cavities. There was nowhere for them to hide. If the great worm returned, the only option would be whether to die screaming in fear or defiance.

When they finally came to a jagged hole that was more than large enough for them to all fit through, Belac almost wept in relief. Leaning over the edge, he stared down at the golden light reflecting off the smooth stone of the corridor below. Belac was so happy, he could have kissed a gnome. *I might actually see the children breathe fresh air!*

Black rock had crumbled down into the corridor where the great worm had bored too close. The drop down would make it challenging to move Brandon, but Belac did not even consider an alternative. The corridor was exactly the kind of thing he had been searching for. That it might present new complications was of scant importance to him. He laid the injured boy down next to the edge.

"Be careful where you step," Belac told the other two children. "It looks like the rock could break away."

Gwen asked, "Is that the way out?" She sounded more scared than relieved.

Belac stood. "It is for us."

Frank simply sounded tired. "How do we get down?"

Belac stepped cautiously around the hole. "I am going to hop down there first." He nodded toward the injured boy. "Then I am going to need you two to lower Brandon down for me. After that, I want you to wait until Gwen jumps down before you come down last."

Petulance livened Frank's voice. "Why do I have to go last?"

Belac turned away from the hole and looked at Gwen deliberately. Her quiet concerned him. She was staring at the hole like it might try to eat her.

Without looking away from the little girl, Belac said, "I don't know if Gwen will actually jump." He waited for her to look at him. "I might need you to push her in."

Gwen's mouth opened in disbelief.

Frank laughed. "I can do that."

Belac turned back to the hole and knelt down next to it. Pain clawed at his ribs. He placed his left hand on the edge and then hopped out into the dark. He used the ledge to slow his fall, but he did not try to hold on. As he dropped down, he imagined the floor below falling away to reveal a rusted spike trap. While there was no trap waiting for him, he did trip on a rock and fall backward. Belac landed on his left hip and shoulder, but it was his right side that pained him most. It felt like the wound was creeping into his abdomen. He stared up at the gaping hole above him. *No going back now.* The ceiling was too high for him to reach even if he jumped.

Belac took a deep breath and forced himself to focus through the pain. He climbed to his feet and then held his light rod aloft. The corridor ran in either direction, perpendicular to the tunnel above. To the right was nothing but darkness and rock. However, to the left, he could make out a turn in the corridor. *No doors. But a turn seems promising.* At the time, he felt like anything was preferable to more of the endless tunnel.

Belac called up to the hole in a hushed voice. "All right. Go ahead and lower Brandon down."

Belac had wanted the children to lower the injured boy down slowly, but once they had him hanging over the edge, the boy slipped from their grasps. Brandon fell through the air limply, his head angling toward the ground. Belac was able to catch the boy, though the effort tore at the elf's wounded ribs. Pain shot through Belac's side, and he almost dropped the boy. Grimacing, Belac moved Brandon away from the hole and laid the injured child on the stone floor.

Belac took a moment to breathe before standing and returning to the hole. "Okay. Now, Gwen."

Gwen looked out over the edge. "Can you stack the rocks up for me? Then, I could just climb down…"

Belac shook his head tiredly. "No, Gwen. I am not going to stack rocks for you. You need to jump."

Gwen was quiet for a moment. "Are you really going to make Frank push me?"

Belac nodded his head resolutely. "Yes. If you don't jump."

Gwen sniffled. "Can I close my eyes?"

Belac nodded and shook his head at the same time. "Just make sure you are standing next to the edge."

Gwen took a small step closer to the edge and then closed her eyes tightly. She brought her hand up to her face, pinched her nose, and took a deep breath like she was about to jump into a lake. Instead of jumping, her legs gave out and she fell forward into the hole.

Gwen was easier for Belac to catch than Brandon had been. However, the little girl tried to wrap her legs around Belac's ribs. As she squeezed the sides of his chest, Belac clenched his teeth and remembered not to drop her. He groaned through his teeth as he pushed the little girl away from himself. Eyes still shut, nose still pinched, breath still held, Gwen squirmed in his arms. Belac set her on the ground and then stepped back. He tripped on a rock and fell backward. He was pretty sure it was the same rock.

Lying on the floor in pain, Belac lifted his head up and searched for the treacherous rock. Once he had located the rock, he rolled onto his side and kicked it. It hurt his foot.

"It's a conspiracy," Belac moaned.

Frank called down from above, "I am coming down now."

"No," Belac ordered. "Wait until I get in position."

"I can do it myself!" Frank insisted.

Belac shook his head as he stood up. "Maybe. But if something goes wrong, and you break your leg, I can't carry you out of here."

"I won't break my leg," Frank argued.

Belac growled. "If you don't wait, I'll break your leg!" he vowed as he positioned himself under the hole. "Okay. Come on down."

Frank jumped and Belac reached out to catch him. Frank was the heaviest of the children, but he was also nimble enough that he may have been able to make the jump safely on his own. Instead of pulling the boy close and risking another assault to his ribs, Belac merely slowed Frank's descent. As Belac lowered Frank to the floor, the shock of an explosion blasted through the corridor. *The monsters found us!* Belac staggered away from the sound even as he turned toward it. *They are coming for the children.* He removed his scabbarded sword. His face hardened with resolve. *They should have just let us go.* He stepped away from the children.

"You two, drag Brandon behind the rocks," Belac ordered without taking his eyes off the corner ahead.

The elf stopped a few paces away from the black debris. Grimy steel scraped as he drew his sword. He tossed the scabbard aside and transferred the sword to his left hand. Snarling at the pain, he pressed his right arm against his wounded ribs. Blood had saturated his silk jacket, and he could feel its wetness on the inside of his wrist. He pressed harder. It felt like fire stabbing into his side, but he knew that he needed the bleeding to stop.

The light in the corridor's corner grew brighter as Belac focused on it. *The distance should give me enough time to measure their numbers.* His grip tightened on his sword. *The corridor should be narrow enough to prevent them from getting behind me.* He set his stance. *I will just keep killing them until they stop coming.*

What came around the corner was not the monsters that Belac had expected. A golden light rod hung from the belt of a muscular orc holding a silvery, cogged mace. Beside him strode a thin man clad in immaculate black.

After turning the corner and seeing what waited for him ahead, the orc muttered something to the man.

The man in black nodded without slowing their advance.

Belac lowered his sword and almost dropped it to the floor. He laughed and cried at the same time as he stumbled to the wall on his left. Leaning his back against the wall, he closed his eyes and took a deep breath. *Vairug. Your ugly face is just about the most beautiful thing I have ever seen.* He slid slowly down the wall until he was seated on the stone floor.

"Hello, Belac," Serath said pleasantly. "It seems as though you have had an interesting night."

Belac laughed painfully. "I hate your face."

Vairug sniffed at the air. "His wound is sour."

Serath knelt down next to Belac and began to unbutton the elf's jacket.

Belac raised his voice. "It's okay kids. We're saved." He looked at the wizard and asked conversationally, "We are saved, right?"

Serath grinned. "You are indeed."

Belac leaned his head back against the wall and closed his eyes again. Serath moved the elf's shirt out of the way so that he could inspect the wounded ribs beneath. Belac's wounds burned fiercely at the man's touch. *Yeah. That has got to be infected.*

"Vairug," Serath spoke professionally. "Your sash."

Vairug slid his cogged mace into a loop on his belt and then untied the crimson sash from around his waist.

Gwen asked timidly, "Are those your friends?"

Serath's smile could be heard in his voice. "That we are," he acknowledged before inquiring, "And who might you be?"

"She's Gwen," Frank answered for her. "I'm Frank. And this is Brandon."

Vairug handed his crimson sash to the wizard. "Are any of the children hurt?"

Belac nodded. "One of them." His voice sounded dead.

Serath tied the middle of the sash into a wadded knot and then pressed it to the elf's side. Belac groaned but the wizard did not ease up the pressure. Serath wrapped the ends of the sash around Belac's chest and then tied them tight. Belac focused on controlling his breathing. When he opened his eyes, he saw that Vairug had moved to help the children.

Looking back to the wizard's handsome face, Belac admitted, "Being a hero does not feel very good."

Serath's smile only made his face more handsome. "Then, that is not why you do it." His gaze shifted to the children.

Twenty-Eight

Serath spoke with an authority that only a wizard would assume. "Stay here and watch over them. As soon as they are able, get them moving back to the city." He was speaking to the orc. "I will go ahead of you and ensure that medical assistance is prepared."

Vairug gestured to the light rod that hung from his belt. "Do you want to take the light with you?"

Serath smiled and shook his head gently. "Thank you for the offer, but I have long since overcome my dependence on the light."

With that, the wizard turned and walked away. *It does not look like he is in a hurry to me.* Belac decided that it was a waste of effort to try to understand a wizard.

Vairug crouched down next to the elf. He stared for a moment and then said, "You wear blood well."

Belac smirked at the orcish attempt at a complement. "We can't stay here, Vairug." He glanced to the corner of the corridor, but the wizard was already gone. "I know Serath said that we should rest for a bit, but this place is not safe. We need to get these children out of here."

Vairug grinned proudly as he studied the elf. Gwen approached trepidly and then poked the orc's cheek with a delicate finger. Vairug growled and turned his head toward the little girl.

Gwen's face lit up. She jutted out her lower jaw and went, "Rawr!"

Vairug laughed silently and shook his head. "You were right to save this one."

Belac understood what Vairug had meant, but the comment made him think of Brandon. *I hope he can still be saved.* Neither of the boys were returning to a happy life. However, if Brandon survived, Frank's might be bearable.

Belac tried not to sound as weak as he felt. "Gwen, hand me my scabbard."

Gwen hurried to do as she had been told.

Belac met the orc's eyes. "I'm serious, Vairug. We need to go." He accepted his scabbard from the little girl and then sheathed his sword. "Can you carry Brandon for me?" He nodded toward the injured child. "He's the one that's hurt."

Vairug nodded solemnly. "I can." He stood.

Belac pushed himself away from the wall and used it to stand. "Frank. It's time to go."

Frank looked up from his younger brother. There were tears in his eyes. "Is he going to die?"

"Not if I can help it," Belac tried to sound reassuring. "Lord Vairdoe is going to carry him for us. There will be people waiting to help him in Cavasca."

Fear crept into Frank's voice. "The orc?"

"Lord Vairdoe," Belac corrected the boy firmly. "Despite what you think he looks like, it will be the noblest of men that carry your brother for you." Belac meant what he said.

Frank nodded shamefully. "I'm sorry, Lord Vairdoe."

Vairug stepped over to the boys. "You should never be sorry for worrying about your brother."

Frank wiped his nose and nodded again. He looked down at his younger brother. "He is so small..."

Vairug knelt to pick up the injured boy. The orc spoke in a warm voice. "I was once smaller." Then he stood with the child in his arms.

Belac raised his voice. "Frank, I want you to hold Gwen's hand and stay between Lord Vairdoe and me until we get out of here."

Frank whined, "What? But why?"

Belac looked at the little girl while gesturing toward the older boy. "Can you make sure that he doesn't wander off for me?"

Gwen nodded dutifully.

Frank walked over and held out his hand. "Here," he said peevishly.

Belac grinned. "You might want to be nice, Frank. Or she might remember that you wanted to push her off the ledge."

Frank looked at the elf as if he had been betrayed. "But… You…"

Belac nodded. "If you are nice enough, she might forgive you."

Frank's gaze jerked toward Gwen. The little girl held her head high and looked away inscrutably.

Belac looked past the two children. "Are you ready, Lord Vairdoe?" He had almost called the orc by his real name.

Belac waited for Vairug to nod before he turned and led the way out. While the elf did not draw his sword, he kept it in hand. *If something comes, it will be up to me to stop it.* Belac breathed against the bandage across his chest. *…At least until Vairug comes over here and clubs it to death for me.*

The corridor was shorter than Belac had expected. They were forced to walk around piles of fallen black rock, but otherwise there was nothing to impede their progress. A growing smell of rotten fruit brought with it a suggestion of where they were. *This must be the other corridor that I could have taken.* He wondered where it would have led him had he followed it instead. Belac shook his head. *It doesn't matter. It's not like I am ever coming back here. I hope the volcano eats this whole place.*

When they reached the larger corridor that ramped up to the surface, Belac found that his speculation was correct. *This is where I first entered this place.* The pack of dead hobbs still lay on the floor where they had been slain while attempting to flee him. Belac wrinkled his nose at them. Turning left, he led the others away from the bloody mess. Gwen walked with her head buried against Frank's arm, not wanting to look at the dead monsters.

As Belac stepped past the burned corpse of a dead hobb, he pointed toward the other corridor and said, "Don't go that way." *Wait a moment…* He glanced back at the orc. "How did you know which way to go?"

Vairug shook his head. "Serath held out his hand and did that wizardly thing that he does."

Belac grinned. "So… You cheated."

Vairug grunted.

Looking at the ramp leading out of the complex, it suddenly occurred to Belac that he had never devised a plan on how to actually escape. *How was I going to get that huge stone slab open?* He looked at the broken chunks of stone that littered the rampway. *I am sure that I would have figured something out.* He scanned the walls on both sides of the ramp as he ascended toward the dark sky above. He found no controls that would have operated the mechanisms that moved the stone barrier.

Belac glanced over his shoulder. "Hey, Vair… Lord Vairdoe." He gestured at the chunks of broken stone. "How did you get through this?"

Vairug sounded uncomfortable with the answer. "Serath stepped on it."

Belac thought that he must have misheard. "He stepped on it?"

"Don't let him step on you." Vairug's tone was dry.

Belac looked again at the rubble that had once been a wall of stone denial. "Uhm… Yeah… Okay."

The night air was humid, but Belac did not care. He breathed in as deeply as his bandage would allow. *Fresh air!* He looked down at the children. They did not seem as appreciative of their freedom as he was. *Humans are strange.* Belac shrugged and went back to examining the forest. Though he could detect no ambush, he was not confident in his ability to do so. *I probably don't need to worry. If there was a trap, Serath and Vairug would have found it on the way in.*

Despite the light rod's golden glow, the night muted the green of the forest. As Belac continued to lead his small group down the winding woodland trail, he concluded that a dark forest was better than a bright cavern. *Somebody just needs to figure out how to make trees without all the green.* His list of questions for Vairug was growing, but Belac knew he should wait to ask them. Once they were beyond the trees and traveling the glade, they could better afford the distraction. *If we can put some distance between us and the tree line, we should have more warning if we are attacked.*

Dark shapes moved through the trees on either side of the trail. Belac's and Vairug's golden lights stretched out into the forest, shifting the shadows around the children. The elf's mind made claws and fangs out of the branches and underbrush. It became harder for him to believe that children could ever be safe in such an environment. He glared at the trees, ready to kill the first one that reached for a child.

Twenty-Nine

Early morning greeted them in the glade. Soon, the light rods would no longer be necessary. Belac was simply glad to get away from the trees. The stars still shone faintly in the cloudless sky, but they were not enough to light the grassy glade. *Lazy moon. I don't know why anybody puts up with it.* Belac narrowed his eyes at the sky. *It does not even show up half the time. When it does, it might not be until the middle of the day! What is the point of that? The moon is not helping anyone in the middle of the day.*

Belac brought everyone to a halt just beyond the tree line. He nodded to the children. "You two go… Uhm… Pee." Then he added, "But make sure you stay on this side of the trees."

Once the children had walked away, Belac stepped closer to the orc and lowered his voice. "Can you lead us back to the city without taking us past the dairy farm or the dead dairy farmers in the glade?"

Vairug nodded. "Yes." The side of his face twitched. "But we will need to trek through more of the forest."

Belac shook his head ruefully. "Of course, we will."

Vairug looked at the child he held in his arms. "The farmers. One of them is their father?"

"Yeah," Belac said sadly. "And the other was their older brother. I'm worried that if Frank finds out what happened, he is going to run off." He glanced past the orc and toward the tree line. "If he does, we can't chase after him."

Vairug frowned.

Belac felt insulted by the frown. "I'm hurt and you have to carry Brandon." He gestured to the boy. "We need to get him to the city as fast as we can. Also, I need to make sure Gwen is safe before that volcano erupts and kills her."

Vairug nodded grudgingly. "We can follow the edge of trees and then cut through the forest early."

"Good." Belac indicated behind the orc. "Here they come."

Gwen hurried to join them first. "Belac, do I still have to hold Frank's hand?"

Guessing at why she did not want to hold the older boy's hand any longer, Belac chuckled. "No, Gwen." He smiled down at the little girl. "Just make sure you stay close to us."

Gwen's pigtails bounced as she nodded. "I promise."

Belac gestured for Vairug to lead, and then waited for Frank. The boy moved with less urgency than Belac would have preferred. *He must be tired. I know I am.*

"Are you hurt?" Belac asked the boy.

Frank shook his head.

Belac pointed the hilt of his sword toward the orc. "Then, stay next to Gwen and follow Lord Vairdoe."

Frank jogged to catch up with Gwen. He reached out to take the little girl's hand, but she stepped away from him, shaking her pigtails.

"It's fine, Frank," Belac assured the boy. "Just keep an eye on her. I don't want either of you getting lost."

Following behind the others, Belac watched the tree line. As the sky brightened, so too did the green of the forest. He thought of the monsters that lurked under the ground below the trees. *What did these people expect? Of course, there are going to be monsters living underneath all that green.*

Belac looked away from the trees. "How did you find us?" The question was clearly intended for the orc.

Frank put forth a guess. "I bet he tracked us!"

Belac narrowed his eyes at the boy.

"I tracked you," Vairug confirmed.

Belac looked at the orc curiously. "In the dark?"

"You left a trail that a blind pup could follow," Vairug replied dismissively.

Belac frowned. "But, how did you even know where to look for me?"

"Marsha," Vairug answered unhelpfully.

"Who's Marsha?" Belac thought that the orc might be trying to confuse him on purpose.

Gwen declared, "That's my mom!"

Belac attempted to fit the piece into the puzzle. "How would Gwen's mother know where to look?"

Vairug considered his answer before giving it. "There was another woman with her. She showed us a note that she had found. It gave us an idea of where we needed to begin our search."

Now, Belac understood why Vairug was being so evasive. *Debra found the letter her brother wrote. Vairug is trying to not bring up the dairy farm.* Belac could reconstruct events from there. *The letter had to have mentioned both Gwen and me. When Debra could not find anyone at the farm, she must have gone back to the city to get help.* He nodded to himself. *I need to stop asking questions about this, or Frank will start asking questions of his own.*

Not wanting to leave the conversation where it was, Belac asked about something else. "Where is Rolan?"

Vairug was quicker to answer the new line of questioning. "He is sleeping on the ship."

Belac did not know why the dwarf would still be sleeping on the ship when there was free wine at the council estate. "Why the ship?"

"Breana," Vairug said as if the answer should be obvious.

Yeah. Okay, that makes sense. Belac was about to ask how they were going to get Breana to the volcano, but then thought of the children. They had no way to know what should not be repeated. *I should probably not talk about our super secret giant-smuggling-plans.* Deciding it was too much effort to parse everything he said, Belac settled into silence.

As the forest began to wake, birdsong flittered into the glade. The smell of moist soil competed with the salt of the sea. Belac stared up at the majesty of Agadon and for a moment, he could almost understand why the people of Cavasca lived there. There was a vitality to the uncanny peninsula that defied the volcano's threat.

Vairug stopped and indicated to a deer trail. "We will need to find a way through here."

Frank looked up at the volcano with confusion and then shook his head. "No. We need to go that way." He pointed off to the southeast.

Belac had hoped that the boy would not be able to find his way home. "We are not going back to the farm. We need to go straight to Cavasca."

Frank argued, "But, I need to tell my dad what happened."

Belac attempted to change the boy's priorities. "Brandon is hurt, Frank. We need to get him to the city as soon as we can."

Frank was unconvinced. He opened his mouth to speak, but could not think of what to say. He stood conflicted, his eyes pleading with the elf.

He is just a little boy that wants to go home. Belac closed his eyes and fought to keep the emotion off his face. When he opened his eyes, he said, "Your family will be waiting for you in the city." *Debra will be there.* While Belac had not lied, he knew that he might as well have.

Frank lowered his head and nodded. "Okay."

Vairug continued into the woods without offering instruction. Belac motioned for Frank and Gwen to follow the orc. The children moved into the trees, leaving Belac to stare at the forest. He did not want to go back in there. To the elf, the tree line seemed like the lower fangs of a monster waiting to bite down. That there was no way out of the glade without braving the forest only made him feel more trapped. Belac's side ached as he took a deep breath. *Any danger that is in there will need to be kept from the children.* He walked into the woods.

As the elf rejoined the others, Gwen asked, "Will my mom be there too?"

Belac smiled at her. "I am sure she will be, Gwen." *That little girl is so cute, it almost makes up for all the green.*

Movement stirred the underbrush to the right of the trail. Belac drew his sword and rushed to put himself between the children and whatever might be coming for them. He held his sword out defensively with the inside of his arm pressed against his side. A deer flashed in and out of sight as it bounded away through the trees.

"You need to calm down," Vairug told the elf. "You are more jumpy than the deer."

Belac gestured weakly with his sword. "You don't know it's friendly."

Vairug glanced back but continued to walk. "It's a deer," he said dismissively.

Belac sheathed his sword. "Sure. But just because it has a friendly name, doesn't mean that it does not want to Eat. Your. Face."

Vairug breathed out loudly. "Belac, it's running the other way."

Belac tucked his right arm tightly to his side. "Maybe it is circling around!"

Frank did not understand the banter. "The deer?"

"Yes, the deer," Belac acknowledged. "Did you see the horns on that thing?"

"They are called antlers," Frank corrected the elf.

Gwen turned around and walked backward so that she could face the elf as she spoke. "I don't think the deer is going to hurt you, Belac."

From the forest, the deer bleated aggressively.

Gwen spun around and grabbed Frank's arm. Her little pigtails flopped side to side as she scanned the shadowed woods.

"Did you hear that?" Belac asked triumphantly. "It's an attack deer!"

Vairug was obviously struggling not to laugh. "It's not an attack deer."

"You don't know!" Belac insisted. "Do you speak crazy-horn-deer?" He did not wait for an answer. "You don't, do you?!"

Vairug shook his head ruefully and elected not to argue further.

Though he led them through a maze of deer trails, Vairug was able to navigate the forest easily. Before long, the density of the forest thinned and the city of Cavasca came into view. The rising sun shone across the red tiled rooves, illuminating the city like a beacon of hope. The vision was unable to bring Belac any great joy. The wound to his ribs had begun to radiate pain that reached all the way to his shoulder and his hip.

If Serath would just make me that flying carpet, I could already be in the city by now. Belac stopped walking. *I bet he has one!* He resumed walking irritably. *I bet he has a super secret flying carpet that he keeps hidden until we are not looking.* He nodded to himself. *That is how he knew he could get to the city before us.* Belac narrowed his eyes at the city in the distance. *Sneaky wizard!*

Once they were safely away from the trees, Belac quickened his stride until he was walking next to the orc. "Serath didn't happen to tell you where we were supposed to go when we got here, did he?"

Vairug shook his head. After a moment, he shrugged and looked to the elf. "The council grounds?"

Belac nodded in agreeance. "People that think they are important probably keep healers nearby." *Besides, I don't know where else to go.*

After a thoughtful moment, Vairug asked, "How do you think the humans are going to react if an orc walks into the city carrying an unconscious child?"

Belac closed his eyes but continued to walk. His entire right side hurt. Every breath he took felt like claws digging into his ribs. *Vairug is right.* Belac stopped walking and opened his eyes. Vairug halted a pace later and turned to face the elf.

Belac slung his sword onto his back and held out his arms. "Yeah. Okay, give him here."

Vairug transferred the injured boy to the elf's arms. "Are you sure you can carry him?"

Belac nodded. "Just stay close in case I drop him or something."

Vairug stepped away and then pulled up his white hood.

Belac frowned. "Everyone has got to know you're an orc by now."

Vairug adjusted his cloak. "It seems prudent to not draw attention to that fact."

Belac began to limp toward the city. "You think the people are going to turn on you?"

Walking beside the elf, Vairug shrugged.

Gwen moved forward and took the orc's gray skinned hand in her own. "Don't worry, Lord Vairdoe. I won't let anybody hurt you."

If I die from my wounds, it will be worth it to have saved that little girl. Belac smiled despite his discomfort.

As they approached the city, it became apparent that the people had been preparing for evacuation. Carts and wagons lined the streets. Luggage, furniture, and everything else that they valued most was strapped down under tarps of canvas and leather. Families stood next to their cargo, waiting for their turn to move forward. Some of the smaller children climbed on the wagons with the restlessness of youth.

Though the city was cluttered with people waiting to evacuate, a path down the center of the street remained cleared. *I hope the whole city is this ordered.* Belac had expected far more chaos during the evacuation. In his mind, he had imagined fire and looting and screaming people running around with their hands in the air.

Belac looked over his shoulder at Frank and motioned with his head for the boy to stay close. As Belac carried Brandon into the city, the people began to quieten. Hushed voices suddenly seemed loud. Belac's azure eyes scanned the crowd. *Go ahead and stare, people. Just don't throw any rocks at us.*

A chant began softly but quickly grew to a startling intensity. "Mel-la-var! Mel-la-var!" The city's roar was so loud that it could be felt in the air. "Mel-la-var! Mel-la-var!"

Belac groaned. *Oh, there is no way my mother does not hear about this.*

Thirty

Belac attempted to walk proudly, but the joint in his right hip refused to cooperate. So, he held his head high and limped as the city called his name.

"Mel-la-var! Mel-la-var!"

Belac would have traded all the cheers for just one person to come and offer to carry Brandon for him.

"Mel-la-var! Mel-la-var!"

The people of Cavasca seemed desperate for gaiety. Forced from their homes, they craved any diversion from the reality of losing their city.

"Mel-la-var! Mel-la-var!"

Belac had become the object of their desperation. He was a hero that had delved into the abyss, fought evil, and rescued the innocent.

"Mel-la-var! Mel-la-var!"

Belac narrowed his eyes in the direction of the council estate and the wizard he expected to find waiting there. *I bet I can guess who told these people what I was doing.*

"Mel-la-var! Mel-la-var!"

Belac had often pretended to be a hero. It had been fun. The adulation had been exciting. The posturing had been a game for him; it was a role he believed everyone wanted him to play.

"Mel-la-var! Mel-la-var!"

This was different. He felt exposed. He felt like the truth of his deeds would show people the truth of who and what he was. *Nobody wants that.*

"Mel-la-var! Mel-la-var!"

By the time he had reached the council estate, Belac was convinced that Serath was to blame for their reception. *He is probably why there was a clear path all the way here.* Once Belac was within the walls of the estate, the chanting continued for a brief time before devolving into general good cheer. Debra was waiting in the courtyard next to a plain woman with flaxen hair.

Gwen ran forward. "Momma!"

Frank scanned the courtyard, confused.

Gwen fell into her mother's arms and began to sob.

Debra rushed over to Belac. Coming to a stop, she covered her mouth with her hands and cried as she gazed down at the injured child. She reached out and gently brushed Brandon's hair away from his tranquil face.

Debra wiped her nose with one hand and waved for the elf to follow with the other. "The dwarf has a room set up." She did not want to take her eyes off the boy. "We need to take him there."

Belac's throat had become so dry that it hurt when he spoke. "Show me where to go."

Debra tore her eyes away from the injured boy and hurried toward a nearby building. Belac followed her as quickly as he was able, but it was obvious that she wanted him to move faster. Debra moved ahead and waited for him in an open doorway. Once Belac was close enough that she was sure he would follow, Debra darted inside the room.

Belac limped after her into an office that had been converted into a makeshift medical station. Two men in red robes stood with Debra next to a cleared, oaken table in the middle of the room. Belac laid Brandon down on the table and then sat in the closest chair he could find. Wood creaked as the skeletal armchair took his weight. His scabbard pressed into his back, but he was too tired to care.

Debra stood between Brandon and the elf, looking from one to the other in indecision. A callused hand palmed her hip and pushed Debra out of the way. She stumbled to the side and then stared down at the offending dwarf indignantly.

Rolan ignored the woman. "Where all are you hurt?" he asked the elf.

Belac lifted his right arm slightly and gestured with his left hand. "It is just my ribs."

Rolan scowled. "Then, why is there a hole in your face?"

Belac touched his cheek and winced. "Yeah, okay. And my face is cut."

"You are covered in blood, Belac," Rolan said impatiently. "I am going to ask you again. Where all are you hurt?"

Belac gestured to his cheek. "It's just the cut on my face," he nodded to his right side, "and the gashes in my ribs." He frowned and shook his head. "And my shoulder and leg don't want to work right." Then he added, "And I have a headache."

Rolan pulled the elf's clothes out of the way to inspect the wounds underneath. "What happened?"

"Hobgoblin claws." Belac reconsidered. "They are more like long, pointy, needle fingers." He groaned as the dwarf peeled the bandage away.

Rolan seemed to ignore the elf's discomfort. "I know what a hobgoblin is," he said testily.

Belac frowned. "Then, why did you ask?"

Rolan shook his head and grumbled.

Belac shied away as the dwarf poked around the wound.

Rolan looked up, his gray eyes meeting the elf's blue. "Serath probably saved your life."

Belac shook his head. "It does not feel like it."

Rolan pressed his thumb into the elf's side.

"Ow!" Belac glared at the dwarf.

Rolan nodded. "The dead don't feel."

Belac narrowed his eyes at the dwarf. *Gonna make you not feel…*

Rolan stepped back and pointed his hand at the elf. "Stay there," he ordered before walking away.

Debra stepped over and gazed down at the elf. Crying had left her face puffy and flushed. She said nothing, but her tear filled eyes begged for answers.

It hurt Belac to look at her. "Brandon?" he asked weakly.

Debra glanced over her shoulder at the men in red robes. "They say that they can help…" She looked back to the elf pleadingly. "Where are Henry and Scot?"

Belac knew that she suspected the answer; knew she feared the truth. What he did not know, was what to tell her. Belac sighed, and then repeated something that he had heard other humans tell each other. "They died bravely."

Debra covered her face with her hands and wept.

"My dad is dead?" Frank asked in disbelief. He looked at his youngest brother lying unconscious on the table. "…They are all dead…"

Belac had not realized that the boy had followed them to the infirmary.

Debra lowered her hands and turned to the distraught child. "Frank…"

Frank ran from the room. Debra chased after him, and Belac began to rise to follow also. Before the elf could fully stand, a strong hand pushed him back down into his chair. Belac groaned at the jostling to his side.

Rolan set a small woven backet on the floor next to the elf's feet. Glass tinkered on top of cloth bandages. "Let them go," he said dismissively. "Leave them alone and let them cry."

Belac stared at the dwarf. He had forgotten how cold Rolan could be. *I need to…* But Belac did not know what he could do.

Rolan reached into the basket and pulled out a brown glass vial. He removed the stopper, then held out the vial. "Here. Drink this."

Belac accepted the vial and sniffed at it. It smelled sickly sweet. He considered asking what it was, but decided that it did not matter. *Besides, Rolan would probably just tell me it is a potion of shut-up-and-drink-it.* He poured the potion into the back of his mouth and swallowed. Despite its sweet smell, the potion tasted bitter beyond compare. Grimacing, he handed the empty vial to Rolan.

Rolan tossed the empty vial into the basket. "Lift your shirt up out of the way."

Belac raised his right arm and reached across with his left hand. He gripped his blouse and jacket and pulled them up to his armpit. Rolan untied the blood soaked, crimson sash that had been used to bandage the elf's wound. He dropped the saturated cloth to the side, letting it fall wetly to the floor. Then Rolan removed the stopper from a clear vial of pink fluid and splashed its contents onto the elf's wounded ribs.

Rolan tossed the second empty vial into the basket. "Keep your shirt up."

Belac nodded lazily. His side was feeling better already. When Rolan proceeded to clean and dress the wound with a fresh bandage, Belac was surprised that it did not hurt at all.

Rolan popped the stopper off another vial and held it to the elf's mouth, conspicuously hiding the vial with his hand. "Here. Drink this."

Belac rolled his head away from the vial. "Whyyyyy…" he said slowly, the word stretching out. *Why… Why is it so hard to say 'why?'* "Whyyyyy…" he said again to test the word.

"You need to drink this, Belac," Rolan insisted.

Belac pushed the dwarf's hand away, getting a glimpse of the vial in the process. "It's green!" *The evil dwarf is trying to feed me green!*

Rolan sighed. "Yes, Belac. But you have to drink it."

"Notdrinkinggreen," Belac slurred. Then he drew out the word, "Whyyyyy…" for no discernable reason.

Rolan reached into the basket and pulled out the empty brown vial. He poured the lime green fluid from the clear vial into the brown one. "See? It's not green." He held the brown vial up for the elf to look at.

Belac leaned forward, his eyes wide. "How did you do that?!" he whispered in amazement.

Rolan shook his head. "Magic. Now, here. Drink this."

Belac almost fell out of his chair trying to lean forward and turn his head to the side, his lips reaching for the vial. Rolan gently pushed him back and helped him drink the medicine. *Why does it still taste green?*

When Rolan stepped away, Belac leaned his head back to relax. The motion made him feel like he was falling backward out of the chair, and he began to flail his arms for balance. Rolan took hold of the elf's wrists and placed his hands in his lap. Then a wet cloth covered Belac's face. It smelled strange, but it felt sublime.

"Just," Rolan chuckled, "Just wait there for a little bit."

The smell of the rag made Belac think of two yellow grizzly bears dancing in a rowboat. "But… Why are the bears wearing hats?"

Thirty-One

Rolan's voice sounded muted and far away. "…I have never given any of that stuff to an elf before." He might have been laughing.

A voice that could have been Vairug asked, "Did you kill him?"

Rolan was definitely laughing now. "No, I didn't kill him."

From the sound of his voice, Vairug must have been smiling. "Maybe you should try again."

Belac mumbled into the cold rag covering his face.

Rolan stepped over and removed the cloth. "What was that?"

Belac took a deep breath to speak, but then let it out. He waited a moment before trying again. "I hope you both die in a fire."

Vairug was smiling. "He seems fine to me."

Belac's head had cleared enough for him to know that he had been drugged. "What did you give me?"

Rolan was making no attempt to hide his amusement. "It was just the essence of a flower seed. I don't know why it made you so loopy."

Vairug contradicted the dwarf. "He thinks it is because you are a skinny elf." He laughed silently.

Belac attempted to narrow his eyes, but his eyelids were misbehaving. He tried to look at them so as to ascertain the problem, but they seemed to move away from him no matter how fast he followed them with his eyes. *Maybe if I can just…* He stuck out his tongue and tried to use it to catch one of the fluttering eyelids.

Rolan snapped his fingers in front of the elf's face. Belac did not like it. He narrowed his eyes at the dwarf.

Belac's eyes widened with surprise. "You fixed em!"

"No," Rolan said, misunderstanding the elf. "But you should be alright by tomorrow as long as you do what you're told. I will help here as much as I can, but then I have got to get back to the volcano. Breana can manage most of what we are doing, but I still need to finish installing the tap. All of this is for nothing if I can't get it set up in time."

All Belac understood was that he was supposed to do what he was told. He didn't really like the sound of that. *Wait… What did he tell me to do?* "Rolan," Belac wanted the dwarf's attention before sharing his suspicions. "I think I might be drugged."

Rolan shook his head and chuckled. "Vairug is going to make sure you get back to your suite. There should be a bath waiting for you there." He held up a small paper packet. "Sprinkle this in the water, and then take a bath." He moved the packet closer to the elf's face. "Do. Not. Eat. This."

Belac pulled his head back. "I am not going to eat my bath water, Rolan." He scrunched his nose and shook his head. "That's disgusting."

Rolan put the packet in the elf's hip pouch and then held up a clear glass vial filled with a thin pink fluid. "Once you're finished with your bath, drink this and then go to bed."

Belac stared at the vial as light refracted from the liquid inside, creating the illusion of a tiny rainbow trapped within. "How did you get that in there?"

Rolan put the vial in the elf's hip pouch and then helped him to stand. "Do you have him, Vairug?"

Vairug's right hand gripped the elf's left arm just under the shoulder. "Come on, you skinny elf."

Rolan stepped back and appraised them. "Maybe make sure he does not kill himself."

"I think you might be asking for too much," Vairug replied sarcastically.

Color blurred around Belac as the orc led him through the estate. Voices and sounds swirled around him like memories tugging at his mind. When he finally stepped into the shadows of his suite, the world began to solidify. The den had been completely rearranged to accommodate a large, copper bathtub of ornate design. The steam rising above the water was only made visible by the light shining through the open front door.

Vairug frowned around his tusks. "They should have left a light on for you." He leaned the elf against the doorframe and marched inside.

"Leave it dark," Belac said before the orc could find a lamp. "Just pull the curtains open a little bit. It is easier to see without so much light."

Vairug checked the bedroom for assassins before returning to the den and pulling back one of the curtains.

Belac moved his head lazily as he searched the entrance to the suite. "Hey. Where is my bag?"

"I saw it on the floor in your room, "Vairug said as he walked back to the elf. "Is that not where it should be?"

"It should be where I left it," Belac replied grumpily.

Vairug smiled. "Then, maybe you should have left it in your bedroom."

Belac narrowed his eyes at the orc.

Vairug reached into the elf's hip pouch and removed the paper packet that Rolan had put there. As the orc opened the packet, Belac was impressed by how much dexterity the orc had developed with his prosthetic hand. Once the packet was open, Vairug shook it over the bathtub and sprinkled tiny, pink beads into the water. He crumpled the empty packet in his gray skinned hand and then turned toward the elf.

Vairug nodded toward the copper tub. "You should get in."

Belac focused on his breathing for a moment in preparation to move.

Vairug seemed in a hurry to leave. "Do you need help getting in before I go?"

Belac shook his head and then walked drunkenly past the orc. "Why are you in such a rush?" he asked suspiciously.

Vairug did not attempt to conceal his motive. "I need to get back to the library. There is still much that can be saved, but they need assistance sorting through the books."

Belac opened the doors to a wine cabinet. It was empty. He glanced at the orc. "Serath turned you into a librarian?"

Vairug shook his head. "The people here do not seem to be able to distinguish the difference between a history and the drivel of philosophers," he critiqued with a frustration that the elf found curious.

Belac opened another cabinet. *Nothing.* He scowled at the empty cabinet.

Vairug continued to explain. "There are too many books to move them all. These people need help prioritizing."

Belac opened the last cabinet. *More nothing.* While he had expected to find the cabinet empty, the reality was still vexing.

Vairug was not finished. "Too many of the fools do not want to abandon the," he spoke in a high and mocking voice, "thoughts of enlightenment and reason." He growled before resuming in his normal voice. "Anyone that needs reason explained to them has no business being a custodian of knowledge."

Belac was so amused by the orc's passion, that he forgot to be annoyed by the empty wine cabinets. "Go." He grinned at the orc. "Go save the books. I'll be fine." *Save the books... Save the wine! There is wine in my duffle bag!*

Vairug nodded, already preoccupied with his mission. He began to leave the suite, but stopped in the doorway. He glanced back with a tusk filled grin. "I am glad you're not dead." Then he left, shutting the door behind himself.

Belac smiled and slowly walked to the bedroom. He stepped inside, searching for his arrant duffel bag. Light creeping past the window curtains created a foreboding atmosphere. Belac stopped in front of a tall, freestanding mirror and met eyes with the elf reflected there. He did not remember his eyes looking so hard. The person who stared back was someone prepared for violence. Belac looked away from the piercing azure eyes. He followed the blood crusted lines of the face down to the ruined clothing he wore. The left arm of the elf's blouse was stained with blood where the jacket's sleeve had been removed. On the other side, the jacket's silky fabric had been blackened and burned across the shoulder and remaining sleeve. Blood darkened the silk of the open jacket and saturated the blouse underneath. *That's what a dragon slayer looks like.*

The thought startled Belac. While it had felt true at its conception, he knew that nothing he had faced came close to the danger of a dragon. He heard Rolan's voice in his mind. *"No one kills a dragon."* Belac stepped away from the mirror.

The elf removed his scabbarded sword and set it on the bed before crouching down next to his duffle bag. It was obvious at a glance that the wine bottles remained inside. Belac grinned at the bottle shaped bulges in the cloth. He dug out a bottle of wine and then stood. The world went black for a moment and Belac had to grab the side of the bed to keep from falling.

Belac waited for his senses to return and then looked at his empty hand. *Where did the wine go?* He searched around him and found the bottle of wine on the floor. *At least it did not break.* He considered how far away the bottle was from him.

Belac pointed at the bottle of wine. "You just stay there for now."

The elf twisted around and sat on the edge of the bed. He kicked off his boots and then took a moment to catch his breath. *That seemed like a lot of effort to just take off my boots.* He reached into his hip pouch and removed the vial of shimmering pink fluid. *I should probably drink this before I forget about it.*

Belac popped the stopper off the vial and downed the potion inside. After a brief search for a place to set the empty vial down, he shrugged and tossed it into the corner of the room. The glass vial clinked across the floor but remained intact.

Belac unbuckled his belt and let it fall back onto the bed. Then he stood and finished undressing. Not knowing if he was supposed to remove his bandages or not, he decided to leave them on. *Less work.* Stepping past his pile of bloody clothes on the floor, he picked up his bottle of wine and stumbled into the den. Steam still rose from the copper tub. It looked inviting, but Belac vaguely remembered his previous bathtub trying to eat him.

Belac pointed his wine bottle at the bathtub. "You better behave."

The elf climbed into the water cautiously, his bottle of wine held ready to club the bathtub at the first sign of aggression. He leaned back in the tub and took a deep breath. The moist air filled his lungs with a relaxing warmth. *Yes, Rolan. It smells nice. But I am not going to try to eat it.* He uncorked the bottle of wine and tossed the stopper aside. *I'm not stupid.* He took a drink of wine.

Thirty-Two

Belac awoke drowning in the bathtub. He shot up, spitting water and flailing his arms in the air. "It's trying to eat me!" the elf shouted as he splashed water wildly.

I knew I couldn't trust the bathtub! He climbed over the side of the ornate copper bathtub and collapsed onto the floor. He kicked at the copper tub. His wet foot slipped across the side harmlessly, the motion rolling him onto his back. He coughed up more water, and then focused on pulling air into his lungs.

Lying in a puddle, Belac stared up into the darkness. He waited for his eyes to adjust, but the room remained black. *Maybe I should have let Vairug light a lamp for me.* His head lulled from side to side as he searched for a lamp, but the room was too dark for him to see anything. *This is what happens when everyone lets the moon do whatever it wants. You get nights so dark that people almost get eaten by their bathtubs.* Even Belac had to admit that his thoughts did not make much sense.

The elf rolled over onto his hands and knees. The night outside, only slightly less dark than the suite's interior, created a pale edging around the curtains. Using the subtle lucence, Belac orientated himself and began crawling toward the bedroom. A wet lock of hair fell down into his face as he dripped water across the floor. He stopped long enough to tuck his hair behind his ear, but he did not bother to retie it.

Once he reached the doorway to the bedroom, Belac used it and the faint glow behind the curtains to find the bed. He crawled up the bedpost and then sat on the edge of the bed. Belac considered lying back and going to sleep, but decided that he should check his wounds first. He reached back and pulled his belt forward, dragging his dagger and hip pouch with it. Belac dug into the pouch, pulled his light rod out, and then struck it against the dagger's modest cross-guard.

Both the ping and the light that filled the room were less than the light rod was capable of, but Belac thought it would be sufficient. He dropped his dagger and belt onto the bed and then stood. *Well, at least I can stand without falling over.* He felt like he had slept forever but was still tired. Stepping over to the mirror, he lifted his bandage up and inspected his reflection.

Thick sludgy blood covered the jagged scars that had once been rent flesh. Belac removed his wet bandage and used it to wipe away the dark blood. He tossed the bandage aside and then ran his fingers over the scars. They were not the only scars he had, but they were definitely the nastiest looking. *It looks like I got into a fight with a bear.*

Belac touched his cheek. The scar there was faint, and he thought it would eventually fade away completely. This led him to spend a shameful amount of time admiring how pretty he was. He pinched his chin and turned his own head left and right. *I don't care how handsome that wizard is. I'm an elf. No human is better looking than an elf.*

Turning away from the mirror, Belac sat down on the floor with his legs crossed under himself. He began pulling things out of his duffle bag until he found a large wooden brush. With a pump of his arm, he held the brush up high over his head victoriously. A bottle of wine rolled across the wooden floor.

Belac pointed his hairbrush at the bottle. "Don't think you can escape!" *Sneaky wine bottle.*

The elf untied his long, black hair and began to brush it out. The thickness of his hair helped, but it was still a chore to remove all the tangles. Some of the hair on the right side of his head felt singed, but he did not think that anyone else would notice.

If I had not just climbed out of a river, I might have lost half my hair when I got set on fire. As he was retying his hair, the light outside the window changed hue. Belac finished tying his hair and then stood. Though faint, warm orange light flickered from the square outside.

A fist hammered on the door to Belac's suite with a force that rattled the door in its frame. The pounding boomed loudly through the dark rooms inside. Belac stepped over to the bed and picked up his scabbarded sword. He pushed the scabbard off the blade and let it fall onto the bed. The impolite banging continued as the elf walked from the bedroom into the den. *Would hobgoblins bother knocking?*

Belac swung his light rod up into his left hand and pressed the end against the cross-guard of his sword, killing the golden light. Using the warm orange glow that shone around the doorframe and window curtains, the elf made his way to the entrance. He slid the bolt to the door open and then stepped back, his sword ready to thrust.

The fist hammering against the door pushed it open into the suite. A startled sailor took one look at the elf and then raised both hands over his head in surrender. The lantern in his right hand swung over and hit the man in the head. The sailor took another step back and tried to hold his hands up higher.

Belac relaxed his stance and pointed with his sword. "I know you."

The sailor was the man who had helped throw Breana off the ship. *What was his name?*

The sailor lowered his hands and nodded. "Captain Rolan sent me and Dringle with a cart." He pointed behind himself with his thumb. "He wants, Captain Rolan that is, he wants us to haul you and the orc's," he was quick to amend himself, "Lord Vairdoe's things to the Tell Her Twice."

"The Tell Her Twice?" Belac asked. "What's that?"

"The Tell Her Twice?" the sailor asked as if he thought the question were some sort of test. "That's the name of the ship. The Tell Her Twice."

Belac laughed. "Rolan named his ship Tell Her Twice?"

The sailor shook his head. "That was its name before he got it. It's an old sea poem." He proceeded to recite,

"Before you sail the sea,

Tell your wife you love her,

Tell her twice.

Before you…"

Belac held up a hand. "Stop. Stop. Stop." *Why do humans insist on making me listen to their bad poetry?* "I get it. It's a nice, 'tell her twice.'"

The sailor shrugged. "Anyhow, we are here to collect your things. The captain said you couldn't carry it around with you, and so we need to load it up before we move the ship."

They are moving the ship? This was news to Belac. "Why are you moving the ship?"

The sailor held out his arms. "They don't tell Kegs nothin."

Is 'Kegs' his name or some kind of sailor title? Belac shrugged. He believed that Rolan would not trust the sailors with his plans.

Kegs gestured toward the elf with his free hand. "Might be you want to get dressed before we cart off your things?"

Belac refused to feel embarrassed. Standing in the doorway completely nude, he pointed with his sword. "That is Lord Vairdoe's suite over there. You can help him load his bags while I get ready."

Kegs nodded agreeably. "Me and Dringle will get right on it." He pointed toward a man standing next to a handcart at the entrance to the square. "We'll be at the cart when you are ready for us."

Belac looked past Kegs to the forementioned cart. A simple two wheeled handcart, the only notable feature was the tall pole that had been affixed to its side. A lantern hung from the pole, illuminating another sailor. *That must be Dringle.* The sailor appeared to be a harder man than Kegs. He stood as if he knew how to use the broad, curved sword that hung from his hip. Kegs too wore a sword, though his was short and easier to overlook. *That does not necessarily make him less dangerous.* Belac took another look at Kegs. *They are worried someone might try to rob them on the way back to the ship.*

Belac gestured to the den. "Or, you two can wait inside. Then you can head out once the sun is up." *They should be less likely to be robbed in daylight.* He suddenly realized how his invitation could be misinterpreted, so he added, "You can wait in the den while I get dressed."

Kegs shook his head. "We're meant to get back as soon as we are able."

Belac shrugged. "The door is open. I am going to go get ready."

Belac turned away and headed back toward the darkened bedroom. Along the way, he struck his light rod against his sword's cross-guard to resummon the golden glow. After stepping into the bedroom, he shut the door behind him to ensure that there would be no misunderstandings.

Stepping over a wine bottle, Belac tossed his sword onto the bed. He sat down on the floor and began pulling things out of his duffle bag. As he collected what he would wear, he selected a black leather vest instead of another silk jacket. While it was not thick enough to turn a blade, he thought the leather would provide more protection than silk against an angry volcano. *The leather might give me enough time to say, "Ow," before the lava kills me.*

Belac dressed in clean clothes and then began to preen in the mirror. Other than the pale blue blouse, he was dressed entirely in black. He held his arms out and twisted side to side. *The blue just makes all the black look less severe. A little touch of color can go a long way.* He wondered if he could trick Serath into wearing a fancy cape.

Once Belac was satisfied with his attire, he stuffed almost everything else back into his duffle bag. His ruined clothes, he left in a pile by the bed next to his dirty boots. He looked at himself in the mirror again, and then he tightened the laces on the sides of his vest before buckling his belt around his waist. *I look even better now.* He grinned at himself. *Who would have thought that was even possible?*

A knock came from the door to the suite. With the front door open and the bedroom door closed, the sound was nowhere near as loud as before. However, Belac recognized the uncouth percussion. *Kegs is here for my bag.* The elf opened the bedroom door and walked into the den.

Kegs was standing just outside the suite. "I know it's not my place to rush you… But, uhm…"

Belac nodded. "But you need to get back to the ship before it leaves you behind."

Kegs nodded in turn. "That id be it."

Belac gestured to the bedroom. "I am going to need help moving this."

Kegs stepped into the suite. "You are not looking to take the bed, are you?"

Belac shook his head. "It is just a bag." He walked into the bedroom and stopped next to his duffle bag. "But it's heavy, and we need to be careful with it," he said after the sailor followed him into the room.

Kegs glanced down at the bulging duffle bag. "What do you have in there? Rum?"

Belac realized that he was about to trust a ship full of sailors with a bag stuffed with bottles of fine wine. He began to narrow his eyes at the sailor, but grinned instead as an idea came to him. He waved the sailor closer.

Belac leaned in like he was sharing a secret and spoke in the same conspiratorial voice he had used on the ship. "Firebombs."

Kegs' eyes went wide, and he immediately retreated away from the bag. He pulled his hands back as if afraid he might touch it. The sailor looked left and right before leaning toward the elf and repeating, "Firebombs?"

Belac nodded seriously. "But you can't tell anyone." He almost laughed and sabotaged his own lie.

Kegs leaned in closer. "Why not?" He looked down at the duffle bag. "Someone might set them off."

Belac let himself grin. He waited until the sailor looked back at him, then the elf tapped the side of his own nose.

Kegs stared back confused.

Belac stepped around the duffle bag and walked to the bedroom door. He stuck his head out the doorway and made a show of searching for eavesdroppers. Then he moved back into the room and stood next to the sailor. Leaning in close, Belac said, "We think that there might be some sticky fingers on the ship." He glanced over his shoulder like he was still worried that someone would hear him. He lowered his voice. "So, the wizard and I are going to set a trap."

Kegs whispered back, "A trap?" and then glanced down at the duffle bag.

"The wizard cast a spell on the bag," Belac said as if confiding. "If this bag gets opened by someone who is not supposed to open it," he put the tips of his fingers together and mimed an explosion, "no more sticky fingers."

Kegs was horrified. "You could burn up the whole ship!"

Belac nodded thoughtfully. "You're right…" He pointed at the sailor. "You should make sure there are a couple barrels of water nearby."

Kegs stared at Belac, obviously thinking that the elf was a madman.

Belac tapped the side of his own nose again and then pointed at the sailor. "Just make sure you don't tell anyone. We wouldn't want the thief to know it's a trap."

Kegs was slowly shaking his head side to side. "What if someone sets it off on accident?"

Belac smiled broadly. "That's the genius of it. It only goes off if someone tries to open it! That wizard is smart."

Kegs began to shake his head faster. "But what if we drop it?!"

Belac nodded agreeably and then looked down at his bulging bag of wine bottles. "Yeah. We should probably be careful with it."

Thirty-Three

Got to save the wine. Belac smiled as he watched Kegs and Dringle push the handcart out of the square like they expected it to explode at any moment. Belac was certain that Kegs had already betrayed his confidence.

Vairug asked, "What did you do to them?"

Belac's azure eyes twinkled in the dawning light of the morning. "I told them a secret."

Unhappy to be awake so early in the morning, Vairug argued, "Then, it is not a secret anymore."

Belac turned toward the orc and tapped the side of his own nose. "Exactly."

Vairug scowled. "You look stupid when you do that."

"I do not!" Belac frowned at the orc. "Besides, humans do it all the time."

Vairug's reply was wry. "And you think humans are a good judge of what is not stupid?"

Belac pointed his finger at the orc with the intention of arguing. However, he quickly realized that he had no argument to make. "That's a good point."

Vairug grunted.

After a moment of consideration, Belac asked, "Do you think I should wink instead?" He gave the orc an exaggerated wink.

Vairug ignored the wink. "I think we should eat breakfast."

Belac's mouth watered at the suggestion. "Yeah! I bet they have great food here."

Vairug's cheek twitched. "You would like to bet?"

Belac narrowed his eyes at the orc. "I am not betting my boots, Vairug."

Vairug waved a dusky skinned hand, indicating that the elf should follow him. "I have breakfast inside."

Belac shook his head. "Let me go get my sword first."

Vairug nodded and gestured toward his own suite. "I will be inside."

The morning light was such that Belac could have crossed the square without the aid of his light rod. However, once he was back inside his suite, he was glad to have the extra illumination. Golden light led the way as the elf returned to his bedroom. Now that he had sent his duffle bag to the ship, his sword and its scabbard were the last of his effects worth keeping. He picked up his sword and inspected the blade. *I should really clean this.* He thumbed the edge. *And sharpen it.* His scabbard was out of reach, so he grabbed the bed's plush top blanket and pulled it toward him. *Or, I could just stick it in its scabbard and worry about it later.* He picked up the scabbard and slid his sword inside.

Belac left the bedroom, but stopped in the den on his way out of the suite. He looked at the ornate copper bathtub, at the sword in his hand, and then back at the bathtub. *Can a sword take a bath?* He considered simply leaving his sword in the bathtub while he went and ate breakfast, but decided that he did not want to soak the leather more than he already had. With a shrug, he exited the suite.

As Belac crossed the square again, he wondered what Vairug would offer for breakfast. *If it is roasted squirrel, I am going to cut off his other hand.* The door to the orc's suite was open, so Belac walked inside without knocking.

Two large table lamps provided the den with a cozy yellow light. The interior was laid out much the same as Belac's had been before being rearranged for his bath. An upholstered sofa and two flanking armchairs surrounded a short table in the center of the room. Two end tables sat next to the chairs and a longer table rested against the back wall. While the wine cabinets were closed, Belac would have bet that they too were empty.

Though Vairug was nowhere to be seen, on the short table waited the breakfast promised. A pitcher and tumblers sat next to three cloth wrapped bundles. Two larger and one smaller, Belac stared at the bundles and wondered what kind of food was hidden under the unbleached cloth.

Belac pitched his voice to carry. "Hey, Vairug. Do you think a sword can take a bath?"

Vairug walked out of his bedroom. "Is this the beginning of a joke?"

"How could it be a joke?" Belac gave the orc a confused look. "What would the punchline be?"

Vairug stopped and gazed up slightly as he considered. "Not in a fight?" he guessed at the punchline.

Belac grinned. "What if it's a blood bath?"

Vairug nodded. "Yes. That is better." He frowned. "Still…" He shook his head. "It is not a very good joke."

Belac leaned his scabbarded sword against an armchair and sat down. "It's your joke," he said with a chuckle.

Vairug set his cogged mace on the sofa and then seated himself in the other armchair. "If it were my joke, it would be funny."

Belac smiled at the orc. "Bloodbath? That sounds like an orc joke to me."

Vairug shook his head. "It should be an axe." He nodded. "Swords are stupid."

"What?!" Belac laughed in disbelief.

"How does an Orcish axe get clean?" Vairug asked.

Holding up a finger, Belac shook his head. "Wait…"

Vairug ignored the elf. "With a bloodbath."

Belac closed his eyes and continued to shake his head.

"That is a much better joke," Vairug stated with confidence.

Belac opened his eyes. "The real joke is you thinking that swords are stupid."

Vairug shrugged. "They are stupid," he insisted seriously. "Swords do not strike with enough force for their weight. They are easy to deflect. Armor or a shield can turn the blade. Even if they do connect with the target, the edge is far too likely to get caught on bone. It is the tip of the sword that is the most dangerous part. If your attacks are limited to a thrust, a spear will always do it better. Spears are lighter, faster, and have greater reach."

Belac was beginning to find the topic less humorous. "Not every attack needs to go through armor or a shield, Vairug."

"True," Vairug nodded, conceding the point. "But why would you want a weapon that only works some of the time?"

Belac shook his head. "It's not that simple. There is a lot of versatility that comes with a sword. They have multiple angles of attack and a wide range of lethal distances. There are ways to move, engage, and maneuver with a sword that you just can't do with an axe or a spear."

Vairug's gray face stared at the elf impassively. "So, what you are saying, is that it requires much more effort for you to accomplish the same thing with a sword as I can by simply swinging my mace?"

Belac frowned. "It's complicated."

Vairug nodded. "Because swords are stupid."

Belac narrowed his eyes at the orc.

"Humans like swords," Vairug added.

Belac leaned back as if he had been slapped.

Vairug laughed silently and gestured to the cloth bundles on the table. "Let's eat."

Belac looked at the cloth bundles, and decided that he was willing to pause the debate until after he had eaten. "What is it?"

Vairug slid one of the larger bundles across the table. "I do not know what it is called." He took the second of the larger bundles for himself and began to unwrap it. "It is bread, and eggs, and cheese, and some kind of fatty meat."

That sounds like food to me. Belac began to unwrap his breakfast. "What is that?" he asked, indicating to the smaller cloth bundle with his chin.

Vairug picked up the small bundle and moved it farther away from the elf. "You get this after you eat that."

Belac frowned but he did not argue. The food that he already had in front of him smelled fantastic. He poured himself a tumbler of water and then began to eat. Whatever the food was called, it tasted even better than it smelled. Once the elf had finished eating his meal, Vairug slid the last cloth bundle over to Belac.

Vairug filled the second tumbler with water while he explained. "Serath said that it would be better if you ate that last."

Belac smiled greedily as he unwrapped the dessert. "You didn't get one?"

Vairug shook his head. "It smells like elf food."

Belac stared down at the bready log, unimpressed. *It looks kind of dry.* He picked the pastry up and sniffed at it. *Smells sweet...* He took a bite and sweet gooey syrup shot into his mouth. He mumbled appreciation unintelligibly as he chewed.

After swallowing, Belac said, "It's like they flipped a sweet bun inside out and trapped all the goodness inside!"

Vairug nodded disinterestedly. "Elf food."

Belac scarfed the pastry down and then immediately regretted not taking his time. He looked at his tumbler of water. He was thirsty, but he did not want to wash the taste out of his mouth.

Belac looked up at the orc. "Is there anymore?"

Vairug shook his head and then drank the last of the water in his own tumbler. He set the empty tumbler on the table. "Are you ready to go?"

Relenting, Belac picked up his tumbler and drank. *I should have kept one of the bottles of wine for breakfast.*

Vairug leaned forward, grabbed his mace from the sofa, and stood. "The others will be waiting on us. We should go join them in the mine."

Belac stood and picked up his sword. "Yeah, okay. But I want to stop and check on Brandon first."

Vairug shook his head. "You cannot."

"What?" Belac asked, confused by the restriction. "Why not?"

"He is not here," Vairug explained. "No one is here. Today is the day that the volcano erupts."

Thirty-Four

"This is uhm..." Belac stared into the empty streets of Cavasca. "This is creepy, Vairug."

The city that had bustled with life only a day before, now stood desolate. A breeze blew through the streets like an echo of the souls that had abandoned them. The absence of voices felt deafening, the emptiness complete.

Vairug seemed unconcerned. "Yesterday morning you were fighting for survival in the dark underground." He looked at the elf with a hint of disdain. "You think that this is creepy?"

Belac nodded, unabashed. "It's... It's the wrongness of it, Vairug. This was a place of life and happiness. Families thrived here." He gestured with both hands in lamentation. "Children once walked these streets." He swept a hand through the air as if it were he who had brushed away the denizens. "Now, everyone is gone."

Vairug was unmoved. "It is nothing but sticks and rock stacked next to the ocean." He shrugged. "Besides, everyone is not gone."

Belac nodded. "I know. Most of those people will find homes somewhere else. It's just..."

"No," Vairug interrupted. "I mean, they are not all gone." He gestured to the city. "There are still people scurrying about."

Belac turned his head to look at the orc. "Really?"

Vairug nodded. "Scavengers, thieves, and those who simply refuse to leave."

Belac reappraised the city. Standing outside the entrance to the council estate, he could not view the entirety of Cavasca. However, he saw no indication that anyone still lingered. He wondered what dark, hidden eyes stared out at him from within the shadowed buildings.

A cold shiver ran up Belac's spine. "Let's get out of here."

Vairug gestured to the left with a gleaming metal hand. "It is this way."

Belac followed, glad to be moving. Standing in place had somehow seemed to pronounce the stillness of the emptied city. The street they took was not one that Belac had been down before, but he felt like he would not have been able to recognize it if he had. The sound of wood breaking carried from somewhere off in the distance, though the elf could not have pinpointed it.

The early sun edged over the red tile rooves of the city, setting Cavasca aglow. While the low buildings still blocked direct light, the coming of dawn reminded Belac that all was not lost. *Someday, that same sun will shine down on those people's new home.* He nodded to himself. *Vairug is right. What is left behind is just sticks and stones piled next to the ocean.* Cavasca was a city no longer. What Belac walked through was nothing more than a corpse.

Vairug turned left again and led Belac to a long stone bridge that reached out over a shallow ravine. Constructed of stones that matched the tan and reddish brown hues of the city, the bridge spanned a river that ran along the base of the volcano. As they crossed the bridge, Belac wondered if the water flowing below him was connected to the rivers he had found underground. Despite its length, the bridge looked sturdy enough to accommodate a freight wagon. *This must be how they got Breana to the volcano.* Belac thought it would be easier to convince the giantess to ride in a cart than it would to get her to wear clothes. Belac grinned, suddenly looking forward to seeing Breana again.

On the other side of the bridge, two men that were clearly some of Rolan's sailors waited next to four draft horses and a covered wagon. *I wonder if that is the escape plan.* The men seemed at ease and prepared for a long wait. However, a short sword hung from each of the men's hips, and their collections of scars became more apparent as Belac got closer.

Belac nudged the orc's shoulder with the back of his hand and then pointed toward the wagon. "Is that how we are getting out of here?"

Vairug nodded. "Once the sword is forged, the wagon will carry us down that road there." He pointed to a rough but serviceable looking road.

Belac traced the road with his eyes. "We are not going back to the docks?"

Vairug shook his head. "Rolan moved the ship up the coast."

Kegs did say they were moving the ship. Belac guessed at the reason. "Is he worried that the volcano will damage it?"

"No." Vairug explained, "He is worried that those who remain in the city will attempt to board once the volcano erupts. Humans are dangerous when they panic."

Belac imagined the ship being swarmed by desperate people. He saw them fighting each other, fighting with the crew, interfering with the operation of the ship, and he saw them continuing to pile on even as the ship succumbed to the fires of the volcano. *I guess Captain Crazy Dwarf knows what he is doing.*

Belac waved to the sailors as he and Vairug walked past them on their way toward a massive mine entrance. Both the portal and the adit were formed of blocked stone that testified to the mine's importance. *I don't care how nice it looks. I still don't want to go back underground. I have had enough of dark tunnels and caverns. I am not a dwarf!*

Entering the mine without complaint, Belac consoled himself with the fact that the mine was lit with oil lamps. *It feels a lot less like walking to my death when I can see where I am going.* Several openings presented paths to both the left and right, but Vairug continued to lead the elf straight.

As they moved deeper into the mine, Belac thought that he could feel the weight of the mountain above him.

The mine's primary ended at a rough wall of dark gray stone and the mouth of a tunnel that almost looked natural. Though the opening was beyond the last of the oil lamps, pale white light shone in the tunnel's mouth. Tall enough for even Breana to walk through comfortably, Belac had little doubt that the tunnel led to their destination.

Be careful," Vairug warned. "The tunnel slopes and the rock is smooth."

Stepping into the tunnel, Belac thought that the orc's concerns were unwarranted. Though the dark gray rock was smooth to the extent of being glossy, the decline was gradual enough that the elf's footing felt sure even in his new boots. However, the cool air emanating from the chamber made him feel like he was walking into a grave.

The length of the tunnel prevented him from seeing more than the floor of the glowing chamber below, but as they continued down, the white light became brighter and brighter. The light was pure and steady in a way that Belac had come to recognize. *Whatever is creating that light has to be magic.* The magical nature of the light was intriguing, but not something that Belac felt was cause for concern. Magic is why they had come.

The chamber came into view as Belac neared the bottom of the tunnel. It was of an irregular shape that made the smoothness of the rock seem strange. Smaller than the courtyard at the council estate but larger than the square outside his suite, the chamber was lit by six arcane objects of beauty. Long stem flowers of translucent blue glass, the alluring objects stood knee high at seemingly random locations in the chamber as if they had grown from the rock itself. Faint white mist poured from the open petals and hung in the air around them.

Much of what else he saw was as Belac had expected. Beyond a row of metal bound barrels, Breana arranged tools on an oversized workbench next to a giant-sized anvil. Rolan was nearby, kneeling beside something that looked like an unfinished metal oven. Nothing about the makeshift smithy seemed out of place except for the forge. A dwarf being involved, Belac had imagined that he would find a massive contraption with cogs and gears feeding a forge of unknowable design. The debarked tree trunk sticking out of the wall and running into the lower end of a large stone trough seemed like a bad joke.

Belac walked into the unnaturally cold chamber and pointed to what he assumed was the forge. "Why is there a tree sticking out of that?"

Rolan stood and turned to face the elf. "The log is hollowed out," he explained. "Mostly, it is just there to act as a conduit while the lava creates a channel, but it should provide some insulation as well."

That sounded like a bad plan to Belac. "Won't the wood just burn up when the lava hits it? I am pretty sure that lava is hot, Rolan. I mean, like really hot."

Rolan shook his head. "The inside is coated with a chemically treated liquid stone. That, and the way that lava crusts as it moves, should be enough to keep the wood from melting or catching on fire before it does its job." He held up a hand and moved it in a tight circle, indicating to the chamber around them. "And the cold should help."

Belac was still unconvinced. "That is a lot of 'should's."

Rolan shrugged. "Yesterday, I made plans that the sun should rise today." It sounded like he was quoting someone.

Belac decided to trust that the dwarf knew what he was doing. He pointed to the peculiar forge. "How does it work?"

Rolan turned and pointed a hand at where the log met the wall. "Once the volcano is more active, pressure will force the magma into the log." His hand followed the improvised tube to the bottom of the stone forge. "Lava will pour out into the basin and then rise up as it fills." He stepped over to the forge and pointed his hand at the other side of the basin. A shallow dip in the lip led to a much smaller section. "The lava flows over there and falls down into a sink that drops the runoff into a chamber below us." He added as an afterthought, "That is how we keep the level regulated." Then he gestured up toward a narrow shaft in the ceiling. "Most of any toxic fumes should be pulled up through there."

Belac's trust was waning. "Most?' 'Most,' of the toxic fumes?"

Rolan shrugged. "You can try not breathing if you want to."

Thirty-Five

"So, I've been thinking," Belac began.

Vairug's cheek twitched. "I do not believe you."

Belac narrowed his eyes at the orc.

Vairug laughed silently and allowed the elf to continue.

"What happens if the volcano doesn't erupt?" Belac asked irritably.

Vairug stopped laughing.

Belac nodded. "If all those people come back, they are not going to just dance in the streets and be glad they get to go home. They are going to be angry. They are going to feel tricked. They are going to want to hunt down the elf, and the orc, and the wizard that lied to them. And then, they are going to want to hang us from a tree and set us on fire."

Now, Vairug looked concerned.

Belac grinned. "But I have a plan."

Vairug's concern only grew.

Belac held out his arms. "I say, that if the volcano doesn't erupt, we tell them that it is because I killed Agadon." He smiled at his own cleverness. "I am The Dragon Slayer after all."

Vairug tilted his head to the side in thought. "That's… That might actually be a good plan."

Serath's rich voice came unexpectedly. "I suspect such a contingency will be unnecessary."

Frowning, Belac turned to the newly arrived wizard. "It's only unnecessary until you are hanging upside down with your hair on fire," he said in defense of his plan.

Serath smiled broadly but did not argue. He instead addressed the dwarf. "Rolan, are you and Breana prepared?"

Standing next to the giantess and her workbench, Rolan turned toward the wizard. "You should ask her." He gave his friend a sly grin.

Serath took a deep breath that was more of a patient laugh. "Lady Breana, lovely giantess and master smith, are you prepared to forge a legend?"

Rolan's grin became a smile as he waited for the giantess to respond.

The wizard's formality amused Breana. "I don't know," she teased. "I am still waiting on a wizard to tell me how he is going to make all of this work."

Serath accepted the giantess's prompt graciously. "When a volcano erupts, it is not the molten lava that kills everything around it. There are explosions of rock, ash, and super-heated gases that rush out. Life is scoured away by the extreme forces released. Ash and rock fall from the sky and cover the devastation in a blanket of death." He let the word 'death' hang in the air for a moment before continuing, "Then, the lava comes to consume what remains."

Belac held up his hand. "I don't like this plan."

Serath smiled at the interruption. "I can mitigate the pyroclastic flow, but the energy will still have to go somewhere."

Breana's amusement had faded away. "What exactly does that mean?"

Belac pointed at the giantess and nodded his support.

Rolan speculated, "It means that this time, it will be the lava that kills everything." He did not sound satisfied with the wizard's plan. "It could kill us too."

Serath frowned at the dwarf.

Belac did not bother holding up his hand. "I don't like this plan either."

Vairug nodded. "This does sound like a bad plan," he agreed dryly.

Breana crossed her arms under her breast unhappily.

Serath waited patiently until he was sure that everyone had finished speaking. "I can hold back the eruption while we forge the sword. The volcano will be active while we work, and we will still be able to extricate ourselves before the lava becomes inescapable."

With open skepticism, Breana asked, "You can hold back a volcano?" She looked to the dwarf for confirmation.

Rolan shrugged. "If he says he can do it, he probably can."

Belac pointed to himself and then at the orc standing next to him. "Is there any reason we have to be here?"

Serath smiled and said, "Yes," in a tone that implied he would not be explaining why.

Belac narrowed his eyes at the wizard.

Serath swept back one side of his long black coat and reached into the bag that hung under his left arm. When he pulled his gloved hand out, he held the milky white ingot of starmetal. He walked over to the giantess and offered her the ingot.

Breana uncrossed her arms and accepted the bar of white metal. "I still think it should be alloyed."

Serath did not argue with her. Instead, he held up a gray metal cylinder similar in size to his thumb. "You will need to use this touchmark." He angled one of the circular sides at the giantess and pointed up with his other hand. "This is how it needs to face in relation to the tip of the sword."

Breana did not take the cylinder. "You would have me put your mark on my work?" There was a challenge in her voice.

Serath shook his head. "It is not my mark. It is a spell. The magic of the blade will not function without it." He moved the metal cylinder into the giantess's field of view. "This side must face up."

Breana nodded grudgingly.

Serath set the cylinder on the giantess's workbench. Then he walked to the center of the room and sat down on the floor with his legs crossed under him. "I suggest you all take a seat." He held his hands out, gesturing to the space around him. "What happens next will be disorienting."

Belac's initial impulse was to reject the wizard's advice. Then he recalled what had happened at the fountain when they had first entered the city. The wizard's tone had sounded much the same. *Serath's suggestions sound a lot like, "Do it or else."* Belac nudged Vairug's arm and then took a seat in front of the wizard.

Vairug shrugged and then sat down with them, creating the third point of a lopsided triangle. Breana crossed her arms again and glared at the back of the wizard's head. Rolan, however, walked over and sat down on the side to Serath's right and Belac's left. Breana redirected her glare at the dwarf.

Rolan pointed his hand at the ground next to himself. "You should probably sit down."

Breana continued to glare at the dwarf.

Rolan sighed and shook his head. He then laid back to stare up at the ceiling with his knees bent. He put his hands behind his head and made himself comfortable.

Finally, Breana joined them. She chose to sit behind the wizard; presumably, so that she could resume glaring at the back of his head.

Serath reached into his bag and removed a brass disc that was no larger than a tea saucer. The small disc had been engraved with patterned, geometric lines that glimmered in the magical white light of the chamber. He set the mysterious disc on the floor in front of himself and then reached back into his bag.

Belac wondered if the patterns on the disc served some purpose other than decoration. "What is that?"

Serath's answer provided no insight. "It is a jelagest."

Belac frowned at the wizard. "You just made that word up."

Serath smiled in return. "In what way would it be relevant if I had?"

Belac narrowed his eyes at the wizard.

Serath held up a small, silver bell palmed in his gloved hand. "You will not be able to hear anything for a time." He flicked his wrist, but the bell made no sound.

"What do you mean?" Belac asked, but he could not hear his own voice. "Hey!" he complained anyway.

The silver bell disintegrated into dust in the wizard's gloved hand. The silvery dust poured through his fingers before dissolving into the ether. Serath reached out and touched the jelagest. Moving his hand in slow deliberation, he turned a flat ring incorporated into the surface of the disc. The nature of the world changed.

All as one, everyone in the chamber began to float away from the floor. Belac flailed his arms as he struggled to achieve some semblance of balance. Vairug froze in place as if terrified to move. Rolan slowly stretched out his arms and legs, somehow managing to maintain his equilibrium. Breana panicked, grabbing at the floor in a desperate attempt to halt her levitation. Her efforts sent her spinning in jerky motions until she collided with Rolan. She wrapped her arms around the dwarf and together they slowly twirled away from the group.

Serath sat cross-legged still. Floating in the center of the room with his forearms resting on his lap and his palms facing upward; his eyes were closed, and his features at peace. The jelagest lay on the floor, unaffected by the alterations it had forced upon reality. Then the world began to shake.

Though the mountain quaked violently, those held in the jelagest's projections felt nothing. Belac found the experience exceedingly odd. He knew he was moving, but there was no sensory input to reconcile the event. He watched as a cloud of dust drifted down the tunnel, only to halt a pace away from the chamber. Absently, the elf recognized that he was floating upside down. *I wonder what would have happened if I had not sat down.*

Serath's bright green eyes opened. His legs uncrossed, and he set his feet on the ground. He stretched out his arm and held his hand over the jelagest with his palm facing toward it. The brass disc rose from the floor and floated up to the wizard's hand. Bringing the jelagest in close to his chest, he took hold of the disc with his left hand and turned the dial on its surface with his right.

All those still floating fell. Belac twisted in the air like a thrown cat and landed on his hands and knees. Though the fall had been frightening, the impact was almost imperceptible. Gradually, he felt pressure return to his body. While the sensation was unpleasant, he found it reassuring as well. It felt like a blanket of reality was being draped over him.

"Why..." Belac began to ask, but he still could not hear himself speak.

Breana stormed toward the wizard, yelling at him silently. She stopped in front of him, pointing aggressively as she continued to berate him.

Serath raised an eyebrow at her.

Wait... Can he hear her?

Breana moved to strike the wizard, but then everyone began to float again. Everyone other than the wizard. Breana attempted to punch him, but all she accomplished was causing herself to slowly turn in the air. She screamed silently and tried to kick the wizard in the face.

Serath waited patiently.

Breana crossed her arms under her breast and smoldered as she continued to rotate in the air. Finally, she said something that no one could hear, and then everyone was lowered to the floor again.

Thirty-Six

The air in the chamber smelled of cooking tree sap.

Rolan chuckled. "It's not my fault you picked a fight with a wizard."

Breana glared at the dwarf and then went back to rearranging her tools. Loudly.

In retrospect, Belac thought that the jelagest had been fun. He wondered if it could do anything else. *Maybe I can get Serath to let me play with it later.* A sharp cracking sound at the forge sent Belac leaping away. He turned around as he landed, and then he stumbled backward away from the awakening forge. He had expected to see hot lava pouring out of the hollowed log, but while the wood had split, the lava continued to flow through the tube inside.

Belac pointed at the log. "It's broken!" Dark sap seeped from the wood.

Rolan waved his hand in a dramatically dismissive manner. "It's fine," he said, drawing out the words.

Belac glanced at the dwarf before looking back to the log again. The log was smoking. "It does not look fine, Rolan!" Flames began to crawl over the log.

Rolan gave the dramatic gesture again. "It's fine." He seemed to be enjoying the elf's distress.

Belac threw his hands up over his head in frustration and then pointed at the burning log emphatically. "It's on fire!" Ashy smoke twisted in the air as it was sucked up into the shaft on the ceiling. Belac held his hands out to his sides. "Am I the only one who sees this?!"

Vairug walked over to the dwarf and pointed toward the now blazing log. "I think your forge might be on fire," he said dryly.

Rolan nodded as if in deep contemplation. "You know? I think you might be right." He turned to the giantess. "Hey, Breana. Do you think the forge is on fire?"

Breana slammed a pair of tongs down on her workbench.

Rolan chuckled.

Belac began to calm down. He pointed at the fire. "So, I guess it is supposed to do that?"

Rolan nodded, his gray eyes twinkling. "The log will burn off, but the tube it helped make will hold up. Once the wood falls off, we can put the fire out."

Belac did not understand why the dwarf had not simply used something that would not catch on fire. "Why not put out the fire now? There is a barrel of water right over there." He pointed toward the row of barrels near the giantess's workbench.

Rolan shook his head. "We don't want to risk any quick temperature changes. Besides, it would just catch on fire again."

The burn time concerned Belac. *I thought we were kind of in a hurry here.* "Won't that take too long?"

Rolan shook his head again. "What's left of the log will fall away soon." He sounded confident.

"How do..." Belac began, but was interrupted by a chunk of burning wood breaking away from the side of the log. Embers scattered across the stone floor where it fell.

Rolan gestured for the elf to follow him. "Come on. I've got a job for you."

Belac followed, though trepidly. *I don't think I want a job.* Rolan walked over to a small barrel standing next to the wall to the left of the forge. He slammed his fist down on one side of the barrel's lid, causing the other side to pop up. He ripped the lid off and tossed it to the side.

The inside of the barrel had been filled with a powdery white dirt. Rolan ran his fingers through the dirt until he located something buried underneath. He pulled out a thin metal scoop and then shook it off before handing it to Belac.

Rolan brushed his hands off on the sides of his splotchy gray trousers and then pointed a hand at the fire. "Wait until all the wood falls off, and then start shoveling."

Belac looked from the fire to the dwarf. "What are you going to be doing?" *Dwarves have got to be better at shoveling than elves.*

"I am going to make the wood fall off faster," Rolan said before turning away from the elf and the fire.

Rolan walked over to the giantess and her workbench. He nudged Breana's thigh and then raised his arm above his head, pointing to something on the workbench. While the dwarf was tall enough to see over the top of the workbench, he would have had difficulty reaching anything too far back.

Rolan said something to the giantess, but Belac could not make out what it was.

Breana handed the dwarf what he had asked for without answering him.

Rolan returned to the forge with a long, hooked rod and a pair of tongs. Using the tools, he stripped the burning log away from the rough tube of flowing lava. Belac had expected the tube to be glowing, but the brownish black stone was dull.

When Rolan was finished, he stepped away and pointed his hand at the pile of burning wood on the floor. "All right. Go ahead and put it out."

Belac began scooping the powdery white dirt onto the flames. The resulting clouds of dust made him sneeze and left a chalky taste in the back of his throat. He continued to throw dirt until the fire was extinguished and then he backed away coughing.

Rolan furrowed his brow. "You didn't breathe in any of the powdery stuff, did you?"

Belac fought to control his coughing. "What?!"

Rolan shook his head. "Ooh. That could be bad."

Belac stared at the dwarf wide eyed. "What?!" *Am I poisoned again?!* "Why didn't you warn me?!"

Rolan chuckled.

Belac narrowed his eyes at the dwarf. Then he sneezed again.

Rolan clapped the elf on the shoulder. "You're fine." He turned toward the giantess and raised his voice. "The forge is ready."

Breana ignored the dwarf.

Rolan walked over to the giantess's workbench and set her tools on the edge. She picked the tools up and moved them back to their proper place without saying anything. Wanting to escape the settling dust, Belac stepped over to the other side of the chamber. It brought him closer to the angry giantess, but he did not think that she would hurt him. *At least, not until after she kills Rolan.*

Rolan took a step away from Breana and held out the thumb and forefinger of both of his hands like he was aligning a picture frame. He made a show of moving around and inspecting the giantess.

Unable to continue ignoring the dwarf, Breana turned her head and demanded, "What are you doing?"

Rolan grinned. "I am trying to figure out which one of your ribs will make you laugh the most."

Breana grinned also, though it was obvious that she did not want to. "Don't you do it, Rolan." She was already struggling not to laugh.

Looking through his fingers, Rolan continued to circle the giantess with his hands held out in front of himself. "I think I found it."

Breana spun around and pointed at the dwarf. "Don't!" Her smile was the brightest thing in the chamber.

Serath interrupted their game. "We should begin to forge the sword."

Breana frowned at the wizard, but then nodded. She looked back to Rolan and pointed at the dwarf again threateningly. Rolan held up his hands in surrender and backed away, but the grin on his face did not look like one of defeat.

Breana donned a thick leather apron before picking up a pair of tongs and a hammer. She used the tongs to lift the white ingot of starmetal, and then stepped over to the volcanic forge. "You still have not explained how this will work," she complained.

Serath moved to the forge and stood to the giantess's left side. The surface of the lava was black and crusted with glowing cracks of deep orange warmth. Bright molten rock poured over the lip on the right side and fell down into the channeled sink.

Serath indicated with his left hand to the basin of lava. "Hold the metal over the lava to heat it." He gestured to the lava pouring over the side. "Hold it over the sink if you need it to cool." He looked up into the giantess's face. "You will need to communicate with me. Let me know when the metal is hot enough or when it has cooled to your liking. The metal will remain at a constant temperature until you request otherwise."

Breana nodded her understanding. "What about when I need only part of the metal to be heated?"

Serath's nod was one of approval. "Simply explain to me what you require. Remember however, that what we are doing is not natural, and that adjustments will need to be made."

Breana gazed at the forge thoughtfully. "I am about to forge magic." Deep emotions of fear, wonder, and resolve colored her words.

"You are about to forge legend," Serath amended encouragingly.

Breana forced herself to smile. Even false, it was beautiful. "Then, let's kill a dragon." She held the ingot over the lava.

Belac watched the giantess work for a while, but it was considerably less interesting than he had anticipated. He had expected fire and sparks as the metal yielded to Breana's hammer. Instead, the giantess took her time getting the ingot to just the right shade of glowing orange before proceeding to slowly shape the metal. Despite the power of Breana's strikes, it quickly became obvious that Belac would not be getting his sword any time soon.

Rolan stood by, waiting in case he was needed. Vairug's attention was far less casual. He watched every movement, every strike, as if each element were deserving of being witnessed. *Maybe it's an orc thing.* While Belac would admit that the forging of a magic sword might be a historic event, he found it oppressively boring.

The elf walked to where his scabbarded sword leaned against the wall. He took the sword in hand and then sat down where it had rested. The scabbard slid from the blade as he pulled his sword free. Setting the scabbard aside, Belac stared at the weapon that had served him so well. *It is a shame this thing is called a 'bastard-sword.'* He held the sword out in front of himself. *I guess I could call it a 'hand-and-a-half sword,' but that is a really awkward name.* He pulled the sword back in and gazed at the center of the cross-guard. *It's my sword. I should be able to call it whatever I want.* He smiled at his conclusion.

Belac stood and walked over to the forge. "Hey, Rolan. Do you have anything I can use to clean and sharpen my dwarf-sword?"

Rolan turned away from the forge. "Your what?"

Belac smiled and held his sword up between them. "My dwarf-sword."

Rolan did not say anything.

Belac moved his sword to the side so that he could lean in as if sharing a secret. "It's crazy lethal," he could barely keep himself from laughing, "but it is also definitely short."

Rolan closed his eyes and shook his head.

Belac continued, "And, no one can really argue if you call it a..."

"All right," Rolan chuckled. "I get it."

"It's a dwarf-sword," Belac insisted happily.

Rolan grinned. "You know, there are going to be dwarves that don't think that name is funny."

Belac laughed a little bit. "Then, I guess we don't have to call them dwarves."

Thirty-Seven

It's like a campfire in reverse. Belac held his hand out to the luminous glass flower. Though the white mist effusing from the open petals was dry, it was so cold that it felt like it seeped into his bones. He took his hand away and sat back on his crossed legs. *It is a shame not all magic is that pretty.* The arcane flower's clean blue elegance pulled at his emotions. His mind's eye looked past the magic of the flower and recalled a blue that had enchanted him more. The elf gazed into light and magic, but what he saw were eyes that could have been the sky.

"You look like you are trying to move that thing with your mind," Rolan commented.

Belac had not been aware of the dwarf's approach. "I miss her," he said without looking away from the glass flower.

"Who?" Rolan seemed genuinely confused. "The woman from the infirmary?"

Belac shook his head. "Emily."

"You knew her for less than half a day." Rolan scoffed. "I have had hangovers that lasted longer than that."

Belac turned his head to look at the dwarf. "She was special, Rolan." Her eyes still haunted him. "There was something about her." He returned his gaze to the flower. "It wasn't even that she was a princess." He did not know how to explain.

"I am not sure that she was a princess," Rolan disclosed casually.

Belac looked back to the dwarf. "Why do you say that?"

"Daikon." Rolan dropped the name without explaining its significance.

Belac remembered the sound of the man's screams as he had burned to death in a back alley. "What does Daikon have to do with Emily?"

"Part of my dealings with Daikon was for information on Emily," Rolan explained. "He said that no one is missing a princess."

Belac frowned. "Why would you trust him?"

Rolan nodded, acknowledging that he should expound. "Daikon was an information broker. He used to be a spy. If someone had lost a princess, he would have known about it."

"He could have lied," Belac said incredulously. *I can't believe I need to explain this!* "Daikon was the most fake person I have ever met."

Rolan shrugged. "That is what a spy is." He shook his head. "I don't believe what he said because I think he was honest. I believe what he said because I think he was smart." He tapped the side of his head and then continued, "If he had wanted to lie, he would not have told me that he knew nothing. He would have made something up to mislead me while still sounding plausible. He would have known that if he told me nothing, I would just keep investigating."

Rolan gave the elf a moment to process before explaining further. "A lot of people think they are smart just because they lie. It makes them feel like they have power over other people. They either degrade the victim and say that they fooled them, or they glorify themselves and say that they outsmarted them. But lying does not make you smart. It just makes you dishonest. A smart liar will tell lies that serve multiple agendas all at once; and the lies will be so grounded in truth, that it is all but impossible to prove they are lies."

Rolan waited again before finishing, "Daikon was a smart liar." Under his breath, he muttered, "The man could have been a politician."

Belac considered the dwarf's words. *I guess he knew Daikon better than I did.* He thought back to the time he had spent in the man's captivity. "He is dead, right?"

Rolan gave a deep belly laugh before answering in a serious tone, "Yes."

Belac recalled the magic potions that the man had forced him to drink. "Are you sure?"

Rolan nodded. "I mailed his skull to someone."

Yeah… Okay, that's pretty dead. Belac nodded his head. "Good to know." He frowned as a question came to him. "But… Why would Emily lie?"

"She was prisoner to a nillanan, Belac." Rolan said as if the answer should be obvious. "If I thought it would get me away from a nillanan, I would tell you I was a princess."

Belac pictured the dwarf in a pink dress wearing a tiara. He grinned. "Would you…"

"Rolan," Breana interrupted. "I have finished shaping the blade. We are going to need the kiln set up."

The appearance of the blade she held left Belac uninspired. "That does not look finished to me."

"She knows what she is doing," Rolan said offhandedly before raising his voice. "Vairug, help me move the kiln."

Breana communicated with the wizard using short terse phrases while Rolan and Vairug walked over to the kiln. Rolan positioned himself on one side of the long metal oven and waved the orc to the other. Vairug squatted down and took hold of his side of the kiln then waited for the dwarf to call time.

Rolan nodded to the orc. "Three, two, one, up."

Vairug and Rolan lifted the kiln together, but then each needed to adjust their hold to account for the other. The orc was able to stop with the long kiln held at shoulder height, but the dwarf was forced to lift his own side up above his head.

After waiting a brief moment to be sure that they each had control over their own end, they carried the kiln over to the forge and lowered it onto the top.

"We need to rotate it a bit," Rolan instructed as they aligned the metal oven with the volcanic forge.

Once he was satisfied with the alignment, Rolan swung open a small door on the side of the kiln. Breana slid the unfinished sword inside and then Rolan shut the door.

Breana stepped away and began to remove her blacksmith apron. "The next part will depend on him." She nodded toward the wizard.

Serath, already seeming to be preoccupied with his task, took a seat on the floor and crossed his legs under himself. He rested his forearms in his lap and closed his eyes.

Breana continued to stare at the silent wizard. "With what he can do, he could be the greatest smith the world has ever seen." She added no scorn to the word 'smith.'

There was a curious note of judgment in Vairug's response. "As long as he has someone else to swing the hammer for him."

Rolan frowned at the orc. "That's not fair, Vairug."

Vairug turned to look at the dwarf directly. "Is it not?" he asked, refusing to back down.

Rolan's frown deepened. "Things are more complicated than you want them to be."

"No," Vairug slowly shook his head in denial. "People make them complicated to justify their own actions."

Belac thought that they were probably both right. Which, in his mind, made for a strange argument. He grinned, remembering something Vairug had once said.

Belac leaned toward the dwarf while looking at the orc. "I bet you won't hit him," he said loud enough for them to both hear.

Rolan scowled at the elf, but Vairug smiled.

Thirty-Eight

Serath rose to his feet almost as if lifted by an outside force. The motion was so fluid that the others would not have even noticed it if not for its speed. His eyes snaped open and he spoke in a commanding voice. "You need to leave."

Belac climbed to his feet. "What? Why?"

"If you stay, you will die." There was no argument in Serath's demeanor. "Breana, get the sword."

Breana was already putting on her leather apron. "We cannot forgo the quench."

Serath nodded toward the kiln. "Both the blank and the sword are prepared."

Breana turned to her workbench and picked up a short, metal crook by its wooden handle. "Rolan, open the kiln." She tossed the metal crook to the dwarf.

Rolan caught the crook and then marched to the kiln expediently. He used the metal crook to hook the oven's door and swing it open "It's open," he called out to the giantess.

Carrying a pair of long-handled tongs, Breana stepped over to the kiln. Rolan held the small door open as Breana reached inside with her tongs. With a smooth motion, she slid a thick bar of glowing steel from the kiln, angling it out in front of her vertically. The metal was so hot that its glow shown pink on the giantess.

"Stand back," Breana ordered as she carried the glowing bar toward the row of barrels.

Belac promptly hopped out of the way. He did not want that burning bar of steel anywhere near him. Breana, holding the bar as far away from herself as she could, raised the glowing metal above a tall, narrow barrel. Fire shot up as she lowered the steel into the barrel. Belac backed farther away.

Breana briefly stirred the contents of the barrel with the steel bar before lifting the dull metal out. She dropped the cooled steel to the side and then returned to the kiln. Rolan held the door open for her again, and her tongs reached inside. With another smooth motion, Breana pulled the sword from the kiln and held it out in front of herself vertically. The starmetal glowed an orange so bright that it was almost yellow, but its emanations still bathed the giantess in pink light.

Breana's caution was noticeably greater as she carried the glowing sword to the barrel of oil. She plunged the blade into the preheated oil and fire shot up to the ceiling once more. After determining that the blade had sufficiently cooled, Breana lifted the sword up and began to inspect the blade. The end that had been held above the oil continued to glow a deep red, but she did not attempt to cool it.

Using her tongs to angle the sword, Breana checked her work. "Serath." She spoke to get the wizard's attention. "I will need you to remove the heat from the tang."

Serath gestured to the kiln. "Bring the sword back to the forge."

Breana hurried over to the wizard and held the sword next to the kiln. "Will this be close enough?"

Serath stepped around the forge to get a better view. "Yes." The glowing metal dulled. He looked into the insane rings of the giantess's eyes. "Now, you need to go."

Breana gave the wizard a single nod of acknowledgement and then turned away. She laid the starmetal sword on her workbench and then began to remove her apron.

Rolan, his rucksack already strapped to his back, pointed his hand at the scabbarded sword leaning against the wall. "Belac, grab your sword."

Belac looked away from the giantess and rushed to do as he was told. Breana wrapped the newly forged sword in her blacksmith apron as she moved toward the tunnel's mouth. Everyone hurried to follow her to the exit. Everyone except the wizard.

Belac turned back to the forge. "Serath, let's go!"

Serath was staring down at the floor as if he could see through the rock. "Go!" he commanded without looking away.

Rolan took hold of the elf's belt and jerked him back. "Move!" he ordered, pushing the elf into the tunnel.

The ground shook under their feet. Belac stumbled but Rolan grabbed his belt again and kept the elf from falling. The entire mountain rumbled around them as unseen forces shifted below them. Once the shaking had subsided, they scrambled the rest of the way through the tunnel. Belac was ready to sprint when they reached the mine's primary. *I am getting out of here!*

"Do not run," Rolan ordered. "If there is another quake, you could fall and break something. Move with purpose, but keep your footing."

Belac looked to the dwarf. "Do you think it's Agadon? I mean, you know, the dragon one."

"There is no dragon," Rolan replied irritably.

The mountain shook again, this time with a violence that threw all four to the ground and then battered against them. The shaking settled into a low, persistent tremor, while the rumble of rock became a storm of sound. Lamps swung on their fixtures, waving light that added to the disorientation. *How are the lamps still burning?* Belac quickly decided that he had more important things to worry about. He crawled to his hands and knees and tried to maintain his balance on the shaky ground. It reminded him of being on the back of a moving wagon. A hand reached under his arm. Breana pulled Belac to his feet while Rolan picked up the elf's scabbarded sword.

Vairug was bleeding from a cut above his left eyebrow. "We cannot stay here!" He began to stumble toward the mine's exit.

Shambling through the tunnel, they rushed toward a black night that had been turned red. The roar of the volcano intensified as they stepped into the salty air outside. Lava flowed down the side of the mountain in hot rivers that lit the night. The sailors were gone. So too were the wagon and the horses. Belac stared at the place where salvation was meant to be waiting, and realized that his chance of escape could be gone as well.

Rolan growled angrily.

"The cowards," Breana said as if unable to believe the depth of the sailors' cravenness.

Vairug was less surprised by the men's desertion. "If they hurt those horses…" he left the threat unfinished.

Belac looked up at the lava spraying into the sky and pouring down the mountain. "I am not worried about the horses, Vairug! I am worried about us!"

Rolan handed the elf his scabbarded sword. "Now, we have to run." He waved for the others to follow him and then he set the pace.

Belac hurried after, more than willing to run from the volcano. *Rolan runs fast for a dwarf.* He glanced over his shoulder at the volcanic mountain raging above them. *Maybe that has something to do with the volcano spraying liquid death into the air like it is trying to set the sky on fire.*

Humid ocean air blew toward them as they ran down the dirt road. To Belac, it felt like the volcano was drawing in breath so that it could roar louder. He now found it easier to understand how a people could mistake a volcano for a dragon. Fire and death, and a fury that would scar the memory of a civilization, Agadon raged in the night.

Belac's endurance began to falter before the relative safety of the ocean could be reached. However, had rising panic not spurred his heart to beat faster, the distance would have proven far less daunting. The road from the mine came to an end at the main road to and from Cavasca.

On the other side lay a dark grassy hill that bordered a rocky shore. Beyond the rocks, waited the ocean and escape. When they crossed the main road, Belac felt his fear begin to relent. Though completely irrational, the road became a perceived barrier between him and the molten lava flowing down the mountain.

Rolan brought everyone to a halt. "Take out your lights. Don't run down the hill."

The dwarf reached into a pouch and took out two light rods. He struck them against each other and then handed one to Breana. Belac and Vairug both dug into their own belt pouches and retrieved a light rod. Vairug struck his light rod against his metal hand, while Belac used the cross-guard of his sword.

Securing their lights as they walked, they continued down the grassy hill and toward a shimmering sea. Black water lit by the radiance of the volcano, the ocean was a peaceful reflection of the chaos behind them. The lights of lanterns shown from a lonely ship waiting beyond the rocky shore ahead. Though the roaring of Agadon persisted, optimism beckoned as Belac neared the waterline.

Rolan growled angrily when they finally arrived at the shore.

Breana pointed at the empty rowboat waiting there. "Are all of your men cowards?" she asked critically.

Rolan marched toward the solitary rowboat. "It seems so." His voice made it clear that there would be a reckoning.

Belac was happy to find a boat. "What's the problem?"

Rolan began to push the boat away from the shore. "There are supposed to be two boats waiting with men to row them." He vaulted into the rowboat as it began to float away.

Breana leapt from the shore into the boat, sending it rocking from side to side. Belac and Vairug hurried into the water, each taking hold of a different side of the boat. Belac tossed his dwarf-sword into the boat and then climbed up after it. Vairug used the elf's weight to help balance the boat while he lifted himself abord.

Belac left his sword lying on the bottom of the boat. "What about Serath?"

Rolan began to row the boat away from the shore. "He will be fine."

Belac gestured to the lava gushing out of the volcano and pouring over the city. "How is that fine?"

Rolan shook his head and continued to row without arguing.

Belac leaned to the side so that he could see around the giantess. He held his hand out toward the ship. "How is he…" The sails of the ship unfurled. Belac rose up in his seat, careful to keep his balance. He pointed to the ship. "Is it just me? Or is that ship moving?"

Rolan glanced behind himself and then growled angrily.

Breana motioned to the dwarf. "Trade seats with me."

Rolan moved the oars into the boat and then shuffled around the giantess as they traded positions. Breana took up the oars and began rowing with fierce determination. The rowboat's change in speed was noticeable. Even after swinging a hammer all day, Breana was still able to row tirelessly. Belac did not know if it was the constitution of giants, or if Breana's will was simply indomitable.

Belac picked up his scabbarded sword and strapped it to his back as they approached the rear of the ship. It was obvious now that the ship was moving. Though, with the wind against them, and the air being pulled in toward the volcano, the ship was sailing slowly.

Rolan passed the leather wrapped, starmetal sword to the elf. "Tuck this into my pack."

"I don't think it is going to fit," Belac said, taking the rolled bundle.

Rolan's focus was already on the deck of the ship. "Just stuff it in there as best you can."

Belac stowed the sword, but he worried that if the dwarf were not careful, the blade would fall into the sea. *I can't think of a better way to get it on board the ship though.* He clapped the dwarf on the shoulder. "It's in."

Rolan nodded and then stood, easily keeping his balance as the giantess rowed.

A finger tapping on Belac's shoulder prompted him to turn and face the orc. "What?"

Vairug pointed toward the shore without answering.

Belac looked past the orc and saw Serath running across the surface of the ocean. Lava hit the waterline behind him, and clouds of steam billowed up into the air. The fires of Agadon shown through the mist in a diffuse light that made the night glow. The wizard sprinted over the water, gaining on the ship.

Belac stared at the black silhouette. "I, ah… forgot he could do that."

Rolan issued directions to the giantess. "Angle us a little more to the left."

As soon as they were close enough, Rolan grabbed a rope ladder on the side of the ship and began to pull himself up. Belac did not wait. He leapt onto the ladder and followed after the dwarf. *If he has to fight to take back the ship, I do not want him to have to do it alone.* When Rolan climbed onto the deck above him, Belac expected to hear shouts and the sound of men dying. However, no alarms were cried out into the night.

Unassured by the quiet reception, Belac hurried up after the dwarf. The sailors on deck stood back as if afraid to act in any way. Rolan was already marching toward the bridge. Looking from the dwarf to the volcano, the frightened men tried to gauge the greater threat. Belac moved slowly toward the bridge, worried that he might disrupt the indecision.

As the dwarf marched onto the bridge, a thin man with an eyepatch held out his hands and stammered, "Rolan…" He gestured to the volcano. "You…"

Rolan pushed the man back. The man waved his arms to keep his balance and then retreated until he was stopped by the ships railing. Rolan pushed the man again, this time dragging a knife across the back of the man's knee as he toppled backward over the railing. The hamstrung man screamed as he fell into darkness.

Still holding the knife, Rolan turned around and shouted, "Don't just stand there! Get this ship moving!"

To a man, the sailors resumed their work. Both of their fears were now aligned, and they welcomed the opportunity to both flee and obey. With renewed vigor, the men proceeded to sail the ship as if the attempted mutiny had never occurred.

Belac turned back to the rope ladder. Vairug was already on board and Breana was crawling over the edge. Belac leaned over the railing and discovered Serath climbing up behind the giantess. Belac grinned. *I think I deserve a bottle of wine for every one of us that is not dead.*

The elf looked away from his friends and gazed out at the city. He watched the buildings being swallowed by rivers of lava. He was now far enough away that he could acknowledge a certain beauty in what he saw. Belac stared at what he had escaped, and decided that it was worthy of legend. In the end, the destruction of Cavasca could not have been more complete had Agadon been a dragon in truth.

Thirty-Nine

"Look at me, Kegs." Belac felt like he was scolding a child. "Just tell me where it is." *It is too early in the morning for this.*

Kegs would not look up from his feet. "It wasn't my fault."

"What was not your fault?" Belac was fairly certain that it was going to be the man's fault.

Though standing on the deck of a moving ship, Kegs behaved like a man trapped in a cage. "They said it was too dangerous."

Belac took a deep breath of salty air to calm his growing frustration. "And why would they think that?" *I bet I can guess.*

"They figured it out!" Kegs whispered as if surprised by the development.

Belac ground his teeth and continued to stare at the man.

Kegs began to speak faster. "It was Dringle." The man nodded as he betrayed his comrade. "He took one look at it, and he knew!" He scanned the deck around them and then lowered his voice. "Said he recognized the shapes."

Belac swept his gaze over the other sailors on deck. Though they were keeping their distance, Belac knew that some would be listening. He also knew that Kegs was lying. *I know he is lying, because I was lying!* Belac glared at the man.

"I told him not to say nothing!" Kegs insisted defensively. "I said, you better not." He nodded as if remembering an actual event. "You better not..."

Belac held up a hand to stop the narrative. He could not take much more of the man's lies. "What did you do, Kegs?"

"It wasn't me!" Kegs was quick to reiterate. "It was Dringle what told everybody." He shook his head. "I said, you better not."

Belac closed his eyes and pinched the bridge of his nose. "Kegs." He opened his azure eyes and stared at the man. "Where is my bag?"

Kegs looked down at his feet again. "They threw it off the docks." He looked up pleadingly. "We was going to leave it sitting on the pier, but we did not want someone to find it and open it up unawares."

"You threw it in the ocean?!" Belac shouted.

The other sailors on deck suddenly found things that needed to be done farther away from the elf.

Kegs continued to plead. "It wasn't me! I swear it! I said, you better not, you better not."

Belac pointed away from himself forcefully. He wanted to strangle the man. However, a small part of him was amused by his own miscalculation. It tickled at the back of his mind and threatened to subvert his anger. Then he thought about all of the precious wine that had been lost, both his and the troves undiscovered. *That sword had better be worth it!*

Kegs fled from the elf. Had Belac possessed even a single bottle of wine, he would have thrown it at the man.

A diabolical thought came to Belac. "Kegs!" he called after the man.

Kegs halted and then turned around slowly like a hound that feared it would be struck.

Belac kept his voice raised. "There was a cache of gold hidden in that bag." He waited until he was sure they had an audience. "That's why it was trapped."

The other sailors began finding reasons to move closer.

Belac continued, "That gold was the crews' bonus for having to face a volcano."

Some of the sailors began to mutter angrily among themselves.

Belac concluded, "You threw away your own fortune."

Kegs looked like his heart had just stopped beating.

Belac turned away and walked below deck, leaving Kegs to explain to his fellows why he had thrown their gold into the harbor. *Now it's time to see this sword that we all almost died for.*

Belac made his way to the hold of the ship. In place of the cargo routinely stored there, Rolan and Breana had set up a workshop. Though storage crates were still present, most of them had been pushed aside to make room for the workspaces. Tall workbenches on the right and short workbenches on the left, it was obvious what space belonged to whom. Past the workbenches, a giant-sized rectangular tent had been set up against the back bulkhead. Loud grinding sounds came from behind the yellowy white cloth of the tent.

Belac studied the tent. To him, it seemed like a rather odd thing to find in the belly of a ship. *I wonder if they are trying to keep the sword secret…* It did not make any sense to him. *Everyone knows why we went to Cavasca. Why would they want to keep it secret now?*

Belac walked over to the tent and pulled back the flap. Rolan was faced away from the opening, pedaling a stone grinding wheel while Breana worked the starmetal blade across it. Both of them had off-white linen scarves wrapped around the lower half of their faces. Breana took the blade away from the grinder and nodded toward Belac. Rolan stopped pedaling and then turned around to see who had entered. Finding Belac, Rolan walked over to the elf and pushed him out of the tent. Though gentle, the dwarf was firm in his direction.

Once outside the tent, Rolan removed the scarf from his nose and mouth. "Don't go in there. The dust from the starmetal will tear up your lungs."

That sounded awful to Belac. "It does not get in your eyes?"

Rolan shook his head. "Eyes don't pull in air." He shrugged. "As long as we flush them every once and a while, it's not so bad."

Belac pointed up. "Why not just do this on deck? It is breezy enough up there to keep the air clean."

Rolan shook his head again, this time with more feeling. "Starmetal is more valuable than gold. It's… It's priceless. We need to be able to re-collect as much of it as we can."

Belac glanced toward the dwarf's side of the workshop. "What are you going to do with it?" He did not see any evidence of the forementioned metal.

The sound of metal rasping began to come from the tent behind Rolan. "We don't have any plans for it yet," he admitted. "But we know it can be used to make magical items."

Belac nodded, returning his attention to the dwarf. "Do you think there will be enough to make another weapon?"

Rolan shook his head. "No. There is not going to be that much of it. We are not removing any more of the material from the blade than we have to."

That all made sense to Belac. "Can I see it?"

Rolan smiled. "You should probably let Breana finish it before you try to take it away from her." He chuckled softly.

Belac tried to not sound overly disappointed. "When will that be?"

Rolan shrugged. "We should have everything fit together sometime this afternoon. I will let you know when it is ready."

Belac nodded acceptingly. "Thanks, Rolan." He turned away to leave but then stopped and looked back. "Would you thank Breana for me?"

"Sure," Rolan acquiesced, "But you should remember to thank her yourself also."

"I will." Belac smiled. "Thanks again, Rolan." He walked away and allowed the dwarf to get back to work. *Now, what am I going to do?*

Belac walked back above deck, half hoping to find Kegs strapped upside down to the main mast. The duplicitous sailor was nowhere to be seen, but Serath was there. The wizard closed the door to the captain's quarters and then began walking toward Belac.

Holding up a hand in greeting, Belac said, "Hey, Serath."

Serath halted in front of the elf and smiled. "Hello, Belac."

Belac tucked a stray lock of hair behind one of his pointed ears. "Can I…" *Don't say, 'play with!'* "Borrow your jelly thing?"

Serath arced an eyebrow. "The jelagest?"

Belac nodded. "Yeah. That's the one."

Serath ran a gloved hand over the trimmed beard around his mouth. "You want me to let you play with an ancient, arcane device of untold power?"

Belac nodded agreeably. *I can't let him know I think this is a bad idea too.*

Serath smiled again. "And what would you do with such a thing? What would you do if you could bend even a small piece of reality to your will?"

Belac had to stop himself from frowning. *This feels like a trap.* "I just want to figure out what all I can make it do."

"Well," Serath's smile broadened, "Far be it from me to impede your curiosity." He reached into his hidden bag and then pulled out the jelagest. Holding the brass disc up at his shoulder, he spoke indulgently. "You will have to keep it below deck. I would not want you to drop it into the ocean."

Belac nodded his agreement and held out his hands.

Serath lowered the jelagest into the elf's hands and then released it. "I will come to collect it later."

Belac looked down at the brass disc in his hands. "How does it work?" He held it up to his ear and shook it.

"You said that you wanted to figure that out for yourself," Serath replied in a mildly patronizing tone.

Belac narrowed his eyes at the wizard. "You could just tell me."

Serath nodded seriously. "I could. But then, you would have no reason to study it." He held out a hand to accept the device's return.

Belac pulled the jelagest to his chest and turned slightly away. "I can do it."

Forty

Belac glared down at the obstinate device. "Do what I tell you!" he commanded, pointing at the brass disc threateningly.

Sitting cross-legged on his cot in the ship's brig, Belac had placed the jelagest directly in front of him. *Now, I know why Serath did not want me to do this above deck.* "He knew I would get mad," Belac pointed angrily at the jelagest, "And throw you in the ocean!"

He had tried spinning the dial on the disc's surface, pressing on the metal plate in the center, and even banging the disc against the wall. Belac could not get the jelagest to work. Begging had come next. He had held the brass disc up to his face and whispered to it as if something might be residing inside. However, nothing he had said could summon the magic of the jelagest.

Belac considered drawing his dagger and using it to pry apart the disc. *Maybe if I can see what's inside…* He shook his head. *It's not mine.* He wondered what would happen if he broke it. *It's magic. Anything could happen.* Even if it did not explode and kill him, Belac was pretty sure that Serath would be more than a little cross.

The markings across the surface of the disc confounded Belac. They looked unlike any language he had ever seen. It was almost as if the characters had been written on top of each other instead of out in a legible line. His slender finger traced the symbols. *Serath had to know that I would not be able to use this.* Belac snatched up the jelagest and hopped off the cot. *I think it's time to go have a talk with that wizard.*

The elf left the brig and then climbed the stairs up to the main deck. Sailors, made lethargic by the midday heat, lounged in the late afternoon sun. Belac scanned the deck for the wizard but did not find him there. In his search, he noticed that the door to the captain's quarters was open. *If Serath is not in there, then there is a sailor that needs his hands cut off.* Belac walked toward the open door, expecting to find the wizard, but prepared to confront a thief.

Serath turned away from the navigation table as the elf entered the room. "Hello, Belac."

Belac held up the jelagest. "How do I make this work?"

Serath smiled pleasantly. "I doubt that you can."

"Why wouldn't you tell me that?!" Belac almost threw the metal disc at the wizard.

Serath moderated his smile. "You said that you wanted to discover that for yourself."

Belac narrowed his eyes at the wizard. "Why won't it work?"

Serath held out his hand. "It will work." The jelagest slipped from the elf's fingers and flew into the wizard's palm. "It simply will not work for you."

Belac frowned. "Why not?"

Serath returned the brass disc to the bag that hung under his long black coat. "Because you, are not a wizard."

Belac wanted to argue, but before he could think of anything to say, Rolan walked into the room behind him. Belac stepped out of the dwarf's way while turning to look at him.

Rolan spoke briskly. "Good. You're both here. The sword is ready."

Belac grinned at the dwarf. "Where are you hiding it?"

Rolan ignored the attempted humor. "Breana wants to be there when you see it for the first time." He nodded to the door. "She has it down in the hold."

Belac rubbed his hands together in anticipation. He glanced back to the wizard. "Let's go."

Serath gestured politely for the others to lead.

Though Rolan wasted no time as he led them to the hold, the dwarf did not move fast enough for Belac. *I finally get to see my sword!* Belac had to stop himself from hopping up and down as he followed.

Oil lamps had been lit in the hold, giving it a warm atmosphere. The softly fluttering lights played against the bare skin of a smiling giantess. Belac wondered if Rolan had chosen that particular ship simply because the hold was large enough that Breana could stand comfortably. *Maybe he just didn't want to have to rebraid her hair every time she bumped her head on the ceiling.*

As attractive as the giantess was, what Belac really wanted to see was what she was holding hidden behind her back. "Is that my sword?!" he asked happily.

Unable to restrain herself any longer, Breana held the scabbarded starmetal sword out in front of herself horizontally. While she said nothing, Belac could almost hear her thinking, "Look what I made!"

It's my sword! A thick, black baldric had been wound loosely around the matching scabbard that housed the blade. More black leather wrapped the hilt, covering the gap between the gleaming steel of the cross-guard and pommel. Though symmetrical, the cross-guard resembled an aggressively clawed thumb and forefinger pinching the side of the scabbard. Belac took in the draconic cross-guard and the blood drop shaped pommel, the symbolism immediately apparent to him. *Blood of the dragon.*

Belac stepped forward and pointed at a thin leather strap that ran over the stylized cross-guard. "Does that keep the scabbard on?"

Breana nodded, handing the sword to the elf. "Rolan did that part." She sounded as proud of the dwarf as she was of the sword. "He crafted everything other than the blade itself."

Rolan grunted. "She means, I did the easy stuff."

Breana beamed down at the dwarf.

The sword was much lighter and shorter than Belac had expected. He fingered the thin leather strap, trying to figure out how to get the blade out of its scabbard.

Rolan reached over and tapped the side of the scabbard. "You have to thumb that snap there."

Belac unsnapped the leather strap and then moved it out of the way. "That is going to make drawing the sword a lot slower."

Rolan shook his head. "Not with practice," he assured the elf. "Besides, you don't need to draw the sword fast. You need to not lose it."

Belac frowned at the dwarf. "A sword is not much use in its scabbard."

Rolan sighed. "This is not something that you run around sword fighting with, Belac. It's a specialized tool with a very specific purpose. Mostly, you are just going to be carrying it on your back. When it comes time to kill the dragon, you are going to have plenty of time to get the blade out of its scabbard."

Belac drew the sword. The solid white blade slid from the black scabbard like the coming of dawn. A slim blade with a matt finish, its simple geometry felt elegant to the elf. Shorter than even his dwarf-sword, the starmetal blade was obviously intended to be wielded with a single hand. *The balance is not really all that much different than a rapier.* Belac's eyes traced from the tip of the blade, down to the arcane marking above the cross-guard. The sharp angles and sweeping lines of the mark would not allow his eyes to follow it. He could feel his mind twisting away from the shape as he attempted to bring it into focus.

Belac moved his gaze to the steel claws of the cross-guard. "I am holding a sword that can kill a dragon," he said, not quite believing it.

Serath refuted kindly, saying, "The sword is not yet prepared. It must still be cleansed in the Tears of The Dead before the ritual can be completed." He gestured to the starmetal sword. "That will not slay a dragon, such as it is."

Belac slid the blade back into its scabbard and then snapped the leather strap in place. "That can't be a real thing."

Serath laughed softly. "Oh, I can assure you it is."

Rolan interjected, "We can worry about that later." He stepped out in front of the elf. "Right now, we should," he put emphasis on the word, "appreciate," then he nodded meaningfully to the giantess behind himself, "that the sword has been forged."

Belac lowered his new sword and looked up at the giantess that had forged legend. "You have proven the honor of giants, Breana." He held the sword back up. "Together, we will slay a dragon."

Breana replied in Giant, her words sounding formal and slightly ceremonial.

Serath's rich voice carried approval. "That was well said, Belac."

Belac glanced around the workshop, realizing that someone was missing. "Has Vairug seen the sword?"

Smiling, Breana shook her head. "I thought you might like to show it to him."

The giantess's smile was so beautiful it almost made Belac forget what they were talking about. *Vairug.* Belac looked to the dwarf. "Do you know where he is?"

Rolan pointed up with his thumb. "He is on the bridge, learning how to sail the ship."

Belac moved his gaze to the giantess. He felt like he should say something more. *'Thank you,' is not enough.*

Breana seemed to understand. "Go," she said encouragingly. "Vairug deserves to see it also."

Belac nodded appreciatively. *I will have to think of a better way to thank her.* Then he turned and ran up the stairs leading out of the hold. Once on deck, he hurried to the short stairs that accessed the bridge.

Climbing the stairs, Belac called out, "Hey, Vairug!"

Vairug turned away from the sailor that he had been speaking with. Grinning around his tusks, he pointed to the sword the elf carried. "Is that Breana's masterpiece?"

Belac thumbed the snap on the side of the scabbard and drew the blade as he walked closer. The nearby sailor backed away quickly. Belac paid the man no mind. He held the sword out in front of himself, its tip pointed up to the sky. "Look at this thing!"

Vairug studied the sword for a moment before declaring, "That is a wicked looking weapon despite the softness of its pale blade."

Belac nodded his agreement. He slid the blade back into the scabbard and held it out in a horizontal display. "It still looks mean when its sheathed."

"I like how the cross-guard rides along the sides of the scabbard." Vairug pointed at the sword. "That should prevent it from snagging on anything." He reached out to take the sword from the elf.

Belac pulled the starmetal sword back. "I would let you hold it," he smiled mischievously, "but you said, you think swords are stupid."

Vairug's frown looked more like a smile.

Forty-One

Once Vairug had finished inspecting the starmetal sword, he had handed it back to Belac. Shortly after, Belac left the orc on the bridge and returned to his cell in the brig. He wanted to retrieve his dwarf-sword and see how his two swords would ride together on his back. The starmetal sword was short enough to be carried on the hip, but its baldric was obviously not designed to do so.

The dwarf-sword lay on Belac's cot as if being used to hold down his blanket. *That sword looks like it is taking a nap.* He kicked the cot to wake the sword up. *Lazy sword.* Belac shook out the starmetal sword's baldric and considered how best to carry it. *It has to go on my back.* His first thought was to wear the two swords crossed on his back, but he quickly found that the baldric had been cut and fixed to the scabbard to facilitate carry on the right shoulder.

The elf slipped the baldric over his head and began to adjust the strap. No matter how much he tried, he could not get the sword to ride high enough for him to draw it properly. *Rolan must have set it up like this on purpose.* Belac reminded himself that the sword was not meant to be used like a normal sword. *I am only supposed to use the sword to slay dragons.* He frowned. *And Serath says that it can't even do that yet.*

Belac picked up his dwarf-sword and strapped it onto his back parallel with the starmetal sword. The added weight of carrying two swords was noticeable, but Belac thought he could get used to it. *The starmetal sword does not really weigh all that much.* He decided that there was probably not a more comfortable way for him to carry the new sword. *Maybe I should get a valet or something.* He pictured a disgruntled young man following him around while carrying a barrel with a collection of swords sticking out of the top.

Belac sat down on the edge of his cot, careful to let the end of his dwarf-sword hang off the side. *I miss my wine.* His attention drifted wistfully around his cell. The starmetal sword on his back made him one of the richest people in the world. And he was sitting in a detention cell.

The elf slapped his hands on his thighs and stood. *There has got to be something more interesting happening somewhere else on this ship.* As Belac left the brig, he glanced back to the cell next to his own. *I hope Ezela and her sister got out of Cavasca safely.* He realized that he would probably never know. He thought of all the people he had met in the lost city of Cavasca. *I will never know what happened to them…*

Belac climbed up the steps to the main deck in search of something more distracting than melancholy. While most of the sailors were on deck, all of them seemed half asleep in the early evening light. *I thought sailors were all supposed to be addicted to gambling and rum.* Disappointed, Belac looked past the shamefully well behaved sailors, and to where Vairug stood at the bow of the ship. Gazing out into the endless sea, the orc appeared lost in thought.

Belac walked over to his friend and joined him in quiet contemplation. When Belac could bear the silence no more, he asked, "Are you as bored as I am?"

Vairug's grin showed his tusks. "Are you so accustomed to danger already?"

Belac frowned at the orc. "I didn't say, I wanted danger."

Vairug gestured to the waters ahead of them. "This. This is peace."

"No." Belac pointed. "That, is the ocean."

Vairug turned to face the elf. "Did you prefer what you found underground?"

Belac was quick to shake his head. "No. That place was awful, Vairug. I was not trapped down there with just the hobbs. There were hobgoblins, zombie-fish-monsters, a big toothy worm thing, and even a fat-troll."

Vairug grinned. "How did you evade the patrol?"

Belac was confused for a moment. *Fat-troll sounds like patrol.* "No." He made sure to enunciate, "A. Fat. Troll." He held his hands up and out. "It was this giant, red brown monster thing with big fat lips and no legs." He remembered the smell of its breath. "It tried to eat me!"

"And you killed it?" Vairug asked, tentatively impressed.

Belac nodded grimly. "I am not food."

Vairug laughed silently. "It sounds as if you waged war on the underground. How many hobgoblins did you slay?"

Belac thought back. "I don't know. There was kind of a lot of them in that village I destroyed."

Vairug stopped laughing. "You destroyed a hobgoblin village?"

Belac nodded. "Yeah. But I only had to fight three of the hobgoblins face to face. I don't know if the ones I set on fire count."

Now, Vairug seem confused. "You only fought three?"

Belac nodded again. "Yeah. And one of those, I did not give much of a chance to really fight back."

Vairug tilted his head to the side in growing confusion. "Then, who killed all the ones in the open field and the others in the passage where you were found?"

Belac frowned for a moment. "Oh! You mean the hobbs. Those evil little round ones." He shook his head. "I don't know how many of those I killed." He shrugged. "It was a lot of them." Then he added, "But those were pretty easy to kill. It was the hobgoblins that were really dangerous. They had these crazy dog heads and long, pointy claws. They were kind of skinny, but they were way stronger than you would expect."

"And you slew three of those creatures?" Vairug asked to assure he understood the facts.

Belac nodded his confirmation. "Unless you count the ones that died in the explosion."

Vairug grinned. "Those were elders."

Belac's brow furrowed. "I thought that they were hobgoblins."

Vairug nodded. "They were. An elder is far more dangerous, but they were all hobgoblins."

"The little ones too?" Belac was still confused. "I thought those were the hobbs."

Vairug shook his head while grinning. "They were all hobgoblins. 'Hobb' is just short for 'hobgoblin.' The smaller ones were the youths."

The youths? Belac suddenly felt like the world was falling away from him. *Youths.* He could see the horrible creatures in his mind. *Children.* He saw them cowering as he cut them down. *They were children.* He saw his blade fall on them as they tried to get away. *I killed children.* He saw the terror in their eyes as they looked up at him. *What have I done…* He could feel the righteousness of his hate. *No…* He could see the small bodies burning as their homes crumbled around them. *I killed children.* He could hear their happy laughter and the sounds of them dying. *I wanted to save the children…*

Forty-Two

Sitting on his cot, staring down at his hands, Belac saw himself killing children. His hands were wet from tears, though he did not remember crying. He did not even remember how he had gotten to his cell. He did remember the children.

Serath spoke as if from another world. "Hello, Belac."

There was a quality to the wizard's voice that cut through the elf's despair. Belac looked up, tears in his azure eyes. "I'm sorry." *I'm so sorry.*

Standing in the doorway to the elf's cell, Serath offered no judgment. "Should you be?"

Belac looked down. He could not meet the wizard's eyes. "You don't know what I have done…"

"That may be true," Serath stipulated. "But, do you know what you have done?"

Belac covered his eyes with the palms of his hands. "I killed children, Serath." The admission tore at his heart. His palms pressed harder into his eye sockets.

Still, there was no judgment in Serath's voice. "Is that the only thing that you have done?"

Belac looked up from his hands. "Have I done something worse?" *What could I have done? What could be worse?*

"Did you not also save children?" There was now a trace of kindness in Serath's words.

Belac shook his head, denying the justification. "But I killed so many…" His mind flashed on the bodies strewn through the gnomish corridor. He remembered how the blood pooling on the floor had stuck to the soles of his boots.

Serath's next question seemed heartless. "Would you trade the lives of the children you saved, to bring back the ones you murdered?"

Belac was appalled by the idea. "Of course not!" *Who would trade the lives of children?* He thought of Gwen sticking out her teeth and growling.

Serath leaned forward, his presence seeming to darken the cell. His green eyes shone bright as he willed the elf to look at them. "Then, consider, Belac. Consider what you have done. Consider the forces that drove you. Consider the consequences."

Serath's eyes seemed to burn into the elf as he continued. "Once you understand why you made your choice, ask yourself if you would make the same one again. If you would not, then dedicate your life to becoming someone who would choose differently." His words became darker. "But if you would do it again, if you understand that what you did was an awful, terrible thing…" the darkness of his words hardened, "That. Was. Necessary." The strength of his voice seemed to reach out and pull the elf closer as Serath concluded, "Then, become someone who can live with it."

Belac could not look away from the wizard. The weight of Serath's words felt like a physical thing. It was as if the air itself had become too heavy. Even after Serath straitened and left the cell, the wizard's presence seemed to linger. Belac did not know what terrible thing the wizard had done, but there was no doubt that it had made Serath who he was.

What about me? What will I become? Belac thought about how the hobbs had pulled Henry down and torn him to pieces next to his savaged son. Then he thought about Gwen covered in mud and clutching her pig protectively. *Would I let her die to spare them?* He knew he would not. Even as he asked himself the question, he knew he would not. He would have done anything to save that little girl. *But they were children…*

Belac struggled to conceive some alternative; a way to save the human children without slaughtering the others. He could think of no way. His only option had been whether or not to abandon the three children he had saved. In his mind, he saw Gwen rushing into her mother's arms. *I would do it again.* He closed his eyes, wishing it were not true. *I'm a monster.*

Panicked shouting pulled him from his private state of contrition. Belac looked up toward the cries of alarm coming from the main deck. Then came a roar so deep, the elf could feel it in his groin. He rushed out of his lamplit cell and sprinted to the shadowed stairs. He looked up at the stary sky waiting above and then began to ascend the steps. From the shadowy stairs he hurried into the glow of lamplight that lit the main deck. Every sailor there stared up into the sky on the starboard side. There, its leathery wings stretched wide, hovered a monster as large as the ship.

"…dragon."

"…gonna die!"

"It's The Danorin!"

"…kill us all!"

"We need to…"

With another deafening roar, fire illuminated the night. Bathed in the radiance of flame, the dragon's dreaded form took shape. Held aloft by massive wings, loomed a body of grandeur and might. A sinuous torso with four legs ending in taloned hands, its long tail balanced a serpentine neck. Blackish blue scales gleamed as inferno sprayed from the dragon's roaring maw. *No one kills a dragon.*

Below the raging dragon, a massive tentacle rose from the ocean in a spray of sea water. Black and slick, the monstrous appendage wrapped around the dragon's lower half and then pulled it down into the rippling depths. *What the...* The ocean churned as the dragon struggled beneath the dark surface of the underwater domain. *Is something trying to eat the dragon?!* Subaquatic light flared, revealing nothing of what transpired in the chaotic conflict. *What eats dragons?!*

A wave rocked the ship, and then violence slammed into the hull. Fragments of broken timber blasted into the sky above the captain's quarters. The stern of the ship lifted up, throwing Belac and the sailors to the deck. One of the men flipped over the railing and went flying off the ship with his arms and legs flailing. The ship settled, and then the stern began to sink.

Belac stumbled to his feet and ran toward the captain's quarters. He had no idea what he could do, but he would not just let the ship sink. The ocean churned around the sinking vessel, throwing sea water onto its sloping deck. As he neared the closed door to the captain's quarters, the stern of the ship began to right itself. The shouts of frightened sailors only grew louder.

Holding his arms outstretched in front of himself, Belac's palms collided with the door. Instead of the door flying open into the captain's quarters, the elf was bounced backward. Belac slapped the bolt open and then pushed his way inside. The interior of the cabin was a wreckage. Everything in the room had been thrown to the port side. Breana, partially buried in debris, groaned as Rolan lifted and shoved a broken crate off of her. Flames blazed among the piles of scattered furnishings, giving light to the disarray.

The back of the room to Belac's left was open to darkness and sea. He stared at the jagged rend in the side of the ship where the floor, walls, and ceiling had been torn away. Behind a rounded wall of distortion, a sphere of modulating force held back the ocean's water. *The jelagest?* From within the distorted field, Serath rose from below, hands held out to his sides, palms facing up. He glided toward the edge of the sphere, his long black coat gently fluttering in the air as if stirred by unseen currents. The growing flames of the wreckage showed a resolve on the wizard's face that caused Belac to take an involuntary step back.

Serath's booted feet landed on the floor of the cabin and then he stepped away from the jelagest's influence. He held his left hand out toward the flames and closed it into a fist. At his command, the fires died, plunging the room into shadows. He scanned the cabin, his green eyes bright in the darkness.

Belac pointed to the open door behind himself. "There's a dragon out there!"

"I am aware," Serath said as a matter of fact. Striding past the elf, he expounded, "Currently, it is being distracted by the kraken that has been trailing us."

Belac followed the wizard out onto the deck. "A kraken?!" He was forced to shout over the frantic sailors. "You mean a giant squid monster?!" *Why would a giant squid monster want to protect us?*

"We need to take advantage of the conflict." Serath halted behind the main mast. He turned his left shoulder toward the sail and raised his right arm into the air, his gloved hand reaching up into the sky as if he was attempting to claim the heavens.

A breeze caught in the sails, drawing Belac's attention up. Dark clouds began to shut out the stars. Then thunder struck as lightning flashed through the gathering storm. The breeze became a wind that filled the sails and moved the ship. Lightning crashed down into the ocean, the concussion violent enough to be felt in the air. The wind continued to increase.

In the aftermath of lightning, only scattered oil lamps held back the blackness of the night. The gaze of every sailor fell on the wizard as they realized it was he who called the storm. Still, the wind continued to increase.

Belac stumbled against the wind, his long hair whipping to the side. Something wooden cracked loudly. Still, the wind continued to increase. *There is no way the ship was designed for this!*

Belac turned away from the wizard and shouted over the wind, "Get ropes on the mast! He pointed up to the billowing sail. "We need to tie that down!"

Some of the sailors nearest to the elf began to relay orders to their fellows, but one of the men stood paralyzed, staring up at the storm filled skies.

Belac grabbed the man and slapped him. "Ropes!" he yelled into the man's face.

The man nodded and replied, though the howling of the wind carried away his words.

Belac released the man and then clapped him on his shoulder. "Go!"

Flashes of lightning fell into the water around the ship, providing more illumination than the sailor's lamps. Belac stared out into the sea. *It looks like the whole ocean is a storm.* In the distance, he saw three tornadoes dancing in a circle as the storm continued to grow. Between black waters and dark clouds, the world was chaos and fury.

Belac turned back to the mast. The sailors had already begun securing lines; tying ropes to the mast and boom in an effort to help brace against the gale winds. Though the wind no longer felt like it was increasing, the speed of the ship continued to accelerate. As the sailors tied off to the railing and anything else they could find, Belac worried that the sails themselves might rip.

Unmoving, Serath seemed unconcerned with the ship or the hazards of the storm. As he stood in place, the world raged around him as if he were the focal point of reality. His will had brought the storm. He would not bend to it now.

Forty-Three

A metal hand grabbed Belac's arm and turned him around to face a gray skinned orc. Lightning flashed around them as if the storm were lashing out at the man who had dared to summon it. Howling wind tugged at their clothing and hair as the ship continued to accelerate.

Vairug let go of the elf's arm and pointed a gray hand at the wizard. "What is he doing?" he shouted over the wind.

How would I know? Belac held his arms out to his sides and shouted back at the orc, "Being a wizard?"

The bow of the ship began to slowly rise up from the ocean. Timber creaked, and a rope snaped. Belac dropped down and put a hand on the deck as the ship shuttered under him. Vairug tried to keep his balance, but he lost his footing and crashed down next to Belac. After a moment, the bow lowered back down slightly, and the shaking subsided into a constant tremor.

The tie in Vairug's hair had come undone and its thick, black strands whipped in the wind. "The ship can't take this!" he shouted to the elf.

Belac did not know what to tell him. "It is going to have to!" he yelled into the wind as he climbed to his feet with the orc.

Vairug moved toward the wizard, fighting the wind as he walked around to the man's front. "Serath, it's too fast! You need to stop! It is too fast!" He grabbed the wizard's coat and shook him. "Serath! You have to stop!"

Serath's right arm dropped down to his side. He shook his head as if coming to his senses. Then his hands came up and slapped the orc's arms away from him with so much force that it knocked Vairug backward. Startled, the orc fell onto his backside.

Serath's words cut through the wind. "You fool!" He gestured furiously to the storm above them. "This is not something that you can set down and then pick back up again!" He unclenched the fist he had made with his left hand and looked down at the fractured porcelain figurine he found there. Then he threw the pieces over the orc's head and into the sea.

Getting to his feet, Vairug rebuked, "You were going to damage the ship!"

Serath closed his eyes and took a deep breath. To Belac, it looked like it required more effort for the wizard to reign in his anger than it had for him to harness the storm. The ship had settled into the ocean, but the wind still blew them onward. Serath stood motionless, his long coat flapping in the wind. Lightning continued to strike in the ocean around them.

When Serath spoke, his words were calm but firm. "The ship. Would have. Been fine." He turned away and began striding toward the captain's quarters.

Vairug watched the wizard walk away, and then he too began to walk toward the stern of the ship. At first, Belac thought that the orc was following after Serath, but Vairug veered right and headed for the stairs to the bridge deck. *I should probably go find out if we are going to die now.* Belac hurried toward the captain's quarters, hoping Vairug would not see it as a betrayal.

The elf halted as soon as he stepped into the room. A lamp had been lit and set on the floor next to Breana. She sat with her back to the wall and her legs stretched out in front of her. A gruesome piece of splintered timber protruded from her lower abdomen. Blood glistened on the wood where it had punctured through from behind her. More blood covered her mouth and upper chest, but the giantess's insane eyes still held life.

We can still save her! Belac did not understand why no one was doing anything. "Rolan! Where is your pack?!"

From where he crouched next to the giantess, Rolan answered, "It's lost." He sounded as if it were he who was lost.

Belac scanned the burned and broken furniture that had been tossed around the cabin. "It has to be here somewhere."

Rolan shook his head. "It's not here, Belac."

Breana gripped one of the dwarf's bloody hands with one of her own. "It's okay," she assured the dwarf and then began to cough.

"No, it's not." Rolan could barely speak. He gazed into the giantess's eyes. "No, it's not."

Breana returned the dwarf's gaze with more joy than the blood could obscure. "...Love you." Her eyes closed and consciousness abandoned her.

It did not seem real to Belac. "Is she..."

Serath shook his head sadly. "No. Though she is fading even now."

Rolan let Breana's hand fall away, and then he stood. He stepped around the giantess, his gray eyes set on the bulkhead to the port side of the door. Rolan advanced inexorably to the wall, kicking a broken chair out of his way. Taking hold of a disguised handle inset on the wall, he roughly ripped off the panel, exposing a hidden compartment and a small wooden coffer inside. After turning the box to the side to make room for its lid, he flipped the top open. His thick fingers dug into the contents and then his fist came up clenching the object he had sought. As Rolan turned around, Serath stepped in front of him.

Serath spoke with both concern and authority. "Do not do this."

"Get out of my way, Serath." Rolan's words were a threat.

Belac did not know whether or not Rolan could kill the wizard, but he was worried that they were all about to find out. *If Serath does not move, that dwarf is going to go through him.*

Serath stepped aside, saying, "This is a mistake, Rolan."

Rolan marched past the wizard. "It is mine to make," he declared without taking his eyes off the dying giantess.

Rolan, his back to the others, placed his palm on Breana's chest. Then he began to whisper loudly in a language that Belac did not understand. Dark and sinister, the words had no place in the world. Harsh sounds, drawn out and deep; whatever the meaning of the words, Belac did not want to know them.

The elf watched as dark scarlet light began to emanate from the concealed space between Rolan and Breana. *This is wrong.* The red nimbus intensified as the dwarf continued his profane diction. Red light coalesced into glowing tendrils that licked at the air around them. A deep rush of sound drowned out Rolan's words before suddenly ending. The ghastly emanations ceased, their departure punctuated by the loss of sound. No longer speaking, Rolan stepped away from the giantess. Breana was dead.

Serath voiced his disapproval again. "She will suffer."

How can she suffer? She's dead…

Rolan did not repent. "She is strong enough."

"And you would force her to be?" Serath pressed. "Will you force her to endure madness and decay?"

Rolan turned around and faced the wizard. "Yes." The conviction in his voice could have crushed kings.

Though muffled in the cabin, wind still howled outside. Lightning crashed as the wizard and the dwarf stared at each other.

What are they talking about? Belac spoke into the relative silence. "Is Breana dead or not?"

Serath nodded. "She is." Then he shrugged. "Mostly."

"What does that mean?" Belac glanced at the convincingly dead giantess. "How can someone be 'mostly' dead?"

Rolan held out his hand, a large ruby resting on his calloused palm. "I have the part of her that matters. I have her mind." He closed his fist around the jewel. "I have her soul."

A soulstone… Belac had thought it was merely a name; something that sounded more impressive than it truly was. The reality of such a thing seemed impossible.

Serath walked out of the cabin, his frustration conveyed without further words. Rolan turned away and faced the lifeless giantess. Belac slowly backed out of the room. *I will just let Rolan grieve… Or whatever you are supposed to do after you trap your lover's soul in a rock.*

There was an explosive sound of cracking wood and then Belac was flying backward. His left shoulder slammed into the deck and his feet flew over his head. He rolled across the deck and then he was flying once more. Flailing, he soared out into the darkness before splashing into the sea. Lightning flashed above the water's surface, but it seemed too far away. As blackness enveloped the elf, he resented that in the end, the ocean and The Deep would have the last word.

Epilogue

The kraken knew why it had been called. Even before the gateway could be opened, it had felt the dark thing waiting above. There were horrors that simply could not be tolerated to exist, forces that could not go unchecked. The restoration of balance had become necessary.

Though the watery depths of the world were vast, they carried with them intrinsic limitations. The dark thing had burned the ocean, then it had moved beyond the kraken's reach. However, patience was a favored tool of the wise. And the kraken, ancient in ways unfathomable, possessed the wisdom of both predator and prey. It had waited, it had searched, and when it had finally located its quarry, the kraken attacked.

In the wake of a sailing ship, the kraken found the dark thing it hunted. And with it, fire and pain. The kraken twisted in the water, spraying ink and eldritch energies in defense. The dragon bit into one of the kraken's tentacles and then violently tore the section off. Despite the pain, the fundamental damage was inconceivable. This was not the way the world was meant to be. No mere beast should have the power to harm a kraken.

The kraken spun away, preparing to grab the dragon as it fled into the sky above. The dragon did not flee. Instead, it rushed forward, its massive wings propelling it through the water. Taloned fingers dug into the kraken's mantle as the dragon locked onto it. Water boiled as the dragon roared, fire burning into the kraken's eye.

The kraken's tentacles reached up blindly, attempting to grab the dragon. With a beat of its wings, the dragon surged away. The kraken swept its tentacles through the water wildly, maddened by fury and pain. Lightning began to crash down from above, its brilliance flashing into the sea. With its remaining eye, the kraken searched for the dragon.

Finding itself alone, the kraken realized that the dragon had escaped. Determined, the kraken chased after the fleeing ship, knowing that the dark thing would be close by. Balance could still be returned to the world.

The ship moved faster than the injured kraken. Had the vessel not crashed into a sea stack, the kraken may have been eluded. The dragon attacked first, somehow sensing the kraken's presence. Darting past the kraken's blind side, the dragon raked its claws across the kraken's flesh.

The kraken wheeled, grabbing for the baneful creature that had wounded it yet again. The dragon evaded, gliding gracefully through the water. Lightning hammered the surface above, sending concussions into the ocean. Steering with leathery wings, the dragon banked behind the side of a rocky sea stack. Swimming past mermaids and men, the kraken pursued the dragon.

The kraken's single eye scanned wreckage and rock, but somehow the dark thing had gotten behind it. Fire and torment slammed into the kraken. The intensity of the unnatural flames burned through the kraken's defenses. And there, as lightning flashed above a darkened sea, an eternal being died.

www.ingramcontent.com/pod-product-compliance
Lightning Source LLC
Chambersburg PA
CBHW020256030826
48979CB00026B/1311/J

* 9 7 8 1 9 5 7 3 2 4 1 6 6 *